Come Clean

Bill James

Come Clean

A Foul Play Press Book

The Countryman Press
Woodstock, Vermont

This edition published in 1993 by Foul Play Press, an imprint of
The Countryman Press, Inc., Woodstock, Vermont 05091

Library of Congress Cataloging-in-Publication Data
James, Bill, 1929–
Come clean / Bill James.
p.   cm. — (Detective Chief Superintendent Colin Harpur novels)
"A Foul Play Press Book."
ISBN 0-88150-243-X : $20.00
I. Title.   II. Series: James, Bill, 1929–   Detective Chief
Superintendent Colin Harpur novels.
PR6070.U23C65   1992
823'.914—dc20   92–39316   CIP

10 9 8 7 6 5 4 3 2 1

Printed in the United States of America
by Arcata Graphics

1

Sitting in a far corner of the club, Sarah Iles slowly became aware of some kind of disturbance over near the door to the street. After a moment she turned her head to observe better what was happening. If she had been quicker, she might have seen more but Sarah had learned a long time ago to be cautious in the Monty. It was a place which could excite her, and she liked it for that, but often part of the excitement was fright.

A man in his twenties must have just come in and now, after a few steps, had sunk down to one knee, as if exhausted or injured, one shoulder propping him against the wall and keeping him from slipping further. His head hung forward, seemingly out of control, and a sheaf of dark hair had fallen over his forehead and obscured part of his face. Oddly, despite her anxieties about his state, and although he was crumpled on the carpet, her mind registered that he wore what seemed a very expensive light grey suit, probably custom made.

Ian had just gone to the bar for drinks and, glancing towards him, she saw he was staring at the man, but made no move in his direction. Nobody else in the club shifted, either, though all of them had seen what was happening. Sarah stood up.

'No,' Ian called to her. 'Stay out of it.'

'Of what?' Very scared, she crossed the little dance square and passed a pool table to where the man remained huddled on the ground. Now, she could make out what was obviously a blood stain under the top pocket of his jacket, and it spread quickly as she watched, like tea through a dipped biscuit. His breathing sounded weak and laboured. As she bent down to him she saw to her relief that Ian had left the bar after all and was at her side. 'What is it?' she asked the man. 'What's happened?'

He did not answer for a moment. Then, without lifting his head, he muttered: 'A drink. Water.'

'Yes, of course,' she said.

'Please.'

'Yes.' She turned to Ian. 'Can you stay with him? I'll go to the bar.' But as she was about to straighten the man reached out suddenly as if to grip her arm and detain her. He could not complete the movement and the effort made him lose balance and almost topple over. To steady him, she put a hand on his shoulder and waited. Before speaking again, he tried to raise his head, but couldn't.

'Listen,' he whispered, 'in case.'

'In case? What do you mean?'

'He nodded his head very weakly a couple of times. 'Yes, in case. A mess.'

'He needs an ambulance,' Ian said, crouching with her.

'Look,' the man muttered, 'some things I just can't take. You're hearing me?'

'Yes,' she said. 'Go on.'

'A silver day. Do you know what I mean? Supposed to be a great day.'

'What?' Sarah asked, bending closer. 'Who do you mean? Which day?'

For a long time he did not answer, seeming to need all his strength to breathe. Then he murmured: 'I'll tell you. But some water – or Scotch.'

She went quickly to the bar and asked Ralph to fill a glass. He did not hurry and, as Sarah waited, she realised with a start that Ian had joined her again. 'No, you should be with him.'

'Stay here.' Ralph said. 'Both of you. No need to intervene any longer. Best keep out of it.'

'Yes, we understand. Don't fret, Ralph.' Ian replied.

When she looked back towards the entrance swing-doors she saw that four or five more men had come in and were grouped around the one on the floor. They looked flushed and excited, as if they had been running. Almost immediately the group began moving, slowly now, across the club towards a door and corridor which led to the wash rooms and lavatories. From the bar, she had trouble making out what was happening and was about to walk back across the room with the drink when Ian and Ralph both said, urgently: 'No, Sarah.' Neither of them touched her or held her back, but she found suddenly that fear had mounted so much that her legs would hardly carry her, and, although she felt ashamed, she did what she was told and waited.

Her first count of the group seemed right: there were four men circling the fifth who was hurt, perhaps helping him, half carrying him now, towards the corridor. He might be on his knees, supported by hands under his armpits and gripping his jacket. The men did not speak and everyone else in the club remained silent and still. The injured man seemed worse and the only sound she could hear was the hideously laboured, rasping efforts as he fought to breathe.

In a minute, they were near the corridor and to enter it had to go single file. One of the men moved ahead, backing into the space, still half-crouched and with his arms stretched out to draw the kneeling, gasping figure after him. Very briefly then, as the circle around him broke up, the man in the centre was clearly visible to her. Again her guess had been right: he was on his knees, but doing nothing to propel himself, and needing to do nothing, because the others were virtually carrying him. The light grey double-breasted suit, white or cream shirt and a tie which was mostly pink, with some dark stripes, seemed a quaintly dandified outfit now. His head hung forward as before and swung out of control when the men moved, as if he might be only half-conscious, or less. She could still make out little of his appearance: there was the dark straight hair across his brow, and he seemed to have a sharp, bony nose and chin. He might be twenty-five. As far as she could tell, she had never seen him before in the club, nor any of the men around him. Two of them wore suits, one good jeans and a T-shirt, the other brown slacks and a brown leather jacket, also fine quality. This one had rapidly receding grey hair and wore rimless spectacles. To her, they seemed the wrong sort of looks for this setting and this incident, like a passed-over clerk's or librarian's. The other face that stuck in her mind belonged to one of the men in suits. His eyes were deep-set and unyielding. Although he could not be much more than thirty, she thought his teeth seemed too white and regular to be real. He had well cared for, very clean-looking dark hair, and immensely powerful shoulders. She found him terrifying.

Now, Sarah thought she discerned some sort of mark on the

7

neck of the injured man, perhaps another wound. His shirt collar seemed stained immediately beneath it, and possibly the pink tie and shoulder of his jacket, as well. Still afraid to go forward, she stood on the foot-rail at the bar and as she did Ian whispered harshly, urgently, one word, 'Lights.' Momentarily, she thought he was addressing her and did not understand what he meant. A second later, she heard someone hit the switches and every bulb in the club went out. So, he had been talking to Ralph.

Ian took her arm and led her to a chair at one of the small tables. Then he moved quickly away, she did not know where. Sitting in the blackness, listening to the appalling wheezing from across the room, and the slither and bumping of the man's knees and feet over the floor as the others continued dragging him, she suddenly felt as if she had been deserted, left on her own. What she had always half feared about Ian all at once looked to be true: she did not know him, was invited into only those parts of his life he chose to show and talk about. There were other parts, and from those she was carefully locked out, until an uncatered-for incident like this forced him to reveal tiny bits more. Perhaps he knew these men and could make a guess at what had happened. Or perhaps – Oh, perhaps almost any bloody thing, but he obviously felt he had to give them cover from her and others in the Monty, and that hurt. She honestly thought she did not care all that much what he was or wasn't, but she wished to know it all. Secrecy between lovers sickened her. Didn't she make a point of being open with him, telling the lot – well, the lot except about Francis Garland, which was a while ago now, and which had become such total ashes finally that she decided it was not worth mentioning?

'It's all right, everyone,' Ralph called. 'Temporary fault. Sit tight.'

Nobody replied. The Monty was heavy with the silence of people minding their own business, a state of mind they would fall into by habit and instinct here. The only sounds were still those from the five men across the room. The noise of breathing had grown less regular and fainter. She heard a door open and then some subdued grunting, as if the four had adjusted their holds on the burden.

'Ian,' she whispered, 'are you still there? Please.' He did not answer. She turned her head, straining to see, and thought she

8

could distinguish Ralph, leaning forward over the bar and gazing up towards the group, but failed to make out a shape for Ian. She was ashamed of feeling the need of him so much, and, although she wanted to call him again, somehow managed to stay silent.

A door slammed shut and the sounds from the five men ended. For a moment an idiotic calm took hold of Sarah, as if the silence and the closed door made everything all right again – now you see it, now you don't, and when you don't it's because it never happened at all, did it? Yes, it did, and it was still happening. Four men had a fifth, hurt, maybe dying, maybe dead, in the lavatory of a back-street club, and, if the men's lavatory was anything like the women's, nobody was going to mistake it for the London Clinic. Some things she could make herself believe for a while, because it was more pleasant to believe them, but not that the Monty would be sweetly back to normal as soon as the lights came on again and the talk re-started and the games of pool.

Ian was suddenly sitting with her on the bench and he gripped her hand. 'You all right?' he asked.

'What was it? Where've you been?'

'Been? Oh, just at the bar.'

'Were you?'

'Just at the bar. Too dark to move.'

'Why did the lights go?'

'Like the pit, isn't it?'

'But who are they, Ian? What the hell's going on?'

'Ralph may know.'

'You don't? You don't, honestly?' The last word came out as an apologetic whisper, an afterthought. Often she felt that she must not press him too hard with questions, perhaps because she did not want to know all the answers, perhaps because she knew he would put up new barriers, making her feel even more shut out.

'Some little crisis. Some bloody stupidity. They shouldn't have come here.' He raised his voice. 'Any hope of a light, Ralph?'

'I'm trying. A minute,' he replied. His voice now came from the other side of the room and as he spoke he switched on a flashlight and shone the beam down to the floor. She had not seen him move from the bar. Ralph walked slowly along the route taken by the group of men, the beam still pointed slightly ahead of him, obviously looking for something. Did he fear traces, unpleasant stains on the Monty's old, worn carpet? The search went as far as the closed door, but Ralph did not open it. 'Yes, a minute,' he said. He sounded anxious. The beam was played carefully over the same ground again, perhaps even slower now, as if he were fixing in his memory the spots that would need attention. 'All very much in order,' he announced, the tone saying the dead opposite. Perhaps he realised that, and when he spoke again he deliberately lightened his voice. 'Yes, all fine.'

The beam moved back towards the bar and in a few seconds all the lights came on. In full, tired splendour the Monty gleamed again. 'Apologies all round,' Ralph cried. 'I'd say the club should stand everyone here a drink after that, wouldn't you? Another power failure, a damned and depressing nuisance. So, what will it be, folks? Arthur, Neville?'

But the two men he spoke to stood up, both looking troubled and obviously eager to get out. One of them made a small gesture to wave Ralph's offer away, and glanced towards the closed door. Then they hurriedly left. Ralph called a genial 'Good night, boys,' after them, which they ignored. He turned: 'Ian? The lady?'

'Yes, why not,' Ian said. 'Brandy again, Sarah?'

For a moment she was on the point of answering him. Because of fear, and because she should not have been in this place at all, and should not have seen what she had seen, she was going to take the drink, cave in to the Monty's nervy ambience again, tag along as a smiling, sipping part of the conspiracy of wise blindness. Then she found she couldn't do it. Instead, she yelled: 'Ralph, a man might be dying behind that fucking door.'

Angrily, Ralph glared at Ian, signalling unmistakably that he regarded him as responsible for Sarah in the club, and that she was deeply out of order and should be kept quiet. 'Oh, I don't think so.'

'Why not go and see?'

'I – .'

'Your place, but you don't go and see. Ian, how can he be like this, how can you be like this, for God's sake? How can any of us?' She found she was yelling, as if to reach everyone in the club and to get through to them, despite the blankness they so carefully built.

'I told you – stupid behaviour, stupid people, they shouldn't have come here. Who wants to get mixed up with them?' Ian replied. 'Look, let's leave now, shall we?'

Again she wavered and was almost on the point of backing down, choosing caution, and agreeing with him. It had become routine: in the Monty there would always be things it was cleverer not to have seen, and things it was brighter not to have heard: the rule was, Just close your eyes once in a while, like in so much of life. Tension never altogether left the Monty and you had better learn how to handle it. Normally, Sarah could handle it: she took a little care, forgot what it was best to forget, yet still got her kicks. She was on a night out, not a course of ethics. No, definitely not a course in ethics.

But tonight she said quietly: 'Ian. I want to see he's all right.'

'Why? You don't know him.'

'What the hell does that matter?'

'It's crazy, Sarah. You're just curious, on the look-out for any damn thing new.'

'Maybe. I'm going to find out, all the same.'

'Please,' he said. 'Take my word.'

'What word?' For a second, she sat plucking up strength. Was Ian right, and did she simply need a new thrill? She certainly could not deny that it was the atmosphere of threat and possible danger which helped draw her to the Monty. Absurd and childish, really, but every time she came into the club looking for Ian she felt that same bright burn of excitement, a sense of risk-taking and freedom and – and a sense of something else she could not define properly, and maybe did not want to. Was it more than the snobby thrill of slumming, an off-colour delight in the seedy raciness of the place and probable villainy of many of its members? Probable? And some more. Ian used to tell her quietly which were crooks, most of them pathetically small-time, but crooks all the same. A few reached middling, and might be waiting the chance to move up, thinking big, walking cocky, but staying put. Occasionally, Ian would introduce her to some of the regulars, and even without help she could have guessed they lived on the wrong side. Mostly, they tried to be cheerful and friendly with her, even charming in their rough style, but, of course, they knew who she was and that eventually she would go home to a police husband rich in braid and commendations, and they did not understand what she was doing in the Monty or why she went on seeing Ian Aston. How could they when she did not really understand it herself? They kept their talk with her short and afterwards stayed at a distance, up near where the five strangers had just passed, beyond the pool tables, so she couldn't hear. One or other of them used to watch her all the time, and she did her best to ignore it.

Their attitude always amused Ian, and so did hers: he could find a laugh almost anywhere. On the whole, she loved this in him, though now and then it might turn her ratty and explosive, but only for a while: she couldn't stay like that with anyone, and especially not with Ian. Usually, she fell easily into harmony with him, thought as he thought, felt as he felt, did what he suggested.

Now, though, she fought off his advice that they should leave and apply the standard Monty veil. Instead, ditching the greasy habit of tact she had acquired here over the months, she stood up.

Even after what she had said, Ian misread the move. 'Good,' he said. 'We're going?'

But she walked quickly past him across the room towards the closed door. For a moment, fear of what she might see on the other side paralysed her and she stood in front of it, defeated. Then, somehow, she forced herself to subdue the dread and reached out and pulled the door fully open. The floor of the corridor was grey tiles and she saw a broad, smudged and broken red line leading along them, like evening cloud pushed about by wind, as if blood had dropped from one or both of the injured man's wounds and then been spread by his dragging knees and feet. Perhaps Ralph had seen something similar, but less clear, on the carpet in the dark. The line of blood led past the Gents and Ladies to the end of the corridor, where a fire exit had been opened. The doors still stood ajar, and beyond she saw a dark yard.

Before terror could disable her again, she went forward, walking awkwardly, one foot on each side of the red trail, like a child avoiding lines in pavement stones. As she neared the door, she became aware of Ian again, following a little way behind. He did not speak, perhaps troubled that she was out alone in front.

She stopped at the open fire doors. The yard lay beyond, black and impenetrable except for a little patch immediately ahead, reached by light from the corridor. She thought she could make out some parked cars, or perhaps wrecks, and possibly a builder's rubble container, but nothing was clear, and the boldness that had brought her this far suddenly began to shrink, just as her courage had wobbled inside the club. Although she still worried about the injured man, and felt indignation that everybody except her wanted to ignore what had happened, she could not bring herself to step out into the darkness of the yards and look for the group. Fear had made a brilliant and total and disgusting comeback. She listened for the laboured breathing but cars were passing not far away and she heard nothing above their engines. In any case, he might not be breathing at all any longer. 'Tell Ralph to get his flashlight,' she said, turning to Ian. She saw then that Ralph had come into the corridor, too, and was not far behind him, still looking angry and very tense. 'Or can you put yard lights on? You're good with switches, Ralph.'

He pushed swiftly past Ian and her and pulled the doors closed. 'You've done remarkably well,' he said. 'Best leave it, now, though, don't you think?'

Ian took her arm to lead her back to the bar. 'The stuff on the floor,' she said. 'Can't you see it, what it is?' She had begun to cry.

'It'll swab out, no problem,' Ralph replied.

'A little water clears us of this deed,' she said.

'What?' Ian asked.

'A quotation Desmond spouts sometimes.'

'Now, what about that brandy?' Ralph boomed, a lovely, mine-host smile in his voice.

Ian still had her gently by the arm 'Yes, come on, Sarah.' She began to move with him, back towards the bar. 'What does it mean?' Ian said.

'That's what I wanted you to tell me.'

'I'm talking about the quotation. What's it saying – the little water? He's got some reading, then, your husband. Is he like those detectives in novels, always able to get a classical reference in when he's discussing burglaries and money with menaces?'

Ralph put the brandies on the bar. 'Did you say with water?'

'No, we were talking about something else.'

'Sorry.'

'Oh, Christ,' Sarah hissed at him. 'I meant swabbing out the blood and swabbing out all trace and memory of what's just gone on here, Ralph.'

'Nothing's gone on here. Whatever happened had happened

before they arrived. They were just passing through. That's obvious. Absolutely nothing took place here.'

'Ralph, you sound like a hypnotist,' she said. 'I want to sit down.' Ian picked up the drinks and they went back to their table. She took a good gulp of the brandy. It tasted smooth and helpful. Ralph must have produced his best. This was a special moment. Only a few people were left in the bar and he served them now with whatever they asked for. The place became almost lively again, in its own seedy way. There was some relieved, edgy laughter from a couple of men she had seen here often before and spoken with briefly once or twice.

For some reason, Ian wanted to continue talking about Desmond, perhaps to take her mind off the injured man and the others. 'I don't really get it with you, Sarah. Never have. Powerful, educated husband, and look at you – Mrs Desmond Iles, nay, Mrs Assistant Chief Constable Iles, down town again among the dross and dawdlers while her better half's at home alone sipping Bovril and reading worthy books. How did it happen, Sarah?'

Her mind was still on the dark, outside yard, preoccupied with trying to gauge why she had turned away, and with trying to rediscover her bits of courage so she could try again, but she said: 'Look, Ian, there's a hell of a lot about him that's great, yes, a lot that's magic.' She realised she was jumping rather too fast to defend him, as if she felt he needed it.

'Don't I know? You're not one to pick a nobody.'

'Ian, I don't want stupid jokes about Desmond or snide talk.'

'No, of course, of course. But –'

'Things can die. Have you ever lived with anybody, I mean for years?'

'Not guilty.'

'It can work, obviously.'

Well, look at the Queen,' he said.

'Maybe if we'd had kids –'

'He didn't want that?'

'You know that instruction on medicine bottles, ''Keep away from children''? Des always says he will.'

'Yes, but –'

She began to find this conversation painful. 'Look, Ian, I don't know why, but I'm here. That's how it is. Let's leave it?' And that's how it had to be. Ian was too genial and sharp-eyed to keep

14

on at her. These were a further couple of the qualities that kept bringing her back to him and the Monty, although half a dozen times or more she had tried to finish it all. He was probably as tough as any of them in the club – but not crooked, he assured her, again and again of that, and she had to believe him – yet he could sense in a moment how she felt and would be careful not to hurt her. It was a change from home. Des would not hurt her, either, not deliberately, but over the years there had been too many times when he failed to see what pain he gave, and how bleak and lifeless things between them had become. That damage was done now, was part of her like a scar, and she did not feel committed enough or interested enough any longer to try to put it right. And so, Ian and the Monty.

She heard Ralph drawing water from the bar tap, and in a moment he came out with a bucket and mop and went to the corridor where the blood trail lay, softly whistling *In a Monastery Garden*.

Perhaps Ian would have been as considerate with any woman he liked going to bed with, but she could convince herself sometimes that it was only for her. She had grown very nifty lately at persuading herself to believe what she needed to believe, and although that sort of comfort never lasted, which sort did?

All the same, what had happened tonight stirred her uneasiness about the Monty. The disaster she had always feared might have come a little closer. 'Ian, wouldn't it be better if we met elsewhere?

'The Monty's part of me.'

'It's got to be dangerous for you – I mean, us two together all the time.'

'Because they want you, too? I suppose so. Yes, you're a cracker, Sarah.'

'Fool. No. Just imagine a prize project goes badly wrong for them one day. Say the police are waiting, an ambush. It happens. The lads here start wondering who's the leak, and your name floats to the top. It would.'

'No. I don't know about their projects, never have, not just because of you. I don't want to. I drink here because I've drunk here from the old days, when the Monty was something else. Why should I let them muck up my way of life?'

'Love me, love the Monty, even if it is tainted?' she asked.

Christ, but she must get a look at that yard, at the rubble container out there and the rest.

'Sarah, sweetie, calm down,' Ian said. 'If there's ever the threat of trouble, I'll pick up early warnings and disappear, don't worry. Ralph would hear and tip me. He's not just owner of this place, he's a mate.'

She said something then which, when she thought about it very soon afterwards, looked to contain a fair degree of clairvoyance. 'Oh, Christ, Ian, you know as well as I do, there are villains in this patch who could scare Ralph dumb, terrify even him. He's still got both eyes and pretty kids. They come first. He wouldn't want more damage.'

He laughed. 'Some black picture of the world! We're not New York or even Peckham.'

'Des says it's harder every day to tell the difference.'

'Police hype. To get their pay up.'

'What did he mean, Ian, the injured man? "A silver day?"'

'Search me. Delirious?'

'It could be. And "in case". In case of what? In case he dies?'

'Might be,' Ian said, 'but Ralph's got to be right, hasn't he? It's obvious something had gone on earlier.'

From the corridor came the healthy, cheerful slap of the mop on the tiles, and Ralph began to let in a bit of tremolo to his whistling. Nearer, there was the nice sound of pool balls clipping one another, and people had begun talking again, even laughing. Everyone appreciated getting back to normality.

Sarah took another drop of brandy. 'I hate it when people keep saying something's obvious. It's because it's not.' But she felt the drink begin to work real comfort on her now, doing just what it had lain waiting in the bottle over all the years improving itself for, smoothing the spiky bits of life, melting trouble and truth away for a time, warming the facts until they melted into something else. She sensed her determination to look outside in the yard begin to fade and she was sliding fast again towards a convenient agreement with Ralph and Ian. They did have a case. It might be easier and simpler, more mature, to let what had taken place fade in her mind. She should not be here and should not have seen it, whatever it was, so she had not seen it. Yes, just close your eyes.

'Sarah, I told him to do the lights because, well, I just thought it would be better all round if you saw as little as possible,' Ian said. 'Occasionally, it can be more comfortable like that. I mean, for you, as much as anyone.'

'Yes, I understand.' As sometimes happened, she began to grow bored with the Monty, its stresses, its concealments, its less than half-truths. 'Ian, can we go to your place now?'

He laughed. 'A minute ago you insisted on staying.'

'I want you.'

'I wish you'd contain yourself.'

'Now I want to contain you.'

What he called 'rough talk' always embarrassed him, which made her use it more. He reddened and glanced about, then whispered, 'Sarah, I –'

'Sorry, I forget they're all angels and shockable virgins here.' She leaned into him on the bench and turned her hand over, to lace her fingers with his. Often in this grubby den she could be as happy as she ever remembered being, happier than since the very earliest days with Des. Ralph, returning to the bar, gave them his fulsome, marriage-broker smile, the old knife scar from under his ear and two or three inches along the jaw-bone looking very pale and creamy in the subdued light, like a line of mayonnaise on a plate rim.

'We'll go soon, now,' Ian said. 'Not quite yet. Things have changed. I don't want it to look as if we're deserting Ralph after the bother, like those other two creeps.'

'No.' That would be one of those important male considerations: the compulsion not just to be loyal but to show the loyalty. In a way it was admirable, and came from real sensitivity. Sensitivity could stop, though, when the person needing it was not regarded as a friend, no matter how bad a state he might be in. Did anyone expect sensitivity to reach a lavatory corridor or an unlit yard? Men laughed at women's inconsistencies, but they weren't all that hot themselves. Anyway, she did not prize consistency very much. Who wanted to be consistently wrong?

'One more drink,' Ian said. He went to the handsome old mahogany bar, with its beautiful brass inlay and lovely, original beer handles, and began chatting and laughing with Ralph as if everything was as well as it could possibly be. Monty's had a good history. Once, apparently, it had been a select meeting place for businessmen, but now business had moved out to the high-tech industrial estates, and this district was entering its second decade of inner city dereliction. Men like Ralph were part of the new scene, maybe men like Ian, too.

She watched the two of them, clearly comfortable with each other, and felt almost envious of the ease and quickness of their conversation. She felt, too, a worry that came her way continually, despite all Ian's assurances: how had he got himself so well in with these sharp-clawed, cagey people? Ralph guffawed at something Ian said and thumped the bar with his fist, in delight. Nice. Such understanding between them. Perhaps Ralph really would look after him if the worst happened. Her doubts might be only the cynicism picked up as a cop wife. All the same, big laughs cost nothing. Comradeship came and went, like happiness, unless it was trained into you, grained into you, the way the police did things: canteen culture.

Watching them, she felt excluded, even resentful, and suddenly realised that the niggling, persistent wish to know the truth was edging its way back again, subduing the brandy and the boredom, and even the fear. She had to smash that shady, smug alliance between the two men. In any case, she never reacted very well to restrictions. After all, social considerations would say she should not be in the Monty at all, but she was. Now, though, she felt irked by the club's own particular inhibitions, couldn't swallow these, either. 'Listen, Ralph, sorry about this, but I'm still bothered. May we borrow your flashlight?' she asked.

'But for what?' he said.

'I'd really like to have a look at that yard. The rubble container.'

'The builder's skip? Why? Nothing out there,' Ralph said. 'They'll be miles away. I heard a car.'

'Not all of them might be miles away.'

Ian was embarrassed. 'Once she's got her teeth into something.'

'This is stupid,' Ralph said.

'Can I borrow it?' she asked.

Ralph looked sullen and tried to sound untroubled. 'Why ever not?'

'Thanks, Ralph.' She stood up at once and took the flashlight from him across the bar. Again she led into the lavatory corridor and again Ian came sheepishly behind her. She pushed the fire doors open and, switching on the beam, stepped out into the yard.

'What are you hoping to find, Sarah?' Ian put a hand on her wrist and helped direct the light slowly around, taking in a couple of vandalised, decaying cars and a newish-looking Montego that might be Ralph's. They all seemed empty. Ian said: 'Who'd hang about in a place like –?'

'Hush,' Sarah told him. She was listening for the appalling din of the injured man dredging into himself for breath, but heard nothing except occasional traffic and the gentle rush and rustle of a few sheets of newspaper whisked by the wind across the yard surface. The beam reached the loaded rubble container and she kept it there, resisting the slight pressure on her wrist from Ian to move it on. 'Let's go closer, Ian.' She began to walk.

'Debris. Ralph's having some outhouses cleared, that's all. They weren't safe.'

'I'd like to look.' She felt as she had felt earlier, afraid, crazily pushy, weak in the legs, wanting to give it all a miss, and determined to keep going and to find out what was wrong. Schizo? Maybe. But sometimes she understood why she had married the police.

They stood alongside the builder's skip, leaning on the side, like languid passengers at the rail of a liner, and she shone the flashlight in. The acrid, depressing smell of rubble and rotten wood hit her and she gazed at old beams, clusters of bricks held together by ancient mortar, slates, splintered rafters. A couple of wooden doors lay on top, overlapping each other and making it hard to see very far in. She reached out with her free hand and tried to shift one of the doors to the side, but it would not budge.

'What? Have you seen something?' Ian asked.

'Can we move it together?'

'Sarah, what for? We're going to get filthy.'

She put the flashlight out and placed it on the ground, to make two hands available. 'Come on,' she said and took hold of one of the doors.

'This is mad.' He gripped it with her, though, and they shoved. The door slid a little towards the far edge of the skip and the other one moved with it.

'A bit more,' she said. They had to lean over further to push again. The doors moved, though much less this time because the

19

top one came up against the skip's far side. 'Right.' She stood back and bent down to pick up the flashlight, then switched on again and hung over the edge, letting the beam reach now into the heart of the container. Her own breathing felt tight. Ian gazed with her.

'So?' he said.

Still leaning over, she moved the whole length of the skip, the light still searching. She switched off and turned to face him. 'All right. Nothing. Nothing but your genuine rubbish. There might have been.'

'Like?'

'You know what like.'

'No.'

'Yes.'

'Honestly, Sarah, I –'

Ralph called from the fire-door exit. 'What the hell are you two doing? Looking for treasure? Come on back in before you hurt yourselves.'

'Yes, we're coming,' Ian said.

'No, let's go to your place now, Ian. I've had enough here.' She took his arm.

'Why not?'

In his bed a little later they tried to put aside the events at the Monty and she said: 'This is no fly-by-night, empty affair. Don't think I don't know exactly what I love in you, Ian Aston.'

'God, what's that mean, all the don'ts?'

'And not just your hands, although your hands seem to know everything there is to know about – Oh, your hands can put everything right, can't they? Like now. Yes, yes, just like now.' She knew she was grinning with pleasure like an idiot at what he was doing to her. One day she must start working on efforts to ration her responsivenss with him: it was such a give-away. 'Your hands are good, and all the rest of it, but it's not everything.' Her own hands reached out silkily under the clothes to him.

'Yours know something, too.' He groaned happily in his quiet, apologetic way.

'You made me gentle and loving, Ian.'

'Only ten minutes ago you were being so tough, shoving chunks of building about.'

'That's what I mean, you change me, make me somebody different. Nobody else can do that.'

'Why you want me?'

'It's part of it.'

'I hope you realise, you'll never make *me* somebody different or change me, Sarah.'

'I don't know so much. This is changing. It's growing.'

'Christ, but you're so crude.' In a little while he said: 'You're responsive absolutely everywhere on your body, you know that? I bet you get a thrill cleaning your teeth, even.'

'Only up and down. Listen, Ian, do we have to wait?'

'No, of course not, love.' He moved towards her.

'Sometimes I like to wait, sometimes, no.'

'Seems reasonable.'

'Tonight, no.'

'Good.'

'Yes, you don't want to wait either, do you?'

'How can you tell?'

When she reached home there was a light on in the front room downstairs and at the kerb an old Viva, the worse for wear. That would probably mean her husband was with Colin Harpur, Detective Chief Superintendent Colin Harpur, head of criminal investigation. Harpur often drove battered-looking cars, hoping they would give some cover, though his big body and head, and thick fair hair jammed up against the top, were almost comically conspicuous in a small vehicle. He was Francis Garland's boss, and worked a good deal with Desmond, too, so presumably had heard most of what there was to hear about her life and ways, though he never gave any sign. None, except, possibly, that he seemed to treat her with special gentleness. Police knew how to sit on secrets, and especially Harpur. The story went that his own marriage and love life had their complications. At any rate, there had been days when she was very grateful for his tender, understanding style with her.

'Sarah's been at bridge, Col,' Desmond Iles said. Both men had stood when she came in and folded down back into the leather chairs now. What could be the sound of a crushed crisp packet came from deep under the cushion of Harpur's. One day

21

she was going to have a big clean-up in this room, and probably the whole house. Yes, definitely, one day: the same sort of target date as for cutting back on her loving warmth in bed with Ian.

'How was it?' her husband asked.

'Fine.'

'Never got to grips with bridge,' Harpur said. 'Bridge, crosswords, chess and the veleta I can't manage.'

'Bridge needs a certain kind of mind,' Desmond told him. 'Subtle, bruising, painstaking. Col, you'd be lovely, unbeatable, on the last. But you're far too charitable. Sarah's goodish all round. Yes.' He turned to her. 'We're chatting policy, love. You know, whether we should advise kiosks to put the Mars bars at the back of the displays, to beat shop-lifters, with the Maltesers at the front, or might it be the other way about? Criminologists are silent on this and Nietzsche only tentative.'

The two men were in shirt-sleeves, drinking tea from the best, real china cups. Desmond had a thing about decent crockery and glass when guests came, even subordinates. His upbringing had been what he called 'wholesome and chintzy'. In front of Harpur was a pad, with a few very brief pencil notes on it.

'Pow-wow? Is there some big police activity ahead, then?' she asked.

'Always,' Desmond said.

'Yes, well, I think I'll have a bath and go to bed now, if you don't mind,' she replied.

'It would be so nice to talk to you for a while,' Desmond said. 'it really would, wouldn't it, Col?' The tone was as close to a plea as she had ever heard from him.

'Grand.' Harpur smiled at her and she was conscious again of his wish to see her happy, or at least unhurt. They said he looked like Rocky Marciano, the boxer, but fair. She doubted that. As she understood things, Marciano was ruthless in the ring. Harpur looked tough, but kindly with it, patient. And, despite what he and Desmond said, he must be bright, too, or he would not have that job in his thirties.

'I'm so tired. Another night?' she said.

'All right, love. We'll probably bog on a bit longer, won't we Col?'

As she crossed the door and moved towards the stairs, she

thought she heard Desmond say to Harpur: 'Yes, bridge, very tiring.'

Sitting in the bath, thinking over the evening, she tasted salt on her lips and became aware, suddenly, that she was weeping. It shocked her. She rarely cried, and when she did she generally knew about it. Now, she hung her head forward something like the injured man's in the club earlier, and let the tears drop into the soapy water, a tiny squall on a grey and white pool.

God, what was this all about? She straightened her neck and swirled the water about with one hand, as if drowning the tears in suds would drown the pain, too. But a mix of sadnesses competed in her head. For a moment downstairs, when Des asked her to stay and she refused, all the pain and aridity of the marriage had closed on her like an illness. Something in her had wanted to please him and almost made her agree. Ten minutes would not have killed her. Simply, though, she had found she could not do it. The chore of speaking to him had seemed too much, much too much tonight, even though Harpur would have been there to help out the talk and prevent any slide into coldness or abuse.

So, was it the hopelessness of things between her and Des that had made her bawl? She could not really believe it. Hadn't she known for long enough about that? Wasn't it now almost fully sublimated into a scar, no more a hurtful wound? The absence of children no longer troubled her, surely? She consulted a marriage counsellor off and on, but this was to help her make up her mind about Ian and the rest of it, not Des.

Perhaps she was crying about Ian, then. It had been all right, it had been lovely, back at his place. That part of it almost always was. Yet tonight those doubts about him, the anxieties, had surfaced again. They were always there, not far out of sight, and at the Monty this evening they had become suddenly more alarming than she could remember them ever before. Did she know him? Could she know him? He held her off, cut off the lights, doused awkward conversations.

She climbed out of the bath, still impatient with herself for growing so gloomy and philosophical, and eager to be in bed and asleep or apparently asleep before Des came up. Briefly she examined herself in the full-length mirror. It wasn't bad, was it?

Another few good years left? Perhaps that was one plus for having no pregnancies. She had stopped crying.

2

Just as Sarah reached her car in the drive next morning she saw Ralph climb quickly from a Montego parked near the house and walk towards her. Panic hit her immediately, and her first terrified, unhinged thought was that he had no right to come up from the Monty to a decent, leafy, pebble-dash road. Christ, it broke the rules: she ran two lives and he ought to stay stuck in that other, down-town version of herself. Boundaries should be respected, at least by him. It was like a rat in the bread bin.

'Mrs Iles,' he said, 'well, I've been waiting for you, obviously. I wasn't sure if you'd be going out, but I waited. I didn't want to call at the house, even after your husband, the senior officer, had left. I had an idea you wouldn't like that.'

'Probably not.'

'This needed delicate handling. Luckily, in business, you get used to summing up a situation.'

'It's a knack, isn't it?'

They were standing near her car and she decided that the sooner they were not the better. She did not want him in the house, so she got behind the wheel of the Panda and opened the passenger door. He joined her and she drove out of the road at once, feeling hopelessly stressed and confused.

Her day had begun badly at breakfast, when she found Desmond civil but very distant, more than usually distant, as if some powerful anxiety gripped him. He was not easily upset, not prone to worry, so whatever it was must be serious. Conceivably, he felt special grief or hopelessness about their marriage this morning, though she doubted it: they had both become toughened to that failure for months now. More likely, Harpur's visit last night signified a delicate and probably messy police problem that he and Des did not feel comfortable discussing in head-quarters, maybe a coming operation, maybe aftermath. Private meetings between the two did happen now and then and the best china came out fairly often these days.

'Is there something you want to talk about, Des?' she had asked, knowing the answer.

'Nothing pressing, love. Is there something *you* want to talk about? The bridge evening?'

'You're not interested in bridge.'

'Right. Not in bridge.' He smiled a bit wearily, a bit sadly. 'Oh, look, forgive the show of self-pity, will you? Put it down to colic.'

She left it at that. Generally they did leave the potentially hurtful topics like that – hinted at, skirted. Still feeling low after he left for work, she rang Margot, the counsellor who helped her occasionally, and was able to make an appointment for later in the morning. God, her marriage problems were getting to be like bad teeth, needing rush treatment at agonising moments.

Always she dressed for full impact when seeing Margot, to make it clear that although she might sound down and desperate there was still plenty of fight in her. Today, she did a thorough job on her hair, improved all key zones with Rive Gauche, and wore pieces of her zappiest jewellery. She reckoned she looked pretty positive in a strained way, but did not feel any better. And when she saw Ralph, she felt much worse.

'I want to make it clear there's nothing to worry about,' he said now, as they drove. 'This is a precautionary visit, very much so. May I say I love your perfume?'

'Have you had breakfast?'

'What?'

'How long have you been there? Dawn? What's so urgent, Ralph?'

'Please, I don't want you to worry. Your breathing, it's very fast.'

'I had school colours for it.'

He sat back and had a nice, long avuncular chuckle about that, tapering it sweetly from very, very amused indeed to just very, very amused. 'Good,' he said. 'I like someone who keeps a sense of humour, regardless.'

'That's the thing about senses of humour, they must be regardless.'

26

'Laughter is certainly an antidote. That's well known.'

'Yes it is.' None of the fear had ebbed and her body was stiffly arched as she drove. Sweat began to run from her head and neck down between her shoulders, and would soon be making a nonsense of the Rive Gauche. For one moment, to her astonishment, she found herself wishing that Des were with her to cope with this man. Absurd as well as feeble: if Des had been around, Ralph would never have shown himself.

He sat half-turned towards her, his knees together, almost touching the gear lever, hands interlaced demurely in his lap. From the corner of her eye as she drove she could just about make out that he was smiling gently, and when he spoke his voice sounded light and friendly. He was making an effort to seem innocuous, and she found it creepy. 'I've known your Ian Aston for years and years,' he said. 'You can't go wrong there.'

'Thanks.'

'Ian's a man I'd always stand by.'

'Grand. I'll just drive around the park and the lake and then take you back to near your car, Ralph. I can't be long. I'm on my way somewhere.'

'Of course.' For a while he grew silent and watched from the side window, apparently content. Then he turned and said: 'You're bound to wonder what all this is about. I understand, perfectly.' He swung away slightly in the passenger seat, so that he was looking from the side window again. When she glanced towards him, she could see only the line of his nose and jaw, with its smooth, white scar. Despite that mark, there was something fine, even noble, about his profile, like a cut-price and darker Charlton Heston. She had noticed that before, in the Monty. Ralph's were the sort of bony good looks her mother had always fancied and found trustworthy, because they were so different from her husband's, Sarah's father. Some of that taste must have been inculcated in Sarah. As if to confirm that life had brought him down a rung or two he said: 'I'm not free to act as I would like, you know, Mrs Iles.'

'Who is?'

'Well, quite,' he said peaceably, 'indeed, who is?' And then his voice suddenly lost its gentleness and became edged with stress and venom. 'Mrs Iles, this is not some fart-arsing dreamy philosophical discussion, you know.' He turned violently in the seat to face her again. 'I'm trying to tell you something, something real, that counts. Do you understand that, you – well, you wife?'

She drew in at the kerb. 'Would you like to push off now?'

'Oh, don't come that, the big, other-age dignity. It went out with the Stanley Steamer.'

'Goodbye,' she screamed at him. The windows were closed but her voice must have reached the pavement, and a couple of old ladies in plastic macs, one pulling a shopping bag on wheels, stared through the glass, in the searching way people looked into ambulances. He was probably right: she had started to act stupidly, putting on the class, like Mrs Desmond Iles of Idylls, Rougemont Place, instead of finding out why he had come, and what he had to say about the situation of Sarah Iles, mistress, and sometimes troublesome guest at his cruddy club. Nerves had done it, nothing else.

He did not leave the car and when he spoke again his voice was back to considerateness and a sort of amiability. 'Believe me, this is not how I see myself, not at all, Mrs Iles, coming out here to frighten someone like your good self. I'm on your side, very much so, I hope that goes without saying. Oh, you have your views of the Monty and of me, I don't doubt it, but there's nothing untoward about the club or myself, nothing dubious or malfeasant, I hope you'll accept that. I'm a family man through and through, doing what I can to give those dear to me a decent life. When I say "on your side" you're going to reply that you have no side, I understand that, but what I mean is I'd do everything I could to save you distress, and Ian.'

She drove on.

'Did you and he discuss that matter of last night, I mean, afterwards?' Ralph asked.

'Not really.'

'Understandable. You have better things to talk about, for heaven's sake. Just an episode, wasn't it, what's called an aberration?'

She felt stifled by the seeping verbiage, desperately looked for a sentence or phrase that meant something to her, like seeking footholds in a swamp. 'Who were those people?'

'At the club?'

'Of course at the club.'

'What I have to tell you is that they've made an identification.'

He sighed and turned towards her. 'Yes, I'm sorry.' The tone was as if he had informed her of a death.

'What? What does that mean, an identification? Who of? Look, we're nearly back to your car. I don't want to go into Rougemont Place again.'

'Understandable, entirely. Park here, briefly. Then I'll walk.'

She drew in again.

'Yes, I had another visit,' he said.

'From one of them?'

'One or two.'

'Which one or two? The one with the false teeth? The grey-haired, balding one?'

'You're observant,' he said, sadly. 'I don't know whether one really wants to stare at people as closely as that.'

'I couldn't help staring, for heaven's sake. Think what was going on.'

'Well, perhaps. Put it another way: best not to be shouting these descriptions around. I mean, wildly. Such glimpses can be very subjective, misleading. We were all under stress. Distortions do take place.'

'When?'

'When what?'

'This second visit.'

'Very early this morning. They were asking about the people who went into the yard last night.'

'They were there when Ian and I – ?'

'These are people who set quite exceptional store upon their privacy, Mrs Iles. The flashlight, and probing into the skip – they watched that, apparently, from wherever they had taken cover and were very discomposed.'

'What identification?'

'They were quite all right with me, I want you to understand that, no untowardness at all.'

'What about malfeasance?'

'What? These are people who like to act in a moderate, professional way, a reasonable way. These are business people, obviously. They don't seek, well, emotive incidents.'

'Emotive?'

'Vigorous, unnecessarily vigorous. Civility up to a point is what they pride themselves on.'

29

'Which point?'

'Well, that's the question, I agree. And they're gifted. That's what I mean, achieving an identification so quickly.'

'Who?'

'Yourself, Mrs Iles. They were able to put a name to you, which means an address as well, clearly. This is what is so regrettable.'

He sounded genuinely hurt and grave, and his eyes were sad, his mouth mournful. There were times when she could almost believe he worried about her, as well as about his skin. She wished now she had taken the trouble to know him better on those visits to the Monty. He was about forty, strong-featured, a bit too charming, when he was doing that turn, but with nothing that she could see in his face to declare he might have a record, had been inside. About that, though, she could only guess. To Des or Colin Harpur his looks might proclaim something very different. She had read in the *Sunday Telegraph* that detectives travelling on a train played a game called CRO – guessing from passengers' looks which had a place in the Criminal Records Office. True, Ian knew Ralph well and liked him, so there ought to be something decent and straight present, ought to be if Ian himself was all right.

'Of course, Mrs Iles, you'll ask how they came to know your name and will suspect I gave it to them. Married to an officer, you will have certainly absorbed a reluctance to take anyone at face value. Please accept that I told them nothing and that they knew it all when they arrived at the club early today.'

She stayed silent.

'It would be simple to identify Ian. He's known to many people – known to and liked by, I might say. But having done that, it was possible by diligence to discover your name.'

'I don't like it. I'm scared, Ralph.'

'I can see.' Perhaps her use of his name in a warm, friendly tone encouraged him: he put out a hand, and seemed about to grip her arm or one of her hands in reassurance, but then drew back, as if still uncertain how she would take it. Possibly he had some sensitivity, or possibly he realised there was no reassurance he could sanely offer. 'They're unhappy that you're the wife of whom you are the wife of, naturally. They regard this as quite phenomenal bad luck.'

'Who for?'

'What?'

'Bad luck – who for?'

Someone in a passing Audi waved and Sarah waved back, though she did not recognise her. Stopping in this street with Ralph, so near the house, could be an unnecessary mistake. Very nervy again, and still offended that he should be up here among Audis and happy gestures, she reacted with what she knew was daft bravado: 'Too bloody bad they're unhappy I'm married. What the hell am I supposed to do about it?'

He had another of his beautifully relaxed giggles. 'Well, exactly. You could put it like that, certainly.' He gazed from the side window once more, in that fashion people had of looking away when they were about to say something crucial, but wanted it to sound offhand and not too heavy, even though it really couldn't be heavier. 'Obviously, what I don't know is how much you talk to your husband, Mrs Iles, and they don't know this either. It's what unsettles them.'

'Yes, we talk, the way people who live together normally do.'

His voice seemed about to plummet away from geniality again, but then almost instantly reverted. 'Mrs Iles, for Christ's sake stop behaving – This is so nice, this conversation, so measured and unblunt, isn't it? We step around the edges like a cow pat in a field. I'm not saying to you, do you talk to the distinguished officer about the next hols in the Gambia or whether the M25 has adequate traffic signs, am I, dear? What I've been sent here to ask you is, have you told your husband what you saw last night at the Monty, and, second, if you haven't told him yet, do you mean to tell him? And did the fellow in the club last night speak to you, the one in the nice suit who had difficulty standing? My impression, admittedly from a little distance, was that he did.'

'I hear they're putting in more and bigger signs on the M25, as it happens, so any discussion of that with Desmond could be immediately obsolete.' She saw him resist rage.

'When I say I've been sent here, I don't mean sent just by them. Ian was very keen I should make matters clear to you, also.'

'Did Ian say the man had spoken?'

'Why do you ask that? Did the man speak?'

'Did Ian say he had?'

'Ian said to ask you. Ian's not behaving altogether in his usual sensible fashion on this. I think he's afraid for you.'

31

'I see.'

'Need I fully itemise for you the dangers Ian is in currently, really as a result of your reactions last night?'

'What dangers is he in? Yes, itemise them.'

'Have you told your husband anything?' he asked, quietly. 'Do you intend to? Or, to put it differently, will you swear that you never will tell him? My own view, and I've given it to them forcibly, I want you to believe that, is that you're not going to tell your husband you've been out in the Monty with someone dubious like Ian, if you'll forgive me, because you're fond of living up in Rougemont Place and attending municipal glitter functions with the Assistant Chief Constable, whatever he's like as a husband. I've indicated to them that you're not likely to broadcast material about certain aspects of your life – let's refer to them as the unconjugal aspects, the spreading yourself aspects. You can't tell him about the incident without telling him why you were there in the first place and who with. They all see the strength of this reasoning, but they're still keen I should put things clearly to you, and return with a satisfactory answer.' And now his tone did break up and he said what he meant. 'Fucking lives are dependent on your answer, not just Ian's – mine, possibly my children's. Your own. For instance, I don't know whether I've been allowed to come up and see you unsupervised. I might have people watching me.'

'Did you tell them you were coming here?' She stared around in horror at this familiar street and at the people in their familiar expensive, casual clothes and expensive cars, trying to spot men who looked wrong and whose only interest was in her and Ralph. She saw nobody who fitted. So was he just pressurising her, or were these observers clever enough to stay unnoticed?

'It's Ian I worry about,' he said.

'It's yourself you worry about.'

'He's so exposed. And his carefree way – very winning in other circumstances.'

'So what dangers?'

'As they see it, he's as much involved as you. He might have overheard remarks from the man on the floor. And he was a part of that inconvenient curiosity about the skip as much as you, Mrs Iles. They don't know it was you who initiated it. You see, it's not that anything was found – well, I don't have to tell you. But the action indicated a frame of a mind, an intervening element. What they don't know is where it might take Ian or you next. Could it lead you into potentially embarrassing conversation with your husband, the officer.'

A yellow Mini sat parked not far ahead of them, the two men in it facing the other way and not appearing to take any notice of her and Ralph, but it made Sarah agitated now.

'So, can you tell me, am I reading things right, Mrs Iles? It's funny, I feel I know you very well, seeing you with Ian so often, and I'd call you Sarah, but somehow I don't believe you'd care for that, like coming to your house.'

'No, I haven't said anything to Des.'

'And not going to?'

'How could I?'

Now, he did touch her, very briefly allowed a hand to brush hers on the steering wheel, then withdrew it. He began smiling again. The teeth were his own and looked after. He was sinister but clean, and with good bone structure. 'What I said. How could you? A love affair is one thing, but breaking an important marriage a somewhat other kettle of fish, surely. Oh, I think so.'

Perhaps. It was the kind of question she usually discussed with Margot, not a drinking-club owner, though neither she nor Margot would have used the word 'important' about this marriage, or anyone's. All the same, Ralph might have a point. 'Will they accept this?' she asked. 'Will they leave Ian alone on the strength of that? And yourself, of course.'

'Don't forget *your*self, Mrs Iles,' he murmured.

'Will Ian be all right now? You say carefree, but if he asked you to come up here –'

'You're upset he didn't come himself, or ring you.'

'Yes. No, but –'

'They said it would be better if I did it, that's all. Ian would have liked to come, believe me.'

'What does that mean? He wasn't allowed? Why? Who are these people? Can they tell him what to do? Did they stop him coming, did they? You mean they're holding him somehow?'

He opened the door. 'I'm going to tell them that it's all right, Mrs Iles – Sarah. I'm going to stress that you've given your word, and that I accept it without question. I'm going to say you heard nothing at all from the man on the floor, and I'll make it clear that you are highly concerned about Ian – that nothing, nothing at all, would make you increase the dangers he faces as a result of last night. It should be obvious to them. What sort of woman would deliberately put in peril the man who – well, someone like Ian? He's young, and ought to have a decent life ahead of him, with use of all his limbs and his faculties, and so on.'

The yellow Mini moved off.

'So, why don't you answer – who the hell are they?' she asked. 'I mean, if you've seen them again, talked to them you must have some idea, even if you didn't last night. You talk as if you know them – know how they work, and so on. And what did happen last night? Was there something in the rubble, was that – ?'

He laughed. 'Nothing beyond what you saw, nothing beyond what you'd expect to find in a builder's skip. As I've said, it's simply that they were a little troubled.'

'They? Who are *they*? Who's the nasty-looking one with the false teeth?'

'That's what I mean, you see: so much aggression and curiosity. And itemising, like that. Take my word, it's foolish. Oh, I don't say it's not understandable. But I'm going to stress to them that you've said it's a closed episode now. They'll believe it, I know. My standing is fortunately long established, sound. But perhaps you could take a little special care of yourself, Mrs Iles. Look about a lot. Be alert to recurrent, unfamiliar faces. Obviously, avoid going alone to deserted, alien spots in darkness. Keep off the stairs of tower blocks on council estates. But, when would *you* be in a tower block? If you're using public car-parks try to get a space on the perimeter, not in the middle of a jungle of vehicles, because jungles are, well, jungles. Don't use multi-storeys at all or public toilets, especially not public toilets.' He eased himself out of the car and stood smiling down at her for a moment before closing the door. His double-breasted suit was steel-coloured, close-fitting, new, possibly Jaeger, and he looked like a pillar of superior ash. 'I trust that I'll not need to intrude again on your life, though, of course, that doesn't mean I shan't be very disappointed if you do not come soon to the Monty again to see us all. Oh dear, my sweet old mother used to warn me so fiercely against double negatives, and yet listen to that!'

'Ian worries about them.'

'What?'

'Double negatives.'

'Continuous discussion between us. Basis of our friendship.' Shutting the door carefully he walked off towards Rougemont Place and his Montego. Once he glanced back and waved cheerfully, still beaming. Something about him reminded her of newsreels of that Prime Minister who came back from seeing Hitler just before the war claiming he had achieved 'peace in our time'.

Sarah had not stopped shaking when she reached Margot's flat high in a recently finished redbrick, waterfront development near Valencia Esplanade, with views over the new marina and as far as Young's Dock, still used by merchant shipping. All coastal Britain was into making part of its dockland bijou and soon there'd be more marinas than hospitals. 'Poor girl,' Margot said, 'you look terrible. You should have called me sooner. Come on, tea first.' They went into her kitchen and Margot filled a kettle. She was about fifty, tall, big and angular at the shoulders and hips, yet surprisingly nimble. Sarah always thought she looked how a woman prison officer ought to, tough but approachable. Sometimes she affected men's half-moon, gold-rimmed glasses worn low on her long, straight nose, and when she had these on she made Sarah think more of the kind of face you met irritably selling rail tickets behind a grille at St Lazare.

'This is something else, not to do with Des. Not much to do with Des, anyway,' Sarah said.

'But to do with Ian?'

'In a sense, yes.' They waited for the tea.

'Strikes me, everything is to do with Ian,' Margot said.

'In a sense to do with Des, as well, I suppose.'

'Is it something we should talk about?'

'I don't know. Perhaps not. No, we mustn't. But perhaps it will come out when we're discussing other things.' She laughed in that loud, spasmodic style she often fell into when feeling especially bad, so as to convince people she wasn't, though it rarely worked, and never with Margot. 'Oh, I don't know where I am, what the hell I'm doing, that's the truth of it.'

They took the tea into Margot's disordered, comforting lounge and sat down opposite each other. Margot had on a voluminous, paisley-patterned house coat, buttoned to the neck, and red and white training shoes. Two cats fought unplayfully in one corner, leaping high on furniture and chasing each other across the top of an old, black, upright piano, spitting committedly and scattering score paper.

'Those buggers make me seem like a witch,' Margot said, and threw a canister of air freshener at them, missing badly. 'It's not like that. Unfortunately, I lack the powers.' The cats glared at her for a moment and then withdrew in a huff.

'Everything says to me I ought to finish with Ian,' Sarah said.

'Yes? Hasn't everything been saying that to you for a long while, everything except your will?'

'There's extra everything now.'

'And could you do it, do you think?'

'I don't know. I've always said I couldn't, haven't I?'

'But obviously things can change: something's happened between you and him, or between you and Desmond?'

'Not between me and Desmond. As ever, it's dead, or dying.'

'Does he think that, too? As I recall, he never used to.' Margot was on a little settee and she swung around so her feet in the trainers hung over one padded arm. The mug of tea she balanced on her stomach. On Sarah's first visit, the informality had shocked her. Now, she recognised it as probably a fairly elementary part of the act, to take any stiffness out of the session, and to do it swiftly: no matter how relaxed Margot might look, she did not miss much.

'No, he still doesn't think it's over,' Sarah said. 'He'd like it all to be as it once was. Yes, he wants me, all the time. I can see that. I feel sorry for him, genuinely, but I can't do it.'

'If you can't you can't.'

Sarah laughed. 'Look, is that really what you're supposed to say, Margot?'

'You mean I should tell you how to put things right, how to make things good with your husband, make all the problems disappear?'

'At least how to try.'

'I will if you want to. But I'm not sure you do.'

'In many ways, Des is a good man. Well, of course he is. I married him, didn't I? He puts up with a lot. He's brave, he's clever, and he's funny, sometimes. I ought to –'

'And, Ian?'

'Who knows what he's really like, or even what he really does?'

For a moment, Margot did not speak. Then she said: 'This

event that's upset you – it's something that makes you wonder more about Ian?'

'Yes, and about myself. I have to ask, am I like a stupid girl, turning down a decent, solid man because he can't reach me, and going instead to somebody I don't know properly, can't know properly, because the mystery and risk of it are attractive?'

'And what answer do you get?'

'Answer?'

'Yes, when you ask yourself this, what do you reply? Do you come clean?'

That was part of Margot's technique, perhaps part of all counsellors' techniques: they let you do the work, hardly told you anything at all, persuaded you into deciding for yourself what you really wanted and into talking about it. What they knew was how to ask questions, and occasionally the procedure annoyed Sarah: she came here looking for guidance, and paying for it, and was prescribed, instead, self-scrutiny. This was counselling? 'The point is, would I want Ian if I could go off tomorrow and live with him, not meet him at the odd, pinched moment in a down-at-heel pool and booze club?'

'Yes, that's the question.'

'Somebody told me just now that I liked the status of my life with Desmond too much ever to give it up for a lover.'

'Oh? There's someone else who knows about Ian and you? I hadn't realised that.' She sounded ratty for a moment. 'Tell me, Sarah, is this related – this person and what he or she said, is it related in any way to the situation that upset you so much?' She took a drink of the tea but had turned her head and was watching Sarah carefully.

'Yes, in a way.' The clarity and speed of Margot's intuitions must explain how she managed to make a living in this woolly, bull-shitting trade.

Margot waited, and Sarah realised she was giving her the chance to say some more. She did not respond and, in a while, Margot asked: 'So, is this person right, do you think, the one who did the diagnosis for you: are you too fond of your privileged style of life to put it on the line?'

'I wouldn't have thought so, not before this. Now, I'm not so sure. I think I may be a bit of a snob.'

'And Ian doesn't fit that social bill, no matter how well he might fit elsewhere?'

Margot liked occasional crudity. It was part of the all-girls-together frankness that she affected.

'Maybe not,' Sarah said. She thought for a second. 'Oh, no, Margot, it's more than that. I don't regard Ian as a bit of rough. I don't need rough, anyway, not my thing at all. Well, I don't think so. But, how can I explain? Try this: it's a tussle between right and wrong. Des is a policeman. He's law and order. I must have wanted that: I married law and order. He's morality. Theoretically at least I'm in favour of morality. All right, I think Des is a policeman who's pulled some dirty tricks in his time, exceedingly dirty, I suspect. In fact, often I feel scared even to wonder. But, speaking generally, he's just about on the side of what we can call good, and he'd say you can't be on the side of good effectively any longer without a tidy armoury of dirty tricks. He's not into fighting with one hand behind his back and the other holding the handbook of the Civil Liberties movement – that's his line.'

'Ian? Is he on the side of good?'

'Who knows?'

'Not you?'

'Not any longer.'

Again Margot paused, obviously waiting for more information. And again Sarah refused to give it. Instead, for the rest of the session she insisted upon talking about her childhood, and Margot listened but made no credible effort to conceal her disappointment and boredom.

At home, Sarah telephoned Ian's flat three times, but could get no reply. She tried the Monty and Ralph answered at once. When she asked if Ian was there he said: 'No, I'm afraid not, madam, not at this moment, though he certainly is a member of the club. Should I say who called? Would you like to leave your number or a message?'

He must have recognised her voice, yet chose to act as if she were a stranger. She did not understand why, though perhaps there was someone nearby in the bar who might overhear, and he wanted no mention of Ian's or her names. 'I might try again,' she said.

'At your service.'

3

Harpur waited for Jack Lamb near a brick-built, Second World War pill box set into the long, earthwork sea wall on the fore-shore, four or five miles up the coast from Valencia Esplanade. Its concrete-lipped weapon slits looked seawards and in 1940, if the enemy had come, the troops here would have tried gloriously to knock him and his tanks back into the mucky water. At low tide the view was wide mud flats, desolate and empty except for an occasional solitary, bent-over fisherman digging bait. Patches of frothy, orange industrial effluent were dotted about the mud today, like a pogrom of ginger cats. Harpur understood that the flat supported uniquely interesting bird life, if you were interested. Fine but heavy rain was being carried in from the sea now, and underfoot the soil had begun to grow sticky.

Lamb had picked this spot. He loved atmosphere and history, possibly environmental mud as well. What he did not like and would not trust was the telephone, so, if ever he or Harpur wanted to say something they had to meet, and to meet where they would not be observed. They used car-parks and art galleries and crowded auction rooms – where they could speak an urgent word or two before separating – and occasionally they came here, the fight-them-on-the-beaches battleground that never was. Informants as a breed felt uneasy about telephones, not just Jack; they were aware how imaginative and crafty people could be at eavesdropping, and how technological, because they were imaginative and crafty at it themselves, and especially Lamb. Harpur had never known a tipster anything like as productive, so if Jack wanted to rendezvous in the mire, in the mire it had to be.

He approached now, huge and unhurried, wearing what appeared to be a Cossack cape, a black beret and wellingtons, like someone ready to play in a one-man Napoleonic war sketch and represent all three main armies. Despite his security obsessions about telephones and meeting places, Jack did not go in for being unnoticeable. How could he at his weight and height? Gazing seawards he murmured: 'Will they never come?'

'I love it here; the tide-mark of nappy liners and knotted french letters.'

They stood under the overhang of the pill box roof, leaning against the brickwork. When fixing the meeting, Lamb had hinted that he was gravely worried about the safety of one of his own occasional sources; these people lived with menace, non-stop, and now and then would come a frenzied cry for help.

But there would be a lot of oblique, general talk before Jack reached this topic. He liked to remind Harpur how indissolubly the two of them were bound together. 'You'll have been concerned, but I'm glad to say the October Stock Exchange dive did me little damage, Colin.'

'Grand.'

'Luckily, I'd unloaded a lot of pictures just before. Some were very cherished, not just by me, by Helen, too, at home. You remember Helen, a sunny, punkish child, familiar with *l'art fang*, and so gifted at ballet and cohabitation? We both felt it a wrench to see some of those works go, particularly the Pre-Raphs. But one gets a feel about the way stocks will behave, and if they do a real plunge it's not long before all sorts of valuables are touched, too. Oh, yes, the crash has reached the salesrooms, you know. Bad. Painful. Renoirs. Bonnards. Picassos not getting to their reserves, and having to be bought in. Mind you, serves the buggers right for putting high, grab-all estimates on everything. Those days are gone. That's what I say, Col.'

'If that's what you say, Jack, that's what you say.' Harpur hated hearing about Jack's commercial life, though he knew as a certainty that fragments of it were above board.

'But pardon me. Sometimes I forget and behave as if you are a part of the business with me. Stupid – and impertinent. You show a friendly, helpful interest, deeply helpful, but how could it be more than that, you an ace lawman? Good God, I'm not here to talk art and profit and loss, am I?'

Harpur waited. He had been through similar introductory

formalities many times before and knew his role was only to digest. These rough reminders were meant by Lamb to soften him up; to proclaim unmistakably, proclaim once more, that the two of them depended on each other and were in each others pockets for ever, one of those unsanctified but brassbound marriages between a copper and his tipster. Harpur did not need telling. He never forgot. It was an uncomfortable feeling, but one shared by most detectives who used informants or grasses or narks or touts or tipsters – whatever ugly name one liked to bless them with. And detectives who lacked these informants, trading whispers for a degree of privileged handling, rarely did much useful in the big, enduring, untidy battle against the darkness. These people inhabited that darkness themselves, either totally or in part, but now and then, for their own purposes and reasons, they might offer to shine a little light into an important shadowy corner where, without their help, police would never see. Politicians and editors who screamed about the perils and unwholesomeness of police dependence on informants might well have a point, one they could go screw themselves with.

'Colin, do you understand how things work, I wonder – the gathering of facts and rumours and hints? Look, I talk to you, but before that can happen there have to be people who talk to me. I don't originate. Well, it's obvious. Do I continue to bore you?'

Oh, God, Harpur thought, so I read things right; someone else wanted protection or a favour, or a bit of special affection and feather-bedding, one of Lamb's mates. He said; 'Jack, I look after you. That's as far as I can go. It's dangerous enough already. What you do about your own informants is not my province.'

Lamb held up an enormous, red-mittened hand to stop him. 'Of course that's up to me. Would I expect you to involve yourself with dirty nobodies, you a public figure, loaded with insignia and kudos? Col, I'm hurt, offended. Give me credit for some knowledge of protocol, will you, please? Please.' A couple walking with a dog despite the rain approached along the sea wall. Lamb watched them carefully, and was silent until they passed.

Then he said; 'This source, the one I'd like to talk about, suddenly isn't around any more. Overnight, gone. Total disappearance. He rang a few days ago and we fixed to meet, but he never shows. So I phone and somebody lifts the receiver and listens but says nothing. Very quiet breather, too. I don't know for certain, obviously, but I'd say this was not my man. He doesn't fool about. Then, almost as soon as I put the phone down, it rings. Naturally, I'm not a listed number, so another mystery. Again nobody speaks. The same master of understatement? Who knows? I've been to have a look at where my source lives but no sign of life. I can't go asking around there. That wouldn't be any good for him or me. So, I don't know what.'

'Are you going to tell me who it is?'

'He could be fine, I realise that. Maybe gone on a quick job somewhere, one he didn't know was coming up, or having a break.'

'But you don't think so.'

'No. He was always reliable. I mean, he's a villain, so when I say reliable it's a bit relative. But it was obvious from his call he had worries. Something was happening that he didn't like, or was going to. He wanted it stopped. So, he would talk to me, expecting I might talk to someone like you. Obviously, he didn't know the name of my contact.'

'Thanks.'

'What do you mean, thanks, for Christ's sake? That's only basic, keeping your identity quiet.'

'Thanks, all the same.'

Jack adjusted his cape. 'Yes, if I want you to look for him, I've got to give you his name, haven't I?'

'You want me to look for him?'

'Col, he knows something, and it will be big. Always in the past, it's been important stuff, accurate stuff. We need to know, I mean, *you* need to know. I haven't a clue what it was.'

Evidently, here was another one who did not talk beyond the basics by telephone.

'And the extra thing; they could have roughed him about,' Lamb said, 'I would like to discover whether he's coughed my name. That could be a hazard.'

'Which they?'

'He runs with Benny Loxton's squadron. Newish recruit. As I understand it, Benny's taken on two people lately – this one, and a boy called Lentle. Robert?'

'So, do I know the missing one?'

'I doubt it. He's small-time, so far. Small-time crook, big-time informant. He's got no record.'

'He *says* he's got no record.'

'I've done a check. Obviously. His name's Justin Paynter.'

'Christ, have the Justin generation reached the age of mature villainy? Remember when crooks were called Bert?' And Jack. 'You're right. I don't know him.'

'Kid about twenty-four. Slight, pale, dark hair falling across his forehead. Dandified, rather. Tailored suits.'

'No.'

'Gifted with cars, and Benny's started letting him do his accounts. He sees a lot. Did. Hear that?'

'What?'

'Curlew. Lovely cry.'

'You really know how a curlew sounds, Jack?'

'Could have been a woodpecker, I supppose, ratty about all the mud and no trees to get stuck into. Or a flamingo, off course?'

The rain had eased and they came out from under the roof projection. A few feelers from the early evening sun penetrated the clouds and caught the sea far out, so it gleamed murky red. The tide was on the way in and Harpur could hear small waves breaking and pushing up slowly, dark and greasy with sewage, towards the wall. 'An address?'

'Yes, I've written it down for you. But we might have a better starting point. There's a tale around, I don't know if you heard it, some street incident up near the Monty a couple of nights ago.'

'Ralphy Ember's place?'

'Near it. Maybe in it, too. I don't know.'

'God, remember the old Monty? Top-drawer membership. Now, Ralphy in charge. What incident?'

'I haven't sorted it out properly, not properly at all. The trouble is, this is another place I can't ask any questions on the spot. Well, obviously, Col.'

'What incident?'

Lamb looked out to sea. 'In its bare, uncompromising way, this bit of coast has a kind of beauty, you know. I've always thought so.' Nimbly, he climbed on to the top of the pill box and gazed out towards the horizon, one hand shading his eyes. 'Remember that poem from school, Col, about stout Cortez, happening on the Pacific and gazing at it eagle-like from a peak in Darien?'

'Yes, you are getting a bit of a gut. Eagle? The mittens are not right.'

43

'All his men in a wild surmise, a really wild surmise. Understandable. You don't find a Pacific every day.' He climbed down. 'This information begins, I gather, with an old lady, sleepless, who looked out of her window late the other night and saw some sort of very serious chase in the street, a young man in what she called "a good serge suit" running from three or maybe four older men, one wearing a leather jacket, one with thinning grey hair. A car was trying to hold the young bloke in its headlights. She doesn't know cars but she said a big old black thing. A couple of the men on foot caught him and started giving real treatment, she thought maybe even a knife, but he broke away and ran again, over towards Shield Terrace, where the Monty is. He looked hurt at this stage, maybe limping and bleeding, the suit stained. They went out of sight then, and that's as much as she knows. Col, it's possible nobody's going to find this lad in time for him to say anything. But worth a try.'

'So what tells you this is your boy?'

'Not all that much, I've got to admit it. Just, he's not about and it's the right age and build, and the smart suit. On top, one of Benny's other lads, a part-timer called Steve Stevens, uses a black Humber Hawk, it's his trademark.'

'A woman sees a knifing and does nothing, asks for no help?'

'I don't think she's sure, Col. And, besides, they hate getting into anything, don't they? So scared of being called as witnesses, and having threatening visits in their prized, door-chained little nests from God knows who, to shut them up.'

'Christ, we can look after people, people who give us information.'

They began walking towards their car. Lamb said: 'I'd be the first to confirm it, you know that. Could I be better looked after? But these people, especially if they're old, Col, they don't seem so sure. What they want is to stay untroubled, and they get very tenacious of life. Although most admire the police, they aren't convinced you can really protect them. Well, they read the papers, I suppose. Their bones are delicate and they have nasty foot problems, so if things did get perilous they can't make a dash. Their answer is to stay under cover. The old really love life but they can't risk seeing much of it, one of those touching paradoxes. I've only heard this myself because she told a neighbour and the neighbour spoke to an acquaintance of mine. Well,

44

you know how information comes. Roundabout, not by the Post Office.'

'Any pictures of this lad, Justin?'

'I'm trying.' He paused. 'Tell me, Col, do you and yours keep an eye at the Monty?'

'Off and on.'

Lamb went silent again. Harpur said: 'You're bothered about Sarah Iles? Yes, I know she shows up there sometimes, poor lost kid.'

'Is that what she is?'

'Along those lines.'

'I can see it makes things sensitive.'

'I know about her and so do some others. But not Iles himself. At least, I don't think so. Who's sure what that bugger knows? Was she in the club when this happened?'

'I don't know. And I told you, I can't say whether the chase actually got into the Monty. I believe lover boy, Ian Aston, was there. Believe. That wouldn't signify, anyway. He's in the club most nights. As far as I can make out, she just rolls up there to see him when she can.'

'Yes, I think that's the arrangement.'

'Is she – ?'

'It's sad, but things aren't right at home. Haven't been for a long while. You know the sort of picture.'

'Don't we all?'

'Yes, well – She's a delightful girl, full of grace and vim. We're all bothered about Sarah. I wouldn't want her landing herself in anything dark.'

'Your Francis Garland used to . . . have a stake, didn't he? It looked a very happy thing.'

'Francis? Only room for one ego long-term there, I'm afraid. But she's a grand girl, Jack.'

'I can believe it. Listen, this Aston – ?'

'Nothing known – like *your* Justin,' Harpur said. 'We've never been able to work out how he lives. He's not short of money, has some style. He takes a job now and then, either selling, or a bit of exterior decorating. Pays his taxes, rarely draws dole. But he couldn't dress the way he does or drive what he does on his earnings.'

'Perhaps I'll make an inquiry or two,' Lamb said.

Harpur shrugged. 'If you like. Be careful. Do you suppose that somebody suspected Justin was talking to you, and that's why he's been taken out?'

'Could be. Could easily be.'

More bird cries came from the flats. 'What's that one, Jack?'

He looked out over the mud again. 'Oyster-catchers. Easy: they fly in dozens.'

After dark that evening, Harpur drove up to the address Lamb had given him for Justin Paynter. When Jack said something, you'd better believe it, even if the tip seemed all instinct and guess, because his instincts and guesses usually turned out more spot-on than supposed hard fact from minor league narks. For a time, Harpur sat in his car and watched the house, a small, old, pretty, stone-built place with a minute front garden, in a grubby, long road, not far from where Harpur lived himself. No lights showed and all the curtains seemed to be across. He gave it an hour, keeping an eye on the street around him, as well as the cottage. In that time, there were no callers and all rooms remained unlit. As far as he could make out, nobody else had observation on the place though plenty of other parked cars stood near, and in the darkness he could not be sure none was occupied. He certainly would not have bet big money on it. Leaving his old Viva, he walked to the end of the terrace and down a lane, to look at the house from the rear. It backed on to a railway line and had a decaying wooden fence at the end of another small yard or garden. He could see no light in the house from here, either.

Forcing apart a couple of planks in the fence he pushed into the garden and stood still, watching and listening. A palsied-looking brown cat yawed away from near two bulging, black plastic refuse bags, one of which had split and dribbled cheerless items on to the rough grass, where rotting cardboard boxes and a scatter of empty beer cans lay. Christ, wasn't this the life, though? To think he might have been wasting his time at home with his feet up, or in bed with Ruth Cotton. Instead, here he was, stalking – stalking what? A grass's grass, or someone who answered the phone, but didn't. Thin stuff? He would concede that.

As he picked his way through the garden to what he guessed would be the kitchen window, a sprinter train charged past behind him, obviously sauced by its own publicity. A roller blind was down but age must have weakened it near the cord and there were a couple of gaping tears. He had no light with him and the room beyond was dark, but he peered through the holes and thought he could make out, scattered on the floor, broken crockery, a frying pan and some other utensils, as though shelves or a cupboard had been cleared in a rapid, crude search. Perhaps Jack Lamb's telephone call to here had come while it was happening.

For half a minute he stood in the shadow of the house, trying to check that he had not been followed. Then, feeling reasonably safe, he tried the kitchen window and a rear door but neither shifted. Every bugger was security-conscious these days, even villains. It could be a right pain. Luckily, someone had been doing a bit of updating, and a modern lightweight ply door and nonsense lock had replaced the solid timber and iron bolt which must originally have been in place here. Harpur applied some concentrated leaning, repeatedly ramming his weight against the lock. Soon, he heard the fragile wood of the frame rip and he gently pushed the door wide.

He felt much better now. For him, it had always been one of the brightest pleasures in police work to enter someone's property on the quiet and look at gear and possessions, trying to sort out a story from them. It fiercely excited Harpur to break down privacy, gave him a sense of intimacy with the target, and occasionally a sense of power over him, sometimes even her. A long time ago he used to consider the pleasure that came from these invasions as like the thinking of cannibals: they wanted to absorb the strengths and virtues of the people they ate, and he wanted to take over for a while the personalities of the suspects who lived in these entered places, so he could know them thoroughly. That was rubbish, really – just a high-flown, fanciful excuse for poking his police nose into someone else's property, often illicitly. A similar sort of eyewash had surfaced recently in a Sidney Lumet film on television, *The Anderson Tapes*, where Sean Connery, as a big-time burglar, compared the joys of opening a safe with those in seducing a woman. These were evasions, sloppy efforts to romanticise or intellectualise what you would do, anyway. And what Harpur meant to do, and continue doing, was to pick thoroughly, secretly and skilfully through a possible villain's private things, hunting a revelation, spinning his drum.

There had been little pleasure just now in the garden, encircled by muck and debris, badgered by train noise. No matter how close to a property, outside was no fun: more laughs on a rubbish tip. But actually to penetrate a house, to break through a portal and get within somebody else's four walls and rooms, reading signs, imagining the life lived there – that thrilled him. At these times he knew he had picked the right job. He loved the finds, the intrusiveness, the risk. If he had not been a cop, he might, indeed, have fancied burglary, like Connery's Duke Anderson; same techniques, same addictive tension. Or maybe psycho-analysis was another possibility, a game where you broke into people's minds not their homes, and shattered cherished, undue privacy that way.

He put on no lights yet but could see more clearly now that he had been right and the kitchen was a wreck. As well as the utensils and smashed crockery, a lot of loose tea, cornflakes and the contents of a cutlery drawer littered the floor. The sink was full of broken crockery, too, as if the cupboard above it had been simply cleared with a few sweeps of the hand. Another cupboard had obviously been sharply tilted forward for a moment so that everything in it fell out and lay on the tiles; an old pair of scales, baking tins, earthenware casserole dishes and jars. It was prob-ably crazy to try to read the message of this shambles but he still felt it looked more like a search than simple vandalism. No aerosol trog-speak defaced the walls, and he could not smell or see urine, or worse. He thought these cupboards had been cleared not just for the sake of destruction but to reveal what might have been hidden in them behind the routine items. The tea had been tipped out of a tin in case it covered something, and the cereal box emptied for the same reason.

He went along the little corridor to the living-room. This, too, had been thoroughly knocked about, or so he thought at first. Then he suddenly realised that, in fact, the damage was confined almost exactly to about one half of the room, the half nearer him. The far side seemed to have escaped. Had the searcher suddenly despaired of finding whatever it was? Or had he been interrupted?

The furniture was all cheap and modern and must have been bought bit by bit, maybe from a junk shop doing reclaimed hire-purchase stuff, with no attempt at matching. All Harpur had learned so far about the occupant of this house was that he did not have much taste, and that he liked tea and could cook a bit. Perhaps his clothes took all the real money. Drawers from a foul, high-gloss sideboard had been turned out on the worn, would-be scarlet carpet. There were cassettes, holiday brochures, bills, a miniature rum, out-of-date raffle tickets. What struck Harpur as especially strange was that on the other side of the room stood a bureau, as shoddy and unhandsome as the sideboard, but clearly left alone during the search. Perhaps it was empty. He crossed the room and opened a drawer. No, it seemed stuffed with newspapers and telephone directories. He opened another drawer. That had clothes in – shirts, ties, a silk white scarf. He stood near the bureau, looking back across the room, trying to work out why there had been no interest in the bureau. There was a sort of frontier roughly in the middle of the faded carpet; one side, chaos, this side, neatness, like hell and heaven, and the great gulf fixed between, which he used to hear about from preachers as a terrified child. A small table with the telephone on it seemed to mark the divide and, after a moment gazing at the room, Harpur stepped to this table and examined the instrument. It was one of those white, plastic, console jobs with a memory device for your half-dozen most used numbers; press one of the six buttons and it automatically dialled pre-set digits. Five of the buttons had small stickers against them, with names on. He saw 'Benny' and 'Ma' and 'Mandy' for the top three and two sets of initials lower down the panel that meant nothing to him. It was the fourth button that had no sticker at all.

He listened carefully again for any sound in the house or outside and then pressed the unlabelled button. In a moment he heard the number ring out and, after another moment, a deep, cautious male voice answered, 'Yes?'

'Ah, Jack,' Harpur said.

'Who is it?' Lamb replied.

'Last time you had a call from this phone it was heavy breathing.'

After a long pause, Lamb said: 'Colin?'

'I'm afraid they've got your number, Jack.'

'You're at Justin Paynter's place?'

'It'll never get into *Ideal Home*, Jack, you made an error.'

'What error?'

49

'Well, to start with basics, using young Justin. That boy's got no idea of security. Your number's only a push button away from anyone who walks in here. He did have the sense not to write your name down, but that's his limit.'

There was another pause.

'Jack, you understand? They don't have to beat anything out of him, supposing he's alive. It's on an electronic plate.'

'Tell me slowly.'

'The other error; ringing him, probably. Looks as if they were searching here when that happened. Your call must have taken them to the phone, brought it to their attention, so when you'd rung off, one of them decided to try its memory bank of numbers. Yours was the only promising one, Jack. That's what I mean about this lad's mad carelessness. They wouldn't be interested in the other five because they'd probably recognise the names and initials – Benny Loxton, Justin's mother, his bird, that sort of thing. So, you get an immediate return call, and the same witty silence.'

'Jesus.'

'They didn't bother searching any more. This room's in two sections, like an ad for "before and after our cleaning service". Obviously they were looking for anything that might tell them who exactly Justin leaked to. Could mean they'd failed to batter it out of him up till then, or perhaps he died too soon. Anyway, there it was, all nicely automated for them. Did you say your name at any stage during these calls?'

'You're joking.'

'But there'll be a simple way of finding which number is dialled by the button. Then, a few tenners to some telephone operator and they can work from a number to a name and address.'

'Yes, I wouldn't be surprised.'

Harpur became silent again for a moment, listening. 'Jack, I don't want to be hanging about here too long. They might have someone watching. Tell me, have you got an emergency exit drill? Somewhere nice and distant, preferably abroad, where you can hole up for a little while, say three or four years?'

Lamb had sounded very edgy earlier. Now, though, his traditional cockiness suddenly rolled back, as it always did when Harpur showed worry about him, a full quota of foolhardy, charmed-life defiance. 'You know, Col, this isn't the first time you've asked me that.'

'Might be the last, Jack, if you don't use it now. These folk are obsessed about secrecy, aren't they? It's clear something enormous is hatching. Anyone endangering it is liable to – '

'We've had these scares so often. And abroad? How do I run my little show from abroad? It might not seem much to you, but it's all I have and it's all mine and it's taken a lot of devoted building over the years.'

'Jack – '

'Don't fret. Think about that pill box, Col. Think about Britishness. How would it have been if this dear old country had panicked in 1940?'

'Jack – I wasn't going to say this, you'll turn sour, but we've had other whispers that something pretty massive is on the cards.'

'Whispers from where?'

To suggest to Lamb that he was not the only one supplying useful information always confused and enraged him. 'Where the hell from, these whispers?' he insisted.

'I can't say now. Iles had some intimations. We've been sweating over them at his house, as a matter of fact. Trying to make some sense out of very little – hints and rumours.'

'Intimations? What sort of ponce word is that, for God's sake? Does it mean anything?'

'Not much at present, as I say. We're trying to puzzle our way through. Iles is worried, and he's not a worrier. Possibly some kind of gang battle building up?'

'You're inventing this lot, aren't you, Col? All the mystery language, "intimations", "on the cards", "hints" – you want to scare me, yes?' Jack must be troubled, or he would never have allowed a telephone conversation to continue this long.

'It's vague, but something's going on, Jack. We're certain. You could be in the middle.'

'But of what?'

'Who knows? This is only an antennae reaction, so far. Christ, you understand that sort of thing – a feel that trouble's around, before you have the facts.'

Lamb did not answer for a while. Then he muttered; 'OK, Col. Yes, I know what you mean and I'm going to believe you're not just teasing. You could be right about taking cover, and I'll think it over.'

'Not for too long.'

'Helen might not want to go.' Again he began to sound assertive and sure. 'She's very fond of this property, you know. Says it cossets her personality. Cossets is the word she uses. Nice? The rooms are large and with helpful, springy board floors, so she can practise her entrechats and so on.'

'Persuasion, Jack. Tell her it's your skin, and there's so much of it to be disarranged.'

'And how do you function as the golden boy detective if I'm not here to feed you?

Now it was Harpur who did not answer.

'Floored you, Col?'

4

'Everything we're getting now, Benny – information. I mean about wiping out Leo Tacette and both his bloody sons – everything confirms what we had at the beginning. It's beautiful,' Macey said. 'What we're seeing is just a grand testament to your careful planning. We all believe, unanimous, that what you deserve, Benny, is congratulations.'

'Congratulations, Benny,' the rest said.

'We're not there yet,' Loxton replied. 'Nowhere near. But it could be shaping, yes.'

'Hear that?' Macey said, chortling. 'Only shaping! What I say again is this shooting party will be beautiful. The only word.'

Loxton, seated in his favourite old bulging and listing armchair, had on full, white-tie evening dress, with a royal blue cummerbund and a yellow carnation in his buttonhole. 'Show me, then, Phil, on the model. We still got that?'

Macey went to his briefcase and brought out a crudely made three-ply representation of what looked like a theatre stage. He stood it on the table. They were in the long, comfortable lounge of Loxton's house on the Loam private estate, almost out into the country.

'Make it quick,' Loxton said. 'Alma's going to be down in a minute, ready for this bloody ball. I don't want her seeing that.'

'Understood, Benny.'

'And don't call me Benny when she's here. I told you, she don't care for it. Just a nickname I picked up in the Navy, being tall. Big Ben, like the clock?'

'And always right,' Macey added.

'Possibly. Anyway, I was christened Theodore.'

'OK, Benny.' Macey now brought from the briefcase three

miniature plastic human figures and carefully arranged them on the wooden stage, in a close group, making sure each was placed correctly. 'That's how we was told original Leo and his sons would be standing, and that's how it still is, Benny, so it's great – the planning's right on the nail. That's important, in view of the fire-point arrangements we had to make. I mean, these three are from a kid's farmyard set, so when I say Leo and Gerald and Lay-waste will be like this, they're not going to be carrying this big whip, or wearing purple riding boots, that's obvious, but these was the best I could get quick.'

'Which is which?' Loxton asked.

'Well, like I said original, the whole thing is going to be run by Gerald, and he'll be here, in the middle, with the microphone.' Macey took a pin from his lapel and stuck it into the model platform between the three figures. 'That microphone is the key to it all. They've got to gather around it in a nice, tight group. So, all of them smack in the rifle sights, extremely neat, extremely open. Gerald will make the main speech from the platform, say what great folks his mother and Leo are, and how it's their silver anniversary, and many of them, the usual heartfelt, family stuff. Gerald can talk. He had education and used to go to the library, it's true, I seen him once myself going in there. But he's only making the speech. The other boy, Anthony – well, Tony, Lay-waste Tony – he's going to do the presentations, one the family's and another from all the friends, what they call friends, the people who run with them, that means. Tony's going to be standing here, behind Gerald while he's making the speech, and the parcels by him on a little table. The present from the family is what's called a censer, made of jade? Very religious. Antique. Oriental, or down that way. It's for burning incense in. Leo and Daphne do much of that? Not that I heard of.'

'The presents don't matter, Phil,' Loxton said.

'No. Well, Gerald says these great things about Leo and Daphne, and all the guests are sitting at the tables clapping and saying 'Hear, hear", and "Give us a song", a seven-course din-ner, pheasant, none of your bubble-stuffed frozen turkey, Leo's paying. But, all right, Benny, that don't matter, either.'

'Alma will be here any time, Phil, that's all.'

'Right. So, Gerald turns for the big moment of the night, and he calls his dad and mum to come on to the stage for the gifts. Then they climb a couple of steps here, look, and they're on the stage, and they walk a few paces till they're near Lay-waste to take the gifts and say something very elevating and reminiscent into the mike about being married twenty-five years.' Macey put a finger on the head of the pin. 'That's why they'll be so close together, like offering theirselves deliberate as targets. It's handsome, inspired. I don't know if Lay-waste ever give anything away in his life before, so maybe he been having training special. He's great on hold-ups and grabbing, and going wild with a handgun, but this got to be geniality. So the four of them, the whole poison family, in such a very neat cluster around Lay-waste, that's Leo, Gerald, Anthony.' Now, he touched each of the farmyard personnel. 'No bodyguards on the stage, just the four of them. Bodyguards would look total bad form, an unforgivable reflection, this being a family affair, family and staff, all trusted. Would Leo show he can't even rely on his own people? No. He've got to be relaxed, you understand, none of the usual muscleshield or he's giving foul offence. They're on a plate.'

'One missing?' Loxton pointed at the toy people.

Macey went over the identifications again; 'Leo with the whip; then, the purple riding boots, Lay-waste; and the one nursing the piglets, Gerald. I haven't got Daphne because we're not interested in her, are we, Benny? The men are the firm. She's spare. Pity she has to be there at all, really, we don't have no quarrel with Daphne, but in silver weddings, you see, Benny, the wife always turns up. It's marriage, isn't it – they're part of it, too? Of course, she could get hit, I can't say different. This is what upset Justin, the idea to kill a woman, and made him act so stupid, trying to leak. There's going to be a lot of bullets, that's bound to be, if we're trying to knock down decisive three people at once, and shooting from a distance.'

Macey pushed over the three farm workers slowly and one at a time and left them lying on the stage. 'We have to take them right out, obvious. Injuries could be all right, if we knew for sure it meant wheelchairs for the rest of their time, or cabbaging their brains, so they're never going to be able to do more evil against us for their firm, but you can't tell with wounds. Doctors have come on such a lot since they let Lord Nelson slip away like that. Our boys won't have time to worry about Daphne, no denying it. They've got to put a real, Quality Street fusillade in there, something irresistible. But that don't give Justin excuse for wanting to grass. It's a pity, but we had to sort him out, no choice.'

'Too right,' Loxton said. 'I'm sad about it, though.' He gazed at the deep green William Morris wallpaper and shook his head slowly in regret.

'Yes, I know, Benny. Well, one of your lads, isn't it?' Macey replied. 'You worry about all of us.'

'That boy, he had such gifts.'

'Sure. But it's done now. Look on the bright side, Benny. Think of this evening, God, but you're going to be the belle of this ball in that gear. What I'd say you resemble is His Excellency some-where, one of them colonies, in the old days, yes, His Britannic Excellency waiting for his rickshaw to take him to the club, but staying so cool even in the cuff-links and waistcoat, and all the maddening heat. Your missus is right. Benny wouldn't do for what you look like tonight. It got to be Theodore, Benny. You need a name with dimensions.'

'Must put on a show. They'll all be there. Mayors and big business, MPs, swagger-stick cops and medieval pussy from the Women's Voluntary Charity is a big call, gets everybody dressing up. Quite right, too. This is what's known as a good cause. I'm definitely in favour.'

'What charity, Benny?' Macey asked.

'What?'

'What charity ball specific you going to?'

'You know, one of them charities – collecting to save some-thing, £60 a double ticket, before the rip-off booze and parking. Me and Alma went last year. She gets very concerned about . . . what's it called? – them needy, yes, that's it, them needy. Or could be whales. Well, a whale got feelings, quite probable. I'm very happy to help. I don't mind turning out in these tiddly clothes, and the smiling at everybody and bent raffles, as long as no chamber of trade jerk turns witty and aloof, you know, smart arse, snide remarks about my business interests, where the money comes from, all that, like they was so spotless, all looking after each other, turning blind eyes. Historians will tell you three-quarters of the House of Lords was bandits or pimps a couple of centuries ago. Only time have given them the nice accents and prize rhododendrons in their grounds. But it upsets

Alma if these pricks get uncivil, I can tell you. Is that humane, to load rough pain on to someone as sensitive as Alma?'

'Diabolical. But you can handle it, I know, Benny. What you give them is that gentle but biting repartee? It seems gentle but when they have a think really it's biting. Everybody says these sort feel that more than smashing their nose with a head-butt. Known as sophisticated.'

'Maybe, maybe,' Loxton replied. 'Tell me about our boys handling the operation.'

'This model's no good for showing it, obvious, Benny, but here you got a long window, high up near the ceiling of the hall, above the little stage,' Macey pointed. 'Our boys are in an eight-floor office corridor next door, higher, looking right down on to that window and the stage. They'll be firing through two lots of glass, but no trouble. Couldn't be better. It's going to be night, so nobody in the office building except an occasional bit of sketchy security. We can handle that, I mean, handle it in a subtle way, we don't want no tangle with security. We don't want any tangle at all, because this is a maximum precision job and the boys will need quiet. The darkness is all right, because the targets will be fully illuminated on that stage, like a spotlight.'

'Bobby and Norman,' Benny said.

The two men nodded.

'Well, you know there's not many people better with a rifle and telescopics,' Macey declared.

'Nobody,' Loxton agreed.

'That's why we brought in Bobby Lentle, obvious. They both say it can be done and they can handle it and get out afterwards. It's going to be a lot neater than Lee Harvey Oswald.' Macey signalled to the two men, inviting them to speak, and went to sit on a low-backed settee while they took over. He was about thirty, big-jawed and powerfully made, with remarkably deep-set eyes that gave him a look of hair-trigger menace. Loxton valued Macey, but had learned to keep him in the background except during bad crises, because he upset people. Of course, there were times when people needed to be upset, or more than that, like Leo and his boys, and then Macey earned his keep. His dark hair was always very well done – skilfully cut and obviously clean – and he spent a packet on clothes, good clothes in fashion, not bin ends, fine suits and such, but he still looked what he was, someone who had shoved his way up from street fighting and chick-enshit villainy to ... Well, to Loxton's prime operations. Somewhere during that career Macey had lost all his front teeth and received a set of false ones that fitted all right but which shone too white and were too even, except for an old Hollywood glamour boy movie, say some pretty moustache like Douglas Fairbanks Junior. Loxton found the teeth a bit of a laugh, but not a laugh he let Macey see.

'Yes, it's on,' Bobby told them. 'We had a dry run. The sighting's perfect.'

'All three? You can do all three?' Loxton said.

Macey stood again and replied for them. 'The weapons they got, they'll be putting God knows how many shells into that little circle in only a couple of seconds. How many is it?'

Norman said: 'We'll be using – '

'I don't want to know,' Benny told him. 'None of the technicalities. If you say it's all right, it's all right. All I got to say is this is going to be the only chance ever of getting the three of them unchaperoned and together. Look, it got to work, got to.'

'We can't get close to even one of them usually,' Macey said. 'Lay-waste's car, it's like Reagan's for protection, you ask me. And anyone geting close that he don't like the look of, Lay-waste's liable to start blasting away like D-Day. But three together, and no retaliation – it's beautiful, no other word.'

'So maybe four,' Loxton said. 'Three, plus one. That's a grief, too, you're right, Phil, but to get them three, I got to be willing to make sacrifices, no way out of that. Daphne, she's not a bad old piece, but she've had a very nice and comfortable run, fat of the land for years, and the thing is, she's one of them, nobody can get away from that.'

'Leo didn't have enough venom on his own to produce them two sons,' Macey said. 'Not even Leo. She helped. She's more than just a pretty old face.'

Loxton spoke sadly: 'Justin – I don't understand why he had to go extreme and consider talking like that. He didn't even know Daphne. A fact, didn't know her at all. Me, I know her, known her for years. Daphne, me, Leo all at Marl View school the same time, not friends, but the same time. Leo always said he never touched her until they was properly married. Well, it's possible. Things was different then, even for someone like Leo. Lived close, the three of us. Great old teacher at the school, Miss Binns, who did a lot for us, tried to keep me and Leo straight, really stuck her neck out. Lovely old duck, really. I still send her a Christmas card with something inside. It didn't work too good, what she tried for Leo and me, things went a bit adrift, what with taking and driving away and the fighting, but she never gave up. Nice. Anyway, that's how far back it goes, so I know Daphne real good and none of us wants her to get any damage, of course not, but she could be slap in the way for them couple of seconds, that's the truth of it.'

'I like that about the teacher, that's real genuine, Benny, and heartfelt, on the side of education, which got to be good, but, like you said, Benny, the truth can be tough,' Macey replied, 'and Daphne could catch one, yes.'

'The thing about Leo, he's the only opposition left. It used to be different when Tenderness Mellick was operating, and Wrighty, and You-know-who. Well, it was what you'd call a community, a working community, a business community, say like the City of London or Hatton Garden and jewellers.'

'Right,' Macey said.

'Them days, things could be spread out, and people kept to their own corner,' Loxton went on. 'There wasn't none of this eyeball to eyeball, because we were all too busy not just watching one another, but two or three or more. Then along comes this thinker, Harpur, and The One Above, Desmond Iles, him with the horns, and suddenly people are disappearing, and now it's just the two of us, Leo and me, and it's a question, who gets the power, who's in control – like after World War Three, only Russia and the States left. One got to see the other off, and the one who goes first and best takes everything.'

'Polarities,' Norman said. He pulled a folded copy of the *Daily Telegraph* from his pocket. 'Did you see this interview with Ronnie Kray, the old London operator, inside now, Benny? He says he had thirty years for killing a couple of villains,' Norman began to read from the paper: "We had to kill them or they would have killed us, I don't think we were evil. There is nothing evil about protecting your own life. It was the same as being a soldier in the war." That's the sort of thinking, isn't it, Benny?'

Loxton did not greatly enjoy the comparison with a Kray, especially the one in a loony jail, but Norman had a point. 'There used to be room for four or five of us operating on this patch. Now there's not even room for two, only one. What numbers can do to you. If I don't finish him, he'll finish me, no question.'

'Pre-emptive,' Norman said, re-folding the paper.

'Most likely,' Loxton replied. 'Leo's had a try. Well, you know – a try at me twice, one very near.'

'Only luck you're still with us, Benny,' Macey told him. 'Leo been difficult, no argument.'

'With dum-dum bullets. I mean, is that civilised?' Loxton asked. 'Them hit you, hole as big as a frisby and more colourful. Can I go on risking something like that? And him so sweet-talking and worried after, saying he heard about the "dastardly attack" – that's his words, "dastardly" – and wanted to offer sympathy. Oh, sure Leo's older now, but that don't make him no kinder. He knows how to run his firm and how to give the orders. Somebody went out and bought them dum-dums, and somebody wrote out the shopping list. And who named the target? That what they call the fucking old school tie? So, it's just like Mrs Thatcher says, the market place – only the sharp ones survive, simple as that. Yes.' He nodded a couple of times, thoughtfully.

'Leo wouldn't be weighing up the rights and wrongs the way you are, Benny, if he had a real chance to finish us,' Macey told him.

'Leo Tacette and his missus going to be at this occasion to-night?' Bobby asked.

'Leo, charity? You crazy?' Loxton replied. 'Leo worries about the whale? I'm telling you he probably never spent even five seconds all his life considering whales, or even the needy. Anyway, who'd let him into a class affair like this? Leo in a penguin suit? You ever seen his collars at all? I seen cleaner coalmen. Leo would be like a fish out of water, a whale out of water.'

Macey laughed first, then the rest quickly afterwards.

'A whale out of water in a penguin suit,' Bobby said. 'Deep-sea fancy dress.' He was solid, going plump, his fair hair cut very short, fresh-faced and clean-shaven, around thirty-five.

Loxton said: 'It would be pitiful to put Leo into a decent social do, cruel to him, and Daphne. Socially, Leo don't even get started, and Daphne less, scratching her arse in public. The only one from our line who might have got there beside me was

Tenderness Mellick, he was really working hard on the mixing, and inviting non-rough elements and even genuine titles and OBEs for amontillado shery and *vol-au-bits* to his big, smart, debt-heavy house up the Enclave, and so on. But this time he can't get away from Gartree, I understand, nor for about twelve years after, even with remission.'

'That's friend Harpur, also,' Macey said.

'He knows too much, thinks too much. Always have,' Loxton agreed. 'But, listen, I didn't want it to get to this situation, having to see off a local boy like Leo, or even blot his sons. And then, losing a good kid like Justin, what seemed a good kid, anyway. I mean he was no age at all, and he knew about numbers, very good.'

'There'll be others, Benny,' Macey said. 'Others, maybe not so leaky.'

'He was talking to Lamb? We know that? I mean, know it.'

'Well, no, not hundred per cent sure,' Macey replied. 'What we know is he used to call him. Like I said, Norman found the number at Justin's place when he had a bit of a look and turn-over up at his place, and traced it to Lamb.'

'No problem,' Norman said.

'You spoke to him?'

'I rang him, but no talk. Speaking didn't seem a good idea, Benny, not at the time.' Norman was about forty, thin, lined, with receding grey hair and rimless classes. He spoke quietly and looked like someone arguing out a tricky point about gays or lady vicars at a serious, top church meeting.

'No, you could be right,' Loxton said. 'That means we don't know whether he've told him about the silver wedding arrangements, nor how many leaks he give Lamb in the past.'

'Well, we aren't certain whether he leaked to him at all, Benny,' Norman replied. 'We gave Justin a lot of very heavy pressure but he wouldn't say why he had Lamb's number. Or, he did say, but what he said was that Lamb was just a mate. It could be. Yes, just about could, although we think Lamb does some big grassing, maybe to Harpur. As a matter of fact, we were seriously asking Justin about Lamb when he broke away, and we never had another chance to work on him because he went under fast after the knife.'

61

'The uncertainty is just another of them risks we got to live with, Benny,' Macey said.

'We can blow all the buggers' heads into hundreds and thousands as long as we got it right and they group at that mike,' Bobby said.

'Certain,' Macey told him. 'Our information – '

'So Mrs Iles, and her stud? I worry about her being at the Monty.' Loxton said. 'Where are we with that? She talk to hubby and we're into difficulty. Police might go poking about at the Monty and maybe find it was Justin. That leads to us. Even if they couldn't prove anything, we'd get limelight, they'd watch us continuous, and no chance at all of giving full attention to the silver wedding. I don't want to miss that, we mustn't miss it.'

'We won't. Don't you fret, Benny,' Macey said.

'Yes, I fret. All right, Mrs Iles is making it with someone else, the most recent someone else, but that don't stop her having conversations now and then with her husband. We certain it was her?'

'It was her,' Macey replied. 'We don't think she talks, not about that, Benny. We don't see how she could. What's she doing in a flop-house like the Monty so late? Who she with? Well, we know who she was with, but does the Assistant Chief? I don't think so. And Panicking Ralphy don't think so. Like you said I asked him to go and say a word or two or two million to Mrs Iles and he tells me it's fine, so confidential. Look, I'd worry myself, otherwise. She saw me there, didn't she, and the other boys. We got no trouble unless Justin comes to light somehow, and that's never going to happen, is it? What they got to go on – no body? They don't even know he's missing. He've moved on, the way people like him do – that's how it looks. He's not walled up in a monastery. All right, his girl's tearful, I suppose, somewhere, but blokes are doing runners every day. Anyway, no bugger can find her. We been looking. Looks like she went to ground as soon as she knew Justin had disappeared.'

'He got a mother, yes?' Loxton asked.

'Wales way. He rings her up once in a blue moon, never sees her. She's not going to be asking questions for a long time yet.'

Loxton still felt uneasy. 'Then, the other things; we sure Justin didn't talk to this Mrs Iles, say something?' he asked.

'Pretty sure,' Macey aid. 'He calls for a drink, and that's about all. This is someone with two knife wounds and he was very poorly, Benny. Would he chat about all that with someone he don't know? And Ralphy's watching and listening, and he don't think no conversation, except the drink.'

'Christ, what else Ralph going to say? He wants this whole thing forgot, like it never happened.'

'He seemed genuine,' Macey said.

'Panicking Ralphy?'

'I mean genuine for somebody like him,' Macey said. 'He would see he's taking a bit risk if he give me bullshit, Benny.'

'If that woman heard something from Justin, she might have a feeling she got to tell her husband, regardless,' Loxton told them.

'We don't think so, Benny. Ralph made things very plain to her and Mrs Iles isn't curious about all that any longer. Ralph knows it got to be watertight or his time's come. He's using his influence, bringing first-class leverage to bear. He don't have no idea about what job we got in mind, but he knows it's something major and grave, our one and only chance, and that we won't take a mess-up on no account, Mrs Iles or anything else. Ralphy talks a lot and a lot of it is big and strong, but he knows it would all stop very sudden if marauders happened to take out his voice box one evening.'

Loxton said: 'And then this piece of consolation Mrs Iles was with at the Monty, Ian Aston? He saw as much as she did, maybe heard something and went out digging around in the builder's skip, yes? So he could have some angle. Suppose he hears from Justin it's a silver wedding, say just those words, he can sniff around and find out it's Leo and Daphne's do and he got something very tidy to sell, yes? He's into that sort of trading, as I hear. Then Leo and the boys put up a bigger security job than the Queen in Armagh.'

'Yes, we'd like to talk to Aston,' Macey replied. 'Well, didn't he see us as well at the Monty? So we been looking, real looking, but he's gone out of sight. Not at his place since that night.'

'That's serious,' Loxton said. 'Gone where? Who the hell's he talking to? Why was they both so damn nosy and interested?' He stopped himself shouting.

'We have Ralph asking around, and off and on we're watching Sarah Iles, in case she leads to him,' Norman told Loxton. 'Our feeling is, he's not going to spill anything because it might bring bother for Sarah Iles. They both need secrecy. We can count on it, Benny.'

'Well, I might pick up a whisper or two at this thing tonight, who knows?' Loxton said. 'Mrs Iles will be there, probably. Others. Maybe Lamb, that bastard, I'll keep an eye and an ear. You going to be at your place, Phil, in case I need to get in touch?'

'Sure, Benny. Look, sometimes I wonder is there a tap on my line – clicks and crazy noises.'

'We all get them, Phil. Maybe yes, maybe no. So, we going to complain to the MP or them Civil Liberties? I wouldn't think so. Just talk very guarded, as ever.'

'Yes, talk guarded. No names, Benny.'

'Am I senile?' Loxton replied. 'Names, for fuck's sake. Names is for postmen. Who's going to be looking after me and Alma at the ball?'

'Me,' Norman said.

'Good. You won't be able to come right in, obvious, but stay as close as you can. Things are getting, well, pretty warm, I'd say. Very warm.'

'Of course, Benny.'

'Don't be edgy about Ian Aston,' Macey told Loxton. 'He'll show, and when he does – ' He stopped as Mrs Loxton entered the room, smiling modestly. She had on a low-necked turquoise silk evening gown, a double string of small pearls in a loose necklace gleaming against her tanned skin. Loxton stood, Macey picked up the model stage and the farm staff and passed them quickly to Bobby Lentle, to put back in the case.

'Well, I must say you're a real team,' Macey declared to Alma Loxton. 'This is going to bowl them over, the two of you together. Theodore was telling us about the gown, Alma, but not even Theodore could do it and you justice in mere words.'

'I give you thanks, Philip Macey,' Alma Loxton replied, in a fine, rounded voice. 'Theodore, we should go,' she said. 'It's only politeness to arrive on time, especially at a charity function. So much effort and work has gone unstintingly and unpaid into the organisation.'

Loxton smoothed down his grand suit. 'I hope there's going to be some top of the charts dancing, not that whiskery ballroom muck again.'

'Oh, so much more elegant,' his wife replied, 'a link with the best of the past, don't you think, Bobby, Phil?'

'It was another era,' Macey replied. 'A time of manners and charm.'

'Lost,' she sighed.

'Now, don't be soulful, Alma,' Loxton said. 'It's going to be a great night.'

He meant it. Despite the kind of rough, snobby moments that he had spoken about to Macey, Loxton loved these big, dress-up social functions. Wasn't he there by right? He had the clothes and the funds to fork out into the begging bowls, and nobody could tell him different.

Oh, yes, a few big-mouths and stirrers might turn up, but generally people were very nice, very friendly. They did not want to dig into your life or your past, and they calculated that if you rated for an invitation you must be wholesome, or as near as anybody successful in business could be. That made Alma happy, and he liked to see her talking and laughing with decent, general company, people who thought protection was what you got from an insurance policy. His wife craved respectability, the way some women craved love or éclairs, and she needed a change now and then from Phil and Norman and the rest, though they were all good boys, as good in their style as anyone here tonight. Sometimes he found it a bit of a laugh, and a bit touching, too, the way Alma longed for acceptance and worked so desperately at it. But he had finally decided, more than a couple of years ago now, that he was stuck with her, so he tried hard to treat her right. She could have been worse.

For the night, even the high-rank police who attended these charity affairs kept quiet about what they knew, or what they half knew, or what they thought they knew, and made no trouble. They came dressed up and hearty, smiling as bright as anyone, and more. In any case, there was a very soothing and very legal gap between what police knew and what they could prove. There was information and there was evidence and, if you had a tidy lawyer, the two never met.

At these affairs, Loxton let it ride if anyone tried provocation, let it ride for now. These social gatherings were to raise money for good works, so who was going to start a rough-house, for God's sake? The greatest of these is charity was what the Bible said, and you had to act according. He did not even do what Phil had suggested, and wipe them out with words. Instead, he just turned away, gave them the full freeze. That was his answer, also like in the Bible – pass by on the other side.

Quite early on at the ball this evening, when he and Alma went for a drink at the bar, Loxton found they were standing close to Jack Lamb and the grinning punk kid, Helen, he lived with these days in that sweet old manor house out near Chase Woods, like a big, crooked, know-all squire. Loxton hated and feared contact with Lamb, always sensing he knew too much about everybody and everything, and still wanted to know more. A talk with him was like an interrogation, except he was cleverer at it than most of the professionals. You had to be on the watch continuous. You never knew what you was giving him. Loxton wanted to leave the bar as soon as he spotted Lamb, but Alma was enjoying herself talking lifeboat collections to a doddery old couple, so he was forced to stay.

There had to be somebody looking after Lamb, maybe Harpur himself. That was the rumour. So, the thing about Jack was you didn't know who you were really talking to when you talked to him. Who was standing behind? And now the bugger might have been getting whispers from Justin Paynter. This was what could definitely be called a sensitive subject. Lamb might be wanting to do some digging on the topic tonight, and drag the whole evening down with business and hinting. That Loxton could do without.

Jack's protector was bound to be a lawman with real power, or he would have gone away for years a long time ago. Instead of that, he put on the style out in this great piece of property and traded paintings worth millions. The manor house had a tall, grey stone wall right around the place and gates with a red and gold coat of arms on them belonging to someone there centuries ago, and over the top of it a Latin motto meaning, In God I trust and we do fucking great together. Or close.

Sod it; Lamb and the girl left some people they had been talking to and came eagerly to greet Loxton and his wife. 'Alma, such a treat,' he said, bending to kiss her on the cheek. 'Theodore, you're looking grand. Do you both know Helen? An art buff and all-round gifted collaborator of mine.'

Loxton had heard that good pictures came and went on the

walls of Lamb's place faster than storm clouds across the moon, proper masterpieces, not painting-by-numbers jobs. Where it came from and where it went nobody except Jack could say, and he didn't. It might be a Picasso with your breakfast, and Kevin Rembrandt by supper time. Jack Lamb said he liked change. Loxton reckoned he liked notes much better, especially fifties in bulk and, if possible, new and hard to trace.

'We always try to get to this occasion, Jack,' Alma gurgled. 'Invariably, such a happy turn-out, and so deeply worthwhile. The best of all worlds, one might say.'

'Exactly.'

'One feels one's self to be among friends,' Alma said, 'all linked year after year by the Christian impulse to help others.'

'Indeed,' Lamb said.

Loxton would say one thing for him – as Alma dished out this horseshit he kept his face dead straight. But perhaps Lamb was not listening much, just watching her, because she could get real excited when talking good works, and her face would light up, making her look lovely again, and so full of life. Although most of what she said at these times embarrassed and bored Loxton inside out, a part of him was forced to admire her. His wife had a real go at things, held nothing back, even if it was almost total balls. He knew then what he used to see in her years ago – the enthusiasm and guts, and the beauty. All right, it was hard to keep going on memories, but didn't all marriages that lasted?

'Are you in art, that sort of line?' Helen asked Loxton.

'Not altogether,' he replied.

'Theodore has various business interests,' Lamb said.

'Fascinating,' the girl cried. 'Such as, Theodore?'

'One thing and the other,' Loxton said, moving a hand about gently in the air to signify.

'Long-established concern and a devoted staff, I know that,' Lamb said. 'Very gifted people, many of them. Philip Macey, Norman, Tommy Vit, sometimes. These people are experts in their fields.'

'Oh, yes,' Loxton replied. He began to feel uneasy.

'Which fields?' the girl asked.

'Absolute experts,' Lamb replied.

'We're so lucky in that respect,' Alma said. 'Contented personnel.'

'No business can thrive without,' Lamb went on.

'Certainly not,' Alma said.

'And are they all in good shape, your people, I wonder?' Lamb asked.

Loxton was not keen on the question, or where it might be leading. 'In good shape? Great. Why not?'

'Oh, Theodore, so brusque. It's very nice of you to inquire, Mr Lamb, Jack,' Alma said. 'Yes, fine. People stay with Theodore. Very little change-over.'

'That's crucial,' Lamb remarked.

'Occasionally a youngster leaves, but the old hands are so wonderfully loyal,' Alma said.

'Yes?' Lamb replied.

Loxton watched him grow alert.

'Restless youth,' Alma said. 'You'll understand.'

'Of course,' Lamb replied. 'Helen, here, was a real nomad. Who's gone from you lately, then, Alma?'

The bugger was no-naming but meant Justin Paynter, for sure, so obvious it became pathetic. And yet Lamb most likely thought he was winning every prize for subtlety. Did he realise how much he might be giving away about himself? The link between them two, Jack Lamb and Justin, really did exist, then? 'Gone?' Loxton said. 'How do you mean,.Jack?'

'Left, as Alma mentioned.'

'Oh, Alma was just talking general, you know. Nobody particular.'

Alma Loxton said: 'But Theodore, I – '

'Yes, she was just talking general,' Loxton declared. 'Ah.' He held up a hand as the band began 'Stardust'. 'Alma knows this is one of my favourites.' He smiled his apologies to Helen and Lamb for breaking up the conversation and immediately walked Alma to the dance floor.

'Are you crazy?' she said.

'It's a waltz.'

'You hate them.'

'That's all right.'

'Why did you leave like that? So rude,' she asked angrily.

'He was fishing, love. I dislike it.'

'I don't understand,' she said.

'About the staff.'

'Jack Lamb, interested in your boys? Why, Theodore? It's not reasonable.'

'Some people trade in information.'

'For heaven's sake, I was only going to tell him – '

'Look, let's leave it, all right?' He found he did not want Justin Paynter's name used, and, simply because it had come into his head, he was conscious of his hand tightening in a fierce spasm on Alma's shoulder. He had not intended that, but it happened. Justin was in the past and he had to stay there, safely forgotten, almost.

She winced and frowned. 'What's wrong?'

'Nothing, love. I'm sorry. Just I don't want any talk about people of mine to someone like Jack Lamb, and that crazy, money-grubbing kid. That's all.'

'Oh, but you're hard on the girl, I think. One should take as one finds, Theodore, surely.'

It really was a charity do tonight. 'Perhaps you're right,' he said. 'Lamb does.'

Desmond Iles and a woman Loxton assumed was his wife danced near them and the Assistant Chief gave him and Alma a lavish smile and mouthed a greeting: 'Wonderful to see you both again.' The woman was slim, blonde, very unhappy-looking, and wearing what looked to Loxton like an exclusive powder blue dress, almost as fine as Alma's. She held Iles as if she wished like hell he was someone different. That figured. Following Iles's gaze, her eyes rested for a second on Loxton and Alma and she gave a tiny smile and a formal nod, though Loxton did not remember ever seeing her before. Then she turned her head away and gazed about at the other dancers.

Loxton and his wife waltzed for a while without talking. Christ, this cruddy music, these ponce steps. He felt like he had aged twenty years since coming on to the floor.

Alma watched him. 'Theodore, there certainly is something wrong. Darling please. You ought to say. I should know about matters that trouble you. It will make you feel better.'

Not exactly. It would make him feel worse, and very exposed. 'I'm fine.' Usually, he liked the way she stuck at things, but now she began to weary him, and to anger him. Why the hell did he bring her to places where she might gab in her friendly, goofy, careless style to the wrong people? She did not know much, of course, as far as he could tell: he always tried to make sure of that, but you could never be certain what might get through to her. Alma was not stupid.

Later in the evening, she went off into a side room to see the raffle drawn with some neighbours they had met at the buffet. Loxton had a saunter alone around the city hall's wide landing and staircases, looking at the coats of arms and the heavy-framed paintings of people who had achieved big things for the area in history. He liked feeling a contact with these old figures in their robes or military uniforms. God knew what some of them might have done to get to the top and stay there long enough to earn a painting. Several with red and blue wino faces and sharp chins looked like they would have strangled their favourite labrador or mother to make it.

One day, when all the opposition was out of the way, such as Leo and Lay-waste and the other son, Loxton might be able to take a rest from the terrible, constant battling in business and become a real part of the decent local leadership, like these boys in the portraits, and like some of the boys with the letters after their names or the titles in front, dancing with their women here tonight. It would be more than just shelling out for charity dances, and bidding in twenties for rubbish at Save the Children auctions. He wanted to create something – say help finance an important public building such as a library or a gallery or a youth centre, a place designed by a good architect, solid and handsome and full of education, if possible. He was less frantic for acceptance than Alma, because he knew there had to be a lot more very rough fighting and earning yet, and Leo had to be pushed right under and held there till the bubbles stopped. But he did want acceptance to come one day.

On the ground floor, wearing a stone mortar board and with a very fat stone open book on his lap, was the seated, stone figure of the man who had been the first chief of the university up the road, and Loxton went down to look at him once more. The figure always fascinated him. Perhaps he was supposed to be reading the book aloud, and his mouth had been done half-open, so you could even see his stone teeth and stone tongue. That must really be something, to be carved to last by a sculptor who knew his trade. In them days it probably meant you had truly made it if you said you was going to get stoned.

As he gazed at this heavyweight old scholar, Loxton heard what he thought for a moment was the muffled scream of a girl, but then decided at once that it was more like a shout of great happiness and relief. He looked around and saw that on the other side of the hall stood a glass-walled telephone box. Inside was the woman he had assumed to be Mrs Iles, with the receiver in her hand. Though he had heard that one noisy yell, he could make out nothing of what she was saying now, but he saw she looked very different from when on the dance floor. Suddenly, Sarah Iles seemed absolutely full of life and joy as she chatted and laughed and listened, and her husband would probably have given a couple of years' pay to make her open up to him like that once in a while. Some hope. Sad, really. As the conversation went on she viewed herself in the telephone box's mirror, and quickly smoothed down some strands of hair with one hand, like she was worried the person at the other end might see her untidy. Part of the skirt of her lovely blue gown was jammed in the door and sticking out, as if she had been in a great hurry to make the call and could not be bothered to free the material. You did not need to be brilliant to guess this was a woman talking to a lover, and a lover who, maybe, she had not been able to see for a time.

Loxton turned his face away in case she glanced towards him and walked up the stairs on the other side, where there were more portraits to look at. Then, after a while, he descended to the hall again and found the telephone free. Quickly, he went in and rang Macey. The air of the box was still heavy and exciting with her scent. 'A bit of a long-shot,' Loxton told him. 'Get up to that lad's place right away, will you?'

'That lad?

'The one we had under discussion recent. The one it been difficult to locate?'

'Oh, *that* lad.'

'I think he might have just had a call from someone pretty fond of him.'

'Ah.'

'Yes. It looks like this person was rushing to make the call at a special time, something arranged, like, so he might be home for an hour or two. Worth a try.'

'Of course. How do you want me to handle it, suppose he's there? What I mean, how serious?'

As he gazed out of the booth at the heavyweight university man and his important book that obviously stood for all learning and so on Loxton considered this: 'Serious. It got to be serious, no question. This lad might have heard some dangerous words the other night, that's the point. He's a liability.'

'Yes, such a liability.'

'That's it. Regrettable he was there, really, but he's in the way, or could be in the way. What I mean, why did he disappear, why's he hiding, if he's not problematical? That's what you got to ask.'

'It's a point.'

'So it's a grave matter, definite. Yes, a grave matter.'

'I understand.'

Iles and his wife were standing with Colin Harpur on the main landing when Loxton returned. 'Benny,' Iles called, 'you look so deserted, forlorn. Don't I know that feeling, though? You need comforting.'

'Alma will be here soon.' Loxton did his best to read from Iles's tone whether he knew anything, but this one was the most two-faced and slippery copper ever, and that title took some winning. 'Have you met Sarah?' Iles asked. 'Sarah, this is Benny Loxton, a real pillar of all our charities. So generous I believe people take advantage of him.'

'You got to do what you can,' he said.

Sarah Iles smiled, briefly again, and shook his hand. Loxton saw that her thoughts were miles away. He wished he knew for certain how many miles, and where exactly.

'Benny, I've been trying to persuade Sarah to put herself forward for the organising committee of this function and similar worthwhile events,' Iles said. 'She needs something to occupy her.'

Yes, he'd heard that, but thought it had been arranged. 'They'd be lucky to get you, Mrs Iles,' Loxton told her.

'Kind,' she replied. 'I'm certainly going to think about it.'

He reckoned that what this meant was that she certainly was *not* going to. Lamb and his girl walked past, on their way to the dance floor, but neither of the police appeared to know him, so maybe that was wrong about him and Harpur. Maybe.

Now, Harpur said: 'Here's Alma, Benny. Looks as if you've cleaned up.'

She was carrying a scarlet teddy bear, half as big as herself, that clashed like hell with the turquoise gown, and a bottle of gin. Alma loved to win and despite her big feelings for charity never gave prizes back to be re-raffled. Yes, she worried about the needy and whales, but there came a limit, so the house was full of crap like this dud bear. Gazing at them and smiling in a way that he probably thought looked so kindly, Iles asked: 'Do you think these two are going off on a private party?'

Loxton and his wife stayed until the end. When they went out to their car, Norman was waiting near. 'All quiet?' Loxton asked.

'No sign of anything at all, Theodore,' he said. 'The police brass just left. A motor-bike cop brought a package for the grey-haired one.'

'Iles. Probably his month's back-handers.'

5

Awaking early, despite their late night at the charity ball, Sarah
Iles felt an immediate rush of joy. Today, she would see Ian.
Generally, it took a while for her mind to get into its stride as she
emerged from sleep, but, this morning, excitement rushed the
change, and she was instantly alert and gloriously happy. Ian
had come back. Thank God she had decided to call him from the
city hall last night. She decided that her life contained no greater
moment of delight than when he answered, and assured her he
was all right. He had been waiting near the telephone and picked
it up at once.

That was not simply luck. Long ago they had hatched an
arrangement for telephoning each other at agreed times if either
had something urgent to say. Mainly, it benefited her, because
Desmond was home at unpredictable hours: she could be ready
to grab the receiver before him, and on an extension. But occasionally, it might be useful for reaching Ian, too: there were
people he badly needed to avoid, and did not always answer his
telephone. The timing told him when it was Sarah.

For days since the Monty incident she had been trying him,
without reply. Somehow, last night at the city hall, she felt
especially desolate without Ian, and the presence of Desmond
and their friends only made it worse: she had company but the
wrong company. At 10.40 p.m., one of their chosen times, she
could not stop herself detouring on her way back from the Ladies
to ring him again. After all those earlier failures, she did not
expect an answer, yet there he was sounding fine. So great and
lovely was the shock that she let out a single, crazy, soaring
whoop of gladness in the telephone box, and when she returned
to Desmond and the others she feared they must see the trans-

74

formation in her. The happiness had been so overwhelming that there was one absurd moment when she felt as if Ian were actually present, and she fussed with her hair in the little mirror, trying to make herself more presentable.

She lay now in bed savouring all the pleasurable surprise of that call, and the sense of huge relief that he was safe and could see her today. Not at the Monty, though, thank you! They had laughed at that notion, joking about what new horrors and complications they might land themselves in if they went back. And, surely, the fact that they could laugh now about it all must be a good sign. Didn't it show that the stress of what had happened there was dropping into the background, was on the way to being forgotten? Thank God for that, too. She had performed her noble, little, pushy bit – her cop-wife duty as she saw it – without result. Let matters rest there. She and Ian had done nobody any damage, discovered nothing that counted, so they could surely be left alone. She dreaded to think she might have put Ian's life in peril, and, for herself, she wanted no more visits from Ralph, or people worse than Ralph. What she did want was the good and contented days and nights with Ian again. At least this crisis had forced her to recognise priorities; nothing much rated against her wish to be with him. When she called last night, Ian said it might not be clever to meet at his place today, so they had settled on a dismal transport café where they ate occasionally, pretty sure it was so drab that they would see nobody they knew there. Maybe it let rooms, too.

Alongside her, Desmond stirred, as if sensing she was awake. Still three-quarters asleep, he turned slowly towards Sarah and put an arm around her waist, drawing himself closer to her. They slept without night clothes and she felt him begin to grow aroused. Muttering irritably, as if he had woken her, she moved away. He grunted in disappointment, but did not pursue her and in a moment turned to face the other direction again. It always made her sad to refuse him, even now, after so many months and so many refusals, but she could not have made love with him this morning. Today belonged to Ian Aston. Not long afterwards she left the bed and quickly dressed.

When Desmond came down to breakfast later he seemed untroubled, so perhaps he had been genuinely asleep and did not recall what had happened. Or he might be ignoring it. At times

75

she thought he deliberately avoided a confrontation, because he feared where it might lead. As ever, he looked pretty good, ready to take the day and bend it any way he wanted: alert, fit, brazen, irrepressible, despite the refusal in bed, youthful, despite the grey hair. Yes, Des was a despite sort of person, she reckoned. He tended to do what he wanted and get what he wanted despite what people might do in efforts to stop him. It was something she used to admire, and still did. Now, though, she admired it less. There was a toughness in him that could sometimes go very close to coldness, harshness.

All the same, she had watched other women in his company and felt sure that many would think themselves lucky to get anywhere near being wanted by him. Occasionally she wished she could still find it a joy, herself. So, why not? Something had died, that was all: no five-act tragedy. It happened in so many marriages, marriages which kept going, regardless. Maybe the absence of children did have something to do with it, but simply as an institution, marriage packed a very big punch. 'A beautiful fellow exists,' she said, working on *The Times* crossword alongside her coffee.

'Yes. Thank you.'

'A clue, berk.'

'Adonis,' he told her. 'The word breaks up into "a don" – slang for a fellow of a university – and "is", meaning exists.'

For some reason, as Desmond explained the answer to her, a recollection of that revered university man in the city hall foyer leapt into her head – existing, but only in stone. Well, no, not just for some reason: she could hardly think of anything today but the delight of making that telephone call and finding Ian at home. She half smiled as she relived the moment now, could almost feel the receiver in her hand again, and the tautness of her dress, caught in the door because of her hurry. When she made that whoop of joy in the booth, had she been half-aware of a man glancing around, comically startled, from near the monument? The vague memory of his shocked face made her smile almost grow into an outright laugh and to conceal it, she bent her head and wrote in Adonis, 'Aren't you the bright one, though, Desmond?'

'Oh, well, yes, but – '

'So why aren't you clever enough to nail people like Benny

Loxton, lording it at the do last night? He's a crook, yes?'

'Of course. On the Nobel prize short-list for extortion and drug dealing, *inter alia*.'

'I suppose in a way it's a giggle to see him decked out like a master of ceremonies, putting on the *gravitas*. In another way it's bloody frightening. Can they do what they like, Des?'

'The world's full of crooks we can't nail, living at the top of the heap, wearing handmade shirts and drinking malt. Just as it's fucking full of blind and intimidated juries and loot-laden, conniving defence lawyers.'

'Are you afraid of him because he's so successful, so well set up socially?'

'Afraid? Well, he *is* formidable. Yes, we go carefully. He's always got the first five digits dialled to his solicitor. I suppose we don't jump on him quite so fast as on a piggy bank burglar.'

'Isn't that disgraceful?'

'Harpur's wife gives him this sort of bad time, you know. Ethics and the whole civil liberties lump.'

'Well – '

'Benny's done time in the past as a matter of fact,' he said, and she saw she had stung him. 'And we might have him again soon. Something epic's brewing up between him and another heavyweight – though what, we don't know. That's what Colin Harpur and I have been trying to discover. Discover? Well, guess at. There's no information yet, just atmospherics and undefined tension. But we both feel it. As it happens, I think things might have started moving at the ball last night.'

'You what? Why, for heaven's sake? I saw nothing.'

He concentrated on his breakfast for a while. 'Sarah, I shouldn't talk about police matters, you know, not beyond the general and routine, such as standard contempt for juries, Queen's Counsel, newspapers and the Home Secretary.'

'Do I gossip?'

For a few moments, she watched him calculate how much he might safely tell her. There had been a time, not all that long ago, when he would never reveal anything. In those days he had quite obviously taken pleasure in secrecy, and drew feelings of superiority from keeping her at a distance. Perhaps this had been one factor that started the gap between them, and then made it wide and permanent. She knew he regretted it now and yearned for the power to interest her, to draw her to him that way and hold her, even if he could not draw her to him and hold her in bed.

This morning she waited for him to cave in and decide to talk, and then when he did his words almost stunned her. 'I don't know if you noticed, but there's a public phone box in the city hall foyer,' he said.

'Is there?' she muttered, her voice suddenly gone to milk and water.

'Benny made a very dark call to one of his people from there.'

'Oh, Desmond, speak plainly. What the hell does dark mean?'

'Alarming.' He hesitated again. 'What sounded like hit instructions.'

She was dazed by what he said. Jesus, had they been monitoring all calls from that box? What for? 'How can you tell?'

'Tell what? That they were hit instructions?'

'That he made such a call.'

Iles did not answer.

'Someone saw him in the box? But how do you know what he said and who he was talking to?'

Iles gazed at her.

In a little while, her mind started working properly again, and she saw with relief – relief for the moment – that it must be from the other end of the line that Loxton's call had been overheard.

'You've got a phone tap going on some crook's house – one of his people?'

'We're keeping an eye and ear open in all sorts of ways, Sarah.'

'But when did you hear about all this – the phone call?'

'I had a report.'

'When?'

'Does it matter?'

She thought for a moment. 'The motor-cycle man who turned up after the ball last night brought you a transcript, did he? It's so urgent?'

'Someone's life, possibly. Yes, it's urgent, we're here to stop hits.'

'But tapping's illegal.'

'Except in specially ordered cases.'

'These are specially ordered?'

'Permission is very rare. It's got to be endorsed by twelve

authenticated virgins, three members of the Magicians' Circle, the Privy Council, a director of a marmalade factory and the religious correspondents of the *Guardian* and *Comic Cuts* – that's two separate papers, though I've heard convincing arguments the other way.'

'So, you haven't got – ?'

'He's extremely careful what he says, possibly suspecting a tap himself.'

'What do you mean, hit instructions?'

'A target to be knocked off because he or she's seen something awkward for Benny, or knows something awkward for Benny, possibly heard something awkward for Benny. That was suggested in the call.'

'But who?'

'Now, Sarah, come on. Could I tell you that, even if I knew, darling? I don't. No names. I understand we can identify Benny's voice, but that's as far as we go. And we didn't have surveillance on the man receiving the call, or we could have followed him.'

'You're saying, these were orders to go out and kill somebody right then?

'That's how it sounds. At about 10.50 – between the tangos and teddy bear raffle – he gave unmistakable instructions for a death.'

'Instructions to whom?'

'Now, now. Naturally, I do know the answer to that, but I'm telling you too much already.'

'To one of his people?'

Iles ate his breakfast.

'Well, obviously,' she said. 'Otherwise, why the tap on his line? But making the call there, in the middle of a dance, as if he's just thought of it – what brought that on, for heaven's sake? He was provoked? What happened? He met someone, heard something?'

'You really mustn't ask about these things, Sarah. You'll get me hanged.' Preparing to go, he stood and put his jacket on, but again she saw that he could not resist having her attention, for once. 'Now, this is the last: it looks as if he'd seen someone else make a call in the same box – probably a woman – and from that he deduced that his target must be at home. They'd been looking for him.'

'My God.' Once more she felt as if she were losing control of her mind and strength. Loxton's call had been about her and Ian?

'Deduced how?'

'Perhaps she looked so pleased. They could be lovers. Benny might have known that.'

'But you've no names?' She guarded against sounding over-anxious.

'No. Not yet.'

'Will you talk to Benny?'

'About what?'

'About the call, of course.'

'We don't know about the call, do we, love? How on earth could we? Permission for taps is hardly ever given, as I told you. Anyway, if we approach Benny he'll realise we're watching him and his.'

Desperately, she tried to dig out from her sub-conscious those memories from last night in the city hall foyer. Yes, surely there had been someone hanging around, a man in full evening clobber gazing reverentially at the seated stone scholar, almost communing with it? And, yes, hadn't he glanced her way when she gave that shriek? She struggled to recall what he looked like, but could bring no face from her memory. Her mind had been too much taken up elsewhere. But why had her brain jumped to Benny Loxton just now when Desmond spoke of a university man as part of the crossword answer? Had she noted him near the monument without being properly aware of it? Perhaps she had scarcely recognised him. There had been only the briefest identification of Loxton for her by Desmond when they were dancing.

She suspected that after the first surprised stare towards her the man in the foyer had deliberately turned his back. His clothes? From when they were all talking together later, she recalled that Loxton had been in a penguin suit and wearing a preposterous blue cummerbund, plus a flower of some sort in his buttonhole. Did the man near the telephone box sport such extras? She could not recall this, either. He was tall, though, no doubt of that, as tall as Loxton.

'But it's terrible.'

'What's terrible is that we can't discover the target's name. We have to wait until we find a – Well, until we hear of some unexplained violence, and then see if it links to Benny.'

'You think it will?'

'Oh, yes. His people do what they're told, and they're good at it, particularly one of them, the one he called. And, before you ask, yes, we've failed so far to nail him, too.'

As soon as Desmond left for work, she telephoned Ian's flat again, but could get no reply. She feared that even if she hung on for one of their special times he would not answer today. Oh, God, it was still hours before they were due to meet, and she could not bear to wait so long before trying to find of he was safe. She stayed in the house until 9.25, one of their chosen moments for calls, but nothing came, and five minutes later drove out to his flat, in a big, handsome Edwardian house, about a quarter of a mile from the Monty. Once, very early on in their relationship, he had offered her a key and she had refused, feeling it would bind her more than she wanted then. He never asked her again.

She ran up the stairs to the second floor and tried his door before ringing the bell. Ian was paranoid about security and had two locks and a top and bottom bolt, yet, to her amazement, the door opened when she turned the knob. Taking one small step into the flat, she softly called his name and listened. There was no answer, nor when she called again, a little more loudly. Then, before she could move any further inside, she heard two or three sets of footsteps on the landing behind her. They seemed to slow down as they came near the door, as if people were looking in, or might enter after her, and for a second she felt too terrified to turn around to find who was there.

When she did, she saw an elderly couple in the doorway glaring suspiciously at her. 'I'm looking for Ian,' she said. 'Do you live here? Have you seen Ian – Mr Aston?'

Long-nosed, gruff and heavy with acrylic cardigans, the woman replied: 'We got keys. We come in to feed the hamster occasional.'

'Oh, yes: Redvers.'

'Name for a hamster, I ask you,' the man said.

'But, please, what about Mr Aston?' Sarah asked.

'We never seen nothing, did we, Trev?'

'Nothing. How could we, that's the point?'

'What happened?' Sarah asked. 'Please.'

'No keys needed now.' The woman glanced down at the Yale

lock and, following her eyes, Sarah saw it had been burst open. The mortice had been forced, as well.

'When?' Sarah said.

'Should you be in there? I mean, whoever you are,' the woman replied. 'All right, knowing about Redvers is all right, but is it all right for you to be in the flat? What, well, is your connection? Don't mind me asking, but he's so particular.'

'He's not here,' Sarah said.

'We don't have no responsibility for the flat, that's admitted, only looking at the hamster now and then, but whether you should be walking around in here – We don't know who's here and who's not, do we Trev?'

'How could we?' He was red-faced, cheerful-looking, short of a few teeth at the edges, dressed in an anorak made up of brightly coloured rectangles, so he resembled the display panel on a switched-off fruit machine. 'People have their private lives. That has to be respected.'

'Did you hear anything?' Sarah asked.

The woman looked down at the locks again. 'Them wasn't opened with a pin.'

'Last night?'

'Just above,' the man said, glancing upwards.

'You live there?' Sarah asked. 'You did hear something?'

'We stayed very put, very put indeed,' he said. 'Noise like that, you don't rush out to look and utter heartfelt reproaches, not in this building, not in this area. It's like I said, privacy. Silence is a living language.' Suddenly, he seemed much less cheerful.

'Yes, of course.'

'We act discreet, always,' he said. 'It's necessary – simple as that. Something go wrong, there's nobody going to look after you. Not these days. Do you know anything about police at all, lady? I don't suppose so, not somebody with top-drawer clothes and shoes like that. But you see, love, police, what do they care? All they want is their free pints round the back and lurking on the motorway, unsafe loads, smoky exhausts and such, clip-boards and the blue light flashing. They worry theirselves about folk in a dump like this? Do me a favour. Elms Enclave, somewhere like that, they might send a crew if there's trouble, because the money's up there and people who can make bother if they don't get no service, power, that sort. You see any influence here and what's known as clout? Qualities like that never took up residence, regrettable.'

'Others heard, likewise, when the door was smashed,' the woman said. 'Did they come to see what was happening? Did they, Trev?'

'This is 1989,' he replied.

'But what about Ian – Mr Aston?' Sarah said. 'Did you hear anything from him?

'We know him, and yet we don't know him, if you understand me,' the woman said.

Yes, Sarah did, very well. 'I must discover where he is.' She took a couple more steps into the flat.

'Careful,' the man cried.

'I must, that's all.'

'She must, Trev. I can see that.'

He grunted and then said, hesitantly: 'Well, yes, we all must. Can we live with our eyes shut for ever? Even kittens do better.'

The two of them had a small discussion in the doorway. 'We ought to come with you, dear,' the woman told Sarah. 'You're from a nice, executive-style home, evident, with lawns and patio. You don't appreciate. Not your territory.'

'Would you? Thanks, oh, thanks.'

The woman came forward and took hold of Sarah's hand in a fierce, brave, terrified grip. 'Sound the advance,' she said, her voice high and tense and weak. 'We don't know him but we like him.'

'Yes, that's Ian,' Sarah replied.

'We heard the noises, but didn't help,' the man said from behind them. 'Do you know a certain word, namely, "recreant"? That's the word that came to me last night. Means yellow. This was late. Now, I'm sick of myself when I think of what went on.'

'We know the way, owing to Redvers,' the woman said. 'But you know the way, too? A friend?'

'Yes,' Sarah replied.

'Why not?' she said. The three of them edged forward slowly, like people in newsreel footage of a wartime food queue. The woman still clasped her hand. Sarah called his name again, as they approached the closed door to the sitting-room. She remembered that other closed door, in the Monty, and felt just as fearful.

83

'Maybe I should go first,' the man said, but made no attempt to come to the front. 'When we open that door, well – '

'Too true,' the woman agreed. But she was the one who reached forward and opened it. Sarah stared past her at the room. For a moment, she thought it looked only untidy, as was usual, with no sign of violence. The three of them advanced a few more cautious steps and stood inside the room, gazing around. 'This doesn't seem right,' the woman said. 'Somehow.'

'What?' Sarah asked, urgently. 'You must tell me. Please. What do you see?'

'Not right at all,' the man said.

'No?' Sarah asked, her voice high.

'No, indeed.' He nodded towards the hamster's cage. It was a barred circular lower area, plus a separate, solid-walled, smaller sleeping compartment on top, like two spacecraft joined. 'Redvers always comes down when he hears us, wanting to be fed.'

'Oh, for fuck's sake,' Sarah shouted, 'is that all? The sodding hamster?'

'Language, *if* you please,' the man replied. 'Leave that sort of talk at home.'

Sarah disengaged her hand from the woman's, went to the other end of the room, and standing in the window bay that overlooked the street, stared about the room again from this new point. Behind an armchair she could now see an overturned dinner plate and around it scattered on the carpet what seemed to be almost a complete pasta meal, the kind of ready-prepared freezer food that Ian lived on in the flat. A fork and spoon were on the floor, too, and a broken wine glass, with a long, red stain nearby. It looked as if the meal had been knocked off a small table with a cloth on it that stood in the bay. Something made her put her hand on the congealed food to check the temperature, though she knew it would be stone cold.

The woman had followed her across the room. She gazed at the mess, and then glanced back towards the broken front door. 'Poor lad,' she said. 'These people, whoever – '

'The table been knocked over and then put back up, you ask me,' the man said. 'We heard all sorts through the ceiling. You ask me, they just went for him. Would he have a chance? There was more than one. These people, they pack hunt, and they would be quick, believe me.'

'Ian's strong,' she whispered, all she could manage, and knowing it was stupid. Somehow, she had to find a fraction of hope, though.

'That's as maybe,' the woman replied, 'but numbers, love. That's what I mean, you're not familiar with this sort of hole. All right, he brought you here for – Well, you came here as a visitor, like, very nice, a new bit of life for you to see and have a bright little time in, and so important for you to get into his own corner for a while, be with him at home, of course it is, but you don't know what it's like to be here non-stop. That's rather a different matter, what's referred to as the nitty-gritty. Things get sorted out here private and sharp, and you'll never read about it in the Court Column. Now, there's very lovely people around here, plenty of them, but other assorted flavours, too, and some of them not leaders on amiability and decorum. It's numbers, all sorts of armament, and just crushing people, finishing them.' She bent down for the plate. 'Don't worry, I'll give it all a clean-up.'

'Where is he?'

'Yes, where is he?' the man said, staring at the hamster cage. Stepping to it he drew a finger softly across the bars a couple of times, without result. Suddenly, he lost all remaining traces of his cheerfulness and looked unbelievably strained, as though this creature had become a kind of omen, and, if it were not here, or if it were dead, everything must be wrong. Sarah tried to reject the notion. Good Christ, where had such a dozy idea sprung from? Just the same, her nerves sang.

Then the man grinned. In one smooth movement, the hamster glided down a plastic chute from the boudoir, stood up on the sawdust with its paws against the bars and pushed a busy muzzle through, sniffing ardently. It was a mixture of browns, dark on top, a lighter waistcoat across the belly, plump, a little rat-like, but stupid-looking.

The woman said: 'Here's my beauty, then.' She picked up a slab of the cold lasagne from the floor and offered it to Redvers through the bars, who immediately snorted and turned away, then careered temperamentally about the cage, kicking up sawdust so that some drifted down on to the carpet.

Sarah left the room and went swiftly through the whole flat alone, still moving slowly and carefully but almost certain she would not find Ian here, and unable to decide whether that was good or bad. If he was somewhere in the flat, why had he failed to answer when she called out?

She was in the kitchen when there suddenly came a high, angry, unbroken whistling from the sitting-room, and, frightened again, Sarah hurried back. The couple had gone and the hamster was clinging suspended to the bars, making this piercing, enraged, unnerving din. The woman had forced the square of pasta through and it lay curled up and ignored on the floor of the cage like a discarded poultice.

'Stop screaming,' Sarah screamed. 'Stop, you bastard. Redvers, please stop.' The creature dropped from the bars for a moment, but then climbed back. Its cry grew louder and more insistent, and holding her hands over her ears Sarah ran weeping from the room and out of the flat.

The man and woman were on the landing, returning with a dust pan and brush. The woman spoke and Sarah took her hands from her ears to listen. 'Don't ever let that Redvers get you down, love. We know him of old. He'll take advantage. His trouble, he don't know when he's lucky. Condominium cage, that's what that sort is called, bought new by Mr Aston, like rich advertising executives in the States, Manhattan, always in condominiums. Mentioned in *Dynasty*. But is Redvers grateful? N.O. Don't know the meaning of the word, you ask me.'

'They got to express theirselves,' the man said. 'Grateful hardly comes into it. This is a beast. Grateful's silly. You want a grateful hen, wasp? It's an inconsiderate noise, yes, inconsiderate, but I wouldn't go beyond that and the point is, who knows what our voices sound like to a hamster? Or music on Radio 1 or that Scharnhorst – no, Strindberg, Scharnhorst was a ship, Redvers got to listen to all that, if it's on the wireless. You ever look at it like that? Live and let live.'

At the transport café, near Osborn Triangle, Sarah took a table in a corner away from the grimy window, but from which she could watch part of the street. Was coming here any more than a bleak, despairing reflex, an attempt to will him to turn up because the arrangement had been made, when all the time she knew he would never arrive, could not? Her mother used to tell her of a woman who, years after the first war finished, walked every day past their house on the way to the railway station to meet her son, long dead in the trenches. Sarah better understood now that sad refusal to accept an agonising truth. But, just the same, wasn't it lunacy to be waiting here? Des said the man who took Benny Loxton's orders did not make mistakes. 'Did not make mistakes,' Jesus, what a feeble, clouding way of putting it. What it meant was that the man who took Benny's orders to kill killed.

Feelings of blame savaged her: twice now she had pointed the finger at Ian, once in the Monty by forcing him to poke about with her in the builder's rubble, and once through phoning him last night. She felt sick: the tea, the guilt and hopelessnesss, the heavy smell of big fry-ups and sweat and cigarettes. Trying the old deep-breathing exercises to dispel nausea only made her take in more of the smoke and grease and her head began to swim.

After an hour and a half and three mugs of tea he had not arrived and she grew distraught. Men coming in for midday dinner stared at her, and some smiled, but there was no teasing or laughing or chatting up. Perhaps she looked too bad for that, too preoccupied and too uninterested in any of them to be mistaken for road fanny.

In this state, she suddenly began to suspect that someone was watching her from outside. It was hard to be sure. She felt so anxious and ill that she knew her mind and perceptions might not be anything like perfect. Had she begun to imagine menace? In the lorry-park opposite, an ancient red van stood among the vehicles of drivers eating here. A man wearing a navy wool bobble hat sat at the wheel, right arm folded back to hide his face, but each time she peered that way through the steamed, dirty café window she thought she could make out his eyes fixed on her. It was only twenty minutes since she had noticed him and the vehicle, but how long had he been there? She tried to force her mind back to when she first arrived here. Was the van in position then? She could not remember, but neither could she recall seeing it arrive.

Again she felt the kind of deep fright that had come in the Monty and in Ian's flat, and again, for a disgusting moment, she considered calling Desmond for help, and never mind the difficulties of explaining why she was hanging about in this place. Yes, as an institution, marriage had some steely power. Its influence seeped pretty thoroughly into every part of life: a husband was supposed to protect his wife, particularly when the husband was police. But one of the drivers had the café pay-phone and, by the time he finished, she had dismissed the notion of ringing Desmond. The logic of her second thoughts was basic, but unanswerable, she thought: could she use him when she would not let him use her?

Instead of telephoning, she tried to watch the man in the van, without making him aware of it. Had they disposed of Ian and now followed Sarah here from his flat to deal with her? What was she into? And what, in God's name, did they imagine she and Ian knew? She would have loved to proclaim that they knew nothing worth knowing and that even if they did they would sit on it, forget it if they could and certainly never try to add to it. All her usual toughness and fight had been scared out of her. She was tempted to go outside and yell this message of surrender across the street at the man in the van, and at anyone else he had with him, Which of those two at Ian's place had said these people moved in packs? Anyway, perhaps such assurances would be too late to save him.

Then, when she next looked up, the man had disappeared from the driving seat. Horribly shocked, she stood quickly and, carrying her tea mug, hurried across the café to get closer to the window and see out better. Standing there, staring at the vehicle, she saw she had been right and the cabin was empty now. Her eyes urgently searched the carpark, but then the absurdity of this dawned on her suddenly: his face had been shielded all the time by his arm and she had no idea what he looked like, how he was built. There were plenty of people walking about between the vehicles, and any of the men could have been the one she wanted. She realised that, stupidly, she had been expecting to see someone like Benny Loxton, tall, burly, stiff-backed, with thinning red hair protruding from under the hat. Yet Benny would not handle a job like this himself. More likely it would be one of those people she had seen in the Monty. Once more she sent her mind rushing back for recollections but it came up with only the dimmest pictures of that group, useless to her now. Although she remembered there had been a greying, clerky-looking man, and another with carefully tended dark hair, she failed to summon up their faces. Had the grey man worn glasses, rimless glasses? She thought so, but that was as far as she could go.

For several minutes she remained transfixed, gazing at the vehicles, unaware of the noise of the café behind her, simply waiting for him to return to his van. In an inexplicable, almost mad way, she felt as if she had been abandoned, because, however threatening this unknown figure, somehow he connected to Ian. It occurred to her that, possibly, this man had not been watching her at all, not watching anybody, only waiting for someone, or whiling away time. She and her long stay in the café might mean nothing to anybody. That thought depressed her, too, more than her fears that she had been under observation. She did not count. Even as a danger of an enemy, she failed to rate.

Then, as she stood there, someone abruptly took her arm very firmly from behind, gripping her at the elbow. She was so startled and scared that the nausea she had kept a hold on till now suddenly grew insupportable and her mouth filled with bitter, regurgitated tea, some dribbling down her chin. She brought the mug up quickly to catch the rest.

'Sarah,' Ian said. 'Who's with you? Where are they?'

As she turned, the mug was still at her mouth and she could hardly speak and hardly even smile; though, when she saw him, a rush of joy went through her as powerful as when she awoke this morning. He, too, was unsmiling. Urgently, she examined his face and head to see if he was injured, but found no wounds. 'Please, Ian,' she said, glancing down at her arm. He had begun to hurt her.

He slackened his grip but did not let go, 'Who's with you? Where are they?' he asked again.

'What? Who do you mean? Nobody here. Are you all right, Ian?'

'He giving you bother, darling?' a driver at one of the tables asked, nodding at Ian.

'What? No, no, thank you. It's all right.'

'You just say,' the man told her.

'I'm fine.'

She led Ian back to her table and now he did let go of her arm and they sat down. 'Ian, you're safe. It's wonderful.'

'I don't know why you're here,' he said.

'But we arranged.'

'For an age ago.'

'I was hoping, that's all. Of course I stayed. How else do I find you?'

'You say you're alone?' He was relentlessly examining the rest of the people in the café and occasionally staring out through the window. The tension he felt seemed to have caused his skin to tighten over his cheekbones, and there were red patches on his cheeks, making him look feverish.

'Of course alone. Who would be with me?'

'I don't know. Who was your friend just now?'

'Which friend?'

Ian pointed with his thumb towards the man who had asked if she was all right.

'I don't know,' she said. 'A knight of the road, a well-wisher. Please tell me what you mean. What's the matter? Why so tense? All I can think of is that you're in one piece, and it's so lovely.' She leaned across the table and gripped his hand. He let her hold his fingers, but made no responding movement with his own.

'I've been watching you, Sarah.'

'Yes, I know. From the lorry-park.' He must have taken off the bobble hat outside.

He almost grinned. 'You spotted me? I must have forgotten you were a cop wife.'

'But why?' Ever since she had known him there came occasional alarming moments when she felt she understood little about Ian, could not read his face, did not follow his motives, and had no notion what he was thinking.

'Yes, watching you since you walked in here.'

'Ian, why? I've been going mad with worry.'

'Have you?' His face remained impassive. When he was relaxed, she found a marvellous warmth and brightness in his looks: dark eyes that would light up with amusement or enthusiasm so easily, and a mouth eager for laughter, or laughing already. It had all been such a change from Desmond. But none of that was available now.

'Why didn't you let me know you were all right?' she asked.

'Why shouldn't I be?'

'I was afraid something terrible had happened to you.'

'Why?'

'What?'

'Why were you afraid?'

'Ian, please, this is turning into cross-questioning.' She tried again for some response from his hand, but still nothing came. 'What the hell are you getting at? We're together, aren't we? Does much else matter? It looked for a while as if that wasn't – '

'Why were you so afraid? We spoke last night. I told you I was all right.'

'Yes, but – Ian, that was last night.'

'So, what's happened?'

His eyes held hers. He was no longer staring at the other customers or out through the window. Small-featured, slightly freckled, fair, he usually had a strikingly cheerful appearance, but today the anxiety of anger, or whatever it was, meant all his face muscles seemed clenched, and he had become forbidding and suddenly older-looking.

'What's happened since last night?' he demanded again.

'Desmond told me – '

The café owner approached. 'I need the table now, folks – for meals, not just tea at this time.'

'Oh. Yes, a meal,' Sarah said. 'We want meals, don't we, Ian?' The thought made her stomach shift dangerously again.

'Sausage, liver, eggs, beans all right? And chips, of course.'

'Of course. Wonderful,' she said.

'Twice?' He looked at Ian, who took no notice.

'Twice,' Sarah said.

When they were alone again, Ian asked: 'Desmond told you what, Sarah?'

'That you could be in appalling danger.'

He was still staring at her. 'What does that mean?'

'People looking for you, darling.'

'How does he know?' He was whispering, but for the next question his normal voice almost broke through, he spoke so violently. 'And how does he know you know me? You've told him everything? You didn't say that last night.'

'Told him?' she said, horrified. 'Is that what's upsetting you?' She tried to laugh, but couldn't really get there. 'Of course I haven't told him, or told anyone.'

'How, then?'

'What?'

'Why else would he tell you I'm in danger? Look, I can see how it would happen, Sarah, and I understand. You got scared after the Monty and – '

'No, Ian, I've said nothing.'

But he would not let it go. 'Listen, Sarah, I get a call from you last night, and half an hour later there's a very heavy posse at my place. That's such bad news. Luckily, I'm eating near the window and see them arrive in the street, so I get out just in time, grub all over the place.'

'Yes.' She felt herself beginning to tremble. 'Ian, what are you saying? I don't understand.'

'Don't understand what?'

'You're accusing me of something?'

Now he did grip her hand, but not with affection. 'Sarah, how is it these people arrive so soon after we speak? Can't you see why that scares me, baffles me? I haven't been in my place for days. Nobody saw me return, I'd swear. But as soon as you've got hold of me there – Listen, are you sure these people are not around here now? Is that why you hung on so long?' Once more he could hardly contain what he was saying in a whisper. 'Christ, Sarah, is this arranged – you'd do that?'

'You think I told them you were home?'

He did not answer.

'Is that what you think? For God's sake, tell me.'

'Maybe not directly. No, not directly.' He released her hand. 'Look, just level with me, will you, Sarah? No melodrama, but this could be life and death. Did you panic and tell your husband about the Monty and me, what we saw and heard, and about finding me last night? I will understand, Sarah, honestly. You're a copper's wife. Not just a copper, the king of the coppers. You think you saw a crime so in your position it's a duty to speak. Habit, instinct. OK, I can wear all that. So, be frank, now, did you tel Desmond – tell him any of it at all?'

'Nothing, I swear.'

Two great plates of food, plus a battery of sauces, were put in front of them.

'Oh, grand,' she said.

'Teas?'

'Oh, yes, teas, too, please.'

'You must have said something, Sarah.'

'Ian, I didn't tell him.' She placed the plate of food so that she need not look directly at it or inhale from it. 'Are you saying that the people who came for you last night were police?'

He looked startled. 'Police? Christ, no. A hit team. Villains. Like the people we saw at the Monty. Maybe the same ones. I didn't wait to identify them. I ran. Didn't even have time to take my car.'

She sat silent and desperately confused.

'I see,' he said. 'You're going to ask how telling Desmond would send a crew of thugs to my place.'

'Well, yes, I – '

'Sarah, you're playing dumb. Look, don't mess me about any more, for God's sake. If I'm under watch here – '

She was crying. 'I don't know what you're talking about, Ian.'

He shook his head in wonderment and anger. 'All right, I'll explain – in case you really don't see it.' He began to whisper very quickly, as if not believing she needed the explanation: 'Sarah, police have all sorts of friends, all sorts of connections. The whole thing runs on deals and understandings, co-operation – taking care of one another. They tip off their mates and vice versa. Some of their mates are a long way on the wrong side.'

She dabbed at her face. The man who had asked earlier whether she was all right caught her eye again. She tried to smile at him, reassuringly. 'You believe Des would co-operate with gangsters, with people wanting to carry out an execution? Desmond? Do you know him? Well, of course you don't. He's never going to – '

'Sarah, there are hidden alliances, and bargains, powerful, very binding agreements, not spelled out, never really referred to, but basic, all the same. Same everywhere. I don't say Desmond is evil. People owe each other secret favours, across the boundaries of right and wrong. These are important debts, and they have to be paid sometime. That's how business works, how the police work. It rolls on and on and can't ever stop. You really didn't know that?'

The café owner brought the teas and she saw him stare at the plates, perhaps hurt that they had not touched their food. 'Great,' she said. Picking up a knife and fork she began to force chips down. Ian ate, too. She almost wanted to laugh. Farce could always find a way in.

'You're right, Ian,' she said abruptly.

He dropped the knife and fork on to the food and stared around again. 'There are people here with you, looking for me?'

'You're right that I sent them to you.'

He lowered his head in sadness and remained silent for a couple of minutes. Then he said: 'Jesus, Sarah, how could you do it? We were so good together, so close and happy. I mean, I said all that to you just now, but I couldn't really believe it. And you're telling me it's true?'

'Loxton saw me phone you and made a guess, that's all. He's bright and he knows about us – from the Monty. He followed with a call to one of his people, and the police heard because they're tapping, but no names.'

'Tapping who?'

'I don't know. One of those who came to your place? Des thinks something big is on the menu for soon, so they're listening all round.'

Ian looked incredulous. 'And your husband told you – told you something as hot as that?'

'Ian, don't you understand: Desmond grabs at any subject we can talk about. There aren't many beyond the crossword puzzle. He wants a full home life. He wants to keep me, don't ask why. To interest me – the way you interest me just by sitting there – he'll talk about almost anything.'

Ian began to eat again. After a while he said: 'It's true?'

'I went to your flat this morning thinking I'd killed you. I sat here for hours thinking I'd killed you.'

'Oh, God.' He munched liver.

'Did I tell you, Ralph came to see me. He said you were in danger, too, so I was already terrified, even before what Des said. Ralph told me you'd sent him.'

'No. But I understand now.' Putting the fork down he reached across the table over the meals to stroke her hand twice. 'It adds up.' He smiled at last, bits of the food jammed around his teeth. 'All the time I was quizzing you, I just couldn't believe you would send them deliberately, couldn't I.'

'Good.'

'Honestly.'

She saw the man who had asked if she was all right smile and nod, happy at their sudden happiness. Gamely, she plodded on through the food. 'Not quite like that pre-sex, lip-smacking banquet in *Tom Jones*,' she said.

'Oh, I don't know. It'll do,' Ian replied.

'Tell me what you see in me,' she said.

'Well – '

'Am I fishing? But tell me, anyway.' Occasionally, she found she did need to hear it.

'You're warm and brave and lively and lovely.'

'That's enough.'

'It's only a start,' he replied.

'I do love love in the afternoon,' she said, not long afterwards. The room was above the café's kitchens and the noise of shouted meal orders, laughter, swearing and clanging utensils reached them through the floor. The beds were singles and they made the best of one of them. 'Truckers generally are not interested in sleeping together,' the proprietor had apologised.

'You lie down,' she told Ian, 'I want to undress you.'

'*I* undress *you*,' he said.

'No, not today. I've been worrying about your body. I thought it was in ruins somewhere. I want to see it's all right.'

'Of course it's all right.'

'Yes, but I want to check for myself, bit by bit. Like an inventory? And kiss it bit by bit to welcome you back.' She pushed him on to the bed and drew his sweater off, then lay with her ear on his chest, listening to his heart. 'That's a lovely sound. A private sound, meant for me.' She turned her head and kissed the spot, a long kiss, her mouth half-open, and passed a hand slowly across his shoulders and neck, brushing his chest hair and nipples. 'Seems fine so far. But this is a preliminary examination only.'

'I'm sorry I didn't trust you, Sarah. I was scared brainless.'

'Shut up about it for now.'

'For now?'

'Well, maybe for ever.'

'But only maybe.'

Yes, perhaps only maybe. He had shaken her, she recognised that, but now was now, and deep thinking and resentment were nowhere on the immediate, fleshly programme.

'I've missed your body, too, Sarah.'

'Well, it's here now, and I wouldn't mind you handling me while I'm doing this. No, I wouldn't mind that at all. Or kissing me, too. No no-go zones.'

'Never have been.'

'Well, I should hope not.' She moved her head down his body a little. 'I hear digestive juices doing their poor best with that avalanche of cholesterol you sent down.'

'As a matter of fact, you feel quite well satisfied yourself.'

'Forgotten the layout of the female body? Your hand's on my stomach, not at all the area where I get to feel well satisfied.' In a moment she said: 'Now, you're talking.' She undid his belt and slowly pushed his trousers and pants down. 'Tricky, this,' she said. 'A kind of obstruction?' She grew more forceful with the clothes. 'So being undressed obviously does do things for you, after all.' She moved her head lower. 'This all looks sound enough, not bloody, and extremely unbowed.' She began to kiss along the length of him, light, fluttering, butterfly kisses, and then closed her lips around the tip and played her tongue delicately, lovingly about the warm contours. All right, one day soon she might want to use that tongue to say things to him that would not be delicate or even loving, but for these minutes it was just a practised instrument of delight. He moved slowly, gently back and forth in her mouth, moaning a little. His fingers had entered her and were lazily, sweetly stroking upwards, in that movement she had told Ian she adored, from him. Since nearly the start of knowing each other they had talked about their preferences, itemised them, catered for them.

'This is too good, too loving,' he said, pulling back from her. 'I'm nearly there.'

She stopped for a moment. 'I wouldn't mind.'

'I mind.'

'Purist.'

'And I can't reach you,' he said. 'I mean, really reach you. And you're still half-dressed.'

She tugged her clothes off and then swung around so that they were lying head to toe. 'Soixante-neuf's as good as a feast,' she said.

'Christ, I might have been still outside in the lorry-park,' he said.

'I would have floated in that direction soon, on tea.' He moved nearer. 'I like that,' she murmured. 'I love that. But you can't hear, can you? You wear my thighs like ear pads. Just don't stop.' When she spoke again she moved her legs quickly: 'Ian, now, now, please.'

He swivelled around in the bed, and touched his mouth to hers – that rich multi-flavour on his breath and lips: herself, him, brown sauce and other traces of the frying-pan plenty. There was a dressing-table mirror alongside the bed and by turning her head slightly she could look at her legs bent up in the air on each side of him as he moved into her. She closed them around his waist for a moment, wrapping him like a parcel with white ribbon, and, among all her other pleasures, that view gave her consolation, seeming to say not just that he had come back to her safely, but that she could hold him, and that he belonged to her. This last bit she did not really believe. How in God's name could she? And did she really want that after what had happened and what had been said? But that was how she forced herself to read it now in the glass. For this afternoon, make the best of things.

'Don't finish yet,' she said.

'No.'

'Don't ever.'

'No. No?'

'I need you there.'

'It's a privilege.'

'And, another thing, I hate to feel you get small.'

'Not small, smaller.'

'It's like the defeat of a hero.'

'Heroes have comebacks.'

'Comebacks. Well, as long as you're sure.'

'Cock-sure.'

Later, when they were dressing, she said: 'Where the hell did you get that van?'

'Which van?'

'The red, knacker's-yard vehicle you were sitting in, of course.'

'I wasn't in a van. What are you talking about, Sarah?' Suddenly, he sounded very alarmed. 'I was on foot, watching you from behind the lorries.'

'Never in a van?' She tried to disguise her own fear.

'No.'

'It's right opposite.' She went to the window and pulled back the curtains a little way. 'Not there now. Oh well, then, could be nothing at all.'

'So what did he look like, whoever was in it?'

'I couldn't see.'

'So, how did you know he was watching?'

'I could see his eyes.'

'Jesus, Sarah, try – '

'I couldn't see anything else.'

'Why? Hair? Moustache?'

'He was wearing a bobble hat and had his arm up.'

'All the time?'

'Yes.'

'Deliberately covering his face?'

'Deliberately? I don't know.'

'Sarah, talk sense. You really think it's nothing at all?'

'Well, who?'

He seemed about to answer but then decide it was not worth the effort. 'We'd better not leave together. Don't hang about.'

'Ian, how shall I – ?'

'I'll contact you.'

'Where can you go?'

'I'll contact you.'

6

'I think we might be worrying about nothing. Bluntly, what hard evidence have we that something big and troublesome is due to hit us?' the Chief asked in his genial, nervous way. Lane was wearing uniform today for a municipal function and looked self-conscious and uncomfortable. Harpur knew how much he hated dressing up, or 'going for a soldier', as he called it.

'That's certainly a point of view, sir,' Iles replied, 'isn't it, Col?'

Harpur said to Lane: 'Let's hope you're right, sir. But Mr Iles and I have these – '

'Bad vibes?' the Chief asked. 'Is it really much more than that? Don't mistake me,' he went on hurriedly, 'I certainly wouldn't undervalue the instinctive perceptions of people as experienced as Desmond and yourself, but –'

'You're too kind, sir,' Iles said. The meeting was in the Assistant Chief's room, one of those informal sessions prized by Lane, who seemed to believe, on no good grounds known to Harpur, that in relaxed conditions Iles would be able to do him less damage. Harpur could just make out, concealed under the latest issue of *Police Review* on Iles's desk, a copy of some heavy-looking book called *Middlemarch*, probably a novel. Iles did not like it put about that he was a reader.

'Yes, what hard evidence? That seems to me the heart of it,' Lane declared.

'"The heart of it",' Iles repeated slowly. There were occasions when he made a meal of writing down and then underlining certain prime phrases used by Lane, but did not do that today, only nodded very emphatically a few times, as if acknowledging unique lucidity and grasp. His contempt for the Chief never diminished, and Lane's ability to cope with him never grew.

'I mean, what are we scared of?' Mark Lane asked, and waved an arm sharply, to rid the room of all ill-based dreads and speculative funk.

'A very fair question, sir,' Iles replied. 'What we're scared of, I suppose . . . yes, this would be a balanced, considered, totally unpurple way to put it, what we're scared of is that some act of inter-gang carnage is being planned which will load our patch with so many corpses, some possibly quite innocent, that we'll look like Sharpeville plus the retreat from fucking Moscow.'

Lane said: 'Yes, but –'

'How do we know this, sir?' Iles replied. 'We don't. Guesswork, and – what was your term? – "instinctive perceptions". Yes, I'll buy that. The *mots justes* as ever. I'll admit to you that occasionally I like to get ahead of the villains, rather than merely cater for aftermath. Perhaps it's an extravagant ambition, even fanciful, but that's how I operate, for my sins.'

Feeling it was time for the straight man, Harpur told Lane: 'There are one or two indicators, sir.'

'Factual?' the Chief asked.

'You're so truly rigorous, sir, I could think you were at Cambridge, not –' As always, Iles pretended to forget Lane's university. 'Elsewhere.'

'Half-factual,' Harpur replied. 'A lad in Benny Loxton's outfit, Justin Paynter, seems to have disappeared, we think because he was about to spill something mighty and had to be stopped.'

As part of the drive to appear casual, Lane was seated on a window sill, legs comfortably apart in front of him, shoes not too clean and his socks crumpled. Lately, he had begun to grow plump on public lunches and dinners and his uniform bulged at the waist and top of his arms. He could have ordered a new one, but seemed to want scruffiness, so as never to look even faintly military. Today, because of the uniform and the strain of talking to Desmond Iles, his round, sallow face was tense, whereas normally he appeared cheerful and good-natured, full of kindliness. Iles sometimes referred to him as Mother Teresa, sometimes as Meals on Wheels. For some reason, which could not be tolerance, he seemed to have given up calling Lane, a Catholic, the Mick.

The Chief looked unimpressed by what Harpur had said: 'I

don't really see the connection, Colin, Someone disappears and we assume he was going to reveal an outrage? Why?'

'He's a known source.'

'Known to us?'

'Not directly, sir,' Harpur replied.

'What does that mean?'

Harpur said: 'Well, sir –'

'Oh, don't tell me: this is a source that feeds one of your sources, whom you can't tell us about, of course, so we're about fifteen steps from the actual truth. God, I hate sources, narks, informants – all that kind of dangerous morass.'

Iles, who was in shirt-sleeves, with his feet on the desk, said: 'That kind of dangerous morass is called detection, sir.' Although he sounded almost as arrogant and imperturbable as ever. Harpur suddenly had the feeling that something might be wrong, as if the ACC were coping with a deeply painful, private trouble. None of the usual relish was evident as he baited Lane.

Bravely, the Chief stuck at it. 'All right, so let's accept that he had something sensitive to reveal, this obscure, far-back nark. How do we know it was a possible gang-war incident?'

'We don't,' Iles replied. 'I'm sorry if I repeat myself. We have no certain knowledge, but it's how things feel to Colin, and also to his informant.'

'Feel?'

Harpur said: 'We might be able to take it a bit further than that today, sir. My tipster thinks the missing man was possibly involved in some sort of recent unpleasantness at or near Panicking Ralph's club, the Monty.'

'What sort of unpleasantness?'

'That we're not clear about,' Harpur replied. 'I'm going to call on him today, see where we get.'

'Violence?'

'It's possible.'

'Have we had any report of that nature?'

'No, sir,' Harpur said.

Lane shrugged and stood, preparing to leave. 'Well, it can't be very much, can it, Colin?'

Wearily, Iles said: 'We're talking about the Monty club, sir, not Lambeth Palace. Monty's is sometimes known as The Collection, because so many customers have records. Ralphy gets a very mixed clientele and does not seek a police presence, no matter what goes on there. Neither do his members. They settle things privately.'

'We've checked hospitals?' Lane replied.

'He might not have reached a hospital,' Iles said. 'Benny has people who are first-aid enthusiasts.'

Lane brushed himself down, achieving an unnoticeable improvement in appearance. He looked like a St John Ambulance man after pushing through a British soccer crowd to treat somebody. 'Benny: what's he doing out of jail, anyway?'

'My wife made the same point this morning, sir, and I couldn't answer then, either.'

'And how is she?' Lane asked, evidently glad to grab a way into routine affability.

'Sarah's very active, sir, very zappy.'

'Yes.' He stepped towards the door. 'We have a lot of workaday crime to deal with apart from the rumour of this future battle and, obviously, what I don't want is a great expenditure of time and ingenuity on something that could turn out to be pursuit of a, well, a chimera.'

He almost whispered the word, probably sensing how much Iles would love it.

'Ah,' Iles said. 'A long time since I've pursued one of those. Tidy turn of speed.'

Harpur said: 'Everything else is going normally, sir. Nothing neglected because of this.'

When the Chief had gone, Iles said: 'Change and decay. What remorseless devastation a job brings when it's too much for the holder. Think of Tamburlaine.'

'Who?'

'Christ, Harpur, what's wrong with you? Tamburlaine.'

'Should I know him?'

'Know him? C. L. J. Tamburlaine. The cardboard box and Christmas novelty firm. That's what I mean, you see: forgotten already.'

The Chief's not so bad, sir.'

'Fine voice – amateur operatics. Fiery yet mellifluous in *The Desert Song*, I'm told. Sad, I feel about him, more than triumphant or vindictive.' Iles's tone changed abruptly, and Harpur went on guard, sensing he had been right to suspect the ACC had some personal pain. 'And, as to everything going normally, Col, I gather we've been doing observations for thefts from the lorry-park at Osborn Triangle.'

'Sir?' What the hell was this about?

'Erogynous Jones came to see me on the quiet earlier with some rather bruising disclosures.'

'Yes, we had him down there keeping surveillance from a van. Not much success.'

'Oh, I don't know.'

'Sir?'

'Col, he tells me he saw Sarah in the drivers' caff opposite. Truckers' Den is it called?'

Harpur would have greatly liked to leave. 'It's all right, sir. Rough but clean. She'd come to no harm.'

'Jones told me she was there for hours.'

'Big meals. Drivers doing long hauls.'

'Eventually, she met a man,' Iles said. 'Or, a man came in and met her.'

'What, a trucker? Tried to pick her up, you mean?'

'Jones had the idea they knew each other well, and that she was very pleased to see him, when he finally showed up. She was obviously waiting for him. Jones couldn't see too clearly at the end because he had to get out of the van and find another viewpoint. He thought Sarah had spotted him.'

'So, is he sure it's her? Erogynous is a great observation man, I know, almost as good as on interrogations, but –'

'He's met her a few times at Force shindigs. No mistake.'

Harpur watched Iles carefully. The Assistant Chief had grown a little paler as he spoke, and his voice was becoming slightly metallic. Otherwise, he seemed reasonably in control, as much as ever.

'–It's odd we should have been talking to Lane about the Monty.'

'Sir?'

'For fuck sake don't keep doing that. You sound like West Point.'

'Why odd?'

'Erogynous says he thinks the man she met is someone called Aston – Ian Aston, on the edge of petty villainy, though maybe no more than on the edge.'

'Yes.'

'Know him?'

'Seen him.'

'He uses the Monty, Jones reckons.'

'Could be.'

'Yes.' Iles mumbled the next words. 'The Truckers' Den has rooms.'

'Yes, sir?'

'Didn't know? Not on your own circuit? They stayed, of course. There appeared to be some sort of row or recriminations, they made it up, and then upstairs to put all to rights. Tell me, is this embarrassing you?'

'Maybe Erogynous –'

'Should have kept it to himself? No, I'm grateful. Col, I think I've been deliberately shutting my eyes. If one's wife is putting it on a plate for somebody, it's better to recognise the fact, wouldn't you say?'

Although Harpur knew Iles liked answers to all his questions he did not give one to that. 'I'll see Jones never breathes a syllable of it.'

Iles smiled. 'He's promised me. But an ACC's wife taking it from a minor crook in a roadies' diner? Makes a ripe yarn, wouldn't you say? He's likely to stay silent?' Iles stood behind the desk and reached for his coat. 'If you're going to see Panicking Ralph I think I'll come with you. You don't mind?'

'Oh, Christ. 'No, of course not.'

In the car, Iles, who was driving, said: 'I found where Aston lives and went up there earlier on. Mind, I want to stress I had no intention of doing anything out of the way, nothing extreme.'

'No, that's hardly worth saying, sir.'

Iles had begun to shake and he gripped the wheel fiercely to keep himself steady. He let the speed drop to about ten miles an hour. 'I'll be great in a minute,' he muttered.

'Of course, sir.'

After a while, he seemed to improve and his driving became normal again. 'Aston wasn't there when I called and, apparently, hasn't been there much at all lately. The place has been broken into, as if people were looking for him. I gather from neighbours nothing was taken. No damage. They said a woman has been sniffing about. It sounds like Sarah: good shoes, beautiful, highly strung, some fucking and blinding. Now, what do I make of that? She's been up there at his flat, so I have to ask, is this a long-term, deep thing, not just a couple of *joie-de-vivre* jumps? Am I going to have to deal with this lad in a very serious way?'

'It must be trying for you, sir.'

'The best you can do, you half-baked arsehole? We're talking about losing a wife, not belonging to the Labour Party.'

'Heartbreaking for you.'

'Of course, you're adulterising Mrs Cotton, so I suppose you might have a different view.' Iles kept his eyes rigidly in front. 'I want Sarah, Col.'

'Of course, sir. She's a great girl.'

'Not of course. She does distribute herself a bit and for my own part I've wandered now and then, as you know. A mistake. To a degree, forced on me, but still a mistake. I'll keep Sarah. Nobody must take her away, Col.' He spoke without much emphasis, but as if it were unarguable. Maybe he feared setting off his frenzy again.

'Women these days, they like to branch out once in a while,' Harpur said. 'It's not just Sarah. They want to live right up to their impulses. We have to adjust. It's only right.'

'Once in a while or twice or three times. Look, Col, I'll try to be reasonable, really try.' He seemed to be losing the battle with himself and now he began to shout in those strange, high, metallic tones, sounding like son of Robocop. He still looked firmly ahead. 'There's no point in tearing one's self to pieces over a bloody woman, no point at all.'

'We all have problems, sir.'

'Sorry, am I hogging the picture? Yes, there's – well, all that stuff: your marriage. I shouldn't go on.' Once again he quietened. 'Erogynous asked in his stylish, roundabout way whether I wanted Aston done over: something fairly disabling, long-lasting and character-forming. It could be handled by a team, but I refused absolutely. One can't let one's own people carry out something like that, it's improper, though the offer was so British of him, gentlemanly.'

'He's coming up on a promotion board, sir.'

'All the same. And he's not even in the Lodge.'

'Some of them enjoy an occasional outing. They say it tones the muscles.'

'Well, I expect I'll work something out privately to cope with Mr Aston.'

'Yes?'

'Oh, much better privately. I certainly don't want anyone dead, Col.'

'No, of course not.'

'What's he like, this Aston?'

'Fair. Baby-faced.'

'Can't compete there, then. If you think about it, I suppose Garland was the same. Could be what she's after these days. Is she proving to herself she can still pull the kids, or at least kid look-alikes? Garland, some kid! Additionally, what interests me, has Aston got anyone else at the same time? I mean, who's transmitting to me altogether, what fraction of the world's leg-over and legs-open population?'

'Something we all have to ask ourselves, these days, sir. Yes. Aids is very democratic.'

'You could sell that as a slogan.'

'Here's Ralphy's.' They went into the club. Although it was mid-morning, Ralph still had his dressing-gown on, an old, heavy, fawn and beige job, with a tasselled sash, like something in an eventide home for the irredeemably naff. Harpur would have expected a much sexier, more colourful item, say shiny yellow or scarlet, with narrow, black trim.

'Old place looking grand, Ralph,' Iles said, gazing appreciatively about. 'Panelling behind the bar. It's a real touch of vener-able quality. Even with the sun shining in, things seem nice. Some clubs in daylight, well, right tips: frowsy carpets, snot on the wallpaper. Here, though, there's a feel of, I wouldn't say opulence, but something decently close to hygiene and odour-lessness. Myself, I don't mind full ashtrays. Better than on the floor, surely.'

'What can I get you, gentlemen?' Ralph asked. He had been talking to them on the customers' side of the bar, but went behind it now and waved a hand at the shelves, showing the range of what was on offer. Iles had his favourite 'old tart's drink', a port and lemon, Harpur cider laced with gin. Ralph drew himself a beer and pulled the dressing-gown tighter around his chest, like a woman worried about showing too much.

'We think we might have had a bit of an incident in the vicinity, Ralph,' Iles told him.

'Yes? Incident? I don't think I can help you in that respect.'

'We're talking to all sorts,' Harpur said. 'Nice type of membership still?'

'Ideal. Decent, homely people, skilled artisan types and their loved ones – looking for a little relaxation, a quiet evening, with perhaps a modest laugh.'

'That's it. Very heartening,' Iles said. 'It's in spots like this that one sees the strength of Britain, the enduring saneness and generosity of spirit.'

'We're talking about five or six nights ago,' Harpur told Ralph Ember.

'Nothing comes to mind,' he replied.

'It might be a false tip,' Harpur said. 'We have to follow every possibility in a matter as big as this.'

'It's that important?' Ralph asked.

'You don't think Harpur would be out of bed so early if it wasn't important, Ralphy? I mean, look at you, still in that bloody horse blanket, and your false teeth in the glass, I bet.'

Harpur felt sorry for Ralph. He could see him urgently trying to work out why this inquiry took an Assistant Chief, and especially an Assistant Chief as malevolent as this one. And also trying to work out how much this Assistant Chief knew about his wife's night-time habits. For somebody with his nickname Panicking Ralph was putting on a very reasonable show.

'What's through there, Ralphy?' Iles asked.

'Toilets.' He prepared more drinks.

Iles walked over and opened the door to the corridor. 'And the fire exit? Where does that come out?'

'A yard we use as a car-park.'

Iles entered the corridor. In a few moments, they heard him push the fire doors open. Harpur said: 'Ralph, I gather that in the old days, when Valencia Esplanade was really something, businessmen and so on used to come through the short-cut from down there and do half their deals in the Monty.'

Ralph welcomed the chit-chat. 'I've got some interesting pictures of it then, one with the mayor of the day standing just about where you are now, Mr Harpur.'

Isles came back. 'How long's the builder's rubbish container been there, Ralph?'

'Few weeks.'

'When was it last emptied?'

'Emptied?'

'Let's put it another way,' Iles said amiably. 'Emptied.'

'Well, I don't know. What sort of important incident?'

Iles sat down with his drink and spoke in very confidential fashion, as to a revered partner. 'We're rather interested in three people, Ralph. First, a lad called Justin Paynter?'

Ralph thought about this. 'No, not a name that means anything. A member?'

'Possibly dis-membered.'

'I don't understand.'

'About twenty-four, five, dark hair, well-dresed.'

'Well, we get a lot like that. I insist on certain standards of turn-out here.'

'Good,' Iles said.

'We wondered whether he'd been involved in any bother here lately – a fight, argument, anything like that,' Harpur said.

'I won't permit fracases or squaring up of any sort, Mr Harpur. That's another factor I'm very strict on. Have to be. A club like this, reputation is so vital.'

'This is very true,' Iles said. 'We heard he could have stepped out of line and found trouble, as a result.'

'Perhaps he did,' Ember said, 'but not here. Not to my knowledge at all.'

Iles took a decorous sip of his port. 'What sort of women do you get in here these days, Ralph?'

Harpur watched Ember trying urgently to sort out the implications of this. Then he replied: 'Oh, an extremely nice class of woman, Mr Iles, I'm pleased to say. What they all know very well is that I won't have slags. Pleasant wholesome women, a full credit to any gathering, quiet dressers, no spitting or blasphemy or scrapping over men, no clawing. Out they go, anything like that, even a hint, and out they stay. Reputation. A place like this, as you said, Mr Harpur – Mr Harpur and I were discussing history while you were outside, Mr Iles – this place has a fine past to be considered, dignitaries of this whole region, makers of it, indeed, meeting in the Monty, sitting here in the old days, talking business and municipal advance, and thank God for them. I see myself as something of a guardian of that history, if that's not vainglorious.'

'Hardly,' Iles said. 'No, I certainly would not term it vainglorious. Would you call it vainglorious, Col?'

'Never.'

Ralph went on, 'Am I going to let easy pieces soil this tradition, pressing their random fannies on the same redolent upholstery? Well.' He took some beer. 'Look, I know this is not White's or the Cavalry Club, but I do insist on sterling standards, on members being spruce and *comme il faut* top to toe, and if possible good with conversation and interesting hobbies, that sort of person. We have people discussing all sorts here, not just playing pool or feeding the fruit machines. You'll hear conversations about great music, such as Elgar and others, or politics, Dr David Owen, summitry. Many's the extremely lively –'

'Does my wife come here?' Iles said.

Ralph was leaning forward, with his elbows on the bar as he talked. He straightened now and pulled the dressing-gown tight again, frowning, half-smiling, while he considered this. 'Would I know Mrs Iles?'

'What I'm asking you, cunt,' Iles replied.

'Your wife?'

Iles sat staring at him.

'But what I mean, I don't think I would recognise your wife, Mr Iles. I take it you're asking if she comes here other than in your company. Obviously, I'd recognise her if you were together, but you mean solo?' Harpur considered Ember was still handling this with flair.

Iles said: 'She's blonde, slim, pretty, thirty-six, looks a bit pent-up, but, then, maybe when she's here she doesn't.'

'And you've reason to think she comes to the Monty? With friends, perhaps?'

'Who exactly was in here the night of this incident with Justin Paynter took place, Ralph?' Iles replied.

'Which incident was that? Who's the boy?'

'Was she here?'

Ralph sighed: 'I'm really out of my depth on this one.'

'Yes?' Iles said. 'Ralphy, please do try not to piss me about, would you?'

'Who are your regulars these days, Ralph? Who might have been in the club that evening?' Harpur asked.

'But which evening, Mr Harper?'

'Five nights ago, maybe six. Say, Tuesday, Wednesday.'

'That's not easy. Well, crowds here most nights, people in and out.'

Iles produced his wallet. 'Here's a picture of my wife.' Harpur could see it cost him plenty to do this, as if delivering up the photograph to someone of Ember's quality soiled her more and put the ACC irrecoverably into Panicking Ralph's hands. Iles did not get up but gave the picture to Harpur, who was standing at the bar, so he could pass it over. Maybe Iles could not bring himself to make the transfer direct.

Harpur glanced at the snapshot. It showed Sarah grinning at the camera in that open, breezy way of hers, wearing what seemed to be a fairly ancient green track suit and trainers. Her fair hair was done in a pony tail and she looked young, relaxed, very beautiful and happy. Anyone could see why a husband would choose this picture of his wife to carry, and why he might be driven to frantic, dangerous rage at the thought of losing her. Harpur handed it to Ralph.

He studied it. 'Very lovely lady, Mr Iles, if I may say.'

'Easy to remember.'

'Not all are as beautiful as Mrs Iles, by no means, but we do see a lot of ladies here, mingling, milling about, dancing, that sort of thing. I find it difficult, even with somebody so grand-looking.'

Harpur thought he could detect sweat shining on Ralph's cheekbones and across his forehead in a thin, unostentatious line. Ember gazed at the picture. He had been holding it up in front of him, but a slight tremor started in his arm and he put the photograph down on the bar near his beer glass and bent forward intently over it. Then he raised his head and faced the ACC squarely. 'On balance, I'd say no, Mr Iles. I don't seem to recognise her, though I admit she could have been in the club some-time, and it's gone from my memory. As you say, one shouldn't forget looks like that, but faces, when you think back, they sort of merge, you know what I mean? When you're seeing them in a changing crowd, and myself busy with running the place and so on.'

'Up here night after night, is she?' Iles asked. 'That the bloody truth of it?'

Ralph handed the picture back to Harpur, who passed it to Iles. 'I've given my considered opinion, Mr Iles, subject to error, I readily concede.'

'Aston,' Iles replied. 'That's the third one we're concerned about. He a member?'

Ralph paused. 'Ian Aston? Yes, I think we do have an Ian Aston.'

'Yes. Regular?'

'Like most of them, Mr Iles, they look in when they feel like it.' He smiled bravely. 'That's the club trade. No one place can expect to keep anybody's custom to itself, unfortunately.'

'Bring women here?'

'Ian? Oh, now and then. Yes, he has lots of friends, women and men. Popular sort.'

'Have you seem my wife with him?'

'With Ian?'

'That's it.' Iles spoke slowly. 'Have you seen the woman in that picture here with Aston?'

'As I said, Mr Iles, I don't –'

'She come up here to find him, meet him?'

'We haven't seen Ian for some little while, as a matter of fact.'

'Why would that be?' Harpur asked, eager to turn the questions to some other topic than Sarah, before Iles went ape again.

'Ian has his business interests, I believe,' Ralph replied. 'Quite a private person – I don't mean stand-offish, anything like that, but discreet? He has to travel now and then. Yes, there are periods when we miss him.'

'When did he disappear?' Harpur asked.

Ralph chuckled. 'Oh, I wouldn't say disappear. Sounds like a fairy tale, a puff of smoke and he was gone, and so on.'

'How long since you've seen him?'

'Now, that's difficult. He didn't say he was going, anything like that. Why should he? Am I my members' keeper, as it were? It's just that you notice after a while that you haven't seen someone. Do you know what I mean? Somebody will say, ''Haven't seen Ian Aston lately'' and then, when you think, you realise you haven't seen him yourself. Like that.'

'Is it about five or six days?' Harpur asked.

'Gone for that period?'

'Yes.'

'Why do you suggest that?' Then Ralph rapped the bar with his fingers and chuckled again. 'Oh, I see, you're still on about that, are you, Mr Harpur – the mysterious incident?'

'That's it. I thought that perhaps Ian Aston was involved, or saw something, and that would explain why he's not about.'

'Involved in what, though, Mr Harpur? Saw what?'

'You tell me.'

'Wouldn't I love to, if I knew what we were talking about? I'm sorry, though, I don't.'

'So it is something like five or six days?'

'I think I've said, I don't know,' Ralph replied, with dignity.

Iles stood suddenly, stepped to the bar and grabbed Ralph by the lapels of his dressing-gown, pulling him forward and holding his face close to Iles's own. 'I asked you a fucking question, Ralphy,' he shouted.

'What?' Ralph gasped. 'Which question, Mr Iles? So many questions, for God's sake. I don't remember.' He did not struggle. A pulse was visibly banging away at the side of his head.

'That's because Mr Oil-on-troubled-waters, here, Harpur, took you off on a long, useless saunter, a digression. What I asked you was if my wife made a habit of coming here to find Aston.'

'Mr Iles –'

'I trust you won't lie to me, Ember, or this knife mark on your face will be the least of your scars.'

'You've had a visit, have you, Ralph, people suggesting you'd better keep quiet?' Harpur asked. 'Darken ship for silent running.'

'Silent about what, Mr Harpur?'

Iles released him. Ralph adjusted the dressing-gown, then drew himself a large vodka and downed it like medicine. He did not offer them anything more.

Iles said: 'They'll know we've called on you, Ralph. Thought of that? They're going to suspect you got in touch with us. You might need some protection. You talk to me, and I'll make sure they're never too busy at the nick to answer your emergency call. Very nasty delays can happen, I know.'

'Suspect I got in touch with you about what, Mr. Iles?'

7

Loxton said: 'Ralphy, what I asked Phil to bring you out here for regarding, we heard you had a visit. This would be Mr Desmond Iles and Harpur, the side-kick? That kind of visit, Ralphy, I can't really be happy about, if I'm frank.' Christ, but Ralph looked bad. You'd think his whole world had suddenly gone right-through-rotten, yet he had to keep feeding on it because that's all there was, like a dog locked in with a corpse. Yes, a dog: the way his head hung down, and the big brown eyes full of nothing, you could say he was a sick dog, and the only thing to have him put down.

Loxton did not want that, not necessarily. Although Ralphy was total nothing, he was local nothing. Ralph Ember had been hanging around so long, and making a fair-to-middling go of things, you had to feel tied to him, sort of, not close, for Christ's sake, not anything that meant much, but you didn't want him knocked over brutal like that, except there was very special reasons. It wouldn't be in order. There could be reasons coming to light, yes, but do nothing hasty, nothing inconsiderate. Of course, Phil Macey might feel different, and Loxton had to see to it Phil was all right. With his mouth open, Ralph could do Phil big damage. Well, with his mouth open Ralph could do them all big damage, and not just the end of the silver wedding party. Things lead to each other, no question, Phil on the police list one day, Loxton himself the next. Ralphy might be nothing – but a nothing with a singing voice.

'What Benny wants to know, why you never told us them two been out to see you,' Macey explained now. 'That would be a simple courtesy, Ralph, you got to agree. You must of known this is the kind of visit we would be interested in. We got the feeling that if we didn't find about that visit by our own ways you would never of told us about it.'

Ralph raised his big, dark-haired head and cried out; 'No, Benny, that's not – '

'What we got is some worries to do with your club, haven't we?' Macey continued, reasonable: no rage or evil in his words yet, but Loxton could feel them not far away. 'I got personal worries, you must of realised that. I mean, we had a troublesome time there. Admitted, it sorted itself out, but them troubles could come alive again, any time, and they could lead to Benny himself, everyone. That's the thing about troubles, they get all over in no time at all, like poison in the blood. When I say "come alive", well, obvious, I don't mean he's ever going to – What I mean is, inquiries, Harpur, that sort of thing, bringing it all back into the forefront, waking up them problems again. People like that Harpur and the crazy one with the grey hair, they don't leave the office for a mugging in the underpass. This got to be important. It's obvious that a visit like that, we would expect to be kept in the picture.'

'I got to say I'm disappointed in you, Ralphy,' Loxton told him. Today he, Phil Macey, Norman and Bobby were dressed for a funeral, Loxton in a heavy, dark three-piece suit, stiff-collared white shirt, black tie and shoes. They were seated around the lounge of his ranch-style house on the Loam private estate, Loxton again occupying his big, lop-sided armchair, looking somehow wilder, less governable, because of the perfect, sombre clothes.

Ralph was hunched forward on the sofa, moving his feet twitchily about in front of him over the carpet, as if trying to kill a very tough bug. People of Ralphy's sort, God, yes, they were a bit of familiar scenery, but Loxton always tried all he knew to keep from getting real involved with such out-and-out, lost dribbles, and then something happens like that up at the Monty, something you could not foresee, no way, and so here he is, not just anywhere, but right into the house, them suede boots and a suit like something from a Don Ameche film, in a room Loxton really thought a lot of: pictures he chose himself, not Alma's florals. Ralph's sitting there, waiting to get his words going, winding up his lies and excuses, shaking and frothing and staring about, like a kid at a nude show, it was disgusting. Get the air freshener going here afterwards.

Loxton went on: 'It's a grief to me, a day like this, when we're in mourning, that I got to be doing this sort of business, Ralphy, sending for you, requesting a conference, urgent. Well, it should not be forced on me, that's the truth, we ought to be allowed to spend time uninterrupted turning our minds to thinking about the much-admired deceased and giving proper respect. Instead of that, all this rush and stress. What it does is unsettle me, Ralphy, and others likewise. This is not just a selfish feeling.'

Fervently, Ember replied: 'Benny, I'm sorry. I wouldn't have had it happen for worlds, take my word, please do, I mean, the unfortunate coincidence of this misunderstanding – and believe me, it's only that, nothing more than a misunderstanding – this misunderstanding with a particular day of sorrow for you, and the others.'

'What misunderstanding?' Macey asked.

'Well, I would certainly have informed you about the call by those two,' Ralph said. 'It was just that I had to make a few inquiries before I contacted you, Benny.'

'That could be reasonable, Phil, a time for extra trawling.'

'That's it exactly,' Ralph said, smiling with gratitude. It made him look so much worse, Loxton thought. What the hell been happening to Ralph, his kidneys on stop?

'What we don't know, how they come to be there at all,' Macey asked. 'I mean, you been in touch with them, Ralph, initiating?'

'Ralph, we're concerned about you, your condition, one way and the other,' Loxton said.

'How they came to be there?' Ralph said. 'You're not asking, did I send for them, surely?'

Macey left his chair and went and stood as if covering the door, a little behind Ralph and to his right. 'What we're asking for starters, Ralphy, is did you send for them?' Macey said. After a moment, Bobby joined him there. Looking at them, the hard bodies behind mourning ties and gleaming shirts, Loxton thought if funeral parlours ever needed bouncers them two would be dead right, yes, dead right. Phil Macey was alongside a print portrait on the wall of a poet, Lord Byron, with great burning eyes that you could see was concerned with big thoughts

115

about Mankind and rhymes. That was quite a contrast with Phil. It took all sorts, though.

Ralph turned his head slowly and with great effort to look towards Macey and Bobby but made his reply to Loxton: 'Benny, would I, for God's sake? Would I invite a contact of that sort? Don't we know each other better than that? Benny, we've seen a lot together these past years. How long would it be?'

Again he was smiling, but in a grieved way now, and it still did not do anything for him, like somebody hearing his dear old mother had passed on and all the money left for neutering cats. 'That's true enough,' Loxton said.

'Yes, we do know you, Ralphy, and you gets scared, unfortunate,' Macey replied. Ralph was still half-turned to watch him and Bobby. 'It's a recognised fact, in the form-book. Nobody's saying you're yellow, nothing extreme, but you expect the worst, like CND, and it makes you jumpy. So, you could of felt a bit frightened, that incident at the club, then myself coming to see you subsequent, all that sort of thing building up, so you're looking for some help, you're looking for guardians. And where do you turn, Ralphy? Well, to the law, of course.'

Loxton said: 'Myself, I got an open mind on this. Phil, he's excited, natural, there could be a lot of time in it for him. Show Phil Macey a couple of high-rank pigs and he's ready to emigrate.'

'Look, pardon seeming to go off the subject a minute,' Macey said, 'because it's not really. I'll show you why, subsequent. But this funeral Benny's attending today, it's his old schoolteacher from way back, just some ordinary retired chalk pusher, that's how it might look to others, but Benny thinks a lot of that very venerable teacher, and he's going to be there to pay last respects. That's the kind of man Benny is, ready to make the selfless effort for somebody who don't really add up to a bar rag. Now, Ralphy, don't you think it would of been the decent thing, a piece of normal politeness, to let a man of them qualities know fast that two top bastards had been sniffing? Don't he deserve that kind of elementary consideration, Ralphy?'

'I do, I do,' Ember cried, 'and I – '

'Benny thinks of others, and others, like you, Ralphy, ought to think of him, same way. Look, he wants us all to go to the funeral, so there's a fine turn-out for this old fart,' Macey went on. 'I mean, that's how some would regard her, this teacher. All right, we need a little team there, anyway, because Leo and his lot could be parading, too. This is Leo's teacher as well. But it's not just in case of trouble Benny asked us to go, that's the point – it's a tribute to this fine old lady schoolie. You see what I mean about the kind of grand person you've hurt by being so inconsiderate, Ralph?' Macey still sounded very calm.

Ember said: 'Not for the world, I wouldn't – '

'Always looked up to the educated kind,' Loxton said. 'Books, fair copies, historical depth, parsing, all that. So, what they there talking to you about, Ralphy, them two gorillas? Which way's it all pointing? We got a legitimate interest in these matters, you got to admit. So, all right, you didn't call them, we accept that, don't we, Phil, so what they there for, what they asking you?'

'It's routine, Benny,' Ralph replied. He tried to relax a little and turned back to look directly at Loxton. 'They've been up before. I know the drill now. They have a squint at the membership list in case there's someone they want to lean on. Simple as that. If you ask me, they're out on a long booze-up, moving through all the clubs, taking a couple of free drinks every time, throwing their weight about for the sake of it. They call it showing the flag, an echo of the Empire. That's how they see themselves, arrogant pair.'

'Nothing about that little incident?' Macey asked.

'Nothing at all.'

'Anybody go out to the yard, Ralphy?' Macey said.

'The yard?'

Loxton, watching him, saw what looked like Ralph trying to work out how much they knew. What he had to keep in his poor, panicky brain was that there had been a tip from somewhere about these police calling, so what they said and did up at the Monty could be known, too. Ralphy probably been through all this sort of questioning and covering with the police already. Stress all ways. No wonder he looked like a day in the life of a nervous breakdown.

'That builder's rubble thing, the skip,' Macey went on. 'Any interest in that? You see the way my mind is going, do you? If you didn't call them, it could be Sarah Iles said something to her husband, regardless. You was supposed to have made her silent, but you might not of done a very good job there, Ralph. And if

117

she mentioned that skip one of them might want to see it. I mean, it don't matter because there's nothing there and never was – would we be so stupid and obvious? – but if they're interested in it it's because they been told something, isn't it? Or could be.'

In a while, Ralph replied, 'Well, yes, I think one of them went out to the yard. Iles. It's a thing about the licence, fire doors, all that. They always do it. It's nothing, Benny.'

'They mention the skip?' Macey asked.

'No interest at all,' Ralph replied. 'Not a word. Why should they? I'm telling you, Benny, it's a social call, a free-loaders' call, dressed up as a routine inspection.'

Loxton, speaking very gently, said: 'My trouble, listening to you, Ralphy, to put it frank but not impolite, I hope, my trouble is, this sounds like a parcel of outright fucking balls. Lies from the word go.'

Ember sat frozen forward, sitting on the edge of the sofa, his head still twisted around to keep an eye on the two by the door, not able to talk for a moment, his breath gone. Briefly then, Loxton feared Ralph might have a stroke.

'You lie to us because you want to stay out of it, don't you, Ralph?' Loxton said. 'You're the poor sod in the middle, yes, lying to everyone I shouldn't wonder, police, us, your aunty, trying anything for the quiet life. The way you always been, the way nearly all the world is.'

'Our tipster says this Iles went and had a good look in that rubbish container, Ralphy,' Macey told him. Sharpness was into his voice now. 'We got someone hanging around constant, inspecting your place, since the incident, well, what you'd expect.'

'Benny, I don't know,' Ralph replied. 'I assumed it was just the usual quick look-over.'

'Do you get the point, though, Ralphy?' Loxton replied. 'The skip itself don't matter. But if he's interested in the skip it must be because his wife told him something. If she told him what she thought about the skip, she've told him all the rest, and we can expect a lot of difficulty. We don't want no difficulty just now, because we got something of considerable importance in view. Let's leave it at that. This is apart from the trouble Phil could have and Norman, they was both up there that night, as you know. And any trouble that comes to them comes to me eventual. I'm the governor. Whatever they're doing they're doing because I told them.'

'They mention any names?' Macey asked.

'Only the past, mayors from way back, that sort of thing. Never your name, Benny, or Phil, or Norman or Bobby. Nothing like that, I swear it.'

'Aston?' Loxton asked.

'Ian Aston? No. Why should they?'

'Because he was there, twat.'

'No.'

'Any other name?' Loxton asked. Had they spoken about Justin Paynter? Well, he couldn't give the name to Ralph, in case they hadn't.

'No names at all.'

Bobby said: 'He's telling us nothing, chief.'

'No, he's telling us nothing, I can't argue.' Loxton replied.

Ralph slewed himself further around on the sofa to look at Bobby: 'How can I tell you anything if there's nothing to tell?'

Now Loxton thought he sounded as if he might weep.

'You touch my heart,' Bobby said.

'We all think you're lying like a lawyer, Ralphy,' Loxton told him, 'that's the tragedy.'

Ralph whispered: 'No, no, Benny. Everything totally straight.'

Macey said: 'Benny, I don't see we can let him go after this. We give him a reasonable chance to speak, and he offers us nothing but shit, it's obvious.' He started to shout. 'Look, he's a peril, not just to me and Norman, but to the whole thing, you know what I mean? He's a witness. He saw the totality, nearly. Well, we thought that didn't matter because he was Ralphy and Ralphy never wanted no trouble from anywhere, so eyes shut, mouth shut, real brilliant discretion. Now, he's talking to police, though. Where are we, Benny? He got to be dealt with, no escape.'

Loxton held up a hand to silence him and tried to speak coolly. 'I don't get into spots where there's no escape.'

Macey said: 'Yes, but – '

'Let me make the decisions, will you, Phil?'

'Of course, Benny, but – '

'That's settled then,' Loxton said. Macey could try to run away with things now and then. He had to learn. 'You see what difficulty I'm in, Ralphy? Listen, you can turn and face me.

They're not going to touch you, I guarantee. But I got to see things from all points of view, their point of view, my own, yours, Ralphy. Yes, I got pressures. Now, why you lie I can't be sure – if it's just to keep clear, or if it's worse. We could find out with a little effort, I know. What I got to bear in mind, this is my home, Alma upstairs having a nap, pictures on the wall of great people, really great, not them jumped-up jerks at the city hall, and one of a great cathedral in France – I don't want ugly acts here. Well, obvious, we could take you somewhere else and see what we could shake out of your turn-up, but I don't think so, not at this moment. As I see it, there's a bargain to be arranged in this situation.'

Immediately, Ralph was interested, eager, pathetic really. Them who give him that name, Panicking, had it right after all. 'A bargain? Yes?'

'A trade-off,' Loxton told him.

'What fucking trade-off?' Macey asked. 'What he got to offer?'

Loxton again held up his hand and would have liked to tell Macey not to get excited because when he did his false teeth slipped half off their anchor, but he held back. Macey had to be kept happy and safe, or as near as possible. 'I'll tell you what I think, Ralphy. I don't think you called them two police and I don't think Mrs Iles been talking to her husband. Your sort, you don't call police, like you said. It don't matter how worried you was, you wouldn't. Good. So, that's one point. And the other one, I've seen Mrs Iles chatting to lover-boy, Aston, and the way she was, she's not going to do something that would break up that carry-on. What she lives for is that love situation, the way women do, I'd give odds.

'So, where do that leave us? Like this: them police know something, but they got it from outside. They have their sources. I can make a guess. We get tips about where *their* information comes from, oh, yes. Enough said. So, anyway, I don't worry very much about Mrs Iles, not at the moment. It could change, but that's how it is now. What worries me the most is this guy Aston. He's the one who could really hurt us. He got no loyalties that one. He's in the buying and selling game, yes? He wouldn't care where he traded information. Not to the police, he's not going to do that, no. Well, he wouldn't get any price, for one thing. But if he goes digging around that incident at your club, going for

120

background, he could come up with an identification of . . . of the central figure. Then he goes and does a bit more digging, and maybe this central figure been talking to friends, and suddenly Aston got some useful, valuable material, material to do with our plans which he could sell so easy to one of our business rivals. You see what I'm saying, Ralphy?'

'Indeed, yes,' Ralph said. 'Sort of industrial espionage.'

'You could call it. We got a really confidential project, and the important thing is it stays that way until a certain date. If anything leaks, anything at all, it's finished. I'd tell you about it, Ralph, but it's so confidential.'

'That's all right, Benny. I understand the ways of business, don't I?'

'Well, of course you do, Ralph. Aren't you a business-man yourself? You can see Aston might really make a mess of things, if he did some good digging and then some good dealing.'

'It's obvious,' Ralph said.

'I was confident you'd see it,' Loxton told him. 'Now, you know Aston pretty well, Ralphy, yes?'

'Not all that well.'

'But a regular at the Monty and so on?'

'Yes. I suppose in that way, I know him.'

'And maybe you've seen some of his friends, contacts, not just women, people who might know where he would hide. People who might even give him a place to hole up.'

'Not sure about that, Benny.'

'You see, I want you to find him for us, Ralphy, really get to work on it. Do it discreet, if you can, but find him. And do it fast. Ask around, go to his haunts, all that. No good up at his place, we been there, and he was already on a runner. But he won't be far away, I'm pretty sure. He's the sort to smell a profit in this situation and he can't resist. With your help we tried to make sure nothing leaked from them two, Mrs Iles and Aston, but we can't be sure it worked, and Ralphy, we got to be sure.'

'It's tricky, Benny.' As Loxton had suggested, Ember was facing him square-on now. There was not much colour left in his face.

'When you find him, Ralphy, just call Phil. We don't ask you to deal with Aston, nothing like that. No need to involve yourself.

Just find him and come on the phone right away. All right? We'll give you numbers and you'll get us on one of them.'

Macey said: 'Yes, Ralph, just stick with him, out of sight, till we get there, in case he moves. You must be able to update us. That'll be neat.'

'I can try, Benny,' Ralph said.

Loxton explained quietly: 'The thing is, you find him and that will show very, very obvious that you don't want to do us damage, Ralph, something which is in doubt for the moment, especially with Phil, because of them police. But if you locate him for us, it says so clear that you're trying to help, and then I can tell Phil to lay off you, I can tell him that entirely reasonable then, can't I? You will be what's called proving yourself. That'll be great and I'll be as pleased as pleased, believe me. But, Ralphy, you fail to come up with where this boy is, so we can talk to him, I'm going to have trouble convincing Phil you're not a big peril as long as you're alive. That's a fact. You see what I'm getting at, Ralph? You understand that Phil can be a bit difficult? I got to accommodate him, and I want to accommodate you, because of knowing you so long. Phil don't go for all that, but never mind, it means something, yes. But you got to prove to all of us it means something, Ralph. And I know that you will. I can feel it.' Loxton stood up and walked across to Ralph and shook his hand. Christ, it felt like a warm fish, but he had really wanted to do that: Ralph wasn't such a bad old toss, and he needed a bit of friendship and warmth. He was suffering.

At the graveside, Loxton stood with Macey, Norman and Bobby close, and felt very glad he had come. There were not many other mourners present. Someone like Miss Binns, unmarried and pretty old, probably had only a few relatives and friends, and the teachers of today would not remember her, though Marl View school was still there. Leo and Daphne, with their sons and a few of their people, had also come out to the cemetery and were on the other side of the grave, Daphne, in a long, dark coat and a hat and veil, holding on to Leo's arm and leaning into him, as if she was really upset. Loxton knew Daphne used to visit Miss Binns right up until she died, taking fruit and magazines. She always had a real heart, Daphne. But it was a bit sad and a bit crazy, really, that about ten of the thin little crowd watching Miss Binns' coffin go down were here because of these old pupils who had turned the wrong way in life. Or that's how she would regard it, anyhow. That might have hurt her bad if she had known. Probably she would have hoped a lot of her old pupils would have come. But although giving education was a great job, it did not make you box-office, alive or dead.

The minister threw some soil down and said about being sure we didn't bring anything into the world and would not be taking anything out. What a fucking useless thought. Amazing what some people got paid for. It was what you had in between that counted, and this bleating minister knew it. He wouldn't be going home in nothing, but a nice new Vauxhall, and he wouldn't be having nothing for his tea, either.

Loxton threw a handful of earth, too, and so Leo had to do the same.

As they all moved away, back to the vehicles, Leo said: 'Grand to see you, Benny, even though the occasion is so painful.'

'Yes, me too, Leo. Daphne, I'm happy you were here.'

'Where's Alma?' Leo asked.

'Well, she didn't know Miss Binns. This is private to the three of us, yes? I brought the boys just to make the numbers up.'

'Yes, the same,' Leo said. 'A tribute to a fine lady.'

'It's been upsetting, and yet somehow nice to think of times gone by,' Loxton remarked.

'Strange to say it, but this has been a good day,' Leo replied. He had on a black homburg hat and with his big, bony, mean nose looked like a middle-grade debt collector. And that was not far out. He did a lot of collecting, but above middle grade, a long way above.

Gerald and Lay-waste Tony stayed very near him and a couple of their other people were with Daphne behind. What they think, that Leo or her was going to get wiped out in a cemetery, with harmless old ducks and a minister nearby and the casket of Miss Binns herself still there, uncovered, only a few yards away? But if you was monsters yourself you thought everybody else behaved like monsters. They had not even heard of decorum.

'Uplifting,' Loxton said. He meant it. Earlier, the funeral service had been in a big old Baptist chapel up near Grant's Hill, quite a nice part. Loxton had felt glad it was not just a hymn and a couple of words from a vicar at the crem. That sort of funeral never seemed to him right, just the least that was decent, as if everybody wanted the dead one gone as fast as could be managed. It lacked. If you were having a funeral, have a funeral, with some time given, and a good service, plus tender memories of the deceased referred to. The minister did well there, and he had really tried to find out something about Miss Binns' life and say something that added up. Of course, there would always be certain people who could not have a funeral, such as troops killed in war or sailors at sea or Justin, and that was very regrettable, but not avoidable, really.

In the chapel he had taken a place at the far end of a pew, against the wall, with Macey next to him and Normal and Bobby immediately behind. Phil was carrying something, and Bobby. Loxton had calculated it would be all right. He could see Leo and Daphne up nearer the front of the chapel, with Gerald alongside them and Lay-waste and a couple of their other people behind.

Although Loxton felt good about the service, it would have been even better in a proper church. Cassocks, stained glass, marble plaques going back to deaths hundreds of years ago, and here endeth the second lesson, all that always excited him, and he loved those big, shining brass stands, like wings on a stalk, for holding the Bible. You got a great sense of top-grade, holy bull-shit in a real church, nonsense polished up with true care and talent.

'Benny, I really feel a part of my life has gone with Miss Binns,' Daphne said. He saw that, under the thick veil, she was near to crying.

'Don't upset yourself, Daph,' Loxton said. She was a friend, whatever, and it hurt him to see her grieving about the past: no point in that. They all stopped near a group of neglected graves where most of the headstones had tilted or fallen and where the ancient jars and flower holders lay abandoned, some broken. It was getting hard to read what was chiselled on the stones be-cause the letters had taken so much weather. If you wanted to be remembered you needed to do something special and get your picture in city hall, or a monument. Miss Binns was remembered today, but would it last? And then Leo and Daphne: they could not count on a great future. It really was a pity about Daphne, she felt things deep. That was womanly, warm.

'Benny, thinking about Miss Binns today, and listening to the Rev, I was recalling some of the things she used to keep on telling us – friendship, looking after each other, decency,' Leo said.

'Yes, true,' Loxton replied.

'These things still mean something.'

'I'd certainly say so.' Loxton had brought the small Beretta pistol with him and gripped it now in his overcoat pocket. Usually, Leo was not a talker. Something could be up. Most people had cleared from the cemetery, just their two groups left. He tried to give Macey a nod, to be ready. Leo's lot could try anything. Decorum? They thought it was a Carib cocktail.

'What I'm saying, Benny, we're the last two, the last two of any real size and substance.' Behind Leo, Gerald smiled a pledge of friendship and understanding, and even Lay-waste tried to look civilised.

'Right,' Loxton replied.

'I believe there's room for two.'

'We've talked about this, Leo and I,' Daphne said. She put the veil back. She had a good, fresh face, with a small nose and mouth and dark blue eyes. It was amazing she still looked so refined and kindly after all those years with Leo, and having two boys like them. 'Why can't we parcel things out, in a civilised style, tell me that? Trade could be shared. For example, you're both interested in making sure the casinos get proper protection, so that could be divided out on a reasonable, fair basis. Other aspects of business the same.'

Lay-waste nodded. 'Why indeed not?'

'That's what we've been discussing, Benny,' Leo said. 'The fighting – it's wasteful, it's perilous, it's out of date.'

'That's certainly a point,' Loxton replied. 'Wouldn't you say, Phil?'

'These are interesting ideas,' Macey replied. 'Undoubted.'

Leo smiled, and looked around at his sons, like to say something really good had happened, even here in a graveyard. 'Well, what I – what we all – would like to propose, Benny, we could arrange talks, yes?' he asked, turning back. He spoke in a voice that was a plea and full of respect.

'Why not?' Loxton replied.

'Grand. That's really businesslike and constructive.'

'Yes, a positive move,' Loxton declared. 'I don't want to sound stupid and sloppy about this, but Miss Binns would be pleased.'

'Oh, yes, indeed,' Daphne cried. 'But not surprised. She always believed good would come out in people, no matter how things looked.'

'She was a godly person, in a true sense,' Loxton said.

'Who'll make contact?' Leo asked.

'I'll call,' Loxton said.

'Grand,' Leo agreed.

'This is truly wonderful,' Daphne said.

'A most promising breakthrough,' Gerald remarked.

They all moved off towards the cars, Loxton indicating to his people that they should stay very close. He still had his hand on the Beretta.

In the car, Macey said: 'What was going on?'

'He been reading *The Godfather*,' Loxton replied. 'Them meetings between the families when people talk sweet and are setting up killings?'

'Yes, I had the idea they wanted to draw us somewhere!'

'Obvious,' Loxton said.

'So why not there, then?' Macey asked.

'They knew we was ready, of course. They want surprise, the tricky bastards. Christ, did you see Lay-waste trying to look like healing the sick and comforting the fatherless?'

Macey said: 'And Daphne, I mean – '

'She's all right,' Loxton said. 'It's desperate she got to go, but Daphne's genuine.'

'I'm glad we came,' Norman said. 'It gives a chance to weigh them up physically, see from close-to, not through a long-distance sight, how they're made.'

8

'I need to see you,' Sarah said.

'Of course,' Margot replied.

'Could it be this afternoon?'

'Why the rush?'

'Margot, something's happened. I'd like to talk.'

'What a counsellor is for. Say four o'clock? Do you want to give me some idea of the crisis now?'

'On the phone?'

'It *is* a bloody cop phone, my dear, isn't it? Surely, that should be secure.'

'Should it?'

'Oh, I see.'

'I was joking.'

'Yes?'

'Well, half. Some strange things have – Sorry, I'm beginning to shout.'

'Take your time, dear.'

'Margot, it's this: suddenly I'm not so sure about Ian.'

'In what way not so sure?'

'Just not so sure.'

'Whether you really want him?'

Sarah was using the guest-room telephone upstairs, squatting on the bed and gazing out over the rear garden.

'Are you still there?' Margot asked.

'What? Yes. Sorry. I thought I saw somebody.'

'Somebody where?'

'Near our bottom fence.'

'In the garden?'

'Yes. The wilderness part – bushes and trees. A movement? But perhaps not. I'm, jumpy, sorry.'

'Are you alone in the house?'

'Yes.'

'Should you tell someone?'

So, even Margot recognised that cuckolded husbands had uses, and ought still to be on call. 'No. It's all right, I'm sure. What was I saying?'

'It was me. You've started doubting whether you really want Ian?'

'He's hurt me.'

'Intentionally?'

Sarah stood up and went to the side of the window, carrying the telephone so she could see better into the garden.

'I asked, was it intentionally?' Margot said. 'Please now, Sarah, is everything all right?'

'No.'

'Not all right? What's wrong? Who is it in the garden?'

'No, I meant not intentionally.'

'Oh, well then – '

'But it makes things worse, much worse. Margot, he didn't know he was doing it, that's what scares me. To him, it was just acting naturally. Ian doesn't trust anybody, me included, or even me especially.'

'If you choose people like – '

'He thought I'd sent some heavies to his place, I mean, a really evil crew.' Once more she caught herself beginning to yell, sob too, now. 'Look, can I tell you about everything later?'

'People like Ian, from what you've said, of course they're going to be edgy and suspicious. Sarah, you run with risk-takers, all that cheap *demi-monde* stuff. It's part of the fun for you, I think, the antidote to Rougement Place. So, expect bad moments.'

'Perhaps.'

'But don't let it upset you.'

'No.'

'I'll see you here at four, then.'

'Yes.'

'What will you do now?'

'Have a walk in the garden. Just to be sure.'

'Sarah, do take care.'

'I'll be fine. I'm OK. It was stupid. My God, who's going to be prowling at nine-thirty in the morning, broad daylight?'

'As I said, you know some very raw people. Well, "know" might not be quite the word.'

'I can't see anyone there now, honestly,' she said, and it was true.

Finishing the call, Sarah watched the garden for a little while longer, then went downstairs, opened the rear door and stepped out. Slowly she crossed the lawn and approached the wilderness. 'Who's there?' she said, in her best, top of the range, jump-to-it voice. There was next to no wind, but what she had seen from the window, or thought she had seen, was a couple of branches of the tall, straggling holly bush lurch sharply, as if they had been brushed against, and perhaps a piece of dark material disappearing behind the foliage, possibly the arm of a man's jacket. Immediately, she had thought it must be Ralph Ember again, in one of his suits, not content to wait outside now, but driven even further this time by special agonies and dreads, ready to load them on to her if he could. God knew, she did not want to see him, but she did not want him lurking, either. Although very scared, she also felt annoyed that he might be on their property: the same sort of resentment as came the other day, when she decided he had no right to crawl his way up into a decent district, and try to fuse the two sides of her life. As Margot said, if you ran with the rough you'd better expect them to show rough.

'Ralph?' she called, quietly. There could be someone over the fence in the garden next door, and they would be asking who the hell was this Ralph that Sarah Iles wanted to find. Carefully, she circled the bush and found nobody. The ground was dry and she could not make out any foot marks behind it. Comforted, she did a good and thorough search of the wilderness and then went back to the house.

And as soon as she had closed the garden door and entered the kitchen she knew someone else was inside with her. Now, she could make out foot marks, faint earth prints crossing the kitchen tiles to the half-open living-room door, reminding her for a moment of those other stains in the corridor of the Monty. That recollection stoked her fears, already fierce. 'Ralph,' she called again, loudly this time, 'Ralph Ember, are you here? What's going on?' There was not much anger left in her now. She decided, suddenly, that she might be safer outside and had half turned to make a run when the living-room door was pulled wide and Aston stood there in his navy anorak and jeans, his voice very harsh.

'Ralph? You're expecting Ralph?' he said, but it was almost a snarl.

The shock made her breathless and for a few moments she stood staring at him, across the kitchen. 'My God, Ian. You make these entrances – the transport café, now here.'

'Why Ralph?' he insisted. 'Why did you think it was Ralph? Ralph, in the house?' The hostility in his voice, and the coldness, also reminded her of those terrible opening minutes at the Truckers' Den.

'What? I'm sorry, you've knocked me off balance.'

'Why Ralph?' he asked again.

'I didn't know who,' she said.

'Yes, but you called his name.'

'He's been up here before, that's all. Not to the house, but in the street. I thought he had come back.' She was stammering. 'Ian, this is – it's wonderful, wonderful.' Forcing herself to break from her frozen pose near the garden door, she ran across the kitchen and put her arms around Ian's neck, pulling his face down hard to kiss him and kiss him again. He hardly responded, but was staring about, very watchfully. In a moment she went on: 'I was going to say this is impossible, but it isn't, is it? You're here and it's ... well, wonderful.' She laughed. 'Oh, where's my bloody vocabulary gone? In my house!' she whispered. 'Who'd have believed it?'

'I couldn't risk the phone again. After last time, who knows who's listening? Who knows who might turn up as a result?'

'Ian, please, I – '

He seemed to relax a little, as if he had begun to believe her account of things. 'I walked here – saw Desmond go to work. I had to get to you, to warn you, Sarah. That's why when you called Ralph's name – Christ, I didn't know what to make of it, nor now.'

'I'm lost. What's going on?'

'Ralph's looking for me. I had a tip he's been asking around, really looking. And others. Sarah, if they're looking for me it's because of what we saw at the Monty. They'll probably know about you, too. I had to come and tell you.'

'I'm still lost.'

He was still gazing about. 'I knew Desmond had gone, but I've looked over the house. You don't mind? I'm very exposed.'

'We're all right here, surely to God.'

'You were on the phone upstairs. I watched you from the garden.'

'Yes.'

'Who to?' Perhaps he noticed how she winced, and softening his tone, he said: 'Sorry. Can I ask, who to?'

She was glad of the brief moment's thought. 'Of course you can, love. No mystery. A shop. Ordering some things. Life goes on.' He was still holding her and she felt so happy now, despite what he had said, that she could not bring herself to recall the talk with Margot about doubts and cooling. All that seemed unbelievable, suddenly. There was something else: occasionally these days she found herself adapting to this other kind of life, using veils, not disclosing it all, shaping the truth. She had never told him about Francis Garland, anyway, but, that apart, she had always been fairly open, until lately. The pressures of the kind of life she had picked were beginning to affect her: changes did happen, were forced on to one. 'Which other people are looking for you?' she asked.

'Men who came into the Monty that night. I recognised them. It's Benny Loxton's people. I couldn't tell you at the time.'

Yes, veils. But that particular veil had not been much use. Even at the Monty she had suspected he recognised the intruders.

'They're searching for me and they must have terrorised Ralph into helping.'

'Ian, I hate to say this and I don't want it, but you ought to disappear, really get away. Somehow, we could keep in touch.'

He grunted. 'I thought of that. Of course I did. But my car's at the flat, if they haven't taken it, and I'm not going back there. They'll be watching the station and Benny has good contacts in taxis and car hire. Besides, can I just walk out on you, Sarah, as things are?' He bent forward and kissed her on the forehead. It was dead, like a kiss from an old aunt, but she smiled up at him. Then he said: 'Besides, there could be some business in this for me. So, sod them.'

131

This was his real reason for staying. She had heard that stubborn tone take over before, and loved him for it, even if it could lead to peril. He did not go under or kowtow. Ian could look at a dire situation, and think of ways to make it work for him. 'Business? What business?'

'Information, tradable information. Sarah, something pretty big is due, that's dead obvious. People will want early signals about it and will pay.'

'Which people?'

'I don't know yet, but I'll find out. My guess is that the injured lad at the Monty had learned too much, or had been talking. Has to be that. It wasn't too hard to identify him and I found out he's got a girl friend, an on-off thing, no big deal. All the same, there's a chance he's said something to her. I drove up to her place a couple of times but she's away in Cyprus or Marbella, or some sun spot, having the grand time, probably with some other bloke. Maybe she's lying low out there, or maybe it's only a holiday and she'll be back. I'm going to keep trying, just roll up on her. She lives in the country, about ten miles. But now, no vehicle. One night, I might sneak back to the flat and see if I can get it. She's important, Sarah.'

'I'll take you. I'll take you today.' It would be compensation after what she had said to Margot, and it might be a chance to bring back some of their old warmth. She longed to put things right and to be part of that fighting, positive side of him.

'No. You're involved enough.'

'Yes, let me. But, Ian, do they know about her?'

'Loxton's people? There speaks the cop wife again. I don't know. Hope not. Things might be tricky for her.'

'And you.'

'Maybe.'

She squeezed his arm. 'Listen, Ian, if you know about her, they know about her.'

'Why I say you mustn't come.'

'I'll put you down nearby. It'll be quite safe. I'm coming to realise I'm not a born risk-taker.' Sarah shifted slightly. 'And I don't like standing here. We're visible through the kitchen window, and you don't look like Des. Not that Des and I ever get close in the kitchen, or anywhere else.'

'Can we go upstairs?'

132

She made sure there was no pause before she answered. 'I should think so. Wait.' She went to lock the garden door and turn the deadlock on the front.

'Are you certain it's OK?' he said.

'Of course.' It was another step. He had come into her house for the first time, and they would make love here for the first time, but what did the venue matter? Although she might have resented Ralph being on their ground, Ian was another matter. Oh, yes, very much another matter. He did not belong either, but she could have wished he did. Perhaps to be with him in the house was a new and bigger betrayal, a special kind of symbolic blow to the marriage, but there had already been enough blows to knock most of the life out of it. She wished she could think of another word than blow, and almost smiled.

As lightly as she could manage she said: 'This is pretty scary, going into our bedroom.'

'It really bothers you?'

'I'm surprised, but, yes, it really bothers me.'

'Well, let's use another one.'

'No. A room's a room, a bed's a bed, nothing more. I shouldn't think I'm the first wife to do this. They say Harpur's lady – Oh, but you don't know these people, and I shouldn't gossip.' By insisting on this room she was again trying to make up to him for what she had said to Margot, but he could not be told that. It was like a re-affirmation, and had to be powerful and glaring, strong enough to rout all scruples. Wow, this fuck had taken on symbolism. But, then, so did many others. Crossing the room quickly, past the unmade bed, she pulled the curtains over. Perhaps the neighbours would be intrigued by that, too, but never mind.

In fact, to coin a phrase, stuff them. She knew what was happening to her and felt almost entirely grateful: the fierce, glory-filled, juvenile disregard for most of those customary restraints among which she usually lived had taken over again. Not bad in someone going on strong for thirty-seven, and before ten o'clock on a chilly morning. So as not to appear ludicrously eager or hungry she took her clothes off at a decently methodical pace, like someone in a general changing room, but it was difficult, and it was a disguise, because she did feel eager and hungry. The conversation with Margot seemed even more unbelievable now. Where were the doubts she had felt about him, and the resentments? Hadn't they been miserably trivial, a reflection on herself, not Ian? She was on one leg, rolling her tights and knickers down, and staggered slightly: could that be the unbalancing impact of penitence – for misjudging Ian, not because she was about to take him into the marriage bed? The thought made her giggle.

'What?' Ian said.

'You're looking very, very well.'

'It's cod liver oil of malt.'

'Oh, thanks. I thought it was me.'

'Well, you do come into it.'

'No. *You* come into it.'

'Oh, God, are you being coarse again? Which side does he sleep on?'

'Why?'

'I'll take the other.'

'*Quelle délicatesse.*'

'What's that mean?'

'It means you're full of surprises, Ian.'

'But you're bothered about it, too. You said so.'

'I was. Now, no. This is my bed and I want my lover in it. What could be more natural than that? It's not complete until you've been here.'

He lifted the duvet and moved in beside her. 'I've missed you rotten,' he said, stroking her face.

'Have you?'

'Rotten.'

'Yes, it hurts, doesn't it? Worse for me. Half the time, I don't know where you are, but you can always find me.' Expertly, she climbed on top of him. 'May I?' She guided him into her, and everything was so right, and such a reproach for all the time they wasted not together.

'Astraddle? You've seen *My Beautiful Launderette*.'

'Actually, I knew about this sort of thing before.'

'That so? Well, it *is* beautiful.'

'Yes, it is.' She began to move on him, slowly.

'Oh, yes, yes, love,' he said. But in a moment he rolled her over, without separating, and kissed her on the ears and neck and nose, gazing down at her. 'I'm so used to looking at you from here.'

'Ian, stay with me,' she whispered. 'Try not to leave me like that again.'

'All right.'

She put her arms around his waist and gripped her own wrist, locking him to her and pulling him harder against her body.

He said: 'Sarah, I – '

'I don't want to talk now.'

'No. Right.'

But after a while she found herself muttering between her fine, animal grunts of pleasure, 'Alive, yes, alive.'

'What?'

'I feel alive.'

'True.'

'In this bed, I don't, usually. But I'm entitled, aren't I?'

'Of – '

'Didn't I say I don't want to talk?'

'*You've* been talking.'

'Bloody nit-picker.' She unclasped her wrist and ran her palms up over his back and shoulders, then down his sides and his hips, beating the bounds, as she liked to think of it, marking out ownership.

He seemed to sense what she was doing: 'And your legs,' he said. 'Haven't I told you how much I like that?'

She wrapped them around him, her heels digging into the back of his thighs.

Later on, when they were resting, she said: 'And speaking of films, this – you and me, here, in this meaningful bed – this is our answer to that flabby and fashionable bloody homily, *Fatal Attraction*, the bloated monogamy ad.'

'Is it? Is that what it is? If it hasn't been on telly I haven't seen it.'

'That lingering shot of the family photograph at the end. Holy smarmy matrimony. God.'

'Yes? It upset you?'

Yes, it had upset her, and she hissed: 'Yanks. What a people. Always have to assert the pieties. Just think of *The Caine Mutiny*.'

'The what? How does that come into it? Bogart? The yellow captain called – ?'

'At the end the supposed great radical lawyer, Jose Ferrer, must suddenly turn round and say the monster Queeg was right all the time, because he was the captain, the law and order man.'

Occasionally, she liked to cut loose, range a bit, to show Ian she had a mind.

But he had a mind, too, in his way. 'I thought law and order was your pay packet.'

That she ignored. 'It's a nothing, burger culture, the States. Christ, they've even got a wine burger.'

'What? Oh, I see, Weinberger.'

'And they – ' Someone rang the door bell very hard and long. They lay silent. The ring was repeated, and then repeated again.

'Who?' he whispered.

She shrugged. 'Not Des. He's got a key.' Play it as a joke, even if she did not feel like laughing: 'Jehovah's Witnesses?'

'It's that bastard, Ralph?'

'Ralph? He wouldn't come here.'

'But no time ago you thought he *was* here. In the kitchen, you did. What goes on, Sarah? Tell me, now, honestly – honestly – it's him?' He gripped her wrist hard, as she had gripped it herself not long ago, to fix her to him and make her feel they belonged to each other, despite everything. That was not his object. He wanted to hurt her. His voice, although so subdued, suddenly had all that roughness and suspicion in it once more.

'Let go,' she told him. 'I'll try to see.'

But he did not release her. 'Wait.'

There was another long peal on the bell and then the sound of someone rapping a glass panel in the door with a coin.

'How do you mean, he wouldn't come here?' he asked.

'Not to the door, for heaven's sake.'

'Where then? He does come here, but not to the door. Is that what you're saying? What goes on?'

'No, he doesn't come here,' she muttered wearily. 'He lurked in the street. Once.' They lay silent again for a few moments. He still held her wrist. 'Gone?' she said.

'Maybe. He could have trailed me here. He's sharp.'

'They've given up,' she said. But immediately then they heard someone try the rear door, and, when it did not open, start to shake it. She reached down to prise his fingers apart. 'Please,' she said. 'I'll try to see.' This time he allowed her to free herself and she swiftly left the bed and went out naked on to the landing, where there was a window overlooking the garden and rear door. Approaching it carefully from the side, she glanced out, and saw

Margot walking hesitantly down the garden towards the wilderness.

Sarah went back to the bedroom. It's all right. One of my friends.' Swiftly, she began to dress. 'I'll have to go and see her.'

'Which friend?'

'Just a friend. Margot.'

'You never mentioned her.'

'Didn't I?' No, there had never seemed a reason to tell Ian she was taking expert advice about her marriage, and there seemed no reason now.

'Why go and see her? She'll give up and leave, won't she?'

'She might be worried. My car's there, so I ought to be in. She'll be puzzled.'

'Well, so bloody what?' After what had been said on the telephone Margot might be perturbed enough to call Desmond. 'I think I'd better see her. Ian, you stay.'

'We shouldn't have gone to bed here. It was bound to turn out wrong.'

'Ian, you sound like *Fatal Attraction*, as if we're being punished for something. It's not the Day of Judgement.'

'Talk sense, will you, for Christ's sake – about us, here, now, not fucking make-believe movies.'

To see Ian so ravaged by panic sickened her and her uncertainties about him were coming to the boil yet again. She went from the room and downstairs. Margot had returned to the front and was ringing the bell once more and, this time, calling Sarah's name softly through the letter box.

She opened the door. 'If you'd shouted before, I'd have come. I thought it was double-glazing, something like that.'

'You're all right?'

'Of course.'

Margot came in. 'Your call – I was damn worried.'

'Yes, I'm sorry.'

Margot spoke rapidly. 'I drove up just to look at the house from outside, check you were all right. I wasn't going to stop, but then, in your road – Sarah, some men hanging about in a car.'

'What men?'

'Lord knows. But as if they were watching the house.'

'Where?'

'Twenty or thirty yards along.'

Oh, God. Again she wanted to scream out and ask what she had let herself in for. Maybe, after all, Ian was right to be so tense and changeable. Fright had started to affect her own ability to think properly. 'You're sure?'

'That's how it looked, Sarah. These were men I wouldn't want hanging about near my house.' Today she was almost smartly dressed, like a manageress or high-calibre secretary, in a light tweed suit and half-heeled shoes, not the trainers. 'They watched my every move, really staring, you know, watched until they saw I'd noticed them. Then, all of a sudden, they became, oh, so very busy, heads down, pretending to examine papers or something.'

Sarah took her into the living-room and they sat down. 'How many men, Margot? What did they look like?'

'Two. One grey-haired but not old. Thin. The other fair, burly. I didn't see him so well.'

Sarah wanted to ask whether the grey-haired man wore rimless glasses, like the one at the Monty, but decided it was best to act dumb.

Margot gazed about the room and then up at the ceiling for a time, as if she could see through it. 'Ian's here, isn't he?' she said, gently.

'What? What are you talking about? In the house?'

'Now, come on, Sarah – the delay in answering, curtains over, and you look like somebody who's just got out of bed, not after sleeping, either.'

'My God, Margot, would I risk – ?'

She smiled at the objections. 'Bringing him here is some sort of symbolic act?'

Sarah gave in. 'Actually, the act felt quite real.'

'Nice.'

'He's in danger, Margot. Those men in the street.'

'They're looking for him?'

'Most likely.'

'And for you?'

'It's possible.' She walked to the window. The sitting-room was in the front of the house, but hedges at the end of the garden prevented her from seeing the road outside. 'Margot, what can I do?'

'They know he's here?'

'I don't think so. No, they'd be there to follow me, in case I could lead to his hiding place. As if he'd tell me.'

Margot stood up and seemed about to cross the room to her. But she remained near her chair. 'Oh, please don't be miserable, Sarah. He's bound to be like that. It's a life and death habit, really it is. There would be nobody he trusts absolutely.' Margot thought for a moment. 'If you drove out, drew them off somewhere, Ian could – '

Sarah held up a hand to silence her. From upstairs had come the faint sound of movement and then a little while afterwards what could have been someone in the kitchen, although she heard nothing on the stairs. Hurriedly, she left Margot and ran up to the bedroom. Ian was no longer there, and his clothes had gone. She checked the other upstairs rooms, without success, and then rushed back down, yelling his name frantically. Margot came out and stood in the hall, her face anxious and sympathetic. In the kitchen, Sarah found the rear door open and she continued out into the garden, but saw nobody. Sprinting across the lawn, she made for the wilderness again, still calling him. Yes, stuff the neighbours. This was two men's names they could puzzle about now, neither of them her husband's. Although she did another search among the bushes and trees she did not find him. The fence was too high for her to look over, but he could have gone that way.

Margot joined her: 'I thought you had doubts about wanting him.'

'What? Which doubts? What are you talking about? Where is he? He could get killed, for God's sake. He doesn't know those people are waiting.'

'They're at the front of the house.'

'The ones we know about are. How many others? This is a gang, you know. Anyway, which way did he leave? He's not here. He might have gone around the side and up the drive into Rougemont Place.'

'Would he?'

Margot's calm and logic enraged her. 'Christ, how do I know?' she shouted and ran back over the lawn, then herself went to the side of the house and up the drive towards the street. Outside, Rougemont Place appeared as terminally sedate as ever. Margot followed again. 'Where?' Sarah asked. 'Where's this car with the men?'

She looked about carefully. 'Gone.'

'Yes, but where was it?'

Margot led her a little way along the road. Sarah scrutinised the ground.

'What are we searching for?' Margot asked.

Sarah was looking for blood, or for any sign of a struggle – a bit of torn clothing, a button. 'I don't know.'

9

Not long after dawn, Harpur stood on the quay-side at Young's Dock, wearing his fire-damage sale camel-hair coat and the round, beige, two-tier Asian cloth hat ceremonially presented to him last year at a racial harmony gathering in the community hall on Ernest Bevin estate. Comfortable and warm, its original was maybe designed for protection against icy blasts pounding down from the Afghan mountains into West Pakistan, and Harpur reckoned it looked decently back-street ethnic, more peasant than those flash, I've-been-Intourist-to-Leningrad, curly, black fur jobs.

The divers waited in their Land Rover near him. Harpur loved the docks, even at this chilly hour, and despite what was going on. The sun, red and weak, had started coming up behind one of a group of moored tug boats, *Destiny II*, the first bits of pale light profiling its stubby, powerful frame. So, what destiny had *Destiny I* met with? Perhaps only age and obsoleteness, which hardly rated as destiny at all, but which were a pain and always liable to get you. Around the bridge and mast of *Destiny II* hung a few strands of morning mist, and more strands rolled sleepily in the breeze across the black water. Once he'd seen a painting of a French port, maybe Le Havre or Fécamp, with the same misty effects, though the ships were sail. If Jack Lamb had been here he could have given the locale and artist right away, might even have had the picture on his wall briefly for a few secret days at some time while he worked a deal.

Harpur saw no activity yet on any docked vessel and the only sounds were a couple of seagulls terrorising another for a fillet of rubbish from a plastic sack, and, further off, a freight train lazily shunting. Things would wake up, soon, thank God. He could tire of romantic desolation. After some tough years, the docks had revived and business seemed good. Across the dock lay a big, well-cared-for Russian timber carrier and, a little way along the wharf, a handsome United States container ship was stacked up, ready to go. Ah, trade, so much more binding than diplomacy. Sights like this could almost make him believe in Thatcherism, though not to the degree where he would disclose it to his children or Megan, especially his children.

The divers sat silent in the back of the vehicle, waiting for more light before they put on their dry suits and went down. Given the choice, he knew they would have left it until much later in the day, when the sun would be higher and offer them an extra foot or two's visibility at twenty feet. But the big American vessel could be moving around by then, as well as *Destiny II* and other tugs, all churning the water. In any case, the Chief wanted this first stage of things done when there were as few people as possible about. Why draw attention? Of course, if there *were* something important on the bottom it would be a crane operation, and that could not be kept discreet.

Iles had said he would probably visit a little later, so, in the mean time, Harpur concentrated on enjoying the scene and absence of stress, pacing the quay to keep his blood on the move. He had nothing to do here except wait. The sergeant with the diving unit would decide when the men should enter the water and what the procedure was to be if they found anything. Harpur would get the report, and until then was a spectator. He liked it that way, felt total non-envy of the divers. It would not be like snorkelling in the Aegean. And, after all, who knew whether they would find anything?

Although Jack Lamb might not be present, it was a tip from him that had brought them all here this morning. At Jack's suggestion, he and Harpur had met yesterday, not this time on the foreshore, but at a sherry party to launch an exhibition of regional works – sculptures, oils and water-colours – in a small privately run art gallery. Jack had brought Helen with him, the once punk child, now moving into chicness, but sent her off to look at pictures, while Harpur and he talked.

'About something perilous?' she asked.

'How would I know anything perilous?' Jack had replied.

'You like this sort of small-time stuff?' Harpur had said. 'Really, Jack?'

'Yes, I do. I even buy. Art's not just about great names, great prices, Col. More to it than Dalis and Brueghels and Hobbemas.'

'That so?'

'You think I sound phoney?'

'I'm always listening.'

'Yes.' They were standing under some gaudy versions of local landscape, all spinach greens and throbbing golds.

'Anyway, Jack, you keep safe?'

'Never a hint of trouble.'

'So far.'

'I'm thinking of renaming my house that, Col. So far is all any of us have.'

'So far and no further?'

'Who knows? Who ever knows?' He smiled at someone and exchanged a couple of words about a London sale.

Harpur reminded himself once more that, without any doubt, Jack did legitimately buy some of the great art that came his way. It was the rest that worried Harpur, and the rest was most. Quite often, Lamb would talk unreservedly and fascinatingly about recent great art thefts – like the Impressionists from the Paris Marmottan Museum valued at around ten million pounds. Of course, talking about them, even in such expert detail, did not mean Jack had ever seen or handled any of these works. You could even argue the reverse: that the frank, full way he discussed them could only mean he was not involved. Would he lay such trails? Anyway, that was how Harpur argued. But there were times when he badly failed to convince himself. At those painful moments, he listed in his head as fast as he could all the items of unequalled information Lamb had fed him, and all the convictions that had come as a result. As to changing house names, Megan, who had begun to learn a little about the importance of informants, once suggested they should call theirs Quid Pro Quo.

Now the girl was away, Jack had said: 'What could be of interest, Col – this has come in roundabout fashion, I admit, and it's taken a long while to reach me – what could be of interest to you, recognising your general anxieties and so on, a pimp I know, I won't give any names, if you don't mind, but a fortnight or so ago this pimp took a heavy beating, trying to get cash out of a trio of clients of one of his girls, a really scientific knocking about that left him blotto near the Lister warehouse at Young's Dock. When he came to it was very much later at night. He didn't feel like trying to move for quite a while, so he just lay there, piecing his components back together, as much as he could, quiet, stoical, like an injured cat, or like a pimp shunning contact with ambulances, police and all the uniforms and questions parade. While he's recovering in the shadows two cars arrive opposite the main doors and one – he thinks a silver Metro, though his observation might not have been too grand, in the circumstances – this query Metro is taken very close to the edge. He's sure there were two people in it, men. The driver lowers all the windows a bit and gets out quickly. He opens the passenger door, unstraps the man, unbuttons an overcoat and pulls it and a scarf off him. My pimp says it looked then as if the man – the docile passenger – was naked. Anyway, the shoulders and top of his back were bare. The driver straps him in again and closes the door. A couple more men leave the other car, a red Sierra, and they push the Metro into the dock, not that it needed three, it was so near. The nude is still strapped, apparently not able to get out, or do anything else. The three stand at the edge for a minute or two, presumably while it filled and sank, then hopped back into the Sierra and are away. My contact thinks – again, only thinks, he claims no more than that – but he thinks he recognised the driver of the Metro as one of Benny Loxton's people, Norman Vardage: rimless glasses, thin grey hair? Heard of him, though I don't know him myself, but apparently that's right.'

'Yes, sounds like Norman.'

'So, there you are, Col. What bets the passenger is Justin Paynter? Looks a bit of an obvious, amateur job, but this was 3.30 a.m., and if they hadn't been spotted the car could stay there for ever undiscovered.'

'Registration numbers?'

'Col, my informant was hardly conscious, one eye almost closed up. You want the earth.'

'They'll have been stolen for the job, anyway, I suppose.'

'Of course.'

Returning at a rush, Helen had cried: 'Oh, you must come and see these flower pieces, both of you. Don't you love plant por-

144

traits, Colin? When they're good, so meticulous, yet warm. Such a gift this man has. I do hope we can have some of them, Jack. The shining pondweed and pyramidal orchid? Yummie.'

'Anything you say, love,' Jack replied. 'Feel incomplete without.'

Harpur had taken the chance to leave.

Now, the sergeant came out of the Land Rover and gazed up, assessing the light. 'Another half an hour, sir.'

If they found someone below, the divers would not bring him up immediately, because a water-weakened body could be easily damaged, and because, if a crane lifted the car with him inside, it would give a virtually intact scene of the crime for examination. Harpur might have preferred it different. A crane operating would bring television and the press, then pressure to say who was in the car, and what the police meant to do about it. And, on that point, Harpur had doubts. To cling on to confidentiality for as long as possible, not even the divers had been told who might be down there. Their orders were to look for a car and a body, nothing beyond.

They were out of the vehicle now in their 'woolly bear' thermals, ready to put on the dry suits and aqualungs. It would be cold below and they might have to stay under for anything up to a couple of hours. 'Will he be still recognisable?' Harpur asked the sergeant.

'Oh, yes, sir, unless he took a bang in the face before, or going in – and the belt should prevent that. The water's pretty chill and it's only two weeks, isn't it? Yes, not too much damage from bacteria. Of course, the windows are open, as I understand it, sir. That means fish and crabs inside. They make for the eyes first.'

'Yes?'

'But I'd bet he'll be reasonably presentable still, – cold water, a shortish period.' Possibly feeling he deserved some reward for this assurance, he asked: 'Anyone we know, sir?'

'What we're trying to ascertain, sergeant.'

'Of course, sir.' He went back to the Land Rover to prepare.

In a few minutes, two of the divers waddled over to the steps leading to the water. Each had a big, underwater flashlight at his belt and a heavy sheath knife strapped to the right calf, the blade to free the diver from entanglements, and the handle for use as a hammer if he needed to break windows. They entered the water and immediately went down, both trailing ropes to the other two divers, who stood on the edge of the dock and waited for pull signals. The sergeant, also all kitted up now, stayed near the steps, ready to go down if there was any trouble. Harpur watched the early rush of large bubbles change to smaller ones as the men went deeper.

Iles arrived in one of the new Granadas. Lately, he had seemed dismally low and brooding, in anguish over Sarah, Harpur guessed, though the ACC had not spoken about her for a while. To butter him up now, Harpur mentioned the half-recalled, misty painting, confident Iles would identify it instantly and so feel warm and superior: it was not that he lived by pictures, like Lamb, but Iles simply knew more or less everything worth knowing and a lot that wasn't. 'Do you remember it, sir?' Harpur asked, and sensed at once that his welfare effort was doomed. To fool Iles took some doing.

'You joking?' he grunted. 'No, you're trying to make me feel good, aren't you, Harpur, doing a bit of therapy, you patronising fart?'

'Sir?'

'Giving me doddle questions, for my morale. Christ, even a gold card jerk as ignorant as you has to know it's *Sunrise*, Le Havre, Monet, 1872 – the picture that began Impressionism. The Volvo estate mob bound for the Dordogne talk of nothing else as they come in there on the car ferry.'

'Yes, I thought Le Havre.'

'Gee. Ever considered taking over the Tate? What the fuck's that on your head?' Iles went to the edge and gazed for a long while at the bubbles. A wedge of grey hair fell forward and he brushed it back langorously with his hand. Harpur had once heard him apologise for that narcissistic gesture, denouncing it as being copied subconsciously from the ex-Cabinet Minister, Michael Heseltine, but here it was again. Iles wore a magnificently cut beige suit, in gamekeeper's tweed, and weighty brown brogues. The whole grand, ageing, *Country Life* profile seemed to proclaim him prime for cuckolding. He came back and stood close to Harpur.

As if picking up his thought Iles asked: 'No chance this could be that charming longcock, Ian Aston, is there, Col?'

'I don't believe so, sir.'

'No. I should be so lucky. One would very much like to think of that decent, grimy, workaday water sluicing all trace of Sarah from his lover-boy flesh. Eel raids on a dead Aston appeal to me.'

'We ought to prepare a strategy in case this does turn out to be Justin Paynter, sir,' Harpur replied, labouring back towards normality. Once before, a long time ago, he had watched Iles driven to appalling frenzy and violence by pain over a woman: not Sarah then, and not a matter of betrayal, but of death. Harpur dreaded seeing anything like that again.

'He's been up the house,' Iles murmured, almost inaudibly.

'Sir?'

'Aston. Did you know that?' Now, Iles seemed to be trying to make his voice conversational, even offhand, like, Did you know the vicar had called?

'Well, no, sir. I wouldn't.'

'Oh, a neighbour informed me. The description's right. Generously told me of seeing him from a window leave our kitchen and go down the lawn and over the fence. Then Sarah, obviously upset and searching for him.'

'Sir, one always has to consider other explanations – the job teaches us that, above all.'

'It's really nice to think all Rougement Place knows Sarah brings her bit of extra home with her, isn't it? A giggle at their parties: "That wife of the fuzz, so democratic and body-bold."' Somehow, he kept control of his tone. 'What's that Byron thing, in "When we two parted", about the lady's light fame? Oh, Jesus, no use asking you, you have difficulty with the *Beano*. He's probably been ploughing my furrow in my own bed.'

'Sir, you can't – '

'Know that? No. I regard it as a very unpleasant likelihood, though, Col, which would be difficult to forgive.'

'I don't – '

'Well, impossible to forgive, really, wouldn't you say, even you, disgustingly temperate as you are?

'Nothing like that ever happened, sir. Probably. You're creating the situation.'

'So, you'll ask why I just don't tell her to get lost – go to him, if he means that much to her.'

'No, sir, I wouldn't ask that. I can see you'd want to keep her.'

'Yes, I'll keep her.'

147

'Sarah isn't someone to – '

'Vic's coming up, sarge,' said one of the men holding a signal rope.

They went and stood alongside him, staring at the water. Harpur had the impression that Iles was trembling, and not from the cold, although he wore no overcoat. More likely, it would be excitement and irrational hope. He wanted this dock to put an end to all his personal troubles through what would be revealed soon. The case they were working on – what there was of it – had ceased to count with Iles and private suffering had taken control. Occasionally, that could happen when police work overlapped a cop's own life, and it meant a sticky situation.

In a little while the diver's head broke surface, and Iles gave a short, impatient gasp. The man finned to the steps, sat and took his mask and fins off, then came up. A little breathless, he leaned against the Land Rover for a moment before speaking. He addressed Harpur: 'A Metro, lying on the passenger side. Geoff's got the registration. He won't be long. Not much more we can do, sir. A man strapped in the front passenger seat, naked. We put both beams on him but were still not seeing much. I thought maybe a wound of some kind in the stomach. Knife?'

Iles said: 'Yes, Vic, it's good work, very good work. But when you lit him, all right, you're not seeing much, but what *did* you see? I mean, colouring, say. How old?'

'It's difficult, sir,' the sergeant said. 'Down there – '

'I know it's difficult,' Iles snarled. 'Let him answer, will you? If I'm talking to you I'll turn your way, so you'll be able to tell.'

'Dark hair, plenty of it,' the diver said. 'Age? Mid-twenties? What I could make out, I didn't recognise him. I don't know about Geoff. Nothing else in the car, as far as I could see. We didn't do any breaking or try to get in.'

'No, that's fine,' Harpur said.

The other diver came out soon afterwards and confirmed it all. He did not recognise the man either, but had memorised the registration.

Iles said: 'Dark hair? You're sure? There was enough light for that?'

Both divers confirmed the man was dark.

Iles turned to the sergeant: 'I'm sorry I barked. No possible excuse, except disorientating envy of people wearing rubber, of course.'

He and Harpur and Iles talked briefly near the Granada. 'Colin, do I recall that Aston's fair? Do I recall! Christ, what verbiage. As if I didn't have the bastard's description burned into my brain.'

'Yes, he is, sir.'

'Ah, well, there'll be other corpses. Where there's death there's hope.' He climbed into the car and was about to drive off. Then he rolled down the window: 'That sounds so bloody smart and unhinged, I suppose. But I do want her, Col, and he's taking her away. It's just normal, unsophisticated hatred.'

'I understand, sir.'

'Oh, kind.'

10

'I think he knows,' Sarah said.

'This is what, instinct on your part? Have there been hints?' Margot was at the window of her flat, gazing out over the new marina, apparently fascinated by something happening far off at Young's Dock, on the other side of Valencia Esplanade.

'And, if he does – Des is not one of your long-suffering types. This is in his own house, his own bed, Margot.'

'I'm not sure –'

'Oh, you'll tell me the venue's unimportant. I said to myself at the time. But it *was* important. I wanted it to happen there, because it would be another step. Margot, it was a real compulsion. God, that sounds so crude, crude and hungry.'

'But you are, or were, hungry.'

'It seemed so right. I don't know if that makes sense to you. Does it strike you as simply spiteful, juvenile, or maybe just anarchic?'

'None of them. I understand.' Margot seemed still enthralled by something at the dock.

Seated near the fireplace, Sarah felt herself grow suddenly loud and ratty, perhaps offended not to have Margot's total attention. 'What the hell are you looking at? You say you understand! Christ, what else can you say, though, Margot? I'm paying you, aren't I? I'm your client. I come here for a nice comforting warm bath of sympathy.'

Margot half turned and said, gently: 'You want me to tell you you're just a treacherous, leg-spread cow? Sorry, I don't believe it.' Then she went on watching whatever it was outside.

'Yes, I felt it was so right, that it said something important. What did it say? I don't know. But I do know that Des will think it couldn't be more wrong. Obviously. A double invasion, wife and nest. I do see that.'

'Yes, I see that, too. If he was a client, I suppose I'd have to give him a warm bath of sympathy, as well. Were those the words?' Now, looking a bit hurt, Margot left the window and came to sit opposite Sarah.

'I'm sorry, Margot. Unforgivable – I mean, about paying you. Rotten of me.'

'But you *are* paying. Maybe it does affect the response. I'm here to try to help you.'

Part of Margot's job must be uncrackable patience, endless tolerance. 'So, have you heard it before?' Sarah asked.

'Someone driven to take a lover into the matrimonial bed? Yes, it's not so rare. Not much chance of hitting originality in sex. What you did, it's like making the big change without making it, like leaving without leaving. Things are reduced to metaphor. It's more comfortable.'

Sarah had worked that out for herself. It helped, though, to know she was not the first.

'A lot of people are at that, men and women. They want the penny and the bun, but not in the oven if they can help it,' Margot said. She nodded towards the window. 'Maybe a tragedy out there. A crane trying to lift something from the bottom of the dock. Perhaps a car?' She did not get up to look again, though. 'What makes you believe he knows?'

'I think Des could play very rough. Some moments, he's not really too balanced. Anyway, who would be balanced about this?'

'But why do you think he knows? He's said something?'

'He's a cop, Margot. When they're suspicious they don't talk. They listen, they watch. He's doing a lot of that. I changed the sheets, well, of course. But it was the wrong day. Did he notice? He's a cop, Margot. My chorus. I went through the house, really checking there was nothing left behind, and footprints from the garden. But neighbours? I don't know.'

'Why?'

'Why what? You mean, why so much effort to conceal things? Do I really want to hang on to Des?'

'Something like that.'

'Yes, I wondered myself.'

151

Margot grinned. 'Half the time you're ahead of me. I can see why you're not sure what you're paying for.' The room was tidier today and Sarah had not seen or heard the cats. Margot looked formal and neat again, too, in a grey skirt and elaborately patterned hand-knitted, multi-coloured cardigan, and half-heel shoes, not the trainers. On the whole, Sarah preferred it like this. A good turn-out in a decent setting seemed to promise more careful consideration of her problems. Rougement Place values would out: she could have done without these continual reminders that buried somewhere in her must be a powerful yearning for order and appearance, perhaps explaining why she had married the police. But then, what explained why she ran so hard and frantically after Ian Aston, nobody's idea of order?

Margot stood and went back to the window, shielding her eyes. 'Talking of police, I think they seem to be running this show in Young's Dock. I'm up early most mornings, and I think there were divers down today. It's a long way, but that's how it looked. Now, I think more divers, the crane, and bobbies keeping people away.'

Sarah joined her. 'Suicide? People drive in occasionally.'

As they watched, a diver surfaced and then two more. In a moment, one of them signalled with a wave to the quay-side. Sarah could hear nothing from that distance, but two cables from the crane into the water seemed to tighten and the jib bent forward, as if taking weight.

'Not how I would do it,' Sarah said. 'Not drowning. Slow. Agonising.'

'Do you think of suicide?' Margot asked, moving away from the window.

Sarah stayed. 'Who doesn't?'

'Yes, I suppose so. There's a time when anyone can feel cornered.'

'Cornered. Good, awful word. There seems to be no right decision.' The crane still appeared to be labouring, though Sarah saw nothing yet to disturb the surface. It looked as if there were a remarkable number of police there, including some in plain clothes.

'You think it's time for decisions, then, Sarah? I'd agree. You're talking about Desmond as if he were an outsider, not your husband: someone you know only through his job. "He's a cop." In a sense, you've already established a gap between the two of you.'

'So, make it real?'

'Doesn't that sound like sense? Doesn't it sound inevitable?'

For a while, Sarah said nothing, watching the crane. An ambulance stood parked not far from it, both its rear doors open. 'Margot, I'm scared.'

'You can't face the thought of a break-up?'

'I mean I'm scared about what's going on at Young's Dock. It's too much fuss for a suicide.'

'Scared? I don't follow.' Margot rejoined her at the window. 'I'll have to buy some binoculars if there's going to be much of this sort of excitement. Can't really make out detail – faces and so on.'

'Scared because Ian's missing, and is being stalked', Sarah said.

Margot stared out at the water in the dock. 'I still don't get it, I'm afraid. You're worried that Ian might be – ? What do I understand by "stalked"?' Margot asked.

'Like it says. Like in a jungle. People want him out of the way, formidable people. A dock's as good as anywhere.'

'Who on earth would do that, Sarah?'

'They might want me out of the way, too, but Ian especially.'

Margot seemed deliberately to turn the talk away from Ian and the dock. 'Obviously, you must take care of yourself, Sarah. What if they're looking for you, too – are more interested in you that you realise?'

'I don't think so. Anyway, all those creeps daren't mess about with me. I'm Desmond Iles's wife.'

Margot glanced at her and Sarah saw her give a small smile: 'Yes, you are.'

'What the hell does that mean?'

'Nothing.'

'That I'm going to stay his wife? Is that what you're saying?' Sarah had begun to shout and Margot's long, plain face grew serious again and looked full of hopeless concern. 'You think I like it, really, don't you, Margot, need to be Mrs Assistant Chief Constable, maybe with something on the side? Oh, look.' Suddenly, Sarah had become aware of the sun glinting now and then on a smooth, silver rectangle just covered by the dark water.

'Yes, a car,' Margot muttered. The crane seemed to pause,

holding the vehicle still virtually submerged. Then the lifting began again and, slowly, the full shape of it could be seen. Streaming and rotating lazily once clear, the car hung over the water for several minutes, as if they were waiting for it to drain. Margot gazed at the vehicle. 'A Metro, I'd say. Sarah, do you recognise it?'

'They'd use a stolen car, for heaven's sake, if they were getting rid of somebody. No, Ian didn't have a Metro.'

'Sorry. I'm a bit of a child about these things. But I'm trying to see the connection.'

'Ian's missing and wanted. There's a car in the dock and what could be a lot of really heavy police – not just bobbies. That's the connection.' She felt herself grow more agitated. 'Margot, I ought to go there. I ought to go there, in case.' She was whispering.

Margot held her arm for a moment. 'I do understand but they're not going to let you near, are they? Not near enough to see the . . . well, to identify anyone. And you might run into all sorts of people who would recognise you. Even Desmond.'

'Yes. But I ought to go. I need to find out who it is. How can I stay here talking? I could say I was driving to bridge at one of these marina flats.' She moved a few steps towards the door, then returned, to continue looking from the window.

Margot said: 'Is that credible – drive across the dock?'

'So I chose to go that way. It's more interesting.'

'Sarah, who's going to –?'

'I don't give a shit whether they believe it or not. I have to be there, that's all. I must know what's happening. What do you mean, you understand? You don't at all.'

But she knew it was all shout and show and that Margot was right: she could not go to the dock. It would be more than blatant – a beacon. Did this ultimate caution, after all the yelling, come from the part of her which liked being Mrs Assistant Chief Constable? The thought depressed her. At any rate, instead of leaving, she remained transfixed at the window with Margot.

After several minutes, the Metro was swung carefully towards the quay, still trailing some black water. The car was on its side and when it had been lowered to a couple of feet above the ground a dozen men in dungarees pushed it upright so that it came down on to the wheels. They unhooked the cables and stood back. Three men in civilian clothes hurried forward out of a waiting group and peered in through the windows. It was too far to tell whether the car contained a body, or bodies, and too far for Sarah to decide whether she recognised any of the police, if they were police. They had opened the front passenger door of the car and all three men were grouped there, gazing in, probably talking to one another occasionally. When they had finished their examination, they stood back and one of them turned and beckoned. A photographer came from the waiting group and began taking shots through the open door and afterwards from all round the car. The ambulance backed slowly towards the Metro, and when the photographer had finished four men came from it, two carrying a stretcher, one of the others with a dark sheet. They had on white coats and she thought she could make out medical face masks. They went to the car's open door and two of them leaned in. She could not see clearly what they were doing, because of distance, and because the car was between them and her, but after a few minutes the two men with the stretcher carried it the couple of steps back to the ambulance. There was what had to be a body on it now, covered by the dark sheet.

'Too late to go there, anyway,' Margot said.

'I will all the same.'

'Sarah, there's no point. You'll discover nothing.'

'Not there,' she said.

Where?'

'I can't just stay here.'

'But where?'

She hardly knew what to answer. 'I know one of the people looking for him.'

'Sarah, in a couple of days the police will say in the papers who it is.'

'A couple of days? Am I suppose to wait?'

'Or Desmond might tell you.'

'Yes, he might, especially if it is Ian. Do I want to hear it like that? Do you think I do, Margot?'

'There'd be no good way of hearing it.'

'That would be the worst.'

They closed the ambulance doors and the vehicle moved slowly away. The group on the quay-side broke up and went to their cars, and they, too, drove off the dock. Sarah recognised none of these vehicles, but that meant little: people like Desmond or Colin Harpur or other senior detectives could be driving any car from the police pool. She left the window.

Margot said: 'Isn't it far-fetched, Sarah? Someone you're fond of is missing, so you assume all this?'

'There's somebody significant in that car.'

'And is Ian significant?'

'He could be.'

She could sense that Margot expected her to explain, but Sarah gave no more.

'And what will you ask this man who's supposedly been looking for Ian,' Margot asked.

'No, not supposedly.

'All right. But what will you ask him?'

'If he found him, of course. If he dropped him in the fucking dock, or if he knows whether someone else did.'

'And, naturally, he's going to tell you. You're only the wife of a chief policeman.'

'I've got to ask him.'

'It doesn't make sense.'

'Not much of what's happening does.'

Margot seemed to give up her protests. 'Who is this you're going to see?'

'Oh, a sort of go-between. A half-crooked nobody, maybe like Ian himself.'

'Yes, but his name? Just in case anything goes wrong. It might be important to know where to start looking.'

'Nothing will go wrong. Do stop fretting. I'm used to this kind of life now. I can look after myself.' She knew she sounded strident again and full of phoney confidence, a frail attempt to conceal her fears, and unlikely to convince a professional like Margot. Well, to hell with Margot, and her cardigan. Leave her to marriage manuals and the cats and the marina.

Sarah drove out to the Monty and, by the time she reached there, all her courage, even her false courage, had slid away. Ralph might be a nonentity, but he had the power to chill her, and to make Sarah wonder why she had ever pushed her way with such determination into his kind of world. She was as much out of place in it as he had been in Rougement Place. Why wasn't she playing bridge somewhere, really playing bridge, or at home trying again to flog her way through Salman Rushdie? She knew there was a very simple answer: she had to discover whether Ian was safe, and he inhabited that same world as Ralph's. The need was obsessive. Once more Margot probably had things right, and it must be morbid fancy to assume that because someone had been recovered from the dock it had to be Ian. Nothing could have stopped Sarah from trying to make sure it was not, though.

At this hour of the afternoon the club would be closed, between lunch-time and reopening in the evening. She parked a little way off and walked the last few hundred yards to the Monty's solid front door, passing the club yard on her way. One side was open to the street and she saw that the builder's rubble container still stood there, still as innocent as ever, no doubt, now loaded to the top. God, if she hadn't been so foolishly and uselessly prying about that none of these anxieties would have come.

Then more anxieties arrived: standing in the porch and about to ring the bell she thought she heard from somewhere deep in the building, perhaps upstairs, a cry of pain and, immediately following, a sound like something or somebody falling heavily to the ground. The cry had been male, she felt almost certain of that, though she could not tell whether it was Ralph. While she was still trying to sort out in her head what might have happened, the sequence of sounds occurred again, though this time the cry struck her as weaker and the noise of a fall louder. Then she heard what seemed to be a few words spoken, again a male voice, and the tone harsh, even savage.

Her fears soared and she drew back from ringing the bell. For a few seconds she thought of turning around, getting back to the car and driving home. Rougement Place and its spruce safety insistently called to her, like a mother seeking a missing child, or the parable shepherd looking for the hundredth sheep. In fact, she left the porch hurriedly and had begun to walk back up to her parking spot, assuring herself that, in any case, Ralph Ember would probably have no news of Ian, when she saw two men leave the club through the rear fire doors and quickly cross the yard. She was looking from the side and from a little behind them, but she felt pretty sure she had seen both these men before, and quite certain that neither was Ralph. One seemed about thirty, dark-haired and with a very powerful-looking body, especially the shoulders. The other looked older, thin, with sparse grey hair, and possibly wearing rimless glasses. Both had on smart, grey suits. Last time she encountered the two it was inside the club, on the night the injured young man appeared, was surrounded by these two and others, and then disappeared.

Before they came out of the yard ahead of her, she turned around and walked at what she hoped was a casual, unostentatious pace, back towards the Monty's front entrance, but did not stop there, in case the men were behind her or glanced down the street and spotted her. She felt weak and terrified. For five minutes she simply kept going, then very gratefully turned a corner and walked another few hundred yards, faster now, before entering a shop. She took her time buying some toffees and a newspaper, occasionally looking out to the street, through the window. The men did not pass. When it came to paying, she found to her shame that her hands were shaking so much she could hardly cope with the coins, and the Pakistani woman behind the counter asked her if she was all right, and whether she would like to sit down for a moment. No, she was not all right, but a chair wouldn't change anything. It was fear of the two men and anxiety about Ian that had taken away control of her muscles, and mostly fear.

Emerging from the shop, she looked about very very carefully, if necessary ready to keep on walking away from the club. But she saw nothing to trouble her in the street and forced herself to go back up to the corner and look from there towards the Monty. The two men were still not in view and so she began to stroll in that direction again, pretending to read bits of her paper, and helping herself to a couple of toffees in the hope that chewing would ease her nerves. Almost everything continued to tell her that she could not handle this situation and should give up the visit and exit while she was able; everything except the need to find out about Ian, and the belief which would not go away, no matter how hard she tried to dispel it, that Ralph might know something after all. This hope gripped her and still fought her fear.

She entered the club yard and saw that the fire doors had been left swinging open when the men hurriedly left. Giving herself no time to develop doubts, she quickly crossed to the doors and entered the corridor where she had seen the blood trail on the tiles at the start of all this. She took a few steps inside, then went back and pulled the doors closed. That bothered her, seeming to cut off escape and commit her to going on into the building. But, if the two men returned, and especially if they returned because they had been secretly observing her, she wanted it to be as difficult as possible for them to get inside.

With the light from the yard excluded now, the corridor was dark and she went gingerly forward past the lavatories. She reached the door to the bar and opened it gently. That brought a little pale light to the corridor from outside through the bar windows, and she felt slightly comforted. Stepping into the bar she stared urgently around. Nothing seemed to have been damaged or disturbed here: the place had obviously been cleaned up after the lunch-time trade and was ready for the evening.

The sounds she heard when at the front door had seemed to come from upstairs and she decided she would have to try to look there. For a moment or two she sat on the bar bench she had last occupied with Ian, assembling her courage, and then made for a door marked Private, behind the bar counter, which she knew gave on to stairs leading to the flat above. She opened this door and stood for a few seconds on the second stair, listening. Ralph had a wife and family living here, yet there was no sound. Slowly, she moved up a few more stairs, then paused again. Although she was tempted to call out, declare her presence, she decided to keep as quiet as she could for at least a short time yet, and put her feet down very softly as she climbed the last stairs to the landing.

There was part of her that kept on saying she was behaving as stupidly and intrusively now as when she pushed herself and Ian into this business at the start: the same tiresome cockiness and stupid nonchalance. Instincts and obsession drove her on, though. Some day she might get back to being just one person again, able to run her life according to reason and consistency and intelligent fear, but that had not happened yet, and she did not really look forward to it very much. She was growing used to this battle in herself between what good sense said, and what her wishes said; knew all the ins and outs of that recurrent fight and how to work it so that her wishes always won. Anyway, were the restraints really good sense? After all, if she – or when she – went back to being one, unified, apparently contented person it would be as the worthy lady of Idylls, Rougement Place, and devoted to Des. That was sensible?

Half a dozen doors gave on to the landing and from the room behind one of them she thought now she could hear breathing, uneven, laboured breathing, occasionally broken by a snore, or perhaps it was a groan. The door stood a little open and she went forward and pushed it gradually wide. She saw an unmade double bed with nobody in it, an old-style pine dressing table littered with cosmetics and lacquers and a couple of pink, narrow, straight-backed wooden chairs with basket-work seats. If it had not been for the noise she would have assumed the room unoccupied. But the sound of someone fighting to breathe had grown louder and seemed to come from the floor on the far side of the bed. Hesitantly, she went in and looked.

Ralph lay close to the bed, his face badly marked, and with blood running from his nose and a cut over the right eye forming a small pool on the purple carpet. Fully dressed in a brown, tired, three-piece suit, he was on his back, unconscious, his eyes closed. For what seemed to her a minute or more he would appear to have stopped breathing and remain utterly still, but then his face would contort and his hand twitch as he strove to pull in air. He was a bad colour, his cheeks greyish-blue and his lips very pale. At school she had learned first aid and she realised almost at once now that Ralph had swallowed his tongue and would choke to death shortly if she did not act. All the same, she hesitated for a couple of seconds: he had always repelled her, his slippery charm, the scar, his impenetrable, high-flown talk, his lying, and she drew back from contact with him.

Again she grew ashamed of herself. Christ, this was a dying man. What did it matter that his face had been marked or that he could stifle you with verbiage? And who was she to take against anyone for lying? She knelt near him and immediately felt the blood on the carpet soak into the knees of her tights. Turning his head towards her she pulled Ralph's mouth wide and put her finger in and tried to hook his tongue forward from out of his throat. It was something she had been shown how to do all those years ago, but shown only on diagrams. She had never needed to attempt it, and diagrams did not prepare you for the unnerving intimacy of poking about deep inside someone's mouth.

At first now she did not succeed and felt herself begin to panic: she wanted to call somebody – a doctor, an ambulance, Desmond

– anyone to rid herself of the responsibility for this life. She knew there was no time for that, though.

Ralph's whole body heaved and momentarily his teeth closed on her finger, as if in a fit, and she cried out in pain. Then he relaxed again, and she felt relief mixed with dread that relaxing meant he had gone and was past fighting for breath any longer. As she fought again to pull this strangely resistant tongue clear, another thought came from somewhere and gave her a sudden sense of hope. She decided that Ralph must have taken this beating because he had failed fo find Ian for those men and whoever ran them – most probably Loxton. They might even have meant to kill him and had been disturbed by the sound of her stepping into the porch.

It followed that, if Ralph had not found Ian, he might be still alive, not in the dock. Even as she struggled with Ralph, she realised that there was no evidence at all for this reading of the situation, and perhaps no logic in it either. It was a guess, but one she could not prevent herself believing, because she wanted to believe it so much. Her mind took that road so often these days.

And then she felt the tongue become freed and she took her finger from his mouth. Her fears that she might be too late persisted, though. Ralph still lay still and she saw no chest movement to signal breathing. Mouth-to-mouth resuscitation she had also learned at school, and actually practised at life-saving classes at the pool. Des had several times told her the police were no longer keen to use it, because of the Aids danger, but she fixed her mouth over Ralph's, held his nose, and began trying to force air and movement back into his lungs.

Thank God, he began to respond almost at once and, after a few minutes, she pulled back and let him breathe unhelped, deeply and regularly now. The frightening colours in his face began to fade and, not long afterwards, she saw his eyelids start to quiver. Drawing one of the horrible pink chairs closer, she sat near him and watched while he gradually came back to consciousness. The blood had spread down from the knees of her tights almost to her shoes and, in the dressing table mirror on the other side of the bed, she saw that her face was streaked with blood, too, picked up when her mouth was on his. Altogether, she must look as if she had been in a road accident and she would need to do some careful cleaning up before she went home. As far as she could tell, no blood was on the rest of her clothes, thank heaven. The tights would have to be junked.

Ralph stirred and opened his eyes. 'Lie still for a little while,' she said. 'You've been knocked about.'

He still looked dazed and seemed to have trouble focusing on her when she spoke. If he could see anything at all, it would be her blood-soaked legs first, and that might trouble him.

After a while he said: 'Mrs Iles?'

'Yes, Ralph.'

'Alone here?'

'I had to see you.'

He tried to get up, supporting himself on his elbow, but did not have the strength and sank back. For a minute or two he closed his eyes again, and she feared he might sink back into unconsciousness. Perhaps he was more badly injured than she could see.

'Ralph,' she said, 'are you listening? Please listen. I don't want to harass you, not now in that condition, but just tell me this one simple thing. You can nod or shake your head if you like. Did you find Ian? That's all I'm here for. I must know.'

He made no movement, his eyes still closed, and she felt even more strongly that unconsciousness had claimed him again.

Panic began to take over once more. 'Two men did this to you, Ralph. You remember? You might know them. Was it because you failed to locate Ian? If you can just tell me that –'

His eyes opened again. 'Where's Margaret?'

'Your wife? I don't know. There seems to be nobody here.'

'She went to pick up the children from school.'

'Nearby? Might she have seen the men, too?'

Now, he did shake his head, but very slightly. 'Ash Tree. Private. Who'd send kids to school in this neighbourhood?'

Even in her present state she found it half-touching, half-comic, to hear his talk snob when blood-bathed and helpless on the floor.

'They mustn't see me like this. God, they come home from lessons on civics and dance and find their father looking like a butcher's shop.' He made another attempt to sit up and this time did better, finishing propped on an elbow. She stood and went closer, to offer him help. He took hold of her hand and with his other one reached up to the bed and gripped the blankets for more support. She pulled and he once more closed his eyes, this time to concentrate on the physical effort, and gradually got himself to his feet. At once he swung round exhausted and sat on the bed, still holding Sarah's hand. For a couple of minutes, he remained with his head hanging forward, occasionally groaning slightly.

'Perhaps they've done you real damage, Ralph. You ought to get a doctor.'

'Sorry about the sound effects. I always let the back row know when I'm suffering. It will pass. We've got a lad who was a nurse lives close, fully trained. I'm going to give him a ring. But Mrs Iles, I don't understand how you are here.'

'I came to ask you about Ian.'

'Yes, but here.' Raising his head now, he waved his free hand, to show he meant the bedroom.

'This is where they beat you up. I found you in trouble.' The bleeding on his face had nearly stopped, but occasionally a drop fell on his trousers or the bedclothes. He watched as if charmed, like a child seeing snow descend for the first time, and eventually released Sarah's hand and fondled the injuries to his nose and eyebrow.

'Please tell me, Ralph. Was it because you couldn't produce Ian for them? It has to be that, has to be. Look, I'm scared frantic about him. Someone's been pulled out of the dock.'

She was crouched down in front of him where he sat on the bed, her face close to his, trying to keep contact with his big, brown eyes, and get past the pain and the secrecy. Never before had she gone so hard for intimacy with a man while totally repelled by the notion of intimacy with him. He did not reply.

'Listen Ralphy, but for me you'd be dead,' she said.

'Dead?' He gave a small smile.

'Yes, bloody dead,' she yelled, 'you ungrateful wreck. I've done you lip service.'

From downstairs came the sound of people moving about and, alarmed in case the men had returned, she straightened up quickly and went on to the landing. She heard a child's voice and then, shortly afterwards, a woman called from below: 'Ralph, What's going on? Who's there?'

Another of those touches of farce at just the wrong time. She had saved a man's life, and now here she was in a bedroom with him when his wife and children returned home, though at least neither she nor Ralph looked as if they had been at a lovers' tryst.

'Mrs Ember,' she said. 'Could you come up? There's been a beating.' But she found that Ralph had managed to stand and make his way from the bedroom and was about to go downstairs. As he began, his wife appeared at the bottom and looked up. 'Ralph,' she cried. 'What?' For a moment, Sarah must have been half shielding him. Now, Mrs Ember obviously saw his injuries, and perhaps she could make out the blood streaks on Sarah's face, too. 'Those animals, Ralph? Yes, those animals. Macey?'

'Macey, Mrs Ember? Who's that?' Sarah asked. She had never seen Ralph's wife before. According to Ian, Ralph did not like her coming into the club: the Monty was his job, with all its rough and dubious elements, and their flat another world, if he could keep it like that. Perhaps that was why Ralph had seemed so disturbed to find Sarah not just on the wrong side of the bar, but in their bedroom. Looking down the stairs, she saw a small, blonde, boyish-looking woman of about her own age, flushed now with anger or fear or the two. She seemed too neat and decorous for Ralph, nearly Rougement Place, and definitely up-town and bone china.

'I'm all right, Maggie', he whispered. 'Take the girls into the yard, would you? Just for a few minutes. I'll spruce up.'

'But who is this woman? Why is she here? She's hurt, too? And, Ralph, the swearing. In front of the girls.'

'It's all right, Margaret. Do what I say.' His wife turned and went out of sight, calling their daughters, and Ralph began to descend the stairs very slowly. Sarah followed. Half-way down he paused and turned: 'Well, I'm grateful, Mrs Iles. I feel it is only right to say that, in the circumstances. One abhors churlishness, oh, above all, churlishness is abhorrent.'

On the whole it pleased her to hear some of the familiar tatty resonance and fart-arsing grandeur stoke his voice again. 'Ralph, you could say more,' she replied. 'Please.'

He stood swaying on the stairs for a moment, his face showing traces again of its former sinister dignity, despite the blood. 'Somebody in the dock?'

'A silver Metro.'

'They didn't mention that.'

'Who? The two who did this?'

'Is this confidential information? Your husband?'

'Who's Macey?'

'That's Margaret talking. Don't take any notice of what she says. Not in the picture at all.'

'Which picture is that, Ralph?'

'A silver Metro means nothing to me.'

'Of course not, but –'

He held up his hand. 'Mrs Iles, I'm convalescing, trying to. Could you go easy?'

'All I want to know about is Ian.'

He sighed for a while and fingered his injuries again. 'All right, I owe you. Accepted.' He turned to face her squarely, a come-clean, partners-together movement. 'What you supposed is correct. I didn't find him, and they thought I hadn't tried. Well, and a bit more: they believe I'm protecting him, putting him wise to the hunt. I'm surprised to be alive.'

'Perhaps I disturbed them. Tell me, would you protect him?'

'As far as I know, he's safe, Mrs Iles.'

'Please, make it Sarah. After all, I've had hold of your tongue.'

He gave a small, creepy, Japanese-style bow that caused a few spots of blood to shower from his nose on to the stair carpet. 'Thank you. So, where is Ian? You've seen him? Why did you come here? Because he'd heard I've been searching for him and told you?' He gave that minute smile again. 'How stupid I am. You're not going to tell me where he is, are you, even if you knew?'

'I should cocoa, Ralph, even if I knew.'

'I'm the enemy.'

'You're –'

'Oh, not big enough to be an enemy to someone like you, I suppose. A nobody. But nobodies often catch the worst of these situations,' he said.

'They've got you terrorised, Ralph, so you're not in control. I'm not blaming you, because you can't help that.'

'Right – a nobody. Ah, well, I suppose I knew that already. Panicking Ralph. What I didn't realise was how much Ian must mean to you.'

'But of course you did.'

'I knew you had something satisfying. Not the seriousness of it.'

She did not answer. In a way he was right. These fears today for Ian had taught her, too, that despite everything, she could not bear to think of him hurt, or worse: could not bear to think of him taken from her. Yet it was only an hour or two ago that Margot had asked why she worried so much over what her husband might know, and suggested she really meant to hang on to him and all he stood for. The confusions that had torn at her for months remained almost as destructive as ever. Only almost, though. Didn't she realise a bit better after watching that crane work and the open doors of the ambulance how much she wanted Ian?

There was no need to let Ralph know any of this. 'Now, listen, thank you, anyway,' she said. 'I'm so much happier than when I arrived. I'm going into your Ladies' room for repairs and then out the way I came in, through the fire doors. You don't need me here. This incident – it's serious, and your wife might want to call the police. I mustn't be about.'

'No, we don't call the police. You know that, and even Margaret knows it. But I understand, Sarah.' He resumed his slow descent of the stairs. 'Stay out of sight until she comes back in, then disappear.'

'Ralph, what the hell's it all about?'

'You'll see the children in the yard. I'd prefer you didn't talk with them. Do you mind? No reflection, absolutely none. How could it be, for heaven's sake, you, from up there, down here? But they're bright, inquisitive. It's surprising what they pick up. Just a friendly, relaxed wave, if I might suggest. A decent but impersonal social gesture, to convey that all is well, and they're not living on the edge of chaos. They're just kids in straw hats.' He went to the bar phone and called his nursing friend. 'Could you come over right away, Harvey, and check I'm firing on all cylinders?'

'Ralph, tell me what it's about,' Sarah said. It might be my life, as well as Ian's. Could you identify these men? I hear this name, Macey. One of Loxton's? Don't I deserve to know?'

'Some of Harvey's balm, a bath and a bit of a lie-down and I'll be fine,' he replied. 'In a couple of hours we're open again. Busy tonight. Super-bingo. Always a very nice, select crowd.'

Strangely, she felt especially tender towards Desmond that evening and suggested they should go out to a restaurant for dinner. His eagerness was touching: people who knew him only through the job would have been astonished at how vulnerable he could seem sometimes.

They were into the main course when she noticed that he had grown extremely uneasy. 'This a place we shouldn't come to?' she asked. 'Another?'

'Could be.'

'Why didn't you say?'

'I didn't know for sure. And it's your night out, your choice. I didn't want to be a wet blanket.' He leaned forward over the food. 'Crooked money backing it. Or, it's being protected.'

'God, how can you tell?'

'The man eating alone behind me.'

'Yes?'

'Leo Tacette.'

'Should I know him?'

'Watch the way the waiters run around him.'

'He owns it?'

'Or he protects it. Harpur would have known they're into this place. I lose track. Should have checked for an update.'

'But, so what, for God's sake, Des?'

'Eating in the same place as a known heavy villain, possibly a place belonging to him? No, it's not a keelhauling offence. Doesn't prove anything.'

'But not whiter than white?'

'One day it might be made to look bad.'

'Why by?'

'Oh, enemies. Or friends. A night like this could end up part of a dossier.'

Tacette seemed to eat little, and was drinking Perrier water. Yes, he did appear proprietorial. Thin, bald, with a small, dense, black moustache, and large straight nose, he spent most of his time gazing about at the other customers. His looks were what she thought of as local: strong, incandescently *lumpen*, weathered, cheerful. He might have made it as chairman of the council. 'At least the food's good,' she said, determined to salvage the evening.

'Great.'

Perhaps Margot would have been able to provide a few words

of seasoned jargon to account for Sarah's wish to be nice to Desmond tonight. Sarah herself put it down to a general happiness now she could believe that Ian was probably all right. And the new certainty that he meant so much to her came into things, too: she felt that would be hurtful to Des, if he knew, and so she wished to show him special warmth and friendliness, the limits of what she could offer.

In the car she had asked: 'What sort of day, Des?'

'Oh, negligible. She waited but that was it: nothing about the dock. In a while he said: 'You?'

'Very steady progress with Rushdie. Page eight in *Shame* now.'

'I think I liked page eight. He's good at page eights. Did you get out at all?'

'The shops, briefly.' That had ended the talk.

Now, they were eating cassaulet, or goose stew as it was given on the no-nonsense menu. Tacette suddenly left his table and, carrying the glass of Perrier, came and stood near theirs. 'Mr Iles, it's a privilege to have you here. I hope everything is to your liking.' He carefully looked towards each of them. Talking seemed a big effort, but he made it.

Desmond nodded. 'Lovely, Leo.'

'Yes, indeed,' Sarah said.

'I'd no idea you had an interest in Chaff, Leo.'

'Really?'

What did that mean, she wondered.

'How long?' Desmond asked.

'We needed to diversify. Actually, this is Anthony's side of things. You know Anthony?' He nodded towards the pay desk where a younger man, bigger than Leo and with very pointed features, stood alongside an older woman. 'And Daphne giving a hand! A real family concern. But these youngsters! Big ideas. They're the future. That's what I hear.'

'Quite.'

Tacette did some ruminating for a while. 'What I mean, look at me and Daphne, coming up to a silver wedding in no time at all. That's how the years go.'

'True. Big celebration?'

'You bet.'

'Nice,' Desmond said. 'When's that?'

'Next month. We would have invited you, naturally, and your

good lady, goes without saying, but I know your protocol wouldn't allow anything like that.'

'Probably a bit difficult,' Desmond agreed.

'I understand. Even at a lower level, I mean tonight, what I'd like, of course, is to have a bottle of Krug on the house sent to your table.'

Desmond said at once: 'Thank you, but – '

'Oh, I know it's an absurdity even to think of your accepting any such thing, worry not.' Tacette nodded gravely as if he regretted this, but mightily approved of police incorruptibility.

Desmond said: 'Well, Leo –'

'Who can ignore the Stalker story, outrageous as his treatment might be? And we'll make sure you get a proper, signed receipt and are charged for every last mouthful! Sorry to sound so damn brutal and grasping, Mrs Iles, but I know the pressures people in your husband's position are under. Might I sit down for a moment, Mr Iles? It's possible I have something of interest.' He did not wait for a reply and drew up a chair. Possibly he felt exhausted after so much conversation. 'Please, you carry on eating as if I weren't here, Mrs Iles.'

'This wise, Leo?' Desmond asked.

'I'll be brief. Only two or three matters.' He glanced around nervously and she realised then that police were not the only ones who had to take care about the company they were seen in.

Leo did not speak at once, though, and the delay was more than his usual hesitancy. Eventually, he said: 'I don't know whether it's all right to be telling you these things in front of Mrs Iles. I mean from the point of view of distressing her, at a meal, and so on.'

'Let's see how it goes, shall we, Leo?' Desmond replied. 'If Sarah's here it looks less like a briefing, only social.'

Leo nodded. 'Perhaps.' He still did not seem comfortable, though, as if he thought there were things she should not hear. 'This is the first item then: Panicking Ralph has taken a beating, I mean, a real beating, possible deep damage, internal.'

Sarah forced herself to keep eating and to keep looking at Leo and Desmond in turn, though she was badly thrown.

'This is this afternoon,' Leo went on. 'My other boy, Gerald, he has a contact, a lad who's done a bit of nursing far back, and he feeds us certain facts now and then. He was called over to the

Monty and found Ralph not too good at all. He says Ralph might have gone under if he'd taken only a little more of it.'

'Robbery?' Desmond asked. 'He surprised someone?'

'Not as I understand. No sign of a turn-over and Ralph's not making a complaint.'

'Ralph doesn't make complaints, not to us,' Desmond said.

'No mention of robbery to Gerald's contact.'

'What then?'

'Mr Iles, we can both makes guesses. Some sort of disciplining?'

'What does that mean?' Sarah forced herself to ask. She tried for a puzzled, innocent smile, as if learning all this for the first time.

'He's gone wrong somewhere,' Leo replied. 'Offended. The thing is, who is he working for?'

'Yes?' Desmond said.

'Not me. I can tell you that.'

'Offended how?' Desmond asked.

'Obviously, that's the problem,' Leo said. A waiter came and asked about drinks. 'Can I at least buy you brandies?'

Desmond said: 'We'll buy you one. Put them on the bill.'

'If you say,' Leo replied.

'So who *is* he working for?' Desmond said.

'Benny?'

'You're not sure?'

'No, not sure.'

'Doing what?'

'Not sure of that either. You know Ralph: free-lance, small-time business commissions now and then. Consultancy matters you could call it, when needed, like the royal family's gynaecologist.'

'Sure,' Desmond said.

Sarah felt some relief for a moment. She finished her cassoulet. The waiter brought the brandies.

'This develops,' Leo went on. 'The nurse lad is patching up Ralph and one of his kids comes into the room and asks about some woman who was there in the afternoon – who left, so it seems, just before the nurse arrived. The kid says the woman was talking to them in the yard, asking their names and what have you, discussing their school, and the child wants to know who she was. But Ralph gets ratty – he's lying there, bandages and lint trailing all ways from him like a maypole, but he throws a real rage, saying he told this woman not to talk to them.'

'I don't get it,' Desmond said. 'She's part of the attack? Hangs about talking to kids?'

'I don't get it either. But something's going on, Mr Iles. Our nursing lad can't ask questions, just keeps an eye open.'

'Ralph knocking off someone's woman? Is this a vengeance thing?'

'So why is she still there afterwards?'

'You ought to be a detective, Leo.'

'The kid says she's a very nice lady, but Ralph is still shouting his head off about it. You know Ralphy: there's his family, and there's the rest of the world, and he thinks they ought to be kept apart. Sanitised they call it?'

'So, what else, Leo?' Desmond asked.

'Else?'

'You said two or three items.'

'No, just about Ralph.'

Sarah had a feeling he had changed his mind and decided to say no more while she was present. In a little while, Leo stood, laboriously made his farewells, and went to the pay desk to join his wife and son.

'So, was that a powerful revelation?' she asked Desmond. 'This man, Ralph?'

'Not much we can do about it unless he wants to bring charges, which he won't. An internal business matter, like a death in the Kremlin.'

'He seemed to think it pointed somewhere.'

'Yes, where, Sarah?'

'God, I don't know.'

'Nor me. Nor him. These people, they love to stir, that's all.' His face became impenetrably shuttered and the topic was closed. She and Desmond talked only gossip for the rest of the meal.

As they were leaving, Tacette came out to the foyer with his wife to say goodbye. 'Daphne so much wanted to meet Mrs Iles,' he said. Sarah saw Desmond immediately grow troubled again as the connections and phoney affability here mounted. He would feel he was being deliberately sucked in.

Dressed in a white silk trouser suit which must have cost a handful, Daphne Tacette began to talk chummily to Sarah about food and the quirks of customers. Round-faced, dyed-dark, full of life, she seemed pleasant enough, unpolished but bright: who the hell expected polish from the wife of a very heavy, career villain? Her conversation was salty and vivid, and Sarah could see why Leo might not be accustomed to saying much. Sarah found chatting with her a treat.

After a few minutes, though, it occurred to her that Daphne might have been brought out deliberately to take her aside, while Leo talked again to Desmond, this time one-to-one. Leo drew him out of earshot, and Desmond was listening carefully, his face now not so much troubled as blank: again that closed-off, professional look he could put on when keeping his reactions private.

'So you've a big day coming?' Sarah said to Daphne.

'Oh, the silver wedding? Frankly, kid, I'll be glad when it's over. So many preparations, and people to be kept sweet. "If you ask her you've got to ask her mother as well" – you know the carry-on."

'But grand to have all the family and friends close around you for the day.'

'Oh, yes. Yes, I suppose that really will be nice, though half of them bore the eyebrows off of me. And maybe it really is something, twenty-five years together. Christ knows how. Matter of keeping your loathings locked away, wouldn't you say? But it gets no easier, that's what amazes me. There's still some good, tough, brainy part of you piping up to ask, "What the hell am I doing with this guy still, putting my life on a plate?" You know what I'm getting at? But, obviously, you've got a distance to go before your silver.'

'Quite a way.'

'Going to make it?'

'Who can tell?'

'And who cares? *Want* to make it? What's so brilliant about a quarter of a century in the same bed, more or less, same hands, more or less, digging their nails into your bottom three nights a week? So, where's he digging them the other four? And then set sail for the gold? Jesus.'

Sarah shrugged.

'I'm prying? If you like, tell me to get lost.'

'It's all right.'

'Somebody else in the frame, dear?'

'Twenty-five years is a very long time.'

'Yes, I am prying. But lucky you. Hang on to it, regardless.'

'Well, I hope it's a wonderful party, and everything goes beautifully. I know you're going to have a really great time.'

'Yes. I sound cynical, but really, love, I'm thrilled to bits.'

On the way home, Sarah asked: 'More disclosures? Big afterthoughts from Leo?'

'Afraid not. As a tipster, he falls dismally short.'

She said: 'But he looked really intense.'

'He was. About nothing much, though.'

'Honestly, Des? He had nothing else interesting?'

'Absolutely.'

'I'll say this for you, when you lie you do give it all you've got. Ever thought of joining the police?'

11

Benny Loxton said: 'Some of my boys was real anxious about this meeting, Leo, I mean, coming here alone and leaving it to you to decide where.' Loxton felt a bit anxious himself, although he was armed. 'They can be fretful, my people.'

The bugger smiled very big and grand over that. 'They don't understand about you and me, Benny – the old days, school, all those years. Good God, this talk is something agreed on at Miss Binns' funeral. Don't they see what that means to you and me?'

'How could they? They're bloody kids. They got no history.' They were sitting opposite each other in Tacette's golf club. God, Leo was a crude-looking item – all that nose and the jumpy eyes, real common. He could have been an MP, or working on the rubbish trucks.

'They think everything's so simple, Benny. Way they see it, there's friends, there's enemies. And friends stick together and enemies try to hurt and kill each other. They wouldn't realise that enemies, well, so-called enemies, you and me, could have a great deal of mutual respect, and might want to come to an accommodation for old times' sake.'

Benny said: 'Vision's what they haven't got even a spot of. They can be good boys every other way, the best, but vision? Not a chance.'

'I remember from school, that text in a frame by Miss Binns' room: "Without vision the people perish." I didn't know what it meant, then, but –'

'There you are. Vision's top priority. Vision's the difference between humanity and the animals, as I see it. A horse or an elk, have it got vision? Not that I heard, Leo. Churchill or Bobby Bartok with his music or them lads who did the bank through sewers in France – what people like that got first and last is great vision. Think of Columbus, Ronny Biggs.'

Somehow, Leo had wangled a membership of this place, out in the back of beyond, and with big clouds of flaky grime from an industrial estate blowing right across the greens, you could watch it, like telly interference. But a decent enough spot with very strong, old-fashioned, wood toilet seats and the chairs in this room real green leather.

Phil Macey had said Loxton was a fool to come and that he was offering a target. Well, Macey would. Even this morning he had still been arguing. Phil saw threats from all ways. He wouldn't turn his back on his mother, and them pictures on the screen of the Metro in the dock had made him worse than ever. In a way, you could understand it. Macey had come right out and yelled it was stupid to be so casual and easy-going about this meeting. Sometimes, he talked like he ran the fucking operation, but he meant well, mostly. If you bought a savage for your team don't ask him to act like baby powder.

'Look, I got to go to this,' Loxton had said. 'Leo got to believe things are coming all right between us, like almost harmony, nothing brewing. He get a whiff of anything and that silver wedding do is somewhere else, with everyone on the look-out, and we're finished. That Metro – it could worry him. He got to be convinced everything's nice.'

'So, how did they find that bloody car, anyway?' Macey had asked. 'I don't like it.'

'I don't like it, either,' Loxton said. 'But they got no identification yet.'

'They will,' Macy replied.

'Let's wait till they do before we start worrying. In any case, I got to play Leo along.'

'Well, of course,' Macey replied. 'Yes, you got to keep up a show, but on ground he picks, Benny? No. A time he picks? No. We got to have participation in the planning, we got to demand parity of influence.'

'It'll be all right,' Loxton had said. 'I can feel it.'

'Yeah, well feeling it, I don't say that don't add up to nothing at all, Benny. You got a great way of getting to things intuitive, I see it plenty of times, and it's great, why this outfit is where it is today, no question. But certain risks – well, one got to invest due forethought, make everything as neat and non-hazard as it can be.'

'My feeling is Leo really wants this agreement, Phil. He's getting to feel old. He's not old, only my age, but some it gets to sooner. So, there isn't going to be no funny work at the meeting.'

'Suppose he've had a whisper?'

'What whisper?'

'Suppose he've had a whisper about what we got lined up for the silver wedding? The surprise. I mean, everybody knows they're having a silver wedding. Just a small whisper would make him worried.'

'He can't have had no whisper.'

'We hope he can't, of course we do. But if he had. We so sure Justin never spoke to anyone? We got to that boy early, very early, but was it early *enough*? He got a girl friend we can't find, he got a mother, there's them people in the Monty. This meeting Leo's setting up could be for them to get in first. You remember what we spoke about before, what's known as pre-emptive? Leo saying to himself, I'll wipe this sod out before he wipes me and mine out? That's the danger.'

'I don't believe it,' Loxton had replied. 'I don't feel it's like that at all. This have got real genuineness in it, on his side, I mean. Daphne been talking to him, maybe – a time for live-and-let-live. I wouldn't be surprised she been thinking like that. She got a nice soul full of decency and calm.'

'Except she hatched Lay-waste.'

'Not out of her soul. Didn't nobody ever tell you how babies was born? A woman can't be blamed for how her kids are. Or not total. Think of Mrs Hitler. I heard she was smiles and sweetness and "Have another slice of applestrudel."'

'Look, Daphne Tacette still got to go in the shooting, most probable,' Macey had said.

'All right, that's obvious. All I'm saying, maybe she been putting some gentle influence.'

Just the same, Macey had not liked it, nor Norman, but Loxton told them discussion was over and he would see Leo where Leo wanted and alone. If you ran an outfit you ran it. You listened to advice, yes, but in the end you had to do what you thought was the best. The best was to let Leo believe he could come closer in a sort of partnership, and also to let him get nice and lulled by hosting and swaggering in his waste-tip golf club.

'I like this place, Leo. It got class.' There were photographs of the Queen and the Duke of Edinburgh on the walls, one with a yellow and green water stain across the bottom, like a flood from an upstairs toilet or something, and a board with the names of captains of the club in gold lettering going right back, people nobody outside ever heard of but glorious years ago in this tripe den. 'There's tradition here, that's the secret, Leo.'

'Reasonable people. A bit loud. Not much spare pussy, not that's worth looking at: arses all corners, like drawing boards, and in tartan trousers. Watery eyes. I can't stand having a woman under me all bloodshot and runny. You'd think you were in bed with a funeral. Now and then you see something dinky by herself out on a green, but there's always a husband having a piss in the bushes. What I was hoping, Benny, was that today these could be talks about talks. That's what the union boys and the diplomats call these kinds of preliminaries. It's a useful formula.'

'Sounds fair enough.' Loxton decided it had been so right to let Tacette fix the meeting here. The place made him real confident, unworried, anyone could see. Loxton had never heard him talk so much before, and he could talk good – top quality accent, proper grammar and everything. You would not have known the only school he been to was Marl View, and they thought he was thick as mud pies even there.

'We want some headings, Benny –' the ground we could cover later in detail. Maybe we'd both like others present then. I'd probably ask Anthony to join us, and you could nominate anyone you want.'

'Today, just see which way we're going?'

'Right.'

'That looks to me real civilised and positive, Leo.' Loxton stood up and went to the big window that gazed out over the last hole and away to other greens in the distance. He watched as the smuts from the factories swooped down on golfers like birds on worms. Or it reminded him of in the Navy, passing some foul old merchantman, spewing its smoke everywhere. 'You've got nobody with you at all, Leo?'

'Not a soul. Same for you?'

'By myself. That was the agreement. Real outlook here. It's a soother.'

'Maybe I could get you membership, Benny. If you were interested.'

'That's very nice of you, Leo.' The bastard would really enjoy being kindly like that, offering a leg up. Who would have believed Leo could have ever got to that situation? Year or two ago he would have been kept out of the Muggers And Threatening Behaviour Club, for being too savage.

'It would cost, one way and the other. You know what I mean?'

'No problem.' Loxton returned to his seat.

Leo leaned forward and spoke quietly, a real confidential, intimate voice, a buddy's voice. 'As I see it, Benny, there's six casinos worth talking about. That's three in the town and then Baize, The Spinning Wheel and The Pimpernel, outlying.'

'Right.'

'There are others in the patch and they might do something one day but just now they're not worth protecting, that's our thinking – more trouble than the take.'

'Accepted,' Loxton said. Yes, Leo was no great talker usually, but when it came to business, and here in the golf club, he could really take off. This sort of thing was obviously what he was made for. In some way he would be a loss. It was a pity he could not have offered a lot earlier to arrange the club membership. Too late now.

'OK, in the town, you hold Black Jack, undisputedly, and we have Cleo's,' Tacette said. 'I don't know the figures, not details, but they ought to be around the same. Say we're taking from each about two hundred grand a year, more if it's a wet summer, or the royal wedding, so everybody's excited and flash with their cash.'

'Near enough.'

Some biggy of the golf club in a purple sweater come in with what seemed to be a golf reporter from a paper and they sat down not far away. This great club star began telling him pretty hearable about his great dramas out on the grass, thirty yard putts, and his ball in a lake, or something like that, the whole fucking bagful, and this kid with the notebook got to write it all down, and cry 'Really?' and 'Fantastic.' Maybe this gorgeous bit of golfing history owned the paper.

Leo came closer still. 'And then we turn to the tricky one in

town, Benny. Well, this is a touchy subject, we'd both agree, but
it has to be faced.'

'Captain Dreyfus?'

'Your people, my people fight over Captain Dreyfus. Christ,
that carnage. Off and on for how long is it? Three years,
four?'

'Since it opened. More like four. Yes, a lot of pain, a lot of
sweat. So regrettable.' Jesus, Captain Dreyfus was one of the
reasons Leo had to go, Leo and especially Lay-waste. They made
that casino a battlefield, Lay-waste turning real fiendish there. It
was funny to be talking to Leo about it like this now, so reasonable and calm. That was never going to be solved, Captain Dreyfus, not until the Tacettes went their way at the silver wedding, if
you could call that being solved.

Leo said: 'Talking of pain and aggro, who did they pull out of
the dock in that Metro?'

'Search me. Some drunk?'

'Maybe. Where was I?'

'Dreyfus.'

'Yes, all right, so we're into bigger cash here, at Dreyfus, much
bigger. This could be up to, what, three-fifty, three-seventy-five
grand?'

'A real peachy place. Brings in your finest big money carriers,
Arabs, of course, and the Chinks, naturally, but all sorts of other
wallets as well. It really pissed me off, Leo, being forced to smash
up a pretty spot of such quality, the tastiest in fitments. But
people like that, they had to be taught unmistakable how much
they needed protection and a guiding hand here. They come in
from London because they been getting a hard time from their
guardians wanting bigger and bigger takes, and because they
hear about development and heavy investment going this way.
All right. However, they had the stupid idea they could do it here
alone, no professional defenders, because they're not in the
capital no more but out among the patsies and nobodies – how
they regard it. They're looking for a saving and we're supposed to
be it. Such a basic error.

'Well, obvious, first thing they need a bit of a revelation that
this is not the home of the brothers Pushover. Or to put it
otherwise, if they thought it was St Francis of Rififi or Oxfam
running this place, they got to find out different. Oh, it hurts, I

know, to do a demolition treatment and, like I said, it's damn regrettable. Only way to let them know the picture, though. They're all right again now, the insurance took care, but you're right, the Dreyfus is still problematical.'

'That's what I mean, Benny, talks about talks. The Dreyfus has to go on any agenda. I don't know it can be resolved, but that's the heart of things.'

'Can't argue.'

'Whether we can protect it together, a straight split.'

'Is Anthony going to wear that?'

'Anthony will do whatever's agreed, Benny. It's only the uncertainty of the situation, the competitiveness, that led to incidents. Once we have a working pattern, Anthony will be as good as gold, oh, yes, as good as gold. Underneath it all, that boy's a natural conciliator, you know, Benny. He loves amity, co-operation. These outbursts, they're deplorable and he knows it and is ashamed, believe me. It's entirely nerves, an essentially gentle spirit put under unbearable strain.' He had on a padre voice now.

'Fine.' Loxton felt strange and a bit solemn and sad – to be talking like this, so level and friendly, and calling that fucker Anthony, like a boutique, instead of Lay-waste, and knowing all the time that none of this chatter mattered because Leo and Lay-waste and Gerald and their whole operation would very soon be deeply unavailable to take from Captain Dreyfus or anywhere else. They had asked for it, especially Lay-waste, but Leo and Gerald, too, and it was coming. Until it came, Benny did not mind discussing collection arrangements and the partnerships and splits, but it seemed spooky, all the same. Never mind, he was comfortable and he felt safe. Was Leo going to try anything in front of a picture of the Queen?

'Or maybe one of us take Dreyfus and the other get all the so-far small-timers,' Leo suggested. 'Nursed along, two or three of them might be into the Dreyfus class themselves in a couple of years.'

'True.'

'No need to decide anything now, Benny. Well, we can't, can we? We both need to consult. It's just a matter of fixing an agenda. So, Captain Dreyfus at the top, yes? Leave Black Jack and Cleo's the way they are, giving no trouble. The minor league stuff for discussion along with Dreyfus? How does that grab you as an outline for the start of casino negotiations?'

'Grand. Tidy.'

'Then, outlying, you're looking after Baize and The Pimpernel. We have The Spinning Wheel. It's two to one, but The Spinning Wheel is bigger, we take about a hundred and seventy-five grand a year protection there. Maybe Baize and The Pimpernel together give you that much? I don't know? A little less? This is the kind of area we could talk about in detail. And, of course, with Baize you've really had to do some work, give active heavy minding now and then, because of the lout gangs who get in there, no sinecure. You see, we could be very understanding about special problems. Benny, what I'm trying to say is, we would be ready to come more than half-way to get a working pattern. You'd find us very, very flexible.'

'That's really something.'

'I don't consider business can be done in any other way. Well, yes, of course, it can be done by confrontation, confrontation and more confrontation. But that's so stupid, so self-destructive and uneconomic. That's the behaviour of another, cruder era.'

'We've thought ditto.'

'Of course you have. So, then, that will be the first stage of negotiations. It's not the main money for either of us, I suppose, but it's where the most bother has come in the past. Obviously, after this, we go on to the grass and coke aspects, where there have also been troublesome misunderstandings, though not so head-on or fierce.'

Leo gave a grand, comfortable laugh, like the two of them was bigger than this crazy fighting and could easy put it all right, man to man.

The king of the golfers had finished his interview and the two of them left, the purple wool gleaming like a bruise for the *Guinness Book of Records*.

'Squabbles like that spill money and blood, Benny, and they draw attention. It's so foolish to send signals to the police.' Leo spoke more quietly: 'As to police, I might be building something with Iles.'

Loxton was shocked and disbelieving. 'Iles? Christ, go careful there. You remember what happened to Cliff Jamieson, the one they called You-know-who? You-knew-who now.'

'Iles was down the Chaff the other night, plus lady.'

'Taking meals? Iles? Can't be.'

'No, of course not. That's too primitive and low. But don't tell me he didn't know we'd bought Chaff. No, he had come on purpose, I'd say. This was introductory. He'll be there again. I'd bet he's looking for a deal, some share of the action. They get an idea of the kind of cash that's going into the casinos and what we're taking for protective services. Meals and drinks – he's not interested, not going to sell his soul for a dozen oysters and a glass of stout, you're right. But talk a few figures with noughts on, that could be different. It generally is with these boys. Not right away in this case, obviously. But in due course.'

'Iles? You sure?'

'Give it a while. We had quite a private conversation. At this stage, some of it has to be confidential. You'll understand that, Benny, I know.'

God, this bastard thought he was chairman of Barclay's Bank.

'Well, I'd say we've made sensational progress here today, Benny. Some ground has been cleared. A few weeks, we could have another meeting for the detailed stuff. I've got a silver wedding coming up, you probably heard, it's no secret, so let me get that out of the way first.'

'No, that right? SIlver wedding! I didn't know. But yes, I suppose it would be about that now. Well, that's to your credit, Leo, that's to be admired, you and Daphne still together and happy, from being kids in school. That's not something you see every day, no, sir.'

'Just a family thing, Benny. You'll understand. That's how she wants it.'

'Best like that, more real, more enjoyable, oh, yes. Intimate. Your boys a few other relations, who else do you need?'

'As soon as that's over – Look, how many people in your outfit these days?' He sat back very relaxed in his green chair again, smiling the good friend smile, and looking like a child abuser just acquitted because the kids had too much trauma to testify. 'Is it all right to ask that, since we're future partners? It's the sort of thing we need to know about each other: I mean, the split, and avail-able manpower.'

'That's all right.' Loxton did not rush to answer, though. What went on? Number, for God's sake, names?

Leo led the way. 'You probably know my side. There's Anthony and Gerald, of course, and then three other full-time lads, Peter Fanton, Ashley Simpson – the one they call In-off, don't ask me why – and Greg Hales. After that, some odd-job people for now and then, heavies mostly, not pay-roll, so they don't rate for splits: Willy Jute, High Pulse Basil, that sort. With you, Phil Macey still, yes, and Norman. Who else, Benny?'

'Lentle – that's Bobby Lentle, you know him? Thirty-five, fair, crew-cut, ugliest sod since Maurice Chevalier, but one of the best. Going a bit fat? He's quite new, but he's settling in very nice, oh yes, he's going to be an asset.'

'No, not a name I know.' Leo smiled a bit bigger. 'Justin with you these days? Justin Paynter?'

Loxton was not ready for that but smiled himself and said at once, no bother or choking on the fucking words because of the Metro: 'Oh, Justin. No, he moved on. What's called mutual. Some things he could handle deft enough, a real natural talent, but some things very slack. Bit naive and forgetful? It comed to a parting, had to. No hard feelings, nothing like that. He was off to London or Wales or somewhere, reckoned he had bids. Could be. There was ability, but he just couldn't get it working full rate, like Edward Heath. Maybe I'll replace him. I don't know. For now like you, we use a lot of part-timers, people looking for something quick and then you don't see them no more. Not the best way, but it works, and no overheads. Steve Stevens, Winston Makepiece – that's Towering Inferno – and Tommy Vit.' He hated telling him these things, even these things that anyone could find out for theirselves easy enough if they wanted to, but soon it would not make no difference. He hated talking to him about Justin Paynter, too, and felt troubled by questions like that, nosy, pushing bastard. Soon, this would not matter either, though.

Three men and their women came a bit too quietly into this lounge and Loxton tensed up for a minute, but they seemed to be genuine golf people, not Mercedes, but maybe big Rover or Audi, and in a while they started gabbling away about tournaments and shoe studs. They knew Leo and called out to him and chatted, like he was something quite sweet-smelling and British Standard. Christ, what sort of outfit must this be? Better check if Sweeney Todd was there in the list of old captains.

'I've enjoyed this,' Leo said, standing. 'I mean, quite apart from the business we've done today, it's good to get together. Should have happened a long time ago.'

'It mustn't go cold again Leo – not let things slide like that.'

They walked towards the door together. Loxton had brought the small Beretta in a shoulder holster and undid one button of his jacket as they went out. Leo noticed that right away and laughed like an idiot. Immediate, he went half on to one knee playing a sniper and made the shape of a pistol with his hand, while he did bang-bang noises from his mouth, popping off at all round the clock. God knew what the people here thought of that little mad show. He must really be sure of himself to believe they would wear it. 'A bit of suspicion still, it's natural, bound to be, Benny,' he chuckled. 'We've lived with it too long, that's the tragedy.' He straightened up and blew on his two fingers, like down a hot barrel at the end of a shoot-out. 'Yes, a long way to go yet, Benny, but we'll get there.'

'Of course, and my very best to Daphne. Give her fullest congrats from me and Alma on the silver wedding, won't you?'

'She'll be touched.'

Macey and Norman were at the house when Loxton returned, both of them looking pretty rough, but he could not talk serious to them immediate because Alma stayed in the room for a while, sounding off about some new millions of needy down Africa way and saying how important it was to send the help and make sure of good organisation, all that. Macey and Norman was nodding like they thought of nothing else, you would expect they might make notes any minute or go to Africa theirselves, taking corned beef. Well, it *was* important, what she said, and he was in favour of helping people having it bad like that, but Loxton wished she would piss off now.

'Some mammoth task,' Norman said.

'A test for all the developed world,' Macey added.

'A matter of conscience,' Norman said. He turned to Loxton. 'We were just saying, Theodore, what a challenge this kind of situation is.'

'The thing is, to force rich governments like our own to face up to this problem, the scale of it,' Macey stated.

When Alma went upstairs to change, Macey said: 'Benny,

maybe they got an identification on Justin from that sodding Metro they pulled out of the dock yesterday. We found out they had a load of heavy police down there, like Iles and Harpur. So, how the hell they find out the car was there and so important? This is one hell of a question.'

'How do you know – Iles and Harpur? And who says an identification? Who told you?' Loxton replied.

'It's right, about Iles and Harpur. We got a rumour and Norm made some calls and done some checking.'

'Checking?' Loxton said.

'It's all right, Benny,' Norman said. 'I was very careful. No invitations to look our way.'

'He got no clothes on, right?' Loxton asked. 'No jewellery, tattoos, scars, missing bits? He's got no record, so they can't do it from fingerprints. Nothing in the car? How would they get an identification so fast? No, it can't be. You did take the coat off him?'

'Of course,' Macey said.

'And it's gone? Blood traces, God knows what.'

'Yes, it's burned.' Macey kept on at what was troubling him. It troubled Loxton, too. 'So, how did they know he was there?' Macey asked again. 'We got a leak? Why Iles and Harpur down there? Far as they knew, this was just some dead in the dock, happens every day. But all the brass on the spot.'

'Who said Iles, Harpur?' Loxton asked.

'We think so,' Norman said. 'I haven't talked to any police, obviously, but docks people around there say one man was grey-haired, in a hell of a good suit and driving a Granada on his own. That has to be Iles. And then a fair, big bloke looking like a boxer, bit scruffy, talking to the divers. Harpur?'

Macey kept on. 'Why they there, Benny? This a leak?'

'How could there be? What you saying, Phil? Who you looking at, for Christ's sake? Who's going to leak? It could put us all in trouble. Talk sense. Only us three knew about him being there. Who else?'

'Yes, only us three,' Macey replied. 'Them people at the Monty –'

Loxton was growing tired of him. 'The Monty don't come into it. Whatever they saw there, they didn't see the car go into the dock, did they?'

185

Alma Loxton came back into the room wearing a topcoat and said she was going to drive to the shops. 'Yes, Norman's right, a challenge to all our governments, and to all of us, personally. Some approach to our MP, immediately, I think, Theodore.'

'That's the kind of thing we been discussing while you were out of the room,' Macey replied. 'As a matter of fact, Theordore said the MP.'

'It would be a worthwhile start,' Norman added.

'Perhaps I'll call into his committee rooms while I'm down there this afternoon,' she said.

'Good notion, Alma,' Loxton told her.

'While the iron's hot,' Macey added.

When she had left again, Loxton said: 'None of this makes no difference. They got no identification, that's obvious, or we would have heard on the radio, in the paper. That Metro's not going to tell them a thing, it was taken miles away, a nowhere car. Even if they did get an i.d. eventual, they might not even know Justin worked for us. He been here no time at all, really.'

'They'd know,' Macey said. 'He'll be on the collator.'

'So?' Loxton asked. 'Suppose he is. Would we kill one of our own people, for God's sake? What kind of sense is that? They'd think Leo's crew – Lay-waste, in one of his little spasms, probably. The fights around the Dreyfus, all that. That's how it would look to them. But, this stage, it don't come into it. They don't know who they got in that car, so relax. What I hear, they're keeping an eye on Leo. Iles been down the Chaff, acting friendly, but that one don't know what friendly is. He been taking a look, that's obvious.'

'I don't like all this – Iles here, Iles there. His wife can tie us to Justin, don't forget,' Macey said. 'We been seen in that club.'

'For Christ's sake, Phil, they don't know it's Justin,' Loxton said. 'And she's not going to talk, anyway. We already decided that, how long ago? Less so now. She going to tell her husband she's into a mucky killing, for God's sake?'

'Yes, well, all right, Benny, but we just got to find that Aston,' Macey said. 'He can sell us, too, and still maybe fuck up the silver wedding arrangements, That jerk Ralph – I still reckon he warned him to get clear. We should of seen him off proper, not just a beating.'

'If you killed him, that's more police activity, yes?' Loxton replied. 'Serious police activity. They'd be all over, and we can't accommodate that just now. A good thumping's enough, for the time being. That's private. Ralphy knows the procedures. In any case, he haven't got the guts to give Aston the tip. He's just useless, that's all, couldn't find a tit on a topless beach. Why he's where he is. Forget him now. Nothing's going to mess up the silver wedding. That's certain.'

Loxton pondered. 'Find Aston? Yes, we ought to. The only way is if we get a whisper, which I agree don't seem likely, or if we watch Mrs Iles, I mean, really watch her, not off and on like before, or hanging about in front at Rougement while he goes out the back way. Them two got to make contact eventual. That's what love's about, yes? Why don't you put Tommy Vit on her, if he's around? Tommy's a real tail, and these days mostly he don't get violent. That other business was nasty, but years ago, and he've definitely quietened. Best thing, he wasn't with you at the Monty with Justin that night, so it's a new face. Ask Tommy just to follow, nothing else, and to get a fix on Aston, same as we told Ralphy, only Tommy will find the bugger. Make it real clear, nothing more than that at this stage. Tell him three times, maybe four. He'll understand. Then. If he locates Aston to come on to us immediate and we'll get there fast and do the rest. Tell him that a few times, too. Tell him, no delay, give us a location immediate.'

Macey and Norman stayed to see the local evening news on television. There was still no name for the body, just a lot of the usual chatter about further inquiries and forensic. The programme took the chance to re-run film from yesterday of the Metro being lifted and Loxton tried to make out Iles or Harpur in the group on the quay-side but failed. That could be panic rubbish. Macey seemed a little better now and had a giggle at the car spinning on the end of the cables, with Justin hidden inside. 'Like a fun-fair,' he said.

Alma returned, very pleased about her interview at the MP's committee rooms. 'Extremely positive response,' she told them. She said she had promised to start any local campaign with a gift of £1000.

'That's reasonable,' Loxton said. 'The boys hung on to hear what news you had, dear, about Africa etcetera.'

'This sort of thing does need someone with drive, like Alma, don't it, Theodore?' Macey said.

'Nobody better,' Norman remarked. 'Happily, there are fine impulses in most people, but those impulses have to be encouraged, released. So much untapped goodness about.'

'What Alma is is what's known as a catalyst,' Macey remarked. 'A real catalyst.'

'Thank you, Philip,' she said.

12

A woman Harpur did not recognise was waiting in his lounge when he went home, but he guessed at once who she was, and, for a moment, felt dazed and appalled at having to face her now. He pushed those feeble reactions to the side: being dazed and appalled did not get you far in this job, or any other, unless you were playing Hamlet.

Megan was out somewhere and the children had been looking after the visitor, chatting and feeding her tea and cake, though she seemed to have drunk and eaten very little. About twenty-five, she was a bit unkempt, modish unkempt, with a blue reefer jacket over grey cords, and beautiful in what Iles would probably call a Pre-Raphaelite way: large-eyed, wan, with long, red-brown hair, the sort of features any man would admire, but which Harpur found somehow unexciting these days. Occasionally, he wondered whether all this new choosiness meant his sex drive was on the fade. In any case, perhaps this girl was not always so pale. She looked anxious and sleepless, her eyes not simply large but wide and staring and over-bright. He could feel sorry for her and, at the same time, reckon she was probably in a condition to do some useful talking.

Hazel said: 'This is Amanda, dad. She has to see your urgently. Why couldn't I be called Amanda? Hazel, for God's sake – it's so chintzy and historical. Which of you picked that? People's aunties in the Boer War were named Hazel, I bet.'

'Girls were called Dolly Grey,' Jill told her.

'Mr Harpur, I saw something on television,' the girl muttered. 'That's why I'm here. I didn't want to go to the nick, not in the circumstances.' She semed about to say more, but glanced at

189

Harpur's two girls and paused. He knew well enough what she had seen, anyway.

'Wise not going to the police station, Amanda,' Hazel said. 'There's currents and cross-currents down there, and you might be far out to sea before you can say, "I want a solicitor."'

'You know who I am, Mr Harpur,' the girl said. 'I can tell. So, you'll understand why I came to your house?'

'Of course.'

'How? How do you know who she is?' Hazel asked, at the top of her voice. 'She said she's never met you. How do you know, then? Are you supposed to be a magician or something now?'

'Amanda's got big trouble, dad,' Jill explained. 'She won't tell us what, but anyone can see it's important.'

'Old laser eyes,' Hazel said.

'I think we'll have you two out of here,' Harpur told the girls. 'Amanda might have something confidential to say.'

'About what?' Hazel asked. 'What on television?'

Harpur said: 'I don't think – '

'I'm only asking about the general area,' Hazel told him.

'She's been trying to get it out of her already,' Jill said.

'Mouth,' Hazel snarled.

Harpur made them leave. At once the girl said: 'Justin Paynter and I were, are, well – '

'Yes. I've been trying to get in touch.'

'How did you know about me?'

He could not say that her name was on a favoured numbers directory at Justin's flat, along with his mother's, Jack Lamb's and Benny Loxton's, because Harpur should never have gone into his flat. 'I picked up some gossip that you were his girl friend.'

For a moment, she gazed at him and her dark eyes tightened and became too sharp and disbelieving to be at all Pre-Raphaelite any longer. 'All right, if that's what you say.' She paused, obviously scared to ask the question that came next, the one he knew was on the way and which he had dreaded from the moment he saw her. 'Mr Harpur, the body taken from the dock? It's Justin?'

So, he withdrew deftly into officialese. 'We've no positive identification yet.'

Again she gazed at him. 'No, but is it? You don't have to treat me like a simpleton.'

'I'm afraid I can't go further just now.'

'Oh, Jesus, what sort of language is that?'

'It's the best I can do. At this stage.'

'At this stage.'

'We're waiting for information.'

She nodded a bit and her jaw twitched. 'What you mean is, you thought it might be Justin when you called up the crane and nothing about the body has made you change your mind?'

That was spot on, but he said: 'We've no positive identification, Amanda.'

'You want me to look at him, so you won't have to bother his mother? Is that why you've been trying to get in touch?'

Yes, they would like her to look at him, though he did not feel like telling her so yet. She might not find him easy to recognise. 'I was trying to make contact with you before any of this at the dock. I needed to ask you a few things.'

'What things?'

'Well, we wanted to trace Justin.'

'And I might be the route. How did you know?'

Again he held back.

'Oh, yes, gossip,' she said.

'That's it. We live on that.'

'Why did you want to trace him?'

'Well, we'd heard he had dropped out of sight.'

'More gossip?'

'Yes.'

'Who does all this gossiping?'

'All sorts.'

'And you don't say which all sorts?'

'If we did, the gossip would stop.'

She sat with her hands clasped in her lap, head bent forward, almost like somebody in prayer, or someone trying to sweet-talk a social security clerk. 'But why would it bother you that Justin wasn't around? He's grown up, entitled to move off.'

'Of course, but some people we like to keep in sight.'

'Why Justin?'

He ignored that. 'How did you get on to me, Amanda? My address?'

She spoke towards her feet. The words came hesitantly, and not very loud. 'Justin told me, if anything tricky happened, you know, if anything went badly wrong with him, to get hold of you because you were straight. Straightish. Exactly what he said was that you were the best around – that's to say, the best copper around.'

She added the last words as if this limiting of the field made all the difference: the best of a shady lot. He was glad he had sent the children out. Otherwise, there would have been some sniggers.

'It was Justin who said see you at your house, not the nick. Privacy for both parties. He gave me the address. I didn't want to disturb your home. I almost came to the station this afternoon, regardless.'

'It's OK. The kids are used to it.' He would not have been at his office because it had been one of his afternoons with Ruth Cotton in a side-street hotel, out of sight, out of line, out of clothes for a few hours. As happened now and then or oftener, she had been saying they must finish, and he felt half-exhausted from arguing, or perhaps it was pleading. Maybe he had managed to patch things again. He was not sure. Often lately he was not sure.

Amanda seemed to have grown more tense. She would need time before they spoke again. 'So, how about some tea for me?' he called to the girls.

'I thought we'd been kicked out?' Hazel shouted from the other room.

'You have. I want tea, not your company.'

'You've been up to my place?' Amanda asked.

'A few times. Neighbours said you'd gone abroad to the sun. Marbella?'

She managed a laugh. 'Some hope. I told them Spain and let them think it was with another guy – to make it look as if I wasn't simply Justin's girl. Suddenly it seemed to me that had become a very dangerous role. But the Mediterranean? So, where's the tan? I just got out of sight as soon as Justin disappeared – not far away, but not visible.'

'You thought you might be next?'

'Does it sound far-fetched? I didn't know what to think, but I wasn't going to hang about wondering. All I knew, Justin runs with Benny Loxton, yes? Or ran. If he's crossed them, everybody close to him has crossed them. Would you take chances? Have you met that Macey? I'm told technically he's sane.' Hazel brought in a mug of tea for him.

'Where's mum?' he asked.

She shrugged: 'At Louise Ettinger's discussing the PLO or the snooker final or the NHS or *The Bonfire of the Vanities* with the rest of the intellectual cream?' She left again.

Amanda lifted her head and looked at him blank-faced. 'Say, then. Would you like me to give an identification? You're sure it's him, aren't you? I'd be a formality. Or does it have to be family?'

'We're – '

She made her voice flat, matter-of-fact: 'Were there wounds on him, Mr Harpur?'

'At this stage, we're not saying anything at all. There has to be a proper examination.' He tried to turn her from these questions. 'I was looking for you to ask whether Justin had said anything to show he was troubled – worried?'

She gave another pained laugh, as if dealing with someone hopelessly naive. 'You couldn't work for Benny Loxton and not feel worried some time. Maybe Justin didn't appreciate what he'd let himself in for.'

'How do you mean?'

'Look, I don't know what their business is, and Justin would never have told me. I didn't ask, and I knew he wouldn't have said, even if I had. Probably, I didn't want to know. All right, I admit that. But I had the idea there were bits of it that might not smell too sweet. Perhaps there are bits in most businesses like that, though. These stories about the City. After all, Loxton was running whatever it was without being pulled in by you and yours, and he's very high profile yet apparently socially acceptable – charity dances and what not – so I assumed it had to be just about all right. Not production of gospel tracts, but OK. As far as Justin was concerned, though, there was a hell of a lot of strain, I could see that. That's what I mean: he was out of his depth.' He watched her wince at the words she had picked.

'What strain, Amanda?'

'I didn't see him all that often, you know. He wasn't crying on my shoulder every day.'

'But some days?'

'Yes, some days.'

'What sort of thing?'

'Look, it is him, isn't it?' She began to cry suddenly as if it had all been locked in for too long. Even now, she covered her face with her hands, clearly ashamed to have given way, and he saw that she wore a garnet ring on her engagement finger. 'Christ, this is my bloke, chucked into mud and filth by a crew of bloody thugs and zombies. What am I doing, sitting here, discussing his way of life when his way of life is over? This is a sort of betrayal, you know that? Mr Harpur, there were some good things about him, but those people just wanted to pull him down and down. Maybe he wouldn't go any further, and that's why what happened happened.' Her voice had become hoarse and loud and when Harpur looked up Hazel and Jill were standing in the doorway staring at her, Hazel almost weeping herself.

'Daddy, what's wrong with her?' Jill said. 'What are you saying to upset her so much?'

'Is there someone dead?' Hazel asked. 'His job's almost always about the dead.'

Amanda wiped her face and tried to smile at them. 'No, it's not because of your daddy, Jill. Something's gone a bit wrong. Some-body I know. It's just for now. I'll be all right soon.'

'I don't believe it,' Hazel said. 'You don't believe it.'

'Yes, I promise,' Amanda told her. She stood up and walked to the girls, then crouched down on bent knees, her face at their level. 'Your dad's trying to help me,' she said.

'Are you sure?' Jill replied. 'Sometimes when he seems to be trying to help people he's really only smarming them along, pretending to be a friend, and aiming to land them in it deeper. That's police. It's called interrogation skills. They have books about it. Worse than selling double-glazing around the doors.'

'I'll be fine,' Amanda said.

'Will she, dad?' Hazel asked.

He could not really give a yes to that. 'We're trying to work things out,' he said.

'You'll never get a straight answer out of him,' Hazel told Amanda.

'Why don't you really help her, dad?'

'I would if I could.'

'Why don't you tell her what it is she wants to know?' Jill asked.

'Because I don't know it myself.'

'You always know it. You act dumb,' Hazel said. She reached out and straightened a sheaf of Amanda's hair, which had fallen across her forehead. Then the two girls turned and left again.

Amanda shut the door and remained standing near it, tall, thin and very tense, but she had stopped weeping.

'Justin's a pointer to something else, is he?' she asked.

'I don't follow.'

'You, a chief superintendent, up at my place looking for him because he's not around? Justin was never that important. You go personally to investigate every missing person, and this one not even reported? It doesn't make sense.'

'What could he point to?' Harpur asked.

'He worked for Loxton.'

'Come and sit down again.' She made a show of refusal, briefly, as though he were trying to seduce her, and then did as he suggested. There did not seem much fight left in her, or much hope. 'I still don't get it,' Harpur said. 'He worked for Loxton. So?'

'So, were you trying to reach Loxton through him?' Once more the conversation suddenly seemed to strike her as wrong, monstrous. She began to yell again. 'I get the idea that a kind of bargain is under way here, you know that? It goes like this – if I answer your questions, you might eventually tell me if Justin's dead. But I've got nothing to bargain with, Harpur. Justin never told me anything.'

'Were you surprised when he disappeared?'

As if afraid of disturbing the children again she glanced towards the door of the other room and when she resumed talking it was in not much more than a whisper. 'He didn't phone. I rang him, eventually, and no answer.'

'He was supposed to phone?'

'Most days he would ring. We were close.' She fingered the ring. It seemed modest, almost poverty-stricken, for someone working with Benny. Perhaps Justin had still not been making very much, or perhaps neither of them liked the flash. 'Mr Harpur, was Justin – all right, was the body in the car, whoever it is, was he alive when it went into the water? They can tell, can't they?'

'Yes, they can tell. We don't know yet.' Probably, she would want to hear he was not, though that would lead back to agonising questions and answers about how he died, and whether there were injuries on the body. There were injuries and it looked to him as if they might have been enough. 'The last time you saw

195

him, or spoke to him, Amanda, did he seem especially troubled? All right, you say he was always troubled working for Loxton, but was it worse?'

'We just talk across each other, don't we?' she said. 'I want to know about Justin, you want to know about Loxton. That's what I mean, a sort of deal, but I don't seem to be getting much out of it. I suppose the question is, can I ever win? I'm sick if you don't tell me, and I'm sick if you do.' Again she glanced towards the door, seemingly to make sure the children were not there. 'You've got women in your life, Mr Harpur – what I hear. Well, obviously, your wife, but the other, as well, which Justin mentioned. So you know how I feel, don't you? Don't you?'

As a sudden kick in the crutch this was not bad. It always shook him when someone talked about Ruth and him like that, even though Harpur knew he was crazy to imagine he could keep her a secret: after all, they used local hotels and his picture appeared on local television and in the papers reasonably often. Although nobody at the hotels ever showed they knew him, and never queried the false names he used, that did not stop them spreading the story. He could not blame Amanda. She was desperate enough to pull any trick, try any pressure.

In any case, even before she chose to launch that one, he had come to feel it must be hellishly worse for her not to know the truth on Justin, and he felt, too, that he could not bear to keep her in this state any longer. Now he had seen how deep her despair went he decided to talk. 'OK, Amanda, we're pretty certain it's him. I've never seen Justin, nor my colleagues, but the circumstantial stuff is strong, I'm very sorry to tell you. We think he was probably killed by a couple of knife wounds before the car went into the water.' In fact, there had been a lot of argument: he and Iles said yes, Garland, as well as the sergeant diver no. The doctors might be able to settle it, ultimately. But he had nothing else to offer as comfort, and she needed it now.

She resumed that very still, head-bent attitude again opposite him, staring down at her shoes. If anything, she had grown paler, even more beautiful and defeated-looking. In a while she said: 'He really was a nobody. For me he was great, but in the outfit, a nobody. Perhaps you know that already. I can't see why he had to be killed. He wasn't big enough.'

'Why I was asking whether he'd said anything. We're puzzled, too.'

'You think Loxton, or his people?'

'I can't say that, I really can't say that. It could be anyone.'

'But you ask about Loxton.'

'Whatever you know, about anybody. We need pointers. When you said they might have been trying to drag him down further – what was that about?'

'A feeling.'

He heard Megan's car draw up, then her footsteps as she entered the house. The children might tell her about Amanda and the weeping, but Megan would never think of coming into the room. Partly, it was because she knew she might disturb a delicate situation. Beyond that, though, she hated having police interviews done at home and preferred to ignore them and the people Harpur saw here. Once, in a lurid, angry moment, she had referred to the kitchen as 'soiled' because he had talked with Jack Lamb there. For this she had apologised later, but he reckoned it was pretty close to what she thought, all the same. Megan believed detective work should be like in the Sherlock Holmes pieces, all magnifying glasses and clever deductions from train timetables. And she believed, too, that there should be a great and obvious gulf fixed between what was legal and what was not.

So, she loathed the way Harpur worked, and referred to him occasionally as the sardonic rat of no-man's land, apparently after some war poem she knew: almost everything could be reduced to literature if you had the reading. What she meant was that, to do his job, he lived and thrived in an undefined, dirty and perilous area between villainy and rectitude, constantly blurring the line separating what was right from what was necessary. And, at a less important level, she did not care for the way he also blurred the line between the office and home, like today. A long while ago they used to have sessions arguing out all these differences, sometimes in a decent, controlled, rational way, but more often ferociously. They did not talk about the problem at all these days: it was too painful and seemed to have come to symbolise all the other differences between them.

Amanda must also have heard Megan come in and, raising her head, watched the door of the room. Harpur took her back to what she had said: 'A feeling?'

197

'Yes.' She turned to look at him. 'There was someone he intended speaking to. I don't know if he did. Would it be you? Is that why he said to come here if there was trouble? Did he talk to you sometimes?'

'No, not me.'

'Well, he had a secret contact outside. He wouldn't discuss these things with me, but there was someone. Do you know who?'

'No. What sort of contact?' It would be Jack Lamb, of course, though Justin had never reached him with whatever it was he had wanted to say.

'I'd have thought you knew him. Wouldn't this be one of your gossips? My impression was, Justin would tell him, and it would reach the police. So either you or one of your colleagues, or a tipster.'

'No.'

'If you say.' She shrugged those thin shoulders. Sometimes he had the feeling that she was out of her depth, too, but sometimes not. She went on: 'He wouldn't talk to me, wouldn't involve me, he always said that. But he did need someone, someone not in Loxton's team. Well, obviously, it was probably something in their business that upset him, offended him. He could get like that. Justin would go so far, but if – That's what I mean, trying to drag him down further, you see.'

'Offended about something that had happened or was going to happen?'

'I had the idea it was a plan, in the future. All I can tell you, he seemed afraid someone would get badly hurt, I mean, really badly.'

'Are you saying killed?'

Again she shrugged, then half nodded. 'Yes, even killed. That was the feeling I had.'

'He said that?'

'No. I told you, he never said things to me, not straight out. It was hints, things I picked up. At the time, I thought I must be manufacturing it, panicking, exaggerating. But this was before the Metro in the dock. Now, when I look back, I can see that nothing I feared then was too black or far out.' She seemed to make a deliberate effort to dredge from her memory and to focus her mind. 'There was something about a woman. I couldn't believe it: a woman to be badly hurt, maybe a woman to be killed? How could that be? How could Justin be mixed up in it? He wouldn't have it, I know he wouldn't.'

'He actually mentioned a woman?'

'He would go on and on, but no detail, just grieving about the spot he'd got into, really, and mutter things like "No need, no need," and then "this poor old duck" or "harmless piece". That's a woman, yes? And I'd say, "Which harmless piece?", and he'd tell me he had to talk about it elsewhere. Yes, elsewhere. That was one of his words. In a way this hurt me. In a way? Of course it bloody hurt me. I'm supposed to be his girl, and I can't know about his worst problems. Lovely, isn't it?' For a second a tiny patch of red appeared in her white cheeks, then subsided, like clouds touched momentarily by evening sunlight. 'He'd say that maybe when he'd discussed it with whoever, he might be able to tell me, but I knew that was eye-wash. His line was he couldn't speak to me about it, or anything hairy, to keep me in the clear. So, he was going to talk to this somebody else, get advice and maybe help.'

'I can understand that.'

'But I believe the real reason he wouldn't speak to me was that he felt ashamed of the work he was in, and didn't want me to know about it. In any case, I'm not in the clear, am I? I'd bet people from Loxton's outfit have been to my place while I was away. He didn't seem to realise they'd have tabs on anyone he knew. It's why I say he was an also-ran: nowhere near sharp enough or knowing enough to be big-time, not in that sort of world.' She seemed about to grow upset again. 'But this sounds as if I'm blaming Justin. I wouldn't, ever, not now. He was doing what he thought the best, I know. I loved him, and he loved me. Yes, he did.' She seemed to expect contradiction. Standing suddenly, she smiled and went on to speak in a tone that was obviously meant to quash argument. 'Now, I'll come with you to see the body. I've done my bit of the bargain, haven't I? Please, Mr Harpur, I must. I'll be fine, I promise.'

By that she meant she would not break down, and she was right. Although Harpur had never seen Justin as he used to be, he knew the water and the fall and maybe a beating had distorted the features, and possibly broken his jaw. The technicians had done what they could, but he still looked like someone who had not died happy and ready. When the morgue man pulled open the long drawer in the tiled wall, Amanda turned her head away quickly as she saw how misshapen the face was now, but made no sound, and after a second resumed her gaze. Her weeping had finished in Harpur's house. Nothing had happened to Justin's eyes, despite what the sergeant had said, but they were shut now and offered her no help in identification. She could do without it, though, and there would be no need to bring the corpse out on to the examination table.

'Yes,' she said, over her shoulder, still looking down at the body. 'Of course it's Justin. Will it really be possible not to bother his mother?'

'She might want to be bothered. People can be possessive about bodies.'

'Yes, I suppose. Some would say he asked for this, running with Benny.'

'No, I don't believe that.'

She turned away and they closed the drawer. 'It's like a filing cabinet,' she said. As they walked back to the car she went on: 'You see, Mr Harpur, I behaved all right. I'll cry later, I expect.'

'You could have cried there. I wouldn't hold you to that sort of promise.'

'No. It was Justin, but it wasn't Justin like I knew him. I'll cry when I think about him as he was.'

'Well, don't cry too much. It's over now.'

'There's something else. I'd like to know he wasn't killed just for grassing, or for trying to grass. It's so contemptible, isn't it?'

'We live by it.'

'I thought it was gossip you lived by.'

'Most grassing is gossip.'

'I want to believe he was acting in a good cause, so to speak.'

'A lot of grassing's in a good cause, if stopping crime is a good cause. Would you prefer a bank to be successfully held up by an armed gang, or have us tipped off and able to prevent it, possibly save life? If there's a saint of grasses I'll put his picture up in my office.'

'Maybe there is,' she muttered.

'Judas?'

But she was too considerate, or squeamish, to spell that out. 'Perhaps if he did it to protect the life of someone it wouldn't be so bad – this woman, whoever she might be. Is that what he was trying to do? I mean, if there is a woman. And will you be able to stop it happening to her, because of Justin? Or has it happened already?'

'Good questions. Let me drive you somewhere.'

'No, thanks. I'm going to stay under cover.'

'Yes, of course, from them. But what if I need to find you?'

'Pehaps I'll be in touch.' She walked away and did not glance back. He thought of the end of *The Third Man* and Harry Lime's woman striding without a smile into the distance, snubbing Joseph Cotton, while the zither frenzies away.

Harpur went home again and had a call from Iles suggesting that the two of them should make an evening visit later on to Benny Loxton, for a talk about the Metro and Justin Paynter. Occasionally, and when it suited him, the Assistant Chief liked to involve himself in the details of an inquiry: what he called 'going walk-about at the sharp end'. Possibly, too, he wanted some distraction from his messy problems at home, and throwing his weight about with Benny might do for the moment. A bit of heart-to-heart terrorising in a good cause often brought the roses back to Iles's cheeks.

Almost as soon as Harpur replaced the receiver, Jack Lamb came through, sounding untypically frail and reversing the charges. 'Forgive me, Colin, but I'm at Heathrow,' he said.

'Going or coming?'

'On our way to Italy,' Lamb went on. 'Long-promised treat. Mother's over from the States and is coming with us.'

'Lovely.'

'Col, I felt such an accumulated yearning to see some galleries – paintings, architecture. Sure, I'm dealing in great art all the time, so it's a bit of a busman's holiday, but I do enjoy viewing works displayed on fine walls and in a grand ambiance. It's one of life's dimensions, or should be. Likewise Helen and mother appreciate that. Perhaps you know the way these pinings can build up and suddenly become well-nigh irresistible?'

'Not the whole breathless Florence bit, Jack, along the sacred Arno?' Megan crossed the hall and made a face when she heard Lamb's name.

'Something akin, Col. Helen's very keen. She saw *Room with a View*: there's a kiss in a field. It's the heat.' Lamb distrusted the telephone and only rarely would he gabble on like this. Normally, he fixed a rendezvous with a couple of code words and rang off. Perhaps he felt safe because he was in a public box far away and would soon be farther still, possibly Florence, possibly Italy, possibly anywhere.

Abruptly ditching the Renaissance man tone, Lamb said: 'I thought it best to get out for a while. Well, your recommendation.'

'Sure.'

'I've got to say, it troubled me seeing that Metro on the screen, swinging on the cable, a dripping, silver tomb. Daft, really. I knew it was there, and probably who was inside, but seeing it – well, I started making these vacation plans. That what they mean by the power of television? Maybe I'm weakening, Col, turning yellow? Mother says I look more twitchy each time she visits. She calls me El Poltroono. There was a time when none of this would have bothered me too much.'

Yes, there was, and not very long ago, either. If events had begun to frighten Lamb, they could be building towards something very sombre. 'I think you're wise, Jack.'

'Yes, well wise often does mean yellow.' Then he brightened. 'Look, we'll be getting our boarding call soon. There's an item.'

'Ah, grand.'

'Would I land you with a phone charge just for pleasantries about Old Masters? And, talking of them, you know Tommy Vit?' Lamb said. 'One of the supreme tails?'

'Yes?'

'And you know, too, that he works for Benny?'

'Now and then. Not staff.'

'The very point. I gather Benny's called him in for something special and urgent. And the fee's special, too. Tommy didn't fancy the job at all, said it was a bit close, that's how I hear it, "a bit close", and had to be bought big. Benny was still willing to pay. This is an important one, Col.'

'What's it mean, "a bit close"?'

'Not sure. So, you're bound to ask who he's supposed to tail.'

'Who's he supposed to tail, Jack?'

'This takes some deduction.'

Christ.

Lamb went on: 'You probably heard, even you people, that

Panicking Ralphy has been around all over looking for Aston, the odd-job man and messenger boy? Some affiliations with Mrs Iles? Familiar with him?'

'So?'

'He's failed to find Aston. Not only that, he took a bad hammering. Benny seemed to think Ralphy might have slipped him a get-clear warning. One story says Ralphy was found injured by a woman upstairs in the club, not his wife, and unnamed so far. What's some outside woman doing in a bedroom at the Monty, for God's sake? This is not a lady belonging to Ralph, we're absolutely sure. Ralphy's very, very family-prone, with a fierce respect for faithfulness, and, well, for what's proper, so when he fucks spare it's always off the premises. What I must ask is, was this visitor Mrs Iles, wanting to know if Ralph had found Ian Aston? Who can tell?'

Harpur pulled up a chair and concentrated very hard.

'This appears to be the picture: Benny wants Aston for some reason,' Lamb said. 'Really wants him. Ralphy's failed, or worse. How else do they find him, Col? Who's he most likely to be in touch with?'

Because Megan might come through the hall again, Harpur did not reply.

'Now, you're playing stupid, yes? You can see, can't you, Col? Oh, someone nearby so you can't talk? It has to be Sarah Iles in case he makes contact – sets up a meeting.'

'Has it?'

'Love – the great imperative. You're going to say too dicey because Iles would spot him if Tommy was behind his wife, no matter how good he is. We all know Iles is smart, too. That might be what "a bit close" meant. Too close to the police, especially to Desmond Iles.'

'But you think he took the job, anyway?'

'Like I said, at a price, Col. That's my information, not from Tommy direct, I have to say, but reputable, very reputable.' Almost everyone who whispered to Jack was that: reputable as a grass, which might not be the same league as saying reputable as a banker or a broker, but something, just the same, and look at the bankers and brokers around, anyway. Lamb's voice faded a little, then came back. 'I'm being summoned. Mother gets masterful at airports. My pimp acquaintance is taking a holiday, too, I hear, since the Metro emerged. The one who saw it go in and spoke to me.'

'I'd have liked to talk to him.'

'What he thought. Why he's going. He says a court appearance would totally destroy his credibility and he sees that as the central asset of his business, after pussy, of course. What you might call *exeunt omnes*. People are growing stressed. Any idea what's behind it all yet? So much activity, but where's it pointing?'

'Yes, where?'

'I thought I'd better talk to you soonest, rather than send a card from Italy, in the circumstances. Tommy Vit can turn nasty, can't he, so you'd want to know where he's operating. I mean, he's not like Macey, nothing so feral, but he's very keen on self-protection and has over-reacted now and then.'

'A long time ago.'

'As far as you know. Just don't run at him or get him in a corner. Well, I leave it with you. Before I go, I'd like to say this: I worry about you, Col. Are you going to be able to manage without me? What will you do for information? Am I leaving you in the lurch?' But Lamb did not wait for an answer and the phone began to whine. To his disgust Harpur found that he did, in fact feel deserted and weaker.

He was due to pick up Iles for the trip to Benny's and, after what Lamb had said, decided he would go up to Rougement Place early for a careful look around. He used the old Viva and took things very gently as he approached Iles's house, *Idylls*, whatever that was supposed to mean. It sounded like super-happiness in the plural, but Iles did not seem to be managing that, poor sod. One of Harpur's daughters said there was a big poem called *Idylls of the King*, but possibly even Iles had been too modest to use the whole title.

Harpur noticed several parked cars, including one quite close to Iles's big drive and standing under trees. It was dark but he had the idea that a man might be sitting alone in the back, folded down low into a corner as Harpur passed, perhaps avoiding the headlights. If he had not been on the look-out Harpur would never have noticed him. The glimpse was so fleeting and indistinct that he had no chance of making even a guess at identification, and he could not say, either, whether observation of Iles's place was under way through the car's rear window. For all

Harpur knew it might be a couple of lovers, the woman lower still on the seat, and out of sight. All the same, this could be a watch, with someone working a fairly sophisticated surveillance trick, the kind of skill that would be second nature to Tommy Vit. People expected that if somebody did an observation from a car he sat behind the wheel with the vehicle facing towards the target, ready to move off fast in pursuit if necessary. A thousand films in the cinema and on television played it like that. But, because it was expected, it was also obvious. On the other hand, if the car had its back to the target, and the watcher kept out of the front seat and used the rear window, the chance of staying undetected was vastly higher. He drove on up Rougement Place and looked into Iles's drive as he passed. Both their cars were there – Iles's plain, blue police Orion and Sarah's white Fiat Panda – so it looked as if she might be at home, and the tail in the right place, if it was a tail. Keeping the Viva at a respectable thirty, he tried to see some more of the Golf and its occupant in the mirror, but there was not enough light. He reached a junction and turned left, out of sight of the Golf, then slowly circled the block.

Eventually, he came around to near the start of Rougement Place again but parked in a side street and decided to walk from there. This took time and made him anxious, but if it was Tommy in the Golf, a reappearance of the Viva would immediately alert him. As he recalled it, the Golf had stood pretty much on its own under the trees, between an Escort estate and a Datsun, each of them a long distance from it. When he had gone a few hundred yards on foot now, he realised suddenly that the Golf was no longer there. The estate car and the Datsun stood as before, but the long space between was empty. He tried to convince himself he had mistaken the bearings and kept on walking. But when he reached the gateway to Iles's drive without seeing the Golf he knew his first notion had been right. This time when he looked into the drive he saw that Sarah's Panda had gone, too.

Harpur ran hard back to the Viva and for the next half-hour toured the area looking for either car, without success. By now they could be anywhere. He felt alarmed but gave up the search and at 8.30, as arranged, he knocked on Iles's door and the Assistant Chief himself let Harpur in.

'Perhaps we should ring Benny and say we're coming,' he suggested to Iles.

'Like hell. Doorstepping is a very precise craft, Col, and shock is one of its main strengths.' He seemed to have been attempting some elementary tidying of the room, which always looked pretty uncared for, and he picked up a couple of newspapers and some chocolate wrappers and put them in an overflowing refuse basket. 'Sarah's gone to bridge again,' he said. 'Or something like that. Who knows? She doesn't stay in very much.' He sounded weary and beaten for a moment. These days he often did.

In the Viva, on the way to Benny's place, Iles added: 'There are certainly times when Sarah and I go out together, you know. We can get on well. There's adequate conversation.'

'Of course, sir. And *The Times* crossword together.'

'Exactly. Not abundant talk, but no venom.'

'More than many couples could say, sir.'

'We were at Chaff, the other night.'

'Ah, Leo's place.'

'I didn't know. He and I had quite a tête-à-tête.'

'Yes, sir?'

'Yes, one or two good and useful disclosures made by him.'

'Yes, sir?'

'Yes, one or two. Could produce something, in due course.'

'Yes, sir?'

'Yes, in due course.'

'Good. Do I need to know about them, sir?'

'Well – '

'In due course?'

'That's it, Col. I'd certainly like you to be in the picture, then.'

'Good.'

As they neared Loxton's place, Iles said: 'I still don't understand how we knew where to look for Paynter in the dock. Or why we should have looked for him in the dock at all.'

'These pieces of information come in, sir.'

'Yes?'

'We're very fortunate.'

'Somebody talked, or somebody saw it happen?'

'These tips, sir, they're not just from one source.'

'That's so?'

'Oh, yes,' Harpur replied. If Iles could sit on stuff, so could he.

When they arrived, Benny's wife answered the bell.

'Wonderful spread here, Alma,' Iles said. 'Your own paddock, too!'

'Why, Mr Iles! Desmond! And a colleague! I don't believe we've met since the charity ball. Such a pleasant affair. Theodore will be so pleased you've called. Do come in. I think a little business meeting may be in progress with staff, even at this time in the evening, but nothing that can't be postponed, I'm sure.' Iles introduced Harpur. She went ahead of them to a closed door on the right and, without knocking, opened it. 'Theodore, dear, imagine who's here?' She pushed the door wide and beckoned Iles and Harpur forward.

In the room, Harpur saw Benny, seated in a listing, bulging old armchair, and Phil Macey and a squat, burly man with fair hair cut very short, on a low-backed settee.

'Theodore,' Iles said. 'Here's a grand, welcoming room. A room of wit and warm fellowship.'

'Isn't it?' Alma Loxton cried. 'The dawn is the time when you should be here, though, Mr Iles. We face south-east and the sunlight creeps in so very gradually from the corner of the bay window and eventually floods the whole room, triumphantly.'

Both Macey and the other man had stood, but Loxton remained in his chair. He had on a three-piece, Prince of Wales check grey suit and a very subdued blue silk tie decorated with small shields. Harpur thought of pictures of fighter aircraft in the war, with their tally of destroyed enemies painted on the fuselage.

'Alma was just on her way to change, Mr Iles,' Loxton said. 'We're going for drinks with friends tonight. You carry on, love,' he said to her. 'I'm sure Mr Iles and Mr Harpur will excuse you and we'll take care of them.'

'Well, a drink for our guests, too?' she asked.

'Yes, we'll see to that,' Loxton said.

'If you're sure, Theodore. I hope you're still here when I come down, Mr Iles, Mr Harpur.'

'Yes, indeed, dear lady,' Iles replied, with a small bow, as she closed the door. 'Delightful woman. You're lucky, Benny. So who's this scalped fucker then?' he asked, nodding towards the fair man and sitting down in a red leather armchair near the big fireplace. 'Does he know who I am, Benny? Has he got it clear?' He faced the stranger. 'Has he told you who I am, gusset face, and where you're likely to be if you err?' Harpur had seen Iles use the same rather brisk, ice-breaking technique before on a new recruit to one of the teams: it was designed to knock a hole in him before he started, and to make Benny, or some other chieftain, look negligible and cowed in the Assistant Chief's presence.

'Robert Lentle's a good friend and associate.'

'It's a prime dossier face, and yet I can't recall seeing it before,' Iles went on. 'Did someone say drinks?'

'Robert's new to this area.'

'I hope you're going to like it,' Iles remarked. 'That you're settling. Is this one to replace Justin Paynter, Benny? Did you have a sort of inkling Justin might sink out of sight, as it were?'

'This is a bit inconvenient, Mr Iles, you calling now,' Loxton said.

'I'll try and make it at dawn next time and catch the triumphant sunrise,' he replied.

'What next time?' Lentle asked

Loxton seemed to realise that Iles and Harpur were not likely to leave and brought them brandies. 'Justin?' he said. 'Oh, he moved on quite a while ago. Wanted to make his own way, I don't blame him. That's youth, isn't it? Where he might be now, I couldn't say. It's easy to lose touch in this business.'

'Easy to lose more than that, Benny,' Iles replied.

'Last I heard, Justin was around Norwich way,' Macey declared, 'seeking a mortgage.'

Harpur said: 'I don't know if any of you heard about a Metro being pulled out of the dock.'

'Extremely nasty,' Loxton replied. 'We thought most likely suicide. Terminal sick, maybe.'

'That's what Benny said soon as we seen it on telly,' Macey added. 'He said, "Got to be some poor devil topping himself, nice new car or not." When you see something like that, you ask what life is about – I mean, if despair can strike, regardless.' He sat down again on the settee.

'They take it out of you, thoughts, don't they, Phil,' Iles said.

'Just a young bloke in there, that's what we heard,' Loxton said. 'That a fact? It makes it all even more tragic, if he had, say, a terminal illness, and a new Metro's not going to make a difference to that.'

'Well, he did have a sort of terminal condition,' Iles told him.

'We've been looking for people who might have seen it happen,' Harpur told them. 'There's almost always someone around the dock, even at night.'

Loxton gave a look of puzzlement. 'What you asking, Mr Harpur? You asking did one of us see this car go into the dock? How would that be? Didn't the television say three in the morning or something like that? Are we going to be at the docks then?' He chuckled.

Iles had a good, rather uproarious laugh at the craziness of this idea, too. 'No, of course not, Benny. But you boys, your company, you're got contacts everywhere. Business knows no boundaries, and doesn't stop for the clock, does it? Whispers. Pointers. That's what we're after.'

Benny said: 'I can say straight off regarding that, nothing, Mr Iles. I don't know about Philip or Robert.'

Macey said: 'Benny's right. Not a murmur.'

'Nothing,' Lentle added. He sat down, too, now.

'You got an i.d. yet?' Loxton asked. 'Easy through the car?'

'Some snags there,' Harpur replied.

'We're still inquiring,' Iles said.

'Terrible. Some kid's parents or maybe his wife wondering where he is,' Loxton remarked.

Iles smiled amiably: 'I suppose we could usefully stop this rubbish now. How the hell does Justin Paynter end up under twenty-odd feet of dirty water in a stolen car?'

'Justin?' Loxton exclaimed.

'One fears so,' Iles intoned.

'But I heard he was in Norwich, looking at properties,' Macey protested.

'What had he done to cross you, Benny?' Iles asked.

'Justin? He was a gem,' Loxton replied. 'Nothing at all against him, except he wanted to move on. He was extremely gifted in property matters, which, as you know, is a very large element in our business.'

'Yes, I heard a lot of the takings were going into building,' Iles replied. 'The docks marina development, isn't it, oddly enough? Didn't one of those London gangs do the same?'

'I see it as a crucial part of our rôle to help the onward progress of the area,' Loxton said. 'A stake in the community.'

'Benny's always talking about that,' Macey added. 'Onward

progress. A stake in the community. These are this company's watchwords. When Benny's talking like this, Mr Iles, I can understand why his wife would like him to be called Theodore, instead. Benny don't seem right, too, like, lightweight.'

'So, was Justin having somebody's missus?' Iles asked. 'That why he had to go? We've seen that before: a youngster comes on to the team, full of juice and gloss, and starts making it with somebody's woman, maybe the boss's. Alma's not past it, not a bit. Faded, but some could still see her a tasty piece, even a kid like Justin. It's quite possible she'd stop jabbering and prosing while she was actually on the job. A lot of them do. It's documented. Kinsey?' Iles smiled again, turning to all three in turn, as if asking for confirmation.

Harpur heard Loxton's breathing accelerate and Macey stood up again.

Lentle said: 'Who do you think you're talking about, you bastard?'

'Talking about? Oh, you know Alma, don't you?' Iles replied, beaming. 'The lady who should have been a duchess, but didn't notice Benny wasn't a duke.'

'It's all right, Bobby,' Loxton said. 'This is just Iles. He stirs. Part of his charm, part of his box of tricks. To get people going, so they talk.'

Macey said: 'Mr Iles got trouble with his own sweet lady, putting it about very tireless, so he thinks all women are like that.'

'We believe it's Justin, so we've got to ask you, Benny, if you can suggest why he'd be dropped in the dock,' Harpur told him.

'But we heard he had two referees for a mortgage and a woodworm survey done, Norwich way,' Macey said.

'What identification?' Loxton asked.

'It's pretty sound,' Harpur replied.

'So what's it to do with Benny, with us?' Lentle asked.

'He worked for Benny,' Harpur said.

'That's fair enough,' Loxton replied. 'I see you got to ask the questions if it really is Justin.'

'Or was he a talker, Benny?' Iles asked.

'A talker? Well, he had schooling, yes. Nice with a phrase.'

Iles said: 'Was he opening his mouth about one of your projects? Who to?'

'Have you thought, I mean, going back to where we started,

that this could still be suicide, even Justin?' Macey suggested. 'This kid was a sensitive kid. Oh, sure, it looked like things was going great, but he could have all sorts of worries. He's got a girl and an old mother, a very old mother, Wales way or the Isle of Man, somewhere that area. There could be things wrong there. He might think to come home to end it at a place he knew. People are like that, sentimental about doing theirselves in, it's well known. Makes them feel comfortable.'

'And drove there naked and with two knife wounds?' Iles said.

'Knife wounds?' Loxton exclaimed. 'That changes the complexion.'

'It did his,' Iles said.

'This sounds very much like a private matter,' Loxton said, 'some enemies Justin had that we never even heard of. He never mentioned nothing like that?' He turned to Macey.

'Nothing. But he could be fiery,' Macey recalled. 'He was a kid, but he could cut loose. Oh, yes. He might of given offence, and this is what he collects. It's bad, out of proportion.'

'Life don't work to proportion, Phil,' Loxton said.

'No, but where's the, well, natural justice of it?' Macey replied.

'Where did it happen, the knifing?' Loxton asked.

'We're not too clear on that,' Harpur replied, 'if we – '

Alma Loxton returned, wearing a long check topcoat in grey, blue and red, like something bought from the wardrobe of *Dr Zhivago*. She waited in the doorway of the room, ready to leave. Loxton stood.

'Can you excuse him, us, now, Mr Iles?' she asked. 'We really must be on our way.'

'Of course,' Iles said, standing, also. 'Our talk's about over, as it happens. A profitable exchange, I think, Theodore?'

'Indeed, yes,' he said.

'You're very kind to fit in with our plans, Mr Iles,' Alma Loxton told him.

'No, if I may say, *you're* very kind, for putting up with us in your lovely house at this hour, you and Theodore,' Iles said.

'But we're delighted,' she cried. 'It's only yesterday that Theodore was saying what a regrettably long time it was since we had bumped into you and your charming wife. Please do give her our regards when you see her. So vivacious, so radiant.'

'Yes, when I bloody well see her,' Iles muttered, as he and

211

Harpur walked down the drive. In the car, Iles said: 'Do we know this boy Lentle's special skills, Col, supposing that's really his name? It might indicate something for the future.'

'He's new to me.'

'Can we ask around?'

'Of course, sir.' But where to ask when Jack Lamb was half-way to Italy or who knew where by now?

'It's a beautiful therapy for me, going into a house like Benny's,' Iles said. 'I'm reminded of why I'm a cop and why I'm willing to be stuck on this skivvy's pay, and why I consent to work with people like the Chief and you, no offence, Col. It's to save the world from Benny, and all the other Bennies. That task needs me. You couldn't do it. Could Lane do it?'

'The Chief has some very strong aspects, sir.'

'Not dress sense, I'd venture, and not wit or far-sightedness or necessary ruthlessness. Good-natured to a fault, a dangerous fault. Is he a saviour, though, Col? Can he harrow hell, defeat evil? Can he recognise it?' He had turned in the front seat to look at Harpur.

'Well, we didn't get very far with Loxton ourselves, sir.'

'We will. He felt a cold wind blowing. I've set my mark on him. He knows it. Those people, if they're left alone, or if they have to deal only with your kind – someone fine and soft and passably decent – they'll come to believe they can do anything, including make the step from being Benny to Theodore, or Theodore OBE, or Sir Theodore, or eventually, through one of his kids, to Lord Theodore of the Docklands, instead of Benny of the Drowned Metro. His wife thinks she's half-way there already, poor, simpering drab. That would be victory for the pit, Col, and enthronement of wrong. It could easily happen. It's happened already. Remember Henry the Fourth?'

'Not all that well.'

'I know you went to a school, because it says so on your papers, but were the teachers there pissed all day? The point is this, Col: if people like Benny are allowed to think that kind of progress might come to pass, they will work the harder and dirtier to make it come to pass. That is a very perilous situation, and one we help create if we don't act effectively. We'd deserve impeachment. Myself, I think Lane should have gone that way a dozen times already, for having a heart of gold and marshmallow teeth. But, when I get myself into the festering, neat lounges of people like Benny, in their half-million quid, tawdry houses, and when I open my mouth and let them get a glimpse of what's blocking their way to the real cream – I mean to respectability and peace of mind – and of what's certain to go on blocking their way for as far ahead as they can see, they lose a vast slab of their bloody arrogance and optimism. I can get through to these people, like an Old Testament prophet crying woe. They hear what I say and think to themselves, "Christ, I'm still just a crook, and this bastard's got me noted." After that, they're always liable to panic and do something stupid and give-away. That's what policing is about, Col, and it's a noble, knuckle-duster job, and a holy joy to be in. It encloses me. Perhaps that's half my trouble at home. All the time I feel like crying out, "Wist ye not I must be about my father's business?"'

'You're into whist, sir? I didn't know that. But Sarah likes bridge. Is that the problem?'

Iles stared at him. Harpur was never totally sure how far he could go with the Assistant Chief, but now and then for self-preservation's sake he had to score a few points against him in retaliation, and try to bring him back to earth.

At Idylls, Sarah's car was still absent. Iles gave no reaction, as if he had known it would not be there yet. 'We'll have a nightcap, Col.'

Harpur might have preferred to go, but decided the decent thing was to wait for her with him: Iles had achieved some happiness through the encounter with Benny and the rest, but it could soon disappear if he were left alone. The Assistant Chief made some cocoa and they sat together in the unkempt living-room.

'It's likely Sarah had a phone call, fixing a rendezvous,' Iles said. 'They've got some sort of code – probably a ring at an exact, specific time. I could have the thing bugged, but what sort of man does that to his wife? Or, I could tail her, but likewise. She's entitled to run free, sod it.'

'You're very tolerant, sir.'

'I don't step into fights I can't handle. If I got tough with Sarah I'd lose.'

'You think she's with Aston now?'

'Where else?'

'A lot of people are looking for him.'

'Aston would tell her where to look.' Noisily he sipped his cocoa. 'I ought to kick her out, I suppose. Or maybe she'll go to him for keeps, if he'll have her. Things are touch-and-go, Col. Still can't face losing her, that's all.'

'It could blow over, sir.'

'Yes: there must be a chance some of these people will find him. Perhaps he could end up at the bottom of the dock, too. I pray constantly about him, in those terms.'

Harpur left at half-past midnight, and she had still not returned. He did another tour of the area, looking for the Golf and the Panda, and found neither. On his way home he dropped into the control room and glanced through the incident reports for the night. None of them sounded like Sarah or Aston or Tommy Vit. It would have been easy enough to bring up the Panda's number on the computer – probably the Golf's too – and ask for patrols to keep an eye open. How did he explain that, though, and especially how would he explain to Iles, if he learned about it? Harpur considered, too, going back to Benny's place and getting him out of bed to ask whether Tommy Vit was on Sarah's tail, and whether he had reported back. That would be real doorstepping. But did he want Benny aware of how much he knew? No, Sarah, running free – in Iles's phrase – would have to look after herself tonight.

13

The call from Ian Aston had brought back almost all the old joy to Sarah, and when she set off to meet him it was with the same sort of excited fearful pleasure that used to grip her at the door of the Monty. They were juvenile feelings, and she recognised it now and then, but they did not let up.

Although he had telephoned when Sarah was alone in the house, Ian would speak only briefly, obviously in case Desmond had the line bugged. And he named no rendezvous point but asked her to go to a pay phone in a suburban street and wait for another call. When she arrived, she saw he had chosen carefully: in this prosperous area, few people would need to use a public box or break everything up for habit cash. It was unoccupied and unvandalised, and she had been waiting inside for only five minutes when he rang again. This time he was ready to talk for longer, but still delayed telling her his address.

'Sarah, love, this isn't to cause alarm, but could you check there's nobody behind you?'

'Behind me?'

'Following.'

'Who?'

'I don't know. Desmond? Or people who know we were at the Monty?'

'Desmond – following me?'

'Who knows what he's found out, Sarah?'

'He wouldn't, whatever he's found out. Desmond? Good God, he'd think it paltry and beneath him to care that much.'

'People do all sorts of things when they're angry and jealous. Please, just look around, outside the box. Remember, we had trouble before.'

She didn't look, because the idea that Desmond might tail her really was absurd and gross, just like the idea that he might bug her calls, but she took a few seconds pretending she had surveyed the street. 'Nothing.'

'Nobody? Not Desmond, nor someone who might work under him, nor anyone else?'

'Ian, it's all right, believe me.'

Then he gave her directions. It was a long run-down road she knew, behind Valencia Esplanade and parallel to it, only a mile or so from Margot's place but to date outside the tarting-up plan for the dockside, and still definitely lacking the chicness and bijou qualities of Margot's area. To avoid pinpointing the house, he asked her to park a distance away and do the rest on foot. She agreed, although it was the kind of district where she would never normally have walked alone in the dark, nor even left the car unattended: but again she reminded herself, if you got into this sort of life, you took the conditions.

'It's lovely to hear you,' he said. 'And even more lovely that I'll see you soon.'

The words were simple and not too original, but, to be told something like that in a voice sounding as if he meant it through and through, she would put up with the mad, tiresome precautions and forgive all Ian's edginess. Even in a phone call to a street box, he could soothe her, warm her, make her feel properly alive again, and nobody and nothing else answered that kind of need. Ten times, and maybe more, she had told Margot what he could do for her, and she always listened full of sympathy, and seemed to understand, but then might suddenly ask, 'So what's keeping you with Desmond and at Rougement Place?' And, if Margot were here now, Sarah knew she would recognise her pleasure at talking to Ian again and going to meet him, but she would also spot the squeamishness over visiting him in the Valencia, and her lack of patience with Ian's endless anxieties and suspicions. Margot would certainly make a meal of all that in her frank, niggling, flat professional voice. Once, she had even grown witty on the subject and said Sarah was only half-and-half in love with the *demi-monde*. Margot could go stuff herself. She might be honest and worth the money, but she was also a top-class pain sometimes, regardless. Sarah said: 'I've been going nuts, Ian, waiting.' The line broke up for a moment.

'Wanting, did you say?' he asked.

'That as well.'

He had rooms at the top of a once stately Victorian house in Tempest Street, now subdivided three or four times, its staircase covered in battered green and gold carpet, the landings dark and littered, and the wallpaper, probably high-quality when new, whenever that was, now hopelessly faded and chipped and scrawled over. The house was full of sounds from behind the closed doors – music, shouting, talk, television voices, pot and pans – but she saw nobody as she hurried up the stairs. He opened his door as soon as she knocked and took her hand to draw her inside. In the poor light from the landing and the little passageway to his rooms he appeared shockingly haggard and pale. He hadn't even smiled yet. For a couple of seconds he remained on the threshold, staring back down the stairs, his body arched and tense, obviously listening for the sound of footsteps above the barrage of noises from the other tenants. Perhaps he looked what he was, a hunted man, and the signs would probably have been familiar to Desmond or Colin Harpur, whose business was with such people all the time, alive and dead.

Then he closed the door and turned and took her in his arms and kissed her, but it was still as if his mind were somewhere else, and his body against hers felt unyielding and ready to move away fast at any moment.

'Nobody came after me, Ian,' she said. 'I took care when I parked and I made sure in the street.' Although none of it was true, she felt a sort of duty to ease his worries, and, besides, she wanted his attention.

'These people, some of them, they're so good at it, Sarah.'

'At what?'

'At staying unseen.'

'Darling, I looked. Nobody's invisible.'

'Close.'

They went into his sitting-room, and he must have sensed her recoil momentarily at the bareness of it, the lack of comfort. There were a couple of straight wooden chairs, a small table, a cheap-jack sideboard, one armchair, a small television set, a spotty wall-mirror, no pictures.

'Makes my other place look luxurious, doesn't it? The hamster wouldn't put up with this, I bet. But it's a transit camp, that's all, love,' he said. 'And a hidey-hole. So far, it's done the job.'

'It's fine,' she replied. And, for a longish second, she had a view of herself occupying this sort of grim dump with him for ever, perhaps always ready to run and find somewhere else because of new threats and fears. It knocked her a bit. So, was she really so sold on comfort and the big house – wedded to them? She felt ashamed and told herself she had been pushed off balance by seeing Ian in this state, and that some of his fears about the future must have reached her.

He went to the window now and, standing at the side, gazed down at the street for a few minutes. Then, coming back into the centre of the room so as not to be seen from below, he went to the other side and looked along the street in the opposite direction. Sarah sat on a straight chair and waited.

'I think it's all right,' he said.

'Ian, I know it is.'

He turned back into the room and now he did smile, so that, for a few minutes, he looked as he did in those early Monty days, full of life and devilment and warmth.

'I like your outfit,' he said. 'Class.'

'What else, coming to see you?' It was a rust-coloured gabardine suit she had bought for some police social occasion, a loose-fitting, male-style jacket and wide-legged trousers. Desmond liked it, too, so she reckoned her taste must be holding its own. Herself, she had been undecided about the suit. Yes, it did look classy and expensive. And that meant you had time to shop and enough money, which probably showed your must be getting on a bit. Mutton dressed as mutton. Surrender.

'I haven't been here long,' he said. 'I have to keep changing addresses. For the moment.'

Her vision of a scared, gypsy life rushed back.

'Why I wasn't in touch sooner, Sarah. I stayed well away for a while.'

'I understand,' she said. 'All I want is for you to be safe. Well, almost all.'

'I had to come back. You. And there was a job I had to do. Have to do. It's not finished yet, but promising. Sarah, this could be the biggy I've been waiting for.'

Now, he not only looked as he used to, he sounded like it, as well. Often she had seen and heard him display this sort of optimism over some vague, confidential project that was supposed to change everything and set him up for ever. It hadn't happened, of course, not yet, but the hope kept coming back, and she had loved that in him. All right, so he was a bit like bloody Micawber, but probably much sexier.

'There's a bedroom?' she asked.

'Décor and furniture by the same gifted consultants. Are we in a hurry?'

'I'm at bridge. Coffee afterwards. No, no hurry. Just I've been missing you.' But there was more to it. She feared that his sudden cheerfulness and confidence could be fragile, liable to break up, and she wanted to make love while he felt good, and while she felt good, because he did. These rooms, this district, the threats he lived with, the fear of someone, or more than one, in the street or on the stairs or into his place again, could throw a chill over both of them at any time. If there was one thing she did not want with him it was fucking that was gloomy. Keep that for home. She was here looking for joy, never mind the crumminess and the perils, or imagined perils, and the dicey future. She wanted her clothes off and his clothes off and for the two of them to be warm and touching and happy and relaxed, but not too relaxed, in a bed, preferably a big bed and preferably a clean bed with nice sheets, but fussiness could be taken too far: this relationship was not after a hygiene award.

'Just let me tell you this,' Ian said, getting into the armchair.

He seemed so full of himself that perhaps it would help to wait and listen.

'Remember I said there could be something in all this for me – I mean, the thing at the Monty, and the scene that was obviously building up, though we couldn't see what it was then?'

'You know now?'

He grinned. 'Like I said, there could be big stuff here, if it's played properly.' For a second, the cocky grin slipped. 'And as long as I'm careful. As long as *we're* careful, Sarah.' He stood up and went to the window again, but at least this time only looked from one side down to the street, and not for very long. The full terror and the obsessiveness seemed to have subsided and, when he came back to the chair, his good spirits had revived. 'I'm going to be in touch with someone who could do me a lot of good, a lot,

219

Sarah. This is a guy really powerful around here. Look, I know I say these things, been saying them for ages, and you could be tired of listening, but this time it's true. This is somebody running an important operation, one of the two biggest operations, locally. That's the whole point. There's just the two of them now and one or other has to go under. Bound to be. That's business.'

'What operation?'

'The thing we saw in the Monty is connected with this battle between them, no question. I couldn't understand how, but I've got it sorted out now. A few things more to fit in, maybe, but minor. This is valuable information, love. It's what I said from the start – someone would pay for this kind of material, and I know who it is. I don't mean just a fee, but if somebody like that sees I can come up with the goods, and these really are the goods, he's going to want to use me for other things in the future. This would be, well, a kind of consultancy, you follow? Something like that, I've always fancied. You're you're own man, but steady work. I don't mean anything crooked. I've never been into that, and I'm not starting it now. All right, this person has some crooked aspects to his business, I can't deny that, but I keep very clear, and I'll go on keeping clear.'

In a way, what he said appalled her, and especially what he avoided saying, but things she could guess at through the gaps and the delicate words he used for frightening realities. Now, she understood better his anxieties and nerviness. To her it sounded as if he was moving into hideously dangerous areas. Yet it obviously excited him, made him feel he was winning at last; the big break. It might involve him in large chunks of self-deception, but who the hell was she to be sniffy about that? 'Which person?' she asked. 'Who are you going to see?'

'Sarah, for your own sake it's better you don't know.' He was intoning, rather, going for gravity. 'Keep out of it, love.'

'I can't keep out of it, can I? If you're in it, so am I. We were both at the Monty.'

'But leave it to me now,' he said.

She saw that what he meant was, Rely on me, I can handle it. And possibly he could.

'I'll just say it's someone at the head of a rich, family business – himself, two sons, a good, close team – and they're going to come out of all this right on top, and it will be because of help from me,

Sarah. That's bound to see Ian Aston all right, I mean, long-term all right, isn't it?'

'Sounds great, yes,' she replied. She assumed he meant Leo Tacette, whom Desmond had described to her at the restaurant, but she let Ian keep up the secrecy, since he wanted it so badly.

'You don't sound really convinced, love,' he said.

'Yes, really. It's just that I don't understand it all, yet.'

'No. How could you? Look, things have been happening.'

He still spoke like somebody full of important information, generously ready to share one or two items with her. Thank you very much.

'I'm not the only one who's lying low. A lot of people are very scared. It's made things difficult. I told you, I wanted to see the girl friend of Paynter, that lad in the Monty, the one they pulled out of the dock. You saw the television? This girl, Amanda, went to ground and she took one hell of a lot of finding.'

'You did it?'

He grinned again. 'Sarah, I had to do this while people were searching for me at the same time. Well, Ralphy. Oh, incidentally, I heard they thought he warned me and got a beating for it. Then someone like you found him.'

'I wanted a lead to you, that's all.'

'It's all right. I understand, love. But Ralph gave me no tips. He was really looking. He meant it. Well, he knows Loxton doesn't mess about. It came very close.' Ian leaned over and touched her hand. This was the first real contact tonight, and it amazed her, disheartened her, that they could sit like this after so long apart, separate, their hunger contained.

He stood up again and this time went to check the lock and chain on the front door. She found that his restlessness, and what he said, had begun to make her as edgy as he was himself. Suddenly, she felt very exposed in these rooms, despite the iron-work on the door. Ian moved to the window once more and spoke while he stood there. 'She wasn't a bit happy that I located her. Well, you can understand. I turn up there out of the blue and she doesn't know who I am, nor why I want to find her. All she knows is that the people who did Justin might want to ask her a few things, and not in a friendly way. It was a job to convince her I wasn't part of their outfit; quite a bit of sweet-talking.'

'One of your fortes. One of many.'

He laughed and came away from the window, to stand near her chair. 'She said she's been to see that cop who works with your husband, the heavy, Mr Clean.'

Harpur?'

'She told him what she told me, but I doubt if he can make anything out of it.'

'He's bright.'

'I believe you, but the thing is, all she could say was that Justin had been very worried about what might happen to some woman in a project due any time now. Yes, possible injuries, or worse, to a woman. This had upset him, and he had wanted to tell some contact and get advice or help, but probably never made it.'

'A woman?' For a few seconds then her fears soared, and she found she was cursing herself for ever straying into the harsh regions where he and Ralph and this girl, Amanda, lived. Couldn't she have settled down to being comfortable and fairly safe and well looked after with Desmond, whatever the deficiencies there might be? 'You mean worried about me?' she asked. 'I'm the woman?'

He laughed aloud. 'Egomaniac,' he said. 'How could it be you? This was before you and I had any involvement.'

'Of course.' She felt reassured, and ashamed that panic had hit her so hard. God, she patronised him and grew bored by his fears, and yet she could collapse like that. 'Who then?'

'Sarah, when he was on the ground in the Monty, Paynter muttered something to you as if he was delirious. You remember?'

'About a silver day. He was going to explain, but passed out.'

'That's right. We didn't understand. Listen, then; the businessman I'm going to see has a silver wedding celebration coming up – a big affair, no secret, with everyone there, all the top people in the outfit.' He stared at her, grinning again, like a prizewinner. 'Sarah, it's a silver day.'

'And his wife will be there,' she whispered.

'Naturally.'

'The woman.' Yes, Daphne Tacette, that rough but delightful character at Chaff.

'They're going to be sitting ducks. The supremacy war could be settled for keeps in a couple of seconds of gun fire.'

'You're talking about assassinations?'

'How it looks.'

'Oh, Christ, Ian, a gang massacre? This is crazy. That sort of thing doesn't happen here.'

But she could not shift him. 'It didn't, because there wasn't enough money around to make it worth while. But it has happened in London, and God knows how often in the States. There've been some changes here. This patch is big league now. We have people about who are mad enough and hard enough and greedy enough and frightened enough of the oppositioin. They could get away with it, or they can convince themselves they would, which is what matters.' He glowed with certainty. 'But you're right, in one way – it hasn't happened and it's not going to happen. Why? Because Ian Aston can let the targets know what's planned. That's what I mean about having something of real class to sell.' His delight in himself made his voice sing, and he still beamed with pride. 'I'm going to be saving this businessman's wife, himself and his sons. He can't be mean with the gratitude, can he? What I've managed to do is transform a very nasty situation into a brilliant one for me, for us.'

He bent down and kissed her on her forehead, then on her mouth, and this time she felt that he was truly close to her, not hag-ridden by worries any more but alight with confidence.

He had forced her to believe him. 'Should you tell the police?' she asked. 'This could be lives, several lives.'

'Perhaps they know. She's told Harpur. He might have worked it out. You say he's bright and they get all sorts of information. But who can tell how they'd play it? You see, Sarah, possibly they'd like it if one of these teams was blasted into nowhere. It might be easier for them to deal with a monopoly.'

She was dazed, unable to keep up with him. 'You believe that? You honestly believe that?'

'I don't know, Sarah. It's hard for you to see things the way the rest of us do, your husband being a cop. But there are all sorts of arrangements, you know. Deals. Understandings. Business is very complicated, very inter-meshed. Nobody can be sure what's going on, these days. Where there's big money there are big, secret contracts. But, what I do know is I've got some high-calibre information and I want to sell it. I'd like as few people as possible in on that. I need to be the one bringing the news to him. You see my point? This is my big opportunity, love. I have to play very cagey.' He kissed her again. 'Now, may I show you the boudoir?'

She stood up. 'We're all right, here?'

He went back to the window. 'Yes. I'm pretty sure. If we'd been going to get trouble it would have come by now. It's clear. You surprise me; I didn't get the idea you were worried.'

'Yes, I'm worried.'

He left the window and went to open the bedroom door and put the light on in there. It looked worse than she had expected, drabber, meaner, dirtier, but at least the bed was a double. He waited in the doorway and, when she joined him, put his arms around her and pushed a hand inside the waistband of her trousers and pants at the back, then down over her bottom to between her legs. It seemed a roundabout route, but never mind. She put her head on one side, so he could kiss her on the neck and ears, and was conscious of her anxieties and resentments starting to turn tail for now.

'You feel good,' he said.

'What's that mean?'

'Well, ready.'

'What's that mean?'

'Excited.'

'You mean wet?'

'Well – '

'I've been sitting there for half an hour, listening to your sodding business prospectus, trying to cope with my love juices.'

'Now try to cope with mine.'

He was improving. A couple of months ago he would never have said anything so basic. 'I will,' she told him, 'but for more than half an hour I hope.'

There was a small noise from one of the flats below, or on the stairs – a bump, as if somebody or something had fallen or shifted suddenly – and he turned his head, and seemed about to go and investigate, but she held him to her, and in a moment they moved together over the tattered linoleum to the bed.

14

Three days before it was all due, Loxton took Phil Macey with him to look at the Roundhouse, site for the silver wedding party and the office tower block next door, where the boys would be. They stayed in the car and did not get too close because, after it had happened, people around here, living and working, would be grilled about strangers showing too much interest in the buildings.

'What I want to be sure, how Norman and Bobby get out,' Loxton said. 'I don't need to see the place they're going to be. If they say it's all right, it's all right. They're the experts. That's something I learned in the Navy, known as delegation. Was the First Sea Lord out there chasing the *Bismarck*? You trusts your people. What you paying them for if you don't trust them? But I got to know they can make it away. That I need to see for myself.'

'It's so like you, Benny, thinking above all of your men. Great. That's the Navy, too, but it's you, Benny Loxton personal, as well.'

'Well, of course. Any leader got to consider his boys' safety, that's basic. Another thing, if them two don't make it out, where do it lead? They wouldn't talk, I know that, not Norm and Bobby, boys like that don't know how to squeal. But they're my staff and it's known. Think of Iles and Harpur the other day, Bobby in the room. They'll be doing some checks on him, believe me. This operation, first thing the police going to think is it's us. We'll have the alibis, yes, they can't prove a dicky bird, but we don't want no cock-up here pointing the finger.'

'They go in the front when the building's still open and they get into a storeroom, third floor, and wait for the night,' Macey told him. 'That's taken care of, the storeroom. Bobby come by a key,

225

don't ask me how. Then when they done the business, they come out from the side doors. They're fixed with bolts inside, not a lock, so no problem. Can you pull up for a couple of minutes? I can show you.'

'One minute,' Loxton said. 'After that we could be in some-body's memory box.'

'Right. Here then, Benny.'

Loxton drew in. It was a side street just outside the city centre, not too busy even now in the middle of the day, and only a short drive to the motorway link.

Macey pointed across the street. 'That's a service lane down there. You can see the side entrance to the office block. It's where they collect rubbish from, deliver all their stuff, that sort of thing.'

There was a truck in the lane, but behind it Loxton could make out a large pair of doors standing partly open at this time.

'Big, wide stairs leading to them inside, easy to get down fast. They're going to have their first vehicle parked here, not no closer than that. It's night, so there's no deliveries, but you never know what could get into this lane, and they might be blocked. So, unbolt the doors and a nice, steady walk from the building to the car here, no running, nothing to make a scene.'

'Carrying the weapons?'

'No. Leave the weapons. They're not traceable.'

'We know that?'

'These boys have had them weapons for God knows how long, but never used in anything where the police collected shells, so no tracing that way. And they was taken from a gun shop, and there've never been anyone ever arrested or charged for it. Them guns just went desperate missing, Benny, those years ago. All right, the police will work back to the shop. But so what? It's miles away, Nottingham, could be. Somewhere like that. Nothing to tie Bobby or Norm. They got to leave them, Benny. They come out here, there could be people, lovers, who knows? You can't walk casual carrying a couple of automatic rifles, even in a cue case.'

'How do we know no arrests?'

'For the gun shop? Norm been over that. He looked at it very, very thorough. Research, it's a strong point with him. Nearly Nobel Prize, but beat at the post by that Einstein: bugger knew the judges. Well, Norm sees it got to be right. It's his balls in the crusher, he get it wrong.'

Loxton drove on.

'They do a few blocks, not more, in the first car, then the switch. That's before the motorway. They drive north, about forty miles, where Bobby's got a place lined up. They leave the car in a hotel park where there's all-night taxis near. They go from there to the overnight place Bobby got, putting down not too close. Next day one of them, it don't matter which, gets back here, train probably, so it don't look as if half your staff have done a gallop because of the shooting, we got to seem normal. The other one comes back next day.'

Loxton drove towards his house. 'What place?'

'What, Benny?'

'What place – the overnight?'

'Something Bobby lined up.'

'Yes, but how? Some bird's place, something like that? Some skawking bird going to shout all round if he stops giving it to her one day?'

Macey was silent for a while.

'Didn't ask?' Loxton said.

'Well, Bobby's pretty good.'

'Good behind a set of sights. I got no evidence he thinks logical, or got a flair for strategy.'

'I'll ask him.'

'Yes, ask him. We don't want no more pussy tied up in this. Hairy enough without that. But, all right, otherwise it sounds good, Phil. Of course there's risks. That's the sort of game.'

'All we got to worry now is this Aston knows too much and gets to Leo. This is big information. This is a big pay packet for him, Benny. You know what he's like, Aston – on the watch for a bit of profit non-stop. I don't know if you heard this, Benny, but it looks like he found Paynter's girl. That's Amanda something. She melted when he went and we been looking for her as well. Then there's a good lead, but when we arrive she've moved on. Far as I can gather, she pulled out because she had a visit, got scared she was on the map. This is a man, this visit, and I had a description and it could be Aston. I got to tell you that, Benny.'

'Shit. That's bad. All sorts of talking, and we don't know what. Sometimes I wonder about this operation, you know? Oh, it's a sweet chance, nobody can say no to that. The dangers pile up, though. Iles, Harpur, this Aston, Mrs Iles, the bloody girl friend.

It all begins to look shaky. And we got Leo making friendly gestures, looking for partnership. Maybe some stage we got to ask, what we sticking our neck out for? Maybe we could live with him, Phil.'

'You believe Leo? Since when you believe one thing that bastard says? Next time you turn up for a friendly meeting you could get blown all ways, and anybody with you. It's a fact, like you said, he's re-running *The Godfather*, acting sweet and pulling what's called coups, planning, lulling, waiting.'

'Well, probably,' Loxton said. 'Even in school they called Leo Two-face. I mean, the teachers as well as the kids.'

'Two's putting it low.'

'He's always thinking. A brain there, the sod.'

'Exactly. He'll have us, we don't have him. We got to go through with it now, Benny. Everything's laid on. Only three days. What we going to tell Bobby, Norman? They're psyched up for it a beauty.'

Loxton nodded. 'How wars start – the preparations, then you got to do it. But you're right. So, what's happened to Tommy Vit? He come up with anything?'

'Nobody seen him. We know he was going up to Iles's place last night, try to get behind Mrs Iles for the first time, but we didn't get no call, and no report back today.'

'Well, he could be sticking close, not able to break off to reach us.'

'All night, all day?'

'He knows his game. You got to leave him play it his way. What I said, delegation.'

'Right. All I worry, he can go fucking bananas something turn a bit tight or provocative. He could do people damage and then just disappear.'

'Damage? We'd have heard something if Mrs Iles was hurt or whatever. Jesus, this is an Assistant Chief's wife.'

'Yes, we'd of heard if people know, Benny. Suppose some love nest, or if he found Aston's place?'

Loxton thought about it. 'What we worrying about? If he done the two of them, we're clear, yes?'

'One way of looking at it.'

'What else do we want?'

'As long as Tommy gets away and don't talk.'

'Tommy would get away.'

When they reached Loxton's house, Tommy Vit was there, waiting for them with Norman and Bobby.

'Well, I'd prefer you didn't come here, not just at this time,' Loxton told him. 'You want contact, there's phones.'

Vit said: 'Yes, phones, but who's listening? I'm fond of phones, one of the great aids to civilised life, Benny, in moderation.'

Loxton said: 'Yes, but coming here – it's not wise, Tommy. You could be – '

'Tailed? Do I get tailed?'

'Observed,' Loxton replied.

'If they're watching your house, you mean? Are they? Why would they be doing that, Benny? I don't think you've levelled with me, you know, about the full menu of perils. It's why I'm here, really.'

The great thing about Tommy, he did not look like a tail, did not look bright enough or hard enough to be anything much. Loxton was always amazed at how dozy and awkward Tommy seemed, like somebody's nephew that they kept quiet about and tried to treat gentle because he wasn't all there. Near forty, he had a round, big-chinned, fair-skinned face with blue, bright eyes that seemed full of happy daftness, and wavy, blond hair, always neat, as if he had really learned to work on that and could give it plenty of time because he wasn't up to anything else. His voice was high and cheerful, unless things turned tight, like a harmless kid's. Half the time Loxton expected him to ask for an ice lolly.

'This fee, it's good, I'm not denying it,' Vit said, 'but I'm not sure it really gets to the heart of things.'

'What's that mean?' Loxton replied.

'He's had some experiences,' Bobby said.

'What happened last night?' Loxton asked. 'This job, it got an element of urgency in it. Did we stress that enough? Why we asked you, Tommy. You're quality. We're looking for developments.'

'Understood,' Vit replied. 'There's angles not catered for, though, difficulties not on the original schedule.'

'Christ, you're getting two and a half grand for this,' Macey said. 'It could be a couple of days' work, not more. It can't be more than three. Who gets paid like that? Jagger?'

'I like to be around to spend it,' Vit replied.

'What difficulties?' Loxton asked.

'This job's awash with big police.'

'You knew about that possibility,' Norman told him. 'If we're interested in the wife of an ACC, there are going to be super pigs involved.'

Loxton made some tea and brought a big cream cake from the pantry. They sat down in a circle in the long lounge. Alma was out somewhere, busy with her campaigning. He cut delicate slices and handed them around with small plates.

'I'm near Iles's place last night, just waiting for a first tickle, that's all,' Vit said. 'I don't know if she's going out, but it's the only place to start. I'm in a hired Golf – '

'We'll see to that,' Loxton said.

'I'll be giving you my expenses claim, yes. Routine. Well then, I'm in Rougement Place, I've got some shadow and I'm backed on, quite a decent spot, so it's all about patience. Then into the street comes Harpur in one of those scrapyard jobs he drives, a Viva, which is supposed to be such a disguise, because it's not a white Jag with its two-tone sounding and Police written all over. You know the way he looks in these vehicles, like an elephant in a horse-box. Spot him five miles off.'

'Harpur was there to collect Iles, I should think,' Loxton said. 'They came here.'

'Yes, well I thought he must be going to Iles's place, what else?' Vit said. 'He drives past, though.'

'Going where?' Macey asked.

'Going nowhere. What's happened is he's seen me, hasn't he, and there's a sudden change of plan? He was going to call on Iles but wants another look at the Golf.'

Loxton said: 'Saw you? How? You're backed on and in tidy cover, you told us.'

'This is Harpur, not Little Miss Muffet,' Vit replied. 'He's been around, you know. He's heard about rear window surveillance.'

Loxton had a think: 'He was expecting to see you there?'

'I considered that, too. Why I said unforeseen difficulties.'

'Expecting how, for Christ's sake?' Macey asked.

'Always gossip about,' Vit told him.

'Already?' Macey protested.

'Some people have very good ears,' Vit said. 'And sensitive stuff travels fastest. That's obvious.'

'It's worrying,' Loxton muttered.

'I reckoned I could see what Harpur was up to. He'll go around the block and come back for another good look into the Golf. Perhaps he wasn't totally sure. Well, I don't want him to be, do I, so as soon as he's round the corner, I move off and get out of Rougement. I park in another street and come back on foot. I find he's done more or less the same and he's ahead of me, walking up Rougement towards Iles's house, known as Idylls, by the way. That's either Tennyson or Malory.'

'What?' Macey asked. 'Who are these? How do they come into it?'

'Oh, Tennyson, of course,' Norman said.

'Yes?' Vit replied. 'Iles pretty literary or what? Harpur is staring over towards where the Golf had been, and I can see he's shaken, but he keeps going up to Iles's gates. He glances into the drive and I feel right away what's happened: Mrs Iles's car has gone while we've both been out of Rougement Place. I also know what's going to happen now, and get under the hydrangeas in somebody's front garden. Harpur runs back down the street, on the way to his Viva, and in a few minutes he's driving up Rougement again, looking for her or me. He comes back after a while to pick up Iles and go to your place, I suppose.'

'So you both missed her?' Loxton asked. 'She could have seen Aston last night and we still don't know where he is.' Again the idea hit him that the job was jinxed. If Tommy Vit could not handle his side of it there must be something wrong.

'Benny, when I took the assignment I knew there was a chance I'd be spotted behind Mrs Iles. But this is different. You must see that. First, it's possible that Harpur, and maybe others, have been alerted that I'm working, so they come looking. I don't know any tail who could cope with that. Every time you move there's an audience.'

'Did you have an audience when you came here today?' Bobby asked.

'No. I'm all right when I'm by myself. I can lose anything behind me. It's when I've got to track someone that I'm exposed, aren't I? Even if they can't see me, they can see her and they know I'm not far off.'

'Do you think she was with him last night?' Loxton asked.

'Could be. She was late back. And she's humming when she gets out of the car.'

'You just waited there?' Loxton asked.

'What else? I don't know where to look for her. I'm good, but not magic. But, Benny, listen to this: I'm out hanging about in Rougement, no car now, and Iles comes down the drive and stands at their gate, looking up and down the street. This is around midnight. Harpur's brought him home and left.'

'Looking for his wife?' Bobby said. 'People can get restless, even someone like Iles. Maybe wanting to see her car as soon as it shows up.'

'Maybe looking for his wife. Maybe just looking, I don't know,' Vit said. 'And I don't know if he spotted me. This is not a street where you see many people on foot, and especially not at night. I got into cover fast, but he came down that drive very quietly. With someone like that, you don't know what he sees. He stood there a couple of minutes, and she didn't show up. Then he went back up to the house. She didn't get home for another hour.' Very thoroughly he wiped some cream from his rosy face with a handkerchief. 'Well, my feeling is, he saw me, Benny. I've got to cater for that from now on. Maybe Harpur had tipped him. I heard those two don't give all that much to each other, but this time it could be different. I'm not too happy. Who would be? You know what Iles can be like.'

Loxton finished his tea. 'What you saying, Tommy? You saying you want a bonus?'

'This turns out to be a lot more tricky than we allowed for, Benny. If I'm going back, this has to be very special rates indeed.' He turned and smiled at Macey. 'I know Phil's going to say they're special already, but this is something else.'

'I would like you to go back, Tommy,' Loxton told him quietly. 'Yes, indeed. This lady is going to lead us somewhere crucial, I know it. We could have been there last night, but all right, bad luck. It happens. I can see your point, about extra trouble, possible trouble. Look, I can go another five hundred. That wouldn't be unreasonable, you get us to this situation we're looking for.'

'That's on top of the expenses?' Vit asked, his eyes shining, and seeming to have nothing in them but helplessness and confusion, but really having quite a lot more than that in them.

'Of course. Fees, expenses, two different categories. Ask the Revenue.'

Vit said: 'I knew you'd see things reasonably, Benny. I very much want to help, but I have to think in business terms. And personal safety terms.' He touched his waves, checking that the whole picture was fine, not just the money.

'I don't believe you've got too much to worry about re personal safety,' Loxton said. 'All right, let's agree Iles saw you. I can believe he did. What does it mean? He knows what you're there for, yes?'

Vit thought hard about that, but the effect on the bugger's face was to make it look even blanker. 'He wants her to lead me to him? You think so, really, Benny?'

'Aston's a man having his wife on a regular basis, right? Not just a man having someone's wife. This is some small-time, tainted nobody getting amongst an Assistant Chief Constable's lady. Everything says Iles knows about it. Everything also says he wants to keep her. Is he going to stand in the way if an expert like you is going to locate this lad and involve him in some very grave damage?'

Macey grinned at this argument and nodded. 'Right, Benny. He wouldn't do any rough stuff himself, but why stop others?'

'Spot on,' Loxton said.

'But how does he know it's just Aston? How can he be sure his wife's not a target, too?' Vit asked. 'I mean, would you be comfortable if somebody was tailing Alma? Forgive the example, Benny, but you see what I mean?'

'Absolutely. Fair point. But, Tommy, he's not comfortable, anyway, is he? He got a wife who's doing him wrong, and he doesn't know how to stop it. So, he'll take a risk or two. We're all in that business, Tommy. If you want something and it's tricky you got to be ready to gamble. Maybe Iles is ready to gamble with his wife. And it is only maybe. He sees it's you and he knows you're a tail, not some heavy. You been hired to follow, not to do injury. He's heard of Tommy Vit, hasn't he? All right, you had a lapse or two ages ago, a spasm, but Iles would realise that's not the way you usually operate. You're an artist, generally, the delicate touch. He could work it out that Aston's the one we want. He'd know that Aston is the boy who does smelly, little deals, runs little, lousy messages and Iles could see someone like

233

that might have give offence, or might be a danger to a major project, and would have to be dealt with. Suddenly, he realises he's in big luck. He wants him out of the way, don't matter what the reason, or who does it, like Phil says, as long as it don't have to be him, although they do say that once upon a time Iles – That's a different yarn, though, very different, and speculation.'

Loxton stood up to show the meeting was over. 'You see my point, Tommy, when I say I don't think you got to worry about the ACC? You and him are on the same side, that's the truth of it. You're doing him a favour. We're all partners. So, you just stick with her, very close, and let us know absolute soonest when he's charted.'

'Great, Benny,' Vit said.

'Phil, get him the extra half-grand, will you, and look after his exes when they come in?'

'It's a treat to do business with you, Benny,' Vit told him. 'A therapy after some of the others.'

'My father had a saying, "The labourer is worthy of his hire,"' Loxton told them.

'Can't fault it,' Macey remarked.

And then, well on into the meeting, Iles suddenly let Lane have it, a crippler, way below the belt, as brutally deft as anything Harpur had ever seen the ACC pull anywhere, which was saying a mouthful. 'This is interesting, sir, what you're telling us about Leo Tacette's silver wedding party, but I know as fact that he's not going through with the celebration at the original venue. Elsewhere, yes. Undisclosed this time. He got wind of something.'

The Chief looked appalled. 'But when did he switch?' Lane demanded. 'I heard it was settled. My information is very recent.'

I hope you didn't pay more than washers for it then, sir,' Iles said. 'There's been a total re-think, forced on Tacette.'

'Colin, have you heard of this?' Lane asked.

'Neither about the original plans nor the change, sir,' Harpur replied. It hurt to say it: these two had moved ahead.

It was another of those off-the-cuff, three-sided gatherings in Harpur's room. Lane had drifted in, obviously excited about something, and asked him to ring Iles and invite the ACC to join them after a few minutes for what he called a '*causerie*'. Lane was like his predecessor, Cedric Barton, in preferring to keep these meetings informal. For no reason Harpur could see, both Chiefs imagined themselves more able to cope with Iles when conditions were relaxed; the ACC usually managed to make a monkey of Lane, whatever the setting, and especially – as things turned out – today.

Lane has his cardigan on, a thing which Iles once alleged had been created in 1941 for a Merchant Navy stoker twice Lane's size by a colour-blind, drunken Knit for Victory lady with frostbite of the hands. Around the office, he rarely wore shoes, and this afternoon he sported thick, loose-fitting cream socks.

Just before Iles joined them, the Chief had asked; 'I was wondering what you and Desmond see as the implications of this boy in the dock. We're going to have to let the name out soon, though I suppose half the world knows it already.' Yes, Lane was obviously pleased with himself about something, voice sturdy, eyes alight, skin shining.

'We haven't really sorted it out yet, sir,' Harpur replied.

Iles, elegant in one of his fine navy blazers with silver buttons, had come in then and sat down, giving a decorous, reassuring smile to the Chief.

'We were discussing the Metro, Desmond,' Lane had continued. 'I was possibly a bit dismissive of the feelings the two of you had that something big could be brewing between the gangs.' He glanced towards Iles, to show regret for his misjudgement and then added hurriedly; 'Certainly this boy, Paynter, could be an indicator of something.'

'Absolutely,' Iles declared. 'An indicator. Of something. Yes, one would go along with that. Yes, definitely of something, sir.'

The Chief, who was standing at the window, had gone on; 'I've picked up a whisper or two, which might have a bearing?'

Iles's grey head came up sharply, and he brought a look of intense interest to his face, possibly to mask disbelief. 'Really, sir?'

'I take it we're talking about possible war between the two main outfits, aren't we?' Lane said. 'Benny Loxton's and Leo Tacette's.'

'Nobody much else counts now, sir,' Harpur replied.

'Quite,' the Chief said. 'This whisper, it's to do with Leo.' He sat on the edge of the desk, and grew suddenly apologetic. 'But perhaps you've heard it. I might be making a fool of myself.'

'You? Oh, I should think not, sir. But tell us what it is, do,' Iles said gently.

And Lane had responded to this encouragement and spoke in the tone of a youngster recounting some mighty achievement to its parents, like making it home by himself on the bus: 'Well, it's the fact that Leo and his wife are coming up for a silver wedding celebration. Few days off, to be exact. It struck me – putting together your apprehensions, and this business at the docks, I wonder if something like a silver wedding party wouldn't be a first class opportunity for anybody wanting to do Leo and his people damage. The whole clan present, people relaxed, boozed, in good spirits, and expecting the rest of the world to be. I went down and had a look around where the party's to take place. There are plenty of possibilities. I'm inclined to think Benny and Phil Macey will have spotted them very early on. The ceremony's in the Roundhouse. Alongside is the Cardinal Street office block. I went up in the lift. There's a perfect line of fire through windows to the Roundhouse platform.'

Harpur had understood then why Lane seemed so proud, and had felt it was totally justified. Lane had done damn well, for a Chief.

'There's sure to be a presentation,' he went on. 'And it will be done on the platform, with everyone who matters in Leo's team nicely grouped, like skittles.'

'Yes,' Harpur had replied. 'A couple of points reinforce that idea. First, we think Benny has just taken on a new boy called Bobby Lentle, who's a crack automatic rifle handler. He might still be sitting on weaponry taken from a gun shop raid at Nottingham in 1981. And Benny already has Norman Vardage, who's bright with a rifle, too.'

'Really?' the Chief said. He had looked again towards Iles, who gave no response. Perhaps Harpur should have been alerted then by the Assistant Chief's indifference, although that was how Iles reacted to almost anything said by Lane.

Harpur had ploughed on. 'There's a second point that could tie in: I'm told Justin Paynter had to be let go because he objected to an operation that might hurt or kill some woman.'

'Ah, even more fascinating,' Lane declared. 'Daphne Tacette? This looks better and better. My God, we could take most of Loxton's people, if we play this properly. Death of Paynter, fire-arms charges, conspiracy.'

It was only then, when Lane had gone as far as he could, and would come out of this looking like undisputed world supreme twat, recognised by all boards of control, that Iles said his piece about the changed location.

'But why?' Lane cried. 'What's happened?'

Iles said: 'As I've indicated, sir, Leo's not an idiot. Nor Laywaste and Gerald. They knew a family party could be a target – knew it from the start.'

'Of course. But my information, from a very good source, is that they had decided on the Roundhouse, nonetheless,' Lane insisted. 'The reservation's made.'

'And that information is undoubtedly correct, sir, basically,' Iles told him. All that's wrong is it's out of date, like . . . oh, like believ ʾg Queen Victoria's still on the throne. They certainly had decided on the Roundhouse. That's no secret.'

'Not?' Lane said.

'Public knowledge, sir,' Iles replied. 'If we had those Chinese wall newspapers it would be on them as well.'

The Chief remained silenced for several seconds. Harpur found it painful to watch. There might come a time, and soon, when Lane would be afraid to open his mouth if Iles were present. Now, when the Chief spoke again he could only fall back on repetition. 'Why this change, then?'

'The Metro in the dock, for a start,' Iles explained. 'That unsettled Leo, though he didn't know the full story, obviously. Then he heard about the arrival of this sniping boy, Bobby Lentle. Routine research; they watch each other's staffs, naturally, like any competing businesses. Gerald dug out the background on Bobby, and it shook Tacette. This is a man already on edge, who had apparently been continually advised by both sons that the Roundhouse was insecure. That clinched it. He's not sure where the party's to be instead, but it doesn't matter, sir, Loxton can't switch his preparations in time. And, in any case, he probably doesn't know about the change. As I understand it, Leo's letting the reservation at the Roundhouse stand, as cover.'

Lane stood again and took a few paces. Pointing as if in horror to a wet patch on the carpet where Harpur had spilled some tea, Iles shouted, feverishly: 'Careful, your lovely socks, sir. God knows what Colin does in here when frustrated. You don't want that stuff getting through to your skin.'

'You've spoken to Leo?' Lane asked.

'At his restaurant,' Iles replied. 'The Chaff. He's bitter about Benny. Well, what else? But especially because there was apparently some seeming move towards what Leo called "friendship and understanding". He meant an alliance, of course, a carve-up. Leo even arranged to take Benny to his golf club for a meeting, letting other members see him, regardless – that rubbish dump for rabble up behind the King Richard Hotel. Leo intended going through with that anyway when we spoke, to keep things looking sweet, but he's very angry.'

'You ate at Leo's restaurant, Desmond?' Lane asked.

'Sort of, sir. Not what you'd be used to. Not the Savoy Grill.'

'Wise to go into a place run by someone like that?' Lane asked, scrabbling for a chance to hit back.

'Ah, the Stalker syndrome. Depends what you hear when you're in there. It means we won't be making cunts of ourselves with three battalions at the Cardinal Street office block, when the party's somewhere else.'

'And he actually spoke to you about marksmen, about possible assassination?' Lane asked.

'Coded, sir, naturally. He talked about Lentle's being "talented", and rightly assumed I knew what the talents were. And he kept off the actual term "assassination", but told me he'd decided not to expose the family "*en masse*".'

Trying to sort out where this new information took them, Harpur said: 'Leo will be scared it's still likely to happen, won't he – either at this new venue, or somewhere else, later? All right, it might not be possible to get the whole outfit next time, but business is about compromise.'

'Yes, he's very scared,' Iles replied. 'I picked up that much. He's afraid that if Benny has committed himself to an attempt he'll go through with it, somehow. Navy resolution.'

'So there must be a chance that Leo could try to get his move in first,' Harpur said. 'Self-defence.'

'Almost certain,' Iles replied. 'Self-defence and rage at the degree of betrayal.'

The Chief grew agitated. 'Something pre-emptive? Where? Christ, I don't want this patch becoming site for a full-scale gang battle. I won't have it. Desmond, how's this to be staged? How?' He never shouted, but his voice had grown high and weak-sounding. His fingers twitched and pulled at the old wool of the cardigan.

Iles stretched out, long-legged and thin in the chair, admiring his pricey-looking, black slip-on shoes. 'I can't help there, sir. Leo was talkative in Chaff, but not that talkative, and not that explicit, either. As I said, coded. I suppose one wouldn't really expect more – not to tell a police officer the way you meant to knock out a rival villain and his disciples. It was put to me simply as a business grievance. But perhaps Colin has ideas?'

'Colin?' the Chief asked, desperately.

'Not at this stage, I'm afraid. In any case, although this is all pretty likely, it is hypothetical, isn't it, sir?' He directed the question to Iles.

'The hanged man's death was hypothetical until the trap door opened,' the ACC replied.

'What the hell does that mean?' Lane muttered. 'Is it one of your fucking stupid quotes, Desmond? Is it Wittgenstein again? What are you saying?'

Iles smiled in very kindly fashion. 'Forgive me. I'm a phrase-monger. My mother used to reproach me for it, too, sir. She thought it arrogant. Arrogant! I? What I am saying, sir, put simply, is that we're liable to get guns on the streets and a fair quantity of degenerate blood shed fairly soon. Now, you'll nat-urally ask, which streets, sir, and to this I regrettably have to say that I don't know. But I suppose a confrontation like that might remove a lot of our problems. In boxes. The buggers could wipe one another out. End of rackets, at least until the arrival of new gangs scenting the pickings here.'

'Desmond, I won't have shoot-outs between villains,' Lane declared.

'I'm not so sure, sir.'

In the evening, Harpur went up again to Rougemont Place, waiting to see whether Sarah Iles came out once more. This time he moved very gingerly, conscious that Tommy Vit might be prowling there. Harpur still could not fathom what had gone on last night. Had Sarah led Vit to Ian Aston? If so, what had happened? Apparently Sarah came back all right, or he would have heard something from Iles. Perhaps Harpur had been mis-taken and the Golf in the shadows had contained no watcher. Had it moved away while Harpur was absent, not because Vit had followed Sarah, but because its owner, living in one of these houses, or visiting, had simply come back to the car and driven off somewhere? That coincidence Harpur could not quite swal-low, but it was possible.

This job would be very tricky. If Tommy had been around last night, he might have spotted Harpur in the Viva and be especially alert now. Harpur was using an Astra station wagon this time, but he still could not risk driving into Rougement Place; supposing he was there, Tommy would be marking every vehicle. Yet if Harpur parked a distance away he might have little chance to get back to the Astra in time to follow Sarah.

As a start, anyway, he decided he had no real option. He left the car as near as he could to the end of Rougement Place and then began to work his way on foot very slowly and carefully up towards Iles's drive again. He did not expect to see the Golf this time, and was right about that; Tommy would probably change his car daily, whether or not he believed he had been spotted. That was basic in his trade.

Thank God for the upper middle classes's love of hedges and large front gardens. Harpur found he could keep off the street itself for most of the time. Perhaps someone in one of these robbable properties would see him and let the dogs loose or, worse still, call the police, but he would have to risk it. He had a pause in one garden and, from behind a couple of hefty shrubs, took a long look at everything parked near Iles's place. There were half a dozen cars, none present when he drove through last night. He could make out nobody in any of them, but it was very dark again and he would not have taken bets. In a minute, he started moving once more, even more slowly and warily now, as he drew near to Iles's house.

He had become very anxious about Sarah, and wondered whether she knew the danger she was in. She was bright, so she presumably had some idea of the hazards, but, if she kept up her contact with Aston, it could mean she did not properly understand where she was treading. Either that, or she had decided she must see him, and to hell with the risks. Almost certainly Sarah would be capable of thinking like that. He had often seen a kind of desperation in her, and maybe this could bring on behaviour that was not always rational: Francis Garland, Sarah's lover for a long while, always said she had something wild about her. Of course, Harpur did not know for certain whether she really was still in touch with Aston. Perhaps she had not seen him during the trip out last night. On that, though, Harpur *would* have taken bets, and he was here only in case she had arranged then to visit him again tonight.

He felt determined to protect her. She was a friend and someone he admired and sympathised with, stuck in that wrong,
bleak marriage. Yes, a friend: Harpur felt almost certain he had
never really considered her sexually, except in that general, un-
committed way he might want any woman as good-looking as
she was. But he worried about Sarah and wished to help her. He
liked her toughness and bounce, and feared they could bring her
to terrible harm. It seemed to him part of his job to stop that
happening, if he could. And there was another part. Sarah might
lead him to Aston, and he needed Aston because he might know
all sorts. Every sign said he did. Why else would Benny want to
find him? Aston might be able to talk about Paynter's death, for
instance. So might Sarah, of course, but if it was possible he
would like to keep her out of all that. Increasingly he felt it would
not be possible, though.

Working his way through the front gardens, he eventually
found himself looking through the hedge into Iles's drive from
the garden next door. Her Panda was there, but not Iles's car. The
ACC must be at a function somewhere. Not knowing what to do
next, he felt his judgement begin to come unstuck and suddenly
he found he wanted to abandon secrecy, ring the front door bell
and ask Sarah to take him with her to Aston. He would explain
the perils she and her lover were in, and it might convince her.
Only might, though; most likely, Sarah would be full of suspicion, convinced he wanted to break her love affair, and return
her to his colleague, her husband, and to proper behaviour. He
couldn't care less about proper behaviour hers or his own, but
would he be able to make her believe that? He doubted it. She had
her view of police, and the Monty and Aston were escapes.
Perhaps Aston was more, but he was that as well.

No, she would not take him voluntarily. But suppose she did
not know. Perhaps the only way he could stay with her and
remain unobserved by Sarah and Tommy Vit might be by hiding
in the Panda. If he could smuggle himself into the back she might
take him to Aston, unaware. He reckoned she probably was not
the kind of fussy woman who would lock up in the drive, so there
must be a good chance. For a while he thought about it, and
almost abandoned the idea; could somebody of his bulk stay
unseen in the rear of that little box? But then he decided he had no
choice, a situation he was growing used to tonight. He pushed

through the hedge and, treading as lightly as he could on the gravel, stepped to the car. He found both doors and the hatchback locked. So, that was how well he understood Sarah. Had any of his assumptions about her tonight been right?

Quickly, he retreated out of the drive the way he had come, and began to make his way back towards the Astra. He felt defeated. The whole expedition had been stupidly conducted, he now realised. He was not even sure why he had needed to approach the house at all, except to check that she had not already gone out. If he had wanted to spot Tommy Vit, it was a wasted trip, and he should have known it would be. Tommy was not in advertising.

For a few minutes Harpur's morale stayed sunk, and his brain refused to operate. Then he slowly recovered. Couldn't this thing be handled much more simply? Why did he ignore knowledge he already had? It was obvious that last night Sarah had driven out of the other end of the road, or he would almost certainly have met her as he came back from circling the block. If she went to see Aston again she must take the same route.

He drove the estate car in the opposite direction around the block to near the junciton where he had turned last night after seeing the Golf. There, he pulled in, switched off his lights, and waited, about fifteen yards from the entrance to Rougement Place. He sank down as low as he could in the car, though he knew that if Vit came up here and had a look it would be all up. But, with any luck, Tommy's interest would be totally taken up with Idylls and Rougement Place.

After only twenty minutes the Panda appeared, with Sarah driving, and turned away from him at the junction. Harpur started the engine, but did not light up yet and stayed where he was. After another couple of minutes a yellow Opel that had been one of the half-dozen cars near Iles's house came out of Rougement Place and followed the Panda. At the wheel was a man who could be Tommy. Harpur gave him a fair distance, then put on his lights and went after both of them. So, if Vit was watching, it indicated that Benny still wanted Aston, and that must mean he did not know about the switch from the Roundhouse and regarded the attack as still on. It meant Sarah Iles was driving to a very sombre situation. Harpur knew he should have had help, and that he should have been armed. But how could he have asked for help to tail the Assistant Chief's wife to a love meeting with a villains' messenger boy and odd-job man? And how would he have explained to the armoury that he might need a handgun to protect her?

They seemed to be driving down towards the Valencia Esplanade area. That would make sense; anyone who wanted to go to ground might choose rooms in one of those big, old, multi-flatted houses, where few tenants remained for very long, and where people did not talk much about who they were or where they had come from, or where they would be moving to next. Harpur still kept far back from Tommy's Opel. It meant a danger of losing them, especially if other vehicles came between, but to go closer would be like lighting up neon to tell Vit he was there. Of course, for all Harpur knew, Tommy had him spotted already. People like Vit were not just good at tailing, they could feel when they were being followed themselves. Well, what else, when they lived by all the gambits? The Panda was far ahead, and could be any one of several sets of rear lights. He had to rely on Tommy to know which and to stay with her. Perhaps he would be so busy keeping track that he would not have time to watch his mirror. Yes, perhaps.

The Opel went suddenly right into Tempest Street, and when Harpur followed, he could see no moving vehicles ahead. For a moment, he feared he had fallen too far back, and that Sarah and Tommy had already left from the other end of the road. Panicked, he was about to accelerate up to the junction when he saw a woman who might be Sarah about a hundred yards off on foot, walking away from him with the striding, sexy, confident lope which was one of her trademarks. Immediately, he pulled into the side and watched her. Soon afterwards, he picked out the Panda parked far up on the other side of the road. A little way behind, but separated from it by several vehicles, stood the Opel, its lights already out.

Sarah turned and ran up the front path of one of the biggest houses and seemed to open the door with a key. She disappeared inside. Immediately then, a man in a long, dark trenchcoat and with a lot of rather gorgeous fair, wavy hair left the Opel and walked unhurriedly towards the house. As Harpur remembered them, the squat build and the layered hair were right for Tommy Vit, and the disarming leisureliness with which he moved. For a moment, he paused in front of the closed door, then bent over the lock, with what could have been a credit card in his hand. In a second he had opened the door and went in after her.

Harpur left the car and approached the house, taking cover behind a parked van. In a ground-floor room he could see an elderly woman lit up by the silver light of a television set, the way three-quarters of humanity continually exhibited itself these days. The floor above seemed totally dark. A young woman and a small child were looking from a window on the storey above that, Harpur decided that Aston, if it was Aston, must be in the attics; two rooms up there had lights showing.

He thought it would be wisest to wait though until Vit left. That should be all right; Tommy was a tail and only turned violent when cornered, or so the dossier said, and the dossiers were sometimes right. His job here would be simply to find Aston, and then tell Benny where he was, strictly a pathfinder. Sarah and her lover were probably in no danger yet, and there would be time to warn them to get out. And time to go with them. That was crucial. He did not want Aston to disappear again. Harpur remained behind the van but prepared himself for some very rapid movement, in case what he saw or heard showed he had read things badly.

After about ten minutes the door opened and Vit came out at the same relaxed pace, made for his car and drove away. He would be reporting to Loxton now what he had found, either on a car phone, or from the first workable booth he came to. His job was over, and it must have been soft money; follow the girl, get an identification of Aston when he opened the door upstairs, observe the layout of the house, make a decent guess at how the rooms were arranged, then brief Benny on the lot. He and his people would come immediately, but Vit would not hang about to watch the action or take part. His chief objects now must be to get well clear and put an alibi together. Tommy was a specialist, and the demarcation understanding would be that his fee did not require him to carry out or watch executions.

Harpur left the Astra and went down a side lane to reach the back of the house. Even in this road, the fire regulations would demand an escape and he had decided to get in that way, if he could. Perhaps there were bells at the front door and perhaps Aston would answer if he rang the right one. But perhaps he would not. This was a man lying low and expecting no callers, except the one already there, who had a key. Some more would certainly be on the way very soon. Tommy could be delivering the invitation at this moment.

Harpur began to climb the escape, moving swiftly and moving quietly, he hoped. It did not matter all that much because he was here mainly to offer help. They ought to be pleased to see him.

At the top storey, the escape became a simple metal ladder leading to a platform outside an unlighted window, with curtains partly across. He went up the ladder and rested for a moment on the platform, then moved close to the window and tried to see inside through the curtain gap. It was a rough bedroom, but, as far as he could make out, unoccupied, thank God. Sarah was entitled to her love sessions, with anyone she liked or loved, but he did not want to arrive in the middle of one, like a divorce snoop. The aim was to look after her, not frighten her frigid. He tried the window but it did not budge. He would have to force the catch, and brought out his pocket knife. This simple burgling skill he had learned years ago, and should be easy enough in this old house, where the wooden frames were getting soft.

While he worked there he thought suddenly that he had heard someone below in the rear yard, and he paused while he listened and looked down. But he located nobody. Intent on speed, he turned back to the window. And then, just as he felt the catch move, the curtains were violently pulled fully open and a flash-light beam from inside the room blinded him momentarily. Someone flung up the window and a man said: 'You? Harpur? Why you? You're in with them? Where are the other bastards?' A large-calibre pistol was pointed at him and he remained very still, crouched low on the platform. There seemed something familiar about the shadowy figure holding the weapon but, for the moment, he could not identify it, nor the voice.

From behind him, he was aware of another man coming fast up the ladder. He snarled at Harpur: 'Keep still. You're covered all ways. Where's the rest? Where?'

'It's fucking police,' the man in the room said. 'Harpur.'

'Police? How police?' the other man grunted anxiously. 'Police, how many? This is a set-up?'

Now, Harpur did recognise them. 'It's Leo, yes?' Harpur asked the man in the room. Without too much success he tried to keep

246

the astonishment and wonder out of his voice. 'And Lay-waste – I mean, Anthony.'

'Get in,' Lay-waste said. 'Into the room.'

Before Harpur could move, though, Leo thrust his small thin body out through the window and searched him quickly for a gun. 'Nothing.'

'Nothing?' Lay-waste said, sounding enraged. 'What the hell is this? You come here clean, a situation like this? You mad or something?'

Harpur jumped into the room. Lay-waste came in after him but then turned and stared back down to the yard, searching.

'I'm alone,' Harpur said.

'You're in this with Benny?' Leo asked, his voice disbelieving. 'You take from Benny? You police taking from Benny? But I thought – '

'I told you you couldn't trust the bastards, and that one bastard above all, Christ, you people, you police, you want a bit of everything,' Lay-waste said. He was bigger than Leo, taller and bulkier, with thick hands, a pointed nose and thin, and sallow, sick-looking skin. He was wearing a navy flak jacket.

'So where is he? Which way are they coming?' Leo asked. Harpur saw he was trembling and had trouble getting his words out.

'Where?' Lay-waste demanded again in a sort of shrieked, scared whisper and, through the darkness, Harpur could make out his arm raised with the pistol in it, as if about to deliver a blow. Then he seemed to change his mind and brought the gun down to his side.

Slowly, his mind still half-baffled and dazed by shock, Harpur had begun to work out what was happening. 'You've got an ambush, with Aston as bait?' Harpur said. 'You'd heard about Tommy Vit and knew Sarah would lead him here, and he'd bring Loxton. Now, you wait for Benny. So, how did you hear about Tommy?'

The door of the bedroom was pushed open and light from beyond reached in. Leo's other boy, Gerald, stood there and stared at Harpur. 'Christ, you with them?' He turnd to Leo and spoke very fast. The two of them were thin and small and big-nosed and bald and might have been brothers, rather than father and son. 'The rest are here, in the street. Four; Benny, Macey,

Norman and the new one – the telescopic sight. They're kitted out. Well, you'd expect. Two handguns, two sawn-offs.'

In the adjoining room behind Gerald, Harpur could see Aston and Sarah sitting upright and stiff, both looking mystified and very afraid. Maybe she had known she would get caught in something like this one day if she went on looking for the risks and the shadows. Yet, although the fear certainly lay there for all to see in her face, pulling her skin tight and making her eyes shine too much, it was not panic. She looked bad, but she also looked as if she could cope. She was still Sarah Iles.

'How are they coming in? Leo asked Harpur urgently. 'Are they following you, up the escape? You're the way ahead, supposed to let them in?'

'I'm alone,' Harpur told him again.

'Alone? Oh, Christ, come on,' Gerald said.

'So, alone wanting what?' Lay-waste asked. They were all whispering now.

'Wanting to look after Sarah Iles,' Harpur told him.

Again Lay-waste raised the pistol, a 9 mm Browning, and this time cracked the barrel down on the side of Harpur's head. He staggered but did not fall. Blood began to run down his face and on to his collar. 'Stop pissing me about,' Lay-waste said.

'Leave it,' Leo told him. 'There are other things.'

'He knows how many people, where they are,' Lay-waste said. 'We have to make him tell us, and what he's doing here, really what he's doing here.'

'It's too late. We deal with it, whatever it is,' Leo told him. 'Harpur, we're defending ourselves here, understand? No option.' He spoke as if foreseeing some court case where Harpur would give evidence, and he hoped this was right, particularly the idea that he might survive.

'Colin,' Sarah said. 'Are you OK? Come and sit down.' She was about to stand and bring him across the room, but Lay-waste swore and told her to remain still.

'Yes, sit down,' Leo told Harpur. 'Stay out of this. You mean it, there are no other police? All we're dealing with is Benny and his crew.' Harpur pinpointed a slight tremor of hope in his voice.

Another two of Leo's people appeared in the room, both carrying handguns. Harpur recognised Ashley Simpson, the one they called In-off, but did not know the other: younger, plumper, and with the sort of face made to look through bars.

'They're coming up the escape,' Simpson said. 'And one waiting at the front door – Norman.'

'We're being hunted, Harpur. You see that? We offered friendship, and we're being hunted, instead,' Leo said. Sweat shone on the round, bald head and along the ridge of his jutting nose. Again he appeared to be anticipating a reckoning, and preparing ways to make the best of it. But, no, they weren't hunted. They had set a trap.

'What are you doing here, Colin?' Sarah said. She sounded as she looked, very frightened, very defeated. 'How?' He could see that what she wanted to ask was whether Iles knew, even whether Iles was here, too.

But she did not ask, and he made no attempt to answer. 'We'll be all right,' Harpur replied. 'Keep still.'

'Yes, listen to what he says,' Gerald told her and Aston. 'Just stay out of it.'

Because they had the door open to this living-room, there would be light showing from the window over the escape now. Unless they hid themselves carefully the light would show up anyone waiting in the bedroom, and they could not count on the sort of surprise Leo had when he confronted Harpur. Four of them went into the bedroom: Leo, Lay-waste, Gerald and Simpson. The other man stayed with Harpur, Sarah and Aston. Harpur had not heard Aston speak yet, but now he said: 'They made me do this. Made me get Sarah to lead them here. She didn't know.'

'Did *you* tell Leo about Tommy Vit?'

'I didn't know he was involved. Leo says Vit was spotted outside Sarah's house.

'Spotted? Who by?'

Aston glanced at Sarah. 'Someone who wanted me out of the way. That's where Leo's tip came from.'

Harpur left it there, and did not press for Iles's name. Christ, though, if Leo was being tipped by Iles and thought police co-operation had been sweetly arranged, no wonder he sounded sick to find Harpur here, apparently footsoldiering for Benny. Routine treachery Leo would always cater for – that was life – but this must look like the darkest sell ever, even for Iles. So, when

Lay-waste talked about 'that one bastard' he had meant the ACC.

Harpur could see the four men in the bedroom, all with pistols in their hands, standing flat against the wall on each side of the window, so they would be invisible for at least the first few key seconds when Benny and his people arrived on the platform. Lay-waste was to the side of the drawn-back curtains and must be able to see part of the way down the escape. The others watched him, trying to read the signs in his face and body.

The man on guard had produced a pistol and turned it towards them. 'No noise,' he whispered, 'No warnings. You understand?'

Harpur nodded, and a small shower of blood fell from his head on to his trouser leg. 'Don't worry.'

All the same, the guard pulled a straight-backed chair around behind Sarah's for himself and sat with the muzzle of the pistol resting on her shoulder and pointed into her neck.

'We understand,' Harpur said. 'You needn't do that.'

'I'll say what I fucking need.'

She gave a very small, stiff grin at Harpur, trying to tell him not to worry. He worried.

It grew very quiet. Harpur strove to hear the sound of footsteps on the escape, but detected nothing. In the bedroom, Leo and his people kept motionless and seemed hardly to be breathing, making no noise. Lay-waste was tilted slightly forward, surveying as much as he could of the escape. Were Benny and his lads already on the way up? Harpur had no way of knowing. The rest of them in the bedroom still studied Lay-waste, using him as eyes.

The danger was that this terrifying silence would stretch and stretch, loading the strain on to everyone's nerves, and then there might come a sudden end when the firing and the yelling and the cursing and, maybe, the screaming began. What was his control like, the bloody tub nobody with the pistol on Sarah's neck? His finger was hooked around the trigger, and his eyes spent part of their time anxiously watching the bedroom group for signs of what was happening, then would switch back and stare at Harpur and Aston and say without more words that if either of them shifted Sarah would die. He looked about thirty, fair, jail pale, dim, jumpy, out of his depth and probably not someone who learned at Sandhurst how to make a safe job of handling small-arms.

And then, abruptly, it started, just as Harpur had feared. Pistol fire fractured the silence. For a second, he was not sure exactly what had happened. Harpur had been intent on watching Sarah and the guard, wondering if he should risk a move, but, when he turned back to look into the bedroom, he saw that Lay-waste had come away from the wall and, standing in the window, was firing down the escape. From the angle, it was obvious that Benny and his people had not reached the platform yet, and Harpur heard at least two bullets hit the metal and ricochet away. Leo was hanging on to his son's arm, apparently trying to hold him back – force him to wait until the targets were nearer. But Lay-waste had never been good on patience and self-control, not a whites-of-their-eyes man. The shooting was very rapid, and Harpur thought he counted five shots. It was not something he could be certain about, or cared much about, because he had heard something much closer. Frightened or excited by the sudden noise, the guard jumped up very quickly, but tried to keep the muzzle of the pistol on Sarah's neck. For a second, he was off balance and lurched a little to the side, knocking his chair over with his legs, his finger still on the trigger, though. As he tried to right himself he shoved Sarah's head lower with the pistol, and for a moment it looked like an execution pose, so that Harpur almost cried out. He knew he had to do something now.

The guard's chair had toppled toward Harpur and lay near him. With two hands, he grabbed at it and then, in the same movement, swung it at the man's head, catching him square on the temple and side of his face before he had recovered from the stumble. Harpur saw the consciousness go out of his eyes at once, and his body start folding. The guard tumbled heavily forward. As he fell, his gun flew out of his hand and went off. Harpur heard the bullet hum and slam into the wall to the left of Aston. The pistol skidded across the floor towards the bedroom.

Harpur moved after it, but Leo must have given up trying to restrain Lay-waste and, standing near the doorway now, he heard the shot and turned, then stooped swiftly and picked up the gun. For a second, he looked as if he might fire at Harpur. The two men stood facing each other, stiff, frozen, Leo holding the weapon out in front of him. But then, almost wearily, almost

251

hopelessly, Leo waved the pistol at Harpur, ordering him to sit again.

'Sarah?' Harpur said. 'Are – '

'I'm fine.' She rubbed her neck and grinned again, almost a smile now. 'Thanks, Colin,' she said, glancing at the guard on the floor. 'But they won't forgive that.'

'We'll be all right,' he said. Could be. Thank God it was Leo who had picked up the weapon, not one of his babies.

Harpur became aware of shouting and groans from below on the fire escape. Yes, it was too late to hold back Lay-waste; he leaned far out over the sill, obviously searching for a target, ready to fire again, if he had anything left.

And then Harpur heard two shots, seeming to come from outside, from below, maybe, and Lay-waste half turned and slid back very fast from the window and on to the floor, his head crashing against the sill as he fell. Leo seemed to sob, then hurried forward and bent down to him. Gerald and Simpson both went to the window now and stared down. 'They're pulling out,' Gerald shouted. 'God, we've blown it. We'll not finish them, Anthony's blown it, the prat.'

'Get an ambulance,' Leo said. He was still crouched over Lay-waste, weeping openly now.

'That dumb fucker,' Gerald replied, staring down at Lay-waste. 'He deserves it. We leave him. Get out. They'll have the bloody SAS here in a minute. We use the front. Norman's probably scarpered with the rest.'

He and Simpson ran back into the living-room, putting their pistols away. The guard had begun to stir and they pulled him upright. Then, supporting him, they tugged the front door of the flat open and Harpur heard them rushing down the stairs. Cars started in the road and roared away.

Harpur found his legs were all right and walked into the bedroom. Leo was trying to stop blood flowing from Lay-waste's neck with part of his own shirt which he had torn off at the front and folded, so that his thin, pale stomach was exposed. Leo's Browning and the guard's pistol lay near the body and Harpur was able to pick up both weapons this time. Lay-waste's was still in his hand, and he took that too.

When Harpur looked below, he could see a man's body lying crumpled on the steps near the bottom of the escape, face down and not recognisable at this distance. Sarah and Aston joined him.

From the floor, Leo said again: 'Please, an ambulance.'

'I've rung,' Aston said.

'Everything will be here in a minute,' Harpur told Leo. Turning to Aston, he muttered: 'Get her out of this place.'

'Right.'

'Eventually, it's bound to be known I was here,' Sarah protested.

'Yes, eventually,' Harpur replied. 'Eventually's better than now.'

Towards dawn he drove out with Iles from Tempest Street to Benny Loxton's place on the Loam Estate.

'Do you know, I wouldn't have been at all surprised to find Sarah there when we arrived at Aston's,' Iles said.

'Yes, sir?'

'There are points in this I don't understand. How did you get there first like that, and your injury?'

'Yes, there are baffling elements, sir. It's the same for all of us. How did Leo know that Tommy Vit had been hired by Benny and would bring all the Loxton outfit into a trap?'

'That is a mystery,' Iles said, 'a real mystery. I agree.'

'Yes, sir? As a matter of fact, I wondered if you'd possibly seen him lurking around your place.'

'You mean did I tell Leo? Christ, you've got a bloody nerve, Harpur. Would anyone be likely to spot a pro like Tommy Vit if he was doing an observation?'

'Well, another pro might, I suppose, sir. And you are on terms with Leo, aren't you?'

Iles discarded that subject. 'I wonder if Sarah will lose some taste for this sort of foolish, shady life now? Two people dead. It's possible, I suppose.'

'Yes, sir?'

'We'll have to see.'

'I think so, sir.'

'She's tough. She goes her own way. That's the trouble. But she's had some very bad sessions lately. Leo told us – Sarah and me – that some woman turned up at the Monty just after Ralph took a beating. Judging by her face as he said it, I reckon that was Sarah. She might come to decide she's had enough of such adventures.'

'Certainly, sir.'

'Ah, you don't think so? No, you're too bloody right. Why can't I hold her, Colin?'

They rang the bell of Loxton's house and after a long while Alma appeared in a dressing-gown. Game as ever, she affected delight at seeing Iles. 'But do come in, gentlemen,' she cried. 'You wish to see Theodore? I'm afraid he's away on a business trip. Yes. You poor people, working such hours. It must be urgent.'

She took them into the big lounge. Nobody who was roused at this hour looked too great, and Alma certainly did not. The time of day, like the time of life, could be a bugger, and occasionally they combined to be a supreme bugger.

'Will you sit down, love,' Iles asked. She looked startled at being addressed like that, and at being offered the hospitality of her own furniture. But she did what the ACC had suggested, and he and Harpur also took chairs.

'Can one offer drinks so early?' she asked, laughing briefly. Harpur saw that she had started to suspect things were not good. Attempting to read their faces, she looked earnestly back and forth at each of them.

'Alma, we had an incident tonight. A dark incident,' Iles said. 'I'm very much afraid two people were killed, a youngster called Anthony Tacette.' He lowered his head, and might genuinely have been upset. 'And, I regret to say, Theodore.'

'That fucking Lay-waste?' Alma cried. 'He killed Benny?'

Harpur felt astonished at her reaction; the swearing, the shrillness of her grief, and, above all, the apparent familiarity with Loxton's rough world. 'It does look like that,' Harpur said. 'So, did you know about all these things, Alma – Lay-waste, the gang battles?' He tried to keep the surprise out of his voice, not eager to sound terminally naïve.

She stared at Harpur, without much warmth. 'Knew about it? I married it, didn't I? I loved Benny, wanted him, and all the rest came as part of the deal. That was the life I took on board with him, so I had to make the best of it. Occasionally I might feel sickened, but I knew I wasn't entitled to. So, I tried to know only as much as I couldn't help knowing, didn't I, and just got on with the washing up and the charities? Do you think I'm some sort of fool? Do you think I believe the Save the Whale movement makes the world go round? But what I knew I didn't make a display of. I would have preferred things to be different and I tried to pretend they really were. Now and then, though, would come a moment when that was impossible. Same sort of thing happens to everybody, I suppose. We all kid ourselves until we can't. "Moment of truth." You've heard of it? Very rough, that can be. Ask the bullfighter with his balls hooked on a horn. But I still had to stick to my *grande dame* act in public. Perhaps Benny and I fought about these things privately. Perhaps I tried to get him to change. I didn't stand a chance. If you live on the proceeds how can you quibble about where they come from?' She wiped her eyes, though Harpur saw no tears. 'And who killed Lay-waste?' she asked.

'We don't know yet.'

'But could it have been Benny?' she persisted.

'It's possible,' Harpur said. It was hardly possible at all, in fact, because everything suggested Loxton died first. One of the others had blazed up at Lay-waste, as a parting shot, and had a big piece of luck. Or it might have been one of their marksmen with a rifle. They had no forensic on the bullet yet. But he knew that this was the reply Alma needed just now, so why not?

'Thank Christ,' she muttered.

'Why do you call him Benny, not Theodore, now he's dead, Alma?' Iles asked.

'Did I? It seems right. I'll miss him like hell, and when I miss him I'll be thinking of him as Benny. Theodore? Oh, that was part of the public relations.'

'We're very sorry about it all, Alma,' Iles said.

'I suppose you wish there'd been more. They could have wiped one another out – both outfits?'

'Indeed not,' Iles replied. 'This is a tragedy, and we are only thankful it is not a greater one.'

'We'll be locking some of them up, anyway,' Harpur said. 'There's another killing, and lesser things.'

Alma stood, still dry-eyed and in command. 'His principal interest in life lately was the kind of charities I've mentioned – not just Save the Whale, but famine and so on. All major needs.'

'He's a loss,' Iles replied. 'Yes.'

A dead loss.

'Shall I see him?' Alma asked.

'In due course, certainly,' Iles said.

She went with them to the front door. 'Yes, patch Benny up and make him look presentable, would you? I couldn't bear to see him all – ' For a second she seemed about to cave in and weep properly. Then her body stiffened and she snapped her head back, like a drill sergeant. 'He was a stickler about appearance. The Navy, you know.'

Mute
Witness

Charles O'Brien

Poisoned Pen Press

Poisoned
Pen
Press

Poisoned Pen Press
6962 E. First Ave. Ste 103
Scottsdale, AZ 85251
www.poisonedpenpress.com
info@poisonedpenpress.com

Printed in the United States of America

Acknowledgments

I would like to thank Tama Baldwin of Western Illinois University for introducing me to the writer's craft and sharing her equestrian experience. William Burton, Johnathan Gash, Patricia O'Connor, and Marilyn Wright read drafts of the novel and contributed much to its improvement. Jennifer Nelson of Gallaudet University and Douglas Baynton of the University of Iowa offered expert advice on issues relating to deafness. Thanks also to Barbara Peters of Poisoned Pen Press for a helpful edit; to Scott Miner, cartographer at Western Illinois University, who assisted with the maps; and to John Dawson, for an attractive, intriguing cover. Robert Rosenwald has been a most supportive and encouraging publisher. Finally, this novel could hardly have been written without the generous help of my wife Elvy, art historian extraordinaire, who carefully read the manuscript at various stages and enriched it with many apt references to the painting and sculpture of the period.

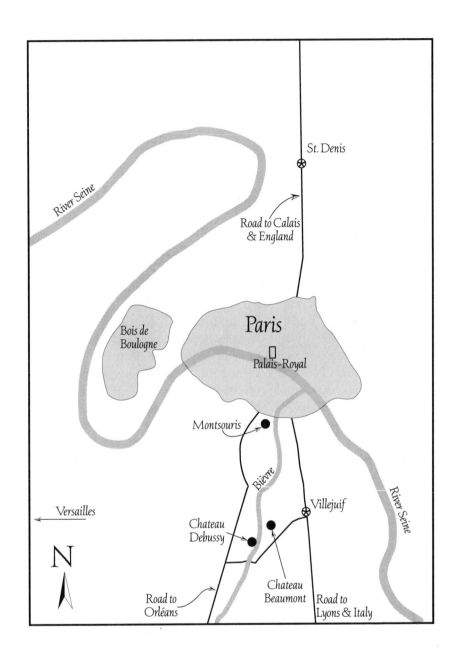

St. Denis

Road to Calais
& England

River Seine

Bois de
Boulogne

Paris

Palais-Royal

Montsouris

Bièvre

Versailles

N

Chateau
Debussy

Villejuif

River Seine

Chateau
Beaumont

Road to
Orléans

Road to
Lyons & Italy

Paris Region 1786

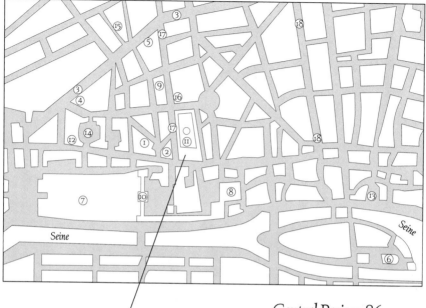

Central Paris 1786

1. Abbé l'Épée's institute for the deaf, Rue des Moulins
2. Anne Cartier's apartment, Rue Traversine
3. The Boulevard
4. Bureau of Criminal Investigation, Rue des Capuchines
5. Café Marcel
6. Cathedral of Notre-Dame
7. Garden of the Tuileries
8. Louvre
9. Michelline du Saint-Esprit's room, Rue Richelieu
10. Palace of the Tuileries
11. Palais-Royal
12. Paul de Saint-Martin's residence, Rue Saint-Honoré
13. Place de Grève
14. Place Vendôme
15. Robert LeCourt's hotel, Rue Thaithout
16. Bibliothèque Royale/Royal Library
17. Rue Richelieu
18. Rue Saint-Denis

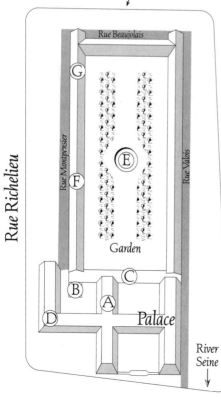

Palais-Royal 1786

A. Palace Theatre
B. Variety Theatre
C. Camp of the Tatars
D. Art Gallery
E. Fountain
F. Café Odéon
G. Theatre of the Little Comedians

Table of Contents

Chapter 1

Paris, Palais-Royal, August 1785

Antoine leaned out the window and smiled with relief. The leaden sky over the city had begun to clear in the late afternoon, offering him hope of escape from a pall of warm humid air. He turned to his companion, who sat listlessly fanning herself, a frown on her face. Something was bothering her, but she refused to talk about it. He was sure it had to do with this evening's scheduled visit to the palace theater in the Palais-Royal. Copywork for him, a meeting with the theater's directeur for her.

"Let's walk to the river, Lélia. It'll do us good."

With a heavy sigh she rose from her chair. "I suppose it would. I feel like I've been in prison."

A few minutes later, Antoine Dubois and Lélia Laplante left their stuffy apartment and strolled in the direction of the Seine. Rain had kept them indoors most of the day. As they reached the left bank, they breathed deeply, taking in fresh summer air scented by pungent whiffs from the city's slaughter house that stood on the opposite bank. Ferries scurried like water bugs back and forth over the glistening surface of the river.

On the Quai de Conti, they stopped for a view of the Pont Neuf, the New Bridge. The broad stone roadway, uncluttered by houses or shops, crossed the downstream tip of the city's central island. Jostled by the crowd coming off the bridge, Lélia gripped her purse with mock anxiety and began recounting an episode she had witnessed a few days earlier in the Palais-Royal, the daring theft of a duke's gold watch in broad daylight.

Antoine listened attentively, relieved that, at least for the moment, she'd forgotten whatever disturbed her.

Arm in arm, they continued along the river on the Quai des Grands Augustins. The book stalls were doing a brisk business now that the rain had ended. Antoine stopped at a stall and began to browse, looking for comic stories he could adapt for the stage. But, Lélia was soon sulking. She had little interest in books. Clothes were another matter. He took her hand. "We have time. Let's go to the Palais-Royal. Look in the shops, have a bit of supper at Café Odéon."

She hesitated for a moment, then agreed. "I'd like that." The lines of worry faded from her brow. Her back straightened. She looked years younger. Nothing satisfied her more than to seek out the latest fashion in the arcades of the Palais-Royal, where celebrated ladies came to be seen. It was enough to gaze at them and to admire or condemn what they wore. They rarely tempted her to buy anything for herself. She had already gathered a large collection of wigs, paste jewelry, and expensive gowns. From admirers, she would say, without blushing.

A flash of doubt seared Antoine's mind. Did he really know her? She hid part of her life from him. Then he gazed at her lively brown eyes, smooth olive skin, full sensuous lips, ample figure. His affection for her flamed up again, as it had in the days of their youth together in Rouen. They locked arms and set off.

Two hours later, they sat themselves down wearily at an outdoor table of Café Odéon, dabbing perspiration from their brows. They ordered wine and cold *soupe aux cerises*. From their vantage point, midway in the Montpensier Gallery, the vast enclosed garden spread out before them. An evening crowd strolled beneath its ordered rows of trees. Lamps were lit. Shops began to close their shutters. Fashionable men and women gathered in elegant cafés in the Valois Gallery, on the far side of the garden, or in the Beaujolais Gallery, off to the left. Common folk thronged to the low wooden stalls of the Camp of the Tatars, off to the right. Antoine could hear barkers calling out their wares. In windows above the arcades, tiny points of light appeared. There the Palais-Royal indulged every taste from chess clubs to richly furnished brothels.

Some of the fashionable crowd drifted into the Odéon. Lélia glanced with interest at a pair of women in the latest striped silk gowns *à la bergère*, their hair worn loose, unpowdered. She preferred a more soignée look in this setting.

Antoine finished his soup and leaned back, twirling the last drops of wine in his glass. He glanced to the right. At the far south end of the garden stood the duke's palace. Through breaks in the foliage, Antoine picked out the top floor of the palace theater and counted the windows to where its office was located. He had to spend a couple of hours there this evening copying script while Lélia talked to the directeur. About what? he wondered. He stole an anxious glance at her. She seemed absorbed in picking up scraps of gossip from nearby tables. But a few minutes later, she glanced at her watch, then frowned. "Time to go."

∞∞∞

"Where's Pressigny? That man! He should be here by now." Lélia's voice echoed in the empty rear entrance hall of the palace theater.

Antoine tried to placate her. "Perhaps he's already in the building. The watchman should know. I'll find him."

"Don't be long," she cautioned. "I don't feel safe here."

"I'll be quick." He set off in the direction of the stage. Though he didn't say so, he placed little hope in the watchman, who had left the outside door unlocked and a pair of oil lamps burning on the wall. The man was known to seek out the theater's nooks and crannies to snatch a drink or a nap.

After a brief, fruitless search, Antoine returned to Lélia. "The watchman has probably left. The building seems deserted."

"I don't want to stand here waiting." Lélia tapped her foot impatiently. "Let's go to the fitting room."

With a lamp in his hand, Antoine led the way down the narrow corridor, then opened the door for Lélia. She smiled as she entered the room and inspected a rack of clothes. "Very good! Michou's altered my costumes for tomorrow's dress rehearsal." The actress glanced toward the adjacent dark wardrobe room. "She must have come and gone."

At the open door behind him, Antoine heard a rustle of silk and swung around. In a pale rose suit richly embroidered with silver, his thick curly hair lightly powdered, Chevalier de Pressigny sauntered toward them with studied nonchalance. "I've come from the variety theater. Devilishly hot. Let's get on with our business." He bowed deeply to Lélia. "Madame Laplante." Mockery danced on his lips. "You wished to speak to me?"

The actress took his measure with cold regard. "Yes, Monsieur le Directeur! We need to clear up a few matters. Right here will do."

Antoine frowned. Lélia surely didn't have just gowns in mind. Her knotted brow was set for battle. With Pressigny it seemed. An uneasy, helpless feeling crept into the pit of Antoine's stomach.

Pressigny sat down, then beckoned the actress to another chair with a crude jerk of the head. Lélia stiffened, her lips tightened. She took off her hat and jabbed the long, sharp pin into the great pile of her hair.

The directeur swung round to Antoine. "Upstairs with you and get to work."

Antoine hesitated, glancing with suspicion at Pressigny. Something was wrong. He searched Lélia's eyes for a clue. "Can I help you, my dear?"

"You'd better leave." She shot him a quick, nervous smile and followed him to the door. It shut with a sharp click behind him.

Antoine climbed the narrow stairway to the first floor and walked out onto the stage. The boards felt gritty beneath his feet, the air musty. The stage hadn't been swept for weeks. He wouldn't complain for fear he'd get the task. He had enough to do. At tomorrow's rehearsal, he'd play the part of a cuckolded clown. He smiled sardonically. Close to the role he played with Lélia at home.

Lifting his lamp, he peered out over the orchestra pit, barely discerning the upper and lower balconies in the distance. During performances, blinded by footlights, he couldn't see them much better. But he'd know an audience was there by the buzz of their conversation, their laughter when amused, their hisses when displeased. After many years on stage, he still found it strange that he couldn't see the faces of the people he entertained, though they could see his.

He glanced into the wings. Dark also. But as he stared, he imagined Annie, his stepdaughter, standing there as if waiting for her cue—a willowy young woman in a long shimmering gown. Yielding to the illusion, he put the lamp aside and beckoned her. He lifted his chin, held out his hand, and began a country dance he'd learned in England. He whirled about the stage, round and round until he felt dizzy...and realized her presence had left him.

For a moment he stood still, sensing the emptiness of the place. How was Lélia doing with the directeur? They were too far away, the walls too thick, to be heard. With a sigh, he picked up the lamp, climbed the stairs to the first, then to the second balcony and made his way to the theater's office. He sat down at the table, mopped sweat from his brow, and picked up his pen.

The clock on the office wall struck ten. Antoine sat still, listening to the resonance of the chimes in his ears and then to the faint, eerie creaking of wooden beams and floorboards. Uneasiness crept over him. Nothing was quite so desolate as an empty theater late at night.

The sultry air dampened to a murmur the sounds from crowds milling in the shopping arcades and gardens in the distance. He walked to an open window. Dark clouds hung low over the city, hiding a crescent moon. He looked down into a deserted palace courtyard, a deep, black pit in the heart of Paris. Beads of light from lanterns at the gate below accentuated the darkness. He felt trapped in this place.

Why did the theater's office *have* to be on the top floor? In the winter, he froze; in the summer, he baked. Drawing a deep breath, he returned to the table, dipped his pen in the ink, and went back to copying the script for tomorrow's rehearsal. He had no choice. Part-time actor, he needed the extra money. He heard his stomach growling.

He bent over the paper, carefully inscribing each letter. The faint light from the oil lamp tired his eyes. He preferred to copy by daylight, but the script had to be ready early in the morning. He finished a line, leaned back, stretched, and glanced round the dingy room, cluttered with unmatched cabinets. Sweat oozed from his body, although he had removed his coat and was working in shirt-sleeves. He had left the door open but the air didn't move. He wiped his hands again, always taking care not to smudge the paper. When Jean de Pressigny directed productions of the Société des Amateurs, he demanded pristine text.

"Finished!" Antoine at last exclaimed. He shuffled the freshly copied papers into a folder and placed it in Pressigny's box. He tapped nervously on the table. It seemed like hours since he had left Lélia and the directeur downstairs. "Need to check my wardrobe," she had said on their way to the theater. He recalled, with a stab of shame, previous evenings when she and the directeur had *checked* her wardrobe. Tonight seemed different somehow. Lélia was so tense, so angry.

Antoine had worn himself out protesting. She would never mend her ways. Last week he had shouted at her so loudly the neighbors had called in the watchmen and sworn they thought he was murdering her. But, he still loved her. Besides, she brought home more money than he did, and she had persuaded Pressigny to hire him. Seasoned flirt. She could be *very* persuasive.

Was this the life he wanted, he asked himself. His love for Lélia seemed so one-sided. She used him as she liked and left him for days at a time. And kept much of her doings secret. If he complained, she reminded him they weren't married. She could do as she pleased.

He should have known better than to join her in Paris three years ago, as if he could renew their old romance. It wasn't working out. Perhaps he should leave her and return to London. He felt a stir of hope. His wife Pauline had died years ago, but his stepdaughter Annie still performed in the city and was his best friend. They could be partners again, side by side on Vauxhall's stage, her supple body sheathed in a bright red acrobat's costume. Together they would bow to loud applause like they used to. If only it were not too late. He might be too old, too lacking in confidence to begin again.

He pulled a leather pouch out of his coat pocket, retrieved an oval silver case, and opened it to a pair of miniature portraits.

Pauline seemed to meet his gaze as he would always remember her in the first years of their marriage—a kind, intelligent, and healthy woman. He touched the broad gold band on his finger, slowly tracing the intertwined *P & A* engraved on its flat surface. His gaze shifted to the portrait of his stepdaughter, Annie. Ten years old then. So much like her mother, fair-haired and comely. And brave. Antoine's mind drifted back to an early summer morning at Sadler's Wells. He had gone to the theater to practice his routine for the evening. Annie had come with him, for she liked to try on costumes in the wardrobe room or play Punch and Judy with the puppets.

As Antoine walked the tight rope, a long pole in his hands for balance, he noticed little Annie watching him, eyes wide, lips parted.

"Can I try it, Antoine?" she called up to him.

Why not, he thought. For her age, she was a strong, agile girl. He found a costume for her and tied the rope a foot above the floor.

She began a slow walk, her face screwed up with determination. She had been watching him more closely than he had realized, for she handled the pole expertly. He stayed near her, steadying her with his hands. After a few successful attempts, she tried to increase her speed. Halfway across, her foot slipped off the rope. With a little shriek she fell into his arms.

Startled but smiling, she looked up at him. "I'll try that again." She didn't fall the next time. Nor the next. She insisted he raise the rope. Before the morning was half over, he had set the rope at twelve feet and tied a net beneath it. She fell a few times but climbed back up to the platform and on to the rope.

At noon, Antoine announced, "Time to go home."

She pouted. "Once more. Let's do the rope together."

He paused for a moment, then consented. It began to dawn on him that he and the girl were becoming partners. He wasn't sure what Pauline would make of it.

Annie went first off the platform, staring straight ahead, body erect. The muscles of her back tightened, working against the weight of the pole. She glided without a misstep to the opposite platform and threw the pole aside. With a squeak of delight she swung around, smiling ecstatically. Her face glistened with sweat.

Suddenly, the vision vanished. "Damn! Today's August ninth! Her birthday's next week!" Antoine struck his forehead a glancing blow. "I'll write to her now." He closed the case, caressing it with the tips of his fingers, and replaced it in his coat pocket.

From a drawer in the table he retrieved the small box of writing paper he stored there. He drew out a sheet and stared at its blank surface. Slowly a feeling of great loss swept over him. How he missed her! He cupped his head in his hands, closed his eyes. Felt pain, felt despair.

Eventually, he straightened, reached out for the pen, dated the paper, and wrote a few lines. Annie seemed so near and yet so far away. A wave of fatigue buffeted him. He was tired and hungry. The pen faltered. He laid it in the ink stand, tucked the letter into the box. He would finish it later.

He drew a fresh sheet of paper from the drawer and initialed it in case the directeur wanted to dictate a new passage for the play. He was usually in such a hurry, so impatient. Antoine bent over the sheet, conjuring up the image of Chevalier de Pressigny. Spoiled, arrogant pup! What on earth could he and Lélia be doing downstairs? In the next moment, he thought he heard footsteps in the hallway. He called out, "Lélia?"

Chapter 2

Sadler's Wells, September 1785

A brisk roll of drums, a piping of flutes thrust through the still, warm air. At Sadler's Wells Theatre in Islington, a few miles north of London, the last act of the evening variety show was about to begin. Anne Cartier, a tall woman in a wide-sleeved, loose, silver costume, climbed to a high platform at the rear of the stage. A wire stretched out tightly before her. For the past half-hour she had amused a large, noisy audience with cartwheels, a slack-rope dance, and acrobatic stunts. Now she squared her shoulders back and stood poised. Her smile tensed. Beyond the footlights, rows of upturned faces stirred with nervous anticipation. She called for the finale. A hush came over the house.

From the orchestra, the trumpeter blew a rousing fanfare. Anne strolled regally back and forth on her wire, singing *Rule Britannia*. Her outstretched arms, like slender silken wings, beat a brisk cadence. The audience surged to their feet, faces flushed with patriotic fervor and strong British ale. Two hundred voices joined in pledging: "...Britons never, never, never will be slaves."

On the last note she saluted, feigned a fall, and back flipped to the stage, landing gracefully on her feet. She bowed deeply. Throwing kisses to her audience, she skipped nimbly from the stage. Loud applause followed her into the wings.

She pulled off her cap, shook loose her thick blond hair, and wove through a crowd of workers in a narrow corridor. At the open door of the women's dressing room she heard loud male voices. Not again! she thought, her jaw clenching in anger. Forcing her way into the room, she saw a fleshy young man in a red waistcoat and tight tan breeches, tearing at the costume of a frightened young dancer, Harriet Ware. A pair of his toadies held the girl by her arms. The other women huddled in a corner at the far end of the room.

Only a month ago Anne had persuaded Mr. Wroughton, the theater manager, to stop the intruders from coming backstage seeking partners for the night. The men gathered instead near the stagedoor after the show, like mongrel dogs lurking behind a butcher's shop. But here they were, inside again.

"Where's the manager?" she asked the stagehands clustered by the door.

"Out with the rest of the company," one of them replied. "At the White Lion, I think. Won't be back for half an hour."

Now she remembered. He'd said she was to join them after her act. She glared at the men. "Help me get that red bastard out of here."

The men shrank back. Jack Roach, the "red bastard," was feckless and clumsy, but when someone crossed him, he always got even.

"Cowards! I'll do it myself." Anne shoved the men aside, picked up an empty chamber pot and swung it with all her force at the bully's temple. For a second he stood stock-still, then fell to the floor like an unstrung marionette.

"Take him away," she shouted to the astonished toadies. In fumbling haste they dragged their fallen leader from the field of battle. The dressing room door slammed shut at his heels.

"Thanks, Miss Cartier," murmured Roach's victim, pale with shock.

Anne put an arm around the young woman's shoulder and led her to a chair. "You'll be all right, Harriet, in a few minutes."

The dancer looked up at Anne with alarm. "Roach might cause trouble for you."

Anne shrugged. "That can't be helped." She took the woman by the hand and met her eye. "We shall not let him treat us like whores."

The dancer took a deep breath, then smiled. "No, we shall not."

Monday evening, September 26th, the doors of Sadler's Wells slammed shut marking the end of the theater season for the year. Outside, Anne Cartier waved to the departing custodian, then gazed fondly at the plain brick building that had been her home for the past three summers. A helter-skelter of images swept through her mind. The dancing dogs. Hercules, the Amazing Strong Man. Tumbling by Matthew, the English Mercury. Lovely Maria's sweet Italian ballads. Anne sighed with nostalgia. Decent, honest people, her friends. She would miss their exuberance, their daring, their generous encouragement. Now they would scatter to London, to Bath, or wherever they could find employment, probably to return to Sadler's Wells on Easter Monday next year for another summer season.

She drew on her cloak. Her life was about to take a new turn. She might not come back here next summer. At least not to dance, or sing, or walk the tight wire. Still, she might see her friends again, but from one of the three-shilling boxes rather than from the wings. Between acts she'd join them for drinks in the garden alongside the theater.

The sound of voices broke into her musing. She turned around. Four persons, faces shadowed, were standing at the edge of the road, involved in a lively discussion. One of them hailed her. "Annie! It's only eleven. The night's young. Join us!"

Anne recognized the voice: Harriet Ware, the young dancer she had saved three weeks earlier from the clutches of Jack Roach. The two women had become good friends. Drawing closer, Anne recognized the others: Louis Fortier, the gentle French strong man, billed as Hercules, who bent iron bars like willow branches; Paulo Napolitano, the Italian high-wire clown; and his wife, the singer Maria.

"Right!" Anne replied. "Let's all celebrate." She twirled her walking stick, then pointed it at Myddelton's Head, the tavern at the end of the street.

Patrons of the theater had filled the inn to overflowing. The noise drove Anne and her friends to an upstairs room overlooking a courtyard. It was a cozy space enclosed by a lightly embossed stuccoed ceiling and linen-fold panelling. A low fire in the stone hearth dispelled the chill of the late September air.

The friends settled around a thick oak table, sharing a bottle of wine. Someone asked Anne if she would move from her cottage now that the summer season was over. She shrugged her shoulders. "I'd like to stay there—it's convenient. My horse has a stall and a pasture in the back lot."

Paulo slipped into his clown's role, grimacing broadly. "You live alone with a horse, Annie? That's no life for a beautiful woman." He threw up his arms in mock anguish. "Find a boyfriend, get married, have *bambini.*" He squeezed his wife, Maria, sitting next to him, then nodded to Louis Fortier. "Our Hercules here is just the man for you."

The giant turned beet red in the face, stared silently into his glass. Everyone knew he was fond of Anne but grew tongue-tied in her presence. Shy with women, he resembled the mythical Greek hero only in his strength. Fortunately, among friends he was good-humored. Screwing up a fierce frown, he muttered, "Someday, Paulo, I shall break you like a twig."

The slender Italian laughed. "A duel! David and Goliath at dawn on the high wire."

While they bantered, Anne glanced at Maria. She had smiled, her eyes bright, as her husband squeezed her. But when he turned his attention away, her face settled into a mask. Thin lines of sadness creased the corners of her mouth and eyes. Anne knew why. She had nursed Maria through a difficult pregnancy, followed by a painful depression. Watching this woman suffer reinforced an attitude that had grown in Anne as an adult. She enjoyed children, but the thought of giving birth to one brought up unbidden anxieties. They could be mastered, she knew, like the fear of falling from the high wire, but she would make the effort only for a very good reason.

Unlike most women, she would enter into marriage and have children only on her own terms. She was legally free. No brother, uncle, or father could force her to take a husband. She lived on her salary and on income from a trust fund. She didn't need any man's money. Furthermore, she enjoyed what she was doing and the friendships that came her way. She could afford to wait for the right man.

Maria's eyes met hers in a searching gaze. Anne started. Maria smiled, as if discerning the thoughts Paulo had prompted. Anne asked herself, was she missing something? A vague, floating distress troubled her. She had witnessed the caresses, the gentle teasing, the close attention between her mother and her stepfather Antoine. Their love carried them through hardships, drew them out of loneliness. Anne glanced sideways at Harriet sitting next to her. The young woman had recently begun to blossom. A blush shone on her cheeks, a certain light in her eyes. A young man had come into her life.

Harriet met her glance, leaned toward her, and whispered, "Why don't you take a lover?"

"For one thing…," Anne broke off for a moment, then continued softly, "the men who have offered themselves thus far seem keener on their own pleasure than on mine." She could have added that she'd learned from her mother to tie love to marriage. Now it was hard to separate them.

The two men, becoming aware the women were not paying attention to them, stopped their banter. Harriet seized the opportunity to mention Jack Roach—he had been seen gambling heavily. No one knew for certain where his money came from. Harriet had heard he bought smuggled goods on the West Country coast and sold them in London.

Anne chuckled, "If he tries to fence a chamber pot, he'll think of me."

Harriet glanced nervously at her friend. "Annie, be careful. Roach is vicious."

Anne patted Harriet's hand. "Thanks for the warning, I can handle him." She paused, staring into her glass. "I'm also thinking of another line of work. When I begin swinging chamber pots, it's time for a change."

"You started out with your father, didn't you. I heard you were partners."

"Stepfather, really. But you're right. I call him father. My real father, Henri, died in a hunting accident when I was a baby. My grandparents say I take after him, their only child."

Anne looked inward, wistfully recalling his image in a portrait. A tall blond young man in riding clothes. She let the image slip away, then turned again to Harriet. "So, I'm fortunate to have had Antoine raise me. A sunny, cheerful man. Kind and encouraging. He trained me as a child on the rope and the wire, while my mother taught me puppetry and to sing and dance. At ten, I joined Antoine on the slack rope. By thirteen, I was in his tumbling act and learning his other tricks."

Anne's mind drifted back ten years. For a few moments she was on stage again at the Vauxhall in London, precariously balanced in a handstand on his upraised arms. He had winked at her, then smiled broadly. As the vision faded, Anne grew pensive. "Antoine moved to Paris a few years ago. At the time, I thought I might enjoy working alone. And I have, most of the time. But I miss him. We still keep in touch. He always sends a greeting on my birthday in August, except this year he seems to have forgotten."

Leaving her glass on the table, she walked to the window and stared out into the murk of the night. She was silent for a few moments, then sighed. Harriet joined her and put a hand on her shoulder. "His note may have been lost in the mail," she said brightly. "It might still turn up."

Anne thanked her with a wan smile. "I'm wondering if he's all right. I don't think he's very happy in Paris."

They returned to the table where their friends were signing one another's playbills from the last performance. Harriet picked one up. "Mademoiselle Cartier, the famous slack-rope artist from Paris," read Harriet aloud. She glanced quizzically at Anne. "How French are you?"

Anne laughed. "French enough, I guess! And I've been to Paris." She explained that the manager had invented the title, thinking it would add a touch of distinction to her act. She was born in England, as were her parents. Her Protestant grandparents had fled from persecution in Normandy. At home she had spoken French as well as English. "And when I was young," she said, fingering her glass fondly, "I spent summers in France with my mother and Antoine acting in the garden theater of a noble family."

When everyone had signed the playbills, a cry went up for a second bottle of wine.

"It's on me," Anne said buoyantly. "I've just found new employment." She shook her mane of hair, letting it fall over her shoulders like a stream of gold in the soft candlelight. Her friends filled their glasses and gathered around her, drinking to her good fortune.

"Who are you going to work for?" Harriet asked.

"Mr. Braidwood, an elderly Scot, who recently moved his school for the deaf from Edinburgh to Hackney, about a mile east of here. I'm helping teach deaf children to speak. He's been training me in some of his techniques—the simple ones at first."

"He's much respected. You are fortunate."

Anne was surprised. "Have you heard of him?"

"I've met him—my parents live in Hackney." She hesitated before continuing. "I'm frankly amazed he'd hire anyone outside his family. He keeps his techniques to himself and his son."

"That's true. But I've promised not to steal his secrets and open up a rival school. He wants me to tutor his younger students when they are sick or away from the school, so they don't become discouraged or lose their speaking skills."

"But why would you want to leave the theater for *that* kind of work?"

"I've been thinking hard about it." She fell silent for a few moments, absently swirling the wine in her glass. "After almost twenty years of theater, I feel a need to do something different and worthwhile. Not just entertain people, but help better their lives." A note of self-doubt crept into her voice. She glanced at her friend. "I'm not sure I've said this as well as I'd wish."

"Don't worry! As an actress, you've learned how to delight people. You'll be an excellent teacher."

Anne shrugged her shoulders. "At least I want to try." She paused. "I enjoy puppetry with children, especially Braidwood's pupils. Two of them, Benjamin and Sarah Brown, have attached themselves to me, watching my lips like a pair of cats staring at a canary. They can speak a little already, and every word they learn gives them pleasure. I'll soon have them taking simple parts in a play."

Harriet took her hand. "You are off to a good start."

"I hope so," Anne said with more assurance than she felt. "I can imagine teaching deaf children for the rest of my life, long after I'd have to give up the slack rope."

As a distant clock struck midnight, Anne finished her wine, got up from the table, and put on her cloak. Harriet drew her aside at the door. "Annie, I'm worried. Jack Roach was loitering outside the theater this evening with a couple of his cronies. Don't go alone—it's late. Let Louis walk you home. He'd love to."

"That's the problem. I don't want to encourage him."

"Then stay the night with me."

"Thanks, Harriet, for the offer." She embraced her friend, then turned to leave. "But the new horse patrol has made the village streets safer." She slashed the air with her heavy, steel-pointed walking stick. "This should keep Roach at a good distance." She stood erect, framed in the open doorway, and waved farewell.

Chapter 3

Parody of Justice

The lights grew faint, the voices and music softer, as Anne put the inn behind her. She felt light-headed from the wine. The good company of friends and her favorable prospects at Mr. Braidwood's institute buoyed her up.

Tapping the pavement with her stick, she started briskly up St. John's Street, passing darkened shops. At New Road she waved to the horse patrol, a pair of coarse-looking men, pistols in their saddle holsters, cutlasses in their scabbards. Near the end of their nightly circuit, Anne thought. They were late, past midnight, and they slumped in the saddle. She was grateful they kept the main roads clear of highwaymen.

At the White Lion Inn in the High Street, the publican held up a lantern and showed his last patrons out the door. They waved back to him, then disappeared into lanes so dark and narrow Anne imagined they had mysteriously walked through solid walls.

The marketplace was deserted except for cats on their nightly prowl, poking into piles of refuse, darting after mice among the stalls. But it was already Tuesday, a market day, and in a few hours the place would bustle. Prosperous villagers would shop at the stalls for duck and cheese, ale and porter, fresh baked bread, and whatever else they needed for a fine dinner on forthcoming Michaelmas Day. On past market days, Anne had seen rough men from the country urge on their fighting cocks while others boxed or wrestled one another until bloody. With a shudder she recalled women and children throwing rotten fruit at some poor wretch in the pillory.

As Anne approached St. Mary's, the parish church in the Upper Street, she shoved the evils of the marketplace out of her mind and thanked God for her blessings. Last Sunday, she had met Mr. Newton, the vicar, a large man with a barrel chest, a square ruddy face, thick silver hair, and a deep, powerful voice that reached easily to the back of the church. She had lingered inside until the congregation left, then told him of her puppetry at Braidwood's institute.

The vicar had listened intently and had seemed pleased. For he had a personal stake in her success. She had earlier mentioned to him her desire for new employment. Aware that Braidwood, a frail man, needed help, the vicar had pressed him to take on Anne. Braidwood had at first been reluctant, preferring a kinsman. But none was suitable.

Newton had argued Anne could quickly be useful. After all, she was an actress, half-way to learning how to teach the deaf, who rely on visual cues and facial expressions. Finally, Braidwood had agreed. Newton had then persuaded Anne this was honorable, godly work, and she could do it full tilt in the winter season while Sadler's Wells was closed.

Thinking of Newton comforted her now as she walked past the church. But the reassurance of his voice faded as the building disappeared in the darkness. She continued a short distance in the Upper Street, then turned right into Cross Street. Not a person in sight. Not a sound from the shuttered cottages along the way. A rat scurried in front of her. She stumbled, recovered her balance, then drew in her cloak against the damp autumn air. At the east edge of the village, she glanced up at the sky. Wispy clouds hung low like wraiths, shrouding a pale moon.

The glow of the wine was wearing off. She grew uneasy in her mind. Harriet's inquiry about Antoine Dubois had sown a seed of anxiety. His image surfaced now, his eyes dark and somber, his hands raised palms upward. He appeared to need her. She couldn't guess why. He was not one to complain. She supposed he hadn't found a good situation. But he could cope with that. He always expected a turn for the better. Something else was wrong that he hadn't mentioned in his letters.

A dog barking in the distance broke the eerie silence. At least one of God's creatures was up and about, she thought; let him be gentle. She quickened her steps, her boots echoing on the cobbled pavement. Spying the humped roof of her rented cottage, she let out a breath of relief and turned onto a dirt path. On the left, a hedge's wall of shadows lined the way to her door. At gaps between the bushes, thin rays of light from the neighbor's porch lantern shafted through the darkness.

Suddenly, midway on the path, a large figure leaped out in front of her. A ray from the lantern revealed a familiar face, jaw outthrust, brow knotted with wrath.

"Bitch! Here's a lesson you'll never forget." Jack Roach swung a thick fist at her face.

She ducked beneath his arm, shoved her stick between his legs and lifted it with all her might. Roach fell to the ground, screaming and writhing and clutching his groin.

As she straightened up, she sensed a man charging toward her from the right. Swinging her stick blindly, she felt it slashing flesh and heard a shriek of pain. Someone rushed up from behind, reeking of tobacco. But before she could turn, he applied a powerful choke hold on her neck. She tore futilely at his arm. Her knees gave way. She couldn't breathe.

Tom Atkinson had been sitting quietly on a bench in front of his house, letting the cool night breeze bathe his face. He had dozed off. Suddenly, sounds of violence woke him. He scurried toward the cottage he rented to the French actress and peered through the hedge. As lights went on in nearby houses, he saw a large man on the ground moaning. A companion staggered about, holding a bloody kerchief to his face, while a thickset man bent over a woman. She lay on her back on the path to the cottage. The man pulled a flask from his pocket, forced open the woman's mouth, poured in several drafts and sprinkled more on her clothes.

Tom could smell gin. Sensed evil going on. What should he do? He was old and sickly, no match for the thickset man. And who was the woman? His neighbor? He couldn't be sure. Better not get involved yet. Let the watchmen sort it out. He crouched down and waited.

Meanwhile, other neighbors had been aroused and were shouting. Within minutes, three watchmen arrived, carrying lanterns and staves. "She attacked Roach," said the thickset man, "and we tried to help him." He went on about Roach wanting sex, a quarrel over the terms and her unprovoked assault on him. "She's Anne Cartier, the Frenchie from Sadler's Wells. You can smell the drink on her." He kicked her with the toe of his boot. "Take her to the jail to sober up. The magistrate can deal with her in the morning."

Atkinson gasped at the name Roach. The bully everyone feared. Something terrible was happening to Miss Cartier. Roach had spread his money freely among the watchmen. Two of them roughly picked her up and carried her away.

While the third watchman was inspecting the scene in the light of his lamp, Tom Atkinson left his hiding place unnoticed and introduced himself.

"Did you see anything?" the watchman asked, lowering his voice to a threat.

"Just heard a racket and saw scuffling in the dark," Atkinson replied cautiously. "What happened?"

"The woman who lives here, the saucy French actress, got drunk and attacked Mr. Roach and a friend. We'll have none of that in Islington." He waved Atkinson away with a curt gesture.

Stunned, his heart pounding, Atkinson slunk back to his cottage, woke his wife and told her what had happened. They sat hunched over the kitchen table, the windows shuttered, the doors bolted and barred. A few embers glowed in the hearth, a single candle threw a fitful light from the mantel.

"Miss Cartier attacked three men twice her size?" Winifrid Atkinson shook her head. "Jack Roach is the villain in this piece." Her brow furrowed in vexation. "We should help her. She's been good to us—carries my groceries from the market. Pays the rent on time. We couldn't ask for a better tenant."

Her husband wrung his hands. "What can we do? The police have her now. She's probably best in jail. Roach and his men are out there in the dark, mad as hornets. Probably keeping an eye on us too. They may suspect I saw something. We'd better stay home."

Winifrid sighed, then pushed her chair back to rise. "We'll have to wait till it's safe to go out in the morning." She rubbed the back of her neck. "Maybe the magistrate will set her free. If he doesn't…, Mr. Newton should be told."

Anne awoke on a bed of straw, nauseous, her head splitting. She raised herself on one arm and looked about. "Where am I?" she wondered aloud, as the first tingling of fear reached her brain. The room was dark. A thin ray of light shafted through a small high window. It must be morning. Her bed lay on an earthen floor near a wooden door. The stench of urine, unwashed bodies, and moldering plaster wafted through the room. She turned toward the wall and retched violently.

What had happened? she asked herself. She lay still on the straw, trying to recall the evening before. It came back slowly. Roach's fist, the shadowy figure lunging at her, the stench of tobacco, the choking. Her neck was sore and she felt pain in her ribs. So, she had been knocked out and brought to this place. But by whom? Was she Roach's prisoner?

She heard a rustling sound. A large shape moved on the opposite side of the room, and then another under the window, and a third even closer. They seemed to be crawling toward her. She sat up, ignoring her headache, and crouched facing them, her back to the wall.

Like curious animals, three women clothed in rags, hair unkempt, their bodies thin and stinking, drew to within a few feet of Anne. One appeared to be young, the other two middle-aged.

"Who are you?" Anne asked in a whisper, the strongest voice she could muster.

The two older women began to babble through toothless gums. Demented, Anne thought. But the younger one appeared sane. Anne turned to her and repeated the question.

"I'm Sarah Parsons, the carter's daughter."

In the next few minutes Anne learned she was in a room of the parish workhouse with persons whom the magistrate had decided to lock up. Sarah was a cripple and a compulsive thief, cast out of her family. The older women were lunatics with no one to care for them.

"Meg looks after us," said Sarah. "She's coming."

A pair of eyes appeared at the barred opening in the door, keys rattled in the lock and a tall, stout woman entered.

"Here's breakfast, girls." She put three small bowls of porridge and some chunks of bread on a rough wooden table to the left of the entrance. "And you," she said, pointing at Anne, "are the saucy actress from Sadler's Wells. The magistrate will see *you* in an hour." She turned away and put her hand on the latch.

"Wait!" Anne cried. "What does he want with me? What's going on?"

"You'll find out soon enough, slut." The door slammed behind her. The three women crawled away toward their bowls.

Anne staggered to her feet, so dizzy she had to lean against the wall. "Got to get help," she muttered to herself, then thought of Harriet, Mr. Braidwood, Mr. Newton. She looked frantically around the room. There was no way to reach them. No way out.

Anne was still leaning against the wall when Meg returned, this time with two women as stout as herself. "I want to contact a friend," Anne exclaimed. "You can't hold me here."

Meg ignored her. "Hold out your arms."

Unthinking, Anne did as she was told. With a practiced gesture Meg snapped on a pair of manacles. Her two companions dragged Anne out of the room, through the yard of King William's Inn, an ancient, half-timbered building, then up a few steps and into a "courtroom" rigged up in the inn's banquet hall. At the far end on a dais sat a black-robed, white-wigged justice of the peace, in front of him a clerk, and to his right the plaintiffs, Jack Roach and his wounded companion. Their supporters sat together on wooden benches to the left. A few more men and women stood on either side of the entrance and watched, mouths agape. Anne recognized Winifrid Atkinson behind a pillar, pale and frightened, out of Roach's sight. Meg jerked Anne forward and made her stand before the judge. She recognized him and her heart sank.

The man in black was the Honorable Thomas Hammer, commander of the local militia and a wealthy landowner. Beneath the wig on his long, narrow head were a pair of thick black eyebrows, a great hawk nose, and a wide clean-shaven jaw. He surveyed the courtroom with cold, shifty, close-set eyes. An unpaid magistrate dispensing local justice for the Crown, he was chosen by the lord lieutenant of Middlesex County from among rich country gentlemen of the area. He sought the support of common folk with generous portions of ale and such official favors as lay in his power.

Anne had heard that Hammer knew little of the law and cared less for its dignity. He had many enemies, but they could not unseat him. Within the wide limits of his discretionary power over minor offenses, he consulted his own advantage and that of his friends and did what harm he could to those in his disfavor. He was distant kin to Roach and, as some suspected, a blind partner in his business enterprises. She noticed the two men exchanging knowing glances as she approached the bar.

The clerk rose to call the court to order but was stopped with his mouth half-open by the crash of Hammer's gavel. "Let's get on with it," shouted the judge. "Every fool knows we're in session." He glanced down at the clerk. "Read the charges."

The clerk adjusted his spectacles and read Roach's rambling account of the clash by Anne's cottage. The justice frowned at the mention of Anne's public drunkenness, lewd solicitation, and battery. Roach's companion, also pressing a charge of battery, removed a bandage from his face and pointed to a deep, jagged wound from ear to mouth.

"What say you to these charges?" roared Hammer, staring fiercely at Anne.

She replied in a strong, steady voice. "Innocent, your honor." As she tried to tell her story, however, she was heckled by Roach and his clique and cut short by Hammer's gavel. The room was bedlam until Anne stopped speaking, drew herself up erect and fixed the magistrate with a withering gaze.

For a moment he fumbled with the gavel, then halted the tumult with a simple wave of his hand. "What do you want?" he asked.

She drew a deep breath. "Postpone this trial until my lawyer can investigate last night's events and call witnesses in my defense."

Another uproar broke out. The gavel pounded furiously. Hammer leaned forward, speaking softly as if addressing a naughty child. "My dear, if you need a lawyer, you shall have one." He gestured to a young man standing in the rear of the room. "Get Boomer, the notary. You'll know where to find him." A roar of laughter broke out among Roach's men.

The young man returned a few minutes later with a bent, bleary-eyed, middle-aged man. He tottered through the court-room in a shabby food-stained coat, pulling up soiled breeches.

"He's drunk," Anne shouted, glaring at Hammer. "I demand my own solicitor, Edward Barnstaple of Jermyn Street, London!"

More hoots and shouts. The gavel pounded out enough silence for Hammer to be heard. "Drunk or sober, Boomer's the best lawyer in Britain." Hammer motioned for the man to approach. A hurried, whispered conference. Boomer shuffled to his seat.

Hammer called out to him. "Sir, how plead you for your client?"

Boomer rose, took a step toward Anne, and cocked his ear.

"Innocent!" she shouted.

He returned to the bar, glanced anxiously at Roach and then at Hammer. "Your honor...," Boomer stammered helplessly. Beads of sweat gathered on his forehead, his voice faded. He dropped down on a nearby bench, shaking violently, unable to speak.

Pandemonium broke out. Anne shifted her weight from one leg to the other, studying tufts of hair growing out of Hammer's ears. He followed her eye, puzzled for a second, then tugged at his wig. He lifted his gavel and restored order again.

"I've heard enough."

Meg's women pulled Anne closer to the magistrate.

"Anne Cartier," he said, "you are herewith convicted of public drunkenness, lewd solicitation, and battery upon two gentle-men of this community." He looked around with a crooked grin on his face. "At noon today you shall be clipped, stripped, and whipped in the marketplace." He paused for a roar of coarse laughter. "Tender as we are to the ladies, we prescribe a soft lashing. Ten strokes with a smooth leather strap." He paused again to allow cries for more, then raised his hand for silence. "Ten's enough. Mr. Roach will apply them to your back." Huzzahs burst out from Roach's clique. Hammer leaned back, looking pleased with himself.

Anne nearly choked with rage, but she stood erect at the bar, outwardly ignoring the tumult. Her stoic posture gradually drew all eyes to her, and the noise died down.

Yielding to her unspoken demand and his own curiosity, Hammer asked if she had something to say.

"Yes, I do." She coolly surveyed the crowd and then looked Hammer in the eye. "This trial is a farce, a crime against the laws of England, and you, sir, are unworthy of your office." Hammer's gavel prevented her from saying more. Roach's men stamped their feet.

Over the din, Hammer screeched, "Contempt of court! Ten more lashes! And you'll hang till sundown!"

Anne paced the cell, jangling her manacles. She was alone. Waves of anger and fear churned in her mind. Was this a bad dream? She had heard of filthy prisons and corrupt judges but she couldn't believe this was happening to her. The stench of the place brought her back to harsh reality. Whatever happened, she told herself again and again, she would hold on to the truth of her innocence. Somehow, she would be vindicated.

As a distant bell struck the half-hour before noon, Meg and her two companions entered the room. "Time to change," she said grimly. "Take off your clothes." She searched the ring on her belt for the key to the manacles.

"No!" Anne crossed her arms defiantly.

"Then we'll tear them off." The three women quickly stripped her, pulled a thin linen skirt over her hips, tied a long halter top on her shoulders and a cord around her waist. Outside the workhouse, they secured her to a bench in a small cart pulled by a donkey. Across the yard Justice Hammer awaited them. Grinning, he raised a crude placard for Anne to see— FRENCH WHORE—and hung it around her neck. The procession set off for the scaffold. The magistrate led the way. His clerk followed, ringing a bell and calling out the court's verdict.

The marketplace was packed with country people, more raucous and excited than usual. In a round pit off to the left, a pair of mastiffs were tearing at each other's throats, saliva mixed with blood dripping from their jaws. Their partisans pressed up against the fence, shaking fists in the air, and urging on the dogs with their curses. To the right, Anne glimpsed a beggar sitting in the pillory, covered with filth.

Snatches of talk reached her as the cart drove through the crowd.

"I know them Frenchies," exclaimed a bald, sallow-faced journeyman in a gray woolen smock and worn leather breeches. "They're wild as alley cats. They'll scratch your eyes out."

"Right," agreed a loutish companion, glancing at Anne, "and she's probably a papist too."

She groaned inwardly and gritted her teeth.

In the center of the marketplace, amid a deafening din, Roach and Hammer called men to tables of free beer and ale, joints of roast beef, wheels of cheese, and freshly baked pies. Anne glanced to her left at a stall of flowers. Harriet Ware, a shopping bag on her arm, was staring with horror at the macabre scene. Their eyes met. Anne mouthed a silent cry for help. Harriet nodded cautiously, as if fearing recognition by Roach's men. She backed out of the crowd and disappeared down a lane.

At the far end of the marketplace stood the scaffold, a temporary platform with two posts supporting a bar between them. A crowd of men and women from the parish workhouses, factories, and nearby farms had gathered there, eagerly awaiting a rare spectacle—Anne being shamed and beaten. It seemed unreal, as if it were happening to someone else. She wanted to scream but the sound stuck in her throat.

At the twelfth stroke of the parish church bell the ritual of punishment began. She was suspended from the cross bar, her toes barely touching the platform. Hammer addressed the crowd like a carnival barker. "What have we here?" he bellowed, pointing to the sign hanging on Anne's chest.

"A French whore!" replied the crowd, clapping their hands.

"And how do good men of Islington deal with whores?" He held up a pair of shears.

"We clip them!" came a thunderous response.

With a flourish Hammer removed the pins from Anne's hair, letting it fall nearly to her waist, glistening in the sun. He gathered it tightly in his hand, then cut it. He held it up to the crowd like a golden trophy. A tear trickled down her cheek. Her lips quivered.

"Behold, whore's hair!" Roach's men whinnied and broke into raucous laughter.

When the crowd quieted, Hammer paced back and forth. He frowned, as if wrestling with a problem. Then he turned to the crowd.

"What do we do with whores who strike and slash gentlemen?"

"Strip and whip them!" roared the crowd.

Hammer beckoned to Roach and handed him the strap. He flourished it, leering broadly, while the magistrate walked up to strip Anne. Her jaw clenched, she pulled hard against the ropes binding her, cutting into her wrists, but they held her fast.

Suddenly, over Hammer's shoulder, she noticed a commotion, as if an enormous wedge were cleaving the crowd. Louis Fortier was plunging toward her, thrusting men left and right, his jaw set in a fierce scowl. In his wake came Mr. Newton in his black clerical suit and Mr. Braidwood, followed by Harriet Ware and Tom and Winifrid Atkinson. Over the crowd's confused babble, Newton's voice thundered again and again, each time louder. "This must stop!"

Hammer swung round from Anne. His eyes narrowed with fury as he recognized Newton. They had clashed before, Anne sensed. Roach pointed with his whip at the advancing vicar, rallying his men who gathered into a block, and tried to stop Fortier's forward thrust. Towering over the bullies, the strongman seized two of them by the hair and banged their heads together. They fell senseless to the ground. With a powerful shove, he scattered the rest like tenpins. Anne sensed Hammer's resolve weaken. He moved away without looking at her.

Approaching the scaffold, the vicar spoke to the magistrate in a low deliberate tone. "You'd better listen to me, Mr. Hammer, or you will certainly hear from the Lord Chancellor."

Hammer quickly surveyed the crowd, his brow furrowed. He might change his tune, Anne thought. Prior to Mr. Newton's intervention, the crowd had been aroused by Hammer's harangue into a common depraved enthusiasm to see her whipped. Now, the crowd broke up into small, confused groups, quarreling with one another. The magistrate shouted for order, but few paid him any heed. Most seemed fascinated or frightened by the French Hercules.

The vicar stepped up on a bench by the scaffold and faced the crowd. "Miss Cartier...," he pointed to Anne, "is a good Christian woman. Born in Britain. Baptized in the Church of England. Honorably employed by Mr. Braidwood of Hackney to teach the deaf. She's innocent of all charges. The victim of an unprovoked assault. At the least, like all of us, she deserves a fair trial."

To Anne's relief, the crowd began to quiet down and attend to the vicar, some of them nodding their heads. A tall gray-haired man in front remarked loudly, she didn't look like any whore he'd ever seen.

Roach's men gathered furtively around their leader, who had abandoned the platform. While Newton went on speaking, Roach looked to Hammer for a signal. None was given. Hammer stood rigid with frustrated anger, unable to speak or act. The vicar had seized the crowd's attention, and drawn in the merchants and their customers from the stalls, many of whom disliked the magistrate.

Roach and his men slipped away, while Newton laid out the affair, gesturing toward Anne, still tied to the crossbar, now more like a martyr than a criminal. He called Braidwood and the Atkinsons forward to testify on her behalf. In conclusion, Newton shook a clenched fist at Hammer and shouted, "Free her." The crowd stirred, then repeated after him, "Free her."

Newton spoke to Louis Fortier, who leaped onto the platform. He untied Anne's wrists and eased her down from the crossbar, releasing her slowly, as if he sensed her will to stand on her own feet. Harriet laid a cloak lightly over her shoulders. Anne leaned on her friend and said softly, "I was headstrong, I should have stayed with you." Harriet caressed her cheek and helped her off the platform to a bench nearby. Mr. Braidwood held a flask of brandy to her lips. She sipped, then pushed the flask aside.

Newton approached her. "Are you well?"

She nodded. "And eternally grateful!"

He threw a tactful glance at her cropped hair. "I wish we could have come earlier. But we needed to organize. It was risky to challenge Hammer in the public market. The crowd's reaction was hard to predict." The vicar exchanged glances with Braidwood. "We'll ask the Lord Chancellor to quash your conviction and deny Hammer a commission of the peace."

Newton leaned forward, his brow knitted with concern. "Roach, unfortunately, is still free. And angry. You must take care."

"I shall." She rose from the bench and embraced him.

Chapter 4

Chateau Beaumont, April 1786

A red lacquered carriage halted at Montrouge on the Orléans highway a few miles south of Paris. Its two black horses pawed the stony roadbed, rattling their harness. A simple coat of arms on the carriage door, a sword slashing a military cape, identified its owner and sole passenger, Colonel Paul de Saint-Martin. He stepped out of the cab and climbed up next to the coachman. The filth of the city was behind them. The colonel took a deep breath of fresh country air. Thin lines of stress faded from his face. The carriage turned left on the road to Chevilly, crossed the Bièvre River, drove north toward Villejuif, and stopped near the village of L'Hay.

The colonel pointed to a vine-covered sign on a post. "This is it, Chateau Beaumont." The coachman nodded, then cracked his whip. The carriage lurched through the open gate and rolled at an even pace down the graveled lane. The rhythmic crunching of wheels and hooves blended with the bird songs of spring. Through the thickening foliage of chestnut trees, the colonel glimpsed the large stone building ahead.

He shivered slightly in anticipation, as if coming home from long absence in a distant and alien land. His father had always been away at court or war. At his death in 1762, his debt-burdened widow sank into deep despondency. Only at Beaumont could young Paul find someone who cared for him: Aunt Marie,

Comtesse de Beaumont, his mother's younger sister. She had chosen his earliest tutors and had directed his moral instruction.

"Be worthy of your name," she had said, as he left for the military academy. Into his hand she had pressed a small book, its leather cover worn and stained. "De Berville's story of the Chevalier de Bayard. Your father's copy." Laying both hands on his shoulders, she had caught his eye. "Serve your king like Bayard, a gentle knight, without fear or reproach, regardless of the evil you encounter. And help the needy, like your namesake, Martin of Tours, who shared his cape with a beggar." A heavy charge to put on a trembling little boy. That was twenty-three years ago, but as clear in his mind as if yesterday.

Nearing the wide iron gates, the carriage slowed down. The curved wings of the chateau reached toward him like arms in welcome. For a few moments he was once again a first-year cadet, fleeing from merciless hazing at the academy. Older cadets had mocked his high principles. "Saint-Bayard," they called him and tried every imaginable trick to corrupt him. On his thirteenth birthday, when they put a prostitute in his bed, he had stolen a horse and escaped to Beaumont.

He had heard not a word of rebuke from his aunt. She negotiated his safe return to the academy, then taught him to win the affection and respect of his peers. "Excel in the military arts and submit to discipline," she had said, "but be your own person." He had grimly followed her advice, at great personal cost, as if all joy had been pressed out of his heart. The first year had been the worst. The following years had been tolerable only because he could retreat during vacations to Beaumont.

The carriage clattered across the cobblestones of the courtyard and halted in front of a porticoed entrance. A servant smiled in recognition, showed him into a reception room, and left in search of the comtesse. He drew his aunt's note from his pocket. An invitation to tea, urgent in tone. A curious message, he thought, wondering what might be troubling her.

Brushing specks of dust off his blue coat and its red cuffs and lapels, he glanced in a mirror. The reflected image startled him—the face of a stranger, with lonely, troubled eyes. He frowned. He had thought he was happy. With a sigh he looked down and inspected the polish on his boots. They shone. Even when visiting an indulgent aunt, he mused, one must be careful of appearances.

She entered as he finished grooming. He bowed to the tall, erect woman striding toward him. A light pink robe hung loosely over a paler muslin dress. They embraced. "It's been too long since my last visit," he said. He stepped back, holding her hands, and gazed at her. "You're as lovely as ever." Her finely etched brow, cheek, and jaw had resisted the ravages of time. Her gray hair was lightly powdered, her complexion clear. And her eyes! Cool gray-blue, discerning, and wise. A genuine jewel of her class, he thought, unlike so many paste imitations.

She returned his gaze. "You seem a little thinner," she remarked. "Are you taking care of yourself?"

He shrugged his shoulders. "Work takes its toll."

"True," she said, "and not only on the body."

He released her hands. "There are remedies—sport, music, and a few good friends."

She hesitated for a second, searching his face. "And women?"

"I measure them by your standard," he bowed slightly, "and, thus far, have found them wanting."

Shaking her head in mock denial, she took his arm. "Come with me to the picture gallery."

They walked between slender Ionic columns into a long room illumined by a soft, northern light filtering through tall windows. Marble busts of Diderot, Voltaire, and other enlightened authors favored by the comtesse stood on pedestals between the windows. A row of family portraits shared the opposite wall with paintings by Watteau, Boucher, and Chardin, hung with an eye for symmetry and balance.

His aunt suggested he might enjoy some quiet time with the collection. How considerate of her, he thought. This was a sacred place, evoking in him a reverence for his ancestors akin to the filial piety of Aeneas toward his father in ancient Rome. Comtesse Marie moved to the far end of the room, opened a cabinet and busied herself, rearranging small precious objects. He was grateful his aunt knew when to leave him alone, and not only in an art gallery. Other relatives badgered him to get married or to connect with influential persons at the royal court and advance his military career.

He was drawn, as many times before, to a portrait of his father in the uniform of a lieutenant-general of cavalry. The intrepid brow spoke of valor; the resolute chin, of decisive action; the proud lift of the head, of indomitable honor. The eyes...Paul wanted to find hidden in them a sign that his father had loved him. But, opaque as ever, they kept their secret. He sighed, then turned away.

He glanced at his aunt, who seemed concerned there was no longer any woman in his life. There had been one, a wife he had learned to love, delicate as a porcelain figurine. She had died in childbirth nine years ago, and the baby with her. His grief lingered, mocking his attempts to suppress it with forced marches and battles in America at the side of the colonists fighting the British.

He felt grief stirring again and sought to distract it, when his aunt caught his eye. He joined her at an excellent copy of Chardin's still-life painting, the *Rayfish*. A soft light from a window in the opposite wall brought out bright yellows, greens, and reds, subtly hidden in the artist's somber palette. The picture drew Paul into its illusion. He smelled the sea beast's oily scent.

His eyes strayed to the window. A worry crept into his mind. He glanced from window to window. They were secured by simple latches. "A professional thief could easily break in here," he said in gentle reproach, "though Chardin's pictures wouldn't interest him. Too difficult to market." He pointed toward an open cabinet. "But he'd surely pick up those gold and silver vessels and that ivory chess set."

"Must I put iron bars on the windows?" his aunt asked, hugging herself as if trapped. "The room would feel like a prison!"

"Strong grillwork and locks needn't be ugly," he replied dryly, adding he would send an architect to advise her.

Her face clouded with doubt. "Can't you get more men to protect our homes from burglars? Nothing seems safe here anymore."

"I've asked for another adjutant," he replied levelly, biting back a sharp retort. She had hit a sore nerve. Rich aristocrats paid no taxes but expected police protection night and day. "'Can't afford it,' Baron Breteuil told me. The thieving's worse in the city." He silently chided himself for the irritation he had felt even though he hadn't vented it. He bowed graciously and offered her his arm. Her eyes warmed. She nodded toward the door. Arm in arm, as if on review, they passed beneath the sightless gaze of their ancestors.

∞∞∞

Tea was ready in her study, a room with a view over a garden in the English style. Here, during the summers as a boy, he had fed the part of himself that was starved at the military academy. Shelves of gold-embossed, leather-bound books covered the walls from floor to ceiling, feasting the eyes as well as the mind. He passed his fingers lightly over Voltaire's *Candide* and Beccaria's *On Crimes and Punishments*. They had taught him to abhor torture and arbitrary arrest and to practice enlightened principles of criminal justice. On a library table stood the large world globe he had often explored. He had been to America in his imagination long before he reached its shores as a soldier.

Comtesse Marie led him through the room, spinning the globe as they passed. A vase of freshly cut daffodils from the garden beckoned them to a small round table set with fine Sèvres porcelain. He smiled with pleasure. Her impeccable taste had always lifted his spirits out of the vulgarity of military company. Servants in pale blue livery attended them, pouring from shining silver pots and offering pastry on silver trays engraved with the Beaumont coat-of-arms.

Having dismissed the servants, his aunt turned the conversation to his forthcoming trip to England. He admitted never having been there, but he felt prepared. He had mastered the language while serving with French forces in America during the recent war. During lulls in campaigning he spoke nothing but English, visiting the homes of American officers he had come to know. When the fighting ended at Yorktown, he was given custody of two captured British officers, Captains James Gordon and William Porter. They became his friends and then his teachers, claiming his English had taken on a colonial accent.

"I'll meet them in London," he said, as his aunt rose to fill their cups again. Looking up at her, he anticipated a question forming in her mind. "May I do something for you there?"

She replied slowly, as if weighing her words. "A painful errand, I fear. Do you recall the Dubois family?"

"I'm not sure I do."

"They were here before the war," she explained. "For several summers they entertained us and taught us English. Antoine Dubois was French. His wife Pauline, English, of French stock. She had a daughter, Anne, from a previous marriage." The comtesse smiled fondly. "Anne! A beautiful girl. Sweet and kind, like her mother. But stronger. Her acrobatics with Antoine were incredible."

Sipping from his cup, the colonel pictured slender limbs cartwheeling elegantly across a green summer lawn. Long blond hair whirling. Shrill, clashing music.

When the war came, his aunt continued, the Dubois family was in London. She lost contact with them. "After the war, I learned from Anne that her mother had died." A pained expression came over the comtesse's face. "Several months ago…" Her voice broke. "Several months ago in Paris, it appears that Antoine killed himself after murdering an actress he was living with."

Saint-Martin leaned forward and stroked her hand. "How shocking it must have been for you!" After a quiet moment he went on, searching his memory. "I recall the case; the city police handled it. At the time, I didn't connect the murder and suicide to the actor at Beaumont years ago."

In a strained voice the comtesse went on with her story. While in Paris recently, she had chanced to learn that the police had searched the city in vain for the actor's next of kin. They were too busy to inquire in England. "That's wrong, Paul," the comtesse said emphatically. She stared at her nephew. "Antoine's stepdaughter *needs* to know."

His aunt's visible distress touched Saint-Martin. He spoke softly. "Give me her last address. I'll start from there and perhaps put a notice in a London newspaper."

"I knew I could count on you." She cast a quick, brilliant smile, then lightly gathered the folds of her gown. "I've already written a message." She rose, picked up a letter on her desk, and handed it to him. "You may read it. I'm inviting Anne to visit me in Paris."

After scanning the letter, Saint-Martin looked up at his aunt. "Any instructions?"

"Use your best judgment about the young woman, whether to extend the invitation. One doesn't know what to expect after so many years." She regarded him quizzically. "You will have time for this, won't you?"

He frowned in mock reproach, then replied gently, "I'll make time."

After tea they walked to an outdoor theater in a clearing among oak trees, delicately crowned with the light green of spring. The slope of the ground formed a shallow amphitheater, enclosed by a low, semicircular stone balustrade. They passed between two stone maidens guarding the entrance—Thalia, the muse of comedy, and Terpsichore, the muse of dance and song—and walked down the center aisle.

"The Dubois family performed there," reminisced the comtesse, gesturing toward a closely trimmed sod stage framed by thick boxwood hedges.

"Tell me about them," the colonel asked as they sat down on a stone bench. He wondered why this family had so deeply touched his aunt.

Comtesse Marie reflected for a few moments, tenderness filling her eyes. "I knew Pauline best," she began. "She came from a Huguenot family that fled to England early in the century and later prospered in the manufacture of fine silver. A beautiful, lively woman, she was fluent in French and English and musically talented. And unconventional! For a few years she performed in London theaters. When Comte de Beaumont and I visited London in 1769, I inquired for someone to tutor me in English. Mrs. Dubois was recommended. She proved to be an excellent teacher and a charming guide to the city. My English improved remarkably. When the comte and I left London after a few months, I realized I didn't want to lose Pauline's companionship. The comte enjoyed her husband and her daughter in vaudeville. He agreed we would all benefit by having the Dubois at Chateau Beaumont for the summer. They came back every year for a decade. Pauline and I grew close. I could confide in her."

"Comtesse de Beaumont? Confide in an *entertainer*?" remarked Saint-Martin hesitantly, unable to grasp how these two women might have a meeting of minds.

She raised her hands in protest. "No *ordinary* entertainer, believe me! but a charming, cultivated lady. In public we acted out what people expected of us, as if on stage. Deference from her, a certain reserve from me. Between ourselves she was Pauline. I was Marie. Like sisters eight years apart. There was even...a family resemblance. Losing her was hard." She dabbed at her eyes.

Saint-Martin allowed her a quiet moment, then asked, "And what of her daughter, Anne?"

His aunt brightened. "I got to know her, riding together early in the morning at Chateau Beaumont. Impetuous. Took risks. She'd jump a stream that sensible riders would wade through. Still, she was a loving daughter. Devoted to Antoine. She liked nothing more than to perform with him. Pauline had educated her, trained her to act as well. She played Puck in the family's production of Shakespeare's *A Midsummer Night's Dream*."

Gazing at the stage, Saint-Martin recalled a willowy green-clad girl dashing through narrow passages in the boxwood, a bright red tassel whirling from her cap.

The comtesse smiled with amusement. "And Antoine was Bottom the Weaver."

"What kind of man *was* Dubois?"

Aunt Marie tapped her cheek with the tips of her fingers, then gazed inwardly, as if recapturing the man's image. "He had black curly hair and a well-formed, muscular body. A lively face, full of sunshine, and quick to smile. Never violent. I can't imagine he would kill himself or anyone else."

A summer face, thought Saint-Martin. How would Dubois look in life's winter weather? In love or war, even decent men sometimes acted like savages. On the other hand, the comtesse was a good judge of men, and she knew Dubois. Soon it was time for him to leave. At the door he assured her, "Before going to London, I'll look more closely at the case. I understand, however, all the evidence pointed to the man. He left behind a confession."

Alone in the carriage returning to Paris, lulled by the clippety-clop of hooves striking stone, Colonel Saint-Martin let his mind drift back to his youth, to the golden-hued summers at Beaumont. Young cousins and their friends were singing, dancing, playing blindman's buff on the lawn, picnicking in the garden. He felt a pang of regret. They had long since disappeared into the social niches he chose to avoid.

He looked lazily out the carriage window toward a setting sun. His nostalgia for the good times at Chateau Beaumont began to mix with a new, unbeckoned thought. A wraith-like, slender form glided gracefully past his mind's eye. "She would be in her late twenties now," he murmured, stroking his chin. "Curious. I can't remember her face." The carriage swayed rhythmically like an infant's cradle. He closed his eyes and saw, dancing toward him, a bright red tassel.

Chapter 5

Searching for Anne

London was bustling on a late Friday morning in a haze of smoke and spring mist. Tradesmen's carts and fashionable coaches packed Jermyn Street as Colonel Paul de Saint-Martin stepped out of a hackney cab. The driver tipped his hat and pointed to a narrow building with an elegant bay. A small engraved brass plaque on the wall quietly announced the ground floor tenant, Mr. Edward Barnstaple, Esq., Solicitor. Saint-Martin glanced at his watch. Fifteen minutes early. He sighed, he hated wasting time. But it was best to wait. He shouldn't give Barnstaple the impression he was eager. The open doors of St. James across the way caught his eye, calling him from the clamor of the street.

Once inside the church he felt his irritation vanish. A pale spring light slanted through the tall clear glass windows, illuminating the spacious room to a cool, soothing ambience. He sat in the back, let his eyes drift upward, and delighted in the richly ornamented, barrel-vaulted ceiling. Excellent plasterwork. He noted a fine limewood carving above the altar, a pelican feeding her young.

"By Grinling Gibbons," remarked the sexton, walking up the center aisle toward him with a mop and a pail in his hands. He had a ruddy, good-natured face.

The man stopped near Saint-Martin and gestured with the mop to a marble baptismal font, carved to the shape of a tree of life. "That's Gibbons' too." Beneath its branches, Eve tempted Adam with an apple while the serpent slithered up the trunk. The sexton nodded proudly at the sculpture. His eyes shifted to the visitor and narrowed with wary curiosity.

The colonel confessed he was French. This was his first visit to an English church. The sexton swiftly took his measure, then smiled kindly, and bade him welcome. "I'll leave you to your prayers," the man said, taking a fresh grip on the mop and pail. He was soon out of sight. A door closed and the church was quiet again.

This brief encounter gave a lift to Saint-Martin's spirit. Since his arrival in London, his days had been spent tediously seeking ways to curb traffic in stolen goods between England and France. He hadn't accomplished much. He learned that British magistrates cooperated poorly among themselves. Why should they do better with foreigners? The most he could hope for was an easier exchange of information between the two countries. He sighed softly. His adjutant, Georges Charpentier, was probably enjoying himself, refreshing his acquaintance with the city's underworld and flirting with buxom barmaids!

A door opened and the sexton reappeared, singing snatches of a hymn. The colonel smiled. The week in London had not been all drudgery. Captains Gordon and Porter, his former prisoners in America, had taken him to a concert almost every evening. And, on Saturday, they had joined the colonel's acquaintance, Mr. Thomas Jefferson, at the Drury Lane Theatre. The American diplomat was on a visit from his post in Paris.

That evening, Mrs. Siddons had taken on the role of Lady Macbeth. A memorable performance. She had played the part, not as a cruel, shrieking harridan—a common fault of the London stage, claimed Gordon—but as a woman of refined sensibility, driven mad by her tragic choice of violence.

The sexton walked through the church again. Moments later the bell tolled eleven. Saint-Martin shifted in his chair; he would wait a few more minutes. Locating Mrs. Dubois' daughter had proven more difficult than expected. He had privately engaged a Bow Street Runner. The search led to the office of Barnstaple, the solicitor who looked after Anne's affairs. In a curt note he had agreed to a meeting in his office, but he had refused to reveal where she lived. Saint-Martin asked himself, why keep that secret? Could she be in prison? God forbid! He rose from the chair and looked for a sanctuary lamp until he recalled he was in a Protestant church. He reverenced the altar anyway and waved to the sexton as he left.

The solicitor's office was small. Piles of books leaned precariously against one another on the floor. A clerk sat on a high stool at a desk by the only window. His pen scratched monotonously. Barnstaple received Saint-Martin with a cool, inquiring gaze, warming to him slowly as he discerned that the Frenchman was a cultivated person of high rank. The colonel, for his part, discovered the solicitor hid a canny mind behind a cherubic countenance. When the two men had settled into tall leather-covered chairs facing one another, Saint-Martin explained the purpose of his visit.

At the news of Antoine Dubois' death, the solicitor appeared shocked. He had known the man and liked him. He disclosed that his stepdaughter, Anne, was living with Mr. and Mrs. Thomas Brown, a wealthy Quaker family, at their country home near Wimbledon. "Their children are deaf," he offered, then added with smiling approval, "she's caring for them temporarily."

Barnstaple called the clerk off his perch and ordered tea, as if he had said enough about his client.

The lawyer's remarks, however, had merely piqued the colonel's curiosity. "Enlighten me, Sir, I had thought Miss Dubois was an actress."

"Cartier, my dear colonel. Anne Cartier. She has kept the name of her father, Henri Cartier, Mrs. Dubois' first husband." The solicitor explained that Miss Cartier, a gifted young woman, had excelled in a variety of theatrical professions, including vaudeville. Last September, having been persuaded of her talent for instructing deaf children, Mr. Thomas Braidwood had hired her to work in his institute at Hackney. Barnstaple's eyes grew bright with admiration. "She talks with her fingers as fast as an auctioneer's patter and the young people seem to understand."

"And what, may I ask, Sir, is her financial situation?"

The solicitor hesitated a fraction. "She lives modestly on what she earns and on income from her mother's legacy that I administer. Her paternal grandparents are also alive and helpful."

"From her name, I assume she's unmarried."

"That is true," said the solicitor as if embarrassed by his client's spinsterhood. "She's attractive and charming. Simply disinclined to marry until the right man appears."

Saint-Martin remembered she was in her late twenties. Surely, English women usually married at a much younger age. He shifted uneasily in his chair. The solicitor was holding back something about Miss Cartier. Granted, he was speaking to a stranger, but his manner seemed more guarded than one would expect even of a cautious solicitor. Saint-Martin left the office convinced he had better probe more deeply into Anne Cartier's life.

Georges Charpentier, Colonel Saint-Martin's right-hand man, sat at a small table in The Sussex, a chophouse on Jermyn Street. Noonday patrons crowded the long, narrow public room. Pink-faced waiters scurried between the tables, taking orders. Voices rose and fell. Dishes clattered. Huge trays of steaming food sailed by the Frenchman's nose, casting a rich aroma of boiled cabbage, roast beef, and spilt ale.

Waiting for the colonel, Georges eavesdropped on conversations nearby. It was an old vice he put to good use during investigations. In a short while he was amusing himself, silently mocking a blathering lawyer's solution to London's crime problem. More public hangings of thieves, the fool had proclaimed. On the back of a menu, the Frenchman rapidly sketched a caricature: first a gallows; then the lawyer hanging from it, his eyes looking toward Brest and Bordeaux and his long tongue lolling out; and finally, a caption, *Primus inter pares*, the first among equals.

When the Frenchman had enough of this sport, he leaned back in his chair and glanced into the mirror to his left. "Georges Charpentier," he said to himself, "you are a handsome devil!" He raised the arched brows above his lively blue eyes, brushed imaginary hair on his bald pate, and admired a pair of large, slightly pointed ears. Forty-five years old? He refused to believe it. Though short and thickset, he was still as agile as a cat. His broad mouth broke into an approving grin.

He turned in the other direction, toward the lunchtime crowd near the entrance. The colonel should come through the door soon. Georges pictured his superior's erect bearing, his level, unblinking gaze. Noble, every inch of him. He was the king's officer even out of uniform, provost of the Royal Highway Patrol for the Paris region. Georges lowered his eyes, studying odd patterns in the battered surface of the table, letting his mind drift back to the Seven Years War. He was with the colonel's father at Minden. August 1, 1759. A battlefield of dead and dying men under a pall of smoke, stinking of gunpowder, offal, and blood. General Saint-Martin lay bleeding beneath his horse. Died of his wounds three years later. Then the general's funeral. Young Paul, a slim lad, barely eleven, by the side of his pale, trembling mother.

"Such is life," Georges murmured softly. He steepled his fingers and turned another page in his memory. After the war, he'd been a trooper for a few years with the Royal Highway Patrol in Normandy, then in Paris. Finally, chief investigator for Antoine Raymond Sartine, Lieutenant-General of Police. Georges smiled with pride. Sartine! The *master* of detection. Nothing escaped his eye. Or his ear. He used to say, "Whenever you see three men speaking together, one of them is mine." Not precisely true, of course, but close enough to the mark.

A burly waiter interrupted Georges' musing. "Will you have a drink while you wait?"

Flashing his best smile, the genial Frenchman asked for an ale. Sartine had taught him to treat servants well. In a short while, the man returned and set a foaming pewter mug on the table. Georges pressed a penny into his hand.

Locking his fingers around the mug, Georges stared into the dark amber liquid, conjuring up Colonel Paul de Saint-Martin. Green as grass at the start three years ago. Provost! A post secured thanks to the reputation of his father and the good will of his distant uncle, Baron Breteuil, Minister for Paris.

Georges took a long draft from his mug, silently commending the English for their ale. He felt good. He had travelled over some rough patches in his life, but now fortune smiled on him. He lifted the mug in a salute to the colonel. Aristocrat, to be sure, but a fine man to work for. Respected subordinates and listened to them, worked hard, and learned fast. He gave Georges an office of his own and comfortable quarters in the provost's residence. And opportunities to earn commissions! They made a good team.

The lawyer holding forth at the nearby table raised an angry voice again above the din. A young waiter fled in confusion. Pity anyone who had to serve him, Georges thought. Behind that bluster hid a small, mean spirit. In comparison, Paul de Saint-Martin was a gem. An imperfect one, Georges granted, for the colonel took his privileges complacently. But he was high-minded and kind. Georges looked around the room, searching for his colonel's match. He found none until Saint-Martin himself came through the door.

"What have you learned from Barnstaple, Sir?" Georges asked, rising from the table. He pulled out a chair for his superior.

"Let's order first, then talk." The colonel looked at the luncheon crowd zestfully attacking heaped plates of food. "I'm starved."

"Here's the menu," said Georges.

The caricature caught Saint-Martin's eye. He stared, puzzled for a moment, then grinned. "Remarkable! Your verdict on the chef?"

Georges laughed with a glance toward the pompous lawyer. Saint-Martin followed the gesture, nodded, and chuckled.

Although the Frenchmen had not yet found anything on an English menu that they cared for, they ventured to order steak pies, Stilton cheese, and small beers. Over lunch, Saint-Martin summed up the impression he had gained of Anne Cartier. "Favorable thus far. But I want to know more about her before I extend an invitation from Comtesse Marie. Barnstaple's holding something back." For a few moments he studied his beer, then turned to his adjutant. "Inquire about Miss Cartier at Sadler's Wells, among her neighbors in Islington, and with Braidwood in Hackney."

While the colonel spoke, Georges leaned forward, attentive, taking up the scent. After a few questions, he pushed back his chair. "I'll find out by tomorrow what kind of woman we're dealing with." He rose to his feet and hurried out the door.

∾ ∾ ∾

Late the next afternoon, as a light drizzle fell upon the city, Colonel Saint-Martin walked from the French Embassy, where he was staying, into Saint James' Park. He badly needed exercise. To his surprise, he found much of the park laid out like a French formal garden, but it was poorly tended. Cattle grazed in a clearing. Brush grew up beneath the tall elms, blocking his view and offering cover to mischief makers. In the evening, he had heard, the park turned into a swarming hive of soldiers and prostitutes.

At the long east-west canal, where he planned to meet Charpentier, his pace quickened. As had his interest in Anne Cartier. Working for the Quaker family spoke well for her virtue. During the war, he had met members of that sect in Philadelphia and had found them to be serious-minded and dependable. Barnstaple's reticence in her regard was perhaps only a lawyer's caution.

The colonel circled the canal once with these thoughts before spying the square figure of Charpentier hurrying toward him. As they met, the adjutant's brow creased with concern. "Sir, I've learned from the young lady's neighbors...she's been in a bit of trouble."

Saint-Martin felt his heart sink. "What's she done?" They set out together on the canal path.

The adjutant's eyes twinkled. "She whacked a gentleman named Jack Roach with a chamberpot."

"What?" the colonel exclaimed, irritated at what seemed misplaced humor. Taking the hint with aplomb, Georges put on a sober face and recounted Miss Cartier's expulsion of Roach from Sadler's Wells.

"More courage than sense," said Saint-Martin dryly, wondering if the rashness of her act was typical. Then noting his adjutant's eyes widen eagerly, he asked, "There's more to the story?"

"Indeed. Roach became annoyed." Georges mimicked the bully, scowling fiercely and shaking his fist. "One night he attacked her at the entrance to her cottage near the theater. She shoved her stick between his legs and almost neutered him! Down he went, howling."

"Quick-witted," remarked the colonel, feeling a tinge of admiration.

"Unfortunately, Sir, Roach's two companions leaped at Miss Cartier. She slashed one of them, but the other knocked her out and planted liquor on her." In graphic detail Georges described her ordeal in the prison and the courtroom and on the scaffold. His face mirrored the horror.

Saint-Martin's outward composure threatened to crack. Raw images from the past were seeping into his mind. The grim, gray barracks of the military academy. The flickering light of candles. A shy young cadet, his only friend, awakened at night by older boys, gagged, stripped, and whipped. Sweating with fear, Paul was made to look on, his arms pinned behind his back, his head held in a vise-like grip. "Watch, or you're next," one of them hissed. They laughed at his tears.

The cadet's suffering began to bleed into the story of Anne Cartier. The colonel stared sightlessly at the ground. He heard the crowd taunting: "French whore! Strip her!" The urge to strike out nearly overwhelmed him. He clenched his fists, grit his teeth.

Unaware of Saint-Martin's agitation, Georges went on with his story. "Roach might have planned originally to knock Miss Cartier unconscious, carry her away, torture, and kill her. The body would never have been found, and he couldn't be blamed. Her resistance forced Roach and Hammer to improvise a scheme for her trial and public punishment. According to Harriet Ware, the town first learned a woman was going to be whipped after the market opened on Tuesday morning."

Saint-Martin had flinched at the word "kill." He stopped in his tracks and glared at his adjutant. "If you're right, then Miss Cartier's life is still in danger."

"Unfortunately. They say Roach always gets even."

Drawing a deep breath Saint-Martin forced himself to recall that, by her solicitor's account, Miss Cartier was now alive and well. He gazed out over the water's calm surface to quiet the unease stirring within him. After a few moments, he resumed the walk. "Who saved her?" he asked.

"Some brave good people. She was lucky!" Georges told the story of her rescue in full, vivid detail. His report concluded as they reached the west end of the canal. Saint-Martin pointed to the right and set off at a brisk pace down the avenue that led to the Queen's Garden.

"What do you make of all this, Georges?"

His adjutant remained silent for several moments, staring into the mist, his brow furrowed in thought. When he finally spoke, he carefully measured his words. "Miss Cartier put herself in harm's way, walking home alone at night when she knew Roach was lurking about."

Saint-Martin didn't dare say what had crept into his mind. Was this violence between Miss Cartier and Jack Roach a bizarre lovers' quarrel? He slowed the pace of the walk, mulling over the idea. "Georges," he asked, filtering anxiety out of his voice, "do you think Miss Cartier might have given Roach any reason to believe she welcomed his advances?"

"Oh, no!" The adjutant protested vigorously. "People at the theater insist she never sold herself to anyone, least of all to him. He's alley scum."

The colonel breathed more easily, as if a weight had been lifted from his shoulders. Extending Aunt Marie's invitation to this young woman seemed feasible now. "Did you find out anything about Mr. Roach?"

"A nasty bug, Jack Roach!" Georges paused, savoring the pun. "I met a former clerk from Hammer's court in Islington." He grinned. "Cost me a pint of ale but he bent my ear for an hour." The man had said Roach was involved with a ring dealing in contraband, one of several persons suspected of receiving gold, silver, and jewels stolen in France. He also informed for corrupt magistrates or paid them off. They protected him.

Saint-Martin drew a deep breath and lengthened his stride, forcing Georges nearly to a trot. He glanced at the older man, smiled indulgently, and slowed down. "Learn what you can about Mr. Roach." The colonel looked into the distance, pursing his lips. "I have some pointed questions for Solicitor Barnstaple."

Saint-Martin found the solicitor at his office the next day, sitting calmly behind his desk, his hands clasped over his ample paunch, a benign expression on his face. The French visitor's investigation of his client Anne Cartier did not perturb him. "It was better you learned about her tribulations by yourself rather than from me." With a warning glint in his eye the solicitor added, "Since Jack Roach is at large, I must take care what I reveal about Miss Cartier."

He leaned forward and met Saint-Martin's eye. "You will not be surprised to hear I have investigated you. The French king's representatives in London insist you are indeed Colonel Paul de Saint-Martin and, what's more, commander of the Royal Highway Patrol for the region surrounding Paris." He leaned back in his chair, arms crossed over his chest. "What can I do for you?"

"We understand one another," replied Saint-Martin. "Perhaps you could tell me, sir, how Miss Cartier has coped with the punishment she received from Justice Hammer and Mr. Roach."

Barnstaple smiled brightly. "She's a resilient young lady. With treatment from Braidwood's physician, she recovered quickly from the shock she had received. As her health returned, however, she became very angry." An ironic tone slipped into Barnstaple's voice. "This was her first personal contact with English criminal justice. She had no idea how venal and cruel it could be. She's a proud woman. The shame was almost more than she could bear." He sighed heavily. "Then depression set in. She realized how vulnerable she was to abuse by rich and powerful men."

"How are her spirits now?" asked Saint-Martin, his chest tightening with alarm.

"Oh, excellent," Barnstaple replied, a bit too quickly. "Her teaching at the Braidwood Institute has been a tonic. The children leave her little time to brood." He explained that the Brown family were caring people. They treated her more like one of the family than a servant, giving her a stall in the stable for her horse. "Riding's good for the spirits," he added with a wink. "Sound body, sound mind."

"Where's Roach?" the colonel asked pointedly. Barnstaple's words were too cheerful. With her assailant at large, Miss Cartier's situation appeared precarious.

The solicitor shifted his weight, adjusting to an uncomfortable issue. He explained the conviction in Islington had been set aside and Hammer deprived of his commission. But Roach and his men were still moving about, "slippery as eels and dangerous as sharks." He grimaced. "Very unpleasant business."

Saint-Martin doggedly pursued the issue. "Has Roach threatened her recently?"

"No," replied Barnstaple. "I would expect him to wait until a half-year or so has passed, hoping that Miss Cartier, and those who care for her, will relax their vigilance. You can be sure Roach has not forgotten! She felled him twice; he hasn't evened the score yet." His lips twisted with irony. "Now would be the right time, let us say, for Miss Cartier to suffer a serious, or even fatal accident. It would hardly be noticed. London is such a crowded and violent place."

"It might be prudent for Miss Cartier to live abroad for a while," suggested Saint-Martin, reaching into his pocket for his aunt's invitation. "She could perhaps become involved in our school for the deaf in Paris. Its director, the priest Charles-Michel, Abbé de l'Épée, has invented a new language for the deaf, trains them for useful occupations. I'm sure Braidwood's heard of him. Miss Cartier could hone skills to bring back later to England." As he handed over the letter, he added: "My aunt, Comtesse Marie de Beaumont, could introduce her to the abbé. She's one of his patrons."

The solicitor read the invitation with care, then returned it. "Braidwood might regard Abbé de l'Épée as a rival," he said cautiously. "Professional jealousy, you know. But, he might also like to learn from Miss Cartier what the abbé is doing for the deaf. Yes, Braidwood would probably write for her." Fortunately, the solicitor explained, the expense of the trip was within her means. Her grandparents, pleased that she would be safe and decently employed, would also help her.

The two men then came to an agreement. Saint-Martin would carry a letter from Barnstaple to Miss Cartier, commending the colonel and his proposal. While Saint-Martin whiled away a few minutes with a cup of tea and *The Gentleman's Magazine*, the solicitor dictated the letter, read it through and signed it. "There you are," he said as he handed it over to the colonel. "That should persuade her."

Barnstaple was indeed a fine fellow! thought Saint-Martin as he left the solicitor's office, pleased with the accommodation they had reached. But before he had taken more than a few steps into the street, he recalled with a start his next task. He must inform the young lady of Antoine Dubois' violent death.

Chapter 6

An Invitation

Under a cloudless sky, two horsemen rode through the lush green English countryside, singing a popular French tune, *Marlborough se va-t-en guerre*, "Marlborough is on his way to war." With his right arm Colonel Saint-Martin vigorously beat the tempo as if he were leading the Sun King, Louis XIV's, army against the great English commander. Charpentier joined in the ghostly chorus, *Il ne se reviendra, il ne se reviendra*, "And he shall not return."

The colonel and his adjutant knew that John Churchill, Duke of Marlborough, had indeed returned victorious to Britain. But that didn't matter. They were enjoying the ride to Wimbledon. The colonel's friends, Gordon and Porter, had lent him a pair of high-spirited thoroughbreds, the finest in their stables.

It was noon when they drew near the Quaker family's country house, a large, square brick building sitting solidly on top of a low hill. At the near prospect of meeting Miss Cartier, a flutter of apprehension disturbed Saint-Martin's high spirits. He began to anticipate the pain she would feel upon hearing the news of her stepfather's death. How fragile was her recovery? he wondered. Could she deal with what he had to say? She and Dubois had seemed so fond of one another.

A servant met them at the entrance and went inside to announce their arrival. The master of the house, Mr. Thomas Brown, a tall, gentle man in plain brown breeches and white shirt, came to the door, a watchful look in his eye. Saint-Martin reassured the man, mentioning Barnstaple's name, then explained his mission. The Quaker listened with growing concern. "This will sorely test Miss Cartier. But I must call her." He glanced down at the colonel's riding boots. "You may wish to change to something more comfortable, while she makes herself ready to see you." He put Saint-Martin in the care of a servant and went looking for Miss Cartier. Georges left to tend to the horses and the saddlebags. They were prepared to stay overnight either with the Browns or at a nearby inn.

In a sitting room a short while later, Saint-Martin stared absently out a window at a meadow carpeted with spring flowers. Tiny beads of perspiration gathered on his upper lip. Had the incident in Islington scarred the young woman, broken her spirit? Footsteps, then a rustling gown sounded behind him. He turned, saw her, and felt a rush of pleasure. She stood in the doorway in a simple yellow muslin dress, head slightly inclined, eyes alive with curiosity.

He sensed she recognized him but wished him to make the first gesture. Bowing, he introduced himself. She smiled and walked toward him with uncommon grace and extended her hand. He kissed it, then drew back a step, taking in her appearance. She was no longer the puckish girl he had earlier known, but a self-assured young woman, lithe, and rather tall, with strong, expressive features. She bore no visible marks of her ordeal, other than the short cut of her golden hair. He breathed an inward sigh of relief.

"Colonel Saint-Martin, why...?" She gazed at him, her eyes perplexed. Finally she asked, "What brings you to Wimbledon?"

"I bear sad news," he replied. "Antoine Dubois is dead." With voice and gesture he tried to cushion the impact of his words, but still they shocked her. She shrank back as if struck. Her eyes widened with disbelief.

For a moment she was speechless, her mind struggling with what he had said. Then she glared at him, as if blaming the messenger. "That can't be," she said in a low, taut voice, clenching her fists. Her eyes left her visitor for a few moments, fixing on some inner vision. Then, her face reddening, she tossed her head. "It's not fair! Antoine was a good man, one who truly cared for me." She eased herself into a chair, dabbing her eyes with a small handkerchief. As she regained command of herself, she glanced at Saint-Martin. Her voice wavered, fighting with her pain. "My real father died when I was only a baby. I've never had any other father, only Antoine. I so wanted to see him, to talk to him again."

She fell into a heavy silence. Her brow furrowed with confusion. Searching for words, she stammered, "What happened to him?"

Saint-Martin felt bound to explain the circumstances of Lélia Laplante's murder and Dubois' unfathomable death, labelled suicide by the Parisian authorities. He spoke evenly, avoiding conjecture.

"He would *never* do that!" the young woman exclaimed at the mention of the murder. The color drained from her face. "Not Antoine! How horrible!" Abruptly gathering her skirt, she rose to her feet and gripped the back of a chair. Rigid, erect, she asked Saint-Martin to continue. The violence of Dubois' death made her grimace. At the end of the report, deep lines of doubt lingered on her forehead. "The police are all alike," she snapped. Her eyes locked on his. "They always blame the victim."

Saint-Martin felt insulted, but he understood her state of mind and responded calmly. "That was surely true in your case, and it might be true in his."

She was still for a few moments. Then she released her grip on the chair and breathed deeply. In the silence between them a clock ticked away minutes of grief and pain, until a quiet calm came over her face.

Meanwhile, Saint-Martin grew convinced his aunt would want to meet this young woman again. When Miss Cartier sat down and glanced expectantly at him, Saint-Martin sensed it was the right moment for the rest of his message. He reached for the valise he had left on a nearby table and handed her the letters from Barnstaple and Comtesse Marie. Reclining in a chair, he watched her grow absorbed in the reading. The hint of a smile softened the creases of anger at her mouth. Her fingers turning the pages were long and strong, her cheeks and forehead lightly tanned by wind and sun. Probably from frequent riding. No slave to fashion, he thought. The natural look was more to his taste than the garish facades of stylish Parisian women.

She looked up from the letters, smiling wanly. "This is generous of your aunt. I'll weigh her offer carefully. It would be a good way to learn more about Antoine's death." She rang for a servant and ordered glasses of a cool local cider. Settling back in her chair, she inquired politely about the health of the comtesse, changes at Chateau Beaumont, and the like. Her voice was low and no longer strained. His replies appeared to spark genuine interest. Her eyes brightened and cleared. She seemed intrigued with the prospect he laid before her.

"I remember the comtesse fondly," she said as the cider arrived. She thanked the servant, then poured for the colonel and herself. "She treated my parents with respect, even allowed Antoine to tease her." She smiled over her glass. "And he was so pleased when the comtesse showed interest in me. After riding early in the morning, we'd have hot chocolate in her room." She glanced at Saint-Martin, as if fearing her remarks had sounded naive.

"She also treated me to morning rides and chocolate," he remarked, putting her at ease with a reassuring smile. "And to uplifting conversation as well. What did you two talk about?"

"Sometimes we'd walk in the gallery and she'd explain the pictures to me. 'Chardin's narrow but honest,' she'd say. Or, 'Boucher's a charming old satyr.' We'd go out into the park. She'd tell stories about the important people she knew. I think the comtesse wanted to open my eyes to the world."

"She has opened mine as well," admitted the colonel, aware of a personal debt of gratitude to his aunt. "I'm sure I've heard many of those stories."

"Comtesse Marie also warned me about highborn men, some of them at least. Love was a game they played. When they came to her chateau, she hid the maids." Her eyes brightened briefly with humor, then shadowed. She shot him an enigmatic glance. "She helped me understand things."

Understand what? Saint-Martin wondered, then smiled. His aunt would have told Miss Cartier how to make her own way in a man's world. While she moved on to other memories of Chateau Beaumont, he lifted the glass to his lips, watching her over the rim while he sipped. Long-buried impressions surfaced in his mind. He had often watched her return from those morning rides, astride a glistening thoroughbred, her cheeks flushed with pleasure. She dismounted with ease, her body supple as a young willow. Her agility, her *grace* came mysteriously from within. He had felt an aching for her. But she was a commoner. His cousins called her the clown's daughter.

"May I pour again?" She was bending toward him, pitcher in hand, a fey look in her eye. She had noticed his distraction.

"I'm sorry," he replied penitently, "for a moment you carried me back to those summers at Chateau Beaumont." He raised his glass.

"To *A Midsummer Night's Dream* out in the park?" she asked while pouring the drink.

"Yes, indeed…," he replied, recalling with a stab of pain the last time he had seen her. Ten years ago. It was the morning he had signed the articles of betrothal to a cousin, a nondescript woman he hardly knew. Sick with self-loathing, he had come to Chateau Beaumont, pleased to find no one but the servants, and walked out into the park.

When he reached the theater, he saw Anne Cartier rehearsing with four of his young male cousins. He stepped back into the shade of a tree and watched. She was clad like a boy in red and green striped tights and shirt. Her body undulated sinuously as if moved by a wicked spirit. A perfect Puck! But the young men were acting from a different script, grabbing at her and chasing her through the boxwood entrances. Finally, they cornered her, then crept up to her like animals in heat.

For a moment he was paralyzed with horror. Was he to stand there and watch them rape her? What matter, his peers would have said; let the boys practice on the clown's daughter. He felt nauseous, but he mastered himself long enough to order the boys out. He recalled staring down at her in shame and despair, but he couldn't speak. He had left abruptly and retched behind a tree.

The polite clearing of a throat brought Saint-Martin back to the present. Behind her glass of cider, Miss Cartier was attempting to suppress a bemused smile. "Indeed, *A Midsummer*

Night's Dream," the colonel repeated hastily, then went on to reminisce about Shakespeare's play. While speaking, he studied her expression. Had she deliberately alluded to the painful incident in the park? No, she seemed pleased with his company. In her blue eyes he detected no reproach or resentment, only the lingering marks of grief for her stepfather.

Gazing at her over the gulf of those many years, he sensed there might be a way across. "Should you accept Comtesse Marie's invitation," he heard himself say, "we could travel to Paris together. My business in London will be finished in ten days. You are welcome to join me then."

His suggestion did not seem to shock her. "I'll think it over and give you an answer tomorrow," she replied, rising from her chair. "Meanwhile, Master Brown has said you are welcome to stay here for the night." She hesitated as if unsure how he would react, then continued, "The children have prepared an hour of entertainment for later in the afternoon. Please join us."

He bowed and said he'd be delighted to come. From the doorway he watched her beckon a servant for him. He watched her cross the hall, climb the stairs, turn, smile, and then disappear.

∾ ∾ ∾

The performance was to begin shortly after tea. Colonel Saint-Martin entered a long room with a high ceiling. On a platform at the far end stood a small puppet theater. Sunlight slanted onto its stage from tall windows in the south wall. The audience of a dozen friends and family chatted softly. Mr. Brown beckoned to an empty seat next to him.

Saint-Martin learned from the Quaker that his children, Benjamin, a boy of ten, and Sarah, a girl of eight, had lost their hearing to a fever four years earlier. "Their vocal organs remained intact," Brown remarked with the detachment of a parent who had long wrestled with a child's disability. "I immediately hired tutors to teach the children to speak properly. But, lacking system and method, the tutors floundered and the children became discouraged. When Mr. Braidwood moved his institute to Hackney two years ago, I enrolled the children with him."

The Quaker's expression grew earnest. A touch of awe crept into his voice. "Braidwood expects Benjamin and Sarah to commit to memory the position of the lips and tongue for each sound they utter. To speak fluently, they need years of training at the institute and constant practice at home."

"That's more discipline than soldiers endure," observed Saint-Martin.

Brown nodded. "And it's hard on the children, even though they realize it's necessary. They are encouraged now that we understand better what they say. We are all happier." Brown glanced up at the puppet stage. "To lighten their burden, our Miss Cartier devises entertainment like today's production of *Punch*. I'm told the children will open and close the curtain and speak the smaller parts. She's reserved Punch to herself."

At four o'clock, from the back of the room came the familiar melody of *Marlborough se va-t-en guerre*. Colonel Saint-Martin smiled, recalling that the English used it in *For He's a Jolly Good Fellow*. He glanced over his shoulder. In a bright yellow costume covered with large red dots, and playing a fife, Miss Cartier strutted up the aisle and onto the platform, followed by the boy and girl in similar attire, beating drums and singing:

Mr Punch is one jolly good fellow,
His dress is all scarlet and yellow,
And if now and then he gets mellow,
It's only among his good friends.

Acting the theater proprietor, little Benjamin faced the audience, bowed three times, and delivered the prologue:

Ladies and Gentlemen, how do you do?
If you are all happy, I'm happy too.
Stop and listen to my merry little play;
If I make you laugh,
Don't forget to pay.

The curtain parted. Punch, armed with his traditional stick, beat his shrewish wife, Joan. A dog, Toby, bit Punch, who turned on the clown Scaramouche, the dog's merry master. A constable then arrested Punch but, in prison, Punch tricked the hangman into hanging himself. At the end Punch, joined by his wife, fought the devil and drove him off the stage. The curtain closed. The children reappeared, their faces beaming with pride. To vigorous applause, they took several deep bows.

Well earned, Saint-Martin thought, as he joined in the clapping. Much effort had gone into this production. He had no trouble understanding the children's speech, though it was a bit oddly inflected. Yet appropriate. Puppets, after all, were supposed to speak in their own way.

Benjamin and Sarah dashed behind the little theater, brought Miss Cartier out front and hugged her. They fetched small baskets of fruit and threw pieces to her. She juggled them and cast them to children in the audience. At the last fruit, an apple, she paused, grinning broadly. With the license allowed to clowns, she tossed it to Saint-Martin. He caught it deftly, smiled to the clown, and handed it to the nearest child. The clown waved to the audience, then came to attention and saluted the French colonel. With a grand gesture, she gathered the children and fifed them out.

Chapter 7

A Ride in the Country

The next morning shortly after daybreak, Colonel Paul de Saint-Martin pulled open the door to the stable and drew into his lungs the rich scent of horses, oiled leather, and fresh hay. Directly ahead of him, the thoroughbreds borrowed from Captains Gordon and Porter stood contented in their stalls, already brushed and fed. A door banged at the far end of the long well-lighted building. A pair of stable boys were cleaning an empty stall. The paved floor was spotless.

From behind came the snap of a buckle. Saint-Martin swung around, startled. A few stalls away, someone dressed in a black English riding cap, red coat, and tan breeches was saddling a fine-boned black thoroughbred. Saint-Martin stared in amazement; he could recognize a prize horse when he saw one. He called out a greeting. The other early riser looked up. It was Anne Cartier.

"You ride like that?" he stammered, accustomed to women riding sidesaddle in long flowing skirts.

She laughed at his consternation. "I do, at least here. It's safer and I can control the horse better. In public, I ride the other way. I'd rather not shock people."

"Mind if I join you?" the colonel asked, marvelling at the woman's self-assurance.

"Please do," she replied, as she walked the thoroughbred past him. "I'll show you the estate. It's lovely this hour of the day."

She was waiting, already mounted, when he led his horse into the paddock. Only then did he notice the pistols holstered on her saddle. She followed his gaze. "They are a matching pair, a gift from my grandfather. His name's engraved on the brass. He thought I might need them."

"Afraid we'll be ambushed?" the colonel asked.

"No, not here." She smiled thinly. "An assassin wouldn't be put off by this." She patted a pistol in its holster, then glanced at Saint-Martin, her eyes an icy blue. "But he'd have to be careful."

They rode down a lane through the meadow behind the house, Miss Cartier leading. "That's a hot-blooded hunter with only a snaffle bit in its mouth, and she's wearing no spurs," the Frenchman muttered to himself. "How will she control the beast? Is she mad?"

They entered a grove of tall oak trees and came to a clearing. "Now, watch," she said. With no apparent movement or command, she urged her horse to a gallop. Holding the reins tightly with her left hand, she pulled the pistol from the right-side holster, cocked and tipped it to the left, and fired at an old clay pot on a tree stump. It shattered.

Incredible, he thought. She and her hunter understand one another perfectly. No need for spurs.

She beckoned him to join her. "I was lucky," she said laughing. "I often miss."

"How did you keep your mount steady? A pistol's report so near will make a horse skittish, even your hunter."

"An old cavalryman who works for my grandfather taught me these tricks." She put the pistol back in its holster. "Come, I'll show you something else."

They dismounted at the far end of the clearing, where Saint-Martin saw a devil, complete with horns, cloven hooves, and gaping mouth, crudely drawn on heavy paper and stretched over a wooden frame that hung from an inclining rope between two thin trees. On closer inspection, Saint-Martin noticed the devil had a long human face with thick black eyebrows and a hawk nose. Justice Hammer, no doubt, judging from impressions Georges had gathered in Islington. There were several holes in the target, one of them precisely between the narrowset eyes. A sudden chill seized the Frenchman's heart.

"I found it in a shed by the house," the young woman said as she pulled the target up the incline. "I've added a few details."

With the second half-cocked pistol in her hand, she released the target, walked rapidly twenty paces, swung around to face the devil coming at her, cocked, aimed, and fired. The shot passed through its heart and echoed through the woods.

"When the king recruits women for the cavalry, I'll recommend you," said Saint-Martin. "May I try a shot?"

She loaded the pistol and handed it to him. "Grandfather Cartier made this one—and its twin—for the Duke of York. Not fancy enough, said His Royal Highness and bought a pair from Wogdon of London."

Saint-Martin gripped the weapon, aimed at the paper demon standing thirty paces away, then fired. The devil lost his left eye. The Frenchman lowered the pistol, nodding with satisfaction. "It's perfectly balanced."

"And reliable," she added. "It has never misfired."

At her gesture, Saint-Martin returned the pistol to its holster on her horse. "Wogdon's guns are good, but you've gotten the best of that bargain." They walked to a bench and sat down side by side. "By the way, where did you learn the trick you played on Mr. Roach in Islington?"

"You've heard about that from Barnstaple, I suppose. It's hardly a secret. If you must know, the trick's part of a routine my father—Antoine—taught me." She flushed, waving a correcting hand. "I mean, we dressed as clowns and did foolish things to amuse people. In the act with the stick, I would just pretend to hit him, but he would double up and howl. The crowd loved it."

She paused, a frown gathering on her face. "Roach jumped in front of me, wild and angry, shouting like a clown. He swung at me." Her jaw tightened as if in pain. "I didn't have time to think; I just fell into my old routine. But I sensed he meant to hurt. I didn't pretend, I hit him as hard as I could. It happened so fast, there wasn't time to scream or to run."

"They could have killed you," said Saint-Martin softly, a brother's concern in his voice. "How do you feel now?"

Her hand rose spontaneously to her neck. "The bruises are gone, but I sometimes have nightmares." She looked at Saint-Martin, as if debating whether to continue, her eyes measuring his empathy. Then she spoke slowly in a low voice. "I dream of the prison or the scaffold and I wake up shaking. Even in the village, where there's no danger, I still look over my shoulder, as if someone were creeping up on me. Roach would attack again if he ever got the chance." She drew a deep breath and smiled nervously. "But that's no reason to hide in a hole. I'll not be chained by fear."

He laid his hand on hers. She let it rest there for a long second, then gently lifted it. They rode back abreast at a trot to the stable.

≪≪≪

In her room later that morning, Anne sat at a dressing table, combing her hair. She glanced down at Comtesse Marie's letter lying in front of her. A tempting invitation. At first she had felt reluctant to accept it. Was there anything belonging to Antoine that she wanted? Did she need to know any more about his life and death in Paris than she already knew? But now her mind was inclining the other way. Intrigued. There appeared to be more to the invitation than met the eye. An underlying urgency. The comtesse really wanted her to come.

She put down the comb and started sifting through a side drawer. Near the top of the pile lay one of her treasures, a miniature portrait of Antoine, a gift to her mother on a wedding anniversary. Anne held it up to the light and caressed it with the tips of her fingers. The broad face beneath the glass was generous and friendly, with large lively eyes and a mouth that broke easily into a smile. He had encouraged her and made her feel confident in herself. "God's given you many talents," he had said. "Don't let people put you down." She had taken his love for granted until he was gone. As she put the portrait aside, she found herself grieving. She brushed away a tear.

From a trunk under the table she pulled out small packets of letters Antoine had written from Paris. Beneath them lay diaries in which he had entered brief accounts of his performances in London. What clear, strong, and well-formed handwriting! She sat back, closing her eyes. He seemed close to her, full of life. He could not have killed himself. Something strange had happened to him in Paris. She felt driven to find out.

She picked up the comb, glanced at the mirror, and began reasoning with herself. She couldn't just run off to Paris. A harebrained idea! others would say. She replaced Antoine's papers in the trunk and snapped the lid shut. On the floor next to the trunk lay Barnstaple's letter to her. It had slipped from the table. Her eye caught the words, "Abbé de l'Épée," and "deaf children." *There* was a reason for going to Paris. A reason her grandparents could understand. If teaching the deaf was going to become her life's work, she should try to learn the method of the master. And this might be her only chance. She'd heard he was an elderly man. Colonel Saint-Martin would see her safely to Paris. Comtesse Marie, her patron, would present her to the abbé.

She got up and paced the room, a spring in her step. Out of her memory rose ever clearer images from Chateau Beaumont years ago. Paul de Saint-Martin had then seemed aloof and distant. Yet he had noticed her. He had always been at a window or door when she returned from morning rides. She had felt his eyes on her during performances in the garden theater.

She stopped at the window and tapped the comb in the palm of her hand, recalling a sunny morning. Just turned eighteen, she had gone alone to the theater to rehearse the part of Puck. All the adults were away for some reason, probably hunting. Four of Saint-Martin's cousins, young males in their mid-teens, joined her, claiming they were Bottom, Quince, Snug, and Snout. They teased her, then chased and jostled her. Sensing danger, she tried to flee. They blocked her escape and closed in on her. Heart pounding, she crouched for a fight.

Suddenly, a harsh command halted them in their tracks. Captain Paul de Saint-Martin, the sun shining upon him, stood at the entrance to the theater looking down. The boys vanished, leaving her shaken and alone on the stage. She looked up at him and was about to speak when she was struck by his expression, lips tight, eyes narrowed to mere slits. He said nothing, turned sharply on his heels, and walked away. He hadn't cared for *her*, but for the family's honor.

She resumed pacing, combing her hair vigorously. Had he changed? He seemed more compassionate than the last time she saw him. Would he try to take advantage of her? She didn't think so. He hadn't in the past. But, now? She conjured up the image of his aunt, Comtesse Marie, and felt reassured, knowing she had sent him.

With a sigh, Anne thought of her grandparents. They would surely shake their heads if they heard she had gone off with a French officer! It would be difficult explaining *that* to them, but she would have to try.

By noon, Anne had made up her mind. The Quaker children had received sufficient instruction from her and would benefit from a change. A substitute from Braidwood's institute would soon take her place. Yes, she would speak to the colonel. But, she must not appear too easily persuaded, too eager to join him. She would make clear to him that she had a mind of her own.

He was waiting for her in the sitting room near the entrance. His eyes brightened when he saw her. He was nervously fingering a button on his coat. She pretended not to notice, but she was pleased to find him a bit anxious. She would need more time to reflect, she told him, and would give him her decision by letter. Nonetheless, they made tentative arrangements to meet in London for the journey to Paris. She walked him to the door, where his adjutant waited with the horses. The colonel swung into the saddle with ease, then engaged her eye so warmly she felt caressed.

She stood at the front entrance, waving as they rode away. In the distance the colonel turned and waved back. How young he seemed for the rank—he could not be more than thirty-five. And so unaffected, despite his privileges. She recalled tossing the apple to him at the children's puppet show. His usual composure had dissolved into a heart-felt smile. For a moment she felt she had peered through a window into his soul. She waved again, softly murmuring, "I'll see you soon."

Chapter 8

On to Paris

Anne Cartier gasped inaudibly as she entered the foyer of the French embassy at Saint James' Park. Stately fluted Ionic columns ringed the large circular room. Soft light sifted down from lunettes in a high domed ceiling. Several footmen in blue livery stood still as statues, while others met guests at the entrance. Gentlemen in pastel velvet suits and ladies in lustrous satin gowns glided across the gleaming marble floor, bowing and curtsying to one another, speaking through barely parted lips. The ambassador, Comte d'Adhémar, was receiving visitors somewhere deeper inside the building.

Glancing at her own plain light brown woolen dress, Anne momentarily wondered if she had walked into the wrong place, perhaps a royal palace. Or should she have used a service entrance? She smiled, reassuring herself. Colonel Saint-Martin had given her clear instructions. She squared her shoulders and walked calmly through the elegant crowd.

At the reception table, the clerk ignored her. She grew apprehensive again. But, forcing herself to be brave, she tapped her foot. He looked up, lips pursed. His eyes narrowed skeptically, reminding Anne she was alone, unpowdered, and dressed well below the mark of the present company.

"Colonel Paul de Saint-Martin was expecting me at noon," she said, adding apologetically, "I'm a little late." The clerk seemed to smirk. For a few moments, he measured her coolly then dispatched a young page with a note. Anne's anger had neared the bursting point, but she cautioned herself not to waste it on clerks.

She stepped back and sat on the edge of a chair with a view of the stairs. If travelling together didn't disturb the colonel, she told herself, it shouldn't bother her. This was her only way to reach Paris and Antoine's grave. And a new career. She couldn't do cartwheels and handstands for the rest of her life.

The page soon reappeared, skipping down the stairs. At a withering glance from the desk clerk, he shifted abruptly to a more stately descent. Colonel Saint-Martin would soon follow, Anne thought. She started to rise, then sat down again, watching for him out of the corner of her eye. She smoothed the folds of her dress. Her heart beat a little faster.

Upstairs in his parlor, Colonel Saint-Martin reclined in a chair, legs crossed at the ankles, reading Miss Cartier's letter a second time. He was relieved. She had accepted Aunt Marie's invitation and confirmed the tentative plan to meet at the embassy. She should be arriving any minute now. Her baggage would go to the coach station. She would stay the night with a friend.

He looked up from the letter, pleased, even morally vindicated. She trusted him. But she wasn't a clinging vine!

> *As I have the means to pay my own*
> *expenses, I shall be no burden to you. I*
> *also have sufficient strength and wit to cope*
> *with travelling to Paris.*

Still nursing some bad bruises to her pride, he thought. She's skittish about men. Well, what matter. He had only to lead her safely to Aunt Marie. She and Miss Cartier could together wrestle with the strange fate of Antoine Dubois.

Out in the hall, a clock chimed noon. He folded the letter, laid it on the side table, and allowed his mind to play. Images from his visit to Wimbledon were soon darting about like minnows in a pond. The clown in bright yellow costume. *And* the toss of the apple! The young woman hearing of Dubois' death, her eyes wide with disbelief.

He steepled his fingers, tapped them lightly. Dubois had won her heart. She *would* try to vindicate him. A hopeless task. The case seemed clear-cut. A crime of passion. How could the police have made a mistake?

His eyes shifted to the folded letter by his side. He opened it again. "Strength and wit," indeed! He sensed she could cope with more than a trip to Paris. He recalled her in the Wimbledon woods, urging her thoroughbred to a gallop, firing her pistol, the pot shattering. A woman of spirit!

The colonel sat up, glancing at his watch. Ten past the hour. He felt disappointed. Had she changed her mind at the last minute? Her grandparents might have convinced her the trip was an unwise idea. He walked to the window, paced the floor several times, stopped abruptly. So be it. He and Georges would depart tomorrow without her.

There were steps outside his door, then a knock and a voice. He opened for a page holding a folded message on a small silver tray. Saint-Martin took the slip of paper and handed the page a half-penny.

As the boy's footsteps faded away down the hall, Colonel Saint-Martin stiffly faced the door, fingering the paper. Then he read, *A Miss Cartier is waiting in the foyer.* "She's come," he said aloud. He felt his life taking a major unpredictable turn. His mind urged caution. Inspecting himself in a mirror, he pulled on a plain buff coat with brown buttons. He would invite Miss Cartier to lunch privately.

A cab brought Anne and Colonel Saint-Martin to the coach station at the George and Blue Boar Inn in Holborn. It was Monday, the 15th of May, a sunny, cool day. The courtyard rang with the shouts and curses of stableboys, porters, and coachmen, with the clatter of hooves and wheels on cobblestones. Several coaches were loading as others arrived or departed. A crowd of passengers waited at the entrance to the inn. Tradesmen pushed through, carrying goods inside.

Georges Charpentier had collected the baggage and was watching with gimlet eye as a porter lifted it onto a Dover coach. Anne and Saint-Martin backed away from the bustle.

Ready for travel, Anne wore her light brown dress and a matching bonnet. She also carried a walking stick which she shifted nimbly from hand to hand. Out of the corner of her eye, she noticed a small, wiry, round-shouldered man in a carter's smock, furtively studying passengers preparing to board a coach nearby. They paid him no attention, heatedly accusing one another of misplacing travel documents. At the call to board, the man drew closer. As the passengers surged forward, jostling one another, he singled out a noisy rotund woman, cut her purse, and darted toward a narrow alley from the courtyard to the street. The victim didn't realize she had been robbed.

Meanwhile, Colonel Saint-Martin had advanced a few steps toward the Dover coach, unaware of what was happening behind him. Anne was more alert. She stepped quickly to her right and tripped the thief with her walking stick. He tumbled head first to the rough stone pavement. Stunned, but still clutching the purse, he rolled over and rested on his elbow, blinking at the steel-tipped stick an inch away from his face.

A pair of steady blue eyes searched him. "Hand me the purse."

He gave it to her without a word.

"Get out of here."

He scrambled to his feet and scurried away.

Anne walked back to the woman who was only now becoming aware of a commotion. "Here's your purse, madam. The thief has escaped."

"Well, thank you, young lady!" the woman stammered. "It's a pity no one caught him. He should be hung!"

"You lost nothing," said Anne over her shoulder, hastening to rejoin the colonel.

The Dover coach was loaded and ready to depart, two pair of horses stamping in their harness. From an outside seat Georges beckoned furiously. Colonel Saint-Martin ignored him and motioned for Anne to come to one side. She balked inwardly at his command but, nonetheless, complied. When they were out of earshot, he asked, with a hint of reproach, why she had not held the thief. "The station master could have brought him to a magistrate."

"Yes, I know," she replied evenly, "and in a fortnight he might have been hung."

Her irony appeared to nettle him. "Hanging's perhaps what he deserved. Do you suppose this was the first time he's snatched a purse? Anyway, he's not *your* concern."

She took a step back and glared at him. "My concern? I had his life in my hands. I *was* his judge! And I had only an instant to decide. He deserved to be punished surely, but not hung." She paused, then added with a teasing smile, "You probably noticed, he didn't get off scot-free. He took a nasty fall that he'll feel for a while."

Returning to the coach, Saint-Martin stole a glance at Miss Cartier. She walked briskly, her brow smooth, free of doubt. He felt his irritation diminish. What the English did with their pickpockets was not his concern. With an indulgent smile, he fell in step with her.

Dozens of swooping gulls escorted the ship through Dover's harbor, their shrill calls echoing across the water. A few miles out in the Channel, white caps crowned the waves. The ship found a favorable steady breeze and steered straight for Calais. The other passengers crowded into the cabin below to sip from flasks they had brought along. Georges Charpentier joined them, hoping to pick up some useful Channel gossip.

Colonel Saint-Martin and Miss Cartier walked the slippery deck amidships, drawing salty air into their lungs, alone except for seamen who were too busy to notice them. England's chalk cliffs receded and the gulls disappeared. The sounds of the sea grew louder. Waves lapped the ship's hull. Wood creaked, rope groaned, canvas flapped against the mast.

Glancing sideways at the young woman beside him, Saint-Martin allowed himself to wonder. Could the Antoine Dubois she loved have changed in a few years into a murderer and suicide? Nothing in his letters had apparently alarmed her. The colonel's curiosity mounted, though he warned himself not to get deeply involved in her affair. Still, this seemed a good opportunity for a gentle probing.

"If it's not too painful," he asked, when she turned his way, "perhaps you could tell me something about Antoine's life with you and your mother."

"It was a good life," she replied, gracefully shifting her weight for balance on the pitching deck. "Both of us loved and appreciated him."

"That speaks well for him. Still, he was handsome and an actor."

She conceded the point with a grudging nod. "He borrowed money and bought expensive gifts. And, he flirted with other women. He and mother quarreled but always reconciled. My grandparents disapproved of him at first, but eventually learned to like him and helped out with money."

Gusts of wind suddenly filled the sails. The ship lurched forward. Anne gripped the railing. The colonel slipped back and forth but quickly regained his footing. They glanced at one another and smiled, sharing the moment.

"How did your mother's death affect him? Was he despondent?"

She knitted her brow in thought for a moment. "At her death, he wept. I recall him grieving but no self-pity or despair. When my maternal grandparents kept him from administering the trust fund my mother left me, he felt hurt. Later, he found lady friends," she added without reproach. "One day he told me I had talent for something better than vaudeville. *And* he wanted to try a new partner." She looked down, studying the ship's deck. "Who can blame him?"

"No one," replied Saint-Martin softly, recollecting the emptiness of his own life after his wife's death. Hopes raised then dashed. He had thrown himself into his duties.

"We kept in touch. After the war, he returned to France to try vaudeville, farce, comedy—the things he was good at." She shrugged her shoulders. "What else he did there, you probably know better than I."

"I doubt it," he replied. "The police interviewed people who worked with him but didn't learn much. He was liked but not successful. Flitted from task to task. Quarreled with his mistress. You can inquire about him when you've visited with my aunt and found your way in Paris. I'll help locate his things."

She thanked him, then leaned on the ship's rail, gazing out over the sea, past the tiny dots of fishing vessels, to the horizon. For several minutes she remained there, still, as if digesting what he had said.

He stood silent next to her, the sea breeze whining in his ears. A few low clouds scudded easterly overhead. Finally, she stirred, and he asked casually what she had done after Antoine left her.

She turned around, resting her elbows on the rail. On her own, she explained, she had tried to become an actress. But she couldn't find good roles without a patron. Off-season she performed in vaudeville at Sadler's Wells. In her spare time, she went back to the puppetry her mother had taught her.

"I made puppets, wrote plays, and presented them." Her face brightened. "One day, after a show, Mr. Braidwood came up to me and asked if I would perform for the deaf children at his school. I discovered I could do some of my vaudeville routines for them as well."

She looked into his eyes as if worried she might be boring a distinguished French army officer.

He smiled, reassuring her, then glanced over her shoulder. "I think we should prepare to debark." He pointed toward the sand dunes of the French coast and the low gray outline of Calais. A flock of gulls was soaring out to greet them.

Calais had a reputation similar to Dover's across the Channel, a port city with more than its share of pickpockets, baggage thieves, greedy innkeepers, and prostitutes. If travellers arrived by midday, they hurried on to Boulogne, a three-hour journey by royal highway. It was a beautiful city with decent inns and a large English colony. Thanks to good weather, Anne and her two companions debarked at one o'clock. Within an hour they were on their way to Boulogne in a rented carriage, Anne and the colonel inside, Georges Charpentier outside next to the driver.

The royal highway soon left the coast and cut directly inland. From the carriage window Anne saw grassy dunes, thickets of low bushes, and groves of stunted trees—a barren place where neither man nor beast seemed to thrive. Farm buildings were decrepit and fences in disrepair. The sun disappeared behind a cover of clouds, leaving the countryside, even the grass on the dunes, looking bleak and gray, a monotone relieved only by splashes of pink spring blossoms on the wild bushes.

Halfway to Boulogne, Saint-Martin closed the book he had been reading and looked in her direction. Anne smiled to herself. Was he going to interrogate her again? No, she thought, it was her turn. "What's it about?" she asked, glancing at the book.

"The Chevalier de Bayard," he replied. "Commander of French forces in Italy early in the sixteenth century. One of our national heroes, the one without fear or reproach."

She stared at him, feigning a look of surprise. "I've heard of Jeanne d'Arc. She's *my* French hero. I didn't know there was another one."

He smiled quietly, searching her eyes, detecting the irony. His brow furrowed as if hurt.

She excused herself gently. "A man truly without reproach is rare in any country."

He handed her the book. "My father's copy. Bayard was his ideal French officer. Brave, loyal to his king, loved by the men serving under him, and respected by his enemies. A gentleman who pursued honor, not money."

The son's ideal, as well, she sensed, opening the book and fanning the frayed pages. "Would you mind telling me about yourself?" she asked directly. She had already learned he was a marquis.

His forehead wrinkled for a moment, as if he seldom needed to explain who he was or what he did. But he quickly recovered his composure. "It's not a secret." For the past three years he had been in charge of the Royal Highway Patrol for the area around Paris. Someone else looked after the city. His expression turned apologetic. "I earned that position." Winking, he added, "By being born into one of the oldest families in France."

"I'm sure you have other qualifications." She leaned back, frowning in mock reproof.

"Baron Breteuil, the Minister for Paris, thinks I can work miracles, in view of the small budget he gives me."

"Do you enjoy what you do?"

He nodded. "I like to work when I can see results. In a regiment of the royal army, I'd be idle." He sighed. "There are too many officers in service now that our country is at peace. Many of them waste their lives drinking, gambling, and chasing women."

"You chase criminals instead." Her voice rippled with amusement. "And keep them from robbing travellers like us going to Paris."

He soberly explained that his troopers had chased the highwaymen away from the roads to the city. His problem now was thieves who looted rich country houses in the outlying area. He needed more investigators. He pointed upward in the direction of his adjutant, whose bursts of laughter drifted into the coach. "Georges is one of the best, but he's the only one I've got. The criminal investigation bureau in Paris can't help. Too busy with the affair of the queen's necklace. I suppose you've heard about that in England, where many of the diamonds disappeared."

"I know that Cardinal de Rohan tried to win the French queen's favor with an expensive necklace. It never reached her."

"A daring scheme!" He explained that the necklace was made of some five hundred large, perfect diamonds commissioned by the jeweler Boehmer and offered to Louis XV as a present for Madame du Barry. The king had declined the purchase. A few years later the cardinal's mistress, Comtesse de la Motte, persuaded him to contract for the necklace on behalf of Queen Marie Antoinette. La Motte would arrange for its delivery. "In fact," Saint-Martin concluded, his voice rich with irony, "she passed it to her husband, who fled to England and sold it off stone by stone."

Anne tapped her cheek, reflecting on the bizarre fraud. "It wouldn't surprise me to hear that Jack Roach's fingers have touched some of them."

"Georges agrees but couldn't find any proof in London."

By the time they reached Boulogne, the colonel had told her quite a bit about himself. For the present, he lived alone in Paris, except for his adjutant and the servants. As he spoke, Anne sensed an engaging simplicity. His peers must wonder about him, perhaps envy him, but he didn't seem to care. He enjoyed work and the company of a few friends. To keep fit he rode, fenced, and played court tennis, and, she guessed, lived moderately.

A fine figure of a man, she had earlier observed. Agile, muscular, and a few inches taller than herself. Stealing a sidelong glance, she admired his fine brown wavy hair, gathered and tied back with a black bow; his brown eyes and long black lashes; his frank, generous expression. Yes, she admitted to herself, a man she could grow fond of.

At dusk the carriage rattled over the cobbled streets of Boulogne into the courtyard of the Auberge Royal, a comfortable old inn, where they were to spend the night. After a simple evening meal in a private room, they remained at the table. Anne opened the box of Antoine's things that Saint-Martin had asked her to bring along. He studied each item—the miniature portrait, the letters, the diaries and odd scraps—encouraging her to reminisce.

Meanwhile, glancing frequently at the miniature, Georges sketched a remarkable life-like portrait. He held it up and asked, "Does this look like a man who would murder a woman and then kill himself?" Saint-Martin looked at the sketch and, hesitantly, passed it on to Anne. She held it to the light, studied it carefully. Georges had shadowed the eyes and given the dead man a menacing smile, lacking in the formal portrait.

"Antoine Dubois?" asked Saint-Martin.

"Yes, but not as I knew him." She handed the sketch to Georges.

"Perhaps it's the face he presented to those who crossed him," Georges remarked. "I questioned people who knew him at Vauxhall. Amiable but touchy, they said."

Prodded by the sketch, Anne's mind drifted back to a summer evening in London during the American war. Feelings were running high against foreigners. While Antoine was on stage at Vauxhall, several scoundrels in the audience had taunted him for his French accent. "Frog," they called him, and "papist." Why hadn't he ignored them and moved on? she wondered. No, he had to give them the finger, the royal shaft. "English dogs," he retorted. The scoundrels pelted him with oranges. He caught several and threw them back. One hit its mark.

Splat! Right between the eyes. His tormentors threatened to storm the stage. A riot seemed imminent. At that moment, she had leapt out of the wings, seized the back of his costume, and pulled him spluttering to safety.

Georges stared at the sketch. "A clown's mask. Hard to penetrate." He pushed back his chair. "Time to speak to our driver." At a wave from Saint-Martin, he left the room wishing Anne good night.

Her gaze returned to the sketch of her father. Was the face he had showed her for so many years also a mask? She passed the sketch to the colonel. He held it with both hands, studying it intently, then met her eye. "Who can tell what a man might do," he said quietly, "if sufficiently provoked."

After several minutes, Saint-Martin looked up from Dubois' papers and turned to Anne. "His letters and other papers reveal little of his mind other than his affection for you. Come to think of it, we have no record of his life before he met and married your mother."

Anne fell momentarily silent, embarrassed by how little she knew about Antoine. He had appeared to live intensely in the present, more disinterested than secretive about the past. "I'm afraid I can't help you. He said he came from Rouen, in Normandy. Had relatives there."

Saint-Martin rose from the table and shuffled through the papers. "I'll write to an acquaintance in Rouen who may be able to help us." He dropped a few of Dubois' letters into his valise. "I'll study these before going to bed." At the door he threw her a preoccupied glance. "Get a good night's rest, Anne."

Lingering at the table, she repeated her name, imitating the way he had spoken it for the first time. She leaned back, hearkening. His footsteps echoed ever fainter in the hall. A candle sputtered and died. The room grew unearthly still, as if sensing the loss of his presence.

Chapter 9

Getting Acquainted

"Comtesse Marie will join you shortly." With a bow the servant left Anne and Colonel Saint-Martin in a small reception room. It was Saturday, the 20th of May. From Boulogne they had reached the town house on Rue Traversine in less than three days, with a stop at the colonel's residence nearby for a change to fresh clothes.

Saint-Martin stood in the center of the room, arms akimbo. "Voltaire has also waited here," he remarked, a touch of awe in his voice.

Anne felt uneasy. She was about to meet a clever aristocratic lady, who had known her only as a girl. She couldn't help wondering what Comtesse Marie would think of her now. She drew little comfort from learning that Voltaire had also been in this room. The famous French writer had surely not been as anxious as she. His *Candide* mocked anyone who irritated him, even kings. Comtesse Marie was too wise to have kept him waiting long.

Hiding her distress, Anne surveyed the room for marks of its mistress. Uncluttered, it spoke of a simple, elegant taste. To the right of the entrance, between a pair of matching chairs, stood a mahogany side table with gilded brass fittings. Cream drapery framed the windows. An intricate Turkish rug lay on the parquet floor. On one wall hung a gold-framed mirror. On another, pastel sketches of country scenes.

Intrigued, Anne walked up to the sketches for a closer look. With a sure, deft hand the artist had created enchanting visions of young lovers at ease by thatched-roof cottages. Shepherd boys lounging in lush pastures played pastoral tunes on pan flutes to their sheep. A girl soared on a swing, while another poured water from a pitcher.

The room's refined taste, Anne sensed, was meant to set the tone for visitors meeting the comtesse, to dispose them to rise to her expectations. Anne stepped back from the sketches, seeing the woman in a new light. Years ago, as a girl, Anne had looked up to her as to a kind, rather distant aunt. Now, from an adult's vantage point, she recognized Comtesse Marie as a woman with power that worked subtly behind a gracious appearance. "Voltaire had waited here." The words echoed again in Anne's mind. And so, no doubt, had other great men.

Anne glanced in the mirror. How common she looked! No lace, no jewelry, no powder or rouge. The pearl grey dress she had chosen to wear—so plain, so out of place in this room. What had she gotten herself into?

Removing her bonnet, she bit her lips for more color, then touched her hair with trembling fingers. The colonel was watching her, thin lines of concern creasing his brow. She began to feel distressed. Her skin tingled. Comtesse de Beaumont would come presently, the servant had said. The waiting seemed to stretch out endlessly, though only a few minutes had passed.

Coming to her side, Colonel Saint-Martin tried to reassure her. "The comtesse will be most pleased to see you again. She still thinks fondly of your mother."

Whistling in the wind, Anne thought. Much had changed since those summers at Chateau Beaumont. Fortunately, the comtesse would not be taken by surprise. From Boulogne the colonel had prudently alerted his aunt by courier of their arrival. She had replied with a brief note to the colonel's residence: she would receive them in her town house.

Footsteps, then voices sounded in the hallway. As the comtesse walked into the room, Anne felt her chest tighten. For a brief moment she could hardly breathe. The comtesse smiled, but her cool gray eyes searched Anne's soul...then softened. She stepped forward and embraced Anne. A warm, but cautious woman, Anne thought, breathing more freely. Fair enough, she was really a stranger in the house, but she was over the first hurdle.

"Let me show you to your rooms," the comtesse said, gesturing toward the door. "We need to get acquainted again." She turned to her nephew. "Paul, I'm sure you have work to do. Come back in the evening for supper." He threw her a knowing glance and took his leave.

Comtesse Marie led Anne to her rooms on the second floor. The parlor reminded her of a privileged servant's apartment, rather like the one she had in Wimbledon. The furnishings seemed modest compared to those in the public rooms, but comfortable. A worn Turkish rug lay on the floor; a pair of upholstered chairs and a tea table stood by the window, which was open to air out the room. She looked out over the street to the jumble of roofs beyond. Traffic rumbled below. To the left of the parlor was a small kitchen with a glazed tile stove, a dry sink, a cabinet, a plain wooden table and two benches. A simple meal could be prepared and eaten there. To the right of the parlor was the bedroom, also lighted by an opened window.

There was a soft knock on the door. A young maid entered, curtsied, and set a large vase of red and yellow tulips on the tea table, then laid out towels, closed the windows, and quietly left the room.

"Now that we are alone, we may speak freely," said Comtesse Marie. They sat down by the window and Anne began to tell her story. When she mentioned her doubting the official version of Antoine's suicide, the countess stiffened. "I have precisely the same feeling." She pressed Anne's hands between hers. "Settle in here over the weekend. I'll show you Paris. And make a few enquiries. I think I know where you might begin to seek the truth."

At the Palais-Royal on Monday morning, the two women found a bank in the Montpensier arcade for Anne's London letter of credit. Leaving the building, Comtesse Marie remarked that they still had some time for shopping. "With new clothes you will look like a Parisian rather than a foreigner and attract less notice as you go about your investigation." She cast a keen glance at Anne's figure. "My dressmaker is only a few steps away in this arcade. She will take your measurements today. I can lend what you may need until she's finished your things."

A few hours later, the two women emerged from the dressmaker's shop. The comtesse turned to Anne. "It's time now to think of ways to learn about Antoine." She pointed with a gloved hand toward the south end of the arcade. "The Théâtre des Variétés Amusantes is the place to start. He and Lélia Laplante often performed there. We'll soon meet its directeur, a Monsieur Bouvin. I've arranged for tea at Café du Foy."

Anne smiled. "Are you thinking of recommending me for a role at his theater?"

"The idea has crossed my mind," the comtesse replied easily. "You will find persons there who knew Antoine." She waved a finger of caution. "But don't reveal he was your stepfather. You don't know how they might react."

Directeur Bouvin arrived at the café shortly after the women, his face flushed from dinner at the Café de Conti. He often dined well, Anne thought, judging from his wide girth. A short man, he carried his chin high in a futile effort to look down on people. Anne was tempted to smile at him, but she held back. There was a certain glint in his eyes. Ruthless and cunning, the directeur was not a man to trifle with.

The comtesse had reserved a private room. Seated between the two women, Bouvin drank brandy to their tea. Feminine charm conspired with the liquor to bring him to an amiable mood. He regaled the women with tales of scandal from the world of Parisian theaters.

The women feigned interest until the comtesse managed to turn the conversation toward Anne. "A gifted performer! She's worked at Sadler's Wells and the Vauxhall in London."

"Really!" Bouvin inspected Anne with a practiced eye.

At a word from the comtesse Anne rose from the table and removed the gauze scarf covering her chest. Leaning back in his chair, hands clasped on his paunch, Bouvin ogled the rise of her breasts. Anne caught his eye, then moved gracefully about the room in the steps of a minuet and an English country dance.

Pausing in front of him, she sang a medley of country airs. Before the end of an hour he had engaged her for a minor part on his stage. As he was leaving, Anne glanced at the comtesse. Her eyes shone with amusement. She mouthed, "Well done!"

∞∞∞

The next morning, feeling almost at home on Rue Traversine, Anne waited again in the small reception room. She and the comtesse had agreed to visit Abbé de l'Épée's institute for the deaf on Rue des Moulins—just a short distance away. Anne glanced once more in the mirror. Out of the scant wardrobe she had brought from England, she had chosen a dark red dress trimmed with black lace. She eyed herself critically, nodded approval, then straightened her black bonnet.

Footsteps echoed in the hallway. Comtesse Marie entered, dressed for the street in moss green and orange. On her arm was a matching green cloak. For a moment, the two women stood reflected in the mirror together, both of them aware of an uncanny resemblance—same height and similar bodies, the comtesse slightly narrower in the shoulders. And similar facial features, though Anne's eyes were blue, the comtesse's gray. They could have passed for mother and daughter, Anne thought, had they gone through more of life together.

"The good man expects us at nine," the comtesse remarked cheerfully, as they descended the stairs to the courtyard. She explained that the abbé opened the institute from seven until noon, Tuesdays and Fridays, to a steady flow of visitors, some of them distinguished foreigners. "Three months ago, Mr. Thomas Jefferson, the American ambassador, came while I was there. A tall man, loose-limbed, with an ambling gait and the most remarkable gray-blue eyes."

Leaving the courtyard, the comtesse paused. Traffic outside was chaotic. Nearby, a wagon had lost a wheel and overturned, dumping its load of charcoal across most of the narrow street. Carts were backed up as far as Anne could see, their drivers screaming at each other.

"Even the sedan chairs are stopped," remarked Comtesse Marie, unperturbed. "We shall walk." She gathered up her skirts. Anne did the same, and the two women threaded their way through a small opening by the cart as oncoming pedestrians yielded place to them.

Once free of the congested traffic, the comtesse continued her story. "While the abbé was busy, I had the pleasure of being Mr. Jefferson's guide." At a glance from Anne, who knew the ambassador was a widower, the comtesse added, "He and I had not been introduced, but I felt I knew him. My nephew, Colonel Paul, met him during the war. They visit occasionally."

A few paces ahead of them, a maid opened a door and without looking left or right threw slop into the street. Comtesse Marie, engrossed in her account of the American diplomat, appeared not to notice. Anne reached out a hand too late to stop her, but the comtesse stepped adroitly over the puddle without losing a syllable of her narrative.

"What an inquisitive mind!" she went on. "Jefferson was fascinated by the hand signing of our students. They seemed especially dexterous and quick that day. In the past, he told me in his halting French, he had believed deaf people were incapable of abstract thought, that they could only understand the meaning of words related to sensory experience, that terms used in philosophy and science—God, Love, Nature—were beyond their capacity. He asked me whether the institute could overcome that basic deficiency. I told him the abbé would fully satisfy his curiosity. And he did." She glanced at Anne. "Just as he will satisfy yours."

In a few minutes the two women reached the institute, one in a row of four- or five-story, plain, stuccoed buildings fronting Rue des Moulins. Abbé de l'Épée met them at the door and bowed, recognizing in the comtesse an important patron. A small round-faced man in a plain black soutane, he was stooped with age.

"Mr. Braidwood has written that you wish to learn something from us," he said to Anne, leading the two women into a narrow room where a demonstration had been prepared. "We are happy to oblige."

The priest directed them to a wooden bench, then nodded to the students. A boy next to Anne signed a question to a girl at the chalk board. Anne missed its meaning until the girl wrote,

"What has Jesus Christ done for us?" Another student at the board wrote, "He has saved us from our sins."

After several such exchanges the abbé signaled a halt and approached Anne. "Do you understand them?" he asked with a doubting smile.

"I'm confused by their signs," she admitted without embarrassment.

"Mr. Braidwood mentioned you might not comprehend. The students are using my own system of conventional signs that transforms the everyday sign language of the deaf into an instrument for expressing the most abstract ideas of science and religion."

He sat down beside Anne, his face brightening with fervor. "Even educated persons used to believe deaf people were a primitive form of human life who could not reason beyond the evidence of their remaining senses. Barely superior to the beasts." He stamped his foot. "Rubbish! With my system their minds and hearts can reach the heights of what is truly human, the knowledge of God and His creation. And sing out His praise. Angels also lack voices. Who would *dare* call them beasts?"

The priest surveyed his students affectionately, his hands signing to them an eloquent tribute. They signed their gratitude in return, grinning at the priest, then at one another.

Épée returned to Anne's bench and sat beside her. "If *you* were diligent, you could learn the essentials of our local sign language in six weeks and master my system in a year."

"I would like to try," she said without hesitation. She had seldom, if ever, met a man of such conviction. And so willing to share what he had invented.

The priest led Anne and the comtesse to the next room. A dozen students sat at plain wooden tables. Their instructor was a slim young dark-haired woman in a gray dress with bits of white lace at the collar and cuffs. Her hands were signing with dazzling speed. "Mademoiselle Françoise Arnaud. She comes from a poor family," whispered the priest to his two guests. "Lost her hearing as a child." He gazed at the young woman, pride in his old watery eyes. "Now she reads and writes Latin and Italian, as well as French, and knows my system better than anyone."

In response to her signs, the students were moving small square metal tiles. They paused for a moment as the visitors approached. The priest touched Anne's arm and pointed out an older boy.

Bending over his shoulder, Anne saw on each tile a letter of the alphabet. The student glanced at her, then rapidly spelled, "How are you this morning, mademoiselle?" Sensing he could read her lips, she faced him and replied, "Very well, thank you." She quickly learned he was André Le Blond, sixteen years old and very bright.

"That young man will soon be going to work in a print shop," the priest remarked. "We place many in that trade."

Looking toward André and two other boys at the table, Anne asked, "May I join them?"

The priest shrugged. "Are you easily embarrassed?" He smiled at the eager faces of the boys. "They look forward to beating a hearing person at this game."

"I'm happy to take on that risk!"

"Good. They'll give you a taste of my system."

For half an hour, perched like a cat on the edge of her chair, Anne watched the shifting tiles. Then, with a broad smile of encouragement, Mademoiselle Arnaud gave her a set. She soon mastered several signs to the obvious pleasure of her young companions. Meanwhile, the priest left the room to speak with Comtesse Marie.

At the end of the lesson, Anne met Mademoiselle Arnaud at her desk and introduced herself, again taking care to face her and to enunciate clearly. The instructor's eyes widened with interest as Anne spoke of puppetry and Braidwood. After a few minutes, Abbé de l'Épée and Comtesse Marie returned and joined the two women.

"Mademoiselle Cartier grasps so quickly!" remarked the young woman in good French. "She has encouraged my students."

The priest studied Anne thoughtfully. "To learn my system you need someone to teach you." He glanced at the instructor, then back to Anne. "If you wish, you may ask her."

Anne turned slowly and faced Mademoiselle Arnaud. "Would you please teach me?"

"Yes." She smiled. "I would like that."

Anne gently drew the young woman's hand to her heart.

∞∾∞∾∞

The evening meal came to an end in an intimate private dining room at Rue Traversine. Candle light from the chandelier, refracted by smooth crystal pendants, gave a warm tone to the pale green panelled walls, on which gilded garlands faintly glowed. A servant cleared the small round table, leaving its centerpiece of yellow tulips. Another filled the brandy glasses. It was a quiet Sunday, more than a week since Anne had arrived. The next day, Comtesse Marie would depart for Chateau Beaumont.

She raised her glass to Anne, who responded in kind. For a few seconds they sipped silently, then exchanged wistful smiles. The years had been bridged, the social distance narrowed. Anne sensed they might now become friends.

Comtesse Marie placed her glass on the table, glancing sideways at Anne. "You've seen Abbé de l'Épée's institute several times this past week. What do you think?"

"I don't know how he manages. He has at least seventy students, many of them penniless, and not enough rooms for instruction. The students lodge in three or four different residences. They might learn better, living together in a larger institute." She paused, feeling her remarks might have sounded presumptuous. But the comtesse was nodding in agreement.

"As a novice," Anne continued, "I find the abbé's method... frankly, cumbersome. But, I see it works. His students read intelligently and learn to think. He helps them earn self-respect. In sum, a wise and skillful teacher."

The comtesse looked thoughtfully into her glass. "Yes, a rare man. He cares for each student, and they return his love." She looked up, her gray eyes now warm with feeling, then gazed at Anne. "Have you thought of where to live?"

"Nearby. I've looked at a room on Rue Richelieu."

"You could live here. The building is usually empty." The comtesse spoke in an offhand manner. "Since my husband's death, I seldom leave Chateau Beaumont. When I come to Paris to visit old friends or the shops in the Palais-Royal, I use only the ground and first floors. You could keep the apartment on the second floor with its own stairway and entrance."

Anne felt a rush of pleasure. "It would suit me very well." She added hesitantly, "I wish to pay rent for it."

"As you like. We can settle on a reasonable sum, I'm sure." Comtesse Marie smiled, taking Anne's hand. "You are doing me a favor. I need to have a person I trust living here." She met Anne's eye. "One whose concerns I share."

Chapter 10

A Private Investigation

A heavy dew had fallen early Monday morning. Paving stones glistened underfoot in the bright sunlight as Colonel Paul de Saint-Martin walked briskly into Place Vendôme. Midway through the vast open space, he stopped in the shadow of the bronze equestrian statue of Louis XIV. As he surveyed the colossal cream-colored facades of the buildings and sensed the unity and regularity of their architecture, he felt lifted by the grandeur of the place. For a moment, with the misery of the poor out of sight and the corruption of the rich out of mind, Paris seemed more than the sum of the people living there.

From Place Vendôme, Saint-Martin made his way to the bureau of criminal investigation on Rue des Capucines. He found the inspecteurs and their staff housed in a warren of small dingy rooms on the ground floor off an inner courtyard. Cabinets and tables crowded the reception room. A thin light seeped through the windows, so dirty they were barely translucent. Unwashed for decades, he thought. He wondered if the inspecteurs gave more careful attention to their cases.

He announced to a clerk that he had come to study Antoine Dubois' dossier. "I have permission from Lieutenant-General DeCrosne."

"You'll have to speak to Inspecteur Jules Mauvert. He had charge of that case."

Mauvert's name rang a bell in the colonel's mind. An inspecteur who prowled among the rich. "Being of service," he was rumored to have said. Hypocrite, thought Saint-Martin sourly. The man was more likely digging up scandal and then selling it, trying to recoup the ten thousand livres he had paid for his position.

A few minutes later, the door opened again and the inspecteur entered, followed by a clerk carrying two boxes. A short narrow-shouldered man, Mauvert wore a black silk suit of the finest quality. From the shop of a society tailor, Saint-Martin surmised. A client, perhaps. The inspecteur's hair was expertly coiffed and powdered. His small beady eyes, protuberant nose, and receding chin reminded the colonel of a crafty rodent.

As the clerk laid a file box on the table in front of Saint-Martin, the inspecteur remarked, "Nothing of interest here, Colonel." He patted the box. "Still, we keep journalists and other hacks from prying into the case. Baron Breteuil's orders. The Duc d'Orléans, owner of the theater where the crime took place, doesn't want any notoriety."

"Rest assured, Inspecteur," Saint-Martin replied, pulling the box toward him, "I shall respect the baron's wish."

Mauvert clasped his hands deferentially. "May I ask why you wish to study the Dubois file?"

"I'm looking for clues. Lélia Laplante and Dubois may have performed at country houses in my district where jewelry was stolen." He lifted a few files, fingered through them, then returned them to the box. "May I bring it to my office? I'll return it soon."

The inspecteur agreed, then pointed to the other container. "You may also examine Dubois's things. Odds and ends. Keep them if you wish. No use to us, and no one has claimed them. My clerk will carry both boxes for you."

Mauvert started to walk away, hesitated, then stared suspiciously at the colonel. "The Minister has also ordered us not to reopen old closed cases without his permission. But, there's no reason to look at Dubois again."

Saint-Martin curbed a surge of impatience. "I understand, Inspecteur. I spoke with Baron Breteuil yesterday." He had explained to the colonel that the resources of the Paris police were committed to ongoing investigations and to the affair of the queen's necklace. Its agents were chasing the thieves all over Europe and were still looking for the jewels.

As he crossed Place Vendôme on the way home, doubt began to stir in Saint-Martin's mind. Mauvert was a clever man. But greedy. A "crime of passion" involving a poor actor like Dubois would have offered little to intrigue him. He could have been hasty, overlooked evidence. The "closed case" might spring open, in spite of the Minister's orders.

At three o'clock that afternoon, Anne Cartier hurried through the courtyard of the colonel's house on Rue Saint-Honoré, stepping carefully to avoid the places where the pavement was uneven. How convenient, she thought, taking in the building with a glance. A large stone town house, three stories high, just a few steps from the royal garden of the Tuileries and a ten-minute walk east to the Palais-Royal. It was also where he worked, she had learned. Once a week, on Fridays, anyone could speak with him. Otherwise, he received people by appointment. Today, he was expecting her, and she was a few minutes late.

He met her at the door with a polite bow. Watching for her, she thought. They hadn't seen one another in over a week. He smiled easily as he ushered her to his office on the ground floor. He was in uniform—blue coat with broad red cuffs and lapels, buff waist coat, and buff breeches. His brown hair was groomed but unpowdered. There was energy in his movements, a bounce in his step that she liked.

She glanced about the room while he gave instructions and a handful of papers to a clerk. Detailed maps of Paris and its environs covered the walls between tall cabinets of speckled mahogany, their brass fixtures embossed and gilded. A large conference table to the right of the entrance and a desk to the left matched the cabinets. From his chair, the colonel had a clear view over the courtyard to the front gate.

After ordering a clerk to fetch coffee, he led Anne into a parlor facing a back garden. Ivy covered the windowless walls of buildings to left and right. A low pavilion closed the garden at the far end. She caught the fresh scent of blooming lilacs.

He showed her to a table near a large open window and gave her the view over the garden. The coffee arrived; the clerk poured and left.

"The flowers will be lovely," Anne said, her eyes wandering over carefully tended beds of budding roses. "A diligent gardener works here."

Saint-Martin gestured modestly to himself. "This is where I feed my spirit." He gazed fondly at the garden and pointed out a damask rose nearly in bloom. "It may be my favorite this spring." He turned back to Anne. "Comtesse Marie stopped here on her way to Beaumont. By her account, you've adjusted well to Paris."

"She's been very helpful." Anne paused to sip from her cup. "She's probably told you I'm going to work at the variety theater—to learn what I can about Antoine."

"A good place to start." His face took on a serious cast. "We'll deal next with Antoine's affairs."

They finished their coffee and went back to the office. A clerk set a small open box on the conference table. On top lay bundles of playbills and manuscripts. "Your father's things—whatever the police and the magistrates thought had no value," remarked Saint-Martin. "They're now yours."

She lifted the box as if its contents were precious, then peered in. "Most of these are from engagements since he left England," she said, browsing quickly. "That's his handwriting." She pointed to a page of dialogue from a comic skit. "He would write out a part even when he planned to improvise."

Opening an oval silver case, she gasped softly. Inside were two miniature portraits, one of herself, the other of her mother. She held them up before her eyes, tenderly regarding her mother's features. Sudden pangs of grief surprised her. She choked. Tears trickled down her cheeks. The portraits were a priceless legacy from Antoine.

She carefully closed the case and put it in her bag. Drying her tears, she glanced again into the box. At the bottom were his pens, ink, blotters, and a small box of blank stationery wrapped in a paper folder. She fingered through the items, then looked up. "His watch and his ring are missing."

Saint-Martin grimaced with disgust. "Snatched by whoever found the body or by police agents. Neither watch nor ring appears on the inventory of his confiscated property."

"Poor Antoine." Anne sighed, her feelings numbed by this petty indignity to her stepfather, robbed in death.

About to close the box, she decided to take a few sheets of the writing paper. Fanning them in her hand, she noticed one sheet was written upon. She pulled it out, stared frozen for a moment, then read aloud:

9 August, 1785, Paris, Palais-Royal:

> *Dearest Annie, partner and friend, you will be reading this, God willing, on August 19, your birthday. I wish you good health and many more years. I am well but have lately wondered if I should stay here. Something strange is going on with Lélia...*

"The birthday greeting I should have gotten," said Anne, her throat thick with feeling. "He wrote it the night he died." She handed the letter to Saint-Martin and walked to the court-yard window, dabbing at her eyes.

"The police might not have noticed it." The colonel studied the letter for a moment, then pointed to the last line. "'*Something strange is going on with Lélia...*' This would seem to confirm their conclusion. The woman was doing something that provoked Antoine to kill her."

With a start, Anne turned from the window. "He didn't kill anybody!" She glowered at Saint-Martin. "Where's Antoine buried? I want to visit his grave."

"I wish that were possible." A pained expression came over the colonel's face. "His body was burned and the ashes scattered."

Anne's eyes narrowed with suspicion. "Was he dishonored?"

"As the law prescribes for a murderer and a suicide, his body was first hanged, then burned."

"Where?"

"Place de Grève, in front of the Hôtel de Ville."

Anne stared blindly at the city map on the wall. This insult to her father's corpse could not hurt him. The law meant to punish her, the dead man's only family and friend. Dreadful images rushed to her mind. A limp body tied to a stake. Antoine's lifeless, bloodied face, his mouth open in a soundless scream. Flickering flames. Anne pressed her temples as if her head were about to burst.

"Are you well, Miss Cartier?" The colonel rose from his chair and hurried around the table toward her.

She stopped him with her stare. "How *can* you be part of such a barbaric system?"

He stepped back, his lips quivering, as if he had been slapped. They tightened to a sharp, thin line. "I'm *in* the system, not *of* it." He paused, mastering his feelings. "If I discover that Antoine Dubois was condemned unjustly, I will do everything in my power to clear his name."

She looked away from him toward Antoine's things on the table. The colonel had brought them to her, had spent the morning studying the dossier. Earlier, he had brought the news about Antoine to her in Wimbledon. With a twinge of shame she drew a deep breath and faced him. "Forgive me, I shouldn't blame you for the evil others have done."

He bowed slightly. She saw hurt in his eyes. He hesitated, then handed her the file on Antoine's case. "Unfortunately," he said in a subdued tone, "It supports the verdict the police have reached. I've found very little in the file that I could challenge."

They sat at the table across from one another while she leaned forward, reading from the file. Suddenly she grew distressed. "Here's Antoine's confession! Or so they claim!" She held up a sheet of paper and began to read aloud:

> The woman I loved has betrayed me, so
> I've killed her. I can't bear the shame of it.
> *A.D.*

She dropped the paper dismissively. "Those are Antoine's initials, but it's not like him at all!"

"That's a copy. The original note is also initialed. Experts in handwriting compared it with other samples of his writing and convinced themselves it was authentic."

Anne protested. "In the note he says he killed her because she was unfaithful. But that doesn't ring true. He must have known long ago what she was like."

The colonel shrugged his shoulders, then gestured toward the open file on the table. "The police culled together whatever supported their first impressions. A crime of passion, they thought. The evidence seemed convincing. Since they hadn't discovered any reason for doubt, they decided the case was solved. And closed."

"Do *you* think the case must remain closed?" Anne was unconvinced.

"New, compelling evidence could force it open. The city police will not search for it. And they will not allow the Royal Highway Patrol to do so." He paused, then measured out his words. "I believe something could be done in private." He rose from his chair. "I'll call in Georges Charpentier. He has studied the matter."

The colonel was gone for a minute, then returned with the short, stocky adjutant. Eyebrows arched, eyes eager, he sat himself at the table, next to the colonel. Anne greeted him with a friendly smile and he replied in kind. At a word from his superior, he began: "There are only two reasonable solutions to the case, a crime of passion, followed by suicide. Or, a double murder by one or more persons known to the victims. There's no evidence of a burglary or a forced entry at the theater. Nor, in the case of Dubois, of any struggle."

Georges reached for the file box. "The police chose the first alternative. Dubois killed Laplante, then jumped out the office window." For a few minutes the adjutant fingered through the file box. "Ah!" he exclaimed, pulling out a paper. "The medical report." He rapidly scanned its contents. "Cause of death," he read aloud, "was massive trauma to the head."

He looked up at Anne. "Do you really want to hear this?"

"Yes," she replied reluctantly. "It's painful but necessary."

"Dubois fell head first from the top floor of the theater into an open outdoor stairwell, fracturing his skull. That probably killed him instantly. As his body tumbled down to the basement landing, his body suffered other fractures and bruises. The examiner identified them without comment. That was enough for Inspecteur Mauvert."

With a sigh Georges shuffled the examiner's report back into the box. He slid down in his chair, folding his hands on his chest. "I wish we could take a closer look at those fractures and bruises than the police did. The examiner lists a bruise to the back of the head that *appears* to have occurred when the body tumbled down the stairs. But it could have been caused by an assassin's club—someone who then threw the unconscious man out a window."

"Right!" interjected Anne. "But we'll never know since his body has been burned." She glanced at the colonel and scowled. "Could that be a coincidence?"

Lines of doubt creased Saint-Martin's brow. "Do you mean the police have deliberately destroyed evidence, preventing a thorough investigation? What do you think, Georges?"

"The investigation wasn't thorough," the adjutant replied. "The police didn't puzzle out the physical evidence because the man was unimportant. They had an authenticated written confession. The writing didn't appear coerced, as if someone were torturing Dubois."

"The experts must be blind!" Anne exclaimed. "If the man had just killed his lover, wouldn't he write with more passion than this?" She thrust the note toward each of the men, her finger jabbing at the text. "This is too tame for Antoine. There's no real grief or remorse. And the hand that wrote it is strong."

"I'll play the devil's advocate," Saint-Martin said cautiously. "Experts can only guess why a man who has committed a murder and is about to kill himself writes his usual steady hand. Perhaps, the deed done and his mind made up, he enjoyed a moment of composure as he wrote out his confession."

"Your experts may say what they like!" Anne glared at him with indignation. "I don't think he killed anyone. I want to explore the idea that someone else killed them both." She glanced at Georges. "Would you help me get started? I'll take the risk."

Georges looked down, tapping his fingers on the table. Then he turned to Saint-Martin. "Miss Cartier could begin by inquiring casually about Lélia Laplante among her acquaintances. I don't think theater people who knew her would be alarmed by the curiosity of a newcomer." Detecting disapproval in the colonel's face, Georges added, "I could back her up in my spare time."

"What spare time!" Saint-Martin growled, as he rose and walked to the courtyard window. Arms folded, he stood there looking out for a few seconds. Then, he turned around and stared first at Anne and then at Georges. "All right, make a few probes. Search for new evidence. You *must* not attract the attention of the police."

He returned to his desk, concern mounting in his face. "And there are others whose attention we don't want if we're dealing with a double murder." He sat down next to Anne. "You may need to speak to me or to Georges. I want to be kept informed. But if you are frequently seen coming to this office, you may arouse curiosity in the minds of certain persons who could do you great harm."

He reached into a desk drawer. "Take this key. You can enter the back way through the garden pavilion. The servants who live there can be trusted."

Anne glanced at him without smiling, took the key, and dropped it into her bag.

Chapter 11

The Variety Theater

Early next morning, the sun barely above the rooftops, Anne stood alone by a fountain in the middle of the vast garden of the Palais-Royal. Around her to the north, east, and west, she saw tall, pilastered apartment buildings rising in regimented order, their uniform facades a fresh cream color. At ground level in the arcades, shopkeepers were preparing for the day's business. To the south, the garden ended at a low arcade of wooden shops and stalls. The Camp of the Tatars, it was called. Beyond stood the duke's palace, an older, irregular, sprawling gray building. Anne slowly turned a complete circle, letting her impressions sink in. This colossal place was designed more for giants than for mere humans.

Her throat tightened. Here Antoine Dubois had lived as well as died. There must be men and women in these buildings who still remembered him. And Lélia Laplante. Where to begin? For a few moments the question overwhelmed Anne, her arms hanging at her side. Thousands of people were milling about in the garden. Countless thousands more were hidden in the shadows of the arcades, in the shops, the restaurants, and theaters. Searching here for traces of Antoine and his Lélia was like looking for needles in a haystack.

Comtesse Marie had guided Anne through the place. Named after the palace at its southern end, she had said. Cardinal

Richelieu had built it, then left it to King Louis XIII. Hence, Palais-Royal. The palace and its grounds passed eventually to Louis-Philippe, Duc d'Orléans, who had transformed them into this bustling commercial and social center.

Anne joined the crowd in the western or Montpensier arcade. She would work her way toward the Théâtre des Variétés Amusantes and her promised job. Dark-skinned Africans in brightly colored robes strolled past her, followed by turbaned Indians. With shame she realized she was staring at them. She began searching for traces of Antoine and Laplante in shops, casually mentioning them without alluding to their violent deaths. Under the gimlet eye of a jeweler she gazed at a diamond studded broach Lélia might have admired. The man hadn't heard of her. In other shops Anne browsed among enormous wigs, miniature portraits, silks, satins and muslins the actress might have inspected. No one knew her by name. An hour passed in fruitless inquiry. Weary and disheartened, Anne told herself to stop. She must save her energy for the place where the murdered actress had worked.

After morning coffee in a small café, Anne made her way to the south-west corner of the Palais-Royal. The new variety theater was housed there in a large plain wooden building. Anne presented herself, repeating "Directeur Bouvin sent me" to a succession of underlings, until she reached his assistant. Recognizing her name, he gave her an ironic look. She reflected tartly on how Bouvin recruited talent. With a scowl, the assistant led her to the stage, chose music she knew, and stepped aside. As she sang and danced, he began to smile with reluctant pleasure. She could sing that very evening during an interlude. He found similar opportunities for her the next several nights as well.

❧❧❧

Anne closed her eyes as if to shut herself out of the hot, tiny dressing room. The smell of powder and the rustle of cloth, the outbursts of shrill irritation, the jostling for space had brought her mind back to London and to some of the reasons for giving up a career in theater. Still, after two evenings, she was becoming familiar with her companions. A few were popular with the public. Others were linked to wealthy patrons. Most were poorly paid and lacked self-respect, especially the dancers and singers of the chorus. She suspected that they sold themselves, informed for the police, or taught song and dance for a pittance.

Her act finished, she removed the powder and rouge from her face. The other women in the dressing room were ignoring her or, with sidelong glances, whispering about her. Anne was not surprised. A stranger who enjoyed Bouvin's favor, she had taken one of the scarce places in the theater company. She pushed back her chair, hung up her costume, and stepped out of the room.

Walking toward the stage, she reflected that she didn't have time to ingratiate herself, even if she could. From a grapevine running back to Bouvin, they might already know—and resent the fact that Comtesse Marie had helped her get the position. Nonetheless, a few of her companions were surely curious about her and would strike up an acquaintance. From them she might learn something worthwhile.

As she watched the show from the wings, a red-haired dancer coming off the stage threw her a friendly smile and a few words of greeting. For the rest of the evening, Anne hovered between stage and dressing room. When the last performance ended, the friendly dancer came up to her. "I'm Henriette Picard. Care to join us for drinks?" They were a small group of women who relaxed after evening shows at the nearby Odéon, a café in the Montpensier arcade.

"I'd be happy to," Anne replied, hoping that Laplante had frequented the place.

Through discreet inquiries over the next several days, Anne discovered that Henriette was well-informed and could be helpful, for she earned extra income selling information to the police and to other parties hungry for scandal. Anne feigned a wish to become acquainted. A risky tactic. The dancer was clever and unscrupulous. But Anne would learn what she could from her.

One evening with Henriette at the Odéon, their conversation turned toward crime in Paris. Anne sipped from her wine glass, then set it on the table. "A woman has to be careful here," she ventured, grasping her opportunity. "I've heard that an actress was murdered last year in the Palais-Royal."

"Lélia Laplante. I knew her." Henriette waved her hands dismissively. "Stabbed, quarrelling with her lover."

"She brought it on herself!" said a woman approaching the table with a glass of brandy in her hand. A singer with a fading voice, Georgette had a tired, worn look on her face. She set the drink down and pulled up a chair. "Lélia'd bed any rich man who'd have her."

"And not just overnight," added Henriette. "She'd move in with him for a week and come back to Monsieur Dubois as if nothing had happened."

Anne leaned back in her chair, lifting the wine glass again to her lips to hide her distress. This gossip threatened to stain her memory of Antoine. Had he lost all self-respect?

Georgette emptied her glass. "I'd have thought he'd take her as she was. Unfaithful and all. But Lélia had a nasty tongue. That could've pushed him over the edge." She sneered. "Even a weak man'll take just so much."

Angered by this slur, Anne glared at the aging singer. "No! He would have left her instead."

Georgette shrugged her shoulders and beckoned to a waiter for another brandy.

Henriette appeared startled by Anne's outburst, began to object, then fell silent.

Regretting the vehemence of her unguarded reaction, Anne inquired in a detached voice, "Was she killed at the variety theater?"

"No, over there." Henriette pointed toward the massive building to the south, faintly outlined by the dim night light of the city. "They were preparing a production at the duke's private theater."

Anne learned that this theater in the west wing of the duke's palace was used by the Société des Amateurs, an association of young noblemen who claimed to foster the performing arts. A few with talent wrote, produced, and acted in their own plays. Others merely dabbled. Most of them mixed a slight interest in the arts with serious gambling, refined carousing, and sophisticated games with women.

The theater was the Amateurs' favorite venue. The palace of the duke, a member of the royal family, lay outside the ordinary jurisdiction of the Paris police and beyond the reach of censors.

The Amateurs rented palace rooms adjacent to the theater for parties following their productions.

The duke was an honorary patron. Embarrassed by the murder-suicide, he had excluded the society from his property for several months. Recently, however, he was persuaded by several prominent businessmen and Freemasons, who shared an interest in the Amateurs, to open the theater to them again.

"Their directeur, Chevalier de Pressigny, will produce a show in a couple of days," said Georgette, the singer. "He's asked our manager for variety acts between plays and during intermissions." She noticed her remark caught Anne's ear. "But he pays poorly and expects us to entertain the Amateurs and their patrons."

She winked at Anne. "You *could* earn real money, depending on what you're willing to do. Few of us go there unless we have to."

"Well, I'll take up his offer," said Henriette with a grimace. "I need the money, and I'll stoop for it." Turning to Anne, she said, "Come with me, I'll introduce you. He'll be happy to fit you in."

About to refuse, Anne stopped, pretended to stifle a cough. A connection had suddenly leapt to her mind. Pressigny! She shuddered, kept her hand pressed to her mouth. According to the police file, Chevalier de Pressigny had charge of the Amateurs' production ten months ago when Antoine died. He was a man she needed to know. "Yes, Henriette, I'll be glad to join you."

Late that night, Anne walked slowly back to her apartment alone, through a dark narrow street. The moon was but a slim waxing crescent. The bells of Saint-Roch struck midnight. A madman's shriek, then a volley of curses punctuated the silence of the city. An ominous quiet returned. Anne stopped as if struck. She felt a tremor of fear. The women's cynical remarks at the Odéon echoed in her mind. Was she being drawn into dangers she might not be able to handle? The events at Islington came back to her. She remembered the pain. Should she quit now?

No, she told herself, she *had* to take these risks. For Antoine's sake. She lengthened her stride. In Islington she had also learned the hard way to trust friends. Harriet Ware. Louis Fortier. Mr. Newton. Here, in Paris, she wasn't alone. She could rely on Comtesse Marie, the colonel, and Georges. Her courage returned. She could deal with the risks.

Chapter 12

The Amateurs, June 1786

Bright sunshine poured into Anne's bedroom as she woke. A good omen, she thought. She walked to the open window, stretched, breathed deeply. A jumble of street noise greeted her. She pulled back the drapes separating her bedroom from the main room. Sunlight flooded the parlor. She had lived here for almost three weeks and it felt like home. She reached for her clothes and planned the day ahead of her.

The Amateurs had called a rehearsal for the morning, a day before the performance. For her small part she would choose something familiar, Rameau's *The Milkmaid's Lament*, perhaps. She practiced the song at the window, her audience a clutter of chimney pots angled helter-skelter on the tile roofs across the street.

Satisfied her voice was ready, she sat before her mirror, comb in hand, considering the next step in her investigation. It soon became clear she must explore the theater and see where the crimes had taken place.

At nine o'clock she joined her companion, Henriette Picard, for coffee at Café Odéon. They chose an outdoor table with a view of the duke's palace. Anne put on her most innocent face and asked again about Lélia Laplante.

"Wouldn't *she* have had a maid with her that night she was killed, to help her with costumes?"

"She couldn't afford a maid. When she needed work done, she hired Michou."

"Michou?"

"A little seamstress."

Anne cocked her head, affecting mild interest. This little Michou might be the kind of person who went unnoticed in a room and could have observed the actress Laplante in unguarded moments.

"An odd creature," continued Henriette, sipping her coffee. "Neither speaks nor hears what you say. Can't read or write either. But she alters garments and paints sets for the stage. She comes cheap. The Amateurs used to hire her." She frowned, as if the little woman were eluding her. "Come to think of it, I haven't seen her in quite a while."

Not a promising lead, Anne thought, but she had to start somewhere. "I might look her up for occasional work. Where does she live?"

"In a garret on Rue Richelieu, a couple of blocks north of here." Henriette reflected for a moment. "If she's not in, try the Hospital of the Holy Spirit on Place de Grève. The nuns look after her."

Midmorning shoppers were now filling the arcades. The two women left the café and walked through the garden toward the palace theater. Henriette pointed to a plain rear door at ground level. "That's where *we're* going, the servants' entrance." They snaked their way through a bustle of tradesmen, artisans, and performers in the back hall, then down a narrow corridor. "This is it," Henriette whispered, stopping at an open door. "Here's where Laplante was murdered!"

An odd-shaped room, it was enclosed on the outside by the thick curved wall of the foundation and, on the inside, by a solid supporting wall. To the right, where the room narrowed, stood a table piled high with boxes. To the left was a large wardrobe where two seamstresses bent over a table at their work. Through the open door, Anne could see herself in a mirror.

Henriette tugged on Anne's sleeve and pointed toward a dressing table up against the foundation wall. "Lélia was probably standing there when she was attacked. It was evening and only Laplante and Dubois were in the theater."

"Wasn't a watchman at the rear door?"

"He didn't see a thing." Henriette rolled her eyes. "He was drunk."

"Then anyone could have come in and..." Anne glanced toward the seamstresses who were talking to one another, ignoring the intruders. She continued in a low voice. "Anyone could have killed Laplante and Dubois and left unobserved."

Henriette shrugged her shoulders. Following Anne's cue, she also lowered her voice. "Nothing was stolen. Why would anyone have bothered to kill them?"

Anne confessed to herself she didn't know.

Her companion pointed toward a pile of cutting shears on a table. "A powerful thrust from one of them killed her." She held up a pair of shears for Anne to see, running her finger to its sharp point.

Anne glanced at the tool and abruptly turned away. She walked around the fitting room, silently fighting the image of Antoine raising such a dreadful weapon. She stepped into the wardrobe. There was a cutting table immediately to the right, bolts of material on nearby counters, and racks of costumes. Daylight poured in through a pair of deeply recessed windows. The seamstresses broke off their conversation and looked up, startled.

"Let's move on," said Henriette. "There's more to see."

They climbed a staircase to the first floor. On the stage, two comedians were rehearsing. Henriette pointed to a slim intense young man off to one side observing the act, chin in hand. "Simon Derennes, assistant to the directeur. There's bad blood between them. Pressigny would like to get rid of him. Or so I've heard. But Derennes is well-connected. Was raised in the palace. Part of the household." Henriette frowned. "Watch out for him."

"Why?"

Henriette glanced over her shoulder, shook her head. "I'll tell you later."

They climbed up to the second balcony, walked into the front row of benches, and gazed over the auditorium toward the stage.

"How lovely!" Anne murmured. Several years ago, it had been renovated in Louis XVI's style, all white and gold. It could seat two hundred Amateurs and guests. She imagined the most distinguished persons reclining on comfortable chairs in the elegant boxes of the lower balcony; the least distinguished, perching on the wooden benches where she stood; the remainder, sitting on padded benches on the main floor.

Henriette beckoned, apparently relishing the role of guide. "We still have a few minutes. Let's see where Dubois killed himself." She led Anne out of the balcony into a narrow walkway. On their left was the open area above the stage, in which hung rows of curtains; on their right, a closed room.

Her ear to the door, Henriette whispered to Anne, "Do you hear anything?"

Anne drew near and listened, then shook her head. Her companion cautiously opened the door. The two women slipped inside an office sparely furnished with a plain writing table, a few wooden chairs and tall cabinets, a shelf of books, and piles of papers. Large transverse beams supported the exposed roof high above them.

Henriette went to a window. "He must have jumped from here. He was found in the morning lying dead in the abandoned basement stairwell below."

Her gorge rising, Anne forced herself to lean over the sill and look down into the courtyard. She quickly pulled back, shuddering, nauseous. Don't faint, she told herself, keep your mind on the investigation. She breathed deeply, then walked to the writing table and stared at its surface, bare except for an ink pot and a rack of pens.

"They found his confession there," said Henriette.

Anne picked up a pen, possibly the one Antoine had used at this table. She tried to imagine how he felt, his hands still stained with Lélia's blood, writing his confession. It all seemed plausible to her now, sitting in his chair with his pen in her hand. Still her mind balked. He could not have killed her. There must be an explanation somewhere.

She began fingering through a pile of paper on the shelf above, searching for Antoine's name. Playbills, notes, scripts, and stage directions were carelessly mixed together.

Her companion shuffled nervously about the room. "We'd better go down to the stage."

"Yes, in a moment," Anne replied, but was too engrossed to stop. She had discovered a small, clasped, leather-bound, gilt-edged book. She was unfastening the clasp when she heard the latch rattle.

Simon Derennes burst in, hair unkempt, clothes disheveled. Dumbfounded, the women glanced at one another. Anne quickly fastened the clasp.

"My book! Have you seen it?" He stared with wild eyes, first at one woman, then at the other, as if he expected them to be where they were. They apparently had not aroused his suspicion.

"Is this it?" Anne volunteered, handing the book to him.

"*Merde*! I *thought* I might have left the damn thing here." He took the book, the wild look vanishing from his eyes. For a moment he stared at Anne, reading her face. "Thank you," he said unsmiling, then turned abruptly and walked away, leaving the door ajar.

"He's strange!" Anne exclaimed in a hushed voice. "Did you see how his hands trembled?"

"That's typical," her companion replied. "They say he drugs himself with laudanum and drinks until he falls on his face. He's charming one day, cruel the next. Likes women. Especially young ones."

Anne had taken an instant dislike to Simon Derennes. A devil! she thought, but curbed her tongue. She started toward the open door. "He's going to wonder what we're doing in the office. Let's get out of here."

A half-hour later, the two women rehearsed before Derennes, Henriette dancing, Anne singing. With cat's eyes, he tracked the movement of their bodies. His feet tapped to their rhythms. His hands no longer trembled. When they finished, he bent over his writing pad, jotting down a note, then looked up. A mocking smile played on his lips. "You are both ready. Be here tomorrow evening at seven sharp."

Anne and Henriette met at the theater the next evening. The manager assigned them the same dressing room on the first balcony with several other women. They were putting on their costumes when the door opened. A handsome gentleman in his early thirties sauntered in, tastefully dressed in a shimmering pale blue satin suit and matching gloves. His lightly powdered hair was thick and curly. His lips, red and sensual.

"Who's here tonight?" he inquired, a cock among hens. Anne had hastily covered herself before noticing Henriette and the other women hadn't bothered. They were snickering at her. The visitor gave slight, teasing smiles to several familiar faces, including Anne's companion. When his gaze reached Anne, it halted abruptly.

"And who is this lovely stranger?" His eyes scanned her body, then lingered on her face.

Henriette spoke up. "Anne Cartier, Sir, she's new at the variety theater."

"Oh!" he murmured, then smiled at her with interest. "We must meet again," he said as he left the room.

"Who was *that?*" she flustered.

"Chevalier Jean de Pressigny, the directeur," replied Henriette softly. "He's in charge of tonight's production." She seemed to sense Anne's irritation. "It's best to go along with him."

As Anne left the dressing room for her performance during the interlude, she looked up to the second balcony for a glimpse of the office where Antoine had worked. A clutter of stage machinery and curtains blocked her view. She had to force her mind back to the task before her.

A small remnant of the audience had remained in the hall chatting with one another. For their entertainment, she had chosen a popular song: a young princess, betrayed by a false lover at court, fled to the countryside into the arms of a virtuous shepherd. An insipid tale set to a charming melody. Dressed in white muslin like the queen's "milk maids" at Versailles, Anne lightly parodied the rustic simplicity fashionable among nobles. Taken by her satirical sallies and vibrant voice, her distracted audience untangled itself from its gossip and gave her several minutes of its attention, then hearty applause.

Leaving the stage, she met Chevalier de Pressigny in the wings. "A bit daring, Mademoiselle Cartier. I like that." He bowed slightly towards her. "I hope we shall have you again on our stage." He drew close, taking her hands in his. "Come to

the palace after the show and meet our members and guests."
For a few moments, he studied her like a fine vase he considered
buying. "Delightful creature! Do come!"

She stepped back, withdrawing her hands. "Perhaps," she
said coolly, though she fully intended to come. It seemed wise
to keep the directeur at a safe distance.

Near the end of the final performance, Anne readied herself
for the reception. Squinting into a mirror, she rubbed powder
and rouge from her face. Muffled voices from the stage mixed
with dressing room chatter. She fought off an attack of nerves.
No need to worry. Georges was coming in disguise. Wear Dido's
costume from Piccinni's *Queen of Carthage*, he had said; he
would recognize the tiara. The reception was a masked party.
Her face concealed, she could move about freely. By the time
she finished dressing, she was the only one in the room. Passing
the mirror, she struck a regal pose and wordlessly pronounced
approval.

As she walked through the hallway to the reception, a man
appeared at her side. "Hello, there." The voice was strange,
but she hoped for a moment it might be Georges. It was,
instead, the assistant directeur in a short Roman tunic, a laurel
wreath in his hair. He seemed sober and courteous, but Anne
noticed with alarm a lecherous glint in his eyes. As she had
only now masked, he must have recognized her coming out of
the dressing room and followed her.

"Let me show you about, Mademoiselle...."

"Cartier," said Anne sharply, as she quickened her pace.

He appeared to alter his expectations. "Sorry, if I seemed
abrupt," he said in a chastened tone. "I did enjoy your performance. May I formally introduce myself? Chevalier Simon
Derennes. I would be honored to be allowed to escort you."
He spoke this plea with good-natured self-irony. Feeling she
had the upper hand and might learn something from him, Anne
took his arm.

They walked masked into a vast hall lighted by a large
chandelier hanging from the ceiling and by hundreds of candles
in sconces on the walls. In the center a band of harlequin revellers
danced in swirls of green, yellow, and red around a life-sized
white marble statue. Standing on a pedestal, the male warrior

was nude save for a Corinthian helmet pushed back from his forehead. One of the revellers with a fife and another with a tambourine goaded the dancers into frenzied gyrations, as if the statue were the focus of a pagan rite. Anne stopped and stared, fascinated by the scene.

"*Diomedes Carrying Away the Palladium of Troy,*" remarked Derennes, nodding to the statue. "Copy of a work by the Swede Sergell, they say." Muscles tensed in mid-stride, his hand gripping a small statue of Pallas Athena, the Greek hero glanced sharply to his right. "He's seen light glinting off the sword of an enemy," said Derennes. A golden glow from the candles bathed the statue's clean, perfectly proportioned features. Anne imagined him alive, alerted to danger. Her head turned instinctively in the same direction.

Catching her eye, Derennes pointed to galleries beyond the hall. "You must see the duke's collection, one of the greatest in France." At the entrance, the young man spoke to a liveried footman who let them pass. They entered a large room with more splendid paintings on its walls than Anne had ever seen before. She raised her mask in wonder.

"Here are my favorites, the Lombard School, especially the Carracci brothers and Guido Reni." Derennes walked up to a cluster of pictures and also lifted his mask. He seemed at ease and engaged with the art before him, as if the painters were his intimate friends. Anne could understand his appreciation of their lovely landscapes and mythological scenes. But what pleasure could he draw from their religious works? He seemed so worldly. When he stepped back from admiring the pictures, she asked about them.

"These artists had to paint what their patrons wanted," he replied. "But Augustino Carracci, like the other two painters of the school, sought beauty above all, even when the subject was religious, like this one." Derennes grasped Anne's elbow and drew her closer to the picture of a man being skinned alive. "Look, two men with sharp knives are peeling off Bartholomew's skin, but he feels no pain. His body still expresses ideal beauty. The mounted officer directs the torture with serene calm. A witness discreetly averts his eyes. From above, a sweet angel offers a martyr's crown to the upstretched hands of the saint."

Stepping back, the young nobleman extended his arms as if calling a blessing on the painting. "There you have it," he exclaimed. "Perfect structure and balance, light evenly diffused, colors toned down. A quiet, harmonious scene that delights our eye."

He savored the pleasure for a moment, then turned to Anne and pointed at the scene with a now trembling hand. "What has *this* to do with real martyrdom? Think of it! The flaying of a man alive. Bloody butchery." He folded his arms in disgust. "Art for the devout indeed!"

Anne was at a loss for words, growing weary of the chevalier's sardonic observations. Much of what he had said made sense, but she detected in him an unhealthy passion for beauty, as if its pleasures were all that mattered.

They hurried past Guido Reni's *Saint Sebastian* with a glance at the martyr's elegant nude body pierced by three arrows. "I want you to see the next one," the nobleman murmured darkly. "It ought to intrigue you." They approached a small painting by Reni of a young woman tied to a pillar, gazing toward heaven. A man held a long pincers at her mouth. "She's Saint Apollina," Derennes remarked. He shot Anne a malign glance that made her shiver. "The man's about to pull out her tongue. The best way to deal with women who use it loosely."

His remark shocked Anne, as if it were a threat aimed at her. Out of the corner of her eye, she observed him closely. Head tilted back, eyes shifting from one painting to the next, he seemed to have altered his attitude. He had had enough of serene beauty, she concluded. His expression had become unfathomable, vaguely menacing. Refusing to be intimidated, Anne cleared her throat to get his attention. "I understand there was a murder here a year ago." She took care to speak as if merely curious, prompted by the scenes of violence depicted in the paintings.

He glanced at her over his shoulder. "It was nothing—a clown's quarrel with an old actress."

His words rang in her mind. "It was nothing." His cheeks were flushed, sunken. His eyes, dark, cold. With a curt motion for her to follow, he left the gallery.

Back in the main hall they fell behind a group of exotic "savages" beating drums and shrieking wild incantations. He touched her arm and pointed toward a deeply recessed doorway. "In here you will find a rare garden of delights." She hesitated, sensing that something wasn't right. He reached for her arm, as if to draw her in. She shook her head and took a step back.

At that moment, a masked pirate appeared suddenly at her side. "Wait a moment," he said. She recognized Chevalier de Pressigny, a note of anger in his voice. "Simon, I need to speak to you. Miss Cartier, would you excuse us."

She watched while Derennes unlocked the door and the two men disappeared into the room. How odd! she thought, that the door had been locked. What had Derennes intended? She shivered, as the possibilities flashed before her mind's eye. Revelers jostled her. She hardly noticed. Why had the directeur intervened? For her sake? He hardly knew her.

While she stood there perplexed, another masked figure in a pirate's costume came up to her. "Dido, I believe. May I be of service?"

She breathed a sigh of relief.

Georges bowed deeply with a flourish of his hat. "I've been following Pressigny, and trying to keep an eye on you as well. Looks like he and I arrived at a critical moment."

Anne described her encounters with Derennes from the rehearsal yesterday up to now.

"I believe he intended to do you harm. The notebook you mentioned must contain guilty secrets. He may suspect you've read parts of it. Pressigny somehow realized what Derennes intended to do and, for whatever reason, stepped in to stop him."

"I shall think better of him from now on."

"Let's see what happens." Georges glanced dubiously at her regal garb. "You must change your costume downstairs. I'll wait here for you. Hurry back before they come out."

Ten minutes later, Anne returned as a shepherd boy. "Any sign of them yet?"

"No. I'm beginning to wonder."

For another ten minutes, they strolled through the hall, keeping the door in sight. Masked men and women gathered around buffet tables of food and wine, or sat in small groups in the hall. Minstrels in Italian costumes filled the air with lilting songs. At the far end of the hall Anne noticed a pair of rooms apparently reserved for gambling and piquant entertainment. She might check them later.

Finally, the recessed door opened. Pressigny edged out, glancing nervously left and right. He locked the door, took a deep breath, and stepped into the hall. Georges and Anne drew close enough to study his face. Beneath his studied nonchalance she could detect the twitching of his mouth and his shifty troubled eyes. He glanced her way but didn't recognize her in the new disguise. He donned his mask and hurried away.

Georges leaned over and whispered to Anne, "I'll follow Pressigny for five minutes and then come back. Keep an eye on the door and stay out of trouble."

Anne resumed the watch alone. She was trying to look inconspicuous, when Henriette Picard approached her in the guise of a Greek goddess. A garland crowned her hair, a low-cut gossamer gown revealed all the contours of her body. "Good Lord," Anne thought. "I'm trapped."

Henriette gripped her by the arm and drew her close. "Who is this charming lad, may I ask?" Brandy had slurred her speech and clouded her vision.

"A humble shepherd, Mademoiselle," replied Anne, lowering her voice. "Would you excuse me, I'm waiting for a friend. You and I must meet on another occasion." At that moment, Anne saw Georges weaving his way through the crowd toward her. "Ah, there he is," she exclaimed, tearing herself loose from Henriette.

Georges appeared puzzled. "Pressigny turned in his costume and left the building. Much agitated."

"Shouldn't Derennes have come out by now? Could he have left by another door?"

"This is the only one," Georges replied. "I know the palace, every inch of it, from the days I worked for Lieutenant-General Sartine. For a month, I investigated a cabal the duke was believed to have organized." He paused, scratched his head, stared fixedly at the door. Suddenly, his face lighted up. "There *is* another way out." He pointed to the recessed doorway. "That leads to a storeroom and a hidden door to the basement. I can guess where he might be. Let's go!"

They took a circuitous route into the basement and, by the light of an oil lamp, made their way through a narrow, moldy passage. Sconces on the wall, draped with cobwebs, resembled mythological beasts. Their candles had yellowed with age and stood askew. Georges stopped at a rampant basilisk whose webbing had been recently disturbed.

"He triggers a lock," Georges said. "There's one like it on the other side. The door's hollow. Turns on a pivot."

Anne gingerly touched the basilisk's serpentine body, the sharp, hooked beak, the malevolent protuberant eyes, the crowned head holding a grimy candle—a cryptic sign for the horror that she suspected took place within.

"Pull down on it."

She did as he asked and a section of the wall slowly swung inward. She stepped cautiously into a dank windowless room. A few candles burned low in the fantastic wall sconces. Others were spluttering out, throwing a fitful light over the room. Pincers, hooks, pokers, and other sinister instruments hung on the walls of massive, crudely cut stone blocks. A brazier stood in a corner of the room, an iron poker resting in the glowing charcoal.

"Is this what Derennes had planned for me?" She stared at the pincers and the hot poker. "Saint Apollina, indeed!" She trembled.

Georges glanced sharply at her. "What's the matter?"

She related to him what Derennes had said in front of Reni's picture of the saint's martyrdom. As she finished speaking, her eye strayed to a white cloth on the floor in the shadow of the brazier. She picked it up—a kerchief. "Pressigny's been here." She showed Georges the directeur's monogram.

"The two men must have come down here from the storeroom. So where's Derennes?" Georges looked about the room. With the toe of his boot he lifted the edge of a square straw mat. "What's this?" He pulled the mat aside, and unbolted and raised a heavy trap door.

A fetid odor from below drove him back reeling. He returned with the lamp and peered into a dark pit.

"Christ!" Georges rubbed his eyes. "A skeleton! A woman, judging from the hair. One of Derennes' victims?"

Anne looked over his shoulder, then stepped back, nauseated. She couldn't speak.

"As best I can judge," Georges continued, "it's been there for some time." He lowered the lamp as far as he could. "Good God! The floor of the pit is littered with small skeletons. Cats or dogs, I think. And there's something moving just beyond the reach of my light."

Anne joined him again at the trap door.

A figure crawled haltingly into the light and looked up. "Get me out of here," Derennes cried, his tunic torn and dirty, his face bruised, his nose bleeding.

"Who beat you and threw you in here?"

"I won't say."

"Did you do this?" Georges brought the light directly over the skeleton.

"No. I never saw her before."

"Liar. What had you planned here for tonight? Candles lighted. A hot poker in the brazier."

Derennes didn't respond at first, then shouted again, "Get me out of here!" He began to whine piteously, covered his face with his hands.

Georges slammed the trapdoor shut and bolted it. His chest heaved with rage. "Damned, abominable liar!"

"Do we call the police?" Anne asked, her voice breaking.

"Not until I talk to the colonel." Georges put the mat back over the trapdoor. "We'll leave Derennes here for now."

Back in the narrow passage, Georges pushed the door shut behind them. "You'd never find it unless you tapped the wall up to the hollow sound."

They returned by way of the stairway up to the storeroom, observing that something had been dragged across its dusty floor. Fresh blood had spotted a sofa-cover, a chair had a newly broken leg. "Pressigny must have beaten Derennes here, dragged him downstairs to the dungeon, and thrown him into the pit."

At the exit to the main hall, Georges leaned on the door for a few moments. "I wonder what drove Pressigny to such violence?" He looked up at Anne. "Is he so fond of you?"

She shrugged her shoulders. "Could be, though I haven't encouraged him. He might have other reasons. Henriette said he dislikes Derennes and wants to expel him from the Amateurs." She gestured with her eyes toward the wall with the hidden door. "He also might have learned what Derennes was doing in the dungeon."

Georges nodded, then picked the lock with a thin tool from his pocket, opened the door, and stepped outside. "The party's going strong. We can get away unnoticed." They walked through a colorful tumult of revellers and out of the main hall.

∽∾∽

The palace theater was dark and empty. From the Amateurs' party came faint echoes of music and laughter. Revellers returning their costumes to the wardrobe shouted in the distance. Georges studied Anne with concern. "This may be our best chance to visit the office upstairs. Are you fit for it?"

"Yes. I'll rest tomorrow." She shook herself awake. "I was looking for a journal or calendar when Derennes walked in."

They climbed stealthily up to the second floor where they found the office door locked. Georges drew the tool from his pocket. "No one is likely to interrupt us." He picked the lock in seconds, then secured it again when they were inside. While Anne rolled a rug against the door sill, he closed the shutters on the window and lit a couple of lamps. "Now to work!" He reached for a shelf of books above the table.

Georges soon found the theater's journal. Its entries began about three years earlier, when Chevalier de Pressigny had taken charge of the Amateurs, bringing order and energy to their enterprises. The journal, in the hand of two or three scribes, recorded each day's events in copious detail. "The police might have looked at this," said Georges, scanning the entries, "but they didn't mention it in their report."

He stopped at the time in 1785 when the murder and so-called suicide took place. "Copy this section, Anne." He pointed to the pages for the month of August. "Something may be hidden there."

For an hour, while Anne worked on the journal, Georges sifted carefully through letters, business records, and unsorted notes. "Nothing here," he sighed, stretching his arms. He shuffled the papers into a semblance of their original order. "We should slip out before the party breaks up."

"Just a minute, Georges, I'm on to something. The pages I've copied refer frequently to a new play for the Amateurs' theater party, planned for August 15, last year, but canceled. Have you seen the manuscript? The title changes from page to page but it's most often, *The Cuckolded Clown: a Tragi-Comedy in One Act.*"

"I'll have a look." Georges walked across the room. "I hadn't thought of checking here." He picked the lock of a cabinet, rummaged through it, and returned to Anne with a thick folder. "This is it."

She skimmed the manuscript, then laid it on the table and leaned back.

"Georges." She lifted up the open journal. "Antoine has written these pages. I recognize his hand." Then she patted the folder in front of her. "He has also written this manuscript." Picking up a sheet, she gathered her breath. "Listen to this."

The one I've loved betrayed me,
so I've stabbed her dead.
Now I too must cease to be.
The shame of it I dread.

"That's the Clown's confession, after he thinks he's killed his mistress. Allowing for the poetry, it's almost identical to Antoine's."

"So?" Georges wrinkled his brow.

"Both the journal and the script were *dictated* to him!" She measured each word. "And so, I believe, was his own confession!"

Georges shrugged. "Or, the Clown's confession was in Antoine's mind when he wrote his own." He anticipated her protest with a shake of his head. "We can't solve the problem now." He quickly calculated. "Tonight's scripts are already here. The Amateurs' next theater party is two months away. They have no reason to go into this cabinet for at least two or three weeks." He picked up the manuscript and a few other samples of handwriting he had selected from the files. "The colonel can surely find someone to study them. I'll put them back before they're missed."

Their work finished, Georges and Anne swiftly restored furniture and papers, doused candles, unlocked the door. Anne peeked out into the hallway. She saw no one, although she could still hear revellers in the building.

"They seem to be making their way to the back exit," said Georges, locking the door. "Let's leave our costumes downstairs and join them."

∞∞∞

Arm in arm, pretending to be tipsy lovers, they staggered past a weary watchman and out of the building. Fresh morning air struck their faces. The thin, blue light before dawn illuminated the great expanse enclosed by the apartment buildings. Small human shapes were soon moving in and out of the arcades. The distant sound of bells announced the first mass of the day at Saint-Roch.

"Anne, shall I walk you home?"

"I would be honored, Sir," she replied in a teasing voice. She took his arm. "How did you join the party?"

He smiled mischievously. "To get into the theater, I picked an invitation from the pocket of a guest. When the lady in charge of the wardrobe left the room unattended, I slipped in and put on a pirate's costume. I checked her list. Pressigny and several others had chosen the same kind of garb." He grinned. "We were enough to capture a small ship. That made it easier for me to follow you."

They set out across the garden. A thought began to nag Anne. "Do you think Derennes might have killed Lélia Laplante and Antoine?"

"Possibly. He has the instinct. The answer might be here." He patted the papers hidden in his coat. "I'll interrogate him when I can slip back into the basement. I want to find out first if he had motive and opportunity."

"And learn the identity of the corpse you just discovered."

"Right. In the meantime, Derennes can't hurt you or anybody else."

Nearing the fountain in the center of the garden, Anne asked, "What will happen to him?"

Georges stared at the fountain. "I think Pressigny wants to get rid of him, finally, secretly. Bur Derennes has water, I saw it running from a pipe into a drain. He could survive for a week or more. The other Amateurs will soon discover he is missing. If they search for him, they won't think of looking in the dungeon. It's unused and almost forgotten. They could prefer Derennes vanish before he creates a scandal and becomes a burden to them." He turned toward Anne. "Don't pity the villain. He was going to put you in that pit with the corpse."

She shuddered, overcome by sympathy for Derennes' victim, someone who'd been tricked as she almost was. "Will Colonel Saint-Martin tell the police?"

"I doubt it. Derennes would claim someone assaulted him. Threw him into the pit. He knew nothing of the corpse. Given his connection to the ducal family, the police would release him." Georges stared again into the fountain, as if its rhythmic pulse could clear his mind for what he had to do. "Derennes is too dangerous to let loose. In the next few days, before the police or the Amateurs find him, he must be moved to a secure place." Georges looked up at Anne, his voice fell to a whisper. "You have seen evidence of his crimes. He will kill you if he can."

Chapter 13

A Cautious Smile

Anne woke later that morning to a dull, throbbing headache. She shuffled to the washstand and splashed water on her face. Drying herself, she glanced in the mirror. Her cheeks looked pale, her eyes red. Too much excitement. Not enough sleep. Touches of powder and rouge would conceal most of the damage.

The evening with the Amateurs had also bruised her nerves. How frequently does one encounter a man like Simon Derennes? Vile monster! He got what was coming to him. Several hours in that stinking black pit! Now, for the first time, it occurred to her, someone might have told him of her unusual interest in Antoine Dubois' case. Henriette perhaps. Well, it could have been much worse. The iron pincers flashed before her. With an effort she shut them out of her mind.

While dressing, she remembered Colonel Saint-Martin was away on a mission. She or Georges could tell him later about Pressigny's assault on Derennes. She tied on a pale blue bonnet and shaped it to shadow her face. The sun would burn hot today. And she must venture out to learn more about the little seamstress they called Michou.

By noon, Anne was at the Foundling Hospital of the Holy Spirit speaking to Sister Justina, a pink-faced, ageless nun. Distracted by a hawker's cry, Anne glanced out the window. In

Place de Grève, a noisy, odorous outdoor market extended from the Hôtel de Ville almost to the banks of the Seine. The nun followed Anne's gaze. "Unwanted infants come from that market and are left at our doorstep. That's why we're here."

Anne had heard that nuns were rich, their convents large as palaces. Some had formal gardens, like Hôtel des Capucines at the north end of Place Vendôme. Anne had seen it with Comtesse Marie. The Foundling Hospital was also large, but crowded into the city's teeming center. The two women sat on a pair of straight wooden chairs in the reception room. A crucifix hung on a wall. The room was otherwise bare. And recently scrubbed. The tile floor gave off a faint scent of lye. Probably typical of the living quarters as well, Anne mused. The nuns didn't appear to spend much money on themselves.

A lingering suspicion on Sister Justina's brow disappeared when Anne said she wanted to employ Michou, the little seamstress. Yes, the nun knew her. Abandoned as an infant at the hospital thirty years ago on the feast day of Saint-Michel, she was christened Michelline du Saint-Esprit and nicknamed "Michou" by the nuns. For years she had been a burden to the hospital until one of the older nuns discovered her talent for sewing.

"She learned to sketch as well," said Sister Justina. With awe in her voice, she explained that Michou's teacher, Sister Madeleine, the daughter of a certain great painter at the royal court, had been a skilful artist herself before entering the convent. "Michou draws beautifully. From her pictures and gestures, we can usually puzzle out what she needs."

"Sounds like much talent still hidden."

The nun agreed. "It's a pity she never learned to read and write. When she was growing up, it didn't seem worth the effort to teach her. She helped in the hospital in the hospital's linen room until she found work in a clothing store."

"I understand she sewed for the actress Lélia Laplante," Anne remarked offhand.

Sister Justina's face turned a deeper shade of pink, her eyes widened. "What happened to that poor woman terrified Michou. She shrank into herself like a mouse trapped in a corner. Afraid the same thing might happen to her, I suppose." The nun let out an exasperated sigh. "And to make matters worse, the police broke into her room—she couldn't know they were knocking on the door! She's stone deaf. They carried her off in manacles. Then that *horrid* little man, Inspecteur Mauvert, asked her questions she couldn't understand. Barked at her, shook his fist, treated her as if she were a criminal. I'd say he scared the wits out of her. She couldn't work for weeks! She's better now, but she still hides from people she doesn't trust."

Anne wondered about the inspecteur's interest in the little seamstress. "Did the police think Michou was somehow involved in the crime?"

"I don't know what they thought," replied the nun. "But, in the end, they decided she didn't know anything and let her go."

Thanking the nun, Anne rose to leave. "Where can I find Michou?"

"At the Théâtre des Petits Comédiens in the Palais-Royal. She's been there since it reopened a month ago."

Freshly painted, the theater graced the north-west corner of Palais-Royal's ensemble of buildings near the Beaujolais portal. The crowds had thinned out in the early afternoon. To Anne's eye, the theater appeared deserted. She approached the service entrance, then smoothed her dress and walked in.

"Michou's with the others, getting costumes ready for this evening," snapped the harried wardrobe manager. "Don't disturb her." He glared at Anne. "She'll have time off in an hour. You can't miss her—the tiny one wearing a white bonnet."

As the manager ran off, Anne retreated to a small café with a view of the theater. Sipping lemonade, she observed the human comedy being played out in the shaded avenues of the garden. The tempo began to increase. Well-dressed men came from dinner at the Café de Conti, business papers stuffed into their pockets. A pair of fashionable women paraded before her, their bodies encased in enormous skirts, their heads covered by great plumed hats. Anne shut her eyes and smiled inwardly in a moment of playful fantasy. Transformed into festive barges, the two ladies glided majestically over the shimmering waters of Versailles' Grand Canal.

In an hour, the theater's service door opened and several working women emerged, blinking in the bright afternoon light. After them trailed a small thin figure in a white bonnet. Anne paid her bill and followed the deaf woman to the center of the gardens.

At the fountain, Michou nibbled on a crust of bread, watching goldfish dart below the glassy surface of the basin. She tossed them crumbs, then danced with delight as they rose to snatch them.

"That's a start," Anne murmured to herself. "At least she's comfortable with fish."

Michou left the pool and walked south toward the "Camp of the Tatars" and its covered rows of temporary wooden sheds and booths connecting the eastern and western arcades near the palace. At midafternoon, the camp's lanes were visited by smaller, quieter crowds than in the evening. The deaf woman moved quickly up and down the rows, looking for free entertainment. Finally, she stopped in front of the Tatar Puppet Theater to watch an outdoor show of *Punch*.

The puppeteer caught Anne's eye; he seemed confused. She nodded and he carried on with the show. Victor Benoit was a man Anne had cultivated as soon as she became acquainted with the Palais-Royal. Watching his performance for the first time, she had sensed an opportunity to supplement her occasional work at the variety theater. Victor could fashion puppets and manipulate them with great dexterity, but he lacked the talent for creative story telling. His plays failed to fascinate and few people came to watch them. Anne had offered to put a little money into the enterprise. She would assume responsibility for writing scripts and directing the productions. Victor had readily accepted.

Entranced with the puppets, Michou had not noticed the silent exchange. Anne came up beside her, stretching to watch the performance. When a dog bit Punch, the little woman shook with laughter. She clapped her hands as Punch tricked the hangman into hanging himself. Gradually sensing Anne's close presence, Michou tried to move away. But the crowd pressed the two women together. They were soon exchanging glances at the amusing turns of the story.

The show ended, the crowd scattered, and Michou left Anne's side without looking back. Her chest tightening with anxiety, Anne wondered if she had gained any measure of the woman's trust. After a few steps, Michou turned and smiled cautiously. Anne replied with a wave of her hand. And breathed more easily.

Chapter 14

Missing Person

Georges stared vacantly out his office window into the garden, stirring sugar into a cup of coffee. As he leaned over his desk, his mind drifted back to last evening in the palace. He smiled at the thought of Miss Cartier. A brave and clever young lady. He and she had worked together as a team. And more than that, he realized. She had been tender towards him, like a daughter, holding his hand and kissing him goodnight. To other women he was merely a passing plaything, a good fellow.

Sipping his coffee, he heard a fluttering on the wall behind him and turned in time to see several sheets of paper floating zigzag to the floor. A breeze from the window was telling him to tidy up. To clear space on the desk for his cup, he gingerly pushed aside stacks of precariously piled folders. He rose from his chair and approached the clutter of police sketches pinned to the walls. Most of them were two or three years old. A dozen missing persons stared blankly at him, as if they had already found death in Paris. What had become of these serving girls, prostitutes, and poor young peasant women? One of them could well be the corpse in the pit with Derennes.

Georges picked up the fallen sheets, his own crude sketches of valuable objects stolen within the colonel's jurisdiction. They revealed a pattern of theft—exotic pieces of jewelry and decorative art bound for London, Amsterdam—anywhere but Paris.

He refreshed his mental image of each object as he pinned its sketch to the wall.

He moved on to pictures of criminal suspects that had come from Paris police headquarters. Comtesse de la Motte and some of her accomplices in the theft of the queen's necklace held pride of place. He removed the pins, crumpled the sheets into small tight balls, and threw them expertly into a basket. The Parlement de Paris had convicted the felons last week. Whipped and branded, the comtesse was now in prison. Georges saved pictures of her husband and other accomplices still at large, as well as the necklace since the police had not yet recovered it.

Enough housekeeping, he thought, stepping back. Now to the business at hand. Had Derennes slept well? Georges was eager to question and then dispose of him, but the more he thought about it, the wiser it seemed to wait until he could speak with Colonel Saint-Martin. A day or two in the pit might persuade the villain to talk more freely. In the meantime, Georges would visit police headquarters. He might learn Derennes' background and find out what he had been doing on the mid-August night in 1785 when Laplante was murdered.

It was late afternoon when Georges returned to the office. After a light supper at his desk, he leaned back in his chair, studying the ceiling. On that night in August, Derennes had been attending the variety theater, a five-minute walk from the scene of the crime, in the company of Chevalier de Pressigny and Monsieur Robert LeCourt, a rich Dutch financier currently living in Paris. The audience was often up and about during several intermissions. Derennes could have easily slipped away from the others to kill Laplante and Dubois. Or, the murders could have taken place shortly after the theater closed. Derennes had ample opportunity. But what could have been his motive? The police files offered no answer.

Frustrated, Georges mumbled a curse. He left his desk and ambled into the garden. Derennes had grown up in the palace, son of an architect in the duke's service. Searching for a hiding place, Derennes had probably studied records in the palace archives that led him to the secret dungeon. Pacing back and forth in the twilight, Georges wondered why Derennes had wanted to attack Miss Cartier? For sadistic pleasure? Why her, rather than a prostitute? Simply because she was alone and the dungeon ready for a victim? Georges was unpersuaded.

He stopped at the garden fountain. Hands clasped behind his back, he leaned over and gazed into the water. Derennes' attack was not random. He'd had his eye on Miss Cartier. Caught her prowling in the theater office, her hands on his book. He'd waited for her outside the dressing room.

Had he feared she was a police agent who might uncover something damaging to him—like the murder of Laplante? Georges returned to his office with the feeling he needed to talk to someone from the ducal household who might have known Simon Derennes. It was still early enough in the evening to pay a visit to an old acquaintance.

In a few minutes, Georges was at the door of Louise Tremblay, retired governess of young girls in the household of the deceased Louis, Duc d'Orléans. Mademoiselle Tremblay, an infirm spinster, lived in a small room in her niece's garret apartment on Rue St. Honoré near Palais-Royal.

"Police business," Georges announced to the niece, and gave his name. "Your aunt knows me." The niece raised an eyebrow momentarily, then showed him into a tiny parlor and went to fetch her aunt. He took in the room's spare, shabby appearance—cracked plaster, no rugs or drapes, plain wooden furniture. Well below the standard Tremblay could have claimed in the duke's employ. The old woman shuffled into the room on her niece's arm, settled into one of the chairs, and motioned for Georges to take the other. The niece withdrew.

"Stiff joints," muttered Tremblay, grimacing with pain, as she crossed her legs at the ankle. "Don't get old." She looked at Georges with a sharp, clear eye. "I *do* remember you—Sartine's man. Investigated a cabal at the palace almost twenty years ago. You had more hair on that occasion." Her lips curled into the hint of a smile. "I couldn't help you then. What can I do for you now?"

"Simon Derennes has disappeared."

"I know. The police were here a few hours ago—that nasty little inspecteur."

"Mauvert?"

"That's him. Wanted to know where Simon Derennes was. I said I hadn't any idea. I've had no contact with him or his family since the old duke died last year. Mauvert never asked what I thought of Derennes."

"But I shall," Georges remarked, settling back in the chair. "How did you come to know him?"

She was silent for a moment. Then she met his eye. "While I served the duke, I seldom talked about family affairs, never to outsiders. Since his death, I feel no obligation to him or his family. He left me a pittance after I had given more than fifty years of faithful service." She lifted her hands palms up. "I'm a beggar. I live on the charity of my niece, who has barely enough for herself and her man." Her eyes clouded and left Georges for a few moments, then turned back to him quizzically. "Who are you working for now?"

"Colonel Paul de Saint-Martin, a provost of the Royal Highway Patrol."

"I've heard of him. Breteuil's kin. An honorable man. Why's he interested in Simon?"

"Derennes may have killed a woman three years ago and has recently attempted to kill another. The colonel wants me to stop him before he kills anyone else." Close enough to the truth, Georges thought.

"Someone should have stopped Simon long ago." Her face hardened in a grim expression. "I'll tell you what I know." The young man was born in 1763, she explained, when she was a fifty-year old governess, pursuing her family's career of service in the Palais-Royal. She grew concerned about Simon when he was seven. The girls she oversaw reported the young boy teasing them maliciously, pulling their hair, stealing their dolls, tormenting their pets. This went on for a while, the governess loath to complain. When she finally brought the matter to the attention of Simon's parents, they became angry and threatened to have her dismissed. They were proud of their son, a handsome boy, who could be sweet and charming. He had also won the affection of the old duke, intrigued by the boy's talent for theater and his precocious appreciation of the palace art collection.

Neglected as well as spoiled by his parents, the boy grew worse. By the time he was fifteen, certain ladies of the palace accused him of killing their pets and harassing their daughters. The old duke wouldn't listen to their complaints. When Simon was twenty, the police suspected him of sadistic attacks on prostitutes and the rapes of young country girls newly arrived in Paris. A magistrate interrogated him, but didn't press charges for lack of evidence. The Société des Amateurs spoke up for him.

"Simon's an artful deceiver," she remarked with a tired voice. "And, secretive. He has hiding places—some of them in the duke's palace—where he practices his vices."

"Derennes, the Amateurs. Pampered parasites, the lot of them!" Georges sniffed with contempt. He leaned forward and held the old lady's hand, then met her eye. "I can assure you, Simon Derennes is nearing the end of his career of deception."

⊗⊗⊗

Early the next morning, Georges approached the Palais-Royal dressed as a carpenter. Questioning Derennes could not wait until the colonel returned. He would be out of town until Sunday evening. Getting into the palace should not be difficult. For the past several years it had been undergoing renovation, and workmen moved about freely.

At the service entrance, he talked his way past the guard. Finding the door to the great hall locked, Georges climbed down into the basement of the theater, then snaked through a dense jumble of sets, stage properties, and discarded furniture to the narrow passage into the palace.

He threaded his way past the exotic brass sconces shrouded with cobwebs until he reached the basilisk, sentinel at the dungeon's secret door. He paused for a moment, ears alert for voices or footsteps. Derennes' disappearance had not yet been announced, but the Amateurs might well be looking for him— though not likely in this musty corridor. Still, Georges didn't want them to find him in the midst of an unauthorized interrogation.

He cautiously opened the dungeon door and stepped inside. His eyes swept the room, looking for changes. He froze. The kerchief Miss Cartier had found was missing. She had thrown it on the floor, Georges was certain of that. He stepped quickly to the trapdoor, not bothering to put on a mask to counter the stench. He heaved up the door and peered into the pit.

Empty, as he had feared. Ignoring the stench, he lowered himself on a rope down to the pit's rough stone floor to search for evidence of Derennes and the corpse. Not a trace. Even the animal remains were gone. He climbed out and searched the dungeon carefully. The iron poker still rested on the brazier, the pincers on the wall.

He paced back and forth, his heart pounding. The clack of his boots echoed off the gray stone walls. Incredible! Someone had removed Derennes and cleared out the pit, then arranged the dungeon to look like nothing had happened! Someone knew what had happened to Derennes and where to find him—in the most secret room of the palace. And only a few hours ago—just before dawn.

Pressigny? Not likely. Probably two men pretending to haul trash in and out of the building. Too much hard work, too little time for one man. So what had Derennes' rescuers done with him? Released him, and he chose to remain in hiding? Or, if they were Amateurs and suspected he was responsible for the corpse and would cause a scandal, they might ferry him out of the country with a new identity, or hide him away as a prisoner, or even secretly kill and bury him.

The Société des Amateurs would want to protect its good name and avoid the displeasure of the duke. LeCourt would be equally concerned. He had invested money and, more important, his reputation, in the Amateurs. They had helped him gain entrance into aristocratic society where he attracted its money to his investments. He also was negotiating on behalf of Dutch bankers with the French government for refinancing its debts. He had good reason to be concerned about scandal involving Derennes, especially a double murder of Dubois and Laplante. Georges was at a loss. He couldn't question either Pressigny or LeCourt without reopening the case again.

Georges stopped, then stared at the open door. His mind raced on. Derennes in hiding? He'd want Miss Cartier dead. And, so just might his mysterious rescuers. He glanced at his pocket watch. Eight o'clock. She'd be at the Tatar Puppet Theater. No time to lose. He must warn her.

∞∞∞

Georges paused for a moment at the entrance to the puppet theater. He had run from the palace and was out of breath. Some theater! he thought, hardly more than a wooden shack. Before him stretched a narrow room with benches for thirty patrons. At the far end, a dark green cloth masked a waist-high plank platform. Kneeling on the platform, her skirt hitched up, Miss Cartier was arranging the strings of a marionette. She recognized him as he walked forward, her expression of pleasure giving way to concern. She jumped nimbly down and met him in the aisle.

"What's happened, Georges?"

"Someone got to the dungeon before I did. Derennes's gone. And so is the corpse. The pit's clean."

She drew him to a bench and sat on the edge, her eyes fixed on him.

He spoke in a low, insistent voice. "Your life's in danger. If he's loose, he will try again to kill you. Even the Amateurs might want you dead, if they are the ones who pulled him from the pit."

"So what am I supposed to do?" She looked at him askance.

"You're free to do as you like, but stay in a safe place." He paused, fearing he might offend her. "And the safest place is the colonel's residence." He proposed she move into a small apartment in the garden pavilion, the one reserved for visitors. She already had a key to the rear entrance.

She rose to her feet, her eyes black with anger. "I'm free, indeed, and I choose *not* to live like a caged or hunted animal." She walked to the platform and leaned against it, glowering at him. "I can take care of myself," she said emphatically. "You are exaggerating the danger."

"Perhaps. But consider the last time you 'took care of your-self,' Jack Roach damned near killed you."

His words had a cold, hard edge. They hit home, he could tell. Her mouth worked with pent-up feelings, struggling to reply. She turned away from him, as if recollecting the shameful punishment she'd received at Islington.

"On that occasion last September," she said, carefully articulating the words, "I recklessly ignored the warning of my friend, Harriet, and paid dearly. I should have spent the night with her." She looked at Georges, clear-eyed and direct. "I count you also as my friend. I shall accept your advice. Staying in the provost's residence over the weekend is certainly the wisest thing to do."

Georges took her hand and stroked it. That confession had cost her a great deal. He felt honored.

The visitor's apartment reminded Anne of a small fortress. The back wall's thick stone blocks shut the provost's property off from an alleyway. She walked through the rooms, opening louvers to catch a slight breeze. It was a warm night. She would have liked to sleep outdoors. The place was safe enough. The bedroom, kitchen, and parlor faced the garden. An older married couple, living in a similar apartment next door, watched the back entrance during the day. Their terrier guarded it by night. She was also under Georges' vigilant eye. From his apartment in the main building, he could survey the entire garden.

Throughout the day, she had had little reason to fear Derennes or anyone else. Guarded by one of Georges' agents, she had kept herself busy at the Tatar Puppet Theater most of the afternoon. The agent watched over her also during her short evening engagement at the variety theater. Chevalier de Pressigny was there with several Amateurs, patrons, and courtesans. Handsome devil! He had stared at her and winked.

Now, however, she sat by herself in the parlor. It was late. Several oil lamps gave off a warm golden light, but the shadows they cast on the walls looked menacing. After the loud music of the theater and the raucous noise of the streets, the room seemed unearthly quiet, its atmosphere heavy and threatening. She felt uneasy. Derennes' attempted deception recalled to mind Roach's assault. The ground she had to cover to clear Antoine appeared more treacherous than she had imagined. She wished for a companion with whom she could share her feelings.

She got up from the chair, threw a thin scarf over her shoulders, and stepped out into the fresh air. Bending over the fountain, she splashed cold water on her face. The terrier approached silently out of the darkness, sniffed and licked her outstretched hands, then disappeared. For several minutes Anne strode back and forth, breathing deeply, and dismissed Roach and Derennes from her thoughts. She looked up. Bright stars patterned the clear night sky, their magnificent display telling of their creator, who wisely governed the affairs of men as well as nature. Her nerves calmed. When she went to bed, she was lulled to sleep by the faint rippling sounds of the fountain.

∞∞∞

Monday morning, Georges was sitting in his office, reading the mail. He had not yet spoken with Colonel Saint-Martin, who had returned home late at night and left again early in the morning. A door slammed. Georges looked up, hearing a familiar voice.

A minute later, Saint-Martin walked in. "I've just come from a conference with the lieutenant-general. He says Chevalier Derennes is missing. He was last seen several days ago at the Amateurs' theater party." The colonel shed his coat and sat down at the desk across from Georges. "The duke's upset. He doesn't want another scandal."

"Does the lieutenant-general suspect foul play?" Georges pushed a pile of letters to the side. "Would he care? Derennes is the worst of a bad lot."

"The lieutenant-general suspects the Amateurs might have decided to get rid of him."

"In that case, they've done a favor to the young women of Paris." Georges crossed his arms on his chest, slouched back in his chair.

The colonel looked down, then slowly pulled off his gloves. "Do you know anything about Derennes that I might relay to the lieutenant-general?"

"As Martha said about Lazarus," Georges replied, lifting his hands, "I know he'll rise on the last day." He smiled inwardly. He enjoyed a game of cat and mouse with his superior.

The colonel pursed his lips. "The lieutenant-general may already know that." He slapped the gloves lightly on his thigh.

"What I have to say may not be for the lieutenant-general's ears." Georges paused, observing the colonel begin to sit up.

"Derennes attempted to seize Miss Cartier while she was investigating the Amateurs' reception at the Palais-Royal." With an apprehensive eye on the colonel's face, Georges related what had happened that night at the palace. "When I returned later to question Derennes, the pit was empty. I've searched all the likely spots but found no trace of him."

"And how is Miss Cartier?" The colonel's brow furrowed.

"Fine." Georges smiled guardedly. "But if Derennes's free, she's in danger. I've arranged for her to stay in the garden pavilion."

Saint-Martin hesitated, as if about to make a remark. But he appeared to change his mind. He rose, clutching his gloves, walked to the window and looked out over the garden toward Anne's apartment. Georges sat in respectful silence.

After a few moments, the colonel cleared his throat, then turned around. He reached for his coat, frowning. "The Amateurs may have rescued Derennes and concealed him. And that corpse you saw in the pit is a matter for the Paris police. But we can't go to them yet. They would realize we are prying into the Laplante case." He paused in the doorway. "My aunt, Comtesse de Beaumont, must know Chevalier de Pressigny. I'll pay her a visit. And you, Georges, try to get better acquainted with Monsieur Robert LeCourt."

The colonel walked through the garden and knocked on Miss Cartier's door. He waited nervously. His imagination conjured up Derennes' iron poker, its white hot point darting like a snake at her face.

The ghastly apparition vanished when Miss Cartier opened the door, a surprised smile on her lips. Saint-Martin bowed, then held her hands for a moment. "Would you step out into the garden with me? I've just learned from Georges what happened Wednesday night at the Palais-Royal. I'm thankful you weren't hurt."

As they strolled between beds of roses, the gravel crunching beneath their feet, Miss Cartier told him her story. Her voice was firm, unruffled. He glanced at her sideways and could detect no damage to her spirit. If anything, she appeared a little more sure of herself, like a promising young officer who has just passed the first test of battle.

At the fountain they listened to the soothing sound of water and enjoyed the warmth of the midmorning sun. The delicate scent of roses in bloom enveloped them, triggering Saint-Martin's chivalrous instincts. From infancy he had been taught to protect women. And *this* was a woman he was growing to like.

"I can imagine the dreadful prospect of that dungeon, what horror might have happened. I would understand if..." He groped for words. "If you decided to be less involved..."

She cut him short. "Colonel Saint-Martin!" Her voice failed momentarily, struggling for words. Her eyes narrowed with resolve. "You can't push me aside. After all, *I* found the source of Antoine's so-called confession in the office."

Startled by her vehemence, he fell silent, then nodded. "Georges just told me. I'm pleased." He added, "I'll give the manuscript to an expert reader." He walked her back to the apartment, keenly alert to the swishing of her gown, the heaving of her chest. He sensed in himself a stirring of affection, a yearning for her. As they approached her door, she turned to him, her jaw taut. "If I must, I'll carry on alone."

"No need to do that," he said gently. "I understand how you feel." She searched his eyes, her expression softened, she moved a step toward him. He reached out his arms and embraced her. "We'll carry on together."

Chapter 15

Chevalier Jean de Pressigny

"Miss Cartier fell into a viper's nest," said Saint-Martin to his aunt. He had ridden into her courtyard at Chateau Beaumont while she was instructing her groom for the day. The sun had barely risen above the trees. The cobblestones glistened with dew. She had just returned from exercising her horse and was dressed in a maroon riding suit. A black leather crop hung from her wrist.

"Viper's nest?" She searched his face, as if she couldn't understand what he meant. She told the groom to care for the colonel's horse. When man and horse were out of earshot, she asked her nephew what had happened.

"Simon Derennes tried to abduct Miss Cartier at Palais-Royal," he replied, then went on to describe Pressigny's conflict with Derennes, the discovery of the latter together with a corpse in the dungeon's pit, and Derennes' disappearance.

"How *is* Miss Cartier?"

"Unharmed and more determined than ever. For safety's sake, she's moved into my garden apartment."

"I didn't expect anything like this, Paul. What have you stumbled upon?"

"It appears that Lélia Laplante and Antoine Dubois were victims of a double murder. That's the theory Georges is pursuing. Secretly." He cautioned his aunt. "For the time being, the Paris police must be kept in the dark."

"Paul, I trust you know what you are doing. Baron Breteuil would be displeased."

"Georges thinks Dubois' death was made to look like a suicide. Miss Cartier's inquiry might have led Derennes to fear she would discover evidence incriminating him, either in killing Laplante and Dubois or in some other unrelated crime. We have the word of a trustworthy witness that Derennes injures and perhaps also kills for the pleasure it gives him."

"Poor Miss Cartier," exclaimed the comtesse shuddering. "So nearly in the clutches of a human beast."

"Whose fangs must be pulled before he can harm her." Saint-Martin's voice threatened to break. He drew a deep breath. "The Amateurs may have saved us the trouble. Derennes had become a potentially serious embarrassment to them. Think of the scandal if the police were to investigate that corpse in the dungeon and arrest Derennes. So, he has vanished, possibly with the connivance of the directeur, Jean de Pressigny, and the principal patron, Robert LeCourt." The colonel paused, seeking his aunt's eye. "We need to know more about these men and what they may have done with Derennes—and the corpse."

For a long minute, Comtesse Marie studied the cobblestones, digesting what she had heard. Finally, she looked up, swinging her riding crop a full circle. "We'll have a bite to eat, then ride over to Chateau Debussy, twenty minutes from here. That's where Jean de Pressigny lives."

"Impressive view!" said Colonel Saint-Martin to his aunt, reining in his horse. They had approached from the east. The morning sun behind them tried fitfully to break through a bank of clouds. Chateau Debussy lay below at the bottom of a long green slope. Four cylindrical towers anchored the corners of the main building, a large gray square structure, flanked by two pavilions and covered with a dull red tile roof.

Beyond the chateau, the land rose gently to the western edge of the estate where it reached a steep chalk ridge partially covered by dark woods. A river, the Bièvre, snaked through the fertile valley, fed a glistening pond in front of the chateau, and went on its way north-eastward toward Paris and the Seine. At least from a distance, the estate appeared well-managed. Near the chateau stood a large greenhouse surrounded by gardens. Stables and work shops seemed busy and in good repair. At midmorning a dozen men were tilling the fields, driving wagons up and down the lanes, and tending cattle and sheep.

The comtesse beckoned her nephew to a grove of trees on a knob of land overlooking the chateau. They dismounted and tethered the horses, then walked to a small shaded clearing facing the chateau. From this closer vantage point, the chateau took on a sinister appearance. The pond now appeared deep and dark, a barrier to entering the building. Its gray walls seemed thicker. It would be easy to hide Derennes there. Or bury him.

Saint-Martin turned to his aunt. "What can you tell me about Chevalier Jean de Pressigny?"

"I have met him a few times, and we have mutual acquaintances." She explained he was a gifted young man with a troubled past. As an infant, he lost an impoverished father who bore one of the great names of the French aristocracy. A few years later, his mother married Comte Philippe Debussy, a man of obscure lineage but much wealth recently acquired in India. "Debussy then bought this property at a bargain price." Comtesse Marie raised her arm in a sweeping gesture over the valley. "He renamed it after himself."

She went on to describe the neglected upbringing of Jean and his younger sister, Claire. The comte never legally adopted them. When their mother passed away, she left her modest estate in her husband's hands. As Jean grew older, he fell into gambling and other costly vices. He demanded his inheritance. Servants reported fierce quarrels. The rascal even spread rumors that Debussy had stolen his legacy.

"I've heard he killed Chevalier Richard de Boisvert in a duel," said Saint-Martin. "For what reason?"

"Jean treated young women like oranges, eating the fruit and throwing away the peel. Boisvert accused him of dishonoring his sister." She sighed. "The king imprisoned Jean in the royal fortress at Vincennes. He was mysteriously released shortly afterwards."

"For a fatal duel, Pressigny should still be in prison," the colonel observed. "He must be connected to a person with great political influence."

His aunt could not name such a person with certainty, but shortly after leaving prison Pressigny joined a masonic lodge that met at the Palais-Royal under the protection of the Duc d'Orléans. Whatever the connection, the young man's behavior seemed to improve. He gave up gambling, became directeur of the Amateurs, and even began enlightened work on the Debussy estate. She pointed toward a marshy area along the Bièvre. Two men were laying a drainage system, using tiles and brick from the old kilns at the foot of the chalk ridge.

Drainage ditches and old kilns, Saint-Martin thought darkly. Convenient for disposing of an unwanted person like Derennes. "I need to get someone into that place," he said as they mounted the horses.

On the way back to Comtesse Marie's chateau, they agreed it was unlikely Pressigny had undergone a religious conversion. "Let's give him the benefit of the doubt," she said with little conviction. "Perhaps he realized his behavior was self-destructive and followed the example of Emperor Joseph, the queen's brother, and nobles who aspire to be socially useful."

"I would be very surprised," he remarked, then asked her, "Would it surprise you to learn, dear Aunt, that Chevalier de Pressigny may have hidden Derennes or his body at Chateau Debussy?"

"No, it wouldn't," she replied with a sigh. "He's a cunning man and a talented actor. He may be cleverly playing a new role."

∞ ∞ ∞

That morning, Anne was in the garden apartment by the window, writing the script of a marionette play for Abbé de l'Épée's institute. She usually devoted these, the freshest hours of the day, to improving her skills for teaching the deaf. She would work at the puppet theater in the afternoon and the variety theater at night.

There was a knock on the door. She looked up startled. Few people knew she was staying at the provost's residence. A young page stood outside with a note from Chevalier de Pressigny.

Would you please meet me at the fountain
in the garden of the Palais-Royal at noon.
I would like to discuss a project that might
appeal to you. Perhaps we could do this
over lunch. The messenger will wait to
receive your reply.

Anne retreated to her parlor and paced the floor, glancing askance at the note. She felt a tremor of anxiety. How had Pressigny found out where she was staying? He must have had her followed. Was he trying to trap her, to find out what she knew about Derennes?

Or did he have something else in mind? She read the note aloud. Its tone was courteous. Reason enough to suspect him. She recalled his preening among the women in the palace theater's dressing room, his scrutiny of her body. Like Jack Roach, he considered women no more than instruments of pleasure. He was elegant and attractive, but she couldn't trust him.

She walked to the window and leaned out, her arms resting on the sill, mulling over the invitation. She could cope with Pressigny. True, he had killed a man in a duel, but he wasn't a deranged murderer like Derennes. He posed a threat to her virtue, not to her life. If he tried to seduce her, the harder she made it for him, the more he would enjoy the effort. She could perhaps trick him into revealing his dealings with the actress Laplante. He had surely known her.

She rose from the sill, nodding thoughtfully. After all, his proposal might be aboveboard. And the fountain, neutral and public, was a safe place to meet. But she would ask for a later date. He shouldn't be allowed to think she was at his beck and call. On the other hand, she *was* free at noon.

Glancing across the garden window toward Georges' office, she wished he were there. He and the colonel wouldn't be back until later in the afternoon. She might as well find out what Pressigny had to say. She sat down at the table and took a plain sheet of paper. "I shall already have eaten lunch," she scribbled, "but I'm willing to hear about your project. I'll meet you at the fountain at noon." She folded the note, handed it to the page, and sent him off.

∞∞∞

Chevalier Jean de Pressigny stood by the fountain five minutes before noon. Mademoiselle Cartier's note had been impudent, but he had received the insult to his rank with amusement. He had discerned her spirit the moment they met in the dressing room. Proud bitch! No fluttering eyelids and simpering smile like the others, but a cool, direct, and steady gaze. No doubt she could play the part his stepfather expected, regal but free of pretense and pomposity.

What a challenge, to break through her facade, to take her down to raw instinct. He imagined subtly enticing her with deference, treating her like a lady. Yes! Then there would be a meeting of minds. He would pretend to long for a simpler, more authentic life, closer to nature. Having won her trust, he would play upon her hidden desires. Yield to nature, he would say, even while dissolving her inhibitions with the artifices of love. In the end, she would come crawling to him naked!

The satisfaction of conquering her would be all the greater, knowing she was the mistress of that prig, Paul de Saint-Martin. Free of danger as well, for the colonel refused to duel! Pressigny shook his fists, amazed by his good fortune. What a prospect to look forward to! He nearly quivered with pleasure, indulging his fantasy to eke out a few more moments of venery.

His eye caught her as soon as she stepped out of the shaded arcade into the open space of the garden. She wore a simple robe, her face shielded from the sun by the brim of a light straw hat. Erect and rather tall, alert and self-assured, she walked toward him with unaffected grace. "Perfect," he murmured to himself. "But, of course, she's an actress and knows I'm watching her." As she drew near, he bowed. "Good day, Mademoiselle Cartier, I'm pleased you could come." She greeted him with polite reserve.

"I'll get right to the point," he said, as they strolled on a graveled path southward toward the palace. "On behalf of the Société des Amateurs, I invite you to join our next production."

He paused slightly to register her reaction. She gestured for him to continue.

"It will take place in five weeks at Chateau Debussy, my stepfather's estate near Paris, to honor the high-born and wealthy notables who patronize us during the year. We offer them a superb meal in the dining hall, followed by entertainment in the chateau's own theater, and conclude with fireworks, games of chance, and other diverting amusements. Since many of our guests prefer not to stay overnight, our program begins early in the afternoon and ends an hour or two after sunset."

"And what would be my part?" she asked with a bemused smile.

"To play a queen."

"What?"

"Yes," he continued, "but not in a drama."

He explained that her role would be to wear the priceless Chanavas jewels, made in India for a very rich and powerful potentate. Comte Debussy had seized them during a colonial war thirty years ago and brought them to France. They were now in the chateau's treasure room, the centerpiece of the comte's remarkable art collection. Because of their value, they were rarely displayed, and then only under glass.

The heat of the day grew uncomfortable, clouds gathered, and rain threatened. They sought the shelter of a row of chestnut trees. Pressigny gestured toward a bench and they sat down, keeping a suitable distance from one another.

Patting his damp brow, he began to explain that recently, while discussing the Amateurs' production at the chateau, Comte Debussy had made a most unusual request. In all the years he had owned the jewels, he had never seen them at their full glory. Chanavas Khan had commissioned them for himself to wear in public. But, insisted the comte, they were really best suited for a beautiful woman in a splendid but intimate setting. The chateau's dining hall and theater were the right places to display them. The Amateurs and their patrons were the right people to see them. What was needed was the right woman to wear them.

"Why me?" exclaimed Mademoiselle Cartier, disbelief written large on her face. "I'm no beauty!"

"True, you have too much spirit in your eyes and too little soft flesh on your bones to have posed as Venus for Monsieur François Boucher. But you have the mind and body to wear the

Chanavas jewels. Trust me. The comte does—at least on this point."

"If I accept this offer, what would I need to do?" Her voice was heavy with suspicion.

"You would be fitted for the role at the chateau in a rich, exotic costume. Bedecked with the jewels, you would accompany my stepfather to the dinner and, afterwards, sit with him in the theater." He raised his hand in a reassuring gesture. "Don't worry, you won't be bored. The count is a diverting companion; he knows many anecdotes and tells them well. From the theater, you would return to the treasure room, the jewels would be put back in their case, and you would be free to do as you please. My stepfather is frail and retires early. He does not expect you to entertain him."

"Would you trust a stranger with such a treasure?" she asked.

He insinuated a playful, mischievous tone into his reply. "When I first had this idea, I decided to get to know you better. I have learned you enjoy the patronage of the Comtesse de Beaumont, an estimable woman with whom I am acquainted, and have the confidence of Colonel Paul de Saint-Martin." With a wink he added, "What finer credentials could I hope for?"

She started, then frowned. Was she surprised, perhaps annoyed that her link with Saint-Martin had been found out? Pressigny discreetly averted his eyes as the young woman struggled to regain her poise.

"I'll consider your offer and give you my reply tomorrow," she replied finally, "together with measurements for the costume, if I accept." To encourage her, he then mentioned the stipend, one hundred livres. She seemed surprised. As well she should, for it was as much as an experienced actress might earn in a month. With that they parted. When she was out of sight, he snapped his fingers, danced a few steps, and walked away with a jaunty air.

❧❧❧

An evening hush came over the garden. Anne was alone in Georges' office, looking out the open window, watching a pair of twittering sparrows at play in the bushes. Rain had cooled the air. She allowed her mind to drift, wondering how the colonel would react to Pressigny's odd invitation. With suspicion, probably. What did the man *really* have in mind? Why didn't he enlist the services of Henriette or another woman at the variety theater? On the other hand, the colonel might welcome an opportunity to pursue an investigation at Chateau Debussy.

Anne continued this debate fruitlessly for a few more minutes, then shrugged. The colonel would soon arrive and could speak for himself. She picked up a crust of bread from the window sill, broke it into pieces, and fed them to the sparrows.

When the bread was gone, she turned from the window and surveyed the adjutant's domain. Georges had shown her into the room, then had gone to fetch his superior. As he left, he gestured to a row of sketches on a wall. If she recognized anyone there, he had said laughing, she should let him know. Dutifully, she studied the faces of several men wanted for murder and other horrendous acts. The evil of their deeds seemed imprinted in their eyes. She thanked God she hadn't met any of them.

She stepped to the left to view the pictures of stolen goods. Georges had said he sketched them himself. The lamps on the wall threw too little light to appreciate his rendering of detail in the jewelry, but certain curious designs caught her fancy— the Z-shaped pedestal of one of the bowls, the serpentine handle of another.

At the sound of steps approaching, she drew back from the sketches. Georges entered, followed by the colonel, who took a chair by the window. Unmindful of the fading light, he sat back, arms crossed, while Anne reported on Pressigny's proposal to her. The colonel's expression remained inscrutable. As dusk filled the room, Georges leaned forward at his desk and lighted the lamp in front of him. Saint-Martin rose and lighted several others. A golden glow spread through the room.

At the end of her report, the colonel raised the questions she had expected. In the discussion that followed, he welcomed the opportunity to carry the investigation into Chateau Debussy. The proposal to wear the necklace was highly unusual, but did not appear threatening. He glanced at Anne. "Comte Debussy's an invalid and has no reason to harm you." He turned to Georges and continued, "I'm sure he'll have the jewels well guarded. She should be in no danger on their account."

"Looks splendid for her," Georges said, "all that money! The dressing up!" He simpered, eye lids fluttering. "I wish Jean had asked me."

"Silly goose!" Anne frowned at him. "Pressigny's giving me an opportunity to pry into his affairs. That's the point!"

Saint-Martin nodded. "Since he has acknowledged that Comtesse de Beaumont and I stand behind you, he's not likely to force his attentions."

Georges winked at Anne. "And I'm sure you can handle his tricks."

She grimaced with mock pain, then turned to Saint-Martin. "I'll send Pressigny a note accepting his proposal." Anticipating an objection, she hesitated. "Could Georges go with me?"

"Yes, incognito." The colonel caught his adjutant's eye. "You have one month, Georges. Arrange to be at Chateau Debussy to work with Miss Cartier. I'll be nearby at my aunt's chateau." Saint-Martin slapped his thigh, preparing to leave.

Anne spoke up. "I think it's safe now to move back to my own apartment. There's been no sign of Derennes. He's either out of the country or held captive by the Amateurs."

"Or dead and buried," interjected Georges.

The colonel rose from his chair. "Keep the key, Mademoiselle. It's still useful."

She jiggled her purse, feeling the key's weight, reassuring herself. "Thank you. I'll be leaving tomorrow."

"The garden apartment will remain free," he said, walking her to the door. "You might need it again."

Alone in the sitting room, Colonel Saint-Martin poured a glass of brandy. He eased himself into a chair and took a sip. The calculating part of his mind liked the idea of prying into affairs at Chateau Debussy. He had smelled something rotten there. It wasn't farfetched to think the Amateurs or their directeur might have hidden Derennes in one of the many caves that must riddle the chalk ridge. Or in the cellars of the chateau. Georges and Anne would find out.

The prospect of her venturing into Pressigny's lair, however, disturbed him. Her role in the Amateurs' reception appeared genuine, but their directeur surely had ulterior motives. That thought agitated Saint-Martin so violently he had to ask himself why.

He discovered he feared for Anne, that she might be violated, stripped of her innocence—as if she were a helpless, naive girl who needed his protection. He scolded himself. She was a mature woman, alert to the sexual games Pressigny played and able to exploit his sensuality. At Chateau Debussy she would need a partner like Georges, not a protector. He gazed into the brandy, aware of a feeling akin to jealousy creeping into his soul.

Chapter 16

Spying

Late the next afternoon, Anne sat sipping a lemonade in the small café by the Théatre des Petits Comédiens. Michou, the deaf seamstress, should soon appear. Over the past several days, Anne had learned the woman's daily routine. She always left her garret on Rue Richelieu a little after dawn and walked the short distance to work. At midday she visited the Palais-Royal, sometimes alone, now and then with two other women from the theater. From their gestures Anne realized they were also deaf. Probably seamstresses like Michou.

After work Michou often wandered in the garden with the same two women until darkness attracted young toughs, prostitutes, and thieves. Then she hurried home like a frightened rabbit. In rare moments of leisure, her favorite pastime was sketching people, animals, and anything else that caught her fancy. Anne occasionally greeted her in passing with a fleeting smile, hoping to gradually appear familiar to her eyes.

Today the women's routine changed. Michou's two friends came from the service door to the table next to Anne's. The café was otherwise empty, except for a waiter. At a signal from Anne, he brought her another lemonade. She paid him and he disappeared into the kitchen. Anne turned her back to the deaf women, then drew a plain snuff box from her bag. The box was empty. She grimaced. The very thought of snuff was repulsive. But inside the lid was a mirror.

Placing the box on the table at her left hand, she adjusted the lid to an angle where she could observe her neighbors. Much of what they were signing to one another meant little to her, but she understood they had just been paid and were through for the day. They were soon joined by two men. Young apprentices, judging from their work clothes. Deaf as well. Wine arrived. The signing grew more animated.

Anne surmised that Michou had also been paid. Within minutes she joined the circle, greeted with smiles and hugs and a glass of wine. The silent conversation continued until the apprentices rose from the table. The circle broke up in a flurry of signing and gestures, and the two men walked out into the garden. Michou's companions from the theater glanced at Anne, who pretended to read a menu.

The older of the two women sat up straight. Her eyes narrowed, searching the room. She signed to the younger one, who reached into a sack at her feet and swiftly moved the contents into Michou's bag.

Anne stared into the tiny mirror. What was going on? She clutched the menu. Her shoulders tensed. Had the women taken something valuable from the theater and passed it to Michou? Hardly surprising. The manager paid them a pittance. Anne recalled his pinched, unsmiling face. He could be ruthless. The women risked being dismissed, then whipped and sent to the workhouse.

Michou closed her bag, a brown cloth sack Anne had not seen before, and waved as her friends went after the men toward the Camp of the Tatars. Clutching the bag, Michou left the Palais-Royal through the Beaujolais portal. Anne followed her to Rue Richelieu, where she turned northward. It appeared she was going to her room.

As she walked on the narrow crowded sidewalk, she glanced left and right like an anxious sparrow. Near the entrance to the Bibliothèque Royale, a barrel fell off a wagon and frightened a horse pulling a cart a few feet from Anne. The animal reared, then charged out of control on to the sidewalk. People leaped out of its way, screaming. With a clatter of hooves, it bore down on the deaf woman. Anne shouted in vain. At the last moment, Michou appeared to detect alarm in the face of an on-coming coachman. She jumped to her right. The cart hurtled past, missing her by inches. But she lost her balance, tripped and fell, knocking her head on the pavement.

Anne rushed up. Michou lay still for a few seconds, then struggled to her knees, a dazed look on her face. A dense, mindless stream of people jostled the two women. Anne lifted Michou and carried her, light as a child, into a corner café and laid her on a wall bench. The proprietor hurried toward them, his arms gesticulating, a protest on his lips.

"We won't be long," Anne said, calming him with a coin. "Some water and a clean cloth, please." Caressing Michou, she wiped dirt from a bruise on her forehead. There were no other injuries she could see. As Michou's daze wore off, panic set in. She touched her chest and seemed momentarily relieved. She'd found her purse. But then she reached frantically for her handbag. Her eyes widened in despair.

Anne leaped to her feet and ran back to the scene of the accident, her hope sinking with every step. Paris was a city of thieves.

But the bag was there, leaning against the library wall. She opened it quickly and saw paints, used brushes, irregular sheets of paper and canvas, and other artist's supplies. Gathered furtively, it appeared, out of fear the manager would object.

Anne closed the sack and hurried back to the café. Michou was anxiously watching the door, sitting upright on the bench. At the sight of her bag, she burst into tears. Anne laid it in her lap, wiped the tears from her cheeks, and hugged her gently. Looking up, Michou gave her a grateful smile.

∾∾∾

The following day Anne was resting on a bench against a plane tree, sheltered from the afternoon sun. The air was warm and still along the Boulevard. Behind her was a depot of the French Guards, where Georges said they should meet. She had been anxious at first about her disguise, a young man's simple brown suit and a short wig. A powder dulled and darkened her complexion.

She relaxed, however, when the uniformed men going in and out of the building took no notice of her. On the Boulevard, coaches clattered by, filling her nostrils with dust. Her eyes darted through the traffic, searching for Georges.

Early that morning he had called at her apartment, saying he needed her later in the day to spy on Robert LeCourt. "He runs the Amateurs from behind the scenes. Puts up most of the money. I've been wondering why."

"Can't one of your agents help?" she had protested. She had planned to spend the day at Épée's institute.

"I try to keep them away from Antoine's case, especially when LeCourt's involved. They might tell the Paris police what we're doing." He had handed her the suit of clothes. "Your costume!" When she had agreed reluctantly, he grinned encouragement. "An actress needs practice. This is like being on stage."

Anne felt relieved when Georges emerged from the crowd, waving his hand.

"You're perfect!" he whispered as she rose to meet him.

"Come here." She led him to a furniture shop next door to the depot. Pointing to their reflection in a display window, she asked, "Who are we supposed to be?"

"A furniture dealer and his son from Rouen." Georges puffed out his chest, every inch the businessman. "We'll use the Norman accent you learned from Antoine."

They did indeed look like a pair of provincial visitors, Anne agreed. Their brown suits were out of style, the coats longer than the present fashion, the buttons larger. Georges' wig added years to his appearance, reminding her that he was old enough to be her father.

They walked to the next corner, where Georges pointed up Rue d'Artois, north of the Boulevard. Financiers, bankers, and other newly rich businessmen had recently built luxurious town houses on its large noble estates. "They're LeCourt's kind of people. He lives nearby on Rue Thaitbout."

"What's happened to the old families who lived there?" Anne had earlier noticed Georges' aversion to the aristocracy.

"They've done very well on profits from dividing their estates and selling off the pieces. Some of them moved across the river into the Faubourg Saint-Germain. Others stayed where they were and renovated their mansions or built new ones." Georges warmed to the topic. "Greedy bastards, crooked as fishhooks! Lieutenant-General Sartine had me investigate one of them. I found an illegal distillery in the basement!"

Turning around, Georges pointed southward at a large, pillared stone building across the Boulevard. "The Italian Comedy Theater, built just a few years ago. The café that LeCourt frequents is a short distance to the east. Gets a lot of late evening business after the shows." They crossed the Boulevard through a moving maze of carriages and pedestrians. A few minutes later they entered a simple two-story building. Over the door hung a weathered sign, Café Marcel.

They found a small marble-topped table for themselves in the main room near the entrance. Anne glanced about, counting a dozen similar tables along the walls and four larger ones in the center. Fewer than half the chairs were occupied in the late afternoon, mostly by merchants and tradesmen reading newspapers or chatting. A few waiters were scuttling about. One of them came by. "Tea and biscuits," Georges said soberly. Anne ordered the same.

Through a wide archway into the next room she could see a bar, more half-occupied tables, and a rack of newspapers on a far wall. Both rooms had once been elegantly decorated. Large crystal chandeliers hung from ceilings that needed fresh paint. Several of the wall mirrors were discolored. The floors were worn near the bar and at the entrance. A steady stream of customers approached the bar and bought wine to take out.

Anne felt at ease. The café's clientele appeared diverse enough to ensure anonymity, her decent bourgeois clothing helped her blend in. Thanks to the mirrored walls she could observe what went on without appearing curious.

"There are rooms upstairs." Georges pointed with his eyes towards a stairway opposite the entrance. "I'll take a quick look. They must be empty now."

When their tea had arrived and the barkeeper was preoccupied by a customer, Georges slipped away, leaving Anne alone at the table.

In the mirror next to her table she checked her posture. She had to remember to sit like a man, spreading her legs and slouching slightly. When ordering, she dropped her voice to a lower register. A harmless deception, she thought, the concealing of one's sex, not to be compared with the evil tricks of a charlatan. People often wore disguises of word, gesture, and dress, pretending to be honest when they were false; wealthy, when they were poor; beautiful, when they were ugly.

She gazed at the men around her, wondering whimsically whether any of them were women in disguise. She half-seriously thought she could pick out one or two. And perhaps a few other imposters.

Georges' return jarred her out of this line of reflection. He sketched a plan of the upper floor. A T-shaped corridor ran from the top of the stairs to the back of the building. The next thing to check, he said, was the newspaper rack. He walked into the barroom, studied the selection of papers, and returned to the table with two of them.

"What's this?" asked Anne, scanning a front page.

"Dutch. Probably the reason LeCourt comes to this café. He reads French, of course, but he gets news from Holland from these two papers and meets a few of his countrymen here." After skimming the papers, Georges returned them to the rack.

Near six in the evening, Anne noticed the tables begin to fill up with wealthier, more stylish customers. As a clock chimed the hour, Georges whispered, "LeCourt just arrived, he's the man in the dark green suit." Anne watched him in a mirror, struck by the simple elegance of his movements. And of his attire. The collar, lapels, and cuffs of his coat were embroidered with delicate silver patterns.

He walked through the barroom, greeting men at tables as he passed by. At the newspaper rack he picked up the two Dutch papers and approached the bar. After a few words with the barkeeper, he received a drink and a key. He tucked one of the papers under his arm, returned the other to the rack, and went upstairs.

"So, this evening he engages a private room," said Georges. "We'll wait and see who comes to visit him."

A question had been forming in the back of Anne's mind. "What's going on, Georges?" she asked doubtfully. "How do you know he's going to meet someone to discuss something we'd want to hear?"

"A professional secret, my dear," he replied grinning. "But I can trust you." He leaned forward—his grin vanishing, and lowered his voice. "LeCourt's barber spies on him for Comptroller-General Calonne. For a little extra money, he also works for me. Yesterday, while peeking in LeCourt's appointment book, he noticed a strange entry for early this evening. Here's a copy." Georges pressed a scrap of paper into her hand.

fncmsd166pm

She studied it, then looked up. "What does it mean?"

"A simple code for Café Marcel, Simon Derennes, 16th of this month, in the evening. *fn* should soon appear."

They sat quietly for a few minutes, drinking their tea. Suddenly, Georges gestured with his eyes toward the barroom. "Watch," he whispered.

A sullen sharp-faced man in a plain brown suit picked up the remaining Dutch paper, read it for a few seconds, then returned it to the rack. When a customer distracted the barkeeper, the sharp-faced man walked quickly upstairs.

"LeCourt surely left a message in that paper," Georges said. "He's covering his tracks."

A few moments later, Georges and Anne also approached the barkeeper. They could have any room except number one; it had been taken. For a couple of *sous*, Georges got the key for number two and put it in his pocket. Anne followed him up the stairs. The two rooms were side by side in the rear of the building. Their windows opened to narrow balconies over a courtyard, enclosed by the blank walls of neighboring buildings.

Georges placed a funnel-shaped device against the wall of number one, trying to hear the conversation between LeCourt and his visitor. The trick failed. Either the wall was too thick or the voices too soft.

While he was preoccupied, Anne stepped out onto the balcony. A narrow ledge jutted out from the café's outside wall, connecting her balcony with the one next door. The ledge was smooth and level but barely visible. The sun had sunk low in the sky. The courtyard was becoming dark.

Anne took a deep breath, climbed over the railing, and shuffled slowly along the ledge to the neighboring balcony. She peered cautiously into the room. The two men sat at a table in quiet, earnest conversation. Only meaningless bits of it came through the closed window.

At a gesture from LeCourt, the other man rose from the table and walked toward the window. Anne pressed her back flat against the wall in the small space between the window and the railing. He pushed open both halves of the window, the right side scarcely a foot away from her. She trembled, certain that he would see her.

"That's too much," she heard LeCourt say. The man muttered under his breath, then closed the window halfway. The half of the window opposite her now served as a mirror, offering a clear view into the room. LeCourt sat with one leg crossed over the other, a glass in his hand. The newspaper lay on the table in front of him. About fifty years old, he was one of the most distinguished-looking men she had ever seen. Dark eyebrows. Finely chiseled handsome face. Thick silver hair. In the room's subdued light, his deepset eyes were inscrutable.

The other man picked up a sheaf of papers, held them close, and squinted at them. Nearsighted, Anne thought. When he finished reading, he took a small notebook from a leather wallet in his pocket and made several entries. He put the notebook and wallet away and looked up at LeCourt. Anne strained to hear.

The financier set his glass on the table. "Remind me, Monsieur Noir, how you found Derennes. From the beginning."

His companion reported that he had slipped into the basement of the palace unobserved, discovered Derennes in the pit below the old torture chamber.

"I had followed him there during the intermission when the English blonde was singing. Knew he was up to something. Afterwards, when he disappeared, I guessed he might have gone back. And there he was. Beaten and out of his mind. Crying that a pirate had attacked him. I also found a woman's skeleton and a mess of animal bones!"

LeCourt stiffened, his dark brow working into a frown. He motioned for the man to continue.

"I searched him. Found the keys to his apartment. Picked up a kerchief belonging to Chevalier de Pressigny." He gave LeCourt a knowing glance. "Pressigny also left his signature on a wardrobe list for a pirate's costume."

LeCourt pursed his lips at the mention of Pressigny. "Why didn't he kill Derennes outright? Why leave him alive to be discovered by you?"

"He probably acted in haste and thought the man was dead." He hesitated a moment for his master to comment. The financier merely nodded. Noir went on to explain how he had moved Derennes and the corpse. Anne could not hear where he had put them.

He pulled a small, leather-bound, gilt-edged book out of his pocket. Anne recognized it immediately from the theater office. "Derennes' journal," he said, handing it across the table to LeCourt. "He's recorded the name of his victim in the dungeon."

LeCourt unfastened the clasp and scanned the pages. "Aha, *she* was the one, I half suspected, ...'s daughter. A pity." His voice had trailed off. Anne could not grasp the parent's name— it was foreign, not French.

Noir pointed to the little book in LeCourt's hand. "Pressigny was also involved in the woman's death."

"The fool!" hissed LeCourt. "Give me the gist of the story." He glanced down at the book and closed it. "Derennes' hand-writing is as bad as his character."

Noir explained that, shortly after leaving the king's prison, Pressigny had seduced the woman at a country estate near Paris and brought her to an Amateurs' party at the palace theater. Growing bored, he handed her over to Derennes, who raped her. She threatened to expose both of them to her father. Derennes strangled her and obliged Pressigny to help move her body to the dungeon and throw her into the pit. Derennes warned him to keep quiet, or they would lose their heads on the block. Afterwards, Derennes borrowed money from Pressigny and never paid it back.

"What a pair!" exclaimed LeCourt, breathing heavily, his face flushed. He soon regained his calm, then opened the book again, paused on a page, and scowled. "Here's last year's incident. The actress and the clown."

Anne's heart leaped at the allusion to Antoine. The story of his death must be in there! She stared at the book, as if to seize it with her eyes.

There was a moment of heavy silence. "Pressigny!" the financier exclaimed again. "I should have left him to rot in prison!" He pressed both hands flat on the table, calming his temper. "I assume he tried to kill Derennes to put an end to extortion. Why didn't he come to me with the problem in the first place? Or, at least tell me, after he had disposed of Derennes?"

The other man waited respectfully silent until LeCourt invited his opinion. "In some ways, Sir, the chevalier is still a boy. He acts on foolish impulses and makes bad mistakes. But you are to him like a stern parent. He does not wish to admit he needs help."

LeCourt shrugged. Then, leaning forward, hands clasped before his mouth, he began speaking in a low voice. Anne drew as close to the window as she dared but could not make sense of what he said. Sounded like Dutch. Finally he put Derennes' journal in his pocket and leaned back in the chair. "By the way, what was Derennes planning to do in the dungeon in the first place?"

Anne's heart skipped a beat.

"To question a young woman he called Dido. He claimed she spied for Pressigny."

"Dido? Sounds odd. Find out who she is. And whether I should be concerned."

"Henriette claims to know. She's holding out for 50 livres."

"Pay her." LeCourt retrieved his glass, took a sip. "Is Derennes safely hidden? I may need to see him."

"Nobody'll find him, and he can't run away. Unconscious most of the time. Spits blood. Has trouble breathing."

"Then we're done," said LeCourt and finished his drink. "Let's stretch." The two men rose from the table and walked toward the window.

Panic gripped Anne. There wasn't time to return to the other balcony. She slid over the railing and crouched on the iron supports beneath the balcony. The two men continued to talk but too softly for much to be overheard. Finally, they left. The window clicked shut. Anne crouched for a few more minutes, then scrambled up onto the balcony.

Her partner appeared at the window and opened it. "What possessed you!" he exclaimed, as he led her into the room the men had vacated. "That was too dangerous. You're lucky LeCourt didn't catch you."

"It was worth the risk," she retorted exuberantly. "You won't believe what I heard!"

When she repeated LeCourt's comments about the corpse in the pit, Georges nodded. "Nalini, daughter of Krishna, steward at Chateau Debussy. That's where Pressigny lives. Her sketch is hanging on my office wall." His eyes moistened, his voice fell. "Lovely girl." He remained silent for a long moment, sorrow working the corners of his mouth. Finally, he glanced at Anne. "We can't tell her father yet, or we'd give ourselves away."

Anne shuddered. In a month she would play her role at the same chateau and most likely meet the young woman's father. She sighed, then moved on to the strange story of Derennes' rescue.

"Pressigny, the pirate!" exclaimed Georges. "The head of the Amateurs assaults his assistant! What's LeCourt going to do about that?" Georges stared at Anne. "And, will he go after you?"

∞∞∞

Georges stood nervously behind her at the door, while she searched for her key. This was the first time she had invited him home. Though he had never married, he had lived off and on with several different women. But he had never known a woman quite so headstrong as this one. Once inside the apartment, his anxiety grew as she took off her coat, shed the wig, pulled the pins out of her hair, and wiped the powder from her face.

"There!" she said, smiling at him. "I'm myself again."

Georges grew more at ease opening a bottle of fine wine, a gift from the Comtesse de Beaumont's cellar. He rarely drank except at meals, so he sipped a glass while they shared cheese and bread at the table. His partner's adventure appeared to have drained her and left her tired and thirsty. After a couple of glasses, she complained it was hot in the room and removed her vest. Her face was flushed and her eyes unnaturally bright. Georges asked if she was all right.

"I'm delighted, Georges," she replied laughing. "We've made headway tonight. If we could only lay hands on Derennes' journal, we'd prove Antoine's innocence." She held out her empty glass. "Let's celebrate!"

He poured a second glass of wine for himself and a third for her. His nerves calmed, and he felt relaxed. She grew livelier as she drank, singing and sharing jokes with him. They finished the bottle and moved toward the chairs by the window. She laid a hand on his shoulder; he tentatively put an arm around her waist. She leaned toward him, parted her lips, closed her eyes and...passed out.

For a moment Georges didn't know what to do. He stood there, wet with sweat, holding her limp in his arms. Then he lifted her up and carried her to the bedroom, laid her down, and covered her. She began to perspire and to shiver. He bent anxiously over her, patting her forehead with a towel.

A few minutes later, she opened her eyes. Disbelief spread over her face. "What happened, Georges?"

"You fainted," he said lamely.

"I guess I spoiled the party." She sat up, eyes heavy-lidded, and leaned against the headboard. "The room's moving. Are we crossing the Channel?" She pressed her fingers against her temples. "Tell the captain I'll walk to France!"

Wondering if she was going to be sick, Georges looked around for a pail. "I'll tell him right away. This evening at the café, I learned you can fly, so I suppose you can also walk on water."

She started to laugh, then stopped, squinting with pain. "Georges, take my head with you. I don't want it tonight." She raised a hand and caressed his cheek. "Gentle Georges," she said. "Best partner."

He kissed her hand and was about to leave when she called out. "It just flashed in my mind the last thing LeCourt said on the balcony: 'Keep a sharp eye on Pressigny, we still need him.'"

Chapter 17

A Precious Bowl

Short of breath, her head aching, Anne hesitated at the rear entrance to the provost's residence. The sun had not yet climbed above the rooftops of Paris. The air was warm and moist. A brief thunder storm had wakened her at dawn. Feeling queasy from too much wine, and a little ashamed, she had skipped breakfast. While she was dressing, a note from Colonel Saint-Martin had slipped under her door, asking her to see him today. She had hurried her toilette and hastened through nearly empty streets to his door.

Was she too eager, she asked herself, glancing at the key he had given her, heavy and black and as long as her hand. No matter, she knew he was an early riser. She bit her lip, opened the door, and stepped inside. He was in the garden in shirt-sleeves, a pair of scissors in his hand, snipping wilted flowers from a rose bush. As she approached, he looked up. A pleased expression came over his face.

"An expert now holds the script you discovered in the Amateurs' office."

Anne flashed a smile, then paused. "I've given more thought to that script." Her breath still short, she measured out her words. "We know that Antoine's alleged confession is almost identical to a passage from the farce, *The Cuckolded Clown*. He *could* have borrowed the passage to explain his suicide. But he could also have simply taken dictation, and it was used to incriminate him. I hope your expert will judge the confession, at the least, to be suspect."

"You can be sure he will examine it critically. He has served me well before."

He bowed and took her arm. "Shall we go to my office?"

On their way through the garden, they stopped to pick a half-dozen yellow roses. He cut the thorns off the stems and handed the roses to her one by one. Tiny drops of dew fell from their petals on to her dress. She chose one of the flowers, inhaled its delicate scent, and offered it to him. He received it with a gracious bow, drew in its aroma, then gestured with it toward the house.

When she had arranged the roses in a vase on his desk, he beckoned her to a chair.

"Are you well? You look pale. What happened yesterday?"

"We learned Derennes is alive!" She went on to report LeCourt's conversation with the sharp-faced Monsieur Noir, withholding the more harrowing details. Georges would present them when he met the colonel later in the morning. And she would be spared a scolding for the risk she'd taken.

"You've confirmed our suspicion," he said. "LeCourt is protecting the Amateurs from the scandal of Derennes' crimes. Perhaps that's good. While in LeCourt's custody, Derennes, whether ill or mad, won't harm anyone. Unfortunately, we can't question him about Antoine's case." He settled back in his chair, examining the roses with a preoccupied air. "LeCourt believes Pressigny was involved in the death of the young woman known as Nalini. But he needs Pressigny, so he's going to protect him. At least for now." He looked up from the roses and glanced at Anne. "Is Pressigny really indispensable to the Amateurs?"

She shrugged her shoulders. "Indispensable to LeCourt at least. His own reputation is at stake. After all, he persuaded the king to let Pressigny out of prison. Picked him to direct the Amateurs. LeCourt wants people to trust his judgment, invest their money with him."

"We may find ourselves jousting with Monsieur LeCourt before this is over." Saint-Martin leaned forward with concern in his eyes. "By the way, if he discovers the identity of the woman whom Derennes was planning to 'question,' you might hear from Lieutenant-General DeCrosne—and so might I."

While he was speaking, Anne's headache returned. Her short supply of good humor diminished. The lieutenant-general could go to hell, she thought, barely concealing her irritation. She stirred in her chair. "Let's talk about what you've found for me."

He nodded patiently, as if he were facing a testy child, then walked round the desk and put before her a copy of a memorandum, dated September 21, 1785. "Georges dug it out of the Paris police archives," he remarked, leaning over her shoulder. She felt the heat of his body and warmed to the thought that he and Georges were taking risks too.

"Start here. Inspecteur Mauvert is reporting to Magistrate Sorin concerning the Laplante case." He pointed to persons questioned by the inspecteur. Anne recognized Henriette Picard and other companions at the variety theater as well as several Amateurs.

"This is what caught my attention." He touched a line with his finger. Mauvert had also summoned a woman called "Michou," who had sometimes assisted Lélia Laplante with her wardrobe. He could not interrogate Michou because she was deaf and simple-minded; could neither read nor write. Between the lines of the memorandum the magistrate had written, "*mute witness, incompetent to testify.*"

"Incompetent? Nonsense! I've met her." Anne stared at the colonel defiantly. "She's scarcely incompetent, but she's terrified of the police and closed up like a clam when Mauvert tried to interrogate her."

Saint-Martin stepped back, lips pursed. "Then we need to know more about her. The magistrate paid her little attention. The Amateurs and their patrons had urged him to close the case as quickly and quietly as possible." He paused, tapping his fingers together. "You've had experience in London dealing with people like Michou."

Anne recalled tutoring Benjamin and Sarah at Wimbledon, children who had heard for several years and had attentive, caring parents. "Michou's more withdrawn, more challenging to reach than the children I taught for Braidwood. But I'm hopeful."

Returning to his chair, he glanced at her with an encouraging smile. "Then see if she can help us."

As Anne rose to leave, he handed her a paper from the desk. "Sorry, I meant to tell you. I've received a report from Rouen. You recalled correctly, Antoine Dubois was born and raised there. We found several of his cousins."

"I see the name Lélia Laplante," said Anne skimming the page.

"Yes, she came from the same parish as Antoine." He frowned. "Their families disowned them when they joined the theater and started living together. They soon clashed and separated, he going to London and she to Paris."

"Why on earth did he live with her when he returned to Paris after the war?" Anne laid the paper on the desk, tapped it lightly. "They surely weren't good for each other."

"Yes, the Paris police would say this report supports their findings."

"Well, I'm not going to stop now." She jammed Mauvert's memorandum into her bag. "I'm eager to learn what the inspecteur's 'simple-minded deaf mute' can tell us."

Michou was among the small knot of people gathered at midday in front of the Tatar Puppet Theater. Victor Benoit was performing a harlequin sketch with the hand puppets. Anne had followed her through the garden and now joined the crowd. Michou beckoned for Anne to join her. When the show ended, they were the only ones left. Anne called to the puppeteer. Would he let them play with the puppets while he waited for a crowd to gather? At first he looked surprised and annoyed. Then, recognizing her, he nodded.

Anne offered a hand puppet to Michou. She frowned slightly and refused, but Anne's repeated gesture reassured her. In a short while, with a little coaching from the puppeteer, the two women were running through simple skits. The pleasure of play transformed Michou. A smile erased the tight lines around her mouth, and her green eyes grew large and luminous.

When a half-hour had passed, Michou laid down the puppets. With a sigh, she mimicked a seamstress at work. Time to return to the theater, Anne thought. They set out together through the garden. As they approached the fountain, Anne pointed to Michou and to herself, then clasped the little woman's hands. Might they meet again?

Michou hesitated, a cautious look in her eyes. Her hands grew tense but she did not withdraw them. She scrutinized Anne for what seemed like minutes. Then, smiling, she pointed to the fountain. They would meet there.

Deeply touched by the woman's trust, Anne cast about in her mind for a way to fix the date.

Apparently anticipating the question, Michou made the sign of the cross, lifted her eyes, folded her hands in prayer.

Tomorrow, Sunday, at the fountain, Anne said aloud, clearly articulating the words.

Michou stared with blank eyes. She couldn't read lips, Anne realized. She also crossed herself and folded her hands. Michou nodded, raised nine fingers, then pointed toward the eastern sky.

"Nine o'clock in the morning," Anne murmured, extending a hand to shake good-bye.

Michou took the hand and pressed it to her heart.

∞ ∞ ∞

Anne entered the mall of the Palais-Royal on a cloudy Sunday morning, thinking Michou had perhaps not really understood their agreement. Or, she might have become ill. Anne was relieved to find her seated on a bench near the pool, surrounded by ducks. She rose quickly, scattering the birds in every direction. Anne put out her hands. Michou took them in hers. How delicate and beautiful they were, Anne observed. Slender yet strong.

To Anne's surprise, Michou seized the initiative. With a gentle smile she beckoned Anne to follow her. She had a routine for this, the only day of the week that was her own. They set off for the river Seine. For an hour they walked on the embankment toward the Pont-Royal, stopping several times to watch boats or to admire the imposing palaces on the other side.

As Michou's shyness receded, she let Anne look at a small book in which she sketched anything that caught her eye. The pages were filled with human faces in rage, ecstasy, repose or pleasure. A bushy-tailed cat arched its back, repelling an inquisitive poodle. Swallows swooped over rooftops. Fashionable men and women strolled in the garden of the Palais-Royal. Beggars sat at a church door. Peddlers showed their wares on a tree-lined boulevard. There were swords and costumes and designs for embroidery and tools of the seamstress' craft.

The sketching was often just a few fine lines, enough to capture a child's hoop or a street lamp. Several drawings were in a nearly finished state. Among them was a sensitive, miniature portrait of an elderly nun, evidently the one who had befriended her.

As the sun broke through the clouds and approached its meridian, Michou indicated it was time to eat. Anne glanced about for a street vendor or a decent café. Her companion smiled and took her hand. Follow me, she gestured.

A half-hour later, barely escaping a summer shower, Anne climbed behind Michou up steep, narrow stairs to her little attic room on Rue Richelieu, a block north of Palais-Royal. Anne welcomed this opportunity for an undisturbed conversation with the little woman. She was far from moronic. If she could express what she knew about Lélia Laplante, she might shed light on the dark mystery of her death.

Watching Michou prepare the meal, Anne leaned back on a wooden chair, lulled by the patter of rain on the roof blending with muted sounds from the kitchen. Michou stirred charcoal, poured water, chopped a carrot, then a stalk of celery. From time to time, she cast a glance over her shoulder, her large green eyes smiling, no longer wary. Anne felt a simple closeness to this person, an undemanding trust.

She hadn't known such intimacy since her mother died and Antoine left her. Alone, she had relied on her own wits. Dodged obstacles in her way. Then the nightmare at Islington: Roach's fist; Hammer, gloating, her long, golden hair clutched in his hand. She saw again the upturned, leering faces. Coarse voices thundered, "French whore." No one had helped her. No one. Until almost too late.

A drawer slammed shut. Anne's demons vanished. She saw Michou bending over a bubbling pot, tasting with a wooden spoon. The aroma of chicken broth hung in the air. Anne *was* not alone. Somehow Michou was leading her out of what she now recognized as personal darkness. Her eyes moistened. Dear God, she thought, this had to be what redemption meant.

When they had finished the meal of soup, bread, and cheese, Michou laid out on the table several thick, well-worn folders of drawings and watercolor paintings. At a quick glance, Anne recognized a few finished pictures from sketches in the notebook. Michou's tutor, the old nun, was lovingly rendered, a white wimple framing her long, thin face with its generous mouth and proud, mischievous eyes.

Thumbing through the folders, Anne realized this was Michou's journal, the fruit of a powerful curiosity. "Incredible," she murmured. By drawing or painting objects, Michou took mental possession of them, adding to the rich treasury of her imagination. Unable to speak with others, she seemed to converse with their images.

Anne looked up, suddenly aware of Michou's scrutiny. Lips parted, she leaned forward with cautious anticipation. Discovered, she flashed a smile, then pushed two miniature portraits across the table to Anne, both highly finished watercolors.

The first depicted the murdered actress, Anne surmised, comparing the image with descriptions she had gathered at the variety theater. As if to please the actress, Michou gave her a long, slender neck, a clear olive complexion. In the eyes and mouth, however, Michou had captured the woman's vanity and guile.

Chevalier de Pressigny was the second portrait, his handsome countenance disturbingly enigmatic. In the lines of his mouth Michou had found playful sensuality; in his eyes, a cold and calculating intelligence.

Anne laid the portraits side by side. When had Michou done them? And why? Perhaps Laplante commissioned them, a gift for Pressigny as directeur of the Amateurs. Or, as lover? Anne shrugged. The actress had not claimed them before she was murdered. She and he might have had a falling out.

Pointing to the portraits, Anne nodded her appreciation. Michou leaned back, smiling, then pulled three more pictures from a file. Anne gave a start—they were extraordinary mosaics. For better light Anne held them up at an angle to the window, one by one, and felt a surge of pleasure. With infinite patience

Michou had pieced together countless tiny colored fragments cut from scraps of heavy paper. Gathered secretly, no doubt, from stage sets.

As Anne gazed at these works, she marvelled at the range of Michou's observations. The first mosaic was a large gilded monstrance she must have often observed at the cathedral. The second depicted a sumptuous carriage. She would have seen many like it outside the theaters where she worked.

The third piece, a strange, richly decorated ornamental bowl, unsettled Anne's mind and set her to wondering. Exquisitely designed, it was the kind of precious object meant for private viewing in the home of a very rich, aristocratic family. How could Michou have seen it? Anne felt certain she had never worked in such a household. And it seemed unlikely she could have committed to memory a complex piece like this one in the course of a fleeting visit.

Could it be the fruit of fantasy? Intrigued, Anne looked closely at the green oval bowl. On its rim sat a human figure poised to throw a three-pronged spear at a sea beast swimming inside. Its broad snout protruded above the rim of the bowl. Its pedestal was a similar exotic sea beast resting on its chest, holding up the bowl with its tail.

It seemed vaguely familiar. Anne lifted up the picture, viewing it from different angles. Closing her eyes, she settled back in her chair and wracked her memory. She was sure she had seen the design recently. She opened her eyes and glanced at her companion. Michou might have copied a precious bowl in one of the art dealers' shops in the Palais-Royal. But Anne hadn't been in such a shop.

Across the table, Michou observed Anne's interest, mistook her curiosity for desire, and offered the picture insistently to her. Embarrassed by the confusion and anxious to please Michou, Anne accepted it as a loan. After embracing Michou and thanking her warmly, Anne took her leave. As she climbed back down the stairs, the picture under her arm, she resolved to discover its source.

∽∽∽

The next morning Anne lay in bed puzzling over Michou's worth as a witness. A bright flash of light startled her. The gilded figure in the picture of the bowl had reflected a ray of morning sunlight. Upon returning to her apartment last night, she had slipped the picture into a frame and hung it on the wall near her bed.

"I've seen it," she said aloud to herself. "But where? In the duke's galleries?" She swung out of bed, took the picture off the wall, and stared at it. Perhaps Georges would recognize it.

He was in his office, gathering his wits over a cup of coffee, idly stirring in a lump of sugar. His eyebrows arched in surprise at her unexpected arrival.

"Look at this." She leaned the picture against a stack of files on his desk. "Michou lent it to me." She described her day with Michou, then pointed to the picture. "Has she seen a real bowl or an illustration? Or has she imagined the bowl?"

Georges glanced at the piece while Anne spoke. "Hard to say," he replied. "I don't recall anything like it at the Palais-Royal." He shrugged his shoulders. "I'd guess it's imaginary." He picked up the picture, pursed his lips, took a closer look. "At least Michou's got a sense of humor. Look at those odd fish!"

Anne lapsed into disappointed silence. Georges wasn't going to be much help. Then the nonchalance suddenly drained from his face. He lurched from his chair and held Michou's picture next to one of his drawings of stolen goods.

"It *is* the same bowl! I guessed wrong. She certainly *has* seen this piece, though her version is twice its size."

Anne rushed to join him. "Tell me about it."

It was stolen about two years ago, he explained, from a chateau near Paris, one of the earliest and most valuable of the recent thefts. "It's five and a half inches high and about as wide, made of jasper and decorated with enamel, pearls, and several large exquisite diamonds. The sea beasts are dolphins." He pointed to the human figure on the edge of the bowl. "That's Neptune. He's the size of your index finger, but he's white gold! Splendid fellow!"

Georges brought Michou's picture back to his desk and laid it in front of Anne. The jeweler Boehmer in Paris had told him that an Italian master goldsmith had made it two hundred years ago. According to Boehmer, if it were legally offered for sale in a good year, it would probably fetch a half-million livres; but a thief wouldn't dare bring it to one of the major art markets.

"He might break it up, then sell the precious parts," suggested Anne, "for far less than the piece is worth."

"Or," Georges added, "he stole it for a wealthy collector who will hide it. Or, it's on its way to a remote market, like India. We looked all over London for it."

Footsteps sounded outside in the corridor.

"Must be the colonel," said Georges. "He's been gone for several days on an inspection tour."

He entered the office, greeting them with a tired voice. Lines of fatigue creased his face. His boots and coat, however, were free of dust. Anne smiled inwardly. He had taken a moment to have himself brushed. After ordering coffee from a servant, he joined Georges and Anne at the desk. They showed him Georges' sketch and Michou's mosaic. Anne related what she had learned.

With a picture in each hand he walked to the garden window. "Michou had to have access to this bowl and time to observe it closely." His face freshening with enthusiasm, he lifted up the pictures, compared one with the other.

"Did she see it before or after the theft?" Georges wondered aloud to Anne. He would inquire at the chateau where the bowl had been stolen. Anne said she would try to extract more information from Michou, though that might prove difficult.

As she rose to leave, her bag jingled. Georges glanced at her quizzically. She flashed him a smile. "My metal tiles! A game I play with Épée's deaf students. Miss Arnaud is expecting me." Halfway to the door Anne paused, reflecting. Perhaps Michou...

Anne glanced at the colonel by the window, absorbed by the mosaic. He appeared unaware of anyone else in the room. She cleared her throat. He looked up, startled, then smiled so sweetly that she flushed with pleasure.

"Shouldn't we try to improve Michou's ability to communicate?" she asked. "I'm on my way to Abbé de l'Épée's institute. I could inquire if he would help her."

"By all means," he replied.

He appeared about to discuss the jasper bowl, but she hurried on. "Michou has no money. Neither has Abbé de l'Épée." She hesitated slyly. "Since she's helping a provost of the Royal Highway Patrol solve a crime, perhaps he would be willing to support her."

He smiled, glanced again at the mosaic, then leaned back against the window. "A good investment, whatever she learns. She's already given us the first clue we've had in two years."

∞∞∞∞

At the Palais-Royal that afternoon, rain forced the fashionable crowd from the garden into the shelter of the arcades. Anne pressed through the dense human mass with little regard for all the full skirts in her way. She was wrestling with a problem. How could she draw information about the jasper bowl from a person who could not speak or hear, read or write? Worse yet, a timid person who was still recovering from brutal interrogation by the police.

An hour ago, Anne had brought Michou to the institute and left her with Miss Arnaud. They would work out a plan of instruction. But that wouldn't prove useful to the investigation for weeks. Gradually a strategy took shape in Anne's mind. Another way to discover what Michou knew.

The door to the Tatar Puppet Theater stood open. The manager, Victor Benoit, was arranging scenery when Anne entered. Through the drawn curtains she saw the stage set for the production of *Pulcinella* that she had arranged for the next several days. Behind the stage on a concealed platform the manager's young assistant was adjusting strings to the marionettes.

Anne closed the door and approached the two men. "Could I have a word with you," she called out.

They glanced at one another, shrugging, then joined her in front of the stage. After they had gone over the day's program, Anne mentioned she would like to bring an "apprentice," the little deaf seamstress, into the company. "At no extra cost to you. I'll bear the expense. But I need the stage to train her—when it's free, of course."

"What can she do, if she can't speak or hear?" asked the manager, his brow creased with doubt.

"She's worked in theaters for years, painting sets and making costumes," Anne replied brightly. "She has talent we could use for the new *Pulcinella*."

Early in the evening, Anne brought her new "apprentice" to the theater and introduced her to the two men. Her eyes darted anxiously from one to the other, but she seemed to feel secure with Anne present. When she understood what she was becoming involved in, she clapped her hands in delight.

Agreement was reached in a nearby café over a glass of wine, and the men went home for supper. The women hurried to Michou's garret, picked up the portraits of Lélia Laplante and Chevalier Jean de Pressigny, and returned to the theater. Anne sat Michou at a table with paints and brushes and put a blank wooden marionette next to each portrait, asking with a gesture if she understood she was to fill in the features. She grinned, then set to work.

∞∞∞

Later that week, Georges was in his office waiting for Anne. They had exchanged notes. He had informed her that the family and servants at the chateau remembered Lélia Laplante, the actress who had played in their theater. She had come without Michou. For her part, Anne reported only that she and Michou were learning to understand one another while Michou made rapid progress in puppetry.

At ten in the morning, when he heard Anne enter the building, he suddenly realized how much he looked forward to seeing her. "Coffee?" he asked, as she shook his hand.

"No thanks. There's something I need to show you. Can you come with me now to the puppet theater?"

"I suppose I could." He stared at her. "What's so urgent?"

"Now's the only time we can have the theater to ourselves. I'd explain more, but it's better you form your own opinion."

Ten minutes later, Georges seated himself on a front bench in the darkened theater while Anne went behind the stage. Soon a thin little figure scurried about illuminating the stage lights. A few minutes more and the curtain was drawn, revealing a dressing room in miniature. An elegant lady stood before a mirror while a small servant arranged her gown. The figures were large, well-formed marionettes, their facial features finely drawn. Georges immediately recognized Laplante and Michou.

There was a knock on the door. The actress dismissed Michou, then opened the door. A male figure entered, his sword identifying his rank, his face clearly that of Chevalier Jean de Pressigny. His hand held a small object wrapped in a cloth. She led him to a table set for two.

At the table he removed the cloth to reveal a tiny replica of the priceless stolen bowl with two cherries.

Georges gasped, speechless.

The actress lifted the bowl and admired it while her companion urged her to eat. They shared the fruit, rocking back and forth, laughing.

Meanwhile, the little servant cowered in a darkened hallway, watching the merry pair through a crack in the door. Finally, they made their way into the next room to a large bed. The door closed behind them. The little servant waited patiently for a while, then hurried to the bedroom door, and peered through a key hole.

Assured the lovers were asleep, the little servant returned to the table. She carefully moved the precious bowl into the light of an oil lamp and studied it from every angle. She then drew a sketch in her pad, replaced the bowl, and slipped out of the room. The curtain fell.

From behind the stage, Anne emerged with Michou in hand. They hugged one another and solemnly bowed to Georges, now on his feet, clapping.

"Fantastic," he shouted. "I can't believe it." Glancing left and right to see if they were alone, he groped for words. "Pressigny and Laplante stole the bowl! We're on to something!"

∞ ∞ ∞

Michou left Anne at the theater door, signing she could find her own way to Épée's institute. With a new bounce in her walk, she disappeared into the crowd. Anne felt profoundly satisfied. Michou had come out of her shell and demonstrated her credibility as a witness.

An hour later, Anne and Georges breathlessly related Michou's revelation to Colonel Saint-Martin at his desk. "Chevalier de Pressigny and Lélia Laplante may have stolen the jasper bowl themselves," Georges concluded, "or received it from the thieves."

While they were speaking, Saint-Martin leaned forward, listening intently. "I'm pleased," he said when they finished. "It appears we have taken yet another step toward solving the series of art thefts. Pressigny and Laplante were involved somehow, and they may lead us to accomplices."

He paused, sat back in his chair, and crossed his arms. "Unfortunately," he added, his brow wrinkling, "Michou's testimony would not persuade an examining magistrate, especially concerning a man as well connected as Chevalier de Pressigny."

"How can you say that?" Anne protested.

He put on a grave, judicial mien. "Suppose I were the magistrate, and I were watching Michou's performance. Why should I accept it as credible evidence? My colleague, Sorin, has declared her a simpleton. In the setting of a puppet theater, she might have thought she was inventing the plot of a play."

"She's depicted a real, stolen bowl, not a phantasy," replied Anne, a testy tone in her voice. "The actress and the directeur of the Amateurs are also real, and what they did is at least plausible."

"Michou *did* work for the actress and for the Amateurs' productions," added Georges. "She must have known Pressigny and would not have mistaken him for someone else."

"Yes," countered Saint-Martin, still playing the devil's advocate, "but she might have a hidden reason to implicate him in a crime he did not commit."

"Come, come, your honor." Georges' voice dripped with mock sarcasm. "Do you suppose they were lovers once and he jilted her?"

The colonel glowered at his adjutant. A moment of icy silence passed before he continued, "Magistrates raise similar questions." His voice lowered. "And we need more than Michou's report to answer them."

Troubled by this discussion, Anne slouched in her chair. She knew Michou, the colonel didn't. While mulling over his remarks, she saw him reach into his desk, bring out a file, and hand it to Georges. "This is the manuscript you stole from the office of the Amateurs," he said with a wry smile. "You can return it now. I've heard from my expert reader."

Anne sat up, lips parted, staring at him expectantly.

"The way the play is put together suggests two different authors," he explained. "Antoine Dubois might have assisted them, but only as a scribe correcting minor faults of grammar. The author of the Clown's confession had to be either Derennes or Pressigny."

"Rogues both." Anne shook her fists. The principal piece of evidence against Antoine was crumbling.

He glanced at her sideways. "You are leaping to a conclusion, a magistrate would say. Antoine Dubois may have adapted the confession in the script to serve as his own."

"Oh, no!" she groaned. "You are *too* cautious, as if a magistrate is listening to your every word!" Angered, her hopes dashed, she spoke through clenched teeth. "I'm encouraged by your expert's report, if not by your opinion." He looked sharply at her but said nothing. She rose abruptly and left by the back way.

Chapter 18

Death of an Actress

At the Tatar Puppet Theater the early July heat had driven the audience away. Victor and his assistant took afternoons off, and Michou tired of the marionettes. On the third of July, the air inside reached the temperature of hell. Anne locked up the building. She and Michou sought the shade of a large linden tree in the garden. Sweat trickling down her neck, Anne stared into the green foliage, mesmerized by the humming of bees above her. Michou sketched listlessly in her pad.

Anne stirred the gravel with the toe of her shoe, discouraged by the slow progress of her father's case. She hadn't seen Georges or Colonel Saint-Martin for a week, not since Baron Breteuil had sent them to inspect a royal highway post in Normandy. They had returned to Paris in the morning, but the colonel went immediately to the lieutenant-general's office. That he had not embraced her view of the reader's report still disappointed Anne. It took an effort of will to put herself in the colonel's place. *Each* piece of evidence, including the expert's report, had to be sound. *She* could leap to conclusions, the colonel could not.

"I see," said a familiar voice, "you've found Michou."

Startled, Anne sat up. Henriette Picard stood before her in an expensive, stylish robe, a poke bonnet on her head, a silk parasol in one hand and an oriental fan in the other. Her eyes shifted inquisitively between Anne and Michou.

Gathering gossip, Anne thought. A sordid way to make a living. She gasped with feigned astonishment. "What a beautiful parasol and fan! From an admirer?"

Henriette waved aside the question, flashing a large paste diamond in the thin beams of sunlight stealing through the leafy canopy. "Is she of much use?" she persisted, glancing at Anne's companion.

"She paints sets and sews costumes for me." Anne pointed toward the distant Camp of the Tatars. "I've a share in the puppet theater." She glanced at Michou, glad that she appeared stupefied by the heat. "It's hard to communicate with her, but she gets the work done. Thanks for the hint."

Henriette waved to an attendant for a chair. "I suppose you know Simon Derennes mysteriously disappeared at the Amateurs' party."

"So I've heard."

"Didn't I see him with you in the picture galleries?"

Anne wrinkled her face in surprise. "Did you?"

Henriette insisted. "Yes, you were looking at the Lombard School in Dido's costume. I recall the tiara."

"Derennes guided me through the Carracci and Reni paintings," Anne conceded, "but I don't know what's become of him." She sought Henriette's eye. "Do you?"

The woman pursed her lips. "They say he's fled the country, or been killed by relatives of women he's ravished." Leaning toward Anne, she lowered her voice to share a secret. "Chevalier de Pressigny must know, but he's not saying." She sat back, fanning her face emphatically. "Not to me at least."

Anne shrugged. Henriette was fishing.

The woman gathered her skirts to leave. "Do you see him often?" A touch of envy seemed to creep into her voice. "I understand he's engaged you for the reception in two weeks."

"Yes, I'll play a small part," said Anne shortly. She didn't wish to elaborate for this woman.

Henriette sucked in a breath. "Well, I'll see you there." She pushed open the parasol and set off toward Rue Montpensier.

Anne stood up and stretched, turning over in her mind what she had just heard. Henriette had spoken to Pressigny but had not learned much. Anne fretted. It was galling to be linked intimately with the dissolute young man. But it was more troubling that someone had paid Henriette to find out the woman who was seen with Derennes the night he disappeared.

Anne felt a touch on her arm and glanced sideways. Michou held up a sketch. A caricature of Henriette as a long-nosed hunting dog wearing a fancy bonnet, sniffing at a languid, half-recumbent Anne. A familiar-looking gentleman, his face dark with menace, led the dog on a leash.

Pointing at the man, Anne mouthed the name LeCourt and mimicked his dignified stance. Michou nodded. She must have seen Henriette working for him. "You read people even better than I thought," said Anne to Michou, ignoring her deafness. "We had better talk to Georges."

Robert LeCourt beckoned to his companion, a few deferential steps behind him. "Monsieur Noir, a word with you please." The two men were walking in the garden of the Palais-Royal. It was early afternoon, rain threatened, and the crowds were thin. "So Henriette Picard spoke with the young English woman yesterday. What's her name again?"

"Cartier. Anne Cartier. The Dido whom Derennes was going to question in the palace dungeon." Noir drew abreast of LeCourt. "Henriette thinks Cartier is gaining the confidence of Chevalier Jean de Pressigny."

"Winning his heart?" asked LeCourt.

The man shrugged. "She doesn't seem to like him. Treats him coolly. But that fascinates him, draws him to her."

"A clever tactic." LeCourt allowed himself a sardonic smile. "Pressigny's a fool. Unfortunately, he's my fool." The financier slowed his pace, absorbed in thought. "Miss Cartier's no ordinary tart. She's become a problem."

The men halted midway through the garden and looked around.

"The inspecteur should arrive at any minute." LeCourt glanced at his watch, then at his companion. "You *did* say two o'clock at the fountain?"

The financier didn't wait for a reply. He scanned the sky, arms akimbo. Dark clouds lowered over Paris. Rain had fallen off and on during the day. He was wearing a plain buff suit without ornament. He wanted to be overlooked. His companion wore an even less noticeable gray. They sought the shade of a chestnut tree where they could observe persons approaching the fountain.

"What else did Henriette tell you?"

"Miss Cartier spends afternoons at the puppet theater in the Camp of the Tatars. Stops for a drink at the Odéon on the way. Evenings, she plays small parts in the variety theater."

"Are you sure she will go to the puppet theater this afternoon?" LeCourt disliked wasting time, but this was a risk he had to take now. He should study this woman for himself and not depend on reports from others.

"She closed it down yesterday. Too hot, I suppose. Today's rain has broken the heat, so she should return. It'll be easy to find her."

"Any friends?"

"She's seen with a small deaf woman who does odd jobs in the theaters. Used to work occasionally for Lélia Laplante."

"Should I be concerned?"

"No. The deaf woman is stupid. But what's going on between Cartier and Jean de Pressigny is another matter. He's invited her to the Amateurs' reception next month. She's to wear the Chanavas jewels from Comte Debussy's collection."

"I've heard that." LeCourt smiled thinly. "I also know she's been seen with Comtesse Marie de Beaumont and her nephew, a provost of the Royal Highway Patrol." His eyes lighted upon a thin figure in black hastening toward the fountain. "Ah, there's Inspecteur Mauvert."

Together the three men walked to Café Odéon and sat inside at a secluded table with a view of the main room. Due to the threat of rain, the outdoor tables were not being served.

Noir pointed to an empty table near the door. "She'll sit there, where we can see her."

They ordered cold lemonade, then sat back to wait. LeCourt turned to the inspecteur. "My companion here, Monsieur Noir, has indicated to you some of my concerns. I'm grateful you could take the time to discuss them privately. I want you to see the woman, Anne Cartier, who is showing an unhealthy interest in last year's unfortunate incident involving the actress."

Mauvert dabbed perspiration from his brow. He had hurried to the meeting. "I can't know every police agent in Paris, but I doubt Anne Cartier's one of them. I'd remember the name."

Noir looked up. "Here she comes."

The tall blond woman took the table he had predicted and ordered a lemonade. She glanced over her shoulder into the room without appearing to recognize anyone. The three men remained hidden from view behind a wall of tall potted plants. Noir sat back, fingering his chin. Mauvert frowned, then whispered, he'd seen her before—the face looked familiar. But he couldn't say where.

LeCourt leaned forward, hands tightly clasped, and stared at the woman. She drank slowly, eyes shadowed, ignoring the bustle of patrons coming and going. Her face was striking rather than pretty. Strong chin, high cheekbones, clear skin. The blond hair took on a brownish tint in the café's subdued light. Her chest rose and fell in the slow rhythm of her breathing. Otherwise, she hardly moved, except to play with the lid of a snuff box.

A tigress in repose, lithe and tawny. A hunter. For a moment, the middle-aged financier was once again a young man in a hot steaming Indian jungle. The tigress had stalked him when he ventured too close to her den. He had escaped, then returned and shot her while she rested unawares.

His mind came back to Anne Cartier. Previously, he had imagined she was a common spy. Her low cunning and sly feminine charms had won a place for herself in Pressigny's fickle heart. Now, LeCourt felt his opinion changing. Miss Cartier was an intelligent, resourceful, and determined woman. A dangerous adversary.

She drained her glass and rose from the table, scanned the room again and left. LeCourt signaled to his man, Noir, who was now sitting up, alert. He waited a few moments, then followed her.

LeCourt pushed away from the table and turned toward Mauvert. "Inspecteur. We must take care. Philippe d'Orléans resents the scandalous deaths of the actress Laplante and her companion in the palace theater. The Amateurs do not want him to be troubled again. By *anyone*. We need to know if this woman Cartier is acting on her own. Or, on behalf of someone in high position who intends, for whatever reason, to embarrass the duke."

The inspecteur pursed his lips, then remarked in a low voice, "Colonel Paul de Saint-Martin called up the records of the case, though it's outside his jurisdiction."

LeCourt sipped from his glass, looking over the rim thoughtfully. "Miss Cartier has apparently tried to draw information from him. No matter. The police records betray no secrets."

"Nonetheless, the colonel *has* cooperated with her."

With growing unease, the financier shifted in his seat. "Indeed! I don't know why. Neither he nor Comtesse Marie de Beaumont appear to have any reason to pry into the incident. And Miss Cartier has no social standing that might influence them."

"A newcomer, I've heard. English. Speaks perfect French." Mauvert paused, weighing an idea. "If you wish, I'll write to an acquaintance of mine in London."

"That sounds like a good first step." LeCourt drew a small purse from his pocket and pressed it into Mauvert's palm. "This is for you."

The inspecteur protested with a wave of the hand but held on to the money. "I'd be happy to serve free of charge."

LeCourt insisted, "Five *louis d'or* to cover expenses. There will be more later."

Mauvert placed the purse in his pocket. "In a month, or sooner, we should know what kind of trick she's up to."

∞∞∞

As she sipped lemonade in Café Odéon, Anne felt she was being watched again. For the past few days, she had had that feeling. Today, Georges had agreed to observe the patrons when she entered. She casually looked around for him. From the back of the room, he caught her eye, then pointed surreptitiously to a table near her veiled by greenery.

Figures had stirred there when she walked in. One of them now bent forward, head craned toward her, face indistinguishable. While she viewed him in the mirror of her snuff box cover, the person never conversed or took a drink. He was still in that posture when she got up to leave. A figment of her imagination? Hardly.

Walking south in the Montpensier arcade, the odd feeling still nagging her, she glanced at the scene reflected in a window and caught a glimpse of a vaguely familiar man's face near a pillar. Was she being followed? Should she keep her appointment with Michou at the Tatar Puppet Theater? She had intended to invite her home that evening for supper. But suppose a trap was being set for her.

To allay her suspicion, Anne stopped at the entrance to a milliner's shop and glanced to the left. The face appeared again in the crowd bustling through the arcade.

She entered the shop, brushed past the clerks, and left by the rear door on Rue Montpensier, then rushed down the street to the café and through the back door, just as Monsieur LeCourt walked out the front, together with a small thin man in a black suit. She looked around the room.

"LeCourt hung on you like a cat watching a canary," said Georges, coming up to her side. "He gave some money to the man in black, Inspecteur Mauvert. I don't like the looks of that. And there was a third man...."

Anne broke in, "The one who followed me in the arcade....I remember his face now. Monsieur Noir. He was with LeCourt upstairs in Café Marcel." Suddenly, a frisson of fear struck her. She imagined snarling dogs circling her, baring their teeth, waiting for an unguarded moment to attack.

By evening a rain shower had cooled the city and a fresh breeze blew through the windows of Anne's apartment. Some of her anxiety from the incident in the Café Odeon had dissipated. Georges had followed her to the puppet theater, where she found Michou touching up the face of a marionette. Yes, she would be delighted to have supper with Anne on Rue Traversine.

An hour later she arrived with a handful of daisies. On this, her first visit, Michou was apprehensive, casting quick, side-long glances about the parlor. Gradually relaxing with a glass of wine, she began to examine the room's spare furnishings. In of wine, she began to examine the room's spare furnishings. In the kitchen preparing an herb omelette, Anne observed her out of the corner of her eye. Suddenly, the little figure grew tense, still. Her gaze had fixed on the three miniature portraits of Anne, her mother, and Antoine which hung side by side on the wall.

As if entranced, Michou rose from her seat and walked up to the pictures. She studied each of them, then compared them to one another. Slowly she turned toward Anne, a stricken expression on her face. Antoine Dubois, she had apparently concluded, was Anne's father. She walked up to Anne, caressed her cheek, and embraced her. With a nod Anne confirmed Michou's assumption. Antoine Dubois, after all, was the only father she had ever known.

After supper, while Michou sat at the table, Anne gave her a blank marionette and the materials to paint it, then placed Dubois' picture next to them. Michou understood immediately and set to work. Before the evening was far gone, she had produced a marionette with a credible likeness to him.

Early the next day, before the Tatar Puppet Theater opened to the public, Anne and Michou climbed onto the platform behind the stage and arranged the strings for three marionettes in a dressing room scene. Victor Benoit soon joined them to prepare the lighting. Anne had told him only that this production was a test for Michou, who had shown unexpected talent in puppetry.

Anne directed Michou to work the marionette representing herself while Benoit worked Lélia Laplante's. When Anne attempted to move the newly painted "Antoine Dubois" into the arms of the actress, Michou waved her hands in protest. Then Anne had her father attack the actress, his arms beating upon her.

Suddenly, a crash echoed through the empty theater. Michou's marionette lay on the stage, its limbs sprawling grotesquely. She had released the strings and rushed from the platform, gesturing to the others to remain. A few minutes later, she returned with another marionette.

An astonishing transformation took place. Possessed by an idea, Michou took command of the stage. She beckoned to the manager to operate "Michou," which she moved into a darkened closet open to the actress' dressing room. "Michou" lay down as if resting, concealed in a jumble of clothes but able to watch whatever happened. She removed "Dubois" from the stage and gave Anne the strings to "Lélia Laplante," who sat at a table. Finally, Michou walked the new marionette into the room. It was "Chevalier de Pressigny."

Michou gestured to Anne that "the actress" should rise. What was clearly a quarrel then took place, with much fist-shaking and foot-stamping. Michou yanked a pin out of her hair and thrust it at her marionette. Anne understood that her enraged "Lélia" should reach into her hair, pull out a long pin, and strike at "Pressigny's" face.

The marionettes had fallen by now into slow motion. Michou's "Pressigny" lifted his left arm to parry the blow. The pin hit his hand; he shook it with pain. He leaned toward the table, seized an object, and struck the actress powerfully in the throat. Confused, Anne asked, "What's that object?"

In reply, Michou reached behind the stage for a pair of scissors. With a fierce expression on her face, she held it up as if to stab Anne, who then let "Lélia Laplante" drop to the floor. The manager raised the concealed "Michou's" arm in horror. "Pressigny" staggered backwards out of the room.

Michou closed the curtain, jumped from the platform, and ran out the door.

There was a moment of silence. "Christ!" exclaimed Victor. "Who would think she could produce a play like *that*?"

Hurrying out, Anne glanced over her shoulder. "Victor, put together a piece for today. I'll look after Michou."

Anne found her friend on a bench under a chestnut tree in the garden, staring down at the gravel, trembling. Anne sat next to her and stroked her gently until she grew calm. She looked up. Anne dried her tear-stained face. Soon the arcades began to bustle with morning shoppers. Anne and Michou rose from the bench and walked together slowly toward the Beaujolais exit like two grieving sisters.

∽∽∽

The sun was still high, but a light breeze cooled the air. Anne and Colonel Saint-Martin walked in his garden, discussing Michou's astonishing performance that morning at the Tatar Puppet Theater. When they reached the fountain, he wondered aloud what Pressigny had said to provoke Laplante's attack. "It's a pity Michou couldn't hear him or at least read his lips." With a cautious glance he asked, "Could you persuade her to tell us more. Perhaps something about the death of Dubois?"

"Not in her present state of mind," Anne replied, feeling pity for her deaf friend. "I've tried, but she balks. Won't touch the marionettes any more. Her memories are too painful." Anne turned to the fountain, listening to the rhythmic splash of water. "For now it's best that she lose herself in her studies at Abbé de l'Épée's institute. She's learning to sign with his method and to read and write."

"Good. She may yet be a credible witness." He sighed. "In any case, we would need more than her testimony to bring Pressigny to court."

"My father is *innocent*," said Anne, suppressing an urge to dispute his point. "Pressigny's the key to proving it." She grimaced at the thought she would be with him soon at the Amateurs' reception.

As they walked back to the residence, she told the colonel she was thinking of bringing Michou with her to Chateau Debussy since she would need a maid. The woman's skill at sketching might also prove useful.

Saint-Martin stopped suddenly and stared at Anne. "Pressigny might know Michou! If he does, he'll suspect you're up to something." He raised a warning hand. "What do you suppose he'll do, if he discovers the sole witness to his crime only an arm's reach away?"

Anne refused to flinch. "He won't notice Michou. She's just another servant in the house. And he doesn't know she witnessed his attack on Lélia."

The colonel's expression hardened.

"Of course," she added with a conciliatory smile, "I'll take sensible precautions. Pressigny can be dangerous."

Before the exchange could grow more heated, a servant walked toward them announcing that coffee was ready upstairs.

Saint-Martin bowed slightly to Anne and extended his right arm. She took it, suppressing a sigh of relief. Quarreling with him was becoming pointless. He spoke from a sense of honor and duty, as best she could judge. She felt his arm, strong from fencing. The pressure of her grip drew his eyes to her. With a smile, he flexed the arm in response.

The servant led them through the house and opened the door to the salon overlooking the courtyard. A foreigner in Paris, Anne could ignore the social convention allowing only a man's wife or mistress the freedom she was enjoying in Saint-Martin's home. While the colonel instructed the servant, she glanced about the room. The furniture was contemporary and comfortable. The sideboard looked English. A Sheraton, she thought. Newspapers, magazines, and theater programs from London were scattered across the mahogany library table. In one corner, four music stands stood in front of as many chairs.

She also noticed a volume of Shakespeare's plays opened to *Macbeth*. Her curiosity aroused, she sorted the programs until she came to a production of the play at Drury Lane Theatre, April 22, 1786.

Smiling amiably, Saint-Martin joined her by the table. "You've discovered my fascination with your great national poet. I'd heard from a friend before going to London that I should not miss Mrs. Sarah Siddons in the role of Lady Macbeth. By happy coincidence, she was playing at the Drury Lane the evening of the day after my arrival."

"You were fortunate. I've also seen her once in *Macbeth*." Anne lifted her eyes, struck her breast.

"Come you spirits that tend on mortal thoughts, unsex me here, and fill me from the crown to the toe top-full of direst cruelty."

"What single-minded evil!" Saint-Martin exclaimed.

Anne rubbed her hands, as if tormented by guilt.

"Out damned spot. Out, I say! Who would have thought the old man to have had so much **blood** *in him!"*

"Well done!" Saint-Martin's eyes smiled with appreciation. "Lady Macbeth was driven by ambition and it destroyed her."

"Perhaps something like her spirit lurks deep within me, *straining* to break out." Ever since realizing Antoine had been murdered, she had sensed in herself a barely conscious, but single-minded, raging passion to avenge a great wrong done to her. An eye for an eye. Thus far she had ignored it, denied it, at least kept it under control. But what would she do, if she were to confront his unknown killer face to face?

The servant returned with a tray set for coffee. The colonel dismissed him, then poured. As he handed Anne a cup, he stared into her eyes. "I see her steely will."

Chapter 19

The Scar

"He's full of surprises," Anne said to Michou, forgetting for the moment that she couldn't hear. Chevalier de Pressigny had sent his own coachman to fetch them. The light carriage, pulled by two horses, rolled rapidly southward on the road from Paris to Orléans, tossing its occupants from side to side. Michou's eyes darted about, viewing the countryside through the open windows. Her mood seemed subdued.

Yesterday afternoon at the puppet theater, Anne had asked Michou, did she think Pressigny knew her? She had thought for a moment, then replied, no, he had never paid attention to her. When she had worked for the Amateurs, she was usually in the wardrobe and out of his sight. If she were with Laplante when he came to visit, the actress sent her away.

Anne had then explained she was going to Chateau Debussy for an investigation. Georges would be with her and the colonel would be nearby. Would Michou come along as Anne's maid? Her skill at sketching might also be needed. She had reacted to the proposal with reasonable apprehension and had asked for time to think it over. Later in the afternoon, she had come to Anne with a sober, trusting face and had agreed.

The carriage left the main highway and soon cut through the chalk ridge above Chateau Debussy. Anne gazed over the vast estate, anxiety gathering in the pit of her stomach. She descended into the broad valley of the Bièvre feeling like Daniel going down into the lions' den.

The seventeenth-century chateau stood in the middle of the valley under a clear blue sky. Its four stout, domed towers appeared to peg it firmly to the ground. The carriage drove along the west bank of the Bièvre in the shade of plane trees, then eased through a passageway in a large gate house. A dark-haired woman inside looked up from her sewing, glanced at the passengers, then nodded. The carriage rolled into an outer courtyard. To the right, Anne glimpsed a busy farmyard flanked by workshops, barns, and stables. The carriage turned to the left, crossed a pond covered with water lilies in bloom, passed under a second, richly decorated gate house, and entered the inner courtyard. The gray mass of the chateau loomed up before her—the roughly cut stonework of the ground floor, the majestic main floor, the mansard roof. Michou's eyes opened wide with awe.

Servants in silver and blue livery escorted the women through a side entrance and up two flights of stairs to their apartment on the mansard floor. The parlor was spacious, comfortably furnished in the style of Louis XV, and recently aired. A large bouquet of freshly cut yellow and lavender freesia stood on the window sill. Through the open doors, Anne saw smaller bouquets in each of their bedrooms. Arms akimbo, she asked herself why a commoner was receiving so much consideration. To groom her for the courtly part she was to play? That perhaps made sense. She felt her skepticism eroding.

While Michou unpacked in her own room, Anne stepped out on a small balcony for a view over the garden to the dark, wooded ridge beyond. Bursting through thick white clouds, the late morning sun fell on rocky outcroppings among the trees, creating an impression of ruined palisades. At the base of the ridge, Anne also discerned the entrance to a cave, like a low gate into a fortress. She half-seriously imagined Simon Derennes hidden inside. A lonely cottage squatted below the ridge in a pool of sunlight. Two small figures walked out of the building to a kiln near the cave.

There was a knock on the door. A man called out her name. With a frisson of apprehension, Anne recognized Chevalier de

Pressigny's voice. What was he up to? If this were a message, why wouldn't he send it with a servant? She threw a hasty glance at herself in the mirror and, smiling politely, opened the door. His face brightened easily when he saw her. He was exquisitely attired in a mauve suit embroidered with silver. Bowing to her without a trace of mockery, he announced that Comte Debussy wished to speak with her. For a moment she felt like a visiting dignitary.

She made herself ready while he waited in the parlor, then they went downstairs to the comte's apartment. The old man sat in an armchair, his legs covered by a thin blue blanket, his feet resting on an upholstered stool. He was idly petting a black cat that had curled up in his lap. Anne stopped at a respectful distance.

"Please come closer, Mademoiselle Cartier, I want to get acquainted." The cat opened two thin yellow slits and yawned.

A large head on a shrivelled body, the comte seemed condensed into little more than mind and will. He reached out thin, cold hands and drew her close. She looked into his eyes, almond-shaped, brown with a golden tint.

For what seemed several minutes, he studied Anne. She walked back and forth, turned left, then right. He said nothing, his brow knitted in concentration. Finally, he reached to a side table, and rang a bell. The cat leapt from his lap. A door opened and the dark-haired woman Anne had glimpsed at the gatehouse entered the room, followed by a maid carrying a large garment bag. As they passed by, the dark-haired woman gave Anne the flicker of a smile.

The comte glanced at the garment bag, then at Anne. "Chevalier de Pressigny has given us an estimate of your size. Claudine has produced this costume. Put it on so we can see if she may need to alter it."

The dressmaker and the maid led Anne to an adjacent room. Until now, she hadn't thought much about what she was to wear. A costly and elaborate costume, perhaps, in the style worn at the opera or formal balls, the skirt wide, the bodice low-cut.

From the garment bag Claudine drew a deep purple bodice over one arm, a mustard yellow skirt over the other, while Anne removed her clothes. Over a silk petticoat she put on the long, full skirt, followed by the short-sleeved bodice with a v-neckline. She glanced at herself and gasped. As an actress, she had worn all kinds of costumes but never one like this. Her midriff was bare to the navel.

She fingered the skirt: thin delicately patterned silk of the finest quality. It lay lightly on her body. Her eyes took in the strong contrast of purple and yellow. In comparison, the pale blues, greens, and pinks favored by the French taste of the day seemed washed out and insipid.

She paced the room, whirled about, bent her body this way and that. The exotic costume let her move freely, unlike the tight-waisted, stiff, layered garments French women wore. And, the bare midriff—designed for a very warm climate—also suited Chateau Debussy under a blazing July sun. Inspecting herself in a mirror on the door, she smoothed the silk over her hips. A nearly perfect fit, thanks to Pressigny's practiced eye. She frowned, as if he had somehow violated her.

Claudine approached from behind and pinched the skirt at the waist. It needed no alteration. Her fingertips caressed the smooth silk falling in graceful folds. She pointed to a chair. "Please sit down. There's more." She tied a yellow turban on Anne's head, then bent down to put a pair of purple slippers on her feet.

Anne gazed at the dressmaker, an intelligent, efficient woman in her forties, rather stout, but fine-featured, brown-eyed, with light brown skin and lustrous black hair. She bore a French given name and carried herself in the manner of a *bourgeoise*. Detecting Anne's curiosity, she stepped back, her brow creased, offended.

"You were sitting at the gatehouse window when we arrived." Anne hastened to say.

"At work on your costume." Claudine held Anne's eye in a level gaze. "I was born in Pondicherry to a French officer and his Indian wife. We came to this country thirty years ago, where I met my husband, Krishna, the steward." She searched Anne's face for a moment, then glanced at the garment. "How do you like it?"

"It's lovely. And unusual. I've never seen anything quite like it."

The dressmaker smiled, her eyes beaming with pride. "In India, it would be worn by a noble lady at the court of a prince, like Chanavas Khan."

"Was it Comte Debussy's choice?"

"Yes. He saw my daughter Nalini wear it three years ago during a masquerade ball at the chateau. With paste jewelry of course. She was stunning. Carried herself like a queen. The comte could hardly take his eyes off her. The costume reminded him of India, where he made his fortune years ago—and of the beautiful women he knew there." Her lips curled slightly in the hint of a sneer. She pointed to the skirt. "I've had to lengthen it. You are taller than she was." She bit her lip, then turned suddenly away.

A heavy silence fell over the room. Anne shivered with horror, recalling Derennes and the corpse in the palace dungeon. "My God," she murmured silently, "I'm wearing the murdered daughter's costume!"

Claudine slowly, methodically folded the garment bag, her neck bent, her features lined with sorrow. The maid wrung her hands and looked down at the floor. Touched by the dressmaker's grief, Anne gazed at her speechless, not knowing what to say.

Claudine pointed toward the door. "We're ready now to let the comte see you."

As Anne emerged from the room, Debussy stared at her for a moment, then rang a bell. A dark-skinned man carried in a highly burnished wooden case which he opened on a nearby table. "Mademoiselle Cartier," the comte said. "This is Krishna, my steward and the faithful guardian of my treasure. He has brought the jewelry to us."

Krishna! Anne felt a surge of compassion for the man. Father of Nalini, Derennes' young victim. And for Claudine, her mother! Watching them carefully, Anne began to sense something prickly in the way they eyed one another. The two were husband and wife—but not friends. Had their daughter's tragedy spawned recriminations and soured their relationship?

At the comte's gesture, the dressmaker laid a cold, heavy necklace on Anne's chest and fastened the clasp behind her neck, fitted a gold tiara on to her turban and bracelets on her arms, wrists, and ankles, and hung pendants from her ears.

"Look at yourself, Mademoiselle," said Debussy, pointing to a full-length mirror on the wall.

She walked toward it, self-consciously squaring her shoulders. "I look a little ridiculous," she mumbled to herself, unaccustomed to acting as a mannequin. But, as she contemplated the jewelry, she found it dazzling. Its Indian creator had adorned the front of the tiara with a sculpted medallion of white jade as large as a man's hand. Behind the tiara, rising above the medallion, Claudine had attached a gold and enamel flower inlaid with several fine emeralds, rubies, and diamonds. Above the flower she had fitted a feather of pearls also set in gold and enamel.

A wide collar of gold links set with dozens of emeralds, pearls, and rubies encircled her neck. Ropes of pear-shaped diamonds cascaded over her chest and stomach. She gasped. Each diamond was at least the size of her thumbnail! She lifted her arms, bending them in front of her. Around her upper arms were matching wide gold bracelets, delicately designed, finely wrought, and as richly studded with irregularly shaped diamonds as were those on her wrists and ankles. She turned first left and then right, glancing in the mirror. Pear-shaped gold pendants, each studded with three exquisite oval diamonds, hung from cords looped over her ears.

The jewelry and costume brought Anne to a regal frame of mind. She turned around and walked back slowly toward Debussy as a gentle light poured through the windows. The precious stones glowed with a touch of the purple from the bodice; the gold glittered. An expression of rapture came over his face. "That will do very nicely, indeed," he said softly. Claudine removed the jewelry and returned it to Krishna. The comte sighed softly, closed his eyes, and motioned everyone out of the room.

∽∽∽

Chevalier de Pressigny lightly touched Anne's arm as they strolled away from the comte's apartment through a wide hallway, its walls hung with tapestry depicting hunting scenes. "Diana's displaying her charms," he said, pointing to the nude huntress in sensual repose. "François Boucher's design."

Studying the work, Anne began to suspect her companion of an ulterior motive, but she corrected herself. Out of the corner of her eye, she noticed his expression seemed almost innocent, suffused with delight in the elegance of the reclining female figure.

As they resumed their walk, Anne fell into thought. Gone was the rude manner he had displayed in the variety theater's dressing room where she had first met him. He was treating her now with respect, perhaps out of deference to Comtesse Marie de Beaumont and Colonel Paul de Saint-Martin. Or as a subtle tactic in a campaign of seduction.

He stopped before a massive door crowned by an ornate pointed gable that two marble nude male slaves struggled to support. Beckoning Anne, he began to pull the door open. "The comte's finest paintings and sculptures are in this gallery. He keeps the jewels and other priceless small objects in the treasury, the round tower room by his sleeping chambers."

Anne recalled with a start the last time a lecherous young man, Simon Derennes, had shown her through a gallery. Wide-eyed, tense, she quickly scanned the hallway for an accomplice. Servants passed by in both directions, but none looked suspicious. A solid, honest-looking older woman approached who appeared to carry some authority in the chateau. The housekeeper, Anne thought, noting a ring of keys on her belt.

As the woman greeted Pressigny, apprehension flickered on his face but vanished almost immediately. "Good afternoon, Madame Soucie," he responded, bowing slightly.

She returned the greeting, then nodded to Anne as if she knew her. Anne felt reassured. With relief she saw through the open door that it was indeed a gallery.

To her right, the large vaulted room stretched at least fifty paces along the chateau's garden side. Light was filtering through window blinds partially drawn to prevent damage to the carpets and tapestries. At an open window, Anne looked out over the garden to its centerpiece, an octagonal oriental pavilion, its reds, yellows, and blacks bleached by the noonday sun. She would visit it later.

They stopped in front of the portrait of a beautiful young seated woman in a full, yellow, silk gown richly brocaded in a floral pattern. Posing in three-quarter profile, a smile on her lips, she cast her eyes down toward a tiger cat that gazed inscrutably at the viewer. It lay on its side to the left of the chair on a thick, cream-colored damask cushion with gold fringe and tassels.

"My mother at the age of thirty," said Pressigny, who had noticed Anne's interest in the picture, "with her favorite pet, Princesse."

Anne moved back a few steps to a better vantage point. The painter was a master, a discerning observer. He had subtly captured the spirit of the woman. With a side glance, Anne detected the mother's fine, well-proportioned, but loveless features reflected in the face of her son. Then she noticed fleeting lines of sorrow about his mouth. She wondered uneasily, did he feel the loss of his mother? Or feign sadness to win sympathy?

"She passed away ten years ago," he replied to her quizzical expression as they resumed their walk through the gallery.

He stopped abruptly and scowled. "Someone's been careless here." A marble statue, the *Faun* by Sergell, rested dangerously close to the edge of its pedestal. Pressigny removed his dress gloves and drew a pair of white cloth gloves from his purse. As he put one on his right hand, Anne noticed with a start the scar on the back of his left hand. When he turned the hand, she saw the scar on its palm. Lélia *had* thrust the hatpin through his hand! The wound must have become infected. Ugly scar tissue had formed where it had been lanced.

Anne stepped back, shaking. In her mind's eye, she saw the raging actress striking at him, the pin penetrating his hand. She struggled with the horror that surely showed on her face, glad that Sergell's statue preoccupied him. By the time he had finished, she felt outwardly calm.

He changed his gloves again, exposing the scarred hand. She couldn't avert her eyes quickly enough.

"Mademoiselle Cartier! You're trembling!" He stared at her with a worried look, then smiled. "Sergell's *Faun* is safe now."

As she walked again at his side through the gallery, she thought of the scars now concealed by a glove. He bore uglier, crippling scars on his spirit.

∞∞∞

The maid closed the door to the corridor, leaving behind a lunch tray of fruit, bread, cheese, and wine on a side table in the parlor. Michou took a portion to her room, where she would eat and rest, then finish unpacking. In what remained of the afternoon, she would practice signing, in which she was making good progress.

Biting into a pear, Anne walked to the window and breathed a sigh of relief. There would be no formal midday meal. She would have time in the afternoon to explore the grounds of the chateau. While eating the fruit, she arranged the freesia in a new rhythm of lavender and yellow. The shocking image of Pressigny's scarred hand slowly ebbed into the remote recesses of her mind.

After lunch she stepped outside into bright sunshine. On the path from the chateau to the garden, she noticed a large-boned woman pruning a pear tree on a trellis. A gray sun-bonnet guarded her face, a plain brown robe covered her body. Although clothed like a peasant, she moved with the unmistakable assurance of an aristocrat. Ah, thought Anne, that must be Claire de Pressigny, the chevalier's sister.

The woman was alerted by the crunch of Anne's shoes in the gravel. Wary, unfriendly eyes glared at her from a face well-formed but scarred by smallpox. Anne walked to a nearby jasmine arbor that overlooked an ornamental kitchen garden. The bright lemon-yellow flowers gave off a pungent vanilla fragrance. "Do you mind if I rest here for a moment?" she asked. "Anne Cartier. I've come for the Amateurs' reception."

Claire shrugged her shoulders, then fixed her attention again on the trellis. She hadn't said a word. Anne heard the sound of hammering in the distance, but no one was in sight.

After several minutes she left the arbor and approached Claire, whose expression remained flint-like. Undaunted, Anne tried to cajole her with friendly questions about the garden. Her responses were cool, terse.

"Would you show me the greenhouse?" Anne persisted. "I've been told you have tropical plants."

Claire consented curtly and set off in the direction of the hammering.

As they entered the building, the sound stopped. A tall, muscular young man looked up at them, a hammer in his hand. He had rough, handsome features, marked by a knife scar on his cheek, black curly hair, and dark flashing eyes. He threw a quick smile at Claire, then an inquisitive glance at Anne.

"René Cavour, our gardener," said Claire. "Mademoiselle Cartier has come for the reception."

Cavour studied Anne for a moment, then spoke in heavily accented French to Claire about the pear trellis. He gave Anne a final glance and returned to his work, a flatbed for potted plants standing nearby. During this brief encounter Anne detected an unmistakably erotic message in the eye contact between the young people.

"Is René French, from the south?" Anne asked, after they had left the entrance hall.

"Italian, from Piedmont," Claire replied, leading the way through an orangery into a room of brilliant flowers. Little by little, she grew more congenial in this place where she felt at home. She pointed to several exotic plants, reciting their Latin botanical names. When they passed a bank of rare orchids and Anne identified a few she had seen in the colonel's home, Claire smiled for the first time.

A mocking smile, Anne thought. "Do you raise medicinal plants as well?" she asked, recalling the comte's wasted appearance.

"We grow the basic ingredient of laudanum right here." Claire led her into a large room of tall plants with bluish purple flowers. *Papaver somniferum*, she explained, a poppy native to southern India. She helped Krishna harvest the sap, from which he manufactured the drug in a solution. "It smells of cinnamon and cloves. Tastes good too. Krishna claims it's medicinal."

"Is that true?" Anne looked askance. From the Vauxhall in London, she knew of young men given over to the drug. They became listless and unreliable and neglected their health.

"Krishna's laudanum seems to ease the comte's pain," Claire conceded.

"Does he make it only for the comte?" Anne's curiosity was aroused.

"No, he also sells it to my brother and his acquaintances."
Claire glanced sideways at Anne. "Like Simon Derennes. You
know him from the palace theater, don't you?"

Anne shrugged noncommittally. She could feel the woman's
probing eyes, her lingering suspicion.

The two women left the greenhouse, Anne striking off in
the direction of the oriental pavilion in the center of the garden.
Claire hesitated at first, then joined her. The low octagonal
structure had a yellow foundation and a red tile pagoda roof.
Black wooden latticework covered four alternate sides; the
others were open. Inside were benches attached to the four
latticed walls and a few wooden chairs. In the middle of the
raised unpainted wooden floor was a trapdoor.

"It opens into a tunnel to the chateau," Claire offered. "It's
fastened tight at both ends." She gestured toward a pair of
benches. The two women sat down facing one another.

"How well do you know my brother Jean?" asked Claire,
barely concealing a smirk.

Refusing to be drawn out, Anne revealed only that she had
performed in one of his productions and he had invited her to
the reception.

Claire frowned, a doubting glint in her eyes. "You know, he
always has his way with women."

Anne shook her gown and rose to leave. "Perhaps with women
of a certain kind."

On the way back to the chateau, Anne went looking for Krishna
to ask if she might have a horse for a ride in the countryside.
She found him seated behind a desk in the chateau's basement
office, wearing a brown suit like a proper Frenchman. A large
account book lay open in front of him. To his right, within
arm's reach, stood shelves of leather-fronted file boxes lined up
in neat rows. To his left, a rack of iron keys hung in an open
cabinet. Light came from high deep-set windows in the thick
whitewashed walls. A musty smell hung in the air.

When she put forward her request, he agreed without question. He penned a note to the stablemaster, blotted it, and
handed it to her with the obliging smile of a proprietor rather
then a servant. She hurried to her room. Comtesse Marie had

lent her a fashionable wine-colored English riding habit embroidered with spangles and silver thread, a black tricorn hat, and boots. The fit was good, just a little tight in the shoulders.

Krishna's note in hand, Anne went to the farmyard opposite the chateau. The stablemaster prepared a riding horse with a sidesaddle for her, then beckoned to a groom working nearby. He should go with her the first time. She wanted to ride alone— she could explore more freely. But, as a guest, she thought it best to comply. She mounted the horse and rode out into the courtyard. The groom followed a length behind. When he seemed about to close the gap, she glanced irritably over her shoulder and increased her speed. He gained ground.

Beyond the courtyard, where the road forked in several directions, she had to stop for a hay wagon. The groom came alongside her on the left. A sharp reproach on the tip of her tongue, she shifted in the saddle to confront him. He winked.

"Georges!" she flustered, choking back the urge to laugh.

"My lady!" He touched the tip of his cap, grinning like a monkey. He pointed to a path winding up to the wooded chalk ridge. She took the lead. When they were out of sight in a small clearing, they dismounted and tethered the horses.

"The stablemaster is one of ours," said Georges, patting his horse. "We were in the cavalry together, so he hired me. He needs extra help for gatherings like the Amateurs." Georges gestured politely toward a crude bench in the shade. "What do you have to tell me?" His eyebrows arched with curiosity.

Sitting on the edge of the bench, Anne eagerly described her visit with Pressigny in the art gallery. "I've seen where Laplante's hat pin went through his left hand," she said in a hushed voice. "The wound became infected and left an ugly scar. That's why he always wears gloves." She settled back on the bench, a question slowly forming in her mind. "Can anyone here treat a wound like that?"

Before replying, Georges looked over his shoulder as if they might be overheard. "Yes, the housekeeper at the chateau, Madame Soucie." He explained she was the stablemaster's wife and had learned the healing arts from her father, a military surgeon. On the estate she treated cuts and bruises and set minor fractures. Nearby villages often called her. "She's also keeping an eye on you," Georges added, clucking softly. "She thought of the bouquet of flowers for your window sill."

"I sensed something between her and Pressigny when we met outside the gallery." Anne grew excited. "He must have gone to her."

"I'll soon find out. She's invited me to supper with the family." Georges got up from the bench, tentatively offered his hand to Anne. Declining with a smile, she sprang to her feet and followed him on a narrow path to a rocky platform at the edge of the ridge. Hidden behind brush growing out of cracks in the rock, she gazed across the valley to the chateau.

"Oh," she murmured, recognizing the balcony of her room. She started to speak. Georges touched her arm, cautioning her. The wind behind them could carry their voices. He pointed to two men stacking tiles at the kiln below.

"They work on Pressigny's projects," he said softly. "See the older wiry one…"

"He's Monsieur Noir, the man we've seen twice with Monsieur LeCourt," she whispered in his ear. "A clever fellow, my shadow in the Palais-Royal."

"A dangerous one," Georges warned. "The servants call him François. He keeps an eye on Pressigny." He pointed toward the short, thickset younger man. "And that's Jacques Gros, Noir's faithful companion. He's brighter than he looks."

After a few minutes, the two men left the kiln and went into the nearby cottage. Georges beckoned Anne forward to the edge of the ridge for a view of the entrance to the caves a short distance beyond the kiln. "I had a stable boy search them when the men weren't around. Lots of sheep shit but no sign of Derennes. And he's not in the chateau. The Soucies would have let me know. Noir has hidden him somewhere else." Georges paused to think for a moment, then shrugged his shoulders. "Let's get back to the chateau."

They untethered the horses and rode back silently. At the door to the stable, they dismounted. Seeing no grooms about, they led the horses to the stalls. Anne wanted to help Georges remove the saddles and feed the horses but he objected, shaking his finger at her. "You're supposed to play the part of a queen.

You'd better start acting like one." He did the chores himself with help from a groom he found sleeping in the hayloft.

While the men were stowing the tackle in another room, Anne wiped the sweat from her horse's glistening neck and admired its rich chestnut color. She found herself hoping to ride it again. With a grimace she stepped back. What a silly notion, to stay at Chateau Debussy a minute longer than necessary! As she left the stable with Georges, she drew a deep breath of fresh air, then sniffed her sleeve. "I'd better wash and change. I shouldn't go to the comte's supper smelling like a thoroughbred."

∞∞∞

The meal was in a small, dark-panelled dining room on the main floor, with only Anne, the comte, and Claire at the table. Thin rays of twilight shafted through the windows. Several candles flickered on the walls. The room momentarily reminded Anne of a poorly lighted stage. And Claire looked like a clown. She had attempted to conceal her facial scars beneath a thick layer of powder.

Loath to appear rude, Anne forced her eyes away from Claire to the marble sideboard where food stood ready. A waiter came with a Sèvres tureen of *potage au cresson* for Anne and Claire, while a second waiter served the comte a cup of chicken broth. The soup was delicious, rich with butter and garnished with water-cress leaves. Anne consumed every bit of it. Claire hardly touched hers. Since she appeared well-fed, Anne thought, she had to be eating somewhere else.

While soup was being served, the comte asked Claire a few polite questions about her day. "It was ordinary, of little interest," she replied curtly.

Unperturbed, he turned to Anne. "Miss Cartier, what have you seen in the gallery?"

"Sergell's *Faun,*" she readily replied. Thanks to Pressigny's preoccupation with the work, she knew it well: a reclining figure, caught at the moment of waking from sleep. Blood seemed to surge through his marble veins. His limbs were poised for action. "What vitality," she observed. "Only the voice is missing."

"I'm impressed that you appreciate the sculptor." A hint of wistful regret shadowed the old man's face. "Sergell's patron,

Bailli de Breteuil, lent me the *Faun*. Unfortunately, he died last year. The statue will pass to his cousin, our Baron de Breteuil, Minister for Paris."

The dish of *haricots verts en vinègre* was served while the comte discoursed on the history of the chateau. It was built in mid-seventeenth-century on the foundations of a medieval castle, hence its irregular shape. Certain passageways and vaulted chambers in the basement belonged to the original building. "The seventeenth-century architect cleared out most of the old moat to gain a dry basement, leaving only a pond in front and adding a tunnel to the pavilion in the garden."

"Why build a tunnel?"

The comte shrugged his shoulders. "The owner's folly. Perhaps he wanted a secret means of escape, should his creditors pursue him."

"Is the tunnel still in use?"

"We keep it locked," replied the comte, glancing maliciously toward his stepdaughter, "lest the gardener sneak through it to abduct our Claire."

A grimace cracked the layer of powder on the young woman's face, but she stared silently at her plate.

Embarrassed, Anne winced at the insult. She regarded Claire with a sympathetic eye. Her marital prospects were indeed bleak. Georges had said she found comfort with René Cavour, the young man in charge of the greenhouse.

The comte turned to Anne. "Your costume should be ready tomorrow morning. See Madame about the final fitting." He looked at her with a lascivious smile. "I look forward to seeing you wear it."

Claire stirred, her lips drawn back in a malign grimace. "Why bother with the costume, Mademoiselle Cartier? For the hundred livres he's paying, you'd display the jewels naked."

Taken by surprise, Anne stared at the woman, then opened her mouth to protest.

The comte stopped her with a wave of his hand. "Ignore my stepdaughter, Mademoiselle, she's witless as well as ugly." The comte glared across the table at Claire.

"Bastard!" shrieked Claire, gripping the table knife near her plate.

Anne looked on, stunned, as the young woman pushed back her chair and began to rise. Instantly the two waiters standing by the sideboard rushed to her side. She hesitated for a second, then tossed the knife with a clatter on the plate.

"Well, we've had a little tantrum, haven't we." The comte spoke to Claire in a low, unnaturally soft voice. "These men will escort you to your apartment and see that you stay there tonight." He turned to Anne as if nothing had happened, smiled thinly, and bade her good evening. He rang a bell. Two footmen entered and picked up his chair to carry him away. His eyes closed; he looked as if he were already a cadaver.

∽∾∽

At the stroke of nine, Anne and Michou were ushered into Comte Debussy's parlor. They found him seated in an arm chair, expecting them. And, in remarkably good spirits, considering his confrontation with Claire at the supper table. Shortly after supper, Anne had dared to send him a request. Could her maid, a gifted artist, sketch the Chanavas treasure? To her surprise, he had agreed. They should come to his apartment in an hour.

"Let us go to the jewels," he said, his voice resonant with expectant pleasure. A tall robust footman carried him from the parlor through his adjacent bedroom to a locked door. Anne and Michou followed. With a key from his belt, the comte opened the door to a large round room. Brown mahogany cabinets lined its walls.

The Chanavas jewelry glittered between two lighted candelabra on a low green velvet-covered table in the center of the room. The two women and the comte settled into chairs around the table. The footman withdrew to his station by the door. Michou glanced shyly at the comte for permission to begin. He nodded to the table. She drew closer and contemplated the pieces, her hands clasped tightly as if she were in church. He studied her with cool regard. After a few minutes, she pulled a large pad out of her bag and set to work, intense concentration creasing her face.

Anne went back to the conversation at the supper table, probing into the comte's renovation of the chateau, a topic of which he was fond. The footman brought a portfolio of architectural drawings from a nearby cabinet. They revealed the chateau's interior as it was when the comte bought it, as well as the new arrangements he had planned and executed. At first glance, Anne could make no sense of the old and new walls, ceilings, and floors. But, with his help she gradually gained a mental picture of what lay behind the present surface.

An hour passed, during which they occasionally glanced at Michou, still absorbed in her task.

"Shall we see what she's done?" asked the comte.

Anne looked over Michou's shoulder, gently interrupting her, and took her sketches to Debussy.

"Quite remarkable," he exclaimed. "She has a draftsman's eye, though her hand needs more training."

"She has sketched everything except the tiara," Anne observed, "saving her favorite piece till last."

"Perhaps she would like you to wear it." He had Anne bring the tiara from the table and kneel before him. When she held it up for him to take, he leaned forward. "Allow me," he said, then ran his hands through her hair, as if arranging it for the tiara. His touch was rough, but she decided not to complain. Suddenly he grabbed her hair and snapped her head back. Their eyes locked in a visceral confrontation. A malevolent grin flashed across his face.

Anne gripped the tiara. The urge to strike him welled up within her. In an instant, like a chameleon, the comte smiled pleasantly and adjusted her head to a comfortable angle. "That will do." He took the tiara from her hands and placed it on her head. She walked back to her chair, trembling with frustrated anger.

Michou shot a frown at the comte, who did not appear to notice, then caught Anne's eye and signed, "I'm sorry." She gazed thoughtfully at Anne for a moment before going back to her sketching.

As if nothing had happened, Debussy continued to discuss the chateau. "Look up there." He pointed to the dark semi-circular lunettes of the domed ceiling. "In one of them is a clever mirror. Standing behind it, Krishna can observe whatever happens here—a useful precaution when I display the treasures." He gestured to several glass cases scattered about the room. "Even distinguished visitors have sticky fingers." A sardonic grin broke through his mask of pain.

When Michou finally laid down her sketchbook, Anne returned the tiara to the table, promising the comte that Michou would send him a finished drawing. Anne left the apartment, troubled by the malice she had experienced from the comte. At her side, Michou clutched her sketchbook, her eyes focused inwardly on the images she had captured.

In the main hall they stepped into a pool of light from the open door of the art gallery. Hearing a familiar voice, Anne peeked inside. Chevalier de Pressigny was holding forth on François Boucher's palette in a landscape painting. Around him had gathered several guests, evidently Amateurs who had arrived in advance of the next day's reception.

Anne sensed Michou sneaking by her through the doorway. Seeing Pressigny, the little woman froze and began to tremble. At that moment, he started to walk toward them. Anne's heart leapt. She yanked Michou out of sight. Anne peeked again, then breathed a sigh of relief. His eyes fixed on a painting, Pressigny had not seen Michou. He and his guests soon left the gallery by the farther exit.

Anne hugged Michou, calming her, and pointed out that the room was now empty. "Don't worry," Anne signed. "He doesn't know you or your secret."

Recalling Michou's love of animals, Anne led her up to the portrait of Pressigny's mother and her "Princesse" on the damask cushion. She stood still before the picture, leaning forward, eyes intent. Then she pulled out her sketchbook and, with a few deft strokes of her pencil, captured the image of the recumbent cat. A pleased expression came over her face. She signed that she would complete the drawing in her room and do a version in color back in Paris. With a start Anne realized Michou was gaining confidence in herself.

Chapter 20

A Stiletto

Georges cooled down in a late afternoon breeze, his back to an open casement window, his hands clasped behind his head. He surveyed the family's common room. Rustic but clean and spacious, a far cry from the filthy cramped quarters of the peasantry or the glittering luxury of the nobility. Large exposed beams supported the low ceiling. The tile floor was level and smooth, the plaster walls freshly whitewashed. Shiny copper kettles and pans stood in good order on shelves near the hearth. The Soucies were simple, honest, hard-working people. He could trust them.

Catching his eye and smiling, Madame Soucie teased him with an apple tart fresh from the oven. "Good," he told himself, "they appear to trust me." He knew, however, they would resist discussing Pressigny's wounded left hand.

A few weeks ago, when Georges had asked Monsieur Soucie about working at the chateau, he had said he wanted to ensure the safety of Mademoiselle Anne Cartier during the Amateurs' reception and to search for Simon Derennes, who had threatened her. Georges hadn't mentioned prying into Jean de Pressigny's criminal behavior. Nonetheless, Soucie might have suspected as much. He knew the young man's crooked past. He also knew Georges worked for Colonel Paul de Saint-Martin, the man responsible for law and order in the area. That Georges was an old comrade didn't make it easier to persuade the stablemaster to cooperate. He had a great deal to lose if he angered the comte.

What had convinced Soucie was Paul de Saint-Martin's personal guarantee, relayed by Georges, of full protection for himself and his family and compensation for any loss he might suffer. The colonel did not give such a promise lightly, Georges realized, for it could mean spending considerably from his reserves of money and influence. It indicated how serious his interest in the Dubois case had become.

Georges had further reassured Soucie with a promise to avoid drawing suspicion to him. The balding thickset colonel's adjutant would become a factotum, helping out as groom in the stables, pot-scrubber in the kitchen, and handyman throughout the chateau.

Only the Soucies knew who he was. Equipped with false discharge papers, he had presented himself to Krishna and the rest of the staff as a recently retired soldier in need of temporary employment. For the few days he expected to be at Chateau Debussy, he had a small room in the upper floor of the stable near the Soucie cottage. To get acquainted with the servants, he usually took his meals in the chateau's kitchen.

This evening, however, he had accepted an invitation to share supper with the Soucies. At a call from Madame, he sat with the family around a thick wooden table laden with her own dark bread, freshly churned butter, cheese, liver paté, salad, and wine. Two of their four children, a boy and a girl who still lived at home, ate silently and listened respectfully to the adults.

Conversation revolved around the years they had spent together in the army, an experience that Madame Soucie partly shared. As a young woman, she and her mother had followed her father, assisting in his medical work on campaigns. In varying degrees, they all had known General Saint-Martin, the colonel's father. Madame Soucie had nursed him briefly at the end of the Seven Years War.

After the apple tart the children were dismissed, the table was cleared and brandy poured. Georges led the conversation toward Madame Soucie's medical practice. She was a sturdy, taciturn woman, but he got her to talk about a few recent cases.

Then he asked about the wound on Pressigny's left hand. The Soucies glanced apprehensively at one another.

"You can tell me the truth," Georges said kindly. He went on to remind them of Colonel Saint-Martin's promise of protection and reward in return for cooperation. A man of honor, he would not let them down. But, if they refused to cooperate, Georges hinted ever so gently, they might be accused of aiding and abetting Pressigny's criminal attempt to escape the king's justice.

For several moments, Madame Soucie stared rigidly at the plate in front of her as if her jaw were locked. Then she glanced at her husband, received a signal from him, and sighed. "I recall when Chevalier de Pressigny came to me." She spoke slowly, measuring her words. "It was this time last year, about eleven in the evening. My husband and I were in bed when the young man pounded on the door. Hurt his hand in an accident, he said."

She had sat him at the table and cut a bloody cloth away from his left hand. An unusually thick hatpin about six inches long had pierced the palm. He told her he had lost his balance and fallen on it. By the time he reached her, the hand had swollen badly and the pin was stuck fast. Her husband poured him a large glass of brandy mixed with a sleeping potion, while she applied a cold compress to reduce the swelling. He fainted the moment she tentatively pulled on the pin! When she finally got it out, she saw it was no ordinary pin. Its shaft was tempered steel.

"A stiletto?" asked Georges.

"Yes," she replied.

"An illegal weapon," her husband added.

"Where is it now?" Georges looked her directly in the eye. "Colonel Saint-Martin is going to want to know."

The corners of her mouth twitched nervously. She took the last sip from her glass. "When Chevalier de Pressigny woke up the next day, he asked for it. I told him it went with the other medical trash into the lime pit. That seemed to satisfy him. His hand was twice its normal size and throbbing. The pain nearly drove him mad." She got up from her chair and began to gather the glasses from the table.

As she reached for Georges' glass, he looked up at her with a guarded smile.

"But you still have it, don't you?"

She froze, his glass in her hand.

Monsieur Soucie furtively glanced at his wife and at a wall cabinet near the hearth.

"That's right," she said at last, then carried the glasses to the sink. She opened the cabinet, retrieved the stiletto from behind a false panel, and brought it to Georges. She sat down again, staring at the table. "At the time, we were sure it wasn't an accident." She glanced at him defensively. "No one asked our opinion, so we kept it to ourselves."

"Why?" He leaned forward, fingering the stiletto.

"It's foolish to get involved in the affairs of the nobility." She spoke with strong conviction.

"A wise rule," he agreed, then laid the weapon on the table between them. "But there are exceptions."

He went on to assure the anxious woman she had done the right thing. The colonel would shield her and her husband from harm. Privately, he began to wonder what would happen to them if Pressigny were arrested. Even if they were to present evidence against him now, they might still be charged with complicity in a criminal act for having failed to denounce him earlier. Could Colonel Saint-Martin really guard them from the wheels of a blind criminal justice?

Madame Soucie didn't seem reassured. "We can't win. If we keep quiet, the police will accuse us of conspiring with Chevalier de Pressigny. If we tell our story to the police, Comte Debussy will turn us out in disgrace or maybe do worse." She paused, reflecting for a moment. "You think he killed the actress, don't you?" She stared at Georges. "Otherwise, why are you here, and Colonel Saint-Martin at his aunt's chateau nearby? And there's probably a brigade of royal troopers in the woods."

With a calming gesture, Georges rose from the table. "Your best choice is to do as I tell you. Alert me if Mademoiselle Cartier's in danger and help me follow Pressigny's movements. In the meantime, tell no one about the stiletto."

Outside the Soucie cottage, Georges took a close look at the weapon, balancing it in his hand. Shouldn't be hard to trace, he thought. Its silver handle was engraved with the initials "*L.L.*"

∞ ∞ ∞

Chateau Beaumont was already dark and the moonlit court-yard deserted. A pair of glowing oil lamps drew Georges to the entrance. He had ridden at breakneck speed, giddy with excitement. The Laplante case was breaking open! Hard evidence finally! He rushed into the chateau, only to learn from a servant that the colonel had not yet returned from a meeting with Lieutenant-General DeCrosne. Georges said he would wait. The servant was not to disturb the comtesse. He showed Georges to the reception room and left him pacing back and forth.

Shortly after ten, Georges heard a horse's hooves on the cobblestones outside, then voices at the entrance, and finally the colonel entered, surprised to find his adjutant waiting. "Have you left Miss Cartier alone?" His brow furrowed in irritation.

"The Soucies will look after her." Georges noticed impatience creeping into his voice. He quickly mastered his feeling, for he saw that the colonel's day in Paris had taken a toll.

"We'll get to that in a minute." Saint-Martin gestured wearily to sit down. A servant removed his boots, collected his sword, brought him fresh hose and shoes, then went for refreshments. The traveller slid back, stretching out his legs. Meanwhile, Georges sat on the edge of his seat.

"Well?" asked the colonel, folding his hands in his lap. He shot a quizzical glance at his adjutant.

"We've found the weapon Laplante used on Pressigny." Georges handed over the stiletto.

Saint-Martin sat bolt upright. "Did you find out who treated him?" He drew his fingers lightly up and down the slender weapon and touched its sharp point.

"Madame Soucie," Georges replied. "Pressigny came to her late that evening, the hatpin still piercing his hand. Before pulling it out, she put him to sleep. He doesn't know she kept it."

"Good work, Georges." The colonel bent over the stiletto's handle and examined Laplante's initials under a magnifying glass. "We will need proof she owned it and had it in her possession," he said, laying the weapon on the gaming table between them. "The Paris police can do that for us later."

The servant returned with a tray of red wine, fruit, bread and cheese, then left. Saint-Martin beckoned Georges to join him. As he poured for his adjutant, he remarked, "For the time being, the stiletto remains a secret."

Georges frowned. "We should hold Pressigny for questioning," he snapped. "Surely we have enough evidence. Soucie's a credible witness. Her story supports Michou's. The police will listen to her."

The colonel stiffened, his eyes grew dark.

Georges rushed on. "I feel in my bones he's about to make a move. Anne or Michou or the stablemaster and his wife may be in danger." He paused, glowering at his superior. "Must we wait for another murder?"

Saint-Martin's lips tightened, his nostrils flared. "I should not have to remind you, Monsieur Charpentier, I must win the lieutenant-general's approval *even* to investigate Chevalier de Pressigny or anyone in his family. To attempt to hold him now would be sheer folly. This afternoon, I spent two hours with DeCrosne, arguing that Pressigny should be questioned in connection with Derennes' disappearance. The lieutenant-general refused. He had handed the matter over to the Société des Amateurs. They were not to be disturbed."

Anger welled up in Georges, overriding the respect he felt for the colonel. The deeper he probed into the case of Antoine Dubois, the more he resented Pressigny and his parasitic kind. "Of course," he spat, "we must respect noble privilege!"

Saint-Martin rose to his feet, his face reddened. "Indeed we must, not because privilege is right, but because it can destroy any rash challenger." He glared at his adjutant. "I detest the evil Pressigny embodies as much as you do, but I must survey his defenses and assemble a force that can overrun them."

Georges shifted in his chair, sullen and unrepentant, wondering who the colonel thought he was talking to, a callow youth?

"If we were dealing with a commoner," the colonel continued, "we could arrest and convict him with the evidence we have. But, Pressigny is protected by several of the wealthiest and most powerful persons in the kingdom."

"Like whom?" Georges asked, goading his superior, who was pacing the floor.

"The Duc d'Orléans, the comptroller general of finance, and the foreign minister," Saint-Martin shot back. "How's that for a start! And, I smell a masonic connection with large amounts of money at risk."

"Is that all?" Georges retorted.

"That's enough!" The colonel stood silent for several moments, slowly shifting his gaze to the checkerboard pattern on the gaming table between them. He stared as if puzzled. "Why do these people protect Chevalier de Pressigny? If this were chess, he would be a pawn. They would gladly sacrifice him. Unless...." He paused again. "Unless he were essential to some grand scheme."

Georges yielded gradually, realizing the futility of further protest. The colonel ordered him back to Chateau Debussy to keep a watchful eye on Miss Cartier, Michou, the stablemaster, and his wife. When he rose to leave, he sensed the colonel's mood changing. His eyes seemed to probe gently for hidden wounds his harsh words might have caused.

Slowly, Saint-Martin raised the stiletto with his right hand, as if swearing an oath. "In due course," he said in a low, calm voice, "Pressigny will pay for his crime."

As horse and rider faded into the night, Colonel Saint-Martin left the entrance and walked to the picture gallery. He felt a strong urge to commune with his father and the philosophers whose spirits inhabited the place. The night watchman locked the front door, then brought a lighted candle and a chair to the gallery.

Saint-Martin sat before the portrait of his father, hearkening to the quiet in the room. The general's features seemed to come alive in the low, flickering light, his brow and his chin still proud and valorous, reflecting the face of battle. He drew a grudging respect from his son sitting silently beneath him.

"Noble privilege." The contempt in Georges' voice rankled in Saint-Martin's mind. Indeed why should anyone respect nobles, much less their privileges? He glanced up at his father. "You died serving a king who cared for nothing but his own pleasure, in a war that was not in France's interest. Most of your peers regarded your valor as eccentric and your chivalry foolish. They kept out of harm's way, loitering in the boudoirs of Paris and cultivating the fine arts of gossip and intrigue."

The dark face seemed unconcerned that others fell so far short of the ideal he had died pursuing. He had ridden into combat in front of his men to rouse their courage. He had shown magnanimity, forgiving fellow officers who had failed him. He had spent his fortune prodigally, aiding the widows and children of men who had died under his command. In his father's features, Saint-Martin now discerned lines of intrepid integrity where he had previously seen only vainglory. He felt strangely moved.

Lieutenant-General DeCrosne had invoked noble privilege to protect the "good name" of the Société des Amateurs. Nobles invoked it to gain offices, titles, and pensions they did not deserve. The colonel sighed. His adjutant had brought home to him what he had long suspected. Today's nobility hadn't the slightest commitment to public service. Its only concerns were pleasure, prestige, and profit. Its honor, no more than elegant posturing.

The disturbing image of Robert LeCourt forced itself into this silent discourse. LeCourt, whose power rested on money. Nobles now groveled before bankers and financiers. The finance minister, Calonne, was beseeching LeCourt and his Dutch bankers to *kindly* help ease the king's debt. Dozens of the most distinguished men at court were pressing LeCourt to invest their money. Whatever he touched seemed to turn a profit.

Saint-Martin shuddered, as if foreseeing a grim future. Clever, ruthless men of money, like LeCourt, would eventually brush aside aristocratic privilege, its foundations rotting away, and take the privileges of power for themselves.

"What should I do?" mused Saint-Martin out loud, seeking contact with his father's eyes. "Retreat?" He paused expectantly for a moment, then answered himself in measured, mocking cadence: "Let the Amateurs have their way, don't probe. That's what all the king's ministers say."

Looking down at the floor, dark and inscrutable in the thin candle light, Saint-Martin experienced a curious sensation. The ground of his life—all that he had assumed to be solid—now seemed to be shaking, like the treacherous surface of a quagmire in a storm. And he was risking rebuke and disgrace. With menace in his voice, the lieutenant-general had warned, "I will not tolerate disobedience."

In the eerie stillness of the gallery, Saint-Martin gazed at his father, yearning silently for reassurance. Time seemed suspended. Then, rapt by the portrait, he sensed the old warrior nodding. *Fiat justitia, ruat caelum.* Let justice be done, though heaven falls.

Chapter 21

Night Games

As Anne stepped out of the picture gallery, she heard an orchestra playing in the distance. With Michou in tow, she followed the sound to a thicket of servants and visitors in the far end of the building. Through an open door, she glimpsed a swirling medley of pink, yellow, and green silk ribbons; pale, filmy gowns; pastel shirts, breeches, and silk hose. A babble of voices rose above the music. She was tempted to linger, to observe the party, but she knew Michou would become anxious.

When they reached their apartment, a page was waiting outside with a message from Chevalier de Pressigny. The music came from his party, a prelude to the next day's reception. Would she sing a few songs for a stipend of twenty livres? There were no further obligations and dress was informal. If she wished, she could stay for dancing and games of chance.

Leaving the page in the hallway, Anne followed Michou into the parlor. She leaned back against the door, reading the message again. Twenty livres. A generous sum! Another trick by Pressigny, no doubt. Two could play that game. She kissed the paper, then let it drop. Whirling about the parlor, flaring her skirt in graceful arcs, she mimicked the dancers she had seen in his apartment. She halted by the window, the small of her back against the sill.

Across the room, Michou picked up the crumpled message from the floor. Though she couldn't read, she mulled over it with growing anxiety. For a moment, she stared at Anne with an expression akin to terror. Then she whirled twice, mimicking Anne's movements, and struck the paper as if with a dagger.

Anne nodded gravely. Her friend realized Pressigny had invited Anne to the party.

Michou slowly shook her head. Tears began to trickle down her cheek.

Some of Michou's terror crept into Anne's own flesh. The host was hardly someone she could trust. With a rush of tenderness, she put a reassuring arm around Michou's shoulder and caressed her, then led her to her room, where she set to work on her sketch of the Chanavas jewels.

Alone again in the parlor, Anne paced the floor, raking her hand through her hair. If she joined the party, she could get to know Pressigny better, explore his apartment. She might even recognize a stolen work of art, like the jasper bowl.

A mirror caught her eye. She strutted like a street-walker and pouted sensuously. Was Pressigny trying to seduce her? Fine. She would sing and dance with him. Then she saw herself growing still before the mirror. A shadow of fear crossed her face. Could she control him? Georges had returned to Chateau Beaumont. She would be on her own.

She glanced at the clock on the wall. It showed eleven at night. The party had only begun. Squaring her shoulders, she went resolutely to the armoire in her bedroom and drew out a gauzy robe and a handful of blue silk ribbons. She dressed quickly, her fingers trembling with excitement.

The page brought Anne into a large salon lighted by a crystal chandelier hanging from the ceiling and by sconces on the wall. She caught sight of Henriette Picard and several other familiar faces from the variety theater. Supplementing their meager income, Anne thought sadly. Laughter rippled across the room. At the far end, a group of musicians seated on a low stage accompanied men and women in a lively gavotte.

Chevalier de Pressigny appeared at her side, his mauve shirt open at the throat. "Delighted you could come!" He flashed her a disarming smile. After the dance, she followed him through the crowd to the stage. He surprised her, proposing they sing a duet. Why not? she thought. Singing was both innocent and safe. And a step toward knowing him better.

Their first song, a popular love ballad by Rameau, began hesitantly but the harmonies were simple and their voices soon blended, his rich baritone with her alto. The words called for her to flirt with him, a task she found dangerously easy. His hair was thick, black, and wavy; his mouth ripe.

Between songs they danced a simple gavotte, she eluding the kisses allowed him by custom. He acknowledged her dexterity with an indulgent smile, his eyes exploring her face, his right arm around her waist. She would have enjoyed his company, were it not that every time he extended his left hand, clothed in a soft, fawn glove, she recalled the scar and shuddered inwardly.

Their act finished to polite applause. He suggested a cool drink outside. They picked up a carafe of white wine and glasses, left the salon, and passed through a small library into a darkened sitting room. A single spluttering sconce feebly lighted a pair of ornamental fig trees standing like sentinels in large urns, flanking the open doors to a balcony. As Anne drew closer, a shaft of pale moonlight revealed a young man and a woman coupled in passionate embrace. At the sight of Pressigny, they smiled, unembarrassed, and yielded the place.

The sounds of the party, now distant and muted, competed with a chorus of crickets on the ground below. The warm still air lay soft on the skin. Anne put her glass on a table, reached for the metal railing, and glanced up toward the hazy moonlit sky. She sensed her companion moving closer. When their bodies touched, she stepped back from the railing and took a sip of the wine. He accepted her gesture without protest. He had learned how to wait, thought Anne, surprised. She had believed him more inclined, like a spoiled child, to grow petulant when denied a pleasure.

As they sat at the table drinking, his tongue loosened. His guests could manage very well without him for a while. She drew him toward theater life, something they shared. He enjoyed vaudeville, he said, fancying especially the tightrope acts. He would like to tie a rope between this balcony and the next and walk across. With training he could do it, she agreed, squinting at him in the dim light. While dancing, she had noticed his excellent balance, perfect coordination, and lithe, muscular physique.

Fingering her glass, she put on a face of innocent curiosity. "What are you preparing for us at the theater tomorrow night?"

"A frothy little thing about a clown cuckolded by his wife and her lover." He pulled his chair closer to hers.

Anne shivered. This could be the very same sex farce she and Georges had discovered in the Amateurs' office. "And what happens to the clown?" She sipped from her glass to mask her feelings.

He grinned waggishly. "You will find out tomorrow night."

For a few moments, he seemed willing to be led on, but he was distracted by a slight rustling noise high above them. Anne involuntarily stepped back. An instant later, a large handful of debris clattered on the tiles where she had been standing. Startled, she glanced up, the crash echoing in her ears.

"Is someone on the roof?" she asked incredulously, recalling it rose high above the mansard floor. It would be difficult to cross even in daylight.

"A large bird or small animal," he replied calmly. "A man can't be up there."

Beneath his reassurance, she detected a note of alarm. "Are we in danger?"

"Yes, if the culprit were to dislodge loose masonry on our heads."

"We'd better move inside." She rose from her chair, the warm stillness of the air now feeling ominous.

In the faint light of the sitting room, he appeared tense and preoccupied, his eyes blank. Entering the salon, they were greeted by slurred shouts and raucous laughter. Anne spied a pink ribbon hanging from one sconce and a pair of pale blue slippers slung over another. Several couples near the stage swung about in a rollicking country dance, out of step with the music. A pride of young men, faces flushed with wine, prowled among the tables, leering at bosoms flaunted by courtesans, including Henriette, who caught Anne's eye and beckoned.

It was time to leave. She started for the door. Pressigny came out of his distraction, caught up with her, and took her hand, bowing slightly. Acting the perfect gentleman, she thought, and bid him a polite goodnight.

The clack of her heels echoed eerily in the corridor to her apartment. No one was in sight. A lone sconce cast a thin flickering light, triggering her imagination. The shadows of grotesque beasts played on the walls; malign spirits lurked in the darkness of the doorways. She slipped into the apartment, carefully locking the door behind her, and breathed a sigh of relief.

Michou was still awake, bent over her table. Anne tiptoed up to her and glanced over her shoulder. Her gallery sketch lay to one side. She was drawing the cat, Princesse, lying on the cushion. Anne tiptoed out, closed the door quietly, and went to her own bedroom. The hour was late, the air very warm and humid. She took off her clothes and lay on the covers, drifting into a deep sleep.

She woke suddenly. Michou stood beckoning in the doorway with a spluttering candle. For a few moments, Anne had no idea where she was. She pulled on a light robe and followed Michou. The clock on the mantel showed one in the morning. She gestured to Anne that she had left her room to check the hall door before going to bed. She had just seen the handle move.

Anne calmed her with a hug, drew close to the door, and listened. At first, she heard nothing. But a few seconds later, there were footsteps and whispers. Her heart pounded. Who could be trying to come in? Several Amateurs had rooms in the mansard. By now they would be drunk on Pressigny's wine.

"Well," Anne said to Michou, "we can't stare at the door all night." She waved her friend to the side and armed herself with an iron poker from the fireplace. Holding her breath, she turned the key, pushed the handle down, then yanked open the door. Michou lifted her candle. A man was leaning against the opposite wall, a sheepish expression on his face. He swiftly raised a finger to his lips.

"Georges!" Anne whispered. She beckoned him into the parlor and closed the door.

"How'd you know I was there?"

"Michou saw the door handle turn and became frightened."

"Sorry. I was making sure the door was locked. I thought you were asleep."

"What's going on?"

"I returned from Chateau Beaumont a half-hour ago. Madame Soucie said Pressigny and his guests were running wild. Krishna's in Paris. The servant girls had come to her for safety. Then she worried about you and Michou. Sent one of Soucie's men up here. I just took his place. That's what you heard."

Anne took the candle from Michou's hand and brought its light close to Georges' face. His eyes were blood-shot and heavy-lidded. A day's growth of beard added ten years to his appearance. She gestured toward chairs by the window where they could enjoy a slight breeze. "It *was* Madame Soucie who treated Pressigny, wasn't it?" she asked confidently.

"Yes," he replied. "And she gave me the stiletto she had pulled out of his hand." He leaned back, folding his arms across his chest. "The colonel has it now. The initials *L.L.* are on the handle."

Anne felt elated. Laplante's stiletto in Pressigny's hand the evening of her death! Could any magistrate continue to blame Antoine Dubois? "What does the colonel want to do with Pressigny?" she asked.

He shrugged his shoulders. A flash of anger hardened his face. "Nothing, for the moment," he remarked dryly. "Keep him in the dark."

"Why not arrest him?" Her hope for Antoine ebbed like an outgoing tide.

Georges shifted in his chair, as if uncomfortable with the question. "That's what I asked him. He said Pressigny has powerful protection. We would need overwhelming evidence against him to persuade the lieutenant-general."

There had been conflict between the two men, Anne realized, and she felt torn. Her heart was with Georges, but her mind with the colonel. She forced a troubled smile. She wanted justice done quickly. But, perhaps the colonel was allowing Pressigny, a little fish, to remain on the line as bait to catch a bigger one. The better she had come to know the dissolute young man, the less she believed he could have killed her stepfather in cold blood. If he were somehow involved, he must have been led by another, much stronger person.

"I shall see at least one of his protectors tomorrow," she said, "Monsieur Robert LeCourt."

"And I'll keep an eye on you." He yawned, then apologized, muttering he'd better take up his post again outside in the corridor.

She stared at him. Lines of fatigue fissured his face. Her eyes moistened. "I don't want you standing out there all night!" She tried to sound exasperated. "You can have this room." She brought bedding into the parlor, spread it out on the floor, and bid him goodnight. Michou slipped away to her room, smiling, clearly relieved Georges would guard the door.

As Anne walked to her bedroom, she felt Georges' eyes upon her. She stopped and slowly turned, calling to mind his concern for her, his standing guard outside her room. He slouched on the bedding, his back against the door, his shoulders slumped forward. She met his eyes. He sat up, expectant. She started. From deep within, the realization suddenly dawned on her that Georges had become a true friend and partner, filling the place in her heart that Antoine had once held. "Sleep well, dear Georges," she whispered with a tired smile. "Tomorrow will be a long day." His tired face broke out in a crooked smile.

∞ ∞ ∞

Her head buried in a pillow, her brain fogged with sleep, Anne heard a voice at a great distance telling her to rise. She rolled over and rubbed her eyes. Georges was standing in the open doorway in livery of silver and blue, a powdered wig on his bald head. "Good God!" she croaked, waving him out. She grabbed for a robe.

As he retreated into the parlor, a maid brushed by him with warm milk, coffee, and bread, announcing breakfast. She stopped abruptly in the doorway to the bedroom, staring at Anne, at her bed, at Georges. "Put down the tray," Anne exclaimed with heat, and pointed to a low table near the door.

Hoping to clear her mind, she shuffled to the wash stand and splashed water on her face.

Georges was soon at the door again telling her to hurry up. "It's past eight!"

She flicked water at him. He ducked back into the parlor. Peering into a mirror, she combed a spiky mop of thick blond hair. Shadows lay under her eyes.

Georges grinned as Anne stepped into the parlor. "You look like one of the Furies. But it's nothing that can't be fixed." He bent forward simpering, could he be of service. Before she could curse him, he waved his hands in apology, then went on to explain that Madame Soucie had suggested him when an extra footman was needed. "You have nothing to fear during the reception. I'll be close by, either outside in the courtyard or in the servants' common room."

He walked briskly to the hall door, lingered briefly, looked back at her. For a moment he dropped his sprightly, jocular mask. She read in his face a longing and a concern that wrenched her heart. He slowly closed the door.

For a few seconds, she stood in the middle of the parlor, shaken by his departure. Then she carried the breakfast tray to the window sill. A pleasant morning breeze caressed her face. She ate standing up, gazing absently out over the garden.

A nagging thought disturbed her. Chevalier de Pressigny would certainly hear that a man had spent the night in her apartment. She shrugged. What Pressigny might think of her hardly mattered. She did feel uneasy about how he might misuse the information. Suppose he brought it back to Paul, blown up into a tawdry affair?

The colonel and Georges had quarreled last night about whether to arrest Pressigny. She sensed other issues lurked in the background. Was she one of them? She liked both men and didn't want them quarreling over her.

She raised a cup of coffee to her lips. An image of Paul came to her mind. A deep, fascinating man. Graceful in his bearing. Kindly as well. She recalled the way he bent forward to catch her words, the warmth of affection in his eyes, even when he and she disagreed. The rumor of an affair behind his back between Georges and herself would upset him. She might lose his respect.

She sighed, then drained the cup. Her imagination was running out of control. One thing at a time. Behind her a door opened. Michou entered the room with an empty breakfast tray. Anne smiled a greeting. First she would see Michou occupied for the day, and next deal with the Amateurs. Any problem with Paul would have to wait.

Chapter 22

A Question of Love

Paul de Saint-Martin rose an hour after dawn and walked to an open window overlooking Beaumont's garden. The smell of damp grass braced him. Men were already at work, trimming the boxwood edges of the flowerbeds before the heat of the sun grew too strong. Several magpies had gathered on the terrace below him. He threw out pieces of dry bread, raising a frantic flapping of wings and a raucous quarrel.

As he watched them scramble for food, the stronger birds shoving aside the weaker, he grimaced. They reminded him of a similar morality among humans. Rich, privileged families in the city's Saint-Germain quarter dined at sumptuous tables while their footmen chased away poor women begging for their garbage. The image chilled him.

He lifted his eyes to the English park beyond the formal garden. A mist hung over the groves of oak and beech, concealing whatever violence nature's creatures might do to one another there. He stood at the window for a few more minutes, allowing the serene beauty of the park to lift his spirits. Then he sat at a desk, rolled back its cylinder top, and picked up a manuscript of his aunt's memoirs.

He had promised to read a chapter before breakfast, an engaging task. As a younger woman, Comtesse Marie had attended the brilliant Parisian salons frequented by Voltaire, Diderot, and other luminaries, foreign and domestic, including, occasionally, the eccentric Rousseau. She also counted among her acquaintances the most distinguished churchmen, military officers, and statesmen of the generation that flourished after the Peace of Paris in 1763. An observer more than a participant, she kept an inner distance from the celebrities around her, recognizing their personal failings, sorting out their ideas in her own mind.

The rays of sunlight crept across the floor, while he slowly turned the pages of the neat, closely written text. He had just finished her reflections on the occasion of Voltaire's death in 1778 when a chambermaid announced that Comtesse Marie had returned from her morning ride. He said he would join her for breakfast. He laid down the manuscript and pondered her opinion of the great philosophe: a Socrates in silk who had chosen exile rather than hemlock. Near the mark, he thought.

He closed the desk, stroking its smooth shiny surface, and glanced at himself in a wall mirror. His aunt would approve. He was wearing the buff breeches of his field uniform, but was otherwise dressed for warm weather in a simple cotton shirt, open at the neck. His face was tanned, his dark brown hair combed back and tied with a black ribbon. In his eyes, however, he detected a glimmer of anxiety. Anne was about to play her part at Chateau Debussy.

At nine o'clock, he followed a servant carrying a breakfast tray into his aunt's room. She was seated at a small round table. Lightly clothed in a soft rose morning robe, her thick silvery hair newly brushed, she could have posed for an intimate portrait. He noticed a touch of rouge powder on her cheeks, a small concession to vanity. While coffee was being poured, she looked at him sideways. "Paul, what brings you to Chateau Beaumont? Merely the pleasure of my company?" She turned her gaze to a basket of biscuits. After a few moments of deliberation, she picked out a currant scone.

"What I say must remain within these walls," he warned.

"Of course," she replied, as if insulted.

"Our investigation into the deaths of the actress Laplante and Antoine Dubois has led us to Chateau Debussy." He paused to take a biscuit. "We've found an opportunity to look inside."

"We?"

He explained what Miss Cartier and Georges were doing at the Amateurs' reception. They had already discovered new evidence linking Chevalier de Pressigny to the actress' death, lifting guilt from Dubois.

"What a risk you've taken, defying the orders of the lieutenant-general of police."

"Does anyone suspect us?" He filled her cup with coffee.

"What have you learned on your recent trip to Paris?"

"Nothing to do with your investigation." She hesitated, as if reluctant to continue. "But you and Miss Cartier are another matter—she is said to be your mistress."

He felt a frisson of embarrassment. Had he been careless? He shrugged, he didn't think so. "Rumor, as so often, is wrong. It's best ignored." He sipped some coffee.

Gazing into her cup, the comtesse remained silent for a few moments. Then she glanced up at him. "Consider Miss Cartier."

"Yes?" he replied, searching for his aunt's point.

She looked at him with reproach. "Is it nothing to be regarded as a man's trophy or his pet?"

He weighed her remark, stung by its sharp edge. "You are right, dear aunt, I should be mindful of her reputation."

"And, of her safety," she added, meeting his eye.

He nodded soberly. "Miss Cartier's a remarkably resourceful person, capable of taking care of herself, and determined to see justice done for her stepfather. I've arranged for Georges and the stablemaster to look after her." Saint-Martin pushed his cup aside, then leaned back. "Is anything else on your mind?"

"Let's stroll in the garden while it's still cool," she replied, throwing a gossamer mauve scarf over her shoulders. She rang for a maid to clear the table.

At the steps down to the formal garden she waved to men trimming the boxwood edges. The cuttings were piled high in a cart hitched to a donkey. She petted the animal as she walked by, then called her nephew's attention to a row of stem roses. They both bent low to smell the fragrance.

An ear-piercing bray suddenly interrupted their pleasure.

"Bottom!" The comtesse wagged a finger at the animal and turned to her nephew. "He expects a piece of sugar when I pet him." She drew a small bag from her pocket. "Sorry, Bottom," she said, palming him a treat.

When she returned to the rose bushes, Paul bowed to her. "Queen Titania! Gulled again by a donkey!"

She smiled quizzically for a moment before catching his meaning. "Shakespeare, of course. *A Midsummer Night's Dream* was one of your favorite summer plays. I recall Antoine Dubois was an hilarious Bottom." A twinge of pain seemed to work the corners of her mouth. She turned her eyes away.

The donkey and his companions soon departed. The comtesse led Paul into the shade of a bower covered with roses and jasmine, one of four at a crossing of gravel paths that divided the garden into four squares. A small fountain in the crossing trickled water into a basin.

"Are you in love with Miss Cartier?" she asked abruptly, when they had seated themselves. For a few moments she looked out at the fountain, while he tried to mask the feelings stirring within him.

He didn't take offense. "I've grown fond of her." He looked up hesitantly for the effect of his words.

His aunt asked gently, "Is she fond of you?"

"I think so. But she guards her feelings closely." His pulse quickened. He walked to the opening of the bower and stared at the fountain, his back to his aunt. "I feel drawn to her. To marriage." He surprised himself; he had not meant to say that. He had not even thought of marrying again. The words lingered in his ears, as he turned to face his aunt. "Miss Cartier's... bracing, like a gust of fresh air. She fascinates me."

Comtesse Marie was silent for a few seconds, then spoke in a low, measured voice. "I dearly wish for you—and Miss Cartier— the mutual love and respect of a good marriage. I believe you love one another, and I'm pleased. But in this matter you must listen to your head as well as your heart. Let me be blunt for a moment. Imagine, Paul, if you married Miss Cartier." She paused, engaging his eye. "She might hurt your career. At best, she could not advance it, having little money and few connections. How much would that matter to you?"

He sat down next to her. "Frankly, it *would* matter. But loving someone like Miss Cartier matters more."

She leaned back against the bench, folding her arms. "And Miss Cartier? She could expect society to ignore her. Or worse. What kind of life would she have?"

"The life she has now," he snapped. "Free from mindless convention." He sought the comtesse' eye and saw there only compassion. "Dear Aunt, you have also chosen your own way. Can you imagine Miss Cartier and I doing that as well?"

His aunt smiled, then smoothed her gown. "You are an army officer, accustomed to giving orders, controlling people." She rose slowly from the bench and faced him. "Miss Cartier is used to managing her own affairs. I believe she'd like to direct an institute for the deaf. If you two married, would you expect her to gladly give up that idea and submit to you like one of your soldiers?" She eyed him askance.

The outdoor theater was deserted—the comtesse had left him with his thoughts. He stood quietly in the entrance between the statues of Thalia and Terpsichore, and listened for sounds lingering from the past. Leaves rustled faintly, like music from an ancient chorus. Sitting on one of the shaded upper benches, he stared at the stage. The questions raised by his aunt might be moot, for marriage with Anne Cartier seemed doubtful. She was fully absorbed in pursuing her father's vindication. And he certainly had enough problems with the Royal Highway Patrol to occupy his mind.

Yet work filled only the mind. He also hungered for companionship, affection, tenderness. Neither nostalgic memories of a sensuous, adolescent Puck, nor distant prospects of marital union with a vigorous, self-assured young woman, met the needs of his heart now. He felt lonely and desolate.

He walked down the grassy aisle to the stage, checking his watch. It was past noon. Anne would be wearing an exotic costume and displaying the jewels. He yearned to see her.

Pacing back and forth across the stage, he began to feel uneasy. He imagined that sybarite, Pressigny, gripping her arm and leading her among the Amateurs. A lamb among wolves! The thought turned his stomach. Suddenly, she appeared to his mind's eye, pressed back against a wall, eyes wide with terror. Young men closed in on her. She opened her mouth in a voiceless scream.

With a strong effort of will he drove these horrid images from his mind. Still, he wondered, could something be going wrong at the reception? He felt a twinge of fear, but he told himself she was safe. Georges was there to protect her. Georges, again! Discharging a duty the colonel wished was his.

He looked out over the empty rows. Could she conceivably prefer Georges to him? He hadn't realized he might meet competition for her affection. Least of all from his own subaltern— rough ugly Georges! Envy stabbed at his heart.

A bell rang. Startled, he glanced about, then realized it came from his aunt's chateau. "Time for dinner," he said aloud to an invisible audience. He stopped pacing and listened until the final peal.

Chapter 23

A Threat

Tension crackled in the air of the small, ground floor ante-chamber. A maid put a pair of purple slippers on Anne's feet, another fitted the turban to her head, while Claudine, the dressmaker, stared critically at her skirt. Anne glanced into a large gold-rimmed mirror and discovered herself biting on her lower lip. Smiling nervously, she raised her arms for the dressmaker, who deftly adjusted the fit of the bodice and gave her a pat of approval.

A knock on the door startled the women. Before a maid could react, Chevalier de Pressigny rushed in and fixed his eyes on Anne. "Excellent, she's ready for the jewels." He turned to Claudine, who nodded in agreement. He left without another word, but Anne understood the reception would soon begin.

Shortly before noon, Krishna came to the door with the burnished wooden box. Two muscular servants stood alert in the entrance. Earlier, the Indian had been a shadowy figure in the background. Now, Anne took note of him, a lean, graying man in his forties. Near her height. Remarkably fit. He was dressed in a patterned white silk Indian costume, a feathered white turban on his head, an ornate, curved knife at his waist. His dark intelligent face gleamed like delicately sculpted mahogany. His facial muscles, however, were taut, and his expression joyless.

Brusquely waving his wife aside, he slipped behind Anne to clasp the necklace around her neck and hang the ropes of diamonds over her shoulders and the pendants over her ears. She felt the heat of his body and smelled his scent, a strong, pleasant musk. He came around in front of her to place the tiara, the ceramic flower, and the ornate feather on the turban. His eyes—amber, like smoldering fire—met hers. He nodded. She held out her arms. He slipped on the bracelets, then bent down to fit other bracelets on her ankles. He rose, surveyed his work, then drew near to arrange the ropes of diamonds across her bosom. In his eyes she detected the hint of a leer. She looked away over his shoulder. His closeness unsettled her.

When he stepped back, she walked to the mirror, keying herself, as if for the stage. The costume fit perfectly, the diamonds sparkled. The maids flitted about her, tucking wayward strands of blond hair into the turban. She wondered whether Comte Debussy would escort her; he could hardly walk. It would look absurd for him to be carried, with her trotting alongside like a gilded poodle.

Krishna smiled politely, proffered his arm and led her to the great hall that looked out over the main courtyard. With a bow he passed her arm to Chevalier de Pressigny. Incredible, she thought. He looked none the worse for last night's party.

Resplendent in a purple linen suit trimmed with embroidered gold flowers, a sword at his side, he nearly danced in anticipation. His eyes darted about, assuring that everything was as it should be. She sensed his tension in the hand gripping her arm as he gave commands to the servants. He stopped for a moment just short of the entrance, held her at arm's length in a shaft of light and gazed at her with a rapt expression. It was for her, she realized, as well as for the jewelry.

Through the open door she surveyed the hall, a starkly simple space that would be cold and austere, were it empty, especially on a gray day. It was now flooded with sunlight, alive and noisy. The Amateurs, their patrons, and their guests milled about, fashionably dressed for a summer feast at a country place, the women in light country gowns, the men in silk waistcoats and breeches, shirts open at the neck.

This hardly looked like a nest of vipers, she murmured to herself, but she knew appearances could deceive. Pressigny leaned toward her, remarking that the white walls of the room had at one time been hung with hundreds of antlers. "They were removed," he whispered. "The comte worships at the altar of Venus rather than Diana."

A gong sounded. Stroking the Chanavas tiara with nervous fingers, she moved forward a few steps until she stood framed in the entrance. A hush came over the hall. All eyes turned toward her. A soft murmur of admiration swelled to a roar. She felt exhilarated. The cold weight on her chest, however, was a reminder that the jewels, not she, deserved the crowd's attention. Yet, she was an actress. It cost her an effort not to compete.

Pressigny guided her through the hall, Krishna following a few paces behind. Wide-eyed, open-mouthed, the Amateurs parted as Anne moved among them. She raised and lowered her head, turned left, then right, bowed, lifted up her arms. She heard audible gasps of amazement, whispered estimates of the jewelry's worth.

The Amateurs and their female consorts admired *her* as well, some glancing slyly, others staring shamelessly. She pretended not to notice, being more concerned to study the men, some thirty of them between twenty and forty years old. Common to all was the self-assurance mounting to arrogance that money and rank could confer. Despite their youth, they seemed jaded. As soon as she passed, the wonder left their eyes. She sensed them incapable of great passion for anything.

"A rather dull lot, wouldn't you say?" Pressigny whispered, as they moved away from an obese, pasty-faced young man, upon whom the jewelry's impact seemed typically shallow.

Surprised he would share this opinion with her, Anne hesitated, struggling for appropriate words. "They may be so accustomed to paste jewelry that they cannot appreciate the real thing. The glitter is nearly the same."

He squeezed her arm and smiled.

Having completed a circuit, Pressigny led Anne into the large pillared vestibule on the garden side of the great hall where a half-dozen of the most prominent patrons had gathered. Quickly scanning the room, she noticed Georges, who nodded to her almost imperceptibly. A few paces away Monsieur Robert LeCourt conversed with three other gentlemen in front of several large pieces of East Indian glazed pottery in niches in the wall. One of them, a tall pale blue vase, had captured his attention. Anne stared: she could not help but admire the studious slant of his head, the elegance of his light green suit trimmed with silver. He seemed even more distinguished than when she had observed him earlier in Café Marcel.

As she drew near, he turned. A frisson of fear warned her. He surely suspected she was the woman Derennes had intended to question in the dungeon of Palais-Royal.

LeCourt gave her a brief, sharp glance, then greeted Chevalier de Pressigny with a few curt words. The young man appeared to stiffen. A question mark flitted across his face before he returned a polite reply. There was an awkward moment.

Then, to Anne's relief, the financier's eyes fastened on the jewels. Lips slightly parted, dark eyebrows raised, he grew engrossed. "May I touch them?" he asked Pressigny, as if unaware of Anne, an arm's length away.

"Of course," he murmured, clearly caught by surprise and loath to refuse his patron.

LeCourt slipped both hands under the necklace, lifting up the diamonds, caressing their smooth, cabochon surfaces, dangling them from his fingers to refract the colors of the spectrum.

His presence was overpowering. Anne felt faint from the heat of his breath, from his hands at her throat. Her body began to tremble, to perspire. She fought back her feelings with a powerful effort of will. Then the memory of crouching beneath him under the balcony at Café Marcel forced itself into her mind. She could barely breathe.

A bell tinkled. A servant was announcing the banquet. LeCourt tore his eyes from the jewels, bowed to Pressigny, and rejoined his companions. Anne's gaze followed him to the door. It swung open and he disappeared. She gulped air, as if freed from a strangler's grip.

∞∞∞

Anne stood for a few minutes in the wide doorway, peering into the banquet salon. The Amateurs and their guests were taking their seats, assisted by a dozen liveried servants in silver and blue. The tables were set with elegant Sèvres porcelain, gleaming silver utensils, and floral arrangements from the chateau's gardens. Large landscape paintings hung on the cream-colored walls. Its lofty, richly textured plaster ceiling gave the spacious room a lively, airy aspect. Two large windows opened to the garden. The graveled terrace outside shimmered in the early afternoon sun.

She walked slowly by the windows, allowing streams of sunlight to play upon the gold and the precious stones she wore. Georges came out of a service entrance, carrying a tray of food to a sideboard. He gave her an encouraging glance. She followed Krishna to a table of honor on a low platform opposite the windows. Comte Debussy, who was now just arriving, beckoned to a seat next to him. He appeared to be in excellent spirits.

He bowed, then lightly touched her arm. "You look lovely, Mademoiselle. I feel we've made the right choice." He inspected the tiara, then the necklace, and finally the lesser pieces, his brown eyes glowing with satisfaction.

Chevalier de Pressigny welcomed his guests, concluding with "Let the banquet begin." There was a scraping of chairs on the parquet floor, a light clatter of silverware, and a growing buzz of conversation. Waiters glided among the tables with bottles of wine.

Anne's frail elderly companion turned away course after course, taking only broth for nourishment. And he paid little attention to the visitors, favoring them with a quick glance from time to time. He seemed pleased with her company. His cheeks gained color and his voice grew lively. Sensing a propitious moment, Anne fingered the necklace and asked when he had acquired it.

He threw her a fleeting smile, then beckoned a waiter who removed the dishes. "As a young man I spent several years with the French East India Company in the Deccan, a region in southern India." He fell into the past. His eyes misted in reverie. "I was helping an Indian ruler, a client of the French king, recover his lands from a usurper, Chanavas Khan. After months of fighting, we laid siege to the khan's palace. In the final assault, he was killed and his treasure discovered."

As he spoke, the tone of his voice grew darker. He glanced at Anne, then fastened his eye on the tiara. "Since I commanded the force, I could claim the jewels." She suspected her question had touched a tender spot.

At a sign from the comte, a servant shifted his chair a quarter turn to face Anne in profile. "I believe the tiara is my favorite." He stroked his chin wistfully. To please him she moved her head slowly back and forth. The deep green of the emeralds, the red of the rubies, the sparkle of the diamonds, and the glitter of the gold splashed on a silver salver in front of her, blending into new living colors. She understood how this beauty could fascinate Debussy.

He looked up at his Indian steward standing impassively behind Anne. "It had actually been found by Krishna, then a boy who had recently entered my service." The Indian glanced at his master, but did not smile.

"A few years later," the comte continued, "when the English and their Indian allies seized most of the Deccan, I returned to France with the jewels." He coughed, complained of a dry throat, and signaled for water.

Anne seized the opportunity to glance toward Georges, now framed by a pair of colossal oriental vases. He had placed himself close enough to Pressigny to overhear his conversation. The comte followed the drift of her eyes, then snorted: "Lazy fellow!" Anne's heart leaped. Debussy wagged a finger in Georges' direction. "He's hiding between two of the finest pieces of East Indian pottery in France." Perceiving he had been noticed, Georges slid back to a sideboard. Anne breathed easier.

Meanwhile, Krishna had begun to fan the comte and Anne. Debussy smiled, remarking that Krishna had returned with him to France and eventually married the daughter of a former French colonial officer and his Indian wife. "Claudine and Krishna have been with me thirty years. Very loyal, both of them."

While listening to the comte speak of India, Anne kept Monsieur LeCourt in the corner of her eye. Unlike many patrons and Amateurs who had brought along mistresses or female companions, he had come alone. He ate and drank very little and did not take part in the general frivolity. Sitting next to him, Henriette Picard glanced furtively at Anne, then bent toward him, veiling her mouth with bejeweled fingers. His eyes turned to Anne. She noticed his lips move slightly.

When the comte paused for another sip of water, Anne inquired about LeCourt, mentioning his singular appreciation of the jewelry.

"He must have good taste," Debussy observed. "But I do not know him personally. He arrived in Paris when I retired to the chateau. We have not met."

Nor, Anne realized, did the comte feel a need to make LeCourt's acquaintance on this occasion, though the man was sitting at a table scarcely ten paces away. Through his illness Debussy had become a recluse, finding satisfaction only in his art treasures.

"I've heard about him," he continued indifferently. "His name suggests a Huguenot family that fled from France to Holland." He shrugged his shoulders. "I'm told he worked abroad for many years in the Dutch East India Company and became rich."

"Why did he come to France?" asked Anne, narrowly avoiding LeCourt's eye.

"Good question, Mademoiselle," Debussy replied. "He represents a group of Dutch investors and financiers. Due to the wretched condition of our royal finances, the king's ministers are 'paying court' to LeCourt." He paused, then smiled when she caught the pun. "They are hoping to borrow money from the Dutch to repay loans we incurred during the American war." He spluttered in disgust, "A fool's errand!"

Anne felt she could safely probe further. "If LeCourt's such an important man of affairs, why does he bother with the Amateurs?"

Debussy spread his hands toward the young noblemen at table before him. "Fools, every one of them. Fish to his bait. As their patron, he entices them and their families to invest in his own dubious financial enterprises. Sugar. Slaves. Exports to Britain. He promises to double their money. For a year or two, they will receive handsome dividends, then nothing. Before they realize what has happened, he will have left the country, much richer than when he arrived." Debussy continued with a sneer. "The French nobility has apparently forgotten how John Law tricked them sixty-five years ago with similar schemes."

A servant approached the comte with dessert, *blanc-manger à l'orange*, and was waved away. The old man was clearly tiring. His eyes had grown heavy-lidded, and his hands trembled. He excused himself with the promise he would join her later at the theater. "Krishna will stay by you." A pair of servants helped the comte through a curtain behind the platform.

Anne had expected to find it hard to talk to the unsmiling Indian who now sat beside her. She was delighted to discover that, while serving the comte some thirty years, he had acquired the language and manners of a French gentleman. He took barely concealed pleasure in filling the comte's place. That happened often, she suspected, in Debussy's decline. He clearly trusted his steward more than Pressigny, his stepson.

Krishna had grown accustomed to his privileged position. After a few glasses of wine, he even indulged in witty remarks about the guests and their companions. Henriette Picard was no stranger to him. "A tart should be sweet," he whispered, nodding toward the woman. "That one sets my teeth on edge."

Anne sensed him leaning closer to her, felt his arm brush against hers. To distract him, she asked about his family.

"We've been content here," he said, drawing back in his chair. "The large gate house is our home." He frowned as if it were painful to continue.

Anne offered silent encouragement.

Krishna stared down at the table in front of him. "We had one child, Nalini, a lovely daughter. Three years ago, she vanished. The police looked everywhere but found no trace of her." The Indian leaned forward, his brow creased with misery. "Is she dead or alive?" he asked himself. "The uncertainty is torture. My wife can hardly bear it." He turned slowly toward Anne and glared at her. His voice fell to a whisper. "Can you imagine how she felt altering Nalini's costume for you?"

Anne recoiled aghast, words failing her. After a few moments, Krishna's gaze seemed to turn inward, as if seeking his lost daughter. Anne regained enough composure to ask, "Do you suspect foul play?" Pressigny might have enticed Nalini away from an Amateurs' reception like this one.

Shrugging his shoulders, Krishna fell into heavy silence. He bent forward, facial muscles twitching beneath the dark skin. He slowly scanned the tables, as if one or more Amateurs might have been responsible for his daughter's disappearance.

Poor man, Anne thought, studying the lines of sorrow in his face. She could hardly ask whom he suspected. Nor could she tell him what she knew without betraying herself. Should he discover the culprit some other way, his reaction might be violent. Though a servant, he could not be abused with impunity. She sensed powerful passions roiling beneath his still surface.

When Krishna's glance reached LeCourt, they exchanged signs of recognition, leading Anne to wonder how closely the two men were connected. For LeCourt knew Nalini's name, and that Derennes had killed her. Why had LeCourt not informed Krishna? Possibly because he too feared Krishna might explode, injuring himself and others and compromising LeCourt's efforts to build up the Société des Amateurs. No wonder the financier seemed tense. He was trying to keep the lid on a boiling pot.

Anne used the distracted silence of her companion to search the room for Georges. She glimpsed him disappearing through a service entrance with a loaded tray. When he returned a few minutes later, the empty tray under his arm, she caught his eye. His slight bow reassured her as he set to work clearing the sideboard.

A gong sounded the hour for dancing. The guests pushed their chairs away from the tables. There was a burst of chatter. All eyes turned toward Anne at the table of honor. She rose gracefully and looked out over the crowd, touching the great necklace and then the tiara, calling attention to their rare beauty.

Krishna escorted her back to the main hall, where an orchestra had assembled. For the opening dance, a stately old pavanne, he handed her over to Chevalier de Pressigny. As the Indian backed away, he pierced Anne with a glance, as if to say, he should have had the honor of the dance. A proud man, she thought, aware of his worth. Anger smoldered in his eyes. Might he resent guarding the treasure *he* had found thirty years ago?

While the second dance was being prepared, she noticed Monsieur LeCourt approaching. He shook Krishna's hand with a peculiar grip, then whispered to him, glancing in her direction. As she had suspected, LeCourt was her next partner in a minuet. He appeared to be unruffled. His posture was elegant, his rhythm perfect. But the palms of his hands felt moist and tiny beads of perspiration gathered above his lip. His eyes fixed on one piece of the jewelry after another. He didn't speak; he hardly noticed her. Strange man! She forced a smile on her face, although she felt ill at ease.

In the last movement of the dance he startled her with a penetrating glance. "May I give you a piece of advice," he said softly, as he drew near to her. "Lélia Laplante's violent death is none of your business." He held her eye as they stepped back from one another. At the final pass he pulled her close and murmured, "Take care, lest you meet a similar fate."

Chapter 24

Farce or Tragedy

From his post at the main door Georges studied the rough cross beams, the high wooden walls of the theater, imagining the ghosts of ancient horses harnessed in this place. A previous owner had cleared several old carriage rooms on the ground floor of the chateau's east wing and built a stage and an auditorium for about eighty spectators. A ramp led to a loge of comfortable chairs reserved for the comte and his favorite guests. The rest of the audience were to sit on upholstered benches.

A door handle rattled behind Georges. A low murmur of voices penetrated the thick oaken door. The guests had arrived and were growing impatient. He surveyed the auditorium: everything was ready. He had helped two ushers arrange the benches under the critical eye of the senior footman in charge while Krishna guarded the jewels. Other servants had lit the wall sconces and the stage lights. They were all waiting now for a signal from Chevalier de Pressigny, who had disappeared behind the stage curtain.

A clock chimed five in the evening. Pressigny reappeared, skipped down the side stairs, barked a command to Georges. He pulled open the doors to the dark, crowded hallway. The Amateurs and their guests streamed into the theater. A few minutes later, Georges stopped the flow for Comte Debussy, carried in a litter by two footmen.

Anne, escorted by Krishna, entered near the last. A stunning sight. During the banquet, Georges had admired her at a distance. But the grandeur of the room, the sunlight pouring through the windows, the noise and clutter of guests and servants had somehow conspired to diminish her brilliance. Now, from the shadow of the hallway, chin high and shoulders back, she stepped into an arc of light. Tall and stately, she wore the feathered turban like an exotic queen. Her body moved with an easy natural grace, her light silk skirt swinging rhythmically with her step. Her purple bodice worked magic in the diamonds of her necklace. Georges recoiled in awe and lowered his eyes, lest he gape like an idiot. He must not distract her. As she moved by, a shiver of delight raced through his body.

⊗∞⊗∞⊗

Walking up the ramp, Anne found Comte Debussy already in his chair, scanning his guests without interest. The old man's face brightened at her approach. He gestured to the seat next to him. For a few moments she posed for the audience, then sat down. The comte edged closer, took her hand, fondled the gold bracelet on her wrist. She resented his touch. Gesturing with her free hand, she drew his attention to the tiara. As she turned her head for him, she furtively glanced over her shoulder, hoping to see Georges. He was standing by the main door, preparing to close it. She felt reassured.

Chevalier de Pressigny walked on stage in front of the curtain, announcing the play they were about to see: *The Cuckolded Clown*, a comedy in one act written by himself.

Anne cringed. It *was* the piece intended for last year's production with Lélia Laplante and Antoine Dubois. Pressigny had not prepared a new play since only a few of his cronies knew what he had written. The sets and costumes had most likely been in storage. She shuddered, recalling the scripts Georges had taken from the office and later returned. That had been risky.

When Pressigny stepped behind the curtain, Comte Debussy cried out with surprising vigor, "Let the play begin." The light dimmed and the curtain rose. "We are never sure what it's going to be until it starts," he whispered to Anne.

She mumbled a response, then stared straight ahead, breathing deeply to calm her anger.

The play began. Anne listened carefully for changes in the script. There didn't seem to be any. It was a sex farce, simple and predictable. An Actress and her Lover barely concealed their liaison from her husband, the Clown, now played by Pressigny himself. When the Clown discovered her unfaithfulness, he entered her darkened room and stabbed her in bed. The lovers, however, had anticipated him and were watching from behind the curtains. The figure in bed was a bag of straw. Unaware of the deception and overcome with remorse, the Clown declaimed a confession and leapt from a window. Instead of smashing onto the pavement, he fell into a wagon of manure passing by. As the wagon pulled away, the lovers leaned out the window and waved.

The audience was amused. Witty innuendo, exaggerated gesture and speech occasionally lifted the production to the level of genuine comedy, and the actors put energy into their roles. Even the comte seemed pleased. Anne, however, felt stricken. The farce mocked the horror of Antoine's death. When she heard Pressigny speak the Clown's melodramatic "confession," she grew rigid. "Callous bastard!" she groaned soundlessly. "May you burn in hell!"

Sensing something amiss, Debussy glanced at her quizzically. She forced a smile until the comedy engaged him again.

At the interlude in the evening's entertainment, the comte caught Krishna's eye. It was time to go. "You will come later with Krishna," he said to Anne. Footmen helped him shuffle down the ramp to a litter and carried him away. Georges opened the door, then stood at attention as they passed through.

A few moments later, Krishna approached Anne. "Let us promenade through the theater." She soon sensed a subtle change taking place in the silent man at her side. Previously, he had seemed to enjoy walking about in his exotic Indian costume and displaying her and the jewels to the Amateurs. Now he appeared preoccupied, as if anticipating trouble ahead. His back stiffened. Thin lines of tension creased his brow.

Unable to account for his shifting mood, Anne grew apprehensive. She had earlier assumed she would return the jewels, change into simpler clothes, then speak with the domestic servants about Krishna's daughter. Now she felt unsure of what lay ahead.

While Georges held the door open, Krishna led her out into the hallway. With a wave of his hand, he beckoned two tall footmen and whispered a few words. They fell in line behind him. He nodded to Anne, and they set off at a brisk pace. She glanced at the Indian's dark, unsmiling countenance, at his hand clutching the large curved dagger. Fingering her necklace nervously, she recalled his sensual touch as he had fastened it. Oddly, his erotic interest had vanished. Something other than a woman's charm preoccupied him now. The thought failed to comfort her. Georges was no longer in sight. She was on her own. Peals of laughter echoed faintly in the dim hallway, then faded away.

∽∾∽

As Anne left the theater, Georges followed her out of the corner of his eye. Then he moved a few steps forward and overheard Krishna tell a pair of footmen, "The comte wants a last look at her." A worried undertone in the steward's voice triggered alarm in Georges' mind. They must be going to the comte's apartment. Following them in the main hall might arouse suspicion, so he hastened to the theater's rear exit.

"Where are you going?" a stern voice asked. "Mind the entrance assigned to you!" The senior footman shook his finger at Georges. He grimaced, clutching his stomach as if in pain, and assured his superior he needed to leave, lest he grow most disagreeably ill and interrupt the performance. The footman drew back, scrutinized Georges sharply, then waved him off with an irritated sigh.

He ran across the courtyard, climbed the service stairway two steps at a time to the main floor, and rushed to the servants' antechamber next to the comte's apartment. "The senior footman ordered me here," he announced to the comte's valet and a pair of upstairs footmen sitting at a plain table. The valet shrugged his shoulders with a look of surprise. "There's nothing to do. The comte has just sent us out." He exchanged knowing glances with the footmen. "He's enjoying the company of the actress wearing his jewels. No telling how long that'll be."

Georges felt his chest tighten. "Is anyone attending the comte?"

"Only Krishna," replied the valet. "He's to keep the actress from running off with the precious trinkets." The footmen snickered. One of them threw a deck of cards on the table. A game got underway among the three.

Georges moved from the table to a chair by the door to the comte's apartment, telling himself Miss Cartier could cope with the invalid nobleman and his cool, dark steward. Through the door he heard a faint, broken murmur of voices. At the table, the card players discussed Monsieur Tétu's recent ascent in a balloon from the Luxembourg Gardens. They inclined to the view that, if God meant men to fly, he would have given them wings.

Suddenly, from within the apartment came the sound of loud voices raised in anger. The men around the table glanced toward the comte's door, then toward one another. They pushed back their chairs, as if about to rise. A hushed silence filled the room. Georges sat on the edge of his seat, ready to spring. Time seemed to stand still. Then the bell rang.

Anne's apprehension mounted as she and Krishna entered the comte's apartment. Drapes were drawn over the windows of the high vaulted salon. A small table was set for two, decorated with a vase of intensely fragrant damask roses. Large lighted candelabra had been placed to the left and right. Two servants stood against the wall. She looked vainly for Georges.

"I would like the pleasure of these jewels for one last time," the comte said wistfully, as he gestured to Krishna, who held a chair for her.

A servant came with a bottle of wine. Krishna poured and stepped back. The comte contemplated the jewels silently for a short while, then looked at Anne and raised his glass. She met his eye and raised her glass. He did not drink, so she merely wet her lips. By this time, she had become cautious. Silly, she thought, but this could be drugged.

After a desultory conversation, the comte lapsed into silence. His mood seemed to change. He signalled for the servants to clear the table and leave.

"Krishna, it's time to remove the jewels from Mademoiselle Cartier." He looked at Anne with mounting lust. She sat upright, her back stiffening.

Krishna placed the burnished wooden box on the table, opened it, approached her. When she tried to rise, he put his hands on her shoulders and pressed her down. "Remain seated," he said, a curious edginess in his voice. "I can manage better." He removed the turban from her head and slipped the bracelets off her arms, wrists, and ankles. As he bent forward to unclasp the necklace and remove the pendants, he stared into her eyes as if trying to read her mind.

What the comte wanted was becoming clear. Her anger toward him grew apace. His eyes opened wide and darkened. His lips parted in a cruel smile, like a cat facing its prey. He clasped his hands and leaned forward.

The box clicked shut.

She jumped to her feet.

"Leaving so soon, Mademoiselle Cartier?" asked the comte playfully. "I'd like to see more of you." He turned to Krishna. "Remove the bodice."

The steward frowned and glanced toward Anne, inviting her to speak.

"That's not in our agreement, Monsieur le Comte," she said emphatically. "I'll deal with the costume myself." Her eyes shifted grimly from one man to the other.

"What a remarkable reaction," murmured the comte through tight lips. "Most actresses would have enjoyed our little sport." He glared at her spitefully. "I would have thought that, having *entertained* one of my servants last night, you might be more *aimable* toward me."

"What happened last night is none of your business and nothing that I need be ashamed of."

Anne's response stung the comte. "Impertinent woman! Will you defy me?" He glared at Krishna. "Do as I told you!"

The steward shook his head, raised a warning hand. "Colonel Paul de Saint-Martin is nearby at Chateau Beaumont. Should any harm come to Mademoiselle Cartier, he would be here with his troopers within the hour."

"I'm a dying man! What do I care about the police!" The comte wagged a bony yellowed finger at his steward. "You miserable black mongrel! You haven't objected to playing with other women. I ought to send you back to India."

"They were willing, Sir." The steward's back had stiffened. His voice was low, his words carefully measured.

The comte weakened. The corners of his mouth twitched nervously. His breathing labored.

Meanwhile, Anne had said nothing. When he now turned to her, she met his eye and he flinched.

"Krishna," he mumbled to his steward, "tell the stablemaster to prepare a carriage for Mademoiselle Cartier. She will be leaving the chateau in an hour." Shifting again to Anne, he added, "Return the costume to the dressmaker before you go. She will have your stipend. Good evening." He pulled a bellrope.

The comte's valet entered the room, his eyes wide with apprehension. "Show her out," ordered Debussy icily, then beckoned the two footmen standing in the doorway. They carried him to his bedroom, Krishna following behind. The valet moved hesitantly toward Anne, who stood still, her anger only beginning to slacken.

"Let me be!" she snapped.

Georges appeared in the doorway. "I'll deal with her," he said to the trembling valet, who scurried gratefully to the comte's bedroom. Georges rushed to her side. "Are you all right?"

"No lasting damage," she replied, then told him briefly what had happened.

He reached for her hand, his eyes tender with concern.

She stepped back, hugging herself. "Please don't touch me— I feel soiled." She attempted a smile. "I'll be better shortly. But I resent the way the comte treated me. He's disgusting if not dangerous." She paused for a long moment reflecting. Something was nagging at the back of her mind.

"Yes? What is it?" Georges asked.

"I'm puzzled by Krishna's behavior. He never threatened me, he blocked the comte's attempt to harm me. Still, I sense he wasn't personally concerned for my health or my virtue."

Georges nodded thoughtfully. "He had a hidden motive for defying his master."

Chapter 25

Aftermath

Anne hurled a pair of shoes into a trunk half full of clothes she had hastily packed. The rest of her things were strewn about the parlor. The humiliation of being ordered out of the chateau was coming home to her. She was folding a shift when Michou touched her arm. A note had slipped under the door.

"Please pick it up," Anne signed, then leaned over the trunk and patted down Comtesse Marie's riding suit. A few days earlier, Anne had tried it on while Comtesse Marie watched. Together they had marvelled at the close fit. The comtesse had worn it as a younger woman. With age she had grown thinner and the costume hung loosely on her.

Anne straightened up, staring into the trunk. Was nobility merely a change of clothes? Or, a title? Marie de Beaumont and her nephew Paul deserved respect. Decent, useful people. But Debussy, Pressigny and the Amateurs? Rubbish in silk stockings! She finished the packing with renewed energy, dropped the lid of the trunk with a thump, and clasped it shut.

Michou handed her the note, a message written by a cramped, shaking hand. Anne went to the window for better light. *Please see me before you depart. Claire.* Intriguing. Did she know what had happened in the comte's apartment? The memory of it rushed back to Anne's mind. The comte's impotent lechery. Krishna's resistance. Perhaps he was merely looking after his master's best interest in keeping the police away from Chateau Debussy. What other reason could there be? She looked out the window, rubbing the back of her neck. Another puzzle. Why this request from Claire? Was she merely curious? She appeared to keep herself informed. It might be prudent to find out what she had heard. Anne glanced at the message again. Its tone was courteous. Surprisingly so, in view of the rude remarks the woman had made at supper last night. Anne looked around the room. The trunk was packed. Next to it stood Michou ready to leave. There was time for a brief visit, Anne thought, and strode toward the door. It was worth the risk. Michou could stay with the luggage.

Claire's apartment at the opposite end of the mansard floor was similar to the one Anne and Michou were vacating. Odd location for a noblewoman and member of the family, Anne thought, as a young maid showed her in. It was as if the comte and his stepdaughter chose to live as far as possible from one another. While waiting for Claire, Anne glanced about the sparsely furnished parlor with amazement. There were no plants or flowers nor any pictures. If Claire had a home, it was elsewhere.

The parlor appeared to serve as a study. Against one wall stood a secretary and next to it a library table, its surface covered with piles of books. Anne inspected the topmost, a volume opened to colored engravings of a trellised pear tree, its fruit and leaves. Bookcases lined another wall from floor to ceiling. Scanning the shelves, she found a few books of recent, fashionable interest, including a worn copy of Choderlos de Laclos' *Les Liaisons Dangereuses*. A gentleman's guide to the art of seduction. "Jean" was inscribed inside the cover. Lent it to his sister, Anne supposed, to feed her starved fantasy.

The rest of the books comprised a botanical library. Anne opened Linnaeus' *Species plantarum*, noting a crest with the name Comtesse de Pressigny stamped on the title page. Claire's mother, most likely. Anne was closing the book when a door opened behind her. Claire approached, looking very different than at last night's supper table. A simple yellow dressing gown lightly covered her shapely body. Free of cosmetics, her face revealed a certain beauty in the soft, early evening light.

"Have you an interest in the Swedish botanist?" she asked with a hint of doubt. She took the volume from Anne and fanned it, raising no dust. Her bible, Anne thought, then glanced at Claire's hands. They were brown and rough. "I'm aware of his reputation," Anne replied. She and Paul had spoken about him a few weeks earlier while they were trimming roses in the garden. "He's the scholar," she said, quoting Paul, "who brought order to our understanding of the plant world." She squirmed inwardly as she heard the pedantic sound of her remark.

Claire looked straight ahead, smiling indulgently, and returned the book to the shelf. "I find plants are better company than most of the people I know." With a brusque gesture she directed Anne to a group of chairs by the window. "I must talk to you." She seated herself across from Anne and waved the maid out of the room.

"I've heard at second hand that you and the comte had a disagreement. Let me guess what happened. He tried to attack you, and you outwitted him. Right?" Without waiting for an answer, she leaned back in the chair, her eyes hard, her arms folded across her chest. "Tell me about it."

The maid brought in a tea tray, giving Anne a few minutes to consider what, if anything, she should say. She fought down an impulse to tell Claire to mind her own business. The woman already knew the basic elements of the story.

Anne agreed with a shrug, then gave Claire a detailed account of the incident. She omitted the comte's snide remarks about Georges spending the night in her apartment.

Claire listened intently, her mouth set in a scowl, until Anne finished. "I owe you an apology," she said. Her expression softened. She leaned forward, rubbing her thighs with her hands. "I was rude to you at the supper table. But I hate the comte and I thought you were his whore!" She appeared to struggle momentarily for self-control, then spoke in a small calm voice. "When I learned you had resisted him, I changed my opinion. I have to say I admire you and wish I had your nerve."

Anne smiled gently, assuring her no offense had been taken for her remarks at supper. "Why do you need more nerve?" asked Anne.

For a moment, Claire stared into her cup, then raised her eyes to Anne. "I feel like I'm in prison, helpless, in the clutches of a lecherous sadistic jailer. Until he grew ill, he had his way with me for years." Her eyes darkened, her chin thrust forward. Anger seemed to roil beneath her icy surface. "If I'd had courage," she said in a low, quiet voice, "I'd have thrown a candelabrum at the old bastard's head."

She rose stiffly from her chair, seized a vase from a nearby shelf, and hurled it at the wall. Anne flinched as it exploded in a shower of tiny pieces. Claire returned to her chair, smiling as if she had done nothing out of the ordinary. But her eyes had become unnaturally bright, her breathing strained.

Was the woman mad? Anne wondered. Should she invent an excuse to leave? She sipped from her cup. Claire did likewise. After a few wordless moments, when Anne sensed Claire's breathing return to normal, she ventured to ask if her brother was of much help.

"He hates the comte as much as I do, but he's concerned only with the Amateurs."

"Could you move away from here?"

"I have no money. The comte has swindled most of my mother's legacy and he controls the rest. The only thing I can do is garden!"

"Perhaps you could turn gardening into a new life." Even as she spoke, Anne realized how unlikely that prospect was, unless Claire could find a sympathetic patron. Comtesse Marie de Beaumont came to mind, but it seemed an unlikely match. Anne rose to leave. "I wish I could be more helpful, but as you know, the comte wants me off the property within the hour! Perhaps we can continue our talk later, somewhere else."

Claire nodded. "I hope so." She saw Anne to the door and took her hand in parting. It felt like the grip of a drowning woman.

Paul de Saint-Martin paced back and forth, mulling over the report his adjutant had just given him. The air felt warm and still in the ground floor parlor at Chateau Beaumont. The colonel had hung his coat over a chair and opened his shirt at the neck. Through the windows he saw a servant lighting lamps in the courtyard. The sun had set. Darkness nearly filled the sky. He glanced down at his adjutant sitting in front of two empty glasses and a bottle of brandy. "I'm concerned about Miss Cartier. That encounter with Debussy and his steward must have upset her. She walked past me with just the ghost of a smile."

Georges looked up and shrugged. "She was tired, didn't want anything to eat, just a bath. When she's rested, she'll tell you what happened first hand. I was in the comte's anteroom and didn't see much." He glanced hopefully at the brandy and the glasses.

Still uncertain about Anne, Saint-Martin sat down at the table and poured for himself and his adjutant. Raising his glass, he met Georges' eye. "Well done! We're now certain Derennes isn't hiding within Chateau Debussy, and we know a great deal more about the Laplante case."

"I'll drink to that." Georges lifted his glass.

The two men settled back in their chairs, sipping their brandy. "We've done what we can here," Saint-Martin said, fingering his glass. "Tomorrow, we'll return to Paris...."

Georges cut in, "And trace the stiletto back to Laplante."

The colonel nodded. "But the first thing on my list for the morning is a ride in the country with Miss Cartier. If she cares to go, of course. I'd like you to have our horses ready, just in case."

"Yes, Sir," said the adjutant, but with a grimace that surprised Saint-Martin. He considered a reprimand but thought better of it. A man as loyal as Georges was entitled to express his feelings. Perhaps it was demeaning to order an old soldier to serve his master's private pleasure with a woman. Or, was envy at the bottom of it? Did Georges resent his riding with Anne? In vain, Saint-Martin sought his adjutant's eye. Conversation lagged while the two men sipped their brandy.

The colonel glanced at his watch. "Ten o'clock. Miss Cartier has rested by now. I'll go to her and hear her report." He took a final sip, placed his empty glass on the table, and bid his adjutant goodnight. Georges looked up but did not respond.

Saint-Martin paused outside Anne's apartment, ran a hand through his hair, then knocked on the door. A young maid opened it and showed him into a parlor. Mademoiselle Cartier was coming out of the bath, she told him. Would he wait? Yes, he said, curbing an impatience that took him by surprise.

The room was plain but tasteful. Four upholstered chairs were placed around a small mahogany table, a pale green sofa stood against a cream-colored wall. Several sconces shed a soft light over a Turkish carpet. As he idly surveyed his surroundings, a curious feeling came over him, a tingling of nerves, a longing to see her, to touch her. Suddenly, unbidden in his imagination, a nude female form shrouded in mist emerged from an emerald pond and glided toward him, water glistening on her body.

At that moment, the maid returned and the vision vanished. Mademoiselle Cartier, she announced, would join him shortly.

∾∾∾

Meanwhile, Anne stepped out of the large copper tub filled with warm water. For this uncommon luxury she had to thank Comtesse Marie, who had seen her return from Chateau Debussy irritated and fatigued. The long soaking bath had dissipated whatever had been disagreeable or insulting to her during the day, especially her confrontation with the comte.

As she towelled herself dry, she realized she had returned to Chateau Beaumont without properly greeting Paul. In truth, she had not wanted to speak to him while she was in a troubled state of mind. Now she looked forward to seeing his honest, handsome face. He would hang on what she had to say, his brown eyes bright and eager.

The sound of footsteps outside distracted her. A few moments later, the young parlor maid opened the bathroom door. "A gentleman, Colonel Paul de Saint-Martin, wishes to speak to Mademoiselle Cartier."

Anne sucked in a breath. Taken by surprise, she recovered as best she could, trying to conceal her pleasure from the maid. "Tell him, I'll join him shortly in the parlor, then come back and do my hair."

Several minutes later, in a thin blue silk house robe, her hair combed back in soft golden waves, Anne sat alone with Paul at the table in her parlor. She had sent the maid away with the wet towels. Paul listened with rapt attention, as she told her story of the Amateurs' reception. She hesitated briefly before passing over Georges' night in her apartment at Chateau Debussy and the comte's invidious allusion to it. She felt uneasy, as if she were hiding something Paul would want to know. And might resent. But she put her mind at rest. These were irrelevant details, nothing he need be concerned about. At least not now. He seemed so happy and…passionate.

∞ ∞ ∞

As Anne related her experience in Debussy's apartment, Paul grew anxious for her safety, then angry. His face burned. "How dare the comte insult you, a young lady under my aunt's protection! If he weren't so ill…." He checked himself, then gazed intently at her. "You taught him a lesson!" He moved forward to the edge of his chair and took her hand. "I'm pleased you returned safely."

She squeezed his hand and smiled. "Could we do something together tomorrow before returning to Paris? An early morning ride perhaps?"

"I'd like that very much." He was delighted she had anticipated his wish. Caressing her hand, their knees almost touching, he sensed the pulsing life within her. Her scent, fresh from the bath, wafted over him. The thin silk garment cleaved to her body, revealing its loveliness. He began to feel lightheaded with desire.

She gently withdrew her hand. "Then it's best to retire now. I've had a tiring day. I want to be fresh for the ride."

He rose reluctant to leave. She walked him to the door. They turned toward one another, as if pulled by a powerful hidden force. "Sleep well, Anne," he said, stroking her cheek.

"And you, too, Paul." She leaned into his caress. Her arms encircled his waist.

He cupped her head in his hands and drew her to his lips. Their bodies pressed together in an intimate embrace. Then, drawing back, they clasped hands.

"Until tomorrow, then." He walked out into the hallway, turned and waved.

"Yes, until tomorrow," she murmured to herself as she closed the door.

Chapter 26

Death in the Night

Shortly after sunrise, a thin morning mist hovered over the low-lying land around Chateau Beaumont. Anne had put on riding clothes and was leaning out the open window of her room over the front courtyard. A moist breeze bathed her face. She shivered slightly. Impressions from yesterday in Comte Debussy's apartment teased her mind. But she could deal with them later. Having rested well, she looked forward to the ride with Paul.

Hooves clattered on the cobblestones. She glanced down. Georges was already at the entrance, holding a pair of eager dark brown thoroughbreds, groomed and saddled. In the distance, a man galloped up the avenue of chestnut trees toward the chateau. Odd, she thought, squinting for a clearer view.

At that moment she heard faint footsteps in the hallway, then a gentle rapping on her door and the voice of Paul calling softly to her. He had seemed greatly relieved when she and Michou returned safely last night from Chateau Debussy. She warmed at the recollection of their embrace, his arms around her, his lips against hers.

She closed the window and brushed dust from her skirt where she had leaned against the sill.

"Anne," he called again from the hallway, a little louder this time.

Biting her lips to freshen their color, her heart drumming, she opened the door.

"Good morning, Anne." He bowed slightly, smiled, then stepped back for her to pass. He was wearing a brown riding suit, an eager, playful expression on his face, as if caught up in the pleasure before him. At the stairway they paused and clasped hands, then descended in step together.

In the foyer they met Georges rushing in, followed by a hatless young groom. "Comte Debussy is dead!" Georges shouted, then glanced at the messenger. "The stablemaster sent him." At a word from Georges, the young man went on to report that the comte had died during the night. Krishna had been found unconscious and bound. The young man hadn't been told if anything had been stolen.

"Chevalier de Pressigny and the others haven't heard the news yet," Georges added with a touch of contempt. "They caroused all night and are still in bed."

Paul stopped in his tracks. Disbelief, then concern spread over his face. He turned to Anne. "Comte Debussy was vigorous when *you* last saw him, wasn't he?"

"In a manner of speaking!" She vividly recalled his lecherous smile. He might nonetheless have died of natural causes, she thought, perhaps of a shock too severe for his frail constitution. But, the violence done to Krishna meant the comte might have been murdered. Unbidden, Anne thought of yesterday's visit with Claire—the vase exploding against the wall. And the day before that, the young woman rising wrathful from the table, gripping the knife.

Paul's jaw stiffened with resolve. "Georges, send the messenger with an order to the Royal Highway Patrol at Villejuif. I want a brigade of five men to join us at Chateau Debussy."

As Paul was about to mount, a flicker of disappointment crossed his face. "I'm sorry this came up, Anne." He drew close to her. His voice grew tender. "We shall ride another day." He took her hand. "Stay with Aunt Marie for the time being and tell her what has happened. Later we'll need a statement from you at Chateau Debussy."

She pressed his hand. "I'll be ready."

He walked back to his horse, staring down in reflection. A pregnant silence came over the courtyard, broken only by the animal's restless snorts. Finally, Paul glanced back at Anne and then over at Georges, who drew his horse near. "I'll wager the jewels have been stolen and Pressigny's somehow involved."

Georges furrowed his brow. "A theft like the others we've had in this area. Like Michou's jasper bowl."

Anne joined the two men by the horses. "Pressigny would steal the jewels, if he thought he could get away with it. He believes Comte Debussy swindled his legacy. And we know how he killed Lélia Laplante. Taken by surprise, threatened, he might also kill the comte."

"Quite likely," Paul agreed. "Many hands could be involved in this affair, including intruders unknown to us." He stroked the horse's glistening neck, paused, then glanced at Anne with an afterthought. "There is something you can do. Ask Michou to work on those sketches of the Chanavas jewels. We may need them." Smiling farewell, he swung into the saddle and beckoned Georges to follow him.

For several minutes after the men had galloped out of sight, Anne stood in the open doorway, staring westward toward Chateau Debussy. She recalled her last impressions of the comte. A wasted body, eyes lit by lust, a voice heavy with sarcasm. Flashes of hot anger raced through her body. His contempt for actresses was like Jack Roach's. Had she not been shielded by the patronage of a police colonel and his highborn aunt, she might have undergone a beating or far worse.

She walked back into the foyer, her anger slowly yielding to more pleasing images: the splendid halls and galleries of Chateau Debussy, the exquisite jewelry and elegant company. At the foot of the stairs she stopped, her hand resting on the bannister. An oriental vase stood on a sideboard, full of cut flowers. She pulled out a withered damask rose and breathed its fading scent.

She started up the stairs. Though Comte Debussy had tried to harm her, she now felt more sad than pleased by his death. Pausing on a step, she gazed at the blotched, pale flower in her hand. A pathetic man, the comte had savored the Chanavas necklace and tiara wistfully, as if for the last time before the final darkness.

∞∞∞

A clap of thunder woke her up. She had fallen asleep in her room, sitting by the open window, the wilted rose in her lap. Droplets of water struck her face as she turned toward the courtyard. Bolts of lightning streaked across the sky. Thunder rumbled again. She stretched, curiously exhilarated by nature's violence. Feeling her gown getting wet, she rose to close the window. A flash of lightning cast an eerie green light over the shining cobblestones. She sucked in her breath. A mounted figure was crossing the courtyard, erect in the saddle even in a driving rain. Paul!

She ran down the stairs and opened the front door just as he pulled the bell cord. Grooms rushed forward to care for his horse. In the entrance hall a footman carried off his dripping cape, his hat and heavy boots, and promised to return with a hot drink. Wiping his face, red with exertion, Paul followed Anne through the hall into a nearby parlor. They sat facing one another at a small table.

In a low voice, from which all feeling seemed to have drained, he told her that a violent crime had indeed taken place at Chateau Debussy. Under cover of darkness, thieves had broken into the treasury in the corner tower and had stolen the Chanavas jewels, knocked Krishna unconscious, and murdered Comte Debussy. Sometime before dawn, they had escaped through the tunnel to the garden pavilion. Servants and members of the family all claimed alibis.

Throughout his report, Anne sat still, listening. The footman arrived with hot, spiced wine and poured a glass for the colonel. Its pungent scent filled the room. Lightning flashed, followed by a deafening crash. Anne declined a glass. Her stomach felt queasy. The late hour. The storm outside. The terse report of violent death.

In a faltering voice she asked, "How did the comte die?"

"Smothered in bed. His eyes wide open. He may have seen his attacker, struggled briefly, but couldn't ring for help. We pried open his fingers. Found this." He took a golden tassel from his pocket. "Madame Soucie searched the chateau in vain for a matching one. We'll keep it a secret. The official report says he was smothered by a bed pillow." He handed the tassel to Anne. "Recognize it?"

She held the object to the light. "It doesn't look familiar. But I don't usually notice tassels." She gave it back to him. "The comte may have been surprised by someone he knew."

He shrugged. "A servant or member of the family, perhaps." He sipped his wine, peering over the rim. "Or, more likely, professional thieves from the city, apparently well informed. We know they crawled over the roof, broke open a louver in the tower, removed a ceiling mirror, and lowered themselves into the treasury on a rope."

"Why kill the comte?"

"I guess he woke up. Perhaps called for Krishna. The thieves would have moved quickly to silence him." A troubled expression came over his face. "I've talked to Lieutenant-General DeCrosne this afternoon. I had to—this is a major case. He's assigned Inspecteur Mauvert to the investigation." He sought her eye. "Does the name mean anything to you?"

She stared at him, dismayed. "Mauvert! The man who investigated Antoine's case. He takes money from LeCourt and spies on me." Her mind raced on. "He'll surely suspect what we're doing here!"

"Don't expect him to be helpful!" With a scowl Paul drained his glass and set it on the table. "I picked him up in Paris. Brought him to Chateau Debussy. Greedy bastard! The main thing on his mind is the fat commission he'll get if he recovers the jewels." Saint-Martin leaned back, gazing sympathetically at her. "He insists on questioning you at the chateau. You may have heard or seen something relevant to the crime."

"Why let him? You or Georges could question me."

Paul shifted uneasily in his chair. "I wish we could do it that way. But Mauvert's demand would seem reasonable to the lieutenant-general. An inspecteur needs to observe the testimony of a witness to judge its credibility. To refuse would only spark suspicion. Mauvert would think we were trying to conceal something." He glanced apologetically at Anne. "I've scheduled the questioning at noon tomorrow. Tell Mauvert no more than he needs to know."

Anne's carriage rattled across the courtyard at Chateau Debussy, splashing through puddles on the glistening paving stones. Opening the window, she tasted the cool fresh air, cleansed by the night's rain. At the main entrance, the carriage stopped with a nerve-jarring screech of brakes and jangle of harness. Moments later, Paul left the building and strode briskly towards her.

She smoothed her soft woolen dress—pearl grey, trimmed with black lace. Another loan from Comtesse Marie's wardrobe. She had argued that an elegant, tasteful, *and* costly costume might win some regard from the inspecteur. Anne dubiously touched the strings of her bonnet. A distant bell rang noon. She was right on time.

Walking beside Paul through the main hall, she sensed anxiety grow beneath his calm, official demeanor. They entered the ground floor room that served as a temporary office. Georges, seated at a table, rose to greet her. Inspecteur Mauvert, reading a file by the window, looked up at her with a tight-lipped, mocking smile. She instantly disliked him, a slim ferret of a man, eyes small, cold, and malicious.

"Colonel Saint-Martin," said the inspecteur, laying the file on the table, "I would like Mademoiselle Cartier to go with us through the chateau, recalling whatever might have bearing on the theft of the treasure and the death of the comte."

The colonel turned to Anne, holding out his arm in a courteous request. She smiled as if pleased to be of assistance.

She led them past Chevalier de Pressigny's apartment, mentioning the debris that fell on the balcony during his party. Mauvert's face lit up; a piece of the puzzle had dropped into place.

Glancing sidelong at him, Anne wrinkled her brow.

The inspecteur noticed her perplexity and explained that the thieves must have loosened a few tiles while exploring the roof for a way into the treasury.

In the main hall, she spoke of LeCourt's fascination with the jewels. "At the reception, I felt they had extraordinary power over him. I could imagine him buying them from the thieves, if not stealing them."

"What a fanciful notion," scoffed Mauvert. "Typical of a woman!" He turned to Colonel Saint-Martin. "Robert LeCourt is a rich banker, a generous patron, and an ardent collector. Hardly the kind of person who deals in stolen goods."

Anne felt a rush of color to her cheeks, a tightening in her throat. Mauvert had turned his back to her and walked several paces ahead. "You little bastard!" she said under her breath. She was about to call after him, that being rich didn't mean LeCourt was honest. But Georges silently mouthed a warning. She bit her lip.

She was still irritated when they entered the comte's apartment. Mauvert asked about her confrontation with him. The colonel had tried to prepare her for this question, but she loathed explaining to the inspecteur how Debussy had insulted her. As she stumbled through her account, a shadow of doubt crossed the inspecteur's face.

She challenged him. "Sir!"

His eyes brightened with malign amusement. "Perhaps Comte Debussy thought you would welcome his playfulness." He pursed his lips in a smirk. "After all, you are an actress. Had spent the night with one of his servants."

Anne flinched as if struck in the face.

The colonel stiffened, glaring at Mauvert.

Before either Anne or Saint-Martin could protest, Georges stepped forward. "Miss Cartier allowed me to sleep in the parlor of her apartment, not the bedroom. I was guarding her and her maid from Pressigny's drunken guests."

Lips parted, speechless, the colonel glanced at Anne, then at Georges.

Mauvert brought a hand to his mouth. "I am so sorry. I didn't mean to offend." Even while he was apologizing, his eyes brimmed with the pleasure his thrust had given him.

She stared at him with thinly veiled scorn.

His brow furrowed in afterthought. "You brought a maid with you, a woman who works at the Tatar Puppet Theater." He spoke in a curious way, as if intending to joust with Anne. "May I speak with her?"

"She can't tell you anything," Anne replied, her tone ironic. Mauvert knew who her maid was. Henriette Picard would have told him.

"I insist." His face took on a smirk.

"Then waste your time." Anne had reached the end of her patience. "The Laplante case, remember? She's Michou, the little deaf woman you called simpleminded."

Mauvert remained silent for a few moments, searching Anne's face, as he had several times during the questioning. "Now I know who *you* are," he said, his voice rising. "In Dubois' coat pocket, we found a silver case with two miniature portraits." He raised a hand as if displaying the case. "You're..."

Anne cut him off. "I'm the young woman, his daughter."

∞ ∞ ∞

"What was wrong with the inspecteur?" asked Anne, still smarting from his rudeness. She glowered at Georges, as if he were somehow responsible.

"He's ill at ease with an attractive young woman who doesn't know her place." A gleam appeared in his eye. "Especially if she has brains."

A servant had withdrawn, closing the door behind him. Georges and Anne were in the investigation's temporary office, alone except for Comte Debussy's black cat, which had followed the servant from the kitchen. The sleek feline meandered about the room, wary, calculating his options. Unmindful of his murdered master, Anne thought. No one, not even the cat, was grieving today.

They pulled chairs up to the table, where a tray of tea and biscuits stood amid a clutter of files. Colonel Saint-Martin was to join them later, after seeing Mauvert off to Paris.

Disarmed by Georges' tact and distracted by the cat, Anne managed a strained smile. "I *had* to stand up to the man! But he'll make trouble for us."

"Can't be helped," Georges said kindly. "The inspecteur had already recognized you and Michou and suspected we were prying into the Laplante case."

As Anne's irritation slowly subsided, her curiosity grew. She glanced at a file box with "Debussy" printed in large letters. "Any progress?"

"Yes, indeed!" Georges rose to open a window, then beckoned Anne. He pointed to the garden pavilion. "That's where the thieves escaped. Someone must have unlocked the trapdoor to the tunnel."

"Pressigny? He watched the evening fireworks from the pavilion."

"Yes, but he claims he never touched the trapdoor. He was with Henriette—she vouches for him."

Anne rolled her eyes upward.

Georges grinned wryly. "By the way, the only keys to the tunnel are in Krishna's office. But Pressigny, or someone else, could have made copies."

They left the window open and returned to their chairs. A soft breeze wafted into the room. Papers fluttered on the table. Georges poured a cup of tea for her and one for himself. His face was grey and lined with fatigue, his clothes rumpled. But he kept a smile on his face. She felt touched by his kindness.

At that moment her eye caught sight of a black furry tail, erect, moving between the file boxes. The cat emerged from an opening in front of Anne, his yellow eyes fixed on the tea tray. Georges cleared the area, set down a saucer of milk, and broke up a biscuit.

"The comte got him half-grown a year ago," Georges remarked. "Called him Orcus. The Roman god of the Underworld, land of the dead. The cook's adopted him." Georges seized the cat by the front legs and drew him up to eye level. Yielding to the firm grip, the cat stared still and silent at his interrogator. "Tell us who killed your master," Georges demanded. "You slept with the comte. You must have seen the whole thing." The yellow eyes blinked. No other response.

Georges loosened his grip and turned to Anne. "When servants broke into the room early in the morning, the cat was on top of an armoire watching the body." He put Orcus in front of the saucer.

Anne lightly stroked the cat's back. He purred, then sniffed the food and set to eating it.

"There's more on Pressigny," Georges continued. "He bribed the butler for the key to the wine cellar. Said he'd serve his guests. That meant he had the basement mostly to himself."

Sipping slowly from her cup, Anne recalled Debussy's architectural plans of the chateau. While Georges looked on and offered advice, she took up a pen and quickly sketched the thieves' most likely escape route. "They left by the private stairway from the comte's apartment to the basement and then on to the tunnel." She added, "Pressigny could have unlocked the doors for them."

"Others could have done the same thing," Georges countered, "and Pressigny has an alibi of sorts. During the evening he was looking after his guests. He spent the night with Henriette."

"She *would* lie for him, wouldn't she."

"I'm sure she would." Georges broke another biscuit for Orcus. "Pressigny remains a suspect. *And* I found a couple more." He paused to bait her curiosity. "The tunnel's wet. There are fresh footprints in the clay floor, including a woman's."

"Claire's?" Anne felt a twinge of apprehension. She had begun to wish the woman well.

"I searched her room. A pair of her shoes have traces of mud and fit some of the prints. She admitted going back and forth in the tunnel with René Cavour, the young gardener, and spending the night with him. A pair of his shoes also matched some of the prints. They claimed they saw two men hurry from the pavilion in the dark about an hour after the fireworks. Could be true. I found other fresh prints I haven't matched yet."

"Did you try Noir and Gros?"

He shrugged. "They have alibis in Paris for the night of the crime. Mauvert needs to check them. None of the shoes in their cottage fit the prints."

Anne glanced at the piles of ledgers and business papers in front of Georges. "Poor man! Do you have to go through all that?"

"I've already found a few choice morsels. Let me show you."

Anne moved around the table to the seat next to his. Orcus quickly curled up in the chair she had vacated.

Patting a large ledger, Georges explained that it contained the chateau's accounts for the past three years. He muttered impishly, "Krishna pays too much for wine!" In the next breath, his voice took on a serious tone. "He buys from a young widow in Rue Saint-Marc, close to Café Marcel. Something else for Mauvert to look into."

There was a knock on the door. Paul, Anne thought, but then she realized he would walk right in.

Georges called out. A courier entered with a sealed packet from Debussy's lawyers. "The comte's last will and testament," remarked Georges, "dated three years ago." He dismissed the courier and turned to Anne. "I've read a lawyer's summary of it in Krishna's office."

For a few minutes Georges scanned the document, occasionally murmuring a phrase. Finally he laid it on the table and pushed it sideways to Anne.

She began reading, then became engrossed. "This looks very strange!" she cried, lifting a page. "Debussy left his jewels and his works of art to the Crown rather than to his heirs."

Georges nodded. "Read on, it gets better."

Her eyes worked to the bottom of the page and fixed on a codicil. She sighed, then looked up from the text. "Too much legal language. Explain it to me, Georges."

He grimaced in mock desperation. "Years after Debussy's return from India, the government claimed he wasn't entitled to his Indian jewels. But they wanted to keep the matter out of the courts, where it would have dragged on forever. He agreed to will his entire art collection to the Crown. They allowed him to enjoy the treasure during his lifetime!"

"An easy bargain for Debussy," observed Anne. "He didn't have a family of his own, and his wife's children meant nothing to him." She settled back in the chair, staring at the comte's will. "Did he leave anything to his heirs and the people working here?"

"They learned three years ago what would happen to the comte's collection. Plenty of time to plan the theft," Georges replied, then added, "The comte was deep in debt. The executors are to sell the chateau and its property to pay off creditors." He waved a hand at the account books. "Nothing is left for the others."

"He must have angered many people," observed Anne, "but no one appears to gain by killing him."

"As far as we know." Georges closed the ledger and pushed it to one side, then handed her a preliminary coroner's report from Monsieur Desault, chief surgeon at the Charité. "The comte's disease of the liver was far advanced, incurable. Murder shortened his life by only a few weeks."

"I see," she said, perusing the report. "If the thieves were from the family or household, they must have known he would soon die. They had to steal the treasure quickly or it would go to the Crown and beyond their reach."

"That's true," Georges said. "And there's another curious thing." He leaned toward Anne and turned a page of the report. "Desault found heavy use of an opiate that the comte's physicians hadn't prescribed. It might implicate Krishna in the theft." He shuffled the coroner's report and the comte's will into a pile. "Who was better placed to supply him with the opiate and control his movements?"

"Have you talked to Krishna?"

"Yes, though he's still groggy." After the fireworks, Georges explained, Krishna had waited in the bedroom while servants helped the comte to retire. The old man dismissed the servants, took a dose of the opiate, and soon fell asleep. Krishna was about to extinguish the candle and leave the room when he heard a strange sound from the treasury. He unlocked the door and stepped inside. That was all he could remember.

"Perhaps he was willing to take a hard knock for the sake of an alibi," Anne observed skeptically. Though he had helped her ward off the comte's advances, she could not entirely trust him. "What did he say about the opiate?" she asked, recalling the tall poppy plants Claire had shown her.

"Krishna prepared laudanum to cut the comte's pain and at least allow him to feel better. The medicines prescribed by his physicians only made him sick."

"A plausible story." Anne leaned back, hands clasped behind her head. "He could also have intended to make sure the comte slept soundly during the robbery. But Krishna couldn't steal the jewels himself if he were going to get knocked out first."

"He would need help from the city. From Masonic brothers. From people he did estate business with. Mauvert will interrogate them."

"And Monsieur Robert LeCourt?"

Georges bowed in mock respect. "He and Krishna both belong to a Masonic lodge that meets in the Palais-Royal. Their patron is the Duc d'Orléans!"

Anne tried to imagine the dark-skinned estate steward in such a lofty social circle.

"In that lodge," Georges remarked, as if reading her mind, "all men are said to be equal."

"So they say," she granted, "but Krishna could not join without a powerful sponsor—like LeCourt." She closed her eyes momentarily, imagining the financier as a puppet master with Jean de Pressigny dancing from one hand and Krishna from the other.

Georges interrupted her thought, shoving an inventory of the stolen goods in front of her. "The thieves knew exactly what they wanted and where it was. Besides the Chanavas jewels, they took the choice pieces from the comte's collection of precious stones. I've marked them in the margin."

While Anne was studying the inventory, Georges interrupted her again. "Here's something I can't understand." He rose from his chair and leaned over Anne's shoulder. She felt the warmth of his cheek. "They stole a few worthless pieces from a cabinet of heirlooms." He pointed to a line and read aloud, "A snuff box, three miniature portraits, an embroidered cushion, and a paste necklace!"

Suddenly, without warning, Paul walked into the room. He stopped in mid-step. Anne looked up, startled. His mouth opened, as if to apologize for intruding into an intimate moment. Anne lowered her eyes to the inventory. Her cheeks burned. Georges stepped back. The cat jumped from the chair and dashed out the door.

An instant later, the colonel recovered his poise and spoke curtly to Georges. "Interrogate the chambermaids again."

A spiteful errand, Anne thought, as Georges left.

Saint-Martin's eyes appeared clouded with pain and anger. He silently studied Anne. "I'll be brief," he said. "I need to question the family."

Slowly, deliberately, Anne stood to face him, as if preparing to listen. She would not let him talk down to her.

Her challenge provoked him. His nostrils flared slightly. "First, I want to bring you up to date." His voice was thick. He cleared his throat. "Tomorrow morning, I'll urge Lieutenant-General DeCrosne to reopen the Laplante case and to hold

Pressigny as a suspect in her murder and in the recent thefts of precious objects."

Anne looked askance. "Isn't he a suspect in Antoine's murder as well? Or, at least, an accomplice?"

"We're still looking for evidence connecting Pressigny to Antoine's death," replied the colonel tersely. "Approaching the lieutenant-general," he added, "is dangerous. Monsieur LeCourt will eventually learn that Michou can testify against Pressigny. She has to be protected. I cannot burden Comtesse Marie with that responsibility. So, I want you to return to Paris tomorrow morning with Michou and stay in my garden apartment." He paused, as if expecting a protest.

Anne waited coolly for him to continue.

"An officer will accompany you. Early in the afternoon, he will pick up Michou's drawings of the jewels and bring them to Paris police headquarters."

Anne heard him out, unblinking. He was right of course. But she felt disappointed in him and resentful. "You may trust me to protect Michou." Unsmiling, she walked to the door, then turned and met his eye. "You were rude to Georges. That was uncalled for." She turned away brusquely and left without allowing him an opportunity to respond.

Chapter 27

Dubois' Killer

In a corner of Saint-Martin's garden, Anne sat at a table with Michou. Above them in a small plane tree nested a family of sparrows. Their song and the faint rustle of leaves calmed Anne's spirit. The anger and disappointment she had carried with her from Chateau Debussy diminished. She glanced fondly at her companion. Michou was giving the finishing touches to a drawing. A sketch stood propped up before her.

Shielded from the midday sun by a veil of clouds, Anne ventured further out into Paul's garden. It had been neglected while he was away. As she cut dead flowers from the plants, she accidentally broke off a large blood-red rose. She brought the flower to the table and laid it in a low glazed pot of water.

Watching the floating rose slowly turn, and its petals spread out, Anne thought of Paul in the garden when she had arrived early one morning. He had offered her a rose's fragrant scent. And her heart went out to him. She regretted now the hurt that her parting words yesterday might have caused him. His rudeness to Georges had *indeed* been uncalled for, but that wasn't like him. Mauvert had insidiously planted suspicion in his mind about her and Georges.

Anne raised her eyes, aware that Michou was looking at her, an expression of concern spreading across her face. Anne smiled back reassurance, encouraging her to return to her work. For the past two days, she had been drawing the Chanavas jewels for the police, who had only an inventory's sparse description to work with. Anne picked up three finished sheets depicting pendants, bracelets, and the necklace, each full scale and meticulously accurate. Michou gave the last touches to the tiara, while the canopy of green leaves above playfully filtered light onto her paper.

A distant bell struck the hour of one. Glancing toward the house, Anne saw Lieutenant Faure of the Royal Highway Patrol at Villejuif coming to pick up the drawings. With a graceful flourish of her pencil, Michou initialed the tiara—she had recently learned the alphabet. She handed it to Anne, who patted the sheets together and gave them to the lieutenant.

"Excellent," he said, scanning Michou's work. He cast a smile to her and turned to Anne. "I'll go directly to the engravers." The Crown, he explained, appreciated Michou's contribution toward the recovery of its stolen treasure. Anne signed his words to Michou, who received them with aplomb. She looked less and less like a frightened bird.

Later in the afternoon, as Anne opened the door to the puppet theater, she fought briefly with her conscience. Paul had strictly enjoined her to stay at home with Michou. But, Anne reasoned, he could not have meant to cage them. She was surely free to walk with Michou in broad daylight through the garden of the Palais-Royal, the elegant heart of Paris, to the Camp of the Tatars. And, if she wished, to spend an hour of the afternoon with Michou in a playful skit of Punch and Judy. What she also intended to do, she admitted to herself, was discover more about the death of Antoine Dubois.

For two weeks she had failed to bring Michou beyond the testimony she had initially given concerning Lélia Laplante's death. Further probing made her morose and withdrawn, like an anxious turtle in its shell. But today she appeared serene, buoyed by satisfaction from her drawings. This might be the moment, Anne thought, to question her again with the help of the marionettes.

While Michou played with a pair of Punch and Judy hand puppets, Anne reassembled the scene of the crime. The

"Michou" marionette cowered in the darkened wardrobe room; the "Laplante" lay on the floor. When she brought in the "Pressigny," Michou immediately took notice. Her face pinched and scowling, she hurried away and sat on a bench. Anne followed, entreating her. Just as Anne was about to lose hope, Michou forced a smile and returned to the stage.

At first she balked, refusing to pick up "Pressigny." Then, with a grimace, she returned him to the fitting room, accompanied by a blank male marionette. "Pressigny" spoke to this companion, who moved off-stage. A servant, Anne thought, going outside on an errand. After a few minutes, he came back with two more blank marionettes, both males. Anne gave Michou a questioning glance. She put aside the strings, stepped out on the stage with one of the blanks, and strutted about, aping the gestures of a fashionable gentleman. She drew an imaginary sword from its scabbard and flourished it.

"A nobleman," exclaimed Anne, instantly suspecting his identity. Fingering the contours of her face, she asked Michou to describe him. With a few rapid strokes on her pad she created a bare sketch of a young man. "Derennes!" Anne shouted.

The two women picked up the marionettes. A trembling "Pressigny" staggered about the room. At center stage, "Derennes" shook his fist at "Pressigny." Finally, "Derennes" led "Pressigny" and the unknown servants from the room, leaving the hidden "Michou" alone in the dark. At this point, Michou threw up her hands. Anne understood the story had become too complicated for the marionettes.

She leaned against the stage, gathering her thoughts. The theater in the Palais-Royal was probably empty, and the back door might be open for tradesmen and workers. A short walk with Michou confirmed her hunch. Inside the theater, two men were noisily repairing benches on the ground floor. The winning smile she gave them was scarcely necessary. To be sure, she could look around. They hardly interrupted their conversation.

Once out of sight of the workers, Michou continued her story. With gestures and sketch pad she revealed she had sneaked out of the fitting room and up the backstage stairway, hoping to find Monsieur Dubois in the office and bring him down to the stricken actress. At the level of the second balcony, she had passed through a large open storage area. Between rows of curtains hanging above the stage, she could see over to the hallway on the opposite side of the theater. The office was open and nearly in full view. Pressigny was sitting slumped behind Monsieur Dubois dictating to him. Derennes was nowhere in sight. After Dubois had written something, Pressigny had ordered him from the office. Two men in the hallway hit Dubois from behind, carried him back into the office, and threw him out a window. Meanwhile, Pressigny had stumbled away.

Acting out the terror she had felt, Michou seized Anne by the shoulders, made her scrunch down. Toward the end of her narrative, she began to shiver; soon she was shaking uncontrollably. Anne held her by the shoulders, rocking and stroking her until calm returned. They dusted themselves off and were about to leave, when Anne heard a new voice downstairs. Peering over the edge of the balcony, she saw François Noir talking to the workers.

"Is the theater empty?" Noir asked.

"Just us," replied a worker, "and a couple of women looking around."

"Are they still here?"

"Don't know," replied the worker. "They may have left."

Anne turned and alerted Michou. The storage area was dark. Drapes drawn over the windows admitted only slivers of light. The two women crept silently into a jumble of coiled ropes, ladders, and stage furniture. Keeping the office still in view, they hid behind a bench. Noir climbed the stairs to the office and stopped in front of the door. He leaned over the edge of the balcony, scanning the area below. Light cast up from the ground floor windows illuminated his face.

Anne felt Michou violently squeeze her hand. In the darkness, she could sense the deaf woman's terror. She nodded yes to Anne's hand on her head: François Noir was one of the two men who had killed her father. Anne felt a rush of sadness but strangely no anger toward Noir, as if he were merely a mindless instrument of Antoine's death. She sensed Michou staring at the man, capturing his sharp features for the marionette's face she would later paint.

Noir unlocked the office door, looked around the room, and left, locking the door behind him. Then, to Anne's dismay, instead of returning as he had come, he walked through the balcony into the storage area and toward the bench that hid the two women. Fortunately, he seemed preoccupied with the office, the stairways, and other lighted areas, and his eyes were unused to the darkness.

He sat on the bench within a few feet of their hiding place. Anne was sure he would hear them breathing, were it not for the workers downstairs roiling the air with their hammering and chatter. Finally, he got up and left. When Anne thought he was gone, she tugged at Michou's sleeve. They stole out of the palace, glancing nervously left and right.

∞∞∞

Eyes cast down, scratching his cheek, François Noir wondered about the two women in the theater. If they had hidden from him, he calculated, they were likely to emerge soon. He hurried to a shaded spot behind a column of the arcade on the east side of the mall.

He felt pleased with himself when he saw them. A strange pair. One quite tall, the other very small, both clothed as commoners in plain grey dresses. He left his hiding place and followed them. When they entered the Tatar Puppet Theater, he hid opposite the entrance and waited. They emerged in a short while, the little one carrying a sketch pad in one hand and a plain wooden marionette in the other.

He stared at the tall one. "Cartier. The English actress. Troublesome slut!" he muttered to himself. He followed the women west on Rue Saint-Honoré to Place Vendôme, where they turned into a narrow passageway behind the residence of Colonel Paul de Saint-Martin.

Noir walked slowly away, wondering why they had hidden from him. What business did they have with a provost of the Royal Highway Patrol? And why did they enter through the back way? He scowled. Could the little one have seen something she shouldn't? Possibly. She used to work for Laplante. The tall one came to Paris later. He quickened his steps toward Café Marcel.

⧞⧞⧞

Passing through the garden with Michou, Anne saw Paul in the salon rising to meet them. He must have just returned from Chateau Debussy. Her heart skipped a beat. "He will not be pleased," she mumbled to Michou, who glanced at her quizzically.

He opened the door for them, his face lined with concern. When she told him where they had gone, his expression quickly changed to anger. With a stiff but courteous gesture, he sent Michou to her room.

Then, eyes flashing, he turned to Anne.

As she approached him, she lowered her eyes slightly, not wishing to provoke him further.

He led her into his office and shut the door. Unsmiling, arms crossed over his chest, he stood behind his desk. "I have insisted Michou live in my home because she may be in danger," he exclaimed, "but you took her to the scene of a crime whose perpetrators are still loose in this city!" He paused, glaring at her. "If it were necessary to expose Michou to danger, I'd have sent an escort of police."

"They would have scared off François Noir, and Michou would not have identified my father's killer." Anne felt a swell of impertinence.

"Your father's killer?"

As Anne described what had happened in the theater, the look in Paul's eyes softened. An amused expression came over his face. He breathed a sigh that released the last of his wrath. "Surely angels must be watching over you two," he finally remarked. "Did Michou get a good look at him? You said the balcony was so dark that he couldn't see you."

She ventured a tentative smile. "Light coming up from the ground floor shone on his face. Michou is drawing his features right now and will paint them on one of the blank marionettes tomorrow." She removed her bonnet and sat down, carefully smoothing the folds of her skirt.

Paul leaned forward, tapping on his desk. "From Michou we've learned that Noir killed Antoine, but it must have been Derennes' idea. Pressigny was too badly shocked to come up with the plan for a scapegoat."

"And too weak to carry it out," Anne interjected.

Paul hurried on. "After killing Lélia, Pressigny called in a servant, presumably Noir, to fetch Derennes from the variety theater."

Anne looked askance. "Why Derennes? He and Pressigny were enemies, even though they worked together."

Paul shrugged. "Perhaps Noir was supposed to find someone else. But Derennes was the one who came. He thought of how to shift the blame for Laplante's death to Antoine. He knew they quarreled about her affairs with other men. He knew about the confession in *The Cuckolded Clown*. Probably wrote it. He put the pieces together. Correct so far?"

"Agreed. Carry on."

"Derennes instructed Noir and Gros to lay in wait for Antoine, then sent Pressigny up to the office to dictate a suicide note, slightly different from the version in the play. When Antoine left the office, Noir and Gros killed him. Derennes had already gone back to the theater...."

Anne interrupted him. "And reported to whom?" The truth leapt at her. A fifth person might have been involved, a man who sent Derennes in the first place. She felt giddy and gasped for breath.

Paul raised an eyebrow. "Something wrong, Anne?"

"I've suddenly realized something." She leaned forward, her clasped hands almost touching his. "Robert LeCourt was at the variety theater that evening, five minutes away from Lélia's dead body. Noir would have gone directly to him."

"That's likely. Noir worked for him."

"And even if Derennes were contacted first, he would not slip away without telling LeCourt what had happened. Derennes hated Pressigny and would want him to look bad in LeCourt's eyes."

Paul sat up and stroked his chin. The room grew unnaturally quiet. "Yes, I see it now. Derennes conceived the plot to scapegoat Antoine, and LeCourt told him to carry it out."

Anne sighed. "How shall we prove it? Derennes has disappeared. LeCourt is above suspicion."

Hands clasped tightly behind her back, eyes closed, Anne stood at the window of Paul's office overlooking the courtyard. It was early Saturday morning, and the aroma of Georges' coffee filled the room. She hardly noticed. Yesterday's experience in the palace theater with Michou had disturbed her sleep. Horrid bizarre images from her dreams still wracked her mind. Noir and Gros in harlequin costume throwing her father out a window. Simon Derennes urging them on, flourishing a white hot poker. Chevalier de Pressigny cowering nearby, blood dripping from his hand.

A shout broke the spell. Anne looked out. The gatekeeper opened for a cart entering the courtyard. In its wake tradesmen scurried in with their wares. The cook and a scullery maid returned from the market, bending under baskets of fruits and vegetables. A pair of urchins began to sweep the cobblestones in front of the stables. Falling in with the common beat of life, Anne raised her eyes to a clear blue sky and ran both hands back and forth through her hair.

She returned to the table and sat opposite Georges. He slouched in his chair, staring glumly into his coffee. She sensed the investigation wasn't going well. It was four days since Debussy's death and the theft of his jewels. No arrests yet.

The Paris police had searched in vain for suspects among the professional thieves and fences of the city. Mauvert and three other inspecteurs had checked everyone involved in the case but found no solid evidence, no sign of the jewels. Anne could imagine who was the most frustrated of all. Inspecteur Mauvert. With every passing day, it seemed more likely the jewels had either left the country or were securely hidden. And there would be no commission.

"Does the colonel have some news?" she asked, trying to break the heavy silence in the room.

Georges could not be drawn out. "I'd better let him speak for himself." He shrugged, his eyes evading Anne's. "I hear him coming."

The door opened and the colonel walked in, a scowl on his face. "I saw the lieutenant-general last night," he said, handing his sword to a servant. He went to his desk and brooded over its smooth brown surface for a few moments.

Then he looked up at Georges and Anne. "DeCrosne called me to his home. Rebuked me for disobeying instructions." He paused, struggling with his feelings. "Mauvert got to the lieutenant-general before me. He's still very much in charge of the Laplante case. DeCrosne has ordered him here this morning to evaluate the new evidence we've gathered."

Anne and Georges looked at him aghast. He nodded grimly, then glanced at Anne. "If he thinks it's worthless or irrelevant to the Debussy case, your father's vindication will have to wait." He mocked the lieutenant-general. "First things first. The police cannot do everything at once."

Glancing out the window, he smiled ironically. "Speak of the devil! Mauvert's just crossed the courtyard. Talking to himself. Appears to be in a vile mood."

Steps sounded in the hallway. The inspecteur entered the room. Pausing for a moment, he glared at Anne, then joined the colonel at the table. Visibly annoyed, he turned to Saint-Martin. "Why's the actress here? I came to find out what *you* have learned in the Laplante case."

Paul bristled. "I've invited Miss Cartier." When everyone was seated, he gestured for her to begin.

Before she could speak, the inspecteur pushed back his chair and began to rise from the table. "I don't have time to listen to this woman," he spluttered in exasperation.

Anne stared at him, trying vainly to catch his eye. Her temper threatened to fly out of control. She cursed under her breath. Georges gave her a sharp kick under the table. She read a mixture of amusement and warning in his eyes and choked back her anger. He raised his hand, masking the wry twist of his mouth.

The colonel rose to his feet, back rigid, lips drawn tight. "Sit down, inspecteur." The words had a sharp, icy edge. "Miss Cartier has discovered evidence concerning Pressigny that escaped you a year ago. You shall hear it from her now!"

A dead silence came over the room. Anne glanced at Georges. He stared at the wall, stone-faced. The inspecteur slid slowly into his chair, lips pinched, eyes mere slits.

"Tell us what you've found, Miss Cartier." Paul gave Anne a quick, encouraging smile and sat down.

Her heart pounded, her voice quivered slightly as she started to speak, but she quickly got a grip on herself. She described how Michou had witnessed Pressigny murdering the actress Laplante and shifting the blame to Dubois. At least part of Michou's story, she continued, was confirmed by the stable-master's wife, who had treated the young man's wounded hand. She concluded with Michou's observation of Noir and Gros killing Dubois.

At the beginning of Anne's narration, the inspecteur had stared sullenly down at the table. When she mentioned Michou, he looked up, his eyes widening. As Anne related the discovery of Laplante's stiletto, he sat on the edge of his chair, fully attentive if skeptical. When she described her stepfather's death, he became visibly disturbed.

After she sat down, he remained silent for a moment, then cleared his throat. His thin lips curled with disdain. "The testimony of an illiterate deaf female has as much weight as the paper I've just scrawled on." He let fall a sheet he had picked up from the table. "The story of the stiletto, however, places Pressigny at the scene of the crime, a coincidence he would find difficult to explain." Mauvert leaned forward, looked directly at Saint-Martin, and spoke each word distinctly, "Nonetheless, Colonel, that case is closed. You *dare* not poke into it." He straightened up, smiling sardonically. "And, what is more to the point, the evidence you have just presented is irrelevant to the murder and theft at Chateau Debussy."

He sat back, appearing to relish a checkmate. Then, to Anne's surprise, Paul calmly rose. "A carriage is outside. We shall adjourn to the Camp of the Tatars."

⊗∞⊗∞⊗

From behind the stage of the Tatar Puppet Theater, Anne observed Mauvert's irritation with keen satisfaction. Paul had seated him in the front row. "This is incredible," the inspecteur muttered, loudly enough for everyone to hear, as he looked about the dark shabby interior. On a bench behind him sat a pair of strangers. Anne soon recognized the elderly priest in a plain, black soutane, engaged in lively, wordless conversation with a young man.

Paul walked up the aisle, stopped in front of Mauvert, and nodded toward the visitors. "Monsieur l'Inspecteur, may I present Abbé de l'Épée, Director of the Institute for the Deaf and Mute, and André, one of his assistants."

Taking a seat to the left of the inspecteur, the colonel remarked, "You've surely heard of the abbé."

Mauvert gave the priest a surly glance. "Why should I?"

Paul appeared surprised, then looked over his shoulder at the cleric and bowed with respect. "He's a well-known authority on sign language. Emperor Joseph, the Queen's brother, admires the Institute and has created a similar one in Vienna."

The inspecteur shrugged his disinterest.

At a word from the colonel, Georges lit the stage lights. A few minutes later, Anne, Michou, and their companions at the puppet theater presented a dramatic version of the tragic fate of Lélia Laplante and Antoine Dubois. Through a peephole in the backdrop Anne could see Mauvert's interest growing. He leaned forward. His mouth opened slightly. Their puppetry had indeed improved with practice.

When the performance had ended and the cast had taken their bows, Abbé de l'Épée sat at Mauvert's right side and spoke softly. "For two months Mademoiselle Cartier, my assistant, and I have been working with Michou. We needed to gain her confidence, for she had been mistreated in the past and had become very shy. She had also suffered severe shock at the death of the actress. I'm not surprised she appeared incapable of testifying a year ago. She is well now, making rapid progress in reading and signing." The priest's voice grew firm and clear. "I can assure you, and if need be, Lieutenant-General DeCrosne, she is a fully competent witness."

Mauvert appeared stunned, his face frozen.

Paul thanked the priest, who then left the theater with his assistant. "Inspecteur, that was the first step—learning the truth about the Laplante case." He gestured to the troupe on the stage, who returned to their marionettes and acted out Michou's observing Pressigny and Laplante with the stolen jasper bowl.

"Do you now see the connection between the bowl and the Chanavas jewels?"

From the stage, Anne looked down at the inspecteur. He appeared to be groping for an answer. Injured pride and rankling resentment struggled plainly on his face. Paul replied for him. "Pressigny's killing of Lélia Laplante, together with his illegal possession of the jasper bowl, strongly suggest he was party to a series of crimes in the Paris region that may include the theft of the Chanavas jewels."

He paced slowly before the stage, hands clasped behind his back. "In these thefts, I see a similar mode of operation. Typically, while visiting a country estate, Pressigny and Laplante, or Pressigny alone, scouted the premises on behalf of a team of professional thieves." He stopped in front of the inspecteur and looked down at him.

Mauvert's mouth worked nervously. "Granted, there's probably enough evidence to charge Pressigny with homicide, but I doubt the lieutenant-general would give permission yet to arrest him." As he spoke, he regained his self-assurance and turned obstinate. "None of this proves he killed Comte Debussy or stole the jewels."

"We don't need proof at this point," countered the colonel, "only reasonable grounds to believe the murders of Laplante and Debussy are connected. I want to proceed with this investigation without having one arm tied behind my back." He locked eyes with Mauvert. "You have found no clues in Paris. The culprits have to come from Chateau Debussy and somehow include the Chevalier de Pressigny."

The inspecteur's face convulsed, as if from inner torment. He slowly exhaled. "Yes, we will need to investigate the affairs of Chevalier de Pressigny."

"And Monsieur LeCourt!" added the colonel, quick as a tiger pouncing on its prey. "François Noir and Jacques Gros, who killed Antoine Dubois, are LeCourt's men. They also work at Chateau Debussy. We must look very closely at LeCourt."

With growing fascination, Anne observed this duel between Paul and the inspecteur. She was expecting Mauvert to deny LeCourt was involved. But the force of his reaction surprised her.

Livid with anger, he sputtered incoherently for a few moments, glaring at Saint-Martin. "You are out of your mind," he managed to say. "LeCourt is a distinguished gentleman with nothing to gain from crime and little reason to know what his servants do on their own." He stood up to leave. His voice grew menacing. "Furthermore, he has powerful friends in the government. You should approach him with great care."

A sign from the colonel indicated the meeting was over. "Inspecteur, remember this, I intend to see justice done, regardless how high I must go to find the guilty ones."

Mauvert stalked out, grim-faced, without saying a word.

Anne climbed down from the stage, relieved that the two men had not come to blows. But the inspecteur had left in such an ugly temper, she feared he might block any further investigation into her father's case. Paul walked up and down the aisle, breathing heavily, his eyes dark with barely contained fury. He beckoned his adjutant, and they joined her in front of the stage.

"Georges, put a close watch on LeCourt," he said harshly, his arms akimbo. "I know he can afford to buy a shop full of jewels, but he can't buy the Chanavas. Maybe that's what he wants! That he's rich may even be reason to suspect him. Can a financier be an honest man?"

He fell into a heavy silence. Then, as if exorcising his anger, he breathed deeply in and out, then let his arms fall. Anne smiled at him sideways. The tension broke. He exchanged glances with her and Georges, and all three leaned back against the stage.

She turned to Paul, a question forming piecemeal in her mind. "Do you suppose the inspecteur expects LeCourt to pay him for protection?"

"I wouldn't be surprised. Money's never far from Mauvert's mind," he replied. "And, Robert LeCourt neglects no one, ever so low, who can serve his purpose. But he counts mainly on Calonne, the comptroller-general of finance, and on rich investors with a personal interest in the royal debt. They need him to refinance loans Dutch bankers gave the king for the war in America. Otherwise, the government will go bankrupt."

Anne shook her head in disbelief. "How can one man become so important?"

"In a crisis, even reasonable men like Calonne will grasp at straws," Paul insisted. "For good measure, through Masonic connections, LeCourt has won favor with the Duc d'Orléans."

"I grant he's mighty," Anne remarked. "But he walks on a slippery slope." She signed to Michou waiting patiently on the stage. It was time to go. Paul and Georges started for the door.

At that moment a trooper burst into the theater, almost running into the colonel. "They're gone!"

"Who?" demanded Saint-Martin.

"Claire de Pressigny and her friend, the gardener." When an early morning fog had lifted, Monsieur Soucie had noticed Cavour's absence from the garden. In the cottage he and Claire had arranged sacks of straw under the blankets on their bed.

While Saint-Martin wrote instructions for the trooper, Georges and Anne walked to the door, followed by Michou. "The two fugitives have as good as confessed," said Georges. "I'll bet they are trying to escape with the treasure."

"They may have found a hiding place in Paris," Anne suggested.

"The inspecteur's agents will watch every person they're likely to contact," Georges replied. "If they're in the city, they'll get caught."

Anne looked askance. Paris was like a gigantic rabbit warren, offering a safe haven to the fugitives. She also felt uneasy with the idea that their flight proved they had committed the crimes. Rather, they might have feared they would be tortured to confess what they hadn't committed. If they had stolen the treasure, why hadn't they fled immediately? Perhaps they were mere accomplices who thought, at first, they could escape suspicion, then fled in panic.

Finished with the trooper, the colonel rejoined Georges and Anne at the door.

"They must have known Mauvert was going to bring them in for questioning," Georges said. "A pity they slipped through our fingers."

Paul stood silent for a moment, then followed them out the door. "But they're Mauvert's prime suspects, not ours. Let him find them."

Chapter 28

Blind Justice

A knock on the door awoke Anne from deep sleep. For a moment she didn't know where she was. She rubbed her eyes, then heard birds chirping. No street noise. Must be the colonel's garden apartment. She pushed open the shutters. The rose beds were still shadowed. It was shortly after sunrise, a cloudy morning, and warm already. She padded to the door to find an embarrassed servant with a note. "Sorry to disturb you, Mademoiselle. The messenger insisted I give this to you immediately." Anne thanked her with a smile and withdrew to read.

"Urgent!!" Georges had scrawled. *"Come to Café Marcel in disguise. I need someone I can trust."*

An hour later, Anne approached the café in the brown smock and breeches of a young artisan, her complexion coarsened and darkened with powder, her hair pinned up and tucked under a cap. In the crowded serving room, she caught sight of Georges at a table sipping coffee. She hadn't seen him in almost a week. He had become LeCourt's shadow.

"What's going on?" Anne asked, sliding into a chair.

"Workmen found Simon Derennes in an abandoned cellar near the Palais-Royal!" Georges replied, shifting toward her. "Thought you'd want to know."

"Dead?"

He nodded. "About a month ago. A thick, heavy door jammed, trapping him inside. Nobody could hear him." He put on a wry face. "*Looks* like he went down there to bury a corpse. God knows why. The police are scratching their heads. So far, they're calling it a suspicious accident."

Anne was stunned. An accident? Never! The Amateurs had hidden the man there for seven weeks. Starved him to death. "LeCourt's mixed up in this," she said in a low voice, recalling what she had overheard on the café's balcony. "The corpse is the one we saw in the pit, isn't it?"

"Krishna's missing daughter, Nalini, as we suspected. He identified her from scraps of clothing and her ring."

A tide of sadness swept over Anne. Since wearing the girl's costume, she had hoped desperately that the corpse might not be Nalini after all. She drew little solace from LeCourt's cruel punishment of Derennes.

Georges' brow creased with concern. "I sense a crisis among the Amateurs. LeCourt's upstairs with Krishna. Trying to calm him down, I suppose. The man was pale with rage!"

"Something dreadful is going to happen." Anne's throat tightened. "Who's next? Pressigny, Michou, me?"

"That's what I'm trying to find out. I want these men followed when they leave." A clock on the wall struck nine. "It can't last much longer." Georges turned to Anne. "You follow LeCourt. He'll probably return to his apartment on Rue Goncourt, but I can't be certain and I still need to keep track of him."

"That should be easy."

"Be home before dark at the latest, or the colonel will be worried."

"Yes, Sir, I understand." She regretted instantly the sarcasm in her voice. There could be danger ahead and Georges was concerned for her.

A few minutes later LeCourt descended, elegant and collected as usual. He picked up a cognac at the bar and sat down to read a newspaper. Probably the Dutch one, Anne guessed.

Krishna came down a minute later, looking neither left nor right, his jaw locked in a fierce scowl. Anne felt sure he was bent on revenge, convinced someone besides Derennes had been involved in Nalini's death. He also ordered cognac and sat down alone, staring inwardly at some dark and bloody vision, clutching his glass as if he would crush it. When he left the café, Georges got up, glanced at Anne, and followed him.

LeCourt put the newspaper to one side, called for pen, ink, and paper. After writing for a while, he picked up the newspaper again, read it while sipping his cognac. A few minutes later, François Noir walked into the café and sat at a corner table with a glass of wine. His eyes casually swept the room. When LeCourt returned his paper to the rack, Noir retrieved it.

Meanwhile, Anne held Noir firmly in her gaze, committing to memory the shape of his body, the lines of his face. He gulped the remainder of his drink, put the newspaper back in the rack, then walked to the door.

Anne found herself in a quandary. What would Georges want her to do? Wait for LeCourt, who was most likely going to return to his apartment? Or, follow Noir, who had just received a secret message? In an instant she had decided. She got up, took a deep breath, and followed him out of the café into the busy street.

∞∞∞

Under a hot midday sun, thousands of people gathered around a raised platform in the large open space of Place de Grève. François Noir slipped behind the crowd, climbed up on a wall, and looked out over the sea of bobbing heads. Anne edged into the crowd where she could watch him without being noticed. His features, in contrast to the excited faces near him, seemed chiseled from stone.

Weaving through congested streets, she had followed him from Café Marcel to the right bank of the Seine. His gait and bearing told her he had served many years in the army. He seemed rather near-sighted and about forty years old, but he was lean and fit. At a shop in the Palais-Royal he had bought an apple, then continued eastward to the Place de Grève.

A sudden roar from the crowd drew Anne's eyes away from Noir. Everyone turned toward the street along the river.

"Here she comes," cried a large, rough-faced woman, giving off a strong stench of fish. She was standing on a crate, craning her thick neck.

Anne felt the crowd give way to the harsh commands of uniformed men. She caught a glimpse of a cart entering Place de Grève. It came close enough for her to see a stocky young peasant woman seated with her arms tied behind her back and her hair cropped short. She was wearing a plain brown robe girdled at her waist. Her mouth was half-open, sucking in air. She stared straight ahead at the platform, her eyes wide with terror.

A shiver of horror ran through Anne's body. The spectacle was going to be an execution!

"What's she done?" asked a thin, older woman standing on the cobblestones next to the fishmonger.

"Killed her baby," replied the woman on the crate, gingerly shifting position as the cart neared the platform. "She was a kitchen maid in the household of a judge. Riche is his name. She had a baby, claimed the judge's son was the father, and demanded money."

The older woman and several by-standers clucked their disapproval.

"The mistress of the house, she's a devout lady," continued the large woman, clasping her fingers together and rolling her eyes heavenward. "She had the servants thrash the girl, then ordered her and her bastard thrown into the street."

The fishmonger looked around at the men and women hanging on her words. She lowered her voice to a loud whisper. "Can you imagine, the slut snuck back into the house with the baby, took a knife from the kitchen, cut the baby's throat, and put the bloody body on the dining room table!" She paused for a moment to share the dreadful image with her audience. Their mouths were agape. "The police caught her as she was about to jump into the river." The fishmonger chuckled, "It didn't take the court long to decide that one."

The woman's words echoed in Anne's ears. A plausible tale, she thought, embroidered by the teller. One of the grooms might have fathered the baby. The young woman's greed might have led her to accuse the judge's son in order to extort money from the family. But Anne withheld judgment. What the girl claimed had the ring of truth. Scullery maids were easy prey for men in noble households.

Thinking of the young woman in the cart made Anne shudder. She too had once ridden past gaping faces on her way to the scaffold. Judge Hammer's hawk-face flashed before her eyes. She banished him from her mind, then glanced at the platform the young woman had mounted. Whatever the provocation, she must have been deranged to have killed her baby.

"What's happening now?" asked the thin, older woman.

"She's tied to the post. A priest is standing in front of her holding up a crucifix." The fishmonger's voice rose a step. "A man in black is pulling a hood over her head, tying it around her neck." A low roar began to swell out of thousands of throats. "He's lighted the faggots...."

Anne could bear no more. She brought her fingers to her ears and turned away from the two women. She found herself staring at Noir. Slouched upon the wall, he was eating his apple as if watching the broiling of meat on a spit in the market. The roar reached a crescendo, then gradually dropped into frenzied babble. Anne sensed people around her shifting from side to side, craning for a glimpse of the flames.

Fantastic figures began to swim before her eyes. They came together in an eerie image of Antoine Dubois, his stiff, dead body tied to a post on the platform, surrounded by huge, leaping tongues of fire. Faint and queasy, Anne staggered out of the crowd into a deeply recessed doorway. She leaned against a wall, her breathing labored.

When she recovered, she saw Noir was on the move again. Apparently sated with the spectacle, he had left his perch and was pushing through the milling crowd toward the river. As he approached, Anne retreated to the back of the doorway and hid in the shadows.

A few moments later she slipped out, tugged her cap down, and followed him across the bridge to the left bank, then south on Rue Saint-Jacques, as if bound to him by an invisible cord.

⚮⚮⚮

At Montsouris, a desolate area just south of the city, Anne began to feel uneasy. She might lose sight of her prey. Noir sometimes disappeared in the lengthening shadows cast by the lowering sun. He led her through small clusters of hovels surrounded by ill-kept gardens in the hollows of the uneven, bushy terrain. The men, women, and children she saw there were wearing rags. Many were deformed.

Giant windmills stood on distant hills like sentinels. In front of her, the land rose to the warren of limestone quarries that had been dug inside the rocky hillside for centuries and later abandoned. She had heard the quarries sheltered smugglers and criminals and, recently, bones from the city's crowded cemeteries.

She glimpsed beggars returning for the evening from their roosts in the city. They joined other, sinister-looking men in small groups around fires, their low murmuring punctuated by bursts of harsh laughter or angry, drunken shouts. She let herself imagine the schemes being laid there, even murder, and the vile tricks and deceit being shared and celebrated. Did the evil, almost palpable here, differ much from what was being plotted or applauded in the drawing rooms of country manors and town houses only a few miles away? Pressigny and the Société des Amateurs came to her mind.

She was jarred from her moralizing by the sudden realization that her man had vanished. He had climbed up a narrow path into a dense grove of stunted trees. Cautiously, she made her way through the grove to a small clearing at the base of a steep limestone bluff. Noir was nowhere in sight.

To the right, a narrow wagon road skirted the bluff, then cut through another grove in the direction of the highway to Paris. In front of her, a rough stone wall closed off the entrance to an abandoned underground quarry. Shepherds and their flocks must have sought shelter there years ago. Someone was still using it, she reckoned. Its large wooden door was in good condition, and the grass in front of it was worn down. A small high window was the only other opening.

She paused at the edge of the clearing. Had Noir taken the road to the right, or had he entered the shelter? She decided to watch the entrance. For what seemed like an hour, she sat there concealed among the trees but saw no one come or go. Meanwhile, the grove grew dark and menacing. Perhaps, she thought, it would be best to give up the chase and return to the city while she still felt safe.

An urge to check the shelter, however, drew her forward. Cautiously, she edged out of the woods and listened. The delicate rustling of leaves mixed with faint sounds from the beggars in the distance. She crept slowly around the clearing to the edge of the bluff and inched her way up to the wall. Quietly, she tried to open the door. It was locked. She glanced up at the small window. Unglazed, but perhaps wide enough for a thin person to squeeze through.

She stepped back, debating her next move. Without warning, a foul-smelling woolen hood fell over her head and jerked tight around her neck. Powerful hands grasped her arms, bent them up behind her back, tied them together, and pushed, half-carried her forward. A heavy key turned in the lock. The door groaned open, then closed behind her.

She shuffled thirty or forty paces through a strong scent of hay and manure. The powerful man halted, renewed his grip on her arms. She winced with pain. He knocked, another door opened. She was shoved into a room, its air heavy with the odor of burning lamp oil.

"Look at what I caught outside," said her captor in a low, coarse voice, tinged with alarm.

The cord was loosened on her neck and the hood pulled off. The ropes on her arms were roughly untied. She found herself standing in the middle of a small, square chamber cut out of the rock. The ceiling was low. The air was musty and damp. A lamp flickered on a plain table between a pair of wooden stools.

Two men were glaring at her. The one who had surprised and overcome her was Jacques Gros—short, thickset, with virtually no neck and a small bald head. At first glance, Anne thought he appeared childish or simple-minded, but this impression quickly changed as she studied his mean, squinting eyes.

The other man was François Noir—taller, older, and slightly stooped. He turned to his companion. "Hold him, Jacques, while I look through his coat."

He found her wallet. "Joseph Beaufort, artisan, Rouen," he said, holding up the false residence card Georges had given her. "What are you doing here?" he asked sharply. "Why did you follow me?"

Lowering her voice, she began to stammer with a heavy Norman accent, "I'm new in Paris. Heard I could make some money if I ran into the right people in Montsouris."

"You've got to do better than that," growled Noir. "Carrying any weapons?"

While the powerful man held her, Noir patted her down. A puzzled expression spread across his face. He pulled off her cap and brought the lamp up close. His eyes brightened.

"I know you!"

He held her jaw with one hand, stared into her eyes, then slowly turned her head left and right.

"The tall bitch from the Camp of the Tatars. With the little deaf woman." His eyes hardened with menace. "Are you working for the police?"

She regarded him coolly and said nothing.

He raised his arm to strike her but changed his mind. He stepped back.

A thought raced through Anne's mind. Break loose. Run for safety. But the heavy man was between her and the first of two doors. Noir would quickly help him. She'd have to bluff her way out.

The older man nodded to Gros, who came up quickly, seized her right arm, and twisted it behind her back again. Her body arched with the pain, as he pushed her toward a door. Noir opened it and Gros shoved her in.

This was a larger, low rectangular chamber warmed by a glowing brazier and lighted by oil lamps. Cloaks, hats, and other clothing hung on pegs on the right wall. Beneath them were racks of shoes—some plain, some fancy—and riding boots. Cabinets and chests of drawers lined the left wall. Near them were stacks of wig boxes. On the wall facing her, a map of Paris hung next to a full-length mirror. A table with wooden chairs stood in the middle of the room in front of the map.

"I'll bet she's a police ferret," said Noir, as he moved slowly around the intruder.

"Let's make her talk," said his heavy companion grinning. Anne stiffened as he lurched eagerly toward her.

"We haven't time for that." Noir had sat down at the table and was observing her intently. He turned to his companion.

"Take her downstairs while I get the horses ready. We'll deal with her when our work is done. That's something to look forward to." With a wave and a crooked smile, he left the chamber.

Gros pushed her roughly around the table toward the mirror. With a touch he released a latch hidden in the wall, and the mirror swung open. They passed through a small room that served as an armory. A wall rack held a half-dozen muskets. Several pistols rested on a gun case; sabres, rapiers, and daggers hung on another wall.

The heavy man lit a torch, then opened a sturdy wooden door and gestured impatiently to her. "Go ahead of me."

By the flickering light of his torch, she could see a steep flight of narrow steps descending into the darkness. She walked down side-wise, plotting a desperate strategy, with each step feeling she had less to lose. As she neared a small landing, she let her left foot miss a step. She fell too fast for Gros to catch her. Down three steps she tumbled, her head grazing the wall. Her body hit the landing with a painful thud and crumbled against the left-side wall. Bruised, dazed, she was alert enough to close her eyes when Gros bent over her. His torch scorched her cheek.

"Damn!" exclaimed the man. "She's a bloody mess." He began to climb over her. "I'll have to haul her the rest of the way down!" While he was still moving forward, she suddenly coiled her body like a spring and thrust her legs upwards, striking him on the left hip. The blow caught him off-balance. With a short, squawking cry and arms flailing, he dove off the landing into the black hole of the stairwell.

On her knees now, Anne listened as his heavy body struck the steps. The sharp sound of splintering bone echoed up the shaft. Thud followed thud until he crashed on the floor of the chamber below. Holding up the torch he had dropped, Anne peered over the edge of the landing. An inert, grotesque figure lay barely visible in the dim light. Panting and trembling, she staggered to her feet. For a moment she thought gratefully of her stepfather. He'd taught her how to fall, to spin a large ball with her feet while on her back, to keep her nerve when performing the dangerous tricks of an acrobat.

Once upstairs, she latched and barred the door to the stairway. At the gun case, she examined the pistols, picked out two that were loaded, and stuck them in her belt. Entering the main room, she glanced about quickly, then closed the door.

In the mirror she saw blood running down her forehead from a ragged scrape at the hairline. Before she could wipe it away, she heard someone in the outer room. She turned around as the door was pushed open. Noir had taken a few steps into the room before he realized she was there.

"Move to the center of the room," she said, aiming a pistol at him. "I know how to use it." Her legs spread for balance, she held the weapon in a two-handed grip. He hesitated. She cocked the pistol, surprised by a growing urge to kill him. He stepped forward, his eyes glancing toward the mirror-door to the armory. "Your thick-necked friend isn't going to help you," she said grimly.

"That ring!" She pointed with the pistol. "Take it off your finger, put it on the table, and step back." She had noticed the simple gold band while he was questioning her. He did as he was told. She took it up and glanced at it, watching him like a hawk.

"Where'd you get it?"

"Bought it from a dealer in the Palais-Royal. Montpensier arcade."

"That's my father's wedding ring," she said in a low voice. "You didn't notice the inscription on the band or take the trouble to file it off."

He seemed surprised. "I don't know what you're talking about."

A practiced liar, Anne thought. But she noticed a glint of anxiety in his eyes. "I'll tell you," she said scornfully. "Someone saw you and Jacques Gros kill my father. But you didn't do it on your own. Pressigny was in shock, so Derennes thought up the confession and the rest of the plan." She paused, holding his eye. "I want you to tell me, did Derennes give the order to kill my father, or did someone else?"

His eyes downcast, Noir appeared to weigh his alternatives. Anne began to feel dizzy. The pistol grew heavier in her hands. He would stall until she collapsed. She couldn't afford to wait.

"All right, you win," he said, lifting his hands palms up in a gesture of capitulation. "I'll tell you."

She felt herself relaxing her grip. The gun wavered.

Suddenly, he lunged at her. Energy seemed to surge through his body and brought color to his face. For a moment, he looked twenty years younger.

Anne pulled the trigger at six paces. The shot entered his left eye, the top of his head seemed to explode. His body arched, then fell back sprawling.

Still holding the pistol with both hands, Anne stood stunned for several seconds, its report hammering in her head. The acrid stench of the powder stung her nostrils. Her eyes smarted. She choked. As the sound ebbed away, so did the nervous tension that had kept her going. She felt panic, an urge to flee, but her legs would not move. Panting, she reached for a chair and sat down.

Her eyes turned away from the body on the floor, a dark pool spreading out from the shattered head. She stared numbly at her father's ring on the table, rubbed it, put it in her pocket. There were odd markings on the map that might make sense later. She rolled it up and put it under her arm.

Leaving the room, she noticed the dead man's coat draped over a chair. A quick search. In one of the pockets was a familiar leather wallet. She gasped. Inside was the notebook she had seen him using at Café Marcel. Should she skim it? No, not now. Her fatigue was almost overwhelming and her head had begun to throb. She tucked the wallet in her shirt and hurried out.

In the stable she found the horses Noir had prepared. Choosing the smaller of the two, a black mare, she threw the map into a saddle bag and rode down the shadowed lane to the highway. She looked up into a clear, fading blue sky. The sun's faint glow hovered on the horizon. She felt like she had climbed out of a grave.

Chapter 29

Murderous Intent

"Where's Miss Cartier?" asked Colonel Saint-Martin, walking away from an open window overlooking the courtyard. He had been watching the departure of several friends, when Georges entered the sitting room.

The adjutant shrugged his shoulders, a puzzled look on his face. "She should have been back hours ago."

"Back?" The colonel frowned. "Where's she been?"

"Helping me."

"Do what?"

"Keeping track of Monsieur LeCourt." Georges hesitated, cleared his throat, wet his lips. "She said she'd keep a safe distance and get back before dark." He stumbled on about LeCourt's meeting at Café Marcel and Krishna's distraught appearance. "I followed him to a pretty widow's wine shop on Rue Saint-Marc. He seems at home. Stayed there all day."

Saint-Martin stared speechless at his adjutant, holding back the urge to throttle him. The man looked so distressed. For the moment there was nothing to do but wait, nursing the hope that she might return at any minute.

Georges glanced at four empty wine glasses on a small table.

"Visitors," remarked Saint-Martin distractedly. "Army officers on duty at Versailles and Mr. Jefferson, the American representative in France." His eyes drifted to the window, drawn by drunken shouts from the street. "We've kept in touch since meeting in America." He waved Georges to a chair and sat facing him. "They had much to say about Monsieur LeCourt. A major player at the royal court. It's uncanny, how his talent for financial trickery wins the confidence of otherwise sensible men."

Georges started to add his jaundiced views on bankers and aristocrats. But Saint-Martin raised a hand to stop—that was enough. His mind wandered anxiously. Could LeCourt have discovered Anne following him and somehow trapped her? She could be lying helpless and in pain, left for dead anywhere in Paris.

He glared at Georges. "How on earth can we find her?" His fist struck the table. The glasses jumped; one tumbled over. He caught it before it rolled off and crashed on the floor. "I'd need the entire royal army for a proper search of the city. With little hope of success."

At that moment a distant knock echoed through the room. Saint-Martin rushed to the window. The gate to the street was thrown open. A rider crossed the courtyard on a small horse, its hooves clattering on the cobblestones. The stranger stumbled as he dismounted, rose uncertainly to his feet, then staggered to the door.

With Georges close behind, the colonel dashed down the stairs and threw open the door. The stranger was leaning against the doorpost.

"Anne?" Saint-Martin caught his breath, confused for a moment by the artisan's clothing and the pistol tucked in her belt. "Good God! What's happened?"

She responded with a weak smile, brushing aside the arm he extended toward her. Erect but unsteady, she walked stiffly into the office. Suddenly, she seemed to wilt and slumped down on a chair.

Saint-Martin gently removed her cap. Smeared with dirt and sweat, streaked with gore, her face was a ghastly mask. "Anne...." Struggling for words, he drew a kerchief from his pocket and dabbed vainly at the encrusted blood. "You've given us a terrible fright."

"Paul," she mumbled, glancing up at him. "Noir's dead... Montsouris."

"Noir? Montsouris?" The colonel drew back, glanced at Georges.

"South of the city, Sir. She must have followed him to the old quarries."

Anne tried to rise on one arm, but fell back. "His book...," she whispered, touching her chest, then passed out.

∞∞∞

Her eyes opened to a darkness broken only by the eerie flickering light of a hidden candle. A heavy silence pressed upon her like a stone weight. Sensations flashed through her body as if she were lying stretched out deep in the cave at Montsouris. She groaned and writhed. Then a hand lightly caressed her cheek, the candle drew near. Michou looked down at her, eyes full of care, and smiled broadly for a few moments. Then she vanished.

Anne realized she was in her own bed in the guest apartment, freshly bathed. When she lifted herself up, her head throbbed, but not more than she could bear. It was bandaged neatly at the hairline. Since the moment Gros had grabbed her, she had acted on impulse and instinct. There had been no time to think. Now, she sat in bed, reflecting. Scenes from the quarry rushed back. The worst was the taut face of Noir rushing at her, the shot shattering his head, and the crashing echo.

She had crossed a threshold. Killed the man who murdered Antoine. She shuddered. Her conscience was clear. She had brought him to justice, but she felt wretched and wished someone else had done it.

To her relief Michou returned with Paul. "You've been unconscious for four hours," he said softly, taking a seat beside her. "Your head wound looked worse than it was. It's clean and should soon heal." His face was lined, his jaw taut. An angry man. But he took her hand and patted it gently. "If you're feeling well enough, tell me what happened."

Michou gave her a sip of water and Anne began to recount the day's events. When she reached the confrontation with Noir and Gros in their den, Paul turned pale. At the end he kissed her hand.

"We are most grateful that you have survived and are well," he said, drawing Michou next to him at the bed. She clasped her hands fervently and bowed to Anne. At a nod from the colonel, she left the room.

Saint-Martin drew his chair close to Anne, his eyes level with hers. His voice quivered with feeling. "The thought that I might have lost you today is almost more than I can bear. You have become so dear to me. I can hardly bring myself to reproach you. Yet I must wonder when you rush rashly into great danger." He paused for a long moment, mastering himself. "Didn't you think of the pain and trouble you might cause others?" His voice fell to a whisper. "Is my concern for you of such little consequence?"

She felt a stab of remorse. She had been too single-minded in her pursuit of Noir to think of anyone else. Had Paul gone off without a word on a dangerous mission, she too would have worried and felt resentful. She drew his hand to her heart. "I'm sorry if I've seemed reckless. But, when I'm on the high wire, or in great danger, I blot out everything but the next step I must take. I promise to improve." She pulled him into a tender embrace and felt his anger subside.

"We must talk more about Noir and Montsouris," he said. "Now there's no time to lose. Georges and I will have a quick supper. Would you want something brought to you?"

"No, I feel well enough. Send in Michou to help me. I'll join you."

As Michou dressed her, Anne recalled Paul's worried look while she was telling her story. Was he anxious what others would think? Gros might have survived his fall and could claim she broke into the cave, surprised and assaulted him and his companion. There were no witnesses. LeCourt and Pressigny would stand behind him. Her imagination now raced out of control. She saw herself arrested by Mauvert. Convicted of murder by the Parlement de Paris. Executed like the young woman on the Place de Grève.

She shuddered violently. Michou, who was tying a blue ribbon around her waist, stepped back. "What's wrong?" she signed.

Looking her in the eye, Anne signed with more confidence than she felt, "A bad dream. It will pass."

∞∞∞

In the parlor, Paul and Georges were seated at table, the map spread out before them, Noir's notebook off to one side. As Anne entered, she overheard them speculating on what others might make of her violence in the quarry, assuming Gros lived to accuse her.

She pulled up a chair. "LeCourt would say I murdered Noir, and Mauvert would agree." The men fell silent, staring at her with uneasy eyes. "My motive? Revenge for the death of Antoine Dubois. They'd claim Noir had nothing to do with it."

Paul signalled to a servant for supper, then turned grimly to Anne. "They'll be too busy defending themselves to attack you. Georges and I have gone through the evidence you brought back from the quarry." He rolled up the map. "We'll study it again after we've eaten."

The meal finished and the plates cleared away, Georges laid out the map again and pointed to several marks in the vicinity of Paris. "These indicate all the places, including Chateau Debussy, where jewels have been stolen during the past three years." He turned to Anne. "You stumbled into a thieves' den."

Then Paul passed Noir's notebook across the table to her. "They appear to have hidden the stolen goods somewhere in the cave. But there's more. Open to the page I've marked."

With growing dismay Anne read LeCourt's plan for a double murder earlier in the evening. He had arranged a confrontation between Krishna and Pressigny in the empty palace theater. If they were to fail to kill one another, Noir and Gros would finish the work.

"You scuttled LeCourt's scheme," Georges broke in, shaking a finger at Anne. "As soon as we discovered what Noir and Gros were supposed to do, we ran over to the Palais-Royal with a few troopers." He shrugged his shoulders. "No sign of the supposed victims. A watchman at the Palais-Royal had noticed them entering the building earlier in the evening. First Krishna, then Pressigny. They haven't been seen since, though they could have left under cover of darkness."

"Krishna has always disliked Pressigny," said Anne. "But why would he confront him now?"

"According to one of Noir's entries," Georges replied, "Pressigny helped Derennes hide Nalini's body in the dungeon. Imagine, if someone put Derennes' diary in Krishna's hands, what would happen?"

"He might try to kill Pressigny." From the Amateurs' banquet Anne recalled the Indian's dark eyes narrowing with suspicion as he looked over the guests and their host. "But why would LeCourt want to pit the two men against one another?"

Georges reflected briefly, then measured out his words. "Suppose LeCourt was behind the theft of the Chanavas jewels, and Krishna and Pressigny had played a part and demanded a share of the profits. LeCourt might feel threatened and order Noir and Gros to silence them."

"That's plausible," said Saint-Martin, leaning back in his chair. He lowered his eyes for a few moments, lost in thought, then roused himself. "I'll ask the Paris police to bring Krishna and Pressigny in for questioning." He turned to Anne, his voice soft with care. "If you're fit, you must tell us how to find the quarry at Montsouris." He glanced at a wall clock. It was two in the morning. "No time for sleep. Georges and I and a couple of troopers must get there before anyone else finds Noir and Gros."

Anne was relieved that they would go without her. The mere thought of the quarry made her stomach roil. Edging between the two men at the table, she located Montsouris on the map, then pointed out the landmarks. Paul took her hand. "We'll find the way, Anne. If Gros is alive and conscious, we'll question him before LeCourt and his allies silence him or tell him what to say. In any case, the cave must be sealed until it can be thoroughly searched." Rising from his chair, he smiled with anticipation. "A treasure is hidden there."

∽∽∽

Anne tossed in bed, unable to sleep, though she felt tired. She threw the thin cover on the floor. No use. The warm, clammy air pressed on her naked body like a sodden blanket. In the distance, a clock struck three. She stared at the ceiling. Her mind followed Georges and Paul through the thieves' den. Noir's body in a pool of blood. Gros, crumbled at the foot of the stairs. The horror gripped her like an obsession.

She forced herself to dwell on the mystery of Krishna and Pressigny. What had really happened? According to Paul's theory, the two men came to the palace theater's office. Krishna accused the chevalier of helping Derennes bury Nalini. Pressigny denied the charge, most likely claiming Derennes' diary could not be trusted. After much heated discussion the two men left the building, each going his own way unnoticed in the darkness. The more she pondered the idea, the less plausible it seemed. Their disappearance didn't make sense.

She got out of bed, stretched, and went to the open window for air. The garden was dark and silent under the new moon. She recalled Krishna's menacing glance at Pressigny during the Amateurs' banquet. An explosive force lurked behind that inscrutable face. He would not walk away from the man he believed had helped hide his daughter's murdered body.

A whiff of fresh air floated through the window. Anne pulled on her shift and walked out into the garden, puzzling over Paul's investigation of the Amateurs' office. He had found no sign of a struggle. But Krishna might have taken his prey unawares or been himself surprised.

At the fountain she surveyed the flowers, their glorious hues lost in darkness. Only a thin light cast by the lamp at her door revealed their shapes. There was better light at the gates to Palais-Royal. Neither Krishna, or Pressigny would have risked dragging a corpse across the palace courtyard.

She drove her fist into the palm of her hand. "There's surely a victim," she exclaimed, her voice resounding in the silent garden. "He must still be in the palace!"

⣀⣀⣀

Through nearly deserted streets she hurried to the Palais-Royal, disguised again as an artisan, face grimy, cap pulled low over her bandaged forehead. She slipped through a gate open for carts hauling rubbish. At the back entrance to the palace theater the door stood ajar. She stole silently past a sleeping watchman and, borrowing one of his oil lamps, worked her way into the basement and down musty corridors until she saw the basilisk sconce. Avoiding its baleful eye, she tapped the wall and heard the hollow sound of a door. She shoved the sconce up, swung the door open on its pivot and stepped into the dungeon. Heart pounding, she lifted the trapdoor and peered into the pit.

A shadowy figure lay inert below. Chevalier de Pressigny or Krishna, she couldn't say. But either one would be too heavy to lift. She lowered herself into the pit, gagging at the stench, and brought her light close to the man's face. Chevalier de Pressigny. Bound, barely breathing. But still alive. Blood trickled from a small knife wound on his neck. He had vomited. Poisoned perhaps. She rushed back upstairs, woke the watchman, and ordered him to call a medical doctor and the Paris police. He gaped bewildered, then protested stupidly, but finally seemed to grasp her meaning.

She strode out into the courtyard, through the Camp of the Tatars, to the large fountain in the center of the garden, a cool, quiet place to plan her next move. Four or five hours ago, she calculated, Krishna had left Pressigny in the pit where Nalini had lain. What would he have done next? Return unsuspecting to LeCourt, the false patron who had prompted him to take revenge upon Pressigny? She nodded, probably.

She gazed up at the hazy moonless sky, allowing her imagination free range. Suppose Krishna had somehow come to suspect LeCourt's plot against him. He would then confront his patron. By either theory, she reasoned, one or the other man might already be dead.

Seated on the basin's rim, she listened to the splashing of water behind her, relentless like the coming dawn. A church bell struck four. She should return to her rooms in the garden pavilion to await word from Paul. He might want her to come to Montsouris. But the rhythm of the water worked hypnotically on her. She felt powerfully drawn to follow Krishna's trail. It could only lead to LeCourt's residence.

∞∞∞

Hidden in the shadow of a wall, Anne crept close to a coach parked in a circle of light at the outer gate. She could barely read the sign over the portal, *Hôtel Goncourt*. Behind her the narrow street stretched like a dark, empty tunnel to a pair of faint lights on the Boulevard. She felt relieved having avoided the city watchmen. They might have picked her up as a suspicious person.

The coach driver, a loud thickset man, appeared to know the gatekeeper. Anne inched closer, straining to hear. The name LeCourt was mentioned: he had given only two hours' notice for the coach to depart shortly after dawn. The gatekeeper spoke a few words in sympathy, saluted the driver, and returned to his room. She dashed to the coach. Seconds later, it lurched forward into the courtyard with Anne curled up in a pile of pads and clothes on the rear luggage rack.

Outside the hotel, wearing a porter's apron from the rack, she mingled easily with grooms, servants, and tradesmen going about their early morning business. A talkative clerk told her that the *Goncourt* rented large suites to wealthy foreign businessmen, some of whom were dealing with the nearby firm of Arthur & Grenard, a major manufacturer of fine wallpaper. LeCourt rented the hotel's entire first floor.

"Ministers of State come to visit Monsieur LeCourt," the clerk boasted. "He's good for the hotel's reputation."

"Will he be travelling alone?" Anne glanced at the waiting coach.

"A dark man was with him when he returned to the hotel last night. The man hasn't left yet. They may be travelling together." The clerk paused, as if aware he had said more than he should to a stranger. His eyes narrowed with suspicion. Anne feared he might challenge her, but a groom leading a horse came between them. She slipped away to a quiet corner near the gate.

By the light of a flickering torch she scribbled an urgent message to Paul, then looked about anxiously, not knowing whom she could trust. Her eyes came to rest on a stableboy, thin but agile, and surely unable to read. He seemed as dependable a courier as she could hope to find. With mounting trepidation, she handed him the message and pressed a coin in his hand, promising him another at his destination. Then she waved him off, shivering as he disappeared in the darkness.

As the sky lightened Anne woke from a brief nap in the stable. The clouds in the east had turned a reddish hue. In the courtyard, servants were extinguishing the night lamps. She heard the coachman muttering to all who would listen that he could have slept another hour. Shrugging his shoulders, the gatekeeper said Monsieur LeCourt was usually punctual. Finally the night manager appeared at the hotel's main entrance on the ground floor and beckoned. Anne joined a small motley crew of porters and climbed upstairs to LeCourt's suite.

A double door opened into a spacious hall. A half-dozen candles offered a faint, flickering light. Others were spluttering out. Inside the door stood a small mountain of luggage. While her comrades carried trunks downstairs, Anne hung back, looking busy, edging close to LeCourt near the door. Wearing a brown suit for travelling, he stood in the light of one of the candles. "Two of my men are missing," he complained to the night manager. "I can't wait any longer. They will have to catch up." LeCourt shifted his weight from leg to leg. Lines of fatigue creased the corners of his mouth. His eyes ticked nervously. Krishna was nowhere in sight.

Anne noticed LeCourt paid scant attention to most of the luggage, but he glanced repeatedly at a large wooden packing box and a valise set apart from the rest. As Anne had calculated, it fell to her and three other porters to carry the wooden box. It was heavy, hurriedly hammered together, and lacked metal reinforcing bands. LeCourt followed them through the corridor, the valise gripped tightly under his arm. At the first floor landing, Anne glanced down through the balustrade. No one stood below.

A desperate plan formed instantly in her mind. She felt a surge of energy. This was the moment. Feigning to stumble, she wrenched the box out of the hands of her astonished partners and tipped it over the balustrade. The box hit the floor with a resounding crack of wood splintering on marble.

Startled, confused, LeCourt rushed to the balustrade. Anne spun round, seized the valise from under his arm and tossed it in the air. It too crashed on the floor below.

Shaking with rage, LeCourt threw a wild glancing blow to Anne's head, knocking her cap off. She shook her thick blond hair, then met his eye.

"You!" he hissed.

"Dubois' daughter," she growled.

"You'll pay for this." He pulled a small pistol from his coat.

∞∞∞

Clutching Anne's message, Colonel Saint-Martin paced back and forth in his office, still in his riding boots. Georges had remained at Montsouris with the troopers, searching for stolen goods and looking after Jacques Gros—alive but unconscious. Saint-Martin had hurried back to Paris, intending to inform the lieutenant-general. But now Anne claimed his attention.

The stable boy stood waiting outside the open door, cap in hand. The boy cleared his throat. Saint-Martin looked up distractedly, handed him a coin, and sent him away. He sat on the desk to read the message again. It was cryptic and alarming:

> Come! Dutchman leaves Hôtel Goncourt
> at dawn. Must see what's going with him.
> Urgent! A.C.

LeCourt departing suddenly from Paris? Suspicious but not illegal. Did Anne suspect he was carrying away the stolen jewels?

Saint-Martin laid the paper on his desk and mulled over his alternatives. Should he call the Paris police? He didn't have authority to search or detain LeCourt. But the word "urgent" worried him. Reckless, impassioned, Anne might actually try to confront LeCourt. He rang for a servant, ordered a fresh horse, and checked the powder in his pistol.

∞∞∞

The colonel and two troopers galloped through the awakening city. The hooves of their mounts struck sparks on the black paving stones. Their clatter echoed in the streets, driving pedestrians into doorways and up against walls. North of Place Vendôme, an odorous caravan of wagons hauling night soil blocked their path. For several precious moments, Saint-Martin shouted and cursed at the drivers. Finally, exasperated, he led his men through narrow side streets, crossed the Boulevard, and found Rue Thaitbout.

In the courtyard of the hotel he leaped from his horse near a coach loaded with luggage. He was striding up the entrance steps, followed by the troopers, when he heard a sound like the snapping of a tree branch. Pistol drawn and cocked, he dashed into the foyer, a large room with a grand staircase at the far end.

The night manager, two assistants, and the coachman cowered against the walls, mouths open in horror at the atrocity before them. Krishna sprawled grotesquely out of a large splintered box, eyes bulging, a tight cord biting into his neck. On the floor near a shattered valise lay glittering diamonds and precious stones, gold bracelets and pendants, an enormous necklace, and a priceless tiara. The Chanavas jewels! Tumbling down the stairs came Robert LeCourt. He hit the bottom with a heavy thud and lay doubled-up, clutching his groin.

Stunned by the sight, Saint-Martin lowered his pistol. Then, looking up, he saw Anne, leaning over the balustrade. Her face was grimy, creased with pain. Smiling thinly, she gripped her side with a bloodied hand and waved to him with the other, as if at the end of a bravura performance.

Chapter 30

Out of Hiding

Triggered by the sun, the little cannon in the garden of the Palais-Royal blasted away, announcing noon on a warm August Saturday. Anne was at work in the puppet theater, arranging for next week's performances. The heat was stifling. She was alone and felt faint. "Time to quit," she muttered to herself. She bent to pick up her purse. A short stab of pain made her gasp.

LeCourt's shot had hit her on the left side. She recalled the look of horror on Paul's face as she waved to him, then collapsed still conscious on the balustrade. He had bounded up the stairs, carried her into a servant's room nearby, then cut the bloodied shirt away from the wound and probed it gently.

"The ball grazed a rib," he had said, wiping grime from her face. "Thank God it missed your heart." Eyes glistening, he had leaned over and kissed her.

At the theater's door, she paused, touching her lips, cherishing the mark of his affection. A week had gone by. The wound in her side, like the hairline scrape on her forehead, had nearly healed. She stepped outside and fumbled in her purse for the key.

A bent old woman in rags approached, hand outstretched like a beggar. In a high, cackling voice she asked, "Could you tell me, Mademoiselle, where I might find Linnaeus, the Swedish botanist?"

Anne fell back a step, staring with astonishment into clear, steady, green eyes. "Claire!" she gasped.

The woman raised a finger to her lips, glancing apprehensively left and right. "I need to talk to you," she whispered. "You might be followed. Move on."

The woman nodded, then shuffled to the far end of the Camp of the Tatars, and returned by a parallel hallway. Concealed in the theater's entrance, Anne worried that Mauvert would catch her aiding a fugitive. She carefully scanned the crowd for anyone coming after Claire. Seeing no one, she beckoned her in.

The women sat on benches, facing one another in the dim light of a small window. Claire pulled the shawl off her head and worked her hand through her hair. In a natural, cultivated voice she said, "I'm grateful. I know you're running a risk with me."

Anne shrugged, unsmiling. "Have you heard? The jewels have been recovered. Your brother and LeCourt have been arrested. Krishna and François Noir are dead."

"I know. Everyone's talking about what you've done."

"They exaggerate, I'm sure." Anne concealed her concern that Paris had its eye on her. LeCourt's powerful friends might be tempted to retaliate. "Let's talk about something else. The Debussy case isn't closed. The Paris police think you and René may have helped the thieves." She sought Claire's eye. "Why did you go into hiding?"

She replied without flinching. "We feared Inspecteur Mauvert was about to arrest us as prime suspects." Resentment filtered through her voice. "We didn't have influential patrons or the money to defend ourselves. The magistrates would have convicted us of stealing the jewels and killing the comte. We'd have been tortured and burned alive on Place de Grève."

Anne shook her head. "I doubt Colonel Saint-Martin would have allowed patrons or money, or the lack of them, to influence the investigation." But to herself she admitted Claire had a point. Once the case had moved into a courtroom, Paul could not have prevented the prosecutor and the judges from making scapegoats of Claire and her friend.

"That may be true," Claire said, "But, the police are still hunting for us and we must hide, even though you have recovered the jewels and the thieves are dead or in prison." She fell silent and glanced restlessly about the little theater, as if unsure what her next step should be.

"What do you want from me?" Anne finally asked, her voice betraying a hint of skepticism.

"Persuade Colonel Saint-Martin to help us." She hesitated, a sly look in her eye. "I can tell him about the theft of jewels in his district and the crimes at Chateau Debussy."

Claire's desire to bargain troubled Anne. "Would you mind telling me? I don't care to run to the colonel on a fool's errand."

Claire hesitated for a few seconds, then began to explain how her brother had used Lélia Laplante to scout wealthy landowners he intended to rob. She had overheard them a year ago, planning a theft and quarreling about shares.

Anne remained silent for a minute, leaning forward, hands clasped. Paul already knew most of Claire's story, but he might think her testimony would strengthen the case against her brother. Nonetheless, before acting on Claire's behalf, Anne felt she needed to voice a suspicion growing in her mind.

She looked Claire in the eye. "Would you swear before a magistrate that you are innocent of the death of Comte Debussy?"

She nodded. "The police think Noir killed him when he stole the jewels."

Anne smiled guardedly. "But you also had motive and opportunity. You went to and from the chateau in the tunnel. What were you doing there?"

Claire looked aside for several seconds, chewing on her lower lip. She sighed. "The thieves left the tunnel and the comte's private stairway unlocked. René and I were curious to find out what they had done. We entered the apartment and found Krishna unconscious on the floor and the comte dead in bed."

Anne gazed coolly at her.

"But we didn't kill him," Claire insisted.

"You should have raised the alarm and helped Krishna. The police wouldn't be hunting you now." Anne was sure she had not heard the whole truth. And, even if she had, she didn't know how she could speak on behalf of the two fugitives to Paul or Georges or, heaven forbid, to Inspecteur Mauvert.

"We were going to seek help. Then I saw my mother's cabinet in the treasury." Claire rose from the bench and walked a few steps to the puppet stage, dabbing at her eyes with a kerchief. "Her heirlooms were there." She leaned on the stage, her back to Anne. "The comte had claimed them at her death. These should be mine, I thought, I'll lose them forever if I don't take them now." She turned around, her face stained with tears. "I was sure his collection of jewels had been stolen. The police would assume my mother's things were taken along with the rest. We brought them back to the cottage and hid them."

Claire's admission stunned Anne. A swell of sadness and disappointment almost overwhelmed her. She had come to like the young woman and hoped for her improvement. Now she appeared doomed. Anne got up from the bench, deciding what she should say, then sought Claire's eye. "But, I wonder...."

Claire looked at Anne expectantly.

"How did you get into the cabinet?"

"I found the key on Krishna's belt."

"Did you take a snuff box, three miniature portraits, an embroidered damask cushion, and some paste jewelry? The items missing from the cabinet's inventory."

"Yes."

"Do you still have them?"

"They are in safekeeping."

"Including the creamy damask cushion?"

Claire's eyes narrowed, grew wary. "Why do you ask?"

"Yesterday, my maid Michou brought me a picture she's working on, a detail from your mother's portrait hanging in the gallery. Her pet cat, Princesse, is lying on a damask cushion with tassels and gold fringe. Michou could not recall exactly the shape and color of the tassels. Suddenly, I thought of the one taken from the comte's hand, which the police have kept a secret."

Claire's lips parted in confusion. "What?"

Anne slowly approached Claire at the stage. "Later that afternoon Michou and I took the tassel to Chateau Debussy and compared it to those in the portrait. Identical. Beyond doubt." She paused, then uttered each word distinctly. "According to the inventory, that cushion was the one in your mother's cabinet."

Rigid, speechless, Claire stared at Anne incredulously.

"Like the police, I assumed the thieves had taken your mother's collection along with the comte's and had used the cushion to kill him. Now I realize that only *you* and René had access to it."

A look of horror spread over Claire's face. By admitting she had entered the treasury and removed her mother's heirlooms, she had confessed to murder. Her hands clenched tightly. Her eyes turned bright and hard.

A shiver of apprehension ran through Anne's body. Was the woman armed?

Claire took a step forward, as if about to spring.

Anne experienced a sense of power, a clearing of her mind, as when she used to step out on the high wire at Sadler's Wells.

Claire stopped, stood still for a few moments, then broke into a thin, self-mocking smile. "I should have known better than try to mislead you," she said, her throat taut, her voice raspy.

Anne folded her arms and waited silently.

"I was leaving the treasury with the pillow. René had gone ahead with the rest of the things. I heard the comte moan for Krishna." Her voice grew thick and slurred. "I feared he would call the guard. Then revenge took hold of me." Her hands rose, gripping an invisible object. "I put the cushion over his face and pressed down until he went limp." She paused, a look of surprise came over her. "I never noticed the missing tassel."

Anne stared at the woman before her. No bent old beggar. Having vented her passion, Claire stood erect, defiant, with the inbred pride of her class.

A seizure of imagination took Anne back to Place de Grève, with Claire instead of the peasant woman in the tumbrel. The crowd roaring. Claire's body lashed to the post, her face straining against fear. The fire, then the screams.

Anne's head throbbed. Her chest tightened. For a moment she could scarcely breathe. Sympathy for a woman who had punished her abuser vied with horror at the killing of a helpless, if evil, old man.

Minutes passed silently.

"What are you going to do?" asked Claire finally, reaching for her shawl. The two women walked side by side toward the exit.

"Nothing for now." Anne unlocked the door. "But I'll not permit an innocent person to be punished for what you did."

Claire gazed at Anne for a moment, then slipped out and disappeared into the crowd.

Chapter 31

Search for Neptune

Anne cupped a hand above her eyes. A bright noonday sun bathed the garden of the Palais-Royal. Paul brushed lightly against her, warding off the jostling crowd. She glanced at him and smiled. He seemed curiously distracted, troubled perhaps by a reflection that had also occurred to her. *What if LeCourt had been a better shot...?* She caught Paul's eye. He responded with an embarrassed shrug that told of his feeling for her.

A pang of conscience struck her. She had not told him of Claire's confession. He would have wanted to know. But it might not be necessary, she hoped. Anyway, his mind was now occupied with another matter.

Michou was walking a few steps behind them, looking at the ground, apparently mulling over the story of Pressigny, Lélia Laplante, and the missing jasper bowl. Its location was still a mystery—the owner had raised the reward to a thousand livres, a year's wages to a working man. With Anne translating, Paul had prodded Michou in vain for new clues that the investigation might have overlooked.

Near the central fountain, they went separate ways: Michou to the shaded bench she loved, promising to search her memory. Paul and Anne turned left to the Café Odeon in the Montpensier arcade and sat outside under an umbrella. Michou would join them when she was ready. Paul removed his hat, patted his brow with a kerchief. Anne fanned herself.

"I questioned Pressigny this morning," he began. "Krishna walked him at knife point from the theater's office down to the palace dungeon. That's why the office appeared undisturbed. He then bound him and stuck him with the point dipped in aconite. The mixture was weak enough to cause a lingering death in the pit. Krishna wanted the man to suffer."

A waiter hovering nearby approached the table. "We'll order shortly," said Paul. "When our friend arrives."

He glanced sideways at the small figure of Michou, who had left her bench and was staring at the fountain. "She may come up with something," he said hopefully, then resumed his account. "At first, Pressigny refused to incriminate himself. But I offered him the prospect of a beheading on Place de Grève. And he talked."

Anne shuddered violently, reminded of painful associations with that place. She choked back a reproof rising from her throat.

Immediately contrite, Paul lifted his hands, palms out. "Sorry," he murmured.

Anne took a deep breath. "No harm done. What did you learn?"

"As we suspected, he helped Noir and Gros reach the roof of the chateau to gain entry into the treasury tower and opened the tunnel for them to leave. Their shoes in the cave matched the prints in the tunnel. All the stolen goods are now accounted for." He tapped his fingers on the table impatiently. "Except the jasper bowl and a few precious stones."

Throughout this conversation, yesterday's encounter with Claire had nagged at Anne's mind. She finally tried to ease her conscience. "By the way, who does the lieutenant-general believe killed the comte?"

"Noir, acting on his own," Paul replied, adding that the lieutenant-general still wanted to question Claire de Pressigny and René Cavour and had issued warrants for their arrest.

Anne felt relieved at least to hear that no innocent living person would be accused of Claire's crime. "But wasn't Noir working for LeCourt?"

"Yes, he was," Paul agreed. "Nonetheless, LeCourt denies playing any part in the Debussy case. He also claims he killed

Krishna in self-defense while recovering the jewels and hired the coach to bring them to the police."

Anne scoffed. "To drive a quarter of a mile through Paris on his errand he needed several trunks of clothing, financial records, and works of art!"

"Lieutenant-General DeCrosne shares your skepticism. That's why LeCourt's under arrest in the fortress at Vincennes." He frowned for a moment. "But Comptroller-General Calonne's working hard to free him."

"He might be released?" she asked. The thought chilled her.

"That's possible, unfortunately." Paul's voice softened. His eyes gently engaged Anne's.

She was still for a moment, then bent forward in distress, her hands covering her face. LeCourt, the man most responsible for Antoine's death, might escape punishment. She imagined him walking about this garden, elegantly attired and coiffed, ladies and gentlemen fawning as he passed. She would walk up to him with her pistol. Bring raw fear to his eyes. "For Antoine," she would say. Then blow his brains out.

She felt a hand on her shoulder. "The Law is clumsy," said Paul softly. "LeCourt may escape its clutches. But decent men will despise and distrust him." His voice brightened. "And there's good news too."

She slowly leaned back. His hand withdrew. She stared at him. "Did Pressigny confess to the murder of Lélia Laplante?"

"Yes, but he claimed self-defense. Derennes came up with the idea of blaming your father. LeCourt approved it." He met her eye. "Lieutenant-General DeCrosne now agrees Dubois was innocent and has promised to clear his name."

Ever since Michou's story of Laplante's death, Anne had been expecting these words. And had struggled to earn them. Now when they were spoken, they stunned her. Tears came to her eyes. She rose from her chair, walked a few steps into the garden, looked up into the clear blue sky. A light breeze caressed her face. For a few moments she let it dry her tears. Then she returned to the table and gazed fondly at Paul. "You drew that promise from him, I'm sure. Thank you."

A smile flickered on his lips. "I promised I'd do my best. But without you...." His eyes lingered for a moment on her face. Then he pointed toward the fountain. "Michou's coming. We'll celebrate Antoine together."

He beckoned the waiter and they ordered sweets. Michou's choice was a dish of fresh raspberries and cream, a treat she had enjoyed recently at the colonel's table. Sitting across from Anne, she ate absentmindedly, pencil in hand, sketching in her book. Anne caught her eye and signed a mild reproach.

Smiling an apology, Michou placed an unfinished drawing of the jasper bowl in front of the colonel. Neptune with his trident and the grotesque dolphins stood in bold relief, the rest of the bowl was faintly outlined. She pointed to the drawing, then signed her opinion that Chevalier de Pressigny would not have passed the bowl on to anyone. He was too fond of it. Anne and Saint-Martin glanced at one another, astonished by her confident expression, eyes bright and unwavering.

"What does she think he did with the bowl?" Paul asked Anne, his gaze fixed on Michou.

Michou looked to Anne, who translated the question.

"Kept it close to him," Michou signed with assurance. Glancing from Anne to the colonel, she clutched her notebook to her chest in mock anxiety.

"But his rooms have been thoroughly searched," countered Saint-Martin.

Michou's face lighted up with a bright intelligence. "It's there," she signed without blinking. "I can find it."

At the exit from the garden, they met a long line of carriages on Rue Montpensier, gleaming in the sunlight. Coachmen stood by in colorful livery. Their fashionable passengers were mingling outside, heads bobbing in animated conversation. Colonel Saint-Martin began to lead Anne and Michou toward his own carriage when he heard his name. With a swift reflex he caught the speaker's eye. The man quickly looked away.

"They are talking about us," Anne whispered, "and they aren't smiling."

"Rumormongers at work," he said in a low voice meant to be heard. "These people," he went on softly, "have little reason to smile. Their investments in LeCourt's business ventures have collapsed since his arrest."

Financial losses were not the only things being discussed, Anne thought. These fine folk were staring at her and at Paul. Was it the clothes they were wearing? His officer's uniform—blue coat, red cuffs and lapels, tan breeches—might attract a glance or two because Paul wore it so well, but it seemed plain compared to what men of fashion were wearing. Her simple blue frock wasn't worthy of notice. Michou stood beneath their line of vision. Something was amiss.

At the carriage next to Paul's, they met a small group dressed in the latest style, the women in narrow-waisted full skirts and towering hats adorned with feathers and silk ribbons, the men in delicately embroidered silk coats in pastel rose, green, and yellow with matching breeches.

"Paul," exclaimed a powdered and painted woman in her forties, attractive but for a small mouth and weak chin. "It's ages since I've been this close to you." She stepped toward Saint-Martin, casting a glance at Anne. "Is this your English..." she paused, pursing her lips, "lady?" The others tittered. "She's the talk of Paris."

"Why?" he asked in English with faintly concealed irony. "For catching a well-connected thief and murderer?" He bowed rather stiffly to the woman. "Miss Anne Cartier, my cousin, Comtesse Louise de Joinville."

Anne uttered a polite greeting in perfect French.

Comtesse Louise arched her brow, scrutinizing Anne's un-varnished features and simple attire, then shifted to Paul. "You do have remarkable taste," she said, a mocking glint in her eyes. "Like our Jean-Jacques Rousseau, you delight in the natural and common or, may I say, primitive."

"You are closer to the truth than you realize," he returned brusquely. "Excuse us, we're on our way to certain official business."

The expression on Comtesse Louise's face had hardened during this exchange. As Saint-Martin turned away, she caught Anne by the sleeve. "You should read this." She handed her a crudely printed sheet from her purse. "It appeared on the streets last night." She left quickly, a fury in swirling silk, and joined her group at their carriage.

Anne scanned the sheet, the color draining from her face.

*Rumor has it that the Provost of the Royal
Highway Patrol for the region around Paris
is enjoying the services of an English whore.
He had better be careful. She is violent as
well as promiscuous. Haled into a London
magistrate's court last year for soliciting and
assaulting a gentleman, she was sentenced
to be publicly stripped and flogged.*

With trembling hands she tucked the paper into her purse.
Paul, who had noticed the incident from a few steps away,
asked what had happened.

"Later," she whispered and climbed into the carriage next
to Michou. They got underway, he sitting opposite the two
women. He asked again about the paper. She handed it over
without looking at him.

"Vile gossip," he muttered, glancing at the sheet. Suddenly
he grew rigid, instinctively reached for the hilt of his sword.
Cold fury filled his eyes. Unable to speak, he shook the sheet
helplessly, as if he would scramble its words. With an explosive
sigh he looked up slowly to Anne, his face a confusion of tender pity and rage. "I'm sorry beyond words." He crumpled the
paper in his fist and threw it on the floor. "You don't deserve this."

She mustered a grateful smile.

He leaned forward and held her hand. "It's a contemptible
lie, but it still hurts that someone has said it." He looked gently
at her. "Scandalmongers have mentioned me from time to time,
and they certainly haven't spared the queen."

"Who is behind this?" She felt a wave of hot anger.

"Mauvert. The rumor surfaced a couple of days ago. Georges
heard it. We didn't know it got into print. Somehow Mauvert
has been in touch with Jack Roach in England, who is both a
police informant and a fence for smuggled goods."

"Mauvert's revenge. What are you going to do about it?"
She pointed to the paper on the floor.

"Ignore it. Otherwise the public will think it's true." He
tore the offensive sheet to pieces and threw them out the window. "I've started to deal with Mauvert. He's not fit to be an
inspecteur and I've said so to Baron Breteuil."

"And the Comtesse de Joinville?" Anne asked, a touch of irony in her voice.

"Ignore my cousin's malice. She's caught up in a society of parasites that breeds envy, spite, and callous contempt for others."

Anne saw the point of Paul's argument, but she could not stir up much sympathy for the woman. "'Common and natural' I take as a compliment, but I don't care to know what she meant by 'primitive.'"

Michou had noticed the offensive sheet and sensed the tension it caused. Eyes clouded with confusion, she stared at Anne.

"Mauvert insulted me," Anne signed, then shrugged it away. Michou's eyes moistened. She leaned over and gave Anne a hug. A shadow of pain lingered on her face, prompting Anne to wonder what insults this small deaf woman had experienced. Michou slumped down in her seat and stared glumly out the window as the carriage passed by a rolling sun-drenched meadow.

After a few minutes she grew absorbed again in her sketch pad, oblivious to the pitching of the carriage. Having sensed Anne's curiosity, she displayed the page she was studying, a free-hand portrait of Chevalier Jean de Pressigny, dark-browed, his face hungry with sensual appetite.

Anne pointed to the sketch and signed, "I agree with you. He's passion's slave."

Michou smiled gratefully and returned to the sketch.

"What are the odds of finding the bowl?" Anne asked Paul.

He shrugged his shoulders. "A few days ago, Inspecteur Mauvert searched the chateau again with a fine-toothed comb." A mirthful grin spread over his face. "When he found nothing, he grew desperate and rushed up to the chalk caves by the kilns. For hours, like a madman, he pawed through centuries of sheep dirt! As he left the caves, you could smell him halfway to Paris."

The image of the soiled detective, otherwise so fastidious in dress and manner, set them to smiling. Then they giggled and finally, losing control, they laughed until their sides ached and tears came to their eyes.

Michou stared at them open-mouthed.

Paul regained his composure as the carriage approached Chateau Debussy. He leaned forward and dabbed the tears away from Anne's face, and she from his.

At the large outer gate house the carriage slowed. Claudine was at the window, clad in widow's black. Her eyebrows lifted as she recognized them. The colonel waved a greeting, then turned to Anne. "I've told Madame Soucie we'd be coming," he whispered. "Seems she's passed the word on to Claudine. They've grown closer since Krishna's death."

Instead of waving them through, Claudine beckoned. With a look of surprise, Saint-Martin ordered the coachman to drive behind the gate house. Claudine came out to meet them, her black hair pulled back in a tight bun. Her voice sounded a plea. "If it's convenient, Colonel, I'd like to speak with you. And with you, Mademoiselle Cartier."

Saint-Martin and Anne exchanged puzzled glances, nodded to one another and then to Claudine. Michou signed she'd be comfortable in the carriage. As they followed the woman into the gate house, Paul whispered to Anne, "She had little to say when I interrogated her."

They were led upstairs to a reception room, tastefully furnished with worn but well-kept rugs and drapes, several upholstered chairs, and a highly polished mahogany table. Framed embroidered pastoral scenes hung on the walls. A pair of vases of fresh-cut yellow freesia stood on the mantelpiece, a mark of Madame Soucie's kindness.

"May I serve you something?" Claudine asked. "Wine? Tea?"

Paul glanced at Anne. "Tea would be fine," she replied, then added her regret at the misfortunes of the family.

Claudine acknowledged with a thin smile. "I pined for years, not knowing what happened to Nalini. My work kept me going. When I buried her remains, I felt released. As for Krishna, I am numb." With a soft sigh, she called a servant girl, said a few words, and waved her off.

Anne searched the woman for signs of grief. Her dark brown eyes had lost lustre. Her shoulders slumped a little. Otherwise she was still the same alert, competent person who had prepared Anne for the Amateurs' reception a few weeks earlier.

"Since my husband's death, I've thought over what I needed to tell both of you. I'm happy you came by today." She sat erect, her hands folded in her lap. "My husband was weak but not a bad man. Unfortunately, he worked for Comte Debussy too long. Took on some of that man's evil ways. Though Krishna was unfaithful—everyone now knows about the pretty widow on Rue Saint-Marc—I still felt obliged to protect him and our home. Now that he's dead, I can speak more freely."

She paused as the servant came with tea and sweet biscuits, then left, closing the door behind her. With evident pleasure Claudine poured from a fine East Indian porcelain pot. She began describing Krishna's gradual, hidden aversion to the comte, his growing resentment at his own common status, especially since he came into contact with Monsieur Robert LeCourt and joined his Masonic lodge. "I knew trouble was on the way."

Anne leaned forward, voicing a recent suspicion. "Had Krishna known LeCourt before?"

"Yes, briefly, in India," she replied. "He was thirteen at the time. He told me about it in an unguarded moment, shortly after LeCourt arrived in Paris. Swore me to secrecy. Comte Debussy never found out." She explained that LeCourt was originally Julien Robert, a young military engineer in Debussy's army when it captured Chanavas Khan's fortress. Familiar with the building, Robert sneaked down to the treasure room, broke into it, and took the jewels. Debussy, guided by Krishna, then just a serving boy in the khan's household, reached the room as Robert was about to leave. When he wouldn't give up the jewels, Debussy shot him and ordered Krishna to make sure he was dead.

But Krishna was afraid to get blood on his hands. Since Robert didn't move, Krishna said he was dead. In the confusion following the battle, Robert escaped, leaving the body of a dead guard in his place. Debussy never learned the truth. Robert changed his name to LeCourt and went on to prosper in the service of native princes and the Dutch East India Company. Arriving in Paris three years ago, he met Krishna, discovered he resented his master, and promised him a well-paid post in his household in Holland.

Claudine sighed. "Krishna never told me *what* he'd have to do for LeCourt!"

"We know now," remarked Saint-Martin. "LeCourt persuaded him to sedate the comte with laudanum and isolate the treasury for the thieves."

Anne reached over and laid a hand on Claudine's. "Your husband was an unfortunate victim of LeCourt's obsession."

She pressed Anne's hand. "Thank you for understanding."

∞∞∞

Pressigny's apartment was empty. After the police had exhausted their interest in it, Madame Soucie had laid sheets over the tables and chairs and packed away the debris of a careless young man's life.

Michou looked about, hands on her hips. "Now I'll find the Neptune bowl," she signed. Her eyes closed for a few moments, as if seeking where a man like Pressigny would hide it. Then, erect, alert, she wandered through room after room, occasionally inspecting plaster copies of ancient works of art covered by dusting-sheets.

Her companions trailing behind her, she entered the sitting room and on to the balcony where Anne had stood with Pressigny. After taking the view over the valley, Michou returned to the room, glancing to the left and to the right at two large urns on low pedestals, each holding a tall ornamental fig tree. Suddenly, she stopped in mid-passage, beckoned frantically, and pointed to a design on the left urn.

"There's Neptune about to cast his trident at a dolphin," exclaimed Saint-Martin, drawing his fingers over crude figures lightly etched into the terra cotta.

"Our bowl's inside!" cried Anne, embracing Michou. "She recognized the motif and knew Pressigny would mimic his cache."

When they had removed the tree, they discovered he had cleverly concealed the bowl beneath a false bottom. Inspection of the other urn revealed a similar hiding place with a small collection of precious stones.

Holding the Neptune bowl for the women to admire, Saint-Martin smiled broadly. "Michou, not Mauvert, has earned the finder's fee." He handed the bowl to Anne and bowed to Michou. "Well done!"

She accepted the compliment with aplomb, then signed to Anne, "I feel blessed."

∞∞∞

An early evening golden light slanted into the coach as it returned to Paris. Anne sat next to Michou. The newly found jasper bowl and the gems, securely packed in a plain wooden box, rested on the floor between them. Paul sat opposite the women, his eyes alert, surveying the countryside. He had kept Michou's discovery a secret at Chateau Debussy, hoping to bring the treasure safely to the nearest highway patrol post in Villejuif. A brace of loaded pistols lay in holsters by his side. One of Soucie's largest and most trusted grooms sat with a short-barrelled musket next to the coachman.

The rhythmic clip-clop of hooves, the jingle-jangle of bells and harness, lulled Anne into musing about the visit with Claudine and about Krishna's death. She looked up at Paul. "LeCourt must have been crazed. He intended to kill off all his accomplices. But why Antoine?"

Paul picked up the thread. "LeCourt believed Pressigny's murderous quarrel with Laplante threatened to undermine the scheme to regain the jewels." The colonel's voice broke slightly. "Antoine Dubois was a convenient scapegoat."

At that point, Michou, who had appeared to be sleeping, rubbed her eyes and signaled her wish to share in the conversation. Anne gave her the gist of it and turned to speak to Paul. Michou tapped her on the shoulder and signed, suddenly, without warning, "Whatever has happened to Debussy's stepdaughter? Suspected in the theft of the jewels, I understand. Are the police still looking for her?" She glanced at the colonel for an answer.

Anne sucked in a breath, then translated Michou's signs.

"One of Mauvert's agents sighted her yesterday, leaving the Camp of the Tatars," Paul replied. "Gave chase, but lost her in the crowd. She hasn't been seen since."

Good God! Anne thought. That was too close. What if the agent had seen Claire leaving the puppet theater! Anne averted her eyes, fearing they would betray her alarm.

"Her friend, René Cavour, is Piedmontese," Paul added. "If they were quick and clever about it, they could reach Italy in a few weeks. The troopers have been alerted, but they have other work to do. The stolen items are recovered; the murderer, Noir, identified. Why bother with two penniless fugitives?"

Anne instinctively shuddered, but her reaction passed unnoticed. The coachman had yelled out, they were approaching the town of Villejuif on a hill just ahead. Leaning out the window, Saint-Martin shouted a command. They came to a halt at a building flying the flag of the Royal Highway Patrol.

"Would you mind waiting?" asked Paul, turning to Anne. "I need a guard to ride with us through Paris. This may take awhile."

"I'll visit the town," Anne replied. "It's a beautiful day." She invited Michou, who shook her head and retrieved her sketch pad. At the entrance to the post, Saint-Martin ordered the trooper on duty to watch the coach.

Anne was still within easy shouting distance of the trooper when a cart pulled by a donkey caught her attention. It was coming toward her at a slow pace. An elderly man held the reins; an old bent woman sat beside him.

Anne recognized Claire de Pressigny. She wore the same disguise as the last time they'd met. Their eyes linked instantly. Claire's body stiffened and tremors of fear worked the corners of her mouth. Inaudibly she pleaded for mercy, her eyes shifting from Anne to the trooper and back to Anne. Although hardly three seconds had passed, Anne grew anxious, fear clutching at her stomach. Would the trooper become suspicious? She gave Claire a nervous smile, then turned away, and didn't look again as the little cart passed her. She held her breath, expecting the trooper to challenge the fugitives. But all she heard was the fading clip-clop of the donkey.

A few minutes later she looked back, eyes scanning the highway to Italy. She let out a sigh of relief. The cart and its two passengers crept slowly southward. Soon they disappeared in the hazy distance. She uttered a soundless *adieu*.

Chapter 32

Departure: August 1786

Anne glanced about the table at familiar faces in the candles' soft golden light. The glittering centerpiece, a delicate silver miniature fruit-bearing shrub, cast dancing shadows on the linen table cloth. Waiters had served a course of sautéed veal, thinly sliced in a rich madeira sauce and garnished with fresh vegetables. Unfortunately, she could not finish it. A touch of sadness had taken the edge off her appetite. She would soon leave this place.

Ignoring convention, Paul had invited Anne, Michou, and Georges, together with Comtesse Marie, for supper at the provost's residence on Rue Saint-Honoré. They were celebrating Anne's birthday, the 19th of August, and her visit that morning to the royal court at Versailles. Though held without fanfare in a modest antechamber, the visit was not secret. The court was buzzing about it.

Paul and Comtesse Marie had presented her to King Louis XVI, a corpulent and rather shy man, but kindly in his manner. With Baron Breteuil at his side, the king had praised Anne's courage and thanked her for recovering the Chanavas jewels. She had stepped forward and placed the burnished box in his hands.

"Please open it," he had said, laying it on a nearby table. Gingerly, she lifted the lid and displayed the jewelry, piece by piece. The king's eyes widened in a long, silent stare. Finally, in a hushed voice, he remarked to Baron Breteuil, "I've never seen the like of it." Then, turning to the courtiers assembled in the room, he added with emphasis, "I believe Mademoiselle Cartier deserves a suitable reward." He took a small, green velvet box from the baron's hand and presented it to Anne.

"May I open it?"

"Please do. I hope you like it."

In the box was a bright cabochon emerald of an extraordinarily pellucid shade of green, set in finely worked gold and hanging on a golden chain. "The work of a French master jeweller," the king had said, then added, "I would have liked to give you a piece of the Chanavas jewelry, but it is best to keep the set intact." Baron Breteuil had leaned forward and laid a heavy velvet purse in her hand. On opening it later, she had discovered a hundred *louis d'or* worth over two thousand English shillings, a small fortune.

The arm of a waiter reaching for her plate jarred Anne out of her reminiscence. Aware that Comtesse Marie was looking her way, Anne fondled the king's emerald hanging from her neck. The two women exchanged smiles.

The comtesse leaned toward Anne. "You and I know each other well enough now to drop titles as your mother and I did years ago. Privately, of course. For I sense that both of us would rather avoid the estrangement and discord that come with openly challenging social conventions. I wish you would call me Marie and allow me to call you Anne. You have so much of your mother's spirit, I feel I've known you as a grown woman for much more than these recent months. I've spoken about this with Paul before supper. He encouraged me."

Anne was touched and pleased and readily agreed. It would take some time to feel comfortable with the new relationship. Marie was her superior, not only in social rank but also in age, judgment, and attainment. To be her friend, Anne realized, was a challenge but one well worth embracing. She also felt she had something to offer Marie: new expectations from life. Marie had perhaps retired too early from society when she still had talents to exercise for herself and others. She could be encouraged to do even more for the deaf—and with them: learn their sign language for a start.

There was hope. Anne observed the comtesse gazing at Michou, who sat erect, alert, benevolently surveying her companions at the table. Her soft yellow silk dress accented the green of her eyes. It was new. She had apparently dipped into the finder's fee for the jasper bowl. Her auburn hair was washed, brushed, and expertly dressed, her pale complexion tinted with discreet touches of rouge. A pleased expression graced Marie's face. Her maids had aided Michou's transformation.

During interludes in the meal, the comtesse made gracious overtures to Michou, who sat silently opposite, a sketch pad by her plate.

"A budding artist," Marie said to Anne, and handed Michou a miniature portrait of herself. Michou glanced repeatedly at the painting and at the woman, and then signed an earnest message that Marie failed to grasp.

Anne explained, "She'd like to paint as well as you."

The comtesse smiled to Michou for the compliment, adding to Anne in a low, respectful voice, "Tell her that a friend of mine painted it."

With the cheese and fruit course, the conversation turned to the recent dramatic events leading up to the arrest of Monsieur LeCourt. Georges held forth on the financier's futile attempts thus far to escape justice. Meanwhile, ignoring her food, Michou hunched over her sketch pad.

"She's been drawing me," whispered Marie to Anne, when Michou finally laid down her pencil. "Would she mind if I looked at what she's done?"

Michou seemed to anticipate her request. Smiling hesitantly, she tore off the top sheet, initialed it, and handed it across the table.

The comtesse exclaimed, "It's extraordinary!" and held up the sketch for Anne to see. Michou had captured the woman's face in a characteristic moment, mouth slightly open, attentive to the conversation.

Michou stared at the comtesse for a minute or two, so intently that Anne began to feel uncomfortable. But Marie calmly accepted her interest and in turn appeared to study Michou. Finally, glancing at the comtesse, Michou signed to Anne, "May I work with her friend the painter?"

Her throat tightening with concern, Anne passed on the request. The comtesse's otherwise animated face turned remarkably still, her gaze fixed on the little woman. Anne held her breath, hoping for Michou, fearing the pain of rejection. A prominent painter could rightly balk at taking on an apprentice like Michou, talented but deaf.

At last Marie smiled and said she would speak to him. She was certain he would agree. Michou signed thank you, her face radiant. Anne uttered a sigh of relief. Marie would undoubtedly pay the artist handsomely.

While Michou and the comtesse arranged a later meeting, Anne turned to Georges across the table. Withdrawn into heavy silence, he was looking at her wistfully. A few days earlier, she had told him and Paul that she would soon return to England. Georges now met her eye, and they raised their glasses together. Anne sensed they had become true comrades. She would miss his droll humor.

He beckoned a waiter to fill his glass. "What will you do in England? Reckon with Jack Roach?" He leaned toward her, unsmiling. "He owes you."

"Indeed he does!" she replied gravely. "My solicitor, Barnstaple, is looking after that account." She paused, glancing into her glass. "I'll spend a month with my grandparents and visit the Braidwood School." She felt a rush of pleasure, momentarily recalling her relatives and friends. "Then I'll come back to Paris and learn more from Abbé de l'Épée. Perhaps someday I'll start a school of my own."

Clearly relieved to hear she would return, Georges asked if she thought she could improve on what the abbé was doing.

"I'd introduce more art and theater into educating deaf children." She made a self-effacing gesture. "Though I'm not an expert, it seems to me his instruction neglects the student's imagination."

"Let me know when you've returned to Paris," said Georges. "Just in case you run into trouble. I could be of some use to you." He raised his glass again in a jaunty salute.

Wearing her travelling clothes, Anne surveyed her apartment. All was in order as when she had arrived, three months earlier. She sent a grateful thought to Comtesse Marie.

A maid came to the open door. "Colonel Paul de Saint-Martin is waiting in the parlor, Mademoiselle."

Anne picked up her handbag and followed the maid downstairs.

Paul bowed as she entered, and they gazed at one another silently for a moment. "Are you anxious?" he asked. "It will take you a week to reach London."

"I'm as ready as one can be." She patted her bag. "Travel documents, a letter of credit, money. And, thanks to you, at least the French highways are safe."

"One of the few things the English envy us for." He laughed. "Tell me about your travelling companions."

"A respectable English couple and their deaf daughter returning to London. Abbé de l'Épée introduced me when they were visiting his institute. Fortunately, we could arrange to travel in the same coach."

Paul seemed relieved. "When shall I see you again?"

"Soon," she replied, fighting back a frisson of anxiety. "In a month, after I visit my grandparents and Mr. Braidwood."

"Please give them my best wishes." He hesitated. "Then it's time we go."

"Not yet." From her bag she pulled out the key he had given her to the rear garden entrance. "I won't be needing this anymore."

A flicker of disappointment crossed his face, but quickly disappeared. He bowed gallantly and took the key.

She touched his arm. "But I don't want to be locked out of your life, so I'm giving you this likeness." She handed him a small box.

He opened it to a miniature portrait of her wearing the Chanavas tiara. He held it to the light. "Lovely! Michou painted it." Chuckling softly, he took a small box from his pocket and gave it to her. It opened to a similar portrait of himself. "I told Michou recently I wished I had something special for you. That same day she brought this painting to me—she had done it while living at my residence."

Anne studied the portrait, her throat choked with feeling. Michou had caught the kindness and nobility of the man. But it was only a likeness, not the presence that she felt so strongly now. And a likeness evoking memories that would inevitably fade.

She glanced up at his face. His eyes moistened. The faint sound of voices drifted from distant parts of the house. They were alone. She reached out a hand. He drew her close to him. They kissed for a long moment, then she stepped slowly back. "Now we must go."

At Porte Saint-Denis, they met the coach to Calais. Oblivious to the London passengers who had already boarded, they locked eyes in a tender, wordless exchange. The postilion shifted impatiently in his saddle. The horses pawed and snorted. Finally, at a call from the coachman, Anne smiled nervously over her shoulder, blew a kiss to Paul. Gathering her skirt, she climbed into the coach. As it drove out, she waved to him. He waved back until the road took a turn and they were parted.

Author's Note

The characters in this novel are fictitious or are treated fictitiously. Streets and places are real except for Chateau Beaumont, Café Marcel, Café Odéon, and Hôtel Goncourt. I have moved Chateau Tanlay from Burgundy to the outskirts of Paris and, with minor alterations, transformed it into Chateau Debussy. I'm indebted to Ambassador Thomas Jefferson for information about the weather in Paris. He recorded it twice daily. The jasper bowl can be seen in the collection of the Grünes Gewölbe, Dresden. The Chanavas jewels are an ensemble of various historic Indian pieces.

Readers wishing to become better acquainted with the Paris of 1786 will find Howard C. Rice, Jr., *Thomas Jefferson's Paris*, Princeton: Princeton University Press, 1976, convenient as well as helpful. For Abbé de l'Épée and the situation of the deaf, I recommend Harlan Lane, *When the Mind Hears: A History of the Deaf*, New York: Random House, 1984. For a good introduction to law enforcement in the eighteenth-century metropolis, read Alan Williams, *Police of Paris*, Baton Rouge: Louisiana State University, 1979. For a more technical, detailed analysis of eighteenth-century French criminal justice, consult Richard M. Andrews, *Law, Magistracy, and Crime in Old Regime Paris, 1735-1789*, New York: Cambridge University Press, 1994. See also E.J. Burford & Sandra Shulman, *Of Bridles & Burnings: The Punishment of Women*, New York: St. Martin's, 1992.

The Royal Highway Patrol [La Maréchaussée], precursor of the modern Gendarmerie Nationale, grew out of the royal army's

military police. In the late eighteenth century its main function was to maintain order in the countryside and on the highways. It numbered almost 4,000 men, spread across France in small detachments. Their provosts were usually retired army colonels. Paul de Saint-Martin would have been an unusually young provost, especially for the region around Paris.

In 1786 there was no longer a theater within the palace of the Palais-Royal. The opera had burned down in 1781 and a temporary Théatre des Variétés Amusants had been built adjacent to the west side of the palace. In *Mute Witness* I have created a small palace theater on the site of the palace chapel. In 1787 the entire west wing of the palace, including the picture galleries and the chapel, was demolished to make way for the present Comédie Française, completed in 1791.